"*An Instance of the Fingerpost* may well be the best 'historical mystery' ever written; it is certainly the best I have ever read . . . rich in nuance . . . Restoration England comes alive in this book."

—*Boston Sunday Globe*

"A superior entertainment. Into the fabric of a solid mystery novel Pears deftly interweaves small human tragedies and the grand events of history; the birth pangs of modern science and the eternal machinations of politics; religious fervor in both its benign and bigoted forms."

—*Houston Chronicle*

"Every sentence in the book is as solid as brick—and as treacherous as quicksand . . . With perfect mastery Pears gradually takes us from an unexplained death in a small college town to a revelation that could shake the foundations of England and the world . . . The book's twists, reversals and red herrings are so neatly executed that you could reread the novel just to savor the subtle tricks of omission and misdirection. Still, amid all the smoke and mirrors, one fact stands out with perfect clarity: Iain Pears has written an impressively original and audaciously imaginative intellectual thriller."

—*Washington Post Book World*

"A whopping-good whodunit . . . [A] potent brew, good to the very last drop."

—*Mirabella*

"A rollicking murder mystery that just happens to enlist such colorful real-life characters as philosopher John Locke, physician Richard Lower, and historian Anthony Wood . . . The writing is elegant, accessible, and tinted with delicate humor . . . Until the final page, it is unlikely that you will be able to guess whodunit."

—*Boston Globe*

(continued on next page)

"The reader encounters medical experiment, theological argument, bibliophilia, and code-cracking, on the way to a thoroughly surprising conclusion. He also encounters some sly comedy . . . The author is unquestionably a learned scholar as well as a nervy and ingenious plot-master."
—*Atlantic Monthly*

"Stylish and memorable . . . Mr. Pears's assured command of period history, language, lore and attitudes is formidable."
—*Wall Street Journal*

"A big, ingenious, intricately plotted fiction that constantly twists around to examine the premises of its own art and craft."
—*Seattle Weekly*

"Successful literary thrillers in the mold of Umberto Eco's *The Name of the Rose* are the stuff of publishers' dreams, and in Pears's novel they may have found a near-perfect example of the genre . . . Pears, with a painstaking, almost forensic attention to detail, constructs his world like a master painter of *trompe l'oeil*."
—*The New York Times Book Review*

"[A] strange, gripping and excellent work."
—*London Free Press* (Ontario)

"Thoroughly satisfying, hard to put down . . . polished entertainment."
—*Philadelphia Inquirer*

"A gripping, expert, and wholly plausible journey to a singularly fascinating time and place."
—*San Francisco Chronicle Book Review*

(continued on next page)

READERS GUIDE ONLINE
www.penguinputnam.com

An Instance of the Fingerpost

IAIN PEARS

BERKLEY BOOKS, NEW YORK

AN INSTANCE OF THE FINGERPOST

A Berkley Book / published by arrangement with
Jonathan Cape, Ltd.

PRINTING HISTORY
Riverhead edition / March 1998
Berkley edition / March 1999

The Penguin Putnam Inc. World Wide Web site address is
http://www.penguinputnam.com

ISBN: 0-425-16772-0

BERKLEY®
Berkley Books are published by The Berkley Publishing Group,
a divison of Penguin Putnam Inc.,
375 Hudson Street, New York, New York 10014.
BERKLEY and the "B" design
are trademarks belonging to Penguin Putnam Inc.

PRINTED IN THE UNITED STATES OF AMERICA

14   13   12   11   10   9   8   7   6

Contents

Historia vero testis temporum, lux veritatis, vita memoriae, magistra vitae.

(History is the witness of the times, the light of truth, the life of memory, the mistress of life.)

—CICERO, *DE ORATORE*

A Question of Precedence

There are Idols which we call Idols of the Market. For Men associate by Discourse, and a false and improper Imposition of Words strangely possesses the Understanding, for Words absolutely force the Understanding, and put all Things into Confusion.

—FRANCIS BACON,
NOVUM ORGANUM SCIENTARUM,
SECTION II, APHORISM VI.

• • •

MY FATHER, GIOVANNI DA COLA, WAS A MERCHANT, AND for the last years of his life was occupied in the importation of luxury goods into England which, though an unsophisticated country, was nonetheless beginning to rouse itself from the effects of revolution. He had shrewdly recognized from afar that the return of King Charles II meant that vast profits would once again be there for the taking and, stealing a march on more timid traders, he established himself in London to provide the wealthier English with those luxuries which the Puritan zealots had discouraged for so many years. His business prospered: he had a good man in London in Giovanni di Pietro, and also entered into a partnership with an English trader, with whom he split his profit. As he once told me, it was a fair bargain: this John Manston was sly and dishonest, but possessed unrivaled knowledge of English tastes. More importantly, the English had passed a law to stop goods coming into their ports in foreign boats, and Manston was a way through this difficulty. As long as my father had di Pietro in place to keep an eye firmly on the accounts, he believed there was little chance of being cheated.

He was long past the time when he took a direct interest in his business, having already converted a portion of his capital into land on Terra Firma to prepare for admission to the Golden Book. Although a merchant himself, he intended his children to be gentlemen, and discouraged me from active participation in his business. I mention this as an indication of his goodness: he had noticed early on that I had little mind for trade, and encouraged me to turn my face against the life he led. He also knew that my sister's new husband was more fitted for ventures than I.

So, while my father secured the family name and fortune, I—my mother being dead and one sister usefully married— was in Padua to acquire the smatterings of polite knowledge; he was content to have his son a member of our nobility but did not wish to have me as ignorant as they. At this point and of mature years—I was now rising thirty—I was suddenly struck by a burning enthusiasm to become a citizen of the Republic of Learning, as it is called. This sudden passion

I can no longer recall, so completely has it left me, but then the fascination of the new experimental philosophy held me under its spell. It was, of course, a matter of the spirit rather than of practical application. I say with Beroaldus, *non sum medicus, nec medicinae prorsus expers,* in the theory of physick I have taken some pains, not with an intent to practice, but to satisfy myself. I had neither desire nor need to gain a living in such a fashion, although occasionally, I confess with shame, I taunted my poor good father by saying that unless he was kind to me, I would take my revenge by becoming a physician.

I imagine that he knew all along I would do no such thing, and that in reality I was merely captivated by ideas and people which were as exciting as they were dangerous. As a result, he raised no objections when I wrote to him about the reports of one professor who, though nominally charged with lecturing in rhetoric, spent much of his time enlarging upon the latest developments in natural philosophy. This man had traveled widely and maintained that, for all serious students of natural phenomena, the Low Countries and England were no longer to be disdained. After many months in his care, I caught his enthusiasm and, having little to detain me in Padua, requested permission to tour that part of the world. Kind man that he was, my father immediately gave his assent, procured permission for me to leave Venetian territory, and sent a bill of credit to his bankers in Flanders for my use.

I had thought of taking advantage of my position to go by sea, but decided that, if I was to acquire knowledge, then it would be best to see as much as possible and this was better done in a coach than by spending three weeks in a ship drinking with the crew. I must add that I also suffer abominably from seasickness—which weakness I have always been loath to admit, for although Gomesius says such sickness cures sadness of spirit, I have never found it to be the case. Even so, my courage weakened, then evaporated almost entirely, as the journey progressed. The journey to Leiden took only nine weeks, but the sufferings I endured quite took my mind off the sights I was viewing. Once, stuck in the mud halfway through an Alpine pass, the rain coming down in torrents, one horse sick, myself with a fever and a violent-looking soldier as my only companion, I thought that I would rather suffer the worst gale in the Atlantic than such misery.

But it would have been as long to go back as to continue, and I was mindful of the scorn in which I would be held if I returned, shamefaced and weak, to my native town. Shame, I do believe, is the most powerful emotion known to man; most discoveries and journeys of importance have been accomplished because of the ignominy that would be the result if the attempt was abandoned. So, sick for the warmth and comfort of my native land—the English have the word *nostalgia* for this illness, which they believe is due to the imbalance caused by an unfamiliar environment—I continued on my way, ill-tempered and miserable, until I reached Leiden, where I attended the school of medicine as a gentleman.

So much has been written about this seat of learning, and it has so little to do with my recital, that it suffices to say that I found and profited greatly from two professors of singular ability who lectured on anatomy and bodily economy. I also traveled throughout the Low Countries and fell into good company, much of which was English and from whom I learnt something of the language. I left for the simple reason that my kind good father ordered me so to do and for no other reason. There was some disarray in the London office, a letter told me, and he needed family to intervene: no one else could be trusted. Although I had little practical knowledge of trade, I was glad to be the obedient son, and so discharged my servant, organized my affairs and shipped from Antwerp to investigate. I arrived in London on March 22nd, 1663, with only a few pounds left, the sum I paid to one professor for his teaching having all but exhausted my funds. But I was not concerned, for I thought that all I needed to do was make the short journey from the river to the office maintained by my father's agent, and all would be well. Fool that I was. I could not find di Pietro, and that wretched man John Manston would not even receive me. He is now long since dead; I pray for his soul, and hope the good Lord disregards my entreaties on his behalf, knowing as I do that the longer he suffers fiery torment, the more just his punishment will be.

I had to beg a mere servant for information, and this lad told me that my father's agent had died suddenly some weeks previously. Even worse, Manston had swiftly moved to take all the fortune and business for his own, and refused to admit that any had belonged to my father. Before lawyers he had produced documents (naturally, forged) to prove this assertion. He had, in other words, entirely defrauded my family of our money—that part of it which was in England, at least.

This boy was, unfortunately, at a loss about how I should proceed. I could lay a complaint before a magistrate, but with no evidence except my own convictions this seemed fruitless. I could also consult a lawyer but, if England and Venice differ in many ways, they are alike in one, which is that lawyers have an insatiable love of money, and that was a commodity I did not possess in sufficient quantity.

It also rapidly became clear that London was not a healthy place. I do not mean the famous plague, which had not yet afflicted the city; I mean that Manston, that very evening, sent round hired hands to demonstrate that my life would be more secure elsewhere. Fortunately, they did not kill me; indeed, I acquitted myself well in the brawl thanks to the fees my father had paid to my fencing master, and I believe at least one bravo left the field in a worse state than I. But I took the warning nonetheless and decided to stay out of the way until my course was clearer. I will mention little more of this matter except to say that eventually I abandoned the quest for recompense, and my father decided that the costs involved were not worth the money lost. The matter was reluctantly forgotten for two years, when we heard that one of Manston's boats had put into Trieste to sit out a storm. My family moved to have it seized—Venetian justice being as favorable to Venetians as English law is to Englishmen— and the hull and cargo provided some compensation for our losses.

To have had my father's permission to leave instantly would have raised my spirits immeasurably, for the weather in London was enough to reduce the strongest man to the most wretched despair. The fog, the incessant, debilitating drizzle, and the dull bitter cold as the wind swept through my thin cloak reduced me to the lowest state of despondency.

Only duty to my family forced me to continue rather than going to the docks and begging for a passage back home. Instead of taking this sensible course, however, I wrote to my father informing him of developments and promising to do what I could, but pointed out that until I was rearmed from his coffers there was little I might practically accomplish. I had, I realized, many weeks to fill in before he could respond. And about five pounds to survive on.

The professor under whom I had studied in Leiden had most kindly given me letters to gentlemen with whom he had corresponded, and, these being my only contacts with Englishmen, I decided that my best course would be to throw myself on their mercy. An additional attraction was that neither was in London, so I picked the man who lived in Oxford, that being the closest, and decided to leave as swiftly as possible.

The English seem to have strong suspicion of people moving around, and go out of their way to make travel as difficult as possible. According to the piece of paper pasted up where I waited for the coach, the sixty-mile trip to Oxford would take eighteen hours—God Willing, as it added piously. The Almighty, alas, was not willing that day; rain had made much of the road disappear, so the coachman had to navigate his way through what seemed very like a plowed field. A wheel came off a few hours later, tipping my chest on the ground and damaging the lid and, just outside a mean little town called Thame, one of the horses broke a leg and had to be dispatched. Add to that the frequent stops at almost every inn in southern England (the innkeepers bribe the drivers to halt) and the journey took a total of twenty-five hours, with myself ejected into the courtyard of an inn in the main street of the city of Oxford at seven o'clock in the morning.

chapter two

FROM THE WAY THE ENGLISH TALK (THEIR REPUTA-
tion for boasting is hard earned) an inexperienced traveler
would imagine that their land contains the finest buildings,
the biggest towns, the richest, best-fed, happiest people in
the world. My own impressions were very different. One
used to the cities of Lombardy, Tuscany and the Veneto cannot but be astonished at the tiny proportions of all settlements
in that country as well as their paucity, for the land is almost
empty of inhabitants and there are more sheep than people.
Only London, *epitome Britannia* and a noble emporium, can
compare with the great cities of the continent; the rest are in
mean estate, ruinous for the most part, poor and full of beg-
gars by reason of the decay in trade caused by the late political turmoils. Though some of the buildings of the
university are fine enough, Oxford has really only a few
streets worth the notice, and you can scarcely walk for more
than ten minutes in any direction without finding yourself
outside the town and in open fields.

I had the address of a small lodging in the north of the
city, on a broad street hard by the town walls, occupied by
a foreign merchant who, at one time, had traded with my
father. It was a sad sort of house and immediately opposite
a site being razed for a new university building. The English
made something of a fuss of this edifice, designed by a young
and rather arrogant man I later encountered who went on to

make a name for himself by rebuilding the cathedral of London after the great fire. This Christopher Wren's reputation is quite undeserved, as he has no sense of proportion, and little ability to construct a pleasing design. Nonetheless, it was the first building in Oxford executed on modern principles, and aroused great excitement amongst those who knew no better.

Mr. Van Leeman, the merchant, offered me a warm drink but said regretfully that he could not provide more, as he had no room for me. My heart sank still lower, but at least he talked to me awhile, sat me by the fire and permitted me to attend to my toilet so that I could present a less alarming appearance when I ventured back into the world. He also told me something of the country I had come to visit. I was woefully ignorant of the place, except for what I had been told by the English of my acquaintance in Leiden, and knew little more than that twenty years of civil war were at an end. Van Leeman disabused me of any notion that the country was now a haven of peace and tranquillity, however. The king was indeed back, he said, but had so swiftly established a reputation for debauchery he had disgusted all the world. Already the strife which had led his father to war and the executioner's block was reappearing, and the outlook was gloomy indeed. Scarce a day passed without some rumor of insurrection, plot or rebellion being talked over in the taverns.

Not, he told me reassuringly, that this should concern me. The innocent traveler such as myself would find much of interest in Oxford, which boasted some of the most notable people in the new philosophy in the world. He knew of the Honorable Robert Boyle, the man for whom I had an introduction, and told me that if I wished to make my way into his society then I should go to the coffee shop owned by Mrs. Tillyard in the High Street, where the Chemical Club had held its meetings for several years, and which, moreover, could be relied upon to provide some warming food. Whether it was a help or a hint, I prepared myself and, begging only permission to leave my bags in his care until I had suitable accommodation, walked in the direction he indicated.

At this time, coffee in England was something of a craze,

coming into the country with the return of the Jews. That bitter bean had little novelty for me, of course, for I drank it to cleanse my spleen and aid my digestion, but was not prepared to find it so much in fashion that it had produced special buildings where it could be consumed in extraordinary quantities and at the greatest expense. Mrs. Tillyard's establishment, in particular, was a fine and comfortable place, although having to hand over a penny to enter took me aback. But I felt unable to play the pauper, my father having taught me that the poorer you appear, the poorer you become. I paid with a cheerful countenance, then selected the Library to take my drink, for which I had to pay another two pennies.

The clienteles of coffee houses choose themselves carefully, unlike taverns which cater to all sorts of low folk. In London, for example, there are Anglican houses, and Presbyterian houses, houses where the scribblers of news or poetry gather to exchange lies, and houses where the general tone is set by men of knowledge who can read or pass an hour or so in conversation without being insulted by the ignorant or vomited on by the vulgar. Thus the *theorem* underlying my presence in this particular building. The *partum practicum* was rather different: the company of philosophers supposedly in residence did not leap up to welcome me, as I had hoped. In fact there were only four people in the room and, when I bowed at one of them—a weighty man with a red face, inflamed eye and lank, graying hair—he pretended not to have seen me. No one else paid much attention to my entrance either, apart from curious looks at one who was so obviously a man of some fashion.

My first venture into English society seemed a failure, and I resolved not to waste too much time on it. The one thing which detained me was the newspaper, a journal printed in London and then distributed around the country, a most novel idea. It was surprisingly frank about affairs, containing reports not only of domestic matters but also detailed accounts of events in foreign places which interested me greatly. I was later informed, however, that they were milk and water productions in comparison to a few years previously, when the passion of faction brought forth a whole host of such organs. For the king, against the king, for Parliament, for the army, for or against this or that. Cromwell, and then the returned King Charles, did their best to restore some form of order, rightly surmising that such stuff merely lulls people into thinking that they understand matters of state. And a more foolish notion can scarcely be imagined, it being obvious that the reader is only informed of what the writer wishes him to know, and is thus seduced into believing almost anything. Such liberties do nothing but convert the grubby hacksters who produce these tracts into men of influence, so that they strut around as though they were gentlemen of quality. Anyone who has ever met one of these English journalists (so called, I believe, because they are paid by the day, like any common ditch-digger) will know just how ridiculous that is.

Nonetheless I read for above half an hour, intrigued by a report on the war in Crete, until a patter of feet up the stairs and the opening of the door disturbed my concentration. A brief glance disclosed a woman of, I suppose, about nineteen or twenty years of age, of average height but unnaturally slim of build: none of the plumpness that endows true Beauty. Indeed, my medical self half-wondered whether she might have a tendency to consumption and might benefit from a pipe of tobacco every evening. Her hair was dark and had only natural curls in it, her clothes were drab (though well cared for) and, while she was pretty enough in the face, there was nothing obviously exceptional about her. Even so, she was one of those people whom you look at, turn away from, then somehow find yourself looking at once more. Partly it was her eyes, which were unnaturally big and dark. But it was more her deportment, because it was so unfitting, which made me take notice. For that underfed girl had the bearing of a queen, and moved with an elegance which my father had spent a small fortune on dancing masters trying to instill in my youngest sister.

I watched with little interest as she walked steadily up to the red-eyed gentleman on the other side of the room, and with only half an ear heard her address him as "doctor," then pause and stand there. He looked up at her with an air of alarm as she began to talk. I missed most of it—the distance, my English and her softness of voice all conspiring to snatch the meaning away—but I assumed from the few fragments I did hear that she was asking for his help as a physician. Unusual, of course, that someone of her servile state should think of coming to a physician, but I knew little of the country. Perhaps it was accepted practice here.

The request met with no favor, and this displeased me. By all means put the girl in her proper place; this is natural. Any man of breeding might well feel obliged to do so if addressed in an inappropriate manner. However, there was something in the man's expression—anger, disdain or something akin—which aroused my contempt. As Tully tells us, a gentleman should issue such a reproof with regret, not with a pleasure which demeans the speaker more than it corrects the offender.

"What?" he said, gazing around the room in a way which suggested he hoped no one would see. "Go away, girl, at once."

She again spoke in a low voice so that I did not catch her words.

"There is nothing I can do for your mother. You know that. Now, please. Leave me alone."

The girl raised her voice slightly. "But sir, you must help. Don't think I am asking . . ." Then, seeing he was adamant, the girl's shoulders slumped with the weight of her failure, and she made for the door.

Why I got up, followed her down the stairs and approached her on the street outside, I do not know. Perhaps, like Rinaldo or Tancred, I entertained some foolish notion of chivalry. Perhaps, because the world had been bearing so oppressively on me in the past few days, I had sympathy for the way it was treating her. Perhaps I was feeling cold and tired, and so sunk down by my troubles that even approaching such as she became acceptable. I do not know; but before she had gone too far, I approached her and coughed politely.

She swung round, fury in her face. "Leave me alone," she snapped, very violently.

I must have reacted as though she had slapped me; I know I bit my lower lip and said, "Oh!" in surprise at her response. "I do beg your pardon, madam," I added in my best English.

At home, I would have behaved differently: courteously,

but with the familiarity that establishes who is the superior. In English, of course, such subtleties were beyond me; all I knew was how to address ladies of quality, and so that was the way I talked to her. Rather than appear a semi-educated fool (the English assume that the only reasons for not understanding their language are either stupidity or willful stubbornness) I decided that I had best match my gestures to my language, as though I actually intended such *politesse*. Accordingly, I gave the appropriate bow as I spoke.

It was not my intention, but it rather took the wind out of her sails, to use a nautical expression beloved of my dear father. Her anger faded on finding itself met with gentility rather than rebuke, and she looked at me curiously instead, a little wrinkle of confusion playing most attractively over the bridge of her nose.

Having started in this vein, I resolved to continue. "You must forgive me for approaching you in this fashion, but I could not help overhearing that you have need of physick. Is that correct?"

"You are a doctor?"

I bowed. "Marco da Cola of Venice." It was a lie, of course, but I was sure I was at least as able as the sort of charlatan or quack she would normally have engaged. "And you?"

"Sarah Blundy is my name. I suppose you are too grand to treat an old woman with a broken leg, for fear of lowering yourself in the eyes of your fellows?"

She was, indeed, a difficult person to help. "A surgeon would be better and more appropriate," I agreed. "However, I have trained in the anatomical arts at the universities of Padua and Leiden, and I have no fellows here, so they are unlikely to think any the worse of me for playing the tradesman."

She looked at me, then shook her head. "I'm afraid that you must have overheard wrongly, although I thank you for your offer. I cannot pay you anything, as I have no money."

I waved my hand airily and—for the second time that day—indicated that money was of no concern to me. "I offer my services, nonetheless," I continued. "We can discuss that payment at a later stage, if you wish."

"No doubt," she said in a way which again left me perplexed. Then she looked at me in the open and frank way which the English can adopt, and shrugged.

"Perhaps we could go and see the patient?" I suggested. "And you could tell me what happened to her as we go?"

I was as keen as young men are to engage the attention of a pretty girl, whatever her station, but I won little reward for my efforts. Although she was not nearly as well dressed as I, her limbs showing through the thin cloth of her dress, her head only as covered as decorum dictated, she seemed not at all cold, and scarcely appeared even to notice the wind which cut through me like a knife through butter. She walked fast as well, and even though she was a good two inches shorter than myself, I had to hurry to keep up. And her replies were brief and monosyllabic, which I put down to concern and preoccupation with her mother's health.

We walked back to Mr. Van Leeman's to collect my instruments and I also hastily consulted Barbette on surgery, not wishing to have to refer to a book of instruction in midoperation, as this does not reassure the patient. The girl's mother had, it appeared, fallen heavily the previous evening and had lain alone all night. I asked why she had not called out to some neighbors or passersby, as I assumed that the poor woman would scarcely have been living in splendid seclusion, but this received no useful response.

"Who was that man you were talking to?" I asked.

I got no answer to that either.

So, adopting a coldness that I thought appropriate, I walked by her side down a mean street called Butcher's Row, past the stinking carcasses of animals hung on hooks or laid out over rough tables outside so that the rain could wash the blood into the gutters, then continued into an even worse row of low dwellings that lay alongside one of the rivulets that run around and about the castle. It was utterly filthy down there, the streams clogged and unkempt, with all manner of refuse poking through the thick ice. In Venice, of course, we have the flow of the sea which every day purges the city's waterways. The rivers in England are left to block themselves up, without anyone thinking that a little care might sweeten the waters.

Of the miserable huts down in that part of the town, Sarah Blundy and her mother lived in one of the worst: small, with the casements boarded with planks of wood rather than paned with glass, the roof full of holes blocked with cloth, and the doorway thin and mean. Inside, however, everything was spotlessly clean, though damp; a sign that even in such reduced circumstances, some pride in life can continue to flicker. The little hearth and the floorboards were scrubbed, the two rickety stools were similarly looked after, and the bed, although rough, had been polished. Apart from that, the room had no furniture beyond those few pots and platters which even the lowest must have. One thing did astonish me: a shelf of at least half-a-dozen books made me realize that, at some stage at least, some man had inhabited these quarters.

"Well," I said in the cheerful way my master in Padua had employed as a means of inspiring confidence, "where is the invalid, then?"

She pointed to the bed which I had thought empty. Huddled under the thin covering was a little broken bird of a woman, so small it was difficult to imagine she was anything but a child. I approached and gently pulled down the covers.

"Good morning, madam," I said. "I'm told you've had an accident. Let us have a look at you, then."

Even I realized instantly that it was a serious injury. The end of the shattered bone had pushed through the parchment-like skin and protruded, broken and bloody, into the open air. And if that wasn't bad enough, some bungling fool had evidently tried to force it back into place, tearing more flesh, then simply wrapped a piece of dirty cloth around the wound, so that the threads had stuck to the bone as the blood had matted and congealed.

"Holy Mary, Mother of God," I cried in exasperation, fortunately in Italian. "What idiot has done this?"

"She did it herself," the girl said quietly when I repeated this last in English. "She was all on her own, and did what she could."

It looked very bad indeed. Even with a robust young man, the inevitable weakness from such a wound would have been serious. Then there was the possibility of rot setting in and the chance that some of the threads would create an irritation in the flesh. I shivered at the thought, then realized that the room was bitterly cold.

"Go and light a fire immediately. She must be kept warm," I said.

She stood there, unmoving.

"Can't you hear me? Do as I say."

"We don't have anything to burn," she said.

What could I do? It was hardly fitting or dignified, but sometimes the task of the physician goes beyond merely tending to physical ailment. With some impatience, I pulled a few pence from my pocket. "Go and buy some wood, then," I said.

She looked at the pennies I had thrust into her palm, and, without so much as a word of thanks, silently went out of the room into the alleyway beyond.

"Now then, madam," I said, turning back to the old lady, "we will soon have you nice and warm. That is most important. First we have to clean this leg of yours."

And so I set to work; fortunately the girl came back quickly with wood and some embers to light a fire, so that I soon had hot water. I thought that if I could clean it up fast enough, if I could reset the broken bone without causing her so much discomfort that she died, if she didn't develop a fever or some distemper in the wound, if she was kept warm and well fed, she might live. But there were many dangers; any one of them could kill her.

Once I began she seemed alert enough, which was a good start, although considering the pain I was giving her, a corpse would have become aware of its surroundings. She told me that she had slipped on a patch of ice and fallen badly, but apart from that she was initially as uncommunicative as her daughter, although with more excuse.

Perhaps the more thoughtful, and those who were more proud, might have walked away the moment that the girl confessed she had no money; perhaps I could have left when it became clear there was no heating; certainly I should have refused outright even to have contemplated the provision of any sort of medicines to the woman. It is not for oneself, of course; there is the reputation of the profession to be considered in these matters. But in all conscience, I could not bring myself to act as I should have done. Sometimes being a Gentleman and Physician do not always coexist easily.

Also, although I had studied the proper way of cleansing wounds and setting bones, I had never had the opportunity to do so in practice. It was very much more difficult than the lectures had made it seem and I fear that I caused the old lady considerable suffering. But eventually the bone was set and the leg bound, and I dispatched the girl with more of my scarce pennies to buy materials for a salve. While she was gone, I cut some lengths of wood and bound them to the leg to try and ensure that, were she lucky enough to survive, the shattered bone would knit correctly.

By this stage I was in no good humor. What was I doing here, in this provincial, unfriendly, miserable little town, surrounded by strangers, such a long way away from everything I knew and everyone who cared for me? More to the point, what was going to happen when, as was bound to occur very shortly, I found myself without money to pay for lodging or food?

Bound up in my own despair, I completely ignored my patient, feeling I had done more than enough for her already, and found myself examining the little shelf of books; not out of interest, but merely as a way of turning my back on her so that I could avoid looking at the poor creature who was rapidly becoming the symbol of my misfortunes. This sentiment was compounded by the fact that I feared that all my efforts and expense were going to prove a waste: even though I was young and inexperienced, I already knew death when I stared it in the face, smelt its breath and touched the sweat it produced on the skin.

"You are unhappy, sir," the old lady said in a frail voice from her bed. "I'm afraid that I am a great trouble to you."

"No, no. Not at all," I said with the flatness of deliberate insincerity.

"It is kind of you to say so. But we both know that we cannot pay you money for your help, as you deserve. And I saw from the look in your face that you are not a rich man yourself at the moment, despite your dress. Where do you come from? You are not from around here."

Within a few minutes, I found myself perched on one of

the rickety stools by the bedstead, pouring out my heart about my father, my lack of money, my reception in London, my hopes and fears for the future. There was something about her that encouraged such confidences, almost as though I were talking to my old mother, not to some poor, dying, heretical Englishwoman.

Throughout she nodded patiently and spoke to me with such wisdom that I felt comforted. It pleased God to send us trials, just as He did with Job. Our duty is to bear them quietly, use the skills He has given us to overcome them, and never to abandon our faith that His design was good and necessary. More practically, she told me I must certainly visit Mr. Boyle; he was known as a good Christian gentleman.

I suppose I should have scorned this combination of puritanical piety and impertinent advice. But I could see that, in her way, she was trying to make amends. She could offer no money, and no service. What she could give was understanding, and in the coin that she had, she paid freely.

"I shall soon be dead, shall I not?" she asked after she had listened to my woes for a good long while and I had exhausted the topic of my hardship.

My master in Padua had always warned about such questions: not least because one might be wrong. He always believed that the patient has no right to confront the physician in such a way; if one is right and the patient does die, it merely makes them morose for the last few days of their life. Rather than composing themselves for their imminent ascent into the Presence of God (an event to be desired rather than regretted, one might think) most people complain bitterly at having this divine goodness thrust upon them. On top of this, they do tend to believe their physicians. In moments of frankness, I confess that I do not know why this is the case; nonetheless, it seems that if a physician tells them they will die, many dutifully oblige, even though there may be little wrong with them.

"We will all die in due course, madam," I said gravely, in the vain hope that this might satisfy her.

However, she was not the sort of person who could be fobbed off. She had asked the question calmly and was plainly able to tell truth from the opposite.

"But some sooner than others," she replied with a little smile. "And my turn is near, is it not?"

"I really cannot say. It may be that no corruption will set in, and you will recover. But, in truth, I fear that you are very weak." I could not actually say to her: Yes, you will die, and very soon. But the sense was clear enough.

She nodded placidly. "I thought so," she said. "And I rejoice in God's will. I am a burden to my Sarah."

Come l'oro nel foco, così la fede nel dolor s'affina. I hardly felt like defending the daughter, but muttered that I was sure she performed her obligations with a happy heart.

"Yes," she said. "She is too dutiful." She was a woman who spoke with a decorum far beyond her station and education. I know that it is not impossible for rude surroundings and coarseness of upbringing to bring forth gentleness, but experience teaches us that it is rare. Just as refinement of thought naturally requires refinement of circumstance, so brutality and squalor in life beget the same in the soul. Yet this old woman, although surrounded by the meanest of states, talked with a sympathy and understanding I have often failed to meet with in the very best of people. It made me take an unwonted interest in her as a patient. Subtly, and without even becoming aware of it, I moved from seeing her as a hopeless case: I may not be able to cheat Death, I found myself thinking grimly, but at least I will make him work for his prize.

Then the girl returned with the little packet of medicines that I had demanded. Staring at me, as though challenging me to criticize, she said that I had not given her enough: but Mr. Crosse the apothecary had allowed her to have two pence credit, when she had promised I would settle the account. I was speechless with indignation at this, because the girl seemed to be rebuking me for some failure on my part. But what could I do about it? The money was spent, the patient was waiting, and it was beneath me to enter an argument.

Maintaining an outward show of imperturbability, I took my portable pestle and mortar and began to grind up the ingredients; some mastick for sticking, a grain of sal ammoniack, two of frankincense, a dram of white vitriol and two grains of niter and verdigris both. Once these were pounded into a smooth paste, I then added the linseed oil, drop by drop, until the mixture had reached the right degree.

"Where is the powder of worms?" I asked, searching in the bag for the final ingredients. "Did they not have any?"

"Yes," she said. "At least I imagine so. But it is no use, you know, so I decided not to buy it. It saved some money for you."

This was too much. To be treated with insolence was one thing and quite common with daughters, but to be questioned and doubted in one's area of skill was quite another.

"I told you I needed it. It is a crucial ingredient. Are you a physician, girl? Have you trained at the best schools in medicine? Do physicians come to you asking for advice?" I asked with a superior sneer in my voice.

"Yes, they do," she replied calmly.

I snorted. "I don't know whether it is worse to be dealing with a fool or a liar," I said angrily.

"Nor do I. All I know is that I am neither. Putting worm powder on a wound is tantamount to making sure my mother loses her leg and dies."

"Are you Galen then? Paracelsus? Perhaps Hippocrates himself?" I stormed. "How dare you question the authority of your betters? This is a salve that has been in use for centuries."

"Even though it is useless?"

While this was going on I had been applying the salve to her mother's wound, then rebandaging it. I was doubtful about whether it would work, incomplete as it was, but would have to do until I could make it up properly. Once finished, I stood up to my full height, and, of course, bumped my head against the low ceiling. The girl suppressed a giggle, which made me the more angry.

"Let me tell you one thing," I said with barely suppressed fury. "I have treated your mother to the best of my ability, even though I was not obliged to. I will come back later to give her a sleeping draft and to air the wound. This I do knowing that I will receive nothing in return but your contempt, although I cannot see that I have deserved it or that you have any right to speak to me in such a fashion."

She curtseyed. "Thank you, kind sir. And as for payment,

chapter three

I HOPE THAT THIS ACCOUNT EXPLAINS THE FIRST
two stages of my progress: my coming to England and then
to Oxford, and my acquisition of the patient whose treatment
was to cause me such grief. The girl herself—what can I
say? She was touched by doom; her end was written, and the
devil was already reaching out his hand to drag her down.
The man of skill can see this, can read a face like an open
book and discern what the future holds in store. Sarah
Blundy's face was deep scored already with the evil that had
gripped her soul and would shortly destroy her. So I told
myself after, and it may be true. But at that time I saw nothing more than a girl as insolent as she was pretty, and as
careless of her obligations to her superiors as she was mindful of her duty to her family.

I need now to explain my further progress, which was just
as accidental although ultimately more cruel in its effects:
the more so because it seemed, for a while, as though fortune
had begun to smile on me once more. I had been left with
the task of paying off the debts she had so impertinently run
up for me at the apothecary's, and I knew that you annoy
apothecaries at your peril if you are concerned with experimental knowledge. Omit to pay, and they are quite likely to
refuse you in the future, and not only them but all their fellows for miles around, so closely do they stick together. In
the circumstances, that would be the final straw. Even if it

was my last penny I could not afford to enter the society of English philosophy as a man of bad credit.

So I asked the way to this Mr. Crosse's shop, and walked halfway along the High Street once more, opening the wooden door in the shop front and going into the warmth of the interior. It was a handsome place, nicely laid out as all English shops are, with fine cedarwood counters and beautiful brass balances of the most up-to-date variety. Even the aromas of the herbs and spices and drugs welcomed me as I moved strategically across the polished oak floor until I stood with my back against the fine carved mantelpiece and the roaring fire in the grate.

The owner, a portly man in his fifties who looked decidedly at ease with life, was dealing with a customer who seemed in no hurry, leaning nonchalantly on the table, chattering quite idly. The customer was perhaps a year or two older than myself, with a lively, active face and bright, if cynical, eyes below heavy, arching brows. In dress he was in a somber garb that steered between the extremes of puritanical drabness and the extravagance of fashion. It was, in other words, well cut but of a tedious brown.

For all that he had an easy manner, this customer seemed very self-conscious, and I discerned that Mr. Crosse was amusing himself at the man's expense.

"Keep you warm in winter, as well," the apothecary was saying with a broad grin.

The customer wrinkled up his face in pain.

"'Course, when spring comes you'll have to put netting over, in case the birds start nesting in it," he went on, clutching his sides in merriment.

"Come now, Crosse, that's enough," protested the man, then began laughing himself. "Twelve marks it cost . . ."

This sent Crosse into greater paroxysms of laughter, and soon both of them were leaning over, helpless and in virtual hysteria.

"Twelve marks!" wheezed the apothecary, before collapsing once more.

I even found myself beginning to giggle with amusement, even though I had not the slightest idea what they were talking about. I didn't even know whether it was considered ill

manners in England to interpose oneself into the merriment
of others, but the fact was that I didn't care. The warmth of
the shop and the open good humor of these two, as they
clung to the counter to avoid slipping onto the floor in their
helplessness, made me want to laugh with them, to celebrate
the first normal human society I had experienced since my
arrival. Instantly I felt restored by it for, as Gomesius says,
merriment cures many passions of the mind.

My slight giggling attracted their attention, however, and
Mr. Crosse attempted to restore himself to the dignified posture that his trade required. His comrade did likewise and
both turned to look at me; a somber silence reigned for a
few seconds, then the younger man pointed at me, and both
of them lost control once more.

"Twenty marks!" cried the young man, waving in my
direction, then banging his fist on the counter. "At least
twenty."

I counted this as being the nearest thing to an introduction
that I was likely to receive and, with some wariness, made
a polite bow in their direction. I half-suspected some appalling joke at my expense. The English love making fun of
foreigners, whose mere existence they regard as an enormous
jest.

My bow to equals—perfectly executed, with just the right
balance between the extended left leg, and the graciously
elevated right arm—nonetheless set them off again, so I
stood with the impassivity of a stoic as I waited for the storm
to pass. And in due course, the gurglings faded, they wiped
their eyes, blew their noses and did their best to appear like
civilized people.

"I must beg your pardon, sir," said Mr. Crosse, who was
the first to regain the power of speech and the grace to use
it civilly. "But my friend here has just decided to become a
man of fashion, and has taken to appearing in public with a
thatched roof on his head. I was doing my best to assure him
that he cuts a very fine figure indeed." He began heaving
with mirth again, and his friend then tore off his wig and
threw it on the ground.

"Fresh air at last," he exclaimed thankfully as he ran his

fingers through his thick, long hair. "Dear Lord, it was hot under there."

At last I was beginning to make sense of it; the wig had arrived in Oxford—several years after it had established itself throughout most of the world as an essential part of elegant masculine dress. I was wearing one myself, having adopted it as a sign, so to speak, of my graduation into the adult world.

I could see, of course, why it caused such amusement, although the understanding was overborne by that sense of superiority felt by a man of parts when he encounters the provincial. When I began wearing my wig myself it took some considerable time to grow used to it; only pressure from my fellows persuaded me to continue. And, of course, looking at it as a Turk or an Indian might were he suddenly transported to our shores, it did seem slightly odd that a man, graced by nature with a full head of hair, should shave much of it off in order to wear somebody else's. But fashionable attire is not for comfort and, as it was profoundly uncomfortable, we may conclude that the wig was very fashionable.

"I think," I said, "that you might find it more comfortable if you shortened your own hair; then there would not be so much pressure under the mat."

"Shorten my own hair? Good heavens, is that how it's done?"

"I'm afraid so. We must sacrifice for beauty, you know."

He kicked the wig roughly across the floor. "Then let me be ugly," he said. "For I will not be seen in public wearing this. If it produces convulsions in Crosse here, think what the students of this town will do to me. I'll be lucky to escape with my life."

"They are the very height of fashion elsewhere," I commented. "Even the Dutch wear them. I think it is a question of timing. In a few months, or maybe a year, you may find that they hoot and throw stones at you if you do not wear one."

"Bah! Ridiculous," he said, but nonetheless scooped the wig up off the floor and placed it more safely on the counter.

"I'm sure this gentleman has not come here to discuss

fashion,'' Crosse said. ''Perhaps he even wishes to buy something? It has been known.''

I bowed. ''No. I have come to pay for something. I believe you extended credit to a young girl not so long ago.''

''Oh, the Blundy girl. You are the man she mentioned?''

I nodded. ''It seems that she spent my money a little freely. I have come to settle her—or rather my—debt.''

Crosse grunted. ''You won't be paid, you know, not in money.''

''So it appears. But it is too late for that now. Besides, I set her mother's leg, and it was interesting to see whether I could do so; I'd learned a great deal about it in Leiden, but never tried it on a living patient.''

''Leiden?'' said the younger man with sudden interest. ''Do you know Sylvius?''

''Indeed,'' I replied. ''I studied anatomy with him; and I have a letter from him with me for a gentleman called Mr. Boyle.''

''Why didn't you say so?'' he asked, and walked to the door at the back of the shop and opened it. I could see a flight of stairs in the corridor beyond.

''Boyle?'' he yelled. ''Are you up there?''

''No need to shout, you know,'' Crosse said. ''I can tell you. He isn't. He went to the coffee house.''

''Oh. No matter. We can go and find him. What's your name, by the way?''

I introduced myself. He bowed in return, and said: ''Richard Lower, at your service. A physician. Almost.''

We bowed once more and, that done with, he clapped me on the shoulders. ''Come along. Boyle will like to meet you. We've been feeling a little cut off up here recently.''

As we walked the short distance back to Tillyard's, he explained that the ferment of intellectual life in the town had ceased to bubble as it had in the past, due to the return of the king.

''But I heard His Majesty is a lover of learning,'' I said.

''So he is, when he can tear his attention away from his mistresses. That's the trouble. Under Cromwell, we eked out our existence here, while all the lucrative places in the state went to butchers and fish sellers. Now the king is back and naturally, all those well-placed enough to take advantage of his generosity have gone to London, leaving a rump of us up here. I'm afraid I shall have to try to make a name for myself there as well, sooner or later.''

"Hence the wig?"

He grimaced. "Yes, I suppose so. One must cut a dash in London to be noticed at all. Wren was back here a few weeks ago—he's a friend of mine, a fine fellow—decked out like a peacock. He's planning a trip to France soon and we'll probably have to shade our eyes just to look at him when he gets back.''

"And Mr. Boyle?" I asked, my heart sinking a little. "He has—ah, decided—to stay in Oxford?"

"Yes, for the time being. But he's lucky. He's got so much money he doesn't have to fish for positions like the rest of us.''

"Oh," I said, greatly relieved.

Lower gave me a look which indicated that he understood perfectly what had been going through my mind. "His father was one of the richest men in the kingdom and a fervent supporter of the old king, bless his memory, as I suppose we should. Naturally, a lot of it was dispersed, but there's enough left for Boyle not to have the concerns of ordinary mortals.''

"Ah."

"A fine person to know, if you are inclined to philosophical knowledge, which is his main interest. If you're not, of course, he won't pay much attention to you.''

"I have done my best," I said modestly, "with some experimentation. But I'm afraid that I am only a novice. What I do not know or understand greatly outweighs what I do.''

The answer seemed to please him mightily. "In that case you will be in good company," he said with a grin. "Add us all together and our ignorance is almost complete. Still, we scratch at the surface. Here we are," he went on, as he led the way back into the very same coffee house. Mrs. Tillyard again approached, wanting another copper off me, but Lower waved her away. "Fiddlesticks, madam," he said cheerfully. "You will not charge a friend of mine for entry into this bawdy house.''

Loudly demanding that coffee be brought to us instantly, Lower bounded up the stairs to the room I had previously selected. It was then that I had the horrible thought: What if this Boyle were the unpleasant gentleman who had turned away the girl?

But the man sitting in the corner whom Lower immediately approached could not have been more different. I suppose I should here pause and describe the Honorable Robert Boyle, a man who has had more praise and honor heaped upon him than any philosopher for centuries. The first thing I noticed was his relative youth; his reputation had led me to expect a man certainly over fifty. In fact, he was probably no more than a few years older than myself. Tall, gaunt and obviously with a weak constitution, he had a pale, thin face with a strangely sensual mouth, and sat with a poise and a degree of ease that instantly indicated his noble upbringing. He did not appear so very agreeable; haughty rather, as though he was fully aware of his superiority and expected others to be as well. This, I later learned, was only part of the story, for his pride was matched by his generosity; his haughtiness by his humility; his rank by his piety; and his severity by his charity.

Nonetheless, he was a person to be approached with care for, while Boyle tolerated some truly dreadful creatures because of their merit, he would not put up with charlatans or fools. I count it as one of the greatest honors of my life that I was allowed, for a while, to associate with him on terms of ease. Losing this connection through the malice of others was one of the bitterest blows I have had to endure.

For all his wealth, reputation and birth, he tolerated familiarity from his intimates, of whom Lower, evidently, was one. "Mr. Boyle," he said as we approached. "Someone from Italy to pay homage at your shrine."

Boyle looked up with raised eyebrows then permitted himself a brief smile. "Good morning, Lower," he said dryly. I noticed then and later that Lower constantly misstepped himself in his dealings with Boyle, as he considered himself an equal in matters of science, but was all too conscious of his own inferiority in rank, and so moved from an excessive familiarity to a respect which, although not obsequious, was still far from assured and comfortable.

"I bring you greetings from Dr. Sylvius of Leiden, sir," I said, "He suggested that, as I was to come to England, you might permit me to make your acquaintance."

I always feel that introductions are one of the most difficult of areas of etiquette. Naturally, they exist, and will always continue. How else could a total stranger be accepted except under the patronage of a gentleman who can vouch for his character? In most circles, however, the mere existence of a letter is enough; if they are read, it is generally after the introductions have been performed. I hoped that a letter from Sylvius, a physician as famous in medicine as was Boyle in chemistry, would ensure me a welcome. But I was also aware that divisions ran deep, and that my religion might well cause me to be rejected. England had only recently been in the grip of fanatical sectarians, and I knew their influence was far from dissipated—my colleagues in the coach to Oxford overnight had informed me with glee of the new persecutory laws against us that the Parliament had forced the king to adopt.

Boyle not only took the letter and began to read it, but also commented on its contents as he progressed, making me ever more nervous as he did so. It was, I saw, rather a long missive; Sylvius and I had not always seen eye to eye, and I greatly feared that much of the letter would be uncomplimentary.

And so it seemed as Boyle read. "Hmm," he said. "Listen to this, Lower. Sylvius says your friend here is impetuous, argumentative and much given to querying authority. Impertinent, and a positive gadfly in his interests."

I made to defend myself, but Lower gestured for me to be quiet. "Family of gentlemen merchants in Venice, eh?" Boyle went on. "Papist, I suppose?"

My heart sank.

"A veritable fiend for blood," Boyle went on, ignoring me totally. "Constantly fiddling with buckets of it. But a good man with a knife, it seems, and a fine draftsman. Hmm."

I resented Sylvius for his statements. To call my experimentation fiddling made me hot with indignation. I had begun methodically and proceeded in what I thought was a rational manner. It was, after all, hardly my fault that my father's summons made me leave Leiden before I had come to any conclusions of substance.

Since it is of some moment to my story, I should make it clear that my interest in blood was no newfound fancy, but by this stage had preoccupied me for some time. I can scarcely recall when the fascination began. I remember once listening to some tedious Galenist lecturing on blood in Padua and the very next day being lent a copy of Harvey's magnificent work on circulation. It was so clear, so simple, and so obviously *true* that it took my breath away. I have not had an experience like it since. However, even I could see that it was incomplete: Harvey demonstrated that the blood starts in the heart, circulates around the body, then returns whence it came. He did not establish *why* it does this, and without that science is a poor thing indeed; nor did he proffer any therapeutic gain from his observations. Perhaps impertinently, but certainly with reverence, I had dedicated many months in Padua and nearly all my time in Leiden to exploring this subject and I would have already achieved some notable experiments had I not obeyed my father's desires and come to England.

"Good," Boyle said eventually, folding the letter carefully and putting it in his pocket. "You are welcome, sir, more than welcome. Above all to Mr. Lower, I imagine, as his insatiable lust for entrails seems to be matched only by your own."

Lower grinned at me and offered the saucer of coffee which had been growing cold as Boyle read. It seemed that I had been put to the test and found adequate. The relief I felt was almost overwhelming.

"I must say," Boyle went on pouring quantities of sugar in his coffee, "that I am all the more pleased to welcome you because of your behavior."

"My what?" I asked.

"Your offer of assistance to the Blundy girl—remember her, Lower?—was charitable and Christian," he said. "If a little unwise."

I was astounded by this comment, so convinced had I been

that no one had paid me the slightest attention. I had entirely misjudged the degree to which the slightest breath of anything can exert fascination in such a little town.

"But who is this girl whom you both know?" I asked. "She seemed a very poor creature and hardly the type who would ordinarily come to your attention. Or have years of republicanism leveled ranks to such an extent?"

Lower laughed. "Fortunately not. People like the Blundy girl are not normally members of our society, I'm pleased to say. She's pretty enough, but I would be reluctant to be known to consort with her. We know her as she has a certain notoriety—her father Ned was a great subversive and radical, while she supposedly has some knowledge of natural remedies. Boyle here consulted her over some herbal simples. It is a pet project of his, to provide the poor with medicines fitting their rank."

"Why supposedly?"

"Many have attested to her skill in curing, so Boyle thought he would do her the honor of incorporating some of her better recipes into his work. But she refused to help, and pretended she had no ability at all. I imagine she wanted payment, which Boyle properly refused to countenance for a work of benevolence."

At least that explained the girl's comment which I had dismissed as a lie. "Why is it unwise to associate with her, though?"

"Her society will do you little credit," Boyle said. "She has a reputation for lewdness. But I particularly meant that she will not prove a lucrative client."

"I have discovered that already," I replied, and told him of the way she had spent my money.

Boyle looked mildly shocked by the tale. "Not the way to grow rich," he observed dryly.

"What is the supply of physicians here? Do you think I could gain some clients?"

Lower grimaced and explained that the trouble with Oxford was that there were far too many doctors already. Which was why, when he had finished a project he was undertaking, and Christ Church ejected him from his place, he would be forced to go to London. "There are at least six," he said.

"And any number of quacks, surgeons and apothecaries. All for a town of ten thousand inhabitants. And you would be at some risk if you did not obtain a university license to practice. Did you qualify at Padua?"

I told him that I had not, having no plans to practice even had my father not considered it demeaning to take a degree. Only necessity made me think of earning money by medicine now. I suppose I phrased it wrongly, for while Boyle understood my predicament, Lower took my innocent remark to indicate a disdain for his own calling.

"I'm sure sinking so low will not taint you permanently," he said stiffly.

"On the contrary," I said swiftly, to repair the accidental slight. "The opportunity is more than welcome, and quite makes up for the unfortunate circumstances in which I find myself. And if I have the opportunity to associate myself with gentlemen such as yourself and Mr. Boyle, I will be more than fortunate."

He was soothed by this remark, and gradually resumed his earlier nonchalance; nonetheless, I had seen briefly beneath the surface, and had a glimpse of a nature which, for all its easygoing charm, was both proud and prickly. The signs vanished as quickly as they had appeared, however, and I over-congratulated myself on my success in winning him over.

To explain myself clearly, I briefly laid out my current position, and a precise question from Boyle induced me to say that I would soon be totally out of funds. Hence my desire to minister to the sick. He grimaced and asked why, precisely, I was in England in the first place?

I told him that filial obligation demanded that I try to reestablish my father's position in law. And for that I suspected I would need a lawyer.

"And for that you need money, for which you need an income. *Absque argento omnia rara,*" Lower said. "Hmm. Mr. Boyle? Do you have any ideas, sir?"

"For the time being, I would be happy to offer you some occupation in my elaboratory," said this kind gentleman. "I feel almost ashamed to offer, as it is far below what a man of your position should do. I'm sure Lower here could find you somewhere to stay at his old lodgings and perhaps, the next time he does a circuit in the countryside, he could take you along. What do you think, Lower? You always say you're overworked.''

Lower nodded, although I detected no great enthusiasm on his part. "I should be delighted with both the help and the company. I was planning a tour in a week or so, and if Mr. Cola wished to come . . .''

Boyle nodded as though all was decided. "Excellent. Then we can tackle your London problem. I will write to a lawyer I know and see what he can recommend.''

I thanked him enthusiastically for his great kindness and generosity. It obviously pleased him, although he affected that it was a mere nothing. My gratitude was entirely genuine; from being poor, friendless and miserable, I had acquired the patronage of one of the most distinguished philosophers of Europe. It even crossed my mind that part of this was due to Sarah Blundy, whose appearance that morning, and my reaction, had swung Boyle into thinking more favorably of me than could otherwise have been the case.

chapter four

WITHIN A SHORT TIME I THUS ESTABLISHED MYSELF in good company and had a vantage point from which to await more money. Eight weeks for the mails to go, another eight to come back, if I was lucky. Add onto that a week or so for the moneys to be arranged, plus some months to sort out my business in London, and I thought I would be in England for half a year at the very least, by which time the weathers would be declining badly. Either I would have to go back home overland, or risk the miserable prospect of a winter sea voyage. Alternatively, I would have to resign myself to another northern winter, and remain until the spring.

But to begin with I was more than content with my position, except where Mrs. Bulstrode, my new landlady, was concerned. Everyone sincerely believed this worthy was an excellent cook, and it was with high hopes—and empty stomach, for I had not eaten properly for two days—that I presented myself at four sharp for what I believed was going to be a fine meal.

If the climate of England was difficult for a Venetian to become used to, then the food was impossible. If quantity were anything to judge by, then I would say that England is indeed the richest country on earth. Even the more modest sort habitually eat meat once a month at least, and the English boast that they have no need of sauces to cover up its stringy texture and unpleasant taste, as the French have to do. Simply roast it and eat it as God intended, they say, firmly believing that ingeniousness in cooking is sinful and that the Heavenly Host themselves tuck into roast beef and ale for their Sunday repast.

Unfortunately, there is frequently little else. Naturally, fresh fruit is often unavailable because of the climate, but the English do not even like preserved fruit, believing it causes the wind, which exhalations they consider a depletion of the body's vital heat. Nor is there much in the way of green vegetables, for the same reason. Rather, they eat bread or, more frequently, drink their grain as ale, of which their consumption is truly stupendous; even the most delicate of ladies cheerfully downs a quart or two of strong beer during a meal, and infants learn insobriety in the cradle. The trouble for a foreigner like myself was that the beer was strong, and it was considered unmanly (and unwomanly) not to drink it. I mention all this to explain why the meal of boiled brawn and three-quarters of a gallon of beer left me feeling not at all well.

My success in attending my patient after the meal had finished was, therefore, of considerable merit. How exactly I managed to prepare my bag and walk to the miserable cottage, I do not recall. Fortunately, the girl was not there, as I had no desire to renew my acquaintanceship with her, but as far as her mother was concerned it was far from lucky; she was badly in need of care and attention, and the girl's absence struck me as being hardly an example of the dutifulness which the old woman had mentioned.

She had slept—in fact she was still drowsy, her daughter having given her some peasant potion of her own devising which, nonetheless, seemed to have been very effective. But she was in considerable discomfort; pus and corrosive matter had suppurated through my binding and caked dry over the wound, giving off an evil smell which filled me with foreboding.

It was a long and distasteful business to remove the bandage, but it was eventually completed and I decided that I would try exposing the wound to the air, having heard the theory that tight warm binding in such cases might very well aid corruption rather than prevent it. Such a view does go against orthodox practice, I know, and the willingness to allow the vapors to swirl round might be considered rash. All I can say is that experiments conducted since by others have tended to support the technique. I was so absorbed in my task that I failed to hear the door creaking open, or the soft pad of feet as they came up behind me, so that when Sarah Blundy spoke, I jumped up with alarm.

"How is she?"

I turned round to look. Her voice was soft, and her manner more appropriate than before.

"She is not well at all," I said frankly. "Can you not attend to her more?"

"I have to work," she said. "Our position is already grave now my mother cannot earn. I asked someone to look in, but it seems they did not."

I grunted, slightly ashamed of myself for not having thought of this as a reason.

"Will she recover?"

"It is too soon to say. I am drying out the wound, then I will rebind it. I fear she is developing a fever. It may pass, but I am concerned. You must check every half hour for signs of the fever getting worse. And, strange as it may seem, you must keep her warm."

She nodded, as though she understood, although she could not.

"You see," I said kindly, "in cases of a fever, one can either reinforce or oppose. Reinforcement brings the malady to a head and purges it, leaving the patient void of the cause. Opposition counters it, and seeks to restore the natural economy of the body. So, with a fever, one can either expose the patient to ice and cold water, or one can wrap her up well. I choose the latter because of her grave weakness: a more strenuous cure could well kill her before taking effect."

She leaned over and protectively tucked her mother in, then, with a surprising gentleness, stroked the old woman's hair into place.

"I'd been planning to do that anyhow," she said.

"And now you'll have my approval for it."

"I am fortunate indeed," she said. She glanced at me, saw the suspicious look in my eye, then smiled. "Forgive me, sir. I mean no insolence. My mother told me how well and generously you acted to her, and we are both deeply grateful for your kindness. I am truly sorry I misspoke. I was frightened for her, and upset about the way I was treated in the coffee house."

I waved my hand, touched strangely by her submissive tone. "That is quite all right," I said. "But who was that man?"

"I worked for him once," she said, still not taking her eyes off her mother, "and was always dutiful and conscientious. I believe I deserved better from him."

She looked up and smiled at me, a smile of such gentleness that I felt my heart begin to melt. "But it seems that we are spurned by our friends, and saved by strangers. So thank you again, sir."

"You are more than welcome. As long as you do not expect miracles."

For a moment we balanced on the brink of a greater intimacy, that strange girl and I; but the moment passed as swiftly as it presented itself. She hesitated before speaking, and it was instantly too late. Instead, we both made an effort to reestablish the correct relations and stood up.

"I will pray for one, even if I do not deserve it," she said. "Will you come again?"

"Tomorrow, if I can. And if she worsens, come and find me at Mr. Boyle's. I will be attending him. Now, about payment," I continued, hurrying on.

I had decided, on my walk down to the cottage that, as there was not the slightest chance of being paid in any case, it would be best to accept the fact with grace. Rather than accept the inevitable, I should turn it into virtue. In other words, I had decided to waive any fee. It made me feel quite proud of myself, especially considering my own impecunious state but, as fortune had smiled on me, I thought it fair to spread my good luck a little further.

Alas, my speech died in my throat before even the end of the first sentence. She immediately looked at me, eyes blazing with contempt.

"Oh yes, your payment. How could I think you would

forget about that. We must deal with that urgently, must we not?''

''Indeed,'' I said, completely astonished by the speed and completeness of her transformation. ''I think that . . .''

But I got no farther. The girl led me through to the damp and squalid little space at the back of the house which was, evidently, where she—or some other animal, I could not tell—slept. On the damp floor was a pallet, hard sacking stuffed with straw. There were no windows at all, and the little space smelled very distinctly of sour water.

With a gesture of the most brusque contempt, she immediately lay down on the bed, and pulled up her thin skirt.

''Come then, physician,'' she jeered. ''Take your payment.''

I recoiled visibly, then blushed scarlet with rage as her meaning became clear even to someone as slow-witted as the beer had made me that evening. I became even more confused as I wondered whether my new friends thought this was my interest in the case. More particularly, I was outraged at the way my fine gesture had been trodden in the dirt.

''You disgust me,'' I said coldly as the power of speech returned. ''How dare you behave like this? I will not remain here to be insulted. Henceforth, you may cater to your mother as you wish. But kindly do not expect me to return to this house and subject myself to your presence. Good night.''

Then I turned round and boldly marched out, even managing—just—to avoid slamming the thin door as I left.

I am more than susceptible to female charms, some might even say overly so, and in my youth I was not averse to taking my pleasures wherever they might arise. But this was not one of those cases. I had treated her mother out of kindness and to have my motives and intentions so abused was intolerable. Even if such was the form of payment I had in mind, it was certainly not the girl's place to talk to me in that fashion.

Seething with fury, I marched away from her hovel—more convinced than before that the girl was as corrupt and foul as her living accommodation. To the devil with her mother, I thought. What sort of woman could she be, to have spawned such a hellish monstrosity? A scrawny little wretch,

I told myself, forgetting I had earlier thought of her as pretty. And even if she were beautiful, what of it? The devil himself can become beauty, so we are told, to corrupt mankind.

On the other hand, a little voice in the back of my mind was whispering critical words into my ear. So, it said, you will kill the mother to have your revenge on the daughter. Well done, physician; I hope you are proud. But what was I meant to do? Apologize? The good San Rocca might be capable of such charity. But he was a saint.

THOSE WHO HAVE SOME INKLING THAT MY COMMAND of the English language by this stage was adequate but by no means sophisticated are no doubt thinking that I am a fraud in recounting my conversations. I admit my English was not good enough to present complex ideas, but then I had no need to. Certainly, in conversations with such as the Blundy girl, I had to do my best in English; although their manner of speaking was usually sufficiently uncomplicated that I could manage perfectly well. With others, the conversation switched as occasion required from Latin and sometimes even French, the English of quality being renowned as linguists of considerable attainment, with a frequent ability in foreign tongues which many other peoples—above all the Germans—could do well to emulate.

Lower, for example, was perfectly at ease in Latin and managed a passable French; Boyle could, in addition, manage Greek and spoke a dainty Italian as well as having a smattering of German. Now I fear Latin is passing out of use, to the detriment of our Republic; for how will men of learning manage when they sacrifice conversation with their equals and have only the ability to talk to their ignorant countrymen?

But then I felt safe in my place, surrounded, as I thought, by gentlemen who brushed aside the prejudices of lesser men. That I was a Roman Catholic occasioned no more than the occasional barbed joke from Lower, whose love of fun sometimes overbalanced into the offensive, and not even that from the pious Boyle, who was as mindful of others' faith as he was fervent of his own. Even a Mussulman or a Hindoo would have been welcomed at his table, I sometimes think, as long as he was pious and showed an interest in experiment. Such an attitude is rare in England, and this bigotry and suspicion is the most serious flaw in a nation which has many faults. Fortunately, my associations meant that I was sheltered initially from its effects, beyond an occasional insult or stone thrown at me in the street when I began to be known.

I should say that Lower was the first man I considered my friend since my infancy, and I fear I misunderstood the English in this respect. When a Venetian calls a man his friend, he does so after long thought, as to accept such a person is all but to make him a member of the family, owed much loyalty and forbearance. We die for our friends as for our family, and value them as did Dante: *noi non potemo aver perfetta vita senza amici*—a perfect life needs friends. Such friendships are justly celebrated among the ancients, as Homer lauds the bond between Achilles and Patroclus, or Plutarch the amity of Theseus and Perithoos. But it was rare among the Jews, for in the Old Testament I find few friends, except David and Jonathan, and even here, David's obligation is not so great that he refrains from killing Jonathan's son. Like most of my station, I had had childhood companions, but put these by me when the obligations of family descended as an adult, for they are a heavy burden. The English are very different; they have friends at all stages of their lives, and maintain a distinction between the obligations of amity and those of blood. By taking Lower to my heart as I did—for I never encountered anyone so close to me in spirit or in interest—I made the mistake of assuming he did the same with me, and acknowledged the same obligations. But it was not the case. The English can lose their friends.

Then such sad knowledge was unsuspected, and I concentrated on repaying my friends for their kindness and, at the same time, advancing my knowledge through assisting Boyle in his chemical experiments, having long and fruitful conversations at all hours and times with Lower and his associates. Although he was serious of demeanor, Boyle's elaboratory positively bubbled with good humor except when work was about to take place, for he considered experiment to be the discovery of God's will, needing to be performed with reverence. When an experiment was to begin, all women were excluded for fear their irrational natures would influence the result, and an air of fervent concentration descended. My task was to take notes on experiments as they happened, to assist in setting up equipment, and to keep accounts, for he spent a fortune on his science. He used—and often broke—specially made glass bottles, and the leather tubes, pumps and lenses he required all consumed huge amounts of money. Then there was the cost of chemicals, many of which had to be brought from London or even Amsterdam. There can be few prepared to spend that much to produce so little in obviously advantageous result.

I must here declare myself as someone who does not for a moment subscribe to the general view that a willingness to perform oneself is detrimental to the dignity of experimental philosophy. There is, after all, a clear distinction between labor carried out for financial reward and that done for the improvement of mankind: to put it another way, Lower as a philosopher was fully my equal even if he fell away when he became the practicing physician. I think ridiculous the practice of certain professors of anatomy, who find it beneath them to pick up the knife themselves, but merely comment while hired hands do the cutting. Sylvius would never have dreamt of sitting on a dais reading from an authority while others cut—when he taught, the knife was in his hand, and the blood spattered his coat. Boyle also did not scruple to perform his own experiments and, on one occasion in my presence, even showed himself willing to anatomize a rat with his very own hands. Nor was he less a gentleman when he had finished. Indeed, in my opinion, his stature was all the greater, for in Boyle wealth, humility and curiosity mingled, and the world is the richer for it.

''Now,'' Boyle said when Lower turned up in midafternoon and we took a break from our work, ''it is time for Cola here to earn the pittance I am paying him.''

This alarmed me, as I had been laboring hard for at least two hours and I wondered whether perhaps I was doing something wrong, or Boyle had not noticed my efforts. But rather, he wanted me to sing for my supper, as the phrase goes. I was there not only to learn from him, but also to teach him, such was the marvelous humility of the man.

"Your blood, Cola," Lower said to relieve my anxiety. "Tell us about your blood. What have you been up to? What experimentations are your conclusions based on? What *are* your conclusions, in fact?"

"I'm very much afraid I am going to disappoint you," I began hesitantly when I saw they were not to be diverted. "My researches are scarcely advanced. I am mainly interested in the question of what the blood is for. We have known for thirty years that it circulates around the body; your own Harvey showed that. We know that if you drain an animal of its blood, it rapidly dies. The vital spirits in it are the means of communication between the mind and the force of mobility, permitting movement to take place . . ."

Here Lower wagged his finger. "Ah, you have fallen too much under the influence of Mr. Helmont, sir. There we will be in dispute."

"You do not accept this?"

"I do not. Not that it matters, at the moment. Please continue."

I regrouped my forces and rethought my approach. "We *believe,*" I started, "we *believe* that it moves heat from the ferment of the heart to the brain, thus providing the warmth we need to live, then vents the excess into the lungs. But is that really the case? As far as I know, no experiments have proven this. The other question is simple: Why do we breathe? We assume that it is to regulate the body heat, to draw in cool air and thus moderate the blood. Again, is that true? Although the tendency to breathe more often when we exercise indicates this, the converse is not true, for I placed a rat in a bucket of ice and stopped its nose, but it died nonetheless."

Boyle nodded, and Lower looked as though he wanted to put some questions, but as he could see I was concentrating and trying to present my case well, he obligingly refrained from interrupting.

"The other thing that has struck me is the way in which the blood changes consistency. Have you noticed, for example, that it alters color after passing through the lungs?"

"I confess I have not," Lower replied thoughtfully. "Although of course I am aware that it changes color in a jar. But we know why, surely? The heavier melancholic elements in the blood sink, making the top lighter and the bottom darker."

"Not so," I said firmly. "Cover the jar, and the color does not change. And I can find no explanation of how such a separation could occur in the lungs. But when it emerges from the lungs—at least, this is the case in cats—it is very much lighter in color than when it goes in, indicating that some darkness is withdrawn from it."

"I must cut up a cat and see for myself. A live cat, was it?"

"It was for a while. It may well be that some other noxious elements leave the blood in the lungs, are sucked out by passage through the tissue, as through a sieve, and are then exhaled. The lighter blood is purified substance. We know, after all, that the breath often smells."

"And did you weigh the two cups of blood to see if they had changed weight?" Boyle asked.

I flushed slightly, as the thought had never even occurred to me. "Clearly this would be a next step," Boyle said. "It may be, of course, a waste of time, but it might be an avenue to explore. A minor detail, though. Please continue."

Having made such an elementary omission, I felt unwilling to continue and lay out my more extreme flights of fancy. "If one concentrates on the two hypotheses," I said, "there is the problem of testing to see which is correct: does the blood shed something in the lungs, or gain something?"

"Or both," Lower added.

"Or both," I agreed. "I was thinking of an experiment, but had neither the time nor the equipment in Leiden to pursue my ideas."

"And that was . . . ?"

"Well," I began, a little nervously. "If the purpose of breathing is to expel heat and the noxious byproducts of fermentation, then the air itself is unimportant. So if we placed an animal in a vacuum . . ."

"Oh, I see," Boyle said, with a glance at Lower. "You would like to use my vacuum pump."

In fact, the idea had not occurred to me before I spoke. Curiously, Boyle's pump was of such fame I had scarcely given it a thought since I'd arrived in Oxford, as I had never dreamt of the possibility of using it myself. The machine was of such sophistication, grandeur and expense that it was known to people of curiosity throughout Europe. Now, of course, such devices are well enough known; then there were perhaps only two in the whole of Christendom, and Boyle's was the better, so ingenious in design that no one had managed to reproduce it—or the results he attained. Naturally, its use was rationed very carefully. Few were even allowed to see it in operation, let alone employ it, and it was forward of me even to bring the subject up. The last thing I wanted was a refusal; I had set myself the task of ingratiating myself into his confidence, and a rebuff now would have been hurtful.

But, all was well. Boyle thought the matter over a while and then nodded. "And how might you proceed?"

"A mouse or a rat would do," I said. "Even a bird. Put it in the bell and extract the air. If the purpose of respiration is to vent fumes, then a vacuum will provide more space for the exhalations, and the animal will live more easily. If respiration requires air to be sucked into the blood, then the vacuum might make the animal ill."

Boyle thought it over and nodded. "Yes," he said eventually. "A good idea. We can do it now, if you like. Why not, indeed? Come along. The machine is prepared, so we can start immediately."

He led the way into the next room, in which many of his finest experiments had taken place. The pump, one of the most artistic devices I had seen, stood on the table. For those who do not know it, then I suggest they consult the fine engravings in his *opera completa;* here I will merely say that it was an elaborate device of brass and leather with a handle connected to a large glass bell and a set of valves through which, propelled by a pair of bellows, the air could be made to pass in one direction, but not the other. By the use of this, Boyle had already demonstrated some marvels, including the disproval of Aristotle's *dictum* that nature abhors a vacuum. As he said in a rare moment of jest, nature may not like it, but if pushed will be made to put up with it. A vacuum—an area of space voided entirely of content—can indeed be created and possesses many strange qualities. As I examined the machine carefully, he told me how a ringing bell placed in a glass chamber will stop making sound as the vacuum is created around it; the more perfect the vacuum, the less the sound. He said he had even constructed an explanation for the occurrence, but declined to inform me of it. I would see for myself with the animal, even if the rest of the experiment did not work.

The bird was a dove, a handsome bird which cooed gently as Boyle took it from its cage and placed it underneath the glass dome. When all was ready, he gave a signal, and the assistant began working the bellows with much grunting and a whooshing sound as air was propelled through the mechanism.

"How long does this take?" I enquired eagerly.

"A few minutes," Lower replied. "I do believe its song is getting fainter, do you hear?"

I regarded the beast with interest, as it was showing signs of distress. "You are right. But surely it is because the bird itself seems unconcerned with making a noise?"

Hardly had I spoken when the dove, which a few moments ago had been hopping around the dome with curiosity, fluttering against the invisible glass walls which it could feel but was incapable of understanding, fell over, its beak gaping open, its beady eyes popping and its legs flailing around pathetically.

"Good heavens," I said.

Lower ignored me. "Why don't we let the air back in, and see what happens then?"

The valves were turned, and with an audible hiss, the vacuum was filled. The bird still lay there, twitching away, although it was clear that it was very much relieved. Within a few moments, it picked itself up, ruffled its feathers and resumed its attempts to fly away to freedom.

"Well," I said, "so much for one hypothesis."

Boyle nodded, and gave the assistant a nod to try it again. Here I must note the extraordinary goodness of this fine man, who refused to use the same animal in more than one series of experiments, because of the torture to the creature. Once it had served its turn, and given itself to the pursuit of humane knowledge, he either let it go or, if necessary, killed it.

Until then, I had never thought such an attitude attachable to any experimentalist other than myself, and I rejoiced to find at last someone whose sentiments were similar to my own. Experimentation must take place, this is certain; but sometimes, when I behold the faces of my colleagues as they cut, I think I see too much pleasure on their countenances, and suspect that the agony is prolonged longer than is necessary for mere knowledge. Once in Padua, a vivisection of a dog was interrupted when a female servant, grieved to hear the beast's piteous cries as it was cut open, strangled it in front of a full audience of students, causing much dismay and protest at the ruining of the spectacle. Of the assembled multitude, I believe that only myself had sympathy for the woman, and was grateful to her; but then I was ashamed of the effeminacy of my concerns which, I think, came from my delight as a child in being read from the life of St. Francis, who loved and reverenced all things in God's creation.

But Boyle came to the same conclusions, although (typically of the man) did so in a far more rigorous fashion than myself and was, of course, uninfluenced by memories of the Assisi countryside. For, just as he believed that a gentleman should show Christian condescension to the lower orders, according to their merits, so men, the gentlemen of God's creation, owed similar courtesy to the animals over whom they had dominion. While not scrupling to use men or animals as was his right, he believed firmly that they should not be abused either. In that, good Catholic and fervent Protestant were in accord for once, and I liked Boyle the more for his care.

That afternoon, we used only a single bird. By means of careful study we ascertained that it was scarcely affected when only half of the air was removed, that it began to show signs of distress when two thirds had gone, and was rendered insensible when three quarters had vanished. Conclusion: the presence of air is necessary for life to continue, although, as Lower said, that did not explain what it did. Personally, I

chapter five

THIS BUSINESS CONCLUDED, LOWER SUGGESTED I might like to dine with some friends, whom he felt I might profit from meeting. It was kind of him and it seemed that the closeness to Boyle that an afternoon's experiment entailed had placed him in a good humor. I suspected, however, that there was another side of his character, a darkness which warred with his natural good nature. For a flickering of a moment, while I laid out my thoughts to Boyle, I had felt a slight unease in Lower's demeanor, although this had never come to the surface. I had also noticed that he had never given his own theories or elaborated his own thoughts; these he kept close to himself.

I did not mind; Boyle was Lower's most important connection among the few gentlemen of standing who could help establish himself in his career and he was naturally concerned lest that patronage be diverted. But I contented myself with the assurance that I presented him with no challenge, and concluded that I could hardly attract his enmity. Perhaps I should have been more sensitive to his concerns, for it was a matter of character not of circumstance which made him uncomfortable.

My position had made me easy with all ranks of life; I admired and was beholden to Mr. Boyle, but in all other respects I considered him my equal. Lower was unable to feel the same; although all are citizens of the republic of learning, he was often uneasy in such company, for he believed himself at a disadvantage due to a birth which, although respectable, gave him neither fortune nor people. Moreover, he lacked the talents of the courtier and in later years he never rose to any position of distinction in the Royal Society while men of lesser accomplishment took on its great offices. This was galling for a man of his ambition and pride but, for the most part, this inner conflict was hidden, and I am aware that he did as much as his nature allowed to assist me while I was in Oxford. He was a man who liked easily, but then was seized by fear lest his affections be abused and exploited by others of a less trusting disposition than himself. The fact that earning position in England is so formidably hard merely heightened this aspect of his nature. I can say this now, as the passage of years has lessened my hurt and increased my understanding. At that time my comprehension was smaller.

It was as a result of his friendliness and enthusiasm, however, that I was led down the High Street that afternoon in the direction of the castle.

"I didn't want to mention it in Boyle's presence," he said confidingly as we marched briskly along in the cold afternoon air, "but I have high hopes of getting hold of a corpse soon. Boyle disapproves."

I was surprised by this remark. Even though some of the older physicians didn't hold with the business at all, and it still caused considerable trouble among churchmen, it was accepted as an essential part of medical studies in Italy. Was it possible that a man like Boyle could disagree?

"Oh, no. He has nothing against anatomizing, but he feels I tend to become undignified about the matter. Which may be true, but there is no other way of getting hold of them without getting permission first."

"What do you mean? Getting permission? Where does this man find the body in the first place?"

"He is the body."

"How can you ask permission of a corpse?"

"Oh, he's not dead," Lower said airily. "Not yet, anyway."

"Is he ill?"

"Heavens, no. Prime of life. But they're to hang him soon. After he's found guilty. He attacked a gentleman and injured him badly. A simple case it is, too; he was found with the knife in his hand. Will you come to see the hanging? I must confess I shall; it's not often a student is hanged, alas. Most of them join the church and get livings . . . I'm sure there's a witticism in there somewhere, if I phrased it rightly."

I was beginning to see Boyle's point of view, but Lower, quite impervious to disapproval when fixed on his work, explained how very difficult it was to get hold of a fresh corpse these days. That had been the one good effect, he said nostalgically, of the civil war. Especially when the king's army had been quartered in Oxford, there were corpses, two a penny. Never had anatomists had such a plentiful supply. I forbore to point out that he was much too young to know.

"The trouble is, you see, that most people who die are sick in some way."

"Not if they have the right doctor," I said, desiring to show myself as witty as he.

"Quite. But it's very inconvenient. The only time we can see what a properly healthy person looks like is if they are killed in some relatively clean fashion. And the best supply of those comes from the gallows. But that is another one of the university's monopolies."

"Pardon?" I said in some surprise.

"Law of the land," he went on. "The university has a right to the bodies of everyone hanged within twenty miles. The courts are so very lax on crime these days as well. Many an interesting specimen gets off with a flogging, and there's only about half a dozen hangings a year. And I'm afraid they don't always make the best use of the corpses they do have. Our Regius professor is scarcely qualified to be a carpenter. Last time . . . well, let's not go into that," he said with a shudder.

We had arrived at the castle, a great gloomy edifice which scarcely seemed capable of defending the town from assault or of providing a refuge for the townspeople. In fact, it had not been used for such a purpose for as long as anyone could remember; and was now the county prison, in which those due to appear at the assizes were held pending their trial—

and pending their punishment afterward. It was a dirty, shabby place, and I looked around with distaste as Lower knocked on the door of a little cottage down by the stream, in the shadow of the tower.

Getting in to see his body was surprisingly easy; all he had to do was tip the guardian a penny, and this old hobbling man—a Royalist soldier who had been given the position for his services—led the way, his keys jangling by his side.

If it was gloomy outside, it was even darker inside, although far from grim for the more fortunate of the inmates. The poorer ones, naturally, had the worst of the cells and were forced to eat food which was barely adequate for keeping body and soul together. But, Lower pointed out, as several were to have body and soul forcibly separated in due course anyway, there was little point in spoiling them.

However, the better sort of prisoner could rent a more salubrious cell, send out to a tavern for food and in addition have laundry done when required. He could also receive visitors if, as was the case with Lower, they were prepared to tip heavily for the privilege.

"There you are, then, sirs," said the warder as he swung open a heavy door leading into what I gathered was a cell for a middle-ranking sort of prisoner.

The man whom Lower hoped to cut into small bits was sitting on a little bed. He looked up in a rather sulky fashion as we entered, then peered curiously, a glimmer of half recognition passing across his face as my friend passed into the thin stream of light that came through the open, barred window.

"Dr. Lower, isn't it?" he said in a melodious voice.

Lower told me later that he was a lad from a good, but impoverished family; his fall from grace had been something of a shock and his position was not sufficiently elevated to spare him from the gallows. And now the time appointed was drawing near. The English rush from trial to sentence with considerable speed, so that a man condemned on Monday can often be hanged the following morning unless he is lucky. Jack Prestcott could count himself fortunate that he had been arrested a few weeks before the assizes arrived to hear his case; it gave him time to prepare his soul, for Lower told me there was not the slightest chance of an acquittal or a pardon.

"Mr. Prestcott," Lower said cheerfully. "I hope I find you well?"

Prestcott nodded and said he was as well as could be expected.

"I won't beat about the bush," Lower said. "I've come to ask something of you."

Prestcott looked surprised that he should be asked a service in his current condition, but nodded to indicate that Lower should ask away. He put down his book and paid attention.

"You are a young man of considerable learning, and I'm told your tutor spoke very highly of you," Lower continued. "And you have committed a most heinous crime."

"If you have found a way of saving me from the noose, then I agree with you," Prestcott said calmly. "But I fear you have something else in mind. But please continue, doctor. I am interrupting your speech."

"I trust you have meditated on your sinful conduct, and have seen the justice of the fate which awaits you in due course," Lower continued in what struck me as being a remarkably pompous fashion. I suppose the effort to hit the right tone made him sound a little discordant.

"Indeed I have," the youth replied with gravity. "Every day I pray to the Almighty for forgiveness, mindful that I scarcely deserve such a boon."

"Splendid," continued Lower, "so if I were to tell you of a way in which you could contribute inestimably to the betterment of all mankind, and do something to cancel out the horrible acts with which your name will be forever associated, you might be interested? Hmm?"

The young man nodded cautiously, and asked what this contribution might be.

Lower explained about the law on the corpses of criminals.

"Now, you see," he went on, scarcely noticing that Prestcott had turned a little pale, "the Regius professor and his assistant are the most appalling butchers. They will hack and saw and chop, and reduce you to a mangled ruin, and no one will be any the wiser. All that will happen is that you will furnish a rarity show for any spotty undergraduate who cares to come along and watch. Not that many do. Now I—and my friend here, Signor da Cola, of Venice—are dedicated to research of the most delicate kind. By the time we are finished, we will know immeasurably more about the functions of the human body. And there will be no waste, I promise you,'' he went on, waving his finger in the air as he got into his stride.

"You see, the trouble with the professor is that, once he stops for lunch, he tends to lose interest. He drinks a good deal, you know,'' he confided. "What's left over gets thrown away or gnawed by rats in the basement. Whereas I will pickle you . . .''

"I beg your pardon?'' Prestcott said weakly.

"Pickle you,'' Lower replied enthusiastically. "It is the very latest technique. If we joint you and pop you into a vat of spirits, you will keep for very much longer. So much better than brandy. Then when we have the leisure to dissect a bit, we just fish you out and get to work. Splendid, eh? Nothing will be wasted, I assure you. All that is required is that you give me a letter specifying as your last request that I be allowed to dissect you once you have met your punishment.''

Convinced that this was a request no reasonable man might refuse, Lower leaned back against the wall and beamed with anticipation.

"No,'' Prestcott said.

"I beg your pardon?''

"I said no. Certainly not.''

"But I told you; you'll be dissected anyway. Wouldn't you at least want it to be done properly?''

"I don't want it done at all, thank you. What's more, I'm convinced it will not be.''

"A pardon, you think?'' Lower said with interest. "Oh, I think not. No, I fear you will swing, sir. After all, you nearly killed a man of some importance. Tell me, why did you attack him?''

"I must hasten to remind you, I have not yet been found guilty of any crime, let alone condemned, and I am convinced I will shortly regain my freedom. Should I be wrong then I might entertain your proposal, but even then I doubt whether I will be able to oblige you. My mother would have the gravest objections.''

This, I suppose, was the time for Lower to return to his theme, but his enthusiasm seemed to have waned. Perhaps he thought the young man's mother would regard being jointed and pickled as bringing still further shame on his name. He nodded regretfully and stood up, thanking the youth for having listened to his request.

Prestcott told him to think nothing of it and, when asked if he needed anything to improve his condition, asked if he could deliver a message to a Dr. Grove, one of his former tutors, asking for the goodness of a visit. He had need of spiritual comfort, he said. Another gallon of wine would be well received also. Lower promised and I offered to deliver the wine, as I felt sorry for the fellow, and I did so as my friend went off to an appointment with a new patient.

''Well, it was worth trying,'' he said in a disappointed tone when we met later on and the conversation returned to the topic of reluctant corpses. I noticed that the rebuff had quite dissolved his cheerful mood of earlier in the day.

''What did he mean about his family having shame enough?''

Lower was lost in contemplation, however, and ignored my remark while he dwelt on his failure. ''What was that?'' he said abruptly when his attention returned. I repeated myself.

''Oh. No more than the truth. His father was a traitor, who fled abroad before he could be held. He would have been executed as well, given the chance.''

''Quite a family.''

''Indeed. It seems that the son takes after the father in more than looks, alas. It is a damnable shame, Cola. I need a brain. Several brains, and I am hindered and obstructed at every turn.'' Then, after a long silence, he asked what I thought the chances were of Sarah Blundy's mother pulling through.

Rather foolishly, I imagined that he wanted a detailed account of the case and the treatment I had provided, so I told him about the nature of the wound, the way I had set the bone and cleaned the flesh, and of the salve I had used.

"Waste of time," he said loftily. "Tincture of mercury is what you need."

"You think? Perhaps. But I decided that in this case, considering the aspect of Venus, she stood a much better chance with a more orthodox remedy . . ."

And then came the first serious indication of the darkness in my friend I have mentioned, for I could not even finish my reply before he exploded with rage, in full public, swinging round to face me, his face darkening.

"Oh, don't be so stupid," he shouted. "The aspect of Venus! What magical nonsense is that? Dear God, are we still Egyptians that we should pay attention to such rubbish?"

"But Galen . . ."

"I don't give a hoot for Galen. Or Paracelsus. Or any foreign magus with his slobberings and mumblings. These people are the merest frauds. As are you, sir, if you drivel on in such a way. You should not be let loose among the sick."

"But, Lower . . ."

"'More orthodox remedy,'" he said, mimicking my accent cruelly. "I suppose some gibbering priest told you that, and you do as you're told? Eh? Physick is too important to be left to the dabblings of a rich man's son like you, who could no more cure a cold than you could a broken leg. Stick to counting your money and your acres, and leave serious matters to people who care for them."

I was so shocked by this outburst, so unforeseen and so very violent, that I said nothing at all in reply, except that I was doing my best and that no one better qualified had offered their services.

"Oh, get out of my sight," he said with the most terrible contempt. "I will have none of you. I have no time for quacks and charlatans."

And he abruptly turned on his heel and marched away, leaving me standing in the street in shock, my face burning red with anger and embarrassment, conscious above all that I had provided cheap entertainment for the mob of shopkeepers all around me.

chapter six

I RETURNED TO MY ROOM IN DEEP DISTRESS TO CON-
sider what I should do next, and try to understand how I had
caused such offence, for I am one of those who naturally
assumes the fault lies in himself first of all, and my lack of
understanding of English ways had greatly heightened my
uncertainty. Even so, I was convinced that Lower's shocking
outburst was excessive, but the temper of the country then
cast all opinions in extremes.

So I sat by the little fireplace in my cold room, with the
feelings of desperation and loneliness, so recently banished,
coming back to plague me once again. Was my acquaintanceship at an end so soon? Certainly in Italy no relation could
survive such behavior, and under ordinary circumstances we
would now be preparing to duel. I intended to do no such
thing, of course, but did briefly consider whether it would be
better to leave Oxford, for my association with Boyle might
well become intolerable, and then I would be friendless once
again. But where could I go? There seemed little point in
returning to London, and less in staying where I was. I was
fixed in my irresolution when feet on the stairs, and a heavy
pounding on the door roused me from my dreary thoughts.

It was Lower. With a grave look on his face, he marched
determinedly in and placed two bottles on the table. I regarded him coldly and cautiously, expecting another round
of abuse, and determined that he should speak first.

Instead, he ostentatiously sank to his knees, and clasped his hands together.

"Sir," he said with a gravity which had more than a touch of the theatrical in it, "how can I ask you to forgive me? I have behaved with the manners of a tradesman, or worse. I have been inhospitable, unkind, unjust and grossly ill-mannered. I offer you my humblest apologies on my knees, as you see, and beg for a forgiveness which I do not deserve."

I was as astonished by his behavior now as I was before, and could find no suitable reply for this contrition, which was every bit as excessive as his violence an hour or so previously.

"You cannot forgive," he continued with an ostentatious sigh as I remained silent. "I cannot blame you. Then there is no choice. I must kill myself. Please tell my family that my gravestone should read, 'Richard Lower, physician, and wretch.' "

Here I burst out laughing, so absurd was his behavior and, seeing that he had cracked my resolve, he grinned back.

"Truly, I am most gigantically sorry," he said in a more moderate tone. "I don't know why, but sometimes I become so angry that I cannot stop myself. And my frustrations over these corpses is so very great. If you knew the torments I go through. . . . Do you accept my apology? Will you drink from the same bottle as me? I will not sleep or shave until you accept, and you don't want to be responsible for me having a beard down to my ankles, do you?"

I shook my head. "Lower, I do not understand you," I said frankly. "Or any of your countrymen. So I will assume this is part of your nation's manner, and that it is my fault for having so little understanding. I will drink with you."

"Thank heavens for that," he said. "I thought I had foolishly thrown away a valued friend through my own stupidity. You are goodness indeed to give me a second chance."

"But please explain. Why did I make you so angry?"

He waved his hand. "You didn't. It was my misunderstanding, and I was upset over losing Prestcott. Not long ago I had a violent row with someone over astrological prediction. The College of Physicians is wedded to it and this man threatened to keep me out of practice in London because I disdain it in public and advocate the new mineral physick. It is a battle between new knowledge and the dead hand of old. I know you did not mean it like that, but I'm afraid the fight I had is too fresh in my mind. The sound of you, of all people, taking their part was too much to bear, so highly do I value you. Unforgivable, as I say.''

He had a way of turning insult into compliment which I was ill-equipped to handle; we Venetians have a reputation for the elaborate nature of both our courtesies and our insults, but they are so formal there is no chance of misunderstanding even the most opaque remark. Lower, and the English in general, had the unpredictability of the uncivilized; their genius is as uncontrolled as their manners, and can make them great or mad. I doubt that foreigners will ever know them, or truly trust them. But an apology was an apology, and I had rarely received such a handsome one; I shook his hand; we bowed solemnly, and toasted each other to bring the argument to a formal conclusion.

''Why do you want Prestcott so much and so urgently?''

''My brains, Cola, my brains,'' he said with a loud groan. ''I have anatomized and drawn as many as I can lay my hands on, and I will soon be finished. I have devoted years to the task, and it will make my name when it is done. The spinal cord, in particular. Fascinating. But I cannot finish without some more, and unless I can finish I cannot publish my work. And there is a Frenchman who I know is doing much the same work. I will not be beaten by some sniveling papist . . .''

He paused, and realized he had misspoken again. ''Apologies, sir. But so much depends on this, and it is heartbreaking to be denied by such stupidities.''

He opened the second bottle, took a long draft from the open neck and handed it to me. ''So there you are. The reasons for my incivility. They combine, I must admit, with an overly wayward temperament. I am choleric by nature.''

''So much for the man who rejects traditional medicine.''

He grinned. ''True enough. I speak metaphorically.''

''Did you mean it about the stars? You think it is nonsense?''

He shrugged his shoulders. "Oh, I don't know. I really don't. Are our bodies a microcosm of all creation? Can we discern movements of the one from studying the other? Probably. It makes perfect sense, I suppose, but no one has ever given me a good and unassailable method for how to do it. All this star-gazing the astronomers do seems very thoughtless stuff, and they will wrap it up so in nostrums and gabblings. And they will keep on finding more of them with these telescopes of theirs. All very interesting, but they become so enthusiastic they've all but forgotten the reason why they're looking. But do not start me on that. I will lose my temper for the second time in the day. So, can we start again?"

"In what way?"

"Tell me about your patient, that most strange widow Anne Blundy. I will give the matter my full attention, and any suggestions I make will be without the slightest taint of criticism."

I was still chary of taking such a risk and so hesitated until Lower sighed and made an elaborate preparation to go back down on his knees.

"All right," I said, holding up my hands and trying to stop myself laughing once more. "I surrender."

"Thank heavens," he said. "For I'm sure I will be rheumatic when I'm old. Now, if I'm right, I believe you said the wound was not knitting?"

"No. And it will turn putrid very rapidly."

"You've tried exposing it to the air, rather than keeping it bandaged?"

"Yes. It is making no difference."

"Fever?"

"Surprisingly not, but it must come."

"Eating?"

"Nothing, unless her daughter has managed to feed her some gruel."

"Piss?"

"Thin, with a lemony aroma and astringent taste."

"Hmm. Not good. You're quite right. Not good."

"She will die. I want to save her. Or at least I did. I find the daughter intolerable."

Lower ignored the last remark. "Any sign of gangrene?"

I told him no, but that there was again every likelihood it might appear.

"D'ye think she would be interested in advancing . . . ?"

"No," I said firmly.

"What about the daughter? If I offered her a pound for the remains?"

"You have met the girl, I believe."

Lower nodded, and sighed heavily. "I tell you, Cola, if I should die tomorrow, you have my full permission to anatomize me. Why it causes such upset I do not know. After all, they're buried eventually, aren't they? What does it matter how many pieces they're in, as long as they die with the blessings of religion? Do they think the good Lord is incapable of reassembling them in time for the Second Coming?"

I replied that it was the same in Venice; for whatever reason, people did not like the idea of being cut up, whether they were dead or alive.

"What do you intend to do with the woman?" he asked. "Wait till she dies?"

It was then that I had an idea and instantly decided to share it. Such was my trusting nature that it never occurred to me not to do so.

"Hand me that bottle again," I said, "and I'll tell you what I'd like to do, if I were only able."

He did so at once, and I briefly considered the momentous step I was about to take. I was hardly in an equable frame of mind; my distress at the bruising I had received, and the relief at his apology were so great that my judgment was unbalanced. I do believe I would never have drawn him into my confidence had his loyalty and friendship been unquestioned; now it had been placed in doubt, the wish to please him and demonstrate my seriousness swept all before it.

"Please forgive the clumsy way I express this," I said when he was leaning back on my truckle bed as comfortably as was possible. "The idea came to me only when we were watching that dove in the vacuum pump. It is about the blood, you see. What if, by accident, there is not enough blood to carry the nutrient? Could a loss of blood mean that there is insufficient to vent the excess heat from the heart?

Might that not be a cause of fever? Also, I have wondered for some years whether the blood gets old with the rest of the body. Like a canal with stagnant water in it, where everything starts to die, because the passageway becomes clogged."

"Certainly, if you lose blood, you die."

"But why? Not from starvation, nor from excess heat, either. No, sir. It is the draining or occlusion of the life spirit present in the blood that causes death. The blood itself, I am convinced, is merely the carrier for this spirit. And it is the decay of that spirit which causes old age. That, at least, is my theory, and it is one where the traditional knowledge you disdain, and the experimental knowledge you applaud, are in perfect agreement."

"At which point, we connect your theoretical preliminary with the practicalities of your case, is that not so? Tell me how you would proceed."

"If you think about it simply it is very straightforward. If we are hungry, we eat. If we are cold, we approach heat. If our humors are unbalanced, we add or create some more to re-create equilibrium."

"If you believe that nonsense."

"If you do," I said. "If you do not, and you believe in the elemental theories, then you rebalance the body by strengthening the weaker of the three elements. That is the essence of all medicine, old and new: to restore equilibrium. Now, in this case, taking away more blood by leeching or scarifying the patient would only make matters worse. If her life spirit is diminished, reducing it still further cannot help her. This is Sylvius's theory, and I believe he is correct. Logically, instead of taking blood away, the only answer should be . . ."

"To add some more," Lower said quickly, leaning forward in his seat with sudden eagerness as he finally grasped what I was talking about.

I nodded enthusiastically. "That's it," I said. "That's it exactly. And not just more, but young blood, fresh, new and unclogged, with the vitality of youth in its essence. Maybe that would allow an old person to repair a wound. Who knows, Lower," I said excitedly, "it might be the elixir of life itself. It is thought, after all, that merely getting a child to share a bed can benefit the health of an elderly person. Just think what their blood might do.''

Lower leaned back in his chair and took a deep draft of ale as he thought about what I had said. His lips moved as he held a silent conversation with himself, going over in his mind all the possibilities. ''You have fallen under the influence of Monsieur Descartes, have you not?'' he asked eventually.

''Why do you say that?''

''You have constructed a theory, and that leads you to recommend a practice. You have no evidence that it would work. And, if I may say so, your theory is confused. You argue by analogy—using a humoral metaphor you do not actually believe in—to conclude that supplying an absence is a solution. That is, adding vital spirit, the existence of which is conjectural.''

''Though not disputed even by yourself.''

''No. That is true.''

''Do you dispute my theory, though?''

''No.''

''And is there any way of finding out whether I am correct except by testing it against result? That is surely the basis of experimental philosophy?''

''That is Monsieur Descartes's basis,'' he said, ''if I understand him correctly. To frame a hypothesis, then amass evidence to see if it is correct. The alternative, proposed by my Lord Bacon, is to amass evidence, and then to frame an explanation which takes into account all that is known.''

In retrospect, looking back over the conversation which I noted diligently in the book which was with me on my travels and which I now reread for the first time in many years, I see many things which were obscured from my understanding then. The English detestation of foreigners leads very swiftly to a wish to ignore any advance which stems from what they consider faulty methods, and allows this proudest of people to claim all discoveries as their own. A discovery based on faulty premises is no discovery: all foreigners influenced by Descartes employ faulty premises, and therefore . . . *Hypotheses non fingo*. No hypotheses here: is that not the trumpet blast of Mr. Newton as he assails Leibniz as a thief for having the same ideas as himself? But at that time I merely thought my friend was using argument as a means of furthering our knowledge.

"I believe your summary of Monsieur Descartes does him scant justice," I said. "But no matter. Tell me how you would you proceed."

"I would begin by transfusing blood between animals— young and old of the same type, then between different types. I would transfuse water into an animal's veins, to see whether the same response was elicited. Then, I would compare all the results to see what exactly the effects of transfusing blood are. Finally, when I could proceed with certainty, I would make the attempt on Mrs. Blundy."

"Who by then would have been dead for a year or more."

Lower grinned. "Your unerring eye has spotted the weakness of the method."

"Are you suggesting I should not do this?"

"No. It would be fascinating. I merely doubt whether it is well founded. And I am certain that it would cause scandal. Which makes it a dangerous business to discuss publicly."

"Let me put it another way. Will you help me?"

"Naturally I should be delighted. I was merely discussing the issues that are raised. How would you proceed?"

"I don't know," I said. "I thought that maybe a bull might serve. As strong as an ox, you know. But good reasons rule that out. The blood has a tendency to congeal. So it would be imperative to transport it immediately from one creature into the other without delay. And we could hardly bring an ox in. Besides, the blood transports the animal spirit, and I would be loath to infuse the bestiality of an ox into a person. That would be an offense against God, who has set us higher than the animals."

"Your own, then?"

"No, because I would need to attend to the experiment."

"There is no problem. We can easily find someone. The best person," he continued, "would be the daughter. She would be willing, for her mother's sake. And I'm sure we could impress on her the need for silence."

I had forgotten about the daughter. Lower saw my face

fall, and asked me what was the matter. "She was so insufferably offensive last time I visited the house I vowed never to set foot there again."

"Pride, sir, pride."

"Perhaps. But you must understand that I cannot give way. She would have to come to me on her knees before I would reconsider."

"Leave that for a moment. Assuming you could do this experiment—just assuming—how much blood would you need?"

I shook my head. "Fifteen ounces, maybe? Perhaps twenty. A person can lose that much without too many ill effects. Maybe more at a later stage. What I don't know is how to effect the transportation. It struck me that the blood would have to leave the one body and enter the other in the same place—vein to vein, artery to artery. I would recommend slitting the jugular, except that it's fearfully difficult to stop it up again. I don't want to save the mother and have the daughter bleed to death. So maybe one of the major vessels in the arm. A band to make it swell up. That's the easy part. It is the transference which concerns me."

Lower got up and wandered around the room, rummaging around in his pockets.

"Have you heard of injections?" he asked eventually.

I shook my head.

"Ah," he said. "A splendid idea, which we have been working on."

"We?"

"Myself, Dr. Willis and my friend Wren. Similar in some ways to your idea. What we do, you see, is take a sharp instrument and push it into a vein, then squeeze liquids straight into the blood, avoiding the stomach entirely."

I frowned. "Extraordinary. What happens?"

He paused. "We have had mixed results," he confessed. "The first time it worked marvelously. We injected an eighth-cup of red wine straight into a dog. Not enough to make it even tipsy, usually, but by this method it turned rolling drunk." He grinned at the thought. "We had a terrible time controlling it. It jumped off the table and ran around, then fell over after bumping into a cupboard of plates. We could barely control ourselves. Even Boyle cracked a smile. The important thing is that it seems a little liquor injected has much more of an effect than when taken through the stomach. So we took a mangy old beast next time and injected sal ammoniack.''

''And?''

''It died, and in some considerable pain. When we opened it up, the corrosion to its heart was considerable. We tried injecting milk the next time to see if we could bypass the need to eat. But it curdled in the veins, unfortunately.''

''Died again?''

He nodded. ''We must have overdone the amount. We'll cut it back next time.''

''I would be fascinated if you would allow me to attend.''

''A pleasure. My point is that we could use the same idea for transferring your blood. You don't want the blood exposed to the air, because it might congeal. So you take a pigeon quill, which can be made very thin and sharp. Put a hole in the end and insert it into Sarah's vein. Join it to a long silver tube, which has a narrow diameter, with another quill in the mother's vein. Wait for the blood to flow, then stop the flow in the mother's vein above the slit. Join the two together, and count. I'm afraid we'd have to guess about how much comes out. If we let the blood flow into a bowl for a few seconds, we'll have some idea of how fast it is going.''

I nodded enthusiastically. ''Wonderful,'' I said. ''I'd been thinking about cupping. This is much neater.''

He grinned, and held out his hand. ''By God, Mr. Cola, I'm glad you're here. You're a man after my own heart, truly you are. In the meantime, which of us is going to see Grove for poor Prestcott?''

chapter seven

I HAVE ALWAYS ACKNOWLEDGED MY DEBT TO LOWER on the mechanics of transfusion. Without his ingenuity, I doubt that the operation could have been made to work. The fact remains, however, that the first suggestion of the idea and the reasoning for it came from myself, and I later carried out the experiment. Until then, Lower's thoughts had revolved solely around the problem of injecting physick into the blood, and he had never for a moment considered the possibility, or potential, of transferring blood itself.

This is a matter for a later part of my narrative, however, and I must stick to my story as it happened. At that moment, my main concern was to offer my services to visit Dr. Grove on behalf of Prestcott, because I still believed that the more members of that society I knew, the better it would be for me. Dr. Grove, certainly, was unlikely to be of much use, and Lower told me he was heartily glad of my offer to go as it spared him a meeting with a man he considered very tiresome. He was an avowed and vociferous opponent of the new learning, and only a fortnight before had delivered a stinging sermon in St. Mary's attacking experimental knowledge as contradictory to God's word, undermining of authority and flawed in both intention and execution.

"Are there many of his opinion in the town?" I asked.

"Dear heavens, yes. There are physicians who fear for their prerogatives, priests frightened of being usurped, and whole hordes of the ignorant who simply dislike anything new. We are on dangerous ground. This is why we must tread carefully with Widow Blundy.''

I nodded; it was the same in Italy, I told him.

''In that case you will be prepared for Grove,'' he replied with a grin. ''Talk to him. He will keep you on your toes. He is no fool—even though he is wrong and, frankly, somewhat tedious.''

St. Mary College of Winchester in Oxford, vulgarly called New College, is a large, shabby building that stands in the east of the town hard up against the walls and the tennis courts. It is very wealthy but has a reputation for being one of the most backward of places. When I arrived, it seemed almost deserted, and there was no indication of where the object of my journey might be. So I asked the one person I saw, and he informed me that Dr. Grove had been ill for some days and was not encouraging visitors. I explained that, while I would normally be willing to leave him in peace, I could not in all conscience do so. Accordingly this man, a short, dark little fellow who introduced himself with a stiff little bow as one Thomas Ken, showed me to the staircase.

The thick oak door of Dr. Grove's room—the English are prodigal with fine wood in this way—was firmly closed, and I knocked, expecting no reply. I did, however, hear a slight scuffling and so knocked again. I thought that I heard a voice; I could not make out what it was saying, but it seemed reasonable to assume that it was inviting me in.

''Go away,'' the voice said with irritation as I entered the room. ''Are you deaf?''

''I do beg your pardon, sir,'' I replied, then paused in surprise. The man I had come to visit was the same person I had seen a few days previously rejecting Sarah Blundy's request for help. I stared uncertainly at him, and he looked back at me, clearly also remembering that he had seen me before.

''As I say,'' I continued when I recovered my poise. ''I apologize. But I couldn't hear very well.''

''Let me repeat myself, then, for the third time. I was telling you to go away. I am feeling much too poorly.''

He was an oldish man, in his early fifties and possibly

more. Broad-shouldered, he nonetheless had that air of decline that sooner or later is sent by the Almighty to touch the shoulder of even the most robust of his creatures, reminding them of their subjection to His laws.

But, *a re decedo.* "I am very sorry to hear you are ill," I said, standing my ground in the doorway. "Would I be right in thinking your eye is causing you distress?"

Anyone could have made this statement, for the doctor's left eye was red and rheumy, inflamed by much irritated rubbing. Quite apart from my reason for being there, the sight aroused my interest.

"Of course it is my eye," he replied curtly, "I am suffering the torments of hell from it."

I advanced a step or two into the room, so that I could see more clearly and establish myself more firmly in his presence. "A severe irritation, sir, producing gumminess and inflammation. I hope you are receiving proper attention. Although I don't think it looks so serious."

"Serious?" he cried incredulously. "Not serious? I'm in agony. And I have a great deal of work to do. Are you a doctor? I don't need one. I have the very best treatment available."

I introduced myself. "Naturally, I hesitate to contradict a physician, sir, but it doesn't look that way to me. I can see from here that there is a coalescence of a brown putridity around the eyelid, which requires medicine."

"That *is* the medicine, idiot," he said. "I mixed the ingredients myself."

"What ingredients were they?"

"Dried dog excrement," he said.

"What?"

"I had it from my doctor, Bate. The king's physician, you know, and a man of good family. It is an infallible cure, tested through the ages. A pedigree dog, as well. It belongs to the warden."

"Dog excrement?"

"Yes. You dry it in the sun, then powder it and blow it into the eyes. It is a sure remedy for all forms of eye complaint."

To my mind this explained why his eyes were giving him

so much trouble. There are, of course, innumerable old remedies in use and some are, no doubt, as efficacious as anything a physician could prescribe—not that this is necessarily saying much. I have no doubt that the mineral physick that so enthused Lower will eventually supplant them all. I had some idea of the sort of prattle that accompanied the recommendation. The natural attraction of like and like; the powdered excrement setting up an affinity with the noxiousness and sucking it out. Or not, as the case may be.

"Far be it from me to question, sir, but are you quite sure it is working?" I asked.

"Surely that means you are questioning it?"

"No," I said cautiously. "In certain cases, it may be effective: I do not know. How long has your eye been troubling you?"

"About ten days."

"And how long have you been treating it in this way?"

"About a week."

"And in that time, has your eye become better or worse?"

"It has not improved," he conceded. "But it may be that without the treatment it would have got worse."

"And it may also be that with another treatment it would have become better," I said. "Now, if I gave you another treatment, and your eye improved, that would demonstrate . . ."

"That would demonstrate that my original treatment has at last begun to be effective and that your treatment was of no significance."

"You want your eye to recover as fast as possible. If you apply a treatment and within a reasonable time there has been no improvement, then one may conclude that, within that time, the treatment does not work. Whether it works next week, the week after or in three years' time does not matter."

Dr. Grove opened his mouth to dispute this line of argument, then suffered another twinge of pain in his eye, which he began once more to rub furiously.

I saw an opportunity both of ingratiating myself and perhaps even of gaining a fee to bolster my resources. So I asked for some water and straightaway began to bathe the foul mess out of the eye entirely, thinking that this alone would probably effect an almost miraculous cure. By the time I had finished, his tortured eye was open once more and, although he was still in some discomfort, he expressed his joy at how much better he felt already. Even more satisfyingly, he attributed it solely to the potion I had applied.

"Now for the next stage," Grove said stoutly as he rolled up his sleeve. "I think five ounces would do, don't you think?"

I disagreed, although I refrained from telling him that I was far from convinced that bleeding ever did anyone much good, as I was afraid of losing his confidence. So instead I suggested the harmony of his body would be better restored by a light vomit after eating—especially as he looked like a man who could easily miss a meal or two with no ill effects.

The treatment concluded, he asked me to share a glass of wine with him, which invitation I declined, having already drunk far too much recently. Instead, I explained my visit to him, thinking that if he did not bring up the incident in the coffee house, I would not do so either. Initially, I had been critical of his behavior; now I knew the girl better, I was more understanding.

"It is about a young man whom I encountered yesterday," I said. "A Mr. Prestcott."

Dr. Grove frowned at the very mention of Mr. Prestcott and asked how I had met him, considering that he was locked in the castle.

"It was through my dear friend Dr. Lower," I said, "who had a . . . message to deliver to him."

"Wants his corpse, does he?" Grove asked. "I swear when I become sick I feel inclined to go back to my family in Northampton, in case Lower turns up at my bedside with an acquisitive glint in his eye. What did Prestcott say?"

I told him that Prestcott had refused outright to countenance the idea, and Grove nodded. "Good for him. Sound boy, although it was easy to see that he'd come to a bad end. Very wayward."

"At the moment," I replied gravely, "he seems very contrite and in need of spiritual comfort. He wants you to visit him, to offer him the solace of religion."

Grove looked as pleased as he was surprised. "The ability

of the noose to make even the worst of sinners embrace God's mercy should never be underestimated,'' he said with satisfaction. ''I will go this evening.''

I liked him for that. He was brusque and certainly of very definite opinions, yet he was also kindly, I sensed, and loved nothing better than for people to disagree with him. Lower told me later that, whatever his failings, Grove never took offense at opinions honestly held, even though he was determined to combat them as much as possible. It meant that, while he was difficult to like, some came to love him.

''He was most anxious to speak to you as soon as possible,'' I said. ''But I would recommend you wait for a day or so. The wind is from the north, and it is known that is bad for an ailment of the eyes.''

''We shall see,'' he said. ''But I must go soon. I was loath to do so unless he called for me himself, and I am gratified he now has. My thanks, sir.''

''Do you know,'' I asked as I peered into his eye once more, ''what the story of his crime was? From the few details I have heard it seems quite peculiar.''

Grove nodded. ''Very peculiar,'' he agreed. ''But I am afraid he was fated to act thus, because of his family. His father was wayward as well. Made an unfortunate match.''

''He disliked his wife?'' I asked.

Grove frowned. ''Worse than that. He married for love. A charming woman, so I am told, but against the wishes of both families, who never forgave him. It was typical of the man, I'm afraid.''

I shook my head here. Coming from a merchant family myself, I was well aware of the importance of not allowing sentiment to cloud one's judgment in marital affairs. As my father had once remarked, if God had meant us to marry for love, why had He created mistresses? Not that he indulged overmuch in this direction himself, for he and my mother were devoted to each other.

''He enlisted on the side of the king when the war broke out, fought with valor and lost everything. But he still continued faithful and plotted against the Commonwealth. Alas, he loved plotting more than he loved his monarch, for he betrayed his king to Cromwell, and almost with disastrous effects. A more evil deed has not been seen since Judas Iscariot sold Our Lord.''

He nodded sagely at his tale. For my part, I found it all very interesting, but still did not understand how Prestcott came to be in prison.

''That is very simple,'' Grove said. ''He is of a violent and unstable disposition; perhaps it is a case of the sins of the fathers being handed down. He became an unruly, ungovernable child and took to bad ways with a vengeance once he was free of family control. He assaulted and nearly murdered the guardian who has looked after him with kindness since his father's disgrace, and there is also a complaint from an uncle that he ransacked that man's money chest on a recent visit. It happens: we hanged an undergraduate for highway robbery last year, Prestcott this year and, I'm afraid, these will not be the last. 'The land is full of bloody crimes, and the city is full of violence.' '' He paused for me to recognize the quotation, but I shrugged helplessly.

''Ezekiel, 7:23,'' he said reprovingly. ''It is a consequence of the turmoil we have been through. Now, sir. I feel unable to insult you by offering you money for your kindness, but perhaps a meal in college would be an adequate recompense? We do fine food, better wine and I can promise excellent company.''

I smiled wanly, and said I would be delighted.

''Splendid,'' he said. ''I am so glad. Five o'clock?''

This was agreed, and I made my farewells to him with as many thanks as I could muster.

The way he waved it aside suggested that he believed I was singularly honored by the invitation. ''Tell me, before you leave,'' he said as I opened the door. ''How is the girl's mother?''

I stopped in surprise at the way he brought the matter up. ''She is not well,'' I replied. ''In fact, I believe she will die.''

He nodded grimly in a fashion I could not decipher. ''I see,'' he said. ''God's will be done.''

And then I was dismissed. I went back to inform Mrs. Bulstrode I would not be dining, then fulfilled my last obligation and took the gallon of wine to Prestcott in his jail cell.

chapter eight

Dinner at New College came as something of a
shock. As my hosts were all gentlemen of education, and
many of them in holy orders, I imagined that I would be
passing a pleasant time in agreeable surroundings. Instead,
the meal was served in a vast and drafty hall, through which
the wind swept as though we were at sea in mid-gale; Grove
was well wrapped up for the occasion and went into considerable detail to inform me of the layers of undergarments he
was wont to don before venturing forth. Had he forewarned
me, I would have done likewise. Even so, I would have been
cold. While the English are used to icy conditions, I am used
to the soft air and balmy weather of the Mediterranean.
Nonetheless, even the lowliest tavern did not possess a bitterness like that hall, which ate through your clothes and flesh
and made your very bones ache with the pain of it.

Even that would have been endurable had food, wine or
company been a compensation. These colleges have the monastic custom of eating in common, with the exception of
the wealthier members who pay to have food sent up to their
chambers. On a raised platform sit the senior Fellows, and
in the rest of the hall are the others. As the food is scarcely
fit for animals, I suppose it is not surprising that they behave
like beasts. They eat off wooden platters, and in the middle
of the tables are vast wooden bowls into which they toss the
bones, when they do not throw them at one another. I ended

up with food splattered over me from Fellows talking with their mouths full, spraying each other with bits of gristle and half-masticated bread.

The wine was scarcely palatable, so I could not even drink myself into oblivion. Instead, I had to listen to the conversation, which was not at all about matters of scholarly interest. I began to realize that, having initially fallen in with Mr. Boyle and Dr. Lower, I had gained an unduly favorable impression, both of Oxford and the English. Far from being concerned about the latest advances of knowledge, the assembly was instead entirely taken up with who was going to gain which preferment, and what the dean of this had said to the rector of that. There was one other guest apart from myself, evidently a gentleman of some standing, and the obsequiousness of their behavior to him was such that I assumed he was a patron of the college in some form. He, however, said little, and I was placed too far away to draw him into conversation.

For my part, I excited little interest and I confess my pride was wounded by it. I had anticipated that someone like myself, fresh from Leiden and Padua, would have rapidly become the center of attention. Far from it. Saying that I did not live in the town and had no position in the church was like confessing to the pox. When it became clear I was a Catholic two members left the hall, and at least one other declined to sit near me. I hated to admit it, since I had become partial to the English by then, but in nearly all respects they were no better than their fellows in Padua or Venice and, apart from the differences in religion and language, could have been exchanged for any group of gossiping Italian priests without anyone really noticing.

But if few paid me much attention, only one was offensive and my reception was neglectful more than hurtful. It was a great shame, however, that the frostiness came from a gentleman whom I was ready to admire without reservation, for Dr. John Wallis was someone I would dearly have liked to count in my society. I knew of him and admired him for his skill in mathematics, which placed him amongst the first rank in Europe, and I had imagined that a man who was the correspondent of Mersenne, who had crossed mathematical swords with Fermat and Pascal, would have been a man of the broadest civilization. Alas, this was not the case. Dr. Grove introduced us, and was shamed by the way that Wallis refused even normal civility to me. Rather, he stared at me with pale, cold eyes that reminded me of a reptile, declined to respond to my bow, then turned his back on me.

This was as we were sitting down to eat, and Grove became excessively cheerful and pugnacious in his conversation to cover up the embarrassment his colleague had caused.

"Now, sir," he said, "you must defend yourself. It is not often that we have an advocate of the new learning amongst us. If you are intimate with Lower, I suppose you must be so."

I replied that I hardly saw myself as an advocate, and certainly not a worthy one.

"It is true, though, that you seek to cast off the knowledge of the ancients, and replace it with your own?"

I said I respected all opinions of worth.

"Aristotle?" he said in a challenging way. "Hippocrates? Galen?"

I said that these were all great men, but could be proven to have been wrong in many particulars. He snorted at my reply.

"What advances? All that you novelists have done is to find out new reasons for ancient practice, and show how a few trifles work in ways other than was supposed."

"Not so, sir. Not so," I said. "Think of the barometer, the telescope."

He waved his hand in scorn. "And the people who use them all come to entirely different conclusions. What discoveries has the telescope made? Such toys will never be a substitute for reason, the play of the mind upon imponderables."

"But the advances of philosophy, I am convinced, will achieve wonders."

"I have yet to see a sign of it."

"You will," I replied warmly. "I doubt not that posterity will verify many things that are now only rumors. In some age it may be that a voyage to the moon will not be more strange than one to the Americas for us. To speak with someone in the Indies may be as usual as a literary correspondence is now. After all, to talk after death could only have been thought a fiction before the invention of letters, and to sail true by the guide of a mineral would have seemed absurd to the ancients, who knew nothing of the magnet.''

''That is a most extraordinary flourish,'' Grove replied tartly. ''Yet I find the rhetoric defective in the suiting of the antitheses and the antipodes. For you are wrong, sir. The ancients did know of the magnet. Diodorus Siculus knew it plainly, as any gentleman should be aware. All we have discovered is a new use for the stone. This is what I mean. All knowledge is to be found in ancient texts, if you know how to read them aright. And that is true in alchemy as in physick.''

''I disagree,'' I said, thinking I was holding my own quite well. ''For example, take cramps of the stomach. What is the usual remedy for those?''

''Arsenic,'' said another further up the table who was listening. ''A few grains in water as a vomit. I took it myself last September.''

''Did it work?''

''I know the pains grew worse first. I must say, I am inclined to believe that letting a little blood was more effective. But its qualities as a purgative are undoubted. I have never passed so many stools so quickly.''

''My master in Padua did some experiments and concluded that the belief in arsenic was a foolish error. The idea came from a book of remedies translated from Arabic and then into Latin by Deusingius. However, the translator made a mistake; the book recommended what it called darsini for the pains, and this was translated as arsenic. But arsenic in Arabic is zarnich.''

''So what should we be taking?''

''Cinnamon, apparently. Now sir, do you defend a long tradition when it can be shown to rest merely on a translator's error?''

Here this other threw his head back and laughed, sending a shower of half-chewed food in an elegant parabola across the table. ''You have justified only the existence of a sound knowledge of classical languages, sir,'' he said. ''No more.

And use this as an excuse to cast away thousands of years of learning so you may replace them with your own feeble scrabblings.''

''I am all too well aware of the feebleness of my scrabblings,'' I replied, still the most civil person there. ''But I do not substitute; merely examine before I accept an hypothesis. Did not Aristotle himself say that our ideas must conform to our experience of things as they are?''

I fear I was becoming reddened with anger by this stage, as I was conscious that he was little interested in a discussion in which reason played a part; while Grove was amiable in his argument, this one was unpleasant in tone and in manner.

''And then?''

''What do you mean?''

''And after you have put Aristotle to your proof? And, no doubt, found him wanting. Then what? Will you submit the monarchy to your investigations? The church, perhaps? Will you presume to put Our Savior Himself to your proofs? There lies the danger, sir. Your quest leads to atheism, as it must unless science is held firmly in the hands of those who wish to strengthen the word of God, rather than challenge it.''

He stopped here and looked around to gather support from his colleagues. I was pleased to see that they did not look on with complete enthusiasm, although many were nodding with agreement.

'' 'Shall the clay say to Him that fashioneth it, What makest Thou?' '' Grove murmured mildly, half to himself.

But his half-spoken quotation roused the young man who had shown me the way to Grove's room that morning. ''Isaiah, 45:9,'' he said. '' 'The price of wisdom is above rubies,' '' he added quietly, being obviously too young and junior to enter into the contest, but reluctant to let the older man speak unchecked. I had noticed that he had tried to take part in the conversation on several occasions, but each time he opened his mouth, Grove had interrupted and carried on as if he wasn't there.

''Job, 28:18,'' Grove snapped back, irritated by the presumption. '' 'He that increaseth knowledge increaseth sorrow.' ''

''Ecclesiastes, 1:18,'' Thomas Ken countered, also showing signs of becoming heated. I discerned that there was some private squabble here, which had nothing to do with me or experiment. " 'Scorners delight in their scorning, and fools hate knowledge.' "

"Proverbs, 1:22. 'Thy wisdom and thy knowledge, it hath perverted thee.' "

The final sally defeated poor Ken, who knew that he could not remember the source of the quotation, and his face grew red under the public humiliation as he desperately tried to think of a response.

"Isaiah, 47:10," Grove said in triumph when Ken's failure was obvious to all.

Ken threw down his knife with a clatter and, hands shaking, stood up to leave the table. I feared that they might come to blows but, in fact, it was all theater. "Romans, 8:13," he said. With icy slowness, he withdrew from the table and marched out of the hall, his footsteps echoing as he went. I believe I was the only person who heard this last comment, and to me it meant nothing. I always found the tendency of Protestants to bandy quotations from the Bible a trifle ridiculous, even blasphemous. Anyway, Grove certainly did not hear, but instead looked pleased with himself for having carried the field.

As nobody else wanted to break the silence, I decided (as a foreigner, and knowing little of what was going on) to try to cover over the affair. "I am not a theologian or a priest," I said, trying to return the argument to rational grounds, "but I have studied the medical arts in my way. And I know that in many cases physick is as likely to kill as to cure. I think it is my duty to find out as much as I can and help my patients the better. It is not impious, I hope, so to do."

"Why would I take your word when it differs from the great masters of the past? What is your authority compared to theirs?"

"Small indeed, and I reverence them as do you. Did not Dante call Aristotle *il maestro di color qui sanno?* But that is not what I am asking. I ask you to decide on the result of experiment."

"Ah, experiment," Grove said with glee. "Do you hold

with the Copernican notion that the earth goes round the sun?''

''I do, of course.''

''And you have performed those experiments yourself? You have made the observations, repeated the calculations, and established by your own labors that it is so?''

''No; I know little of mathematics, alas.''

''So you *believe* it is true, but you do not know? You take Copernicus's word for it?''

''Yes. And that of those experts who accept his conclusions.''

''Pardon me for saying so, but it appears to me that you are just as bound to authority and tradition as a man who subscribes to Aristotle or Ptolemy. After all your protestations your science is also a matter of faith, not in any way distinguishable from the old learning you so despise.''

''I judge by results,'' I said pleasantly, for he was clearly enjoying himself, and it seemed churlish to spoil his entertainment. ''And by the fact that the experimental method has produced good results.''

''This experiment of yours, it is the core of the new medicine, for example?''

I nodded.

''But how do you reconcile it with the notions of Hippocrates which you physicians seem to think are so important?''

''I do not need to,'' I said. ''I see no conflict.''

''Surely you must?'' Grove said in surprise. ''For you have to substitute proven treatments for others which might be better, but might well be worse. Rather than trying first and foremost to cure your patients, you experiment on them to see what result is obtained. You use patients to gain your knowledge, not to make them better, and that is a sin. Bartolomeus de Chaimis says so in his *Interrogatorium sive confessionale,* and he has been seconded by the best authorities ever since.''

''Clever argument, but untrue,'' I said. ''Experiment is there to improve treatment for all patients.''

''But if I come to you with an illness, I do not care for all patients. It matters not to me if others are cured when I die proving a treatment does not work. I want to be healthy, yet you say your wish for knowledge is greater than my need for health.''

"I say nothing of the sort. There are many experiments which can be carried out without endangering the patient.''

"But you are still setting aside Hippocrates. You are deciding to use treatments not knowing whether they will work or not, and that breaks your word.''

"Think, sir, of a patient for whom there is no remedy. That person will die. In that case, an experiment which gives the chance of health is better than none at all.''

"Not so. Because you might well be hastening death. That is not only against the oath, it is against God's law. And the law of men, if it be murder.''

"You are saying that no improvement in medicine is permissible? We have what we have been given by our forebears and can hope for nothing more?''

"I am saying that by your own admission the experimental method is corrupt.''

It was hard, but still I remembered my manners. "Perhaps. But I treated you today and you show much improvement. You may dispute the source, but not, in this case, the result.''

Grove laughed and clapped his hands together with pleasure and I saw that he was really only amusing himself, seeing how far I could be provoked. "That is true, sir, very true. My eye is much better, and I am grateful to the new philosophy for that. And I will trust you on the dangers of any substance you dislike, and avoid them entirely. But,'' he said with a sigh as he confirmed that his wine glass was empty, "our meal is over, and with it our discussion. A pity. We must talk more on this during your stay in our university. Who knows? I might even persuade you of the error of your ways.''

"Or I you?''

"I doubt it. No one has ever succeeded before. But I would be happy to hear you try.''

Then everybody stood while a young scholar read out thanks to the Lord for the food (or maybe it was for having survived it) and we all shuffled out. Grove accompanied me across the courtyard to see me out, pausing briefly at the entrance to his stair to pick up a bottle which had been left there. "Splendid," he said as he clutched it to his breast. "Warmth on a cold night."

I thanked him for his hospitality. "I am sorry if I annoyed either you or your colleague, Dr. Wallis. I did not intend it."

Grove waved his hand. "You certainly did not annoy me, and I wouldn't worry about Wallis. He is an irascible fellow. I don't think he liked you very much, but do not concern yourself: he doesn't like anyone. However, he is not a bad man; he has offered to visit Prestcott for me, as you say I should spare my eyes, which is kind of him. Now, here we are, Mr. Cola," he said. "Goodnight to you."

He bowed, then turned rapidly round and marched off to his room and his bottle. I stood watching him for a moment, surprised by the sudden dismissal, so unlike the lengthy formalities of Venice; but then there is nothing like a north wind in March for curtailing civilities.

chapter nine

IT WAS NOT UNTIL THE NEXT MORNING THAT I REAL-
ized a catastrophe was in the making; the earlier part of the
day was spent commiserating with Lower on the loss of his
corpse.

He took it in good part; as he said, his chances of getting
his hands on Prestcott's body had been small, so it gave him
a little satisfaction to know that the university wouldn't be
getting it either. Besides, he'd quite liked the lad, although
he, and most of the members of the town, did think that the
way he had maltreated Dr. Wallis was quite unseemly.

To explain briefly—and this succinct account was the result of piecing together innumerable accounts until I understood what had happened—the escape of Jack Prestcott from
the king's justice was partly my doing. I had delivered the
message about the lad wanting a visitor, and Dr. Wallis, the
very man who had been so rude to me at dinner, had gone
in Grove's place because of my medical advice. It was a kind
act, both to Grove and to Prestcott, and I felt ashamed for
deriving some small amusement from the result.

Wallis had asked that the prisoner be unshackled so that
he might have more ease in prayer, and was left alone with
him. About an hour later, still swaddled in his thick black
gown and heavy winter hat, he had emerged so distressed at
the imminent loss of a fine young life that he had scarcely
been able to speak, merely tipping the jailer two pence and

asking that Prestcott be allowed an undisturbed night's sleep. Reshackling could wait until the morning.

The jailer, who would undoubtedly lose his place as a result, had obeyed and it was not until after five the next morning that the cell was opened. Whereupon it was discovered that the person on the little cot was not Prestcott, but a bound and gagged Dr. Wallis who had, so he related, been overpowered by the young criminal, tied up and stripped of his cloak and hat. It had been Prestcott who had left the previous evening and who had won, as a result, nearly ten hours' start on any pursuers.

This intelligence caused a wonderful sensation; the population at large of course enjoyed the majesty of the law to be made ridiculous but was aggrieved at the loss of a hanging. On balance, admiration for the audacity outweighed the disappointment; the hue and cry set off to find him, but I suspect that most were not wholly displeased when they came back empty-handed.

Having appointed myself Grove's physician, I was naturally dispatched by Lower to examine his eye once more so that I could pick up gossip on the matter. However, the thick oak door leading to his room was firmly shut and locked, and this time there was no reply when I beat on it with my stick.

"Do you know where Dr. Grove is?" I asked of a serving woman.

"In his room."

"There is no answer."

"He must be still asleep."

I pointed out that it was nearly ten o'clock. Did not Fellows have to rise in order to attend chapel? Was it not unusual for him to be still asleep?

She was a surly and unhelpful woman, so I appealed to Mr. Ken, whom I saw walking around the other side of the quadrangle. He looked concerned, because he said it was Grove's particular pleasure to take the roll at chapel, and persecute latecomers. Perhaps his illness . . . ?

"It was only an inflamed eye," I said. "He was well enough to dine last night."

"What medicine did you give him? Perhaps that accounts for it?"

I did not like the suggestion that I might be responsible for making him ill, if he was so. But I hardly felt like admitting that my cure—which I had used as an example of the superiority of experimental medicine the previous evening—was merely water and eau de cologne.

"I hardly think so. But it concerns me; is there any way in which we can open this door?"

Mr. Ken talked to the servant and while they went in search of another key, I stood outside the door, and pounded again to see whether Grove could be roused.

I was still pounding when Ken reappeared with a key.

"Of course, it will be of no use if his own is in the lock, you know," he said as he knelt down and peered through the keyhole. "And he will be very angry indeed if he returns to find us here."

Ken, I noted, looked alarmed at this prospect.

"Perhaps you want to retire?" I suggested.

"No, no," he said uncertainly. "We have no love for each other, as you may have noticed, but in all Christian charity I could not abandon him if he were ill."

"You have heard about Professor Wallis?"

Mr. Ken suppressed a twitch of very unzealous merriment just in time to maintain his somber countenance. "I have indeed, and it shocks me that a man of the church should be treated in such a shameful fashion."

Then the door was open, and all thought of Dr. Wallis was banished from our thoughts.

That Dr. Grove was *corpus sine pectore* was indisputable, and it was apparent that he had died in considerable pain. He was lying on his back in the middle of the floor, face creased up, mouth open, with dried saliva dribbling out of one side. He had vomited and emptied his guts in his last moments, so there was an insufferable stink in the room. His hands were clenched so they more resembled claws than human hands, with one arm outstretched along the floor, and the other at his neck, almost as though he had tried to extinguish himself. The chamber itself was in total disarray; books lying on the floor, papers scattered about, so that it looked as if he had flailed around violently in his last moments. Or, as Lower later pointed out, maybe he was just untidy.

Fortunately, dead bodies do not trouble me greatly, although the shock of seeing this one and the horrible circumstances of its arrangement distressed me. But the sight terrified Mr. Ken. I half-thought he almost made the sign of the cross, and only stopped himself in time to preserve propriety.

"Dear Lord protect us in our time of sorrows," he said with a shaking voice as he saw the outstretched body. "You," he said to the servant, "run and fetch the warden quickly. Mr. Cola, what has happened here?"

"I am at a loss to say," I replied. "The obvious explanation would be a seizure, but the clenched hands and expression of the face would not indicate that. It looks as though he was in some great pain; perhaps the state of the room is a result of that."

We looked quietly at the poor man's corpse until the sound of steps on the wooden stairs roused us. Warden Woodward was a small, alert-looking man who maintained a great degree of self-possession when he saw what was within the room. He had a small mustache and beard in the old Royalist manner but, I was told, was in fact a Parliament man, who had hung onto his position not because he was a great scholar—the college paid little attention to that—but because he was a marvelous man with the money. As one fellow remarked, he could make a dead pig yield up a perpetual profit, and for that the college respected him.

"Maybe we should have a more definite opinion before we proceed," he said after he heard Ken and myself explain what we had found. "Mary," he went on, addressing the servant who was still standing in the background, ears flapping, "go and find Dr. Bate in the High Street, if you please. Tell him it is urgent, and that I would be grateful for his immediate attendance."

I almost opened my mouth to speak here, but again said nothing. To be passed over so rapidly did not please me, but there was little I could do about it. My only hope was that, my services not required and this a college matter, I would not be expelled from a most interesting situation. Lower, for one, would find it hard to forgive me if I returned without the story complete in all particulars.

"It seems clear to me," the warden said in a definite tone of voice that brooked no contradiction as we waited, "that the unfortunate man had a seizure. I can think of little else to be said. We must of course wait for confirmation, but I have no doubt it will be forthcoming."

Mr. Ken, one of those obsequious prelates who made a point of agreeing with anyone more powerful than he, nodded fervently. Both of them, in fact, seemed excessively eager to reach this conclusion, but it was mainly because of my sense of pique, I think, that I ventured my own opinion.

"Might I suggest," I said tentatively, "that the particulars of this business be examined more thoroughly before such a conclusion is adopted?"

Both looked at me with reluctance as I spoke. "For example, what ailments had the man complained of in the past? Did he, perhaps, drink too much the previous evening? Had he taken some physical exertion which strained his heart?"

"What are you suggesting?" Woodward said, turning round, stony-faced, to confront me. I noticed that Ken turned pale at my words as well.

"Nothing at all."

"You are a malicious man," he replied, taking me entirely by surprise. "Such an allegation is entirely without foundation. For you to bring it up at a time like this is monstrous."

"I know of no allegations, nor am I bringing them up," I said, completely astonished, yet again, by the unpredictability of the English. "Please assure yourself of my entire innocence on that. I simply wondered . . ."

"It is obvious even to me," Woodward continued vehemently, "that this was merely a seizure. And, what is more, it is a college matter, sir. We thank you for raising the alarm, but do not wish to trespass further on your time."

Which statement was obviously a dismissal, and a somewhat offensive one. I took my leave with more politeness than they.

chapter ten

I HAD ALMOST FINISHED MY TALE, MY FELLOWS IN
the coffee house enthralled by the account. It was, after all
about the most exciting occurrence to have happened in the
town since the siege and, as everybody involved was known
to my audience, doubly interesting for that. Lower immedi
ately started wondering whether he might offer to examine
the body himself.

We were trying to persuade him that the chances of being
allowed to anatomize Dr. Grove were slight, and he was pro
testing that such an idea had never crossed his mind, when
he looked up behind me, and a faint smile flickered across
his face.

"Well, well," he said. "What can we do for you, child?"

I looked around, and saw Sarah Blundy standing behind
me, pale and tired. Behind her, the woman Tillyard was com
ing into the room, scolding her for her impertinence. She
took hold of her arm, but Sarah threw it off angrily.

It was clear she had come to see me, and so I looked a
her coldly, as she deserved, and waited to hear what it was
I knew already: Lower, I was sure, had talked to her, and
stated the price of her mother's life. Either she made amend
for her behavior, or her mother died. It was, I think, a smal
fee.

She dipped her eyes in an attempt to be modest—such
eyes she had, I thought, very much against my will—and

said in a low, quiet voice: "Mr. Cola. I would like to offer you my apologies."

Still I said nothing, but continued to look frostily at her.

"My mother is dying, I think. Please . . ."

It was Dr. Grove who saved the old woman's life, then. If it hadn't been for the memory of his behavior in exactly the same setting a few days back, I would have turned away and made Tillyard throw her out as she deserved. But I wasn't going to give way so easily this time.

"Do you think for a moment I should lift a finger to help her? After the impudence you have showered on me?"

She shook her head humbly, her long dark hair cascading around her shoulders. "No," she said almost inaudibly.

"So why come?" I said doggedly.

"Because she needs you, and I know you are too good a man to abandon her because of my fault."

Praise indeed, I thought sarcastically as I made her wait in anguish and suffering a few more moments. Then, as I saw Boyle coolly appraising me, I sighed heavily and stood up. "Very well, then," I said. "She is a good woman and I will come for her sake. Having a daughter like you must be suffering enough for her."

I left the table, scowled at Lower's look of smug self-satisfaction. We walked across the town barely exchanging a word. Try as I might, I could not but feel pleased, and not because of having won a cheap victory. No; my pleasure was due solely to the fact that I could now conduct my experiment, and perhaps even save a life.

I had not been in the cottage more than a few moments before any further thoughts about the daughter dissipated entirely. The old woman was pale and restless, tossing and turning in her bed in delirium. She was also fearfully weak, and had a fever. At least the wound had not turned gangrenous, which had been my worst fear. But it was not mending either: skin, flesh and bone were not knitting, even though, by this time, there should have been very distinct signs that natural healing was taking effect. The splints still held the bone in place, but this was useless if her frail and weakened body would not look after itself. I could not make it do so, if it refused to act in its own interest.

I sat back and stroked my chin, my brow furrowed as I tried to come up with some other, more conventional treatment, some drug or some salve, which might help the old woman. But my mind was a blank. I want it understood that I tried to think of all possibilities which would obviate the need for my experiment: I did not rush into the attempt recklessly. Lower was right in saying the project should first be essayed on an animal. But there was no time, and no alternative that either I, or Lower when I asked, could suggest.

And the girl knew, as well as I did myself, how limited were my resources. She squatted down on her haunches in front of the fire, cupped her chin in her hands and gazed calmly and intently at me, for the first time a look of grave sympathy on her at my evident dismay.

"Her chances of recovery were not good, even before you came," she said softly. "Because of your kindness and skill she has lasted longer than I thought possible. I am grateful to you for that, and my mother has long been prepared for her death. Do not reproach yourself, sir. You cannot defeat God's will."

I looked at her carefully as she spoke, wondering whether there was some sarcasm or condescension in her voice, so used was I to rudeness from her. But there was none: she was speaking only with gentleness. Strange, I thought; her mother is dying, and she is comforting the physician.

"But how do we know what God's will is? You may be sure of it, but I was not brought up so. Maybe I am supposed to think of something that will aid her."

"If so, then you will do so," she answered simply.

I agonized with myself, hardly daring to say, even to a girl like this who could not possibly even begin to understand what I was proposing.

"Tell me," she said, almost as though she could see my indecision and hesitation.

"For a long time I have been pondering a form of treatment," I began. "I do not know if it would work. It might very well kill her more quickly than an executioner's blade. If I tried it I could be your mother's savior, or her killer."

"Not her Savior," the girl said seriously. "She has no need of another. But you could not be her killer either. No one who tries to help could be anything but her benefactor, whatever the outcome. It is the wish to help which is important, surely."

"The older you become, the more difficult it is to heal a wound," I said, wishing I had made this point to Grove the previous evening, and surprised at the wisdom of her remark. "Something a child would shrug off in a matter of days may be enough to kill an old person. The flesh becomes tired, it loses its resilience, and it eventually dies, freeing the spirit which abides within."

The girl, still squatting, looked impassively at me as I spoke, neither shifting restlessly, nor showing signs of incomprehension. So I continued.

"Or it may be that the blood grows old by constantly coursing through the veins, until it loses its natural strength, and becomes less effective in conveying the nutrients for the heart to ferment the vital spirits."

The child nodded at this, as though I had said nothing that surprised her; whereas in fact, I had advanced some of the latest discoveries and, for good measure added an outlandish interpretation that would already have had my elders shaking their heads in dismay.

"Do you understand me, child?"

"Of course," she said. "Why shouldn't I?"

"It surprises you that I say the blood circulates through the body, no doubt?"

"That could only surprise a physician," she said. "Any farmer knows it."

"How do you mean?"

"If you bleed a pig, you cut the main vein in its neck. The pig bleeds to death and produces soft white meat. How else could all the blood come out of one slit unless it was all connected? And it moves of its own accord, almost as though it is being pumped, so must go round and round. That is all obvious, isn't it?"

I blinked, and stared at her. It had taken practitioners of the medical art the better part of two thousand years to make this astounding discovery, and there was this girl saying she knew it all along. A few days ago, I would have been furious at her impudence. Now I merely wondered what else she—

and the country folk she mentioned—might know if only people troubled to ask them.

"Ah. Yes. Very well observed," I said, thrown off my path as I struggled to remember what I'd been talking about. I looked at her seriously and took a deep breath. "Anyway, what I propose is to give your mother fresh, new blood, to give her the restorative power of a woman very much younger than she. It has never been done before, never even thought of, as far as I know. It is dangerous, and would be scandalous if it were publicly known. And I do strongly consider that it is the only chance your mother has of continuing in this life."

The poor girl looked stunned at what I had said, and I could see a look of strained apprehension on her face.

"Well?"

"You are the physician, sir. It is in your hands."

I took a deep breath, realizing that I had half-hoped the girl would start to abuse me again, accusing me of flouting the Law of God or some such and thus relieve me of the burden I had so cavalierly taken on. But I was not to escape my fate so simply. I had staked my good character, my expertise, on what I had said, and there was no going back.

"I will have to leave you and your mother alone for a while and go and consult Lower, whose assistance I will require. I will be back as soon as possible."

I quit the hovel, and left Sarah Blundy kneeling by her mother's bed, stroking the old lady's hair and singing a song in a low, soft voice. A comforting and gentle sound, I thought as I left; my own mother had sung to me thus when I was ill, and stroked my hair in the same way. It had reassured me in my illness, and I offered up a prayer that it did the same for the old woman.

chapter eleven

I FOUND LOWER HARD AT WORK DISSECTING A BRAIN;
such work—later given to the world as his *Tractatus de
corde*—occupied him greatly during his days, and he had
prepared many fine sketches of its anatomy. He was not
pleased when I burst in to demand his assistance and again
I saw him in bad humor.

"Can't it wait, Cola?" he asked.

"I don't think it can. Not for long, at least. And in return,
I can offer you one of the most enjoyable of experiments."

"I do not experiment for enjoyment," he said curtly.

I studied his face, bent over the table as it was, with one
of his dark locks of hair hanging over his eye. There was a
set about the mouth and cheeks that made me concerned that
one of the moods of passing blackness was upon him.

"It is also a charity, and I beg you not to turn me away,
for I need help and you are the only person steady and wise
enough to give it. Do not be angry, for I promise to repay
your kindness tenfold later. I have examined Widow Blundy
and there is little time."

The obsequiousness of my manner disarmed him, for he
grimaced and, with a show of reluctance, put down his knife
and turned toward me.

"She is as bad as the girl's face indicated?"

"She is. She will die very soon, unless something is done.
We must try the experiment. She must be given blood. I have

examined the almanac; the sun is in Capricorn, which is good for matters of the blood. Tomorrow will be too late. I know you are doubtful of such details, but I am disinclined to take risks.''

He growled at me angrily as my manner made it clear that I would brook no refusal and not leave him in peace.

''I am not convinced this is a sound idea.''

''But she will die otherwise.''

''It is probable she will die in any case.''

''So what is there to lose?''

''In your case, nothing. In my case, the risk is more substantial; my career and my family depend on my making my way in London.''

''I don't see the problem.''

He wiped his thin knife on his apron and washed his hands. ''Listen, Cola,'' he said, turning to face me when he had finished, ''You have been here long enough to know of the opposition we face. Think of the way that idiot Grove assailed you at New College last night on exactly this question of experimental treatment. He has a point, you know, loath as I am to admit it. And there are many worse in a position to do me harm if I give them the slightest chance. If I take part in this operation, the patient dies and it becomes known, then my reputation as a physician will be damaged before my career has even begun.''

''You have doubts about the experiment I am proposing?'' I asked, trying another approach.

''I have the very gravest doubts about it, and you should have as well. It is a pretty theory, but the chances of the patient surviving the application of it seem small indeed. I must admit,'' he said reluctantly, making me sure I would win, ''it would be fascinating to try.''

''So if there was no fear of it becoming generally known . . . ?''

''Then I would be delighted to assist.''

''We can swear the daughter to silence.''

''True. But you must also swear that you too will say nothing. Even when you are back in Venice, if you published a letter saying what had taken place, you would land me in the most serious difficulty unless it was all done properly.''

I clapped him on the back. "Have no concerns," I said, "for I am not a publishing man. I give my word that I will not say anything unless you give me express permission."

Lower scratched his nose as he thought this over, then, grim-faced at the risk he was taking, he nodded his agreement. "Well, then," he said. "Let us be about it."

THAT IS HOW IT HAPPENED. EVEN NOW I LIKE TO THINK that he had no occult motive in insisting on this arrangement. He was prompted by the simplest self-interest and I think it was only later that, swayed by the siren words of his friends in the Royal Society, he came to prefer fame to honor, and advancement to friendship. Then he exploited my honesty and trust most basely, using my silence for his own ends.

At the time, however, I was overjoyed and grateful to him for taking such a risk on my behalf.

To be frank, I would have preferred to have conducted my experiment in better surroundings, and with more witnesses present to note what we were doing. But such an option did not exist: Mrs. Blundy could not be moved and, quite apart from Lower's fears, finding other qualified persons to participate would have taken too much time. So Lower and I alone walked, seriously and silently, back to the little hovel, where we once more found the sick woman and her daughter.

"My dear child," said Lower in his most friendly and reassuring fashion, "do you understand fully what my colleague has proposed? You understand the dangers, both to yourself and to your mother? We may be linking your souls and your lives together, and if it fails for one, it may be catastrophic for the other."

She nodded. "We are already linked as closely as mother and daughter can be. I told her but don't know how much she understood. I'm sure she would refuse, because she has always accounted her own life of little value, but you must ignore that."

Lower grunted. "And you, Cola? You wish to proceed?"

"No," I said, doubtful now the moment had arrived. "But I think we must."

Lower then examined the patient and looked grave. "I

certainly cannot fault your diagnosis. She is very ill indeed. Very well, then, let us begin. Sarah, roll up your sleeve, and come and sit here.''

He gestured to the little stool beside the bed, and when she was sat, I began wrapping a ribbon round her arm. Lower got to work uncovering the thin scrawny arm of the mother, and wrapped another ribbon—a red one this time; it has stuck in my mind—around her upper arm.

Then he took out his silver tube and two quills, and blew through them to make sure there were no blockages. ''Ready?'' he asked. We both nodded grimly. With a neat and experienced movement, he slipped a sharp knife into the girl's vein and inserted one quill into it, with the end pointing against the flow so that the natural movement diverted the blood out into the air; then he slipped a cup under it and began to collect the liquid. It poured in a ruby red rush into the bowl, faster than either of us had anticipated.

He counted slowly. ''This can hold half a gill,'' he said. ''I will just see how long it takes to fill, and then we can guess more or less how much we are taking.''

It filled swiftly, so much so that it overflowed and the blood began to splash on the floor. ''One and an eighth minutes,'' Lower called loudly. ''Quickly, Cola. The tube.''

I handed it to him as Sarah's lifeblood began splashing on the floor, and I inserted the other quill into the mother's vein, the other way around this time so that the new blood would flow in the same direction as her own and not set up turbulence. Then, and with surprising gentleness, as the girl's blood began to flow copiously out of the silver tube, Lower moved her over, and connected the tube to the quill protruding out of the mother's arm.

He peered intently at the join. ''It seems to be working,'' he said, barely managing to keep the surprise out of his voice. ''And I can see no sign of coagulation. How long do you calculate we should wait?''

''For eighteen ounces?'' I did the calculations as swiftly as I could while Lower counted. ''Ah, about ten minutes,'' I said. ''Make it twelve to be sure.''

Then silence fell, as Lower counted intently to himself, and the girl bit her lip and looked worried. She was very brave, I will say that: not a sound of complaint or worry came from her throughout the entire proceeding. For my part, I was in a state of anxiety, wondering what the result would be. There were no effects either way to start off with.

"... Fifty-nine, sixty ...," Lower said eventually. "That'll do. Out we come," and he pulled the tube out and put it on the floor, expertly putting his finger over the mother's vein and pulling out the quill. I did the same for the girl and then we both busied ourselves in bandaging their arms to stop the bleeding.

"Finished," he said with satisfaction. "How do you feel, my girl?"

She shook her head, and breathed deeply once or twice. "A bit dizzy, I think," she said faintly. "But all right."

"Good. Now you sit down quietly." Then he turned his attention to the mother. "No change there," he said. "What do you think?"

I shook my head. "Not better, not worse. But of course, it may take time for the youthful blood to have its effect."

"Whatever that effect might be," Lower murmured. "Normally in a case like this one would recommend a strong emetic, but I hardly think that would be wise at the moment. I think the only thing to do, my dear sir, is to sit and wait. And hope and pray. Your treatment will either work, or it will not. And that's an end of it. It's too late to change our minds now."

"Look at the girl," I said, pointing out how she had begun yawning mightily; she was also pale about the face, and complained of feeling lightheaded.

"That's just the blood loss. We have tapped her spirit, and so she is obviously reduced. Lie down, my girl, beside your mother, and sleep awhile."

"I must not. I have to look after her."

"Don't you worry about that. Cola here will want to watch her progress, and I will send someone I know after, so we can be informed of any developments. So get yourself into bed with her, and don't worry. What a day, Cola! What a day. First Dr. Grove, then this. I am quite fatigued by the excitement of it all."

"What?" Sarah said. "What about Dr. Grove?"

"Hmm? Oh, you know him, don't you? I'd forgotten. He's dead, you know. Cola here found him in his room this morning."

The girl's composure, apparently untouched by the blood loss and even by the thought of her mother dying, was affected for the first time by this news. She turned even paler than she already was, and we noticed, to our great astonishment, that she shook her head sadly, then curled up on the bed and buried her face in her hands. Very affecting and surprising, but I noticed that, for all her distress, she did not ask what had happened.

Lower and I exchanged glances, and quietly decided that there was nothing we could do: the tapping of her blood had weakened her, and the starvation of her womb had let slip the humors held in it, causing the body to react with all the symptoms of hysteria.

My friend was splendid, revealing a kindness and skill which his flippant exterior did not suggest, and which made the darkness of his occasional rage all the more perplexing to me. Having assured ourselves that there was enough food and heating, and acquired warm bed clothing for our patient, there was little else to do. We wished her well, and left. I came back a few hours later to see what progress had been made. Both mother and daughter were asleep, and I must say that the mother looked the more at peace.

chapter twelve

BY THE TIME I JOINED LOWER THAT EVENING AT
Mother Jean's—a woman who ran a cookhouse not far from
the High Street and offered edible food for only a small
amount of money—he seemed in a far better mood than he
had been earlier.

"And how is your patient?" he cried from his table as I
walked into the small, crowded room, full of students and
the more impecunious of Fellows.

"Largely unchanged," I said, as he pushed an undergraduate aside to make room for me. "She is still asleep, but her
breathing is easier and her complexion more sanguine."

"So it should be, considering," he replied. "But we must
talk of this later. May I introduce you to a good friend of
mine? A fellow physician and experimentalist? Mr. da Cola,
I present you to Mr. John Locke."

A man of about my age with a thin face, supercilious expression and long nose raised his head from his platter for a
second, muttered something and then descended back into
the food.

"A brilliant conversationalist, as you see," Lower continued. "How he can eat so much and remain so thin is one of
the great mysteries of creation. When he dies he has promised me his body so I can find out. Now, then. Food. I hope
you like pig's head. Tuppence, with as much cabbage as you

can eat. Beer a ha'penny. There is not much left, so you'd better shout the good mother over."

"How is it prepared?" I asked eagerly, for I was starving. I had quite forgotten to eat in the excitement of the day, and the prospect of a nice head, roasted with apples and liqueur, and perhaps with a few shrimp as well, made me salivate with anticipation.

"Boiled," he said. "In vinegar. How else?"

I sighed. "How else, indeed? Very well."

Lower called the woman over, ordered on my behalf, and presented me with a tankard of beer from his jug.

"Come, Lower, tell me what is the matter. You have a look of great amusement on your face."

He raised his finger to his lips. "Hush," he said. "It is a great secret. I hope you are not doing anything tonight."

"What would I be doing?"

"Excellent. I wish to repay you for your consideration in allowing me to assist you this afternoon. We have work to do. I have received a commission."

"What sort of commission?"

"Look in my bag."

I did as I was told. "A bottle of brandy," I said. "Good. It is my favorite drink. After wine, of course."

"You would like some?"

"Most decidedly. It will wash the taste of boiled pig's brains out of my mouth."

"That it would. Look at it carefully."

"It is half empty."

"Very observant. Now look at the bottom."

I did as I was told. "Sediment," I said.

"Yes. But there is sediment in wine, not in brandy. And this has a granular appearance. What is it?"

"I've no idea. What does it matter?"

"It came from Dr. Grove's room."

I frowned. "What were you doing there?"

"I was asked to attend. Mr. Woodward, who is a distant relation of Boyle—everyone is a distant relation of Boyle, as you will discover—asked his advice, and he declined to assist on the grounds that this was not an area in which he could claim competence. So he asked me to go in his stead. Naturally, I was delighted. Woodward is an important man.''

I shook my head. It was already clear what was going to happen. Poor Grove, I thought. He never had time to escape to Northampton. ''I thought he'd called in someone else. Bate, wasn't it?''

Lower flipped his fingers contemptuously. ''Old Grandfather Bate? He won't even leave his bed if he thinks Mars is in the ascendant, and his only treatment is leeching and burning herbs. It would take his entire training even to see poor old Grove was dead. No; Woodward is no fool. He wants the opinion of someone who knows what he's talking about.''

''And your opinion is . . . ?''

''That's the clever bit,'' he said craftily. ''I examined the body briefly and decided further investigation was required. Which I will do this evening, in the warden's kitchen. I thought you would like to be there. Locke wants to come as well and if Woodward provides some wine, we should have a most instructive time.''

''It would be a great pleasure,'' I said. ''Although are you sure I would be allowed? Warden Woodward did not seem a very welcoming man, when we met.''

Lower waved his hand dismissively. ''Don't worry about that,'' he said. ''You did meet him in distressing circumstances.''

''He was offensive,'' I said, '' in accusing me of giving countenance to slanderous tales.''

''Really? Which ones?''

''I don't know. All I did was ask whether the poor man might have undertaken some physical activity. Woodward turned dark with anger and accused me of malice.''

Lower rubbed his chin, a faint smile of understanding on his face. ''Well, well,'' he said. ''Maybe it was true, then.''

''What?''

''There was a little scandal,'' this man Locke said, for he had finished his food now and was prepared to give his attention to other things. ''Nothing too serious, but someone put it around that Grove was fornicating with his servant. Personally, I thought it unlikely, given the source of the story was Wood.''

"What do you mean?" I asked.

Locke shrugged, as though unwilling to continue. Lower, however, would have none of this decorum.

"The servant in question was Sarah Blundy."

"I must say that Grove always struck me as an upright man, well able to resist the wiles of someone like her," Locke said. "And, as I say the tale originated with that ridiculous man Wood, so naturally I discounted it."

"Who is Wood?"

"Anthony Wood. Or Anthony à Wood, as he likes to style himself, as he has delusions of quality. Have you not met him? Don't worry; you will. He will seek you out, and suck you dry. An antiquary of the most burrowing sort."

"Not so," said Lower. "I insist on justice. In that field he is a man of excellent abilities."

"Maybe so. But he is a pernicious gossip, and a melancholic little bundle of envy; everybody is less deserving, and succeeds only through connection. I'm sure he believes Jesus only got his job through family influence."

Lower cackled at the blasphemy, and I surreptitiously crossed myself.

"Now, Locke, you are upsetting our papist friend," Lower said with a grin. "The point is that Wood lives a monastic life with his books and manuscripts and rather took up with the girl in some way. She worked for his mother as a servant, and poor Wood felt greatly deceived by her."

Locke smiled. "Only Wood, you see, would have been at all surprised by such things," he said. "But he did find the girl a position with Grove and then constructed these notions about them. As he is malicious, he started spreading this around the town, with the result that Grove was forced to dismiss the girl to guard his good name."

Lower poked him in the arm. "Hush, my friend," he said. "For here is the man himself. You know how sensitive he is to being talked about."

"Oh, Lord," said Locke. "I can't take it. Not with food. I must apologize, Mr. Cole."

"Cola."

"Mr. Cola. I hope to see you later, perhaps. Good evening, gentlemen."

He rose, bowed swiftly and headed for the door at an un-civil speed, bowing to an absurdly scruffy man shambling toward us.

"Mr. Wood, sir," cried Lower civilly, "do sit down with us, and meet my friend Mr. Cola, of Venice."

Wood was already about to do so in any case, without being asked, and squeezed in alongside me, so that the smell of his unwashed clothes became quite impossible to ignore.

"Good evening sir, good evening, Lower."

I could see why Locke had been in such a hurry. Not only did the man smell, not only was he bereft of any elegance, even wearing his spectacles in public, as though he had for-gotten he was no longer in a library, but his presence in-stantly cast a pall of gloom over what had previously been a jolly table.

"I understand you are an historian, sir," I said, trying to make polite conversation once more.

"Yes."

"That must be very interesting. Are you of the univer-sity?"

"No."

Another long silence, broken eventually by Lower pushing back his chair and standing up. "I have to prepare," he said, quite ignoring my panicked looks of entreaty that I should not be left alone with Mr. Wood. "If you would join me at Mr. Stahl's in Turl Street in half an hour or so . . ."

And with a quiet twitch of amusement which indicated he knew full well the trick he was playing on me, Lower walked off, leaving me with only Mr. Wood for company. He, I noticed, did not order any food; rather he collected the plates of the others and scoured them for bits of fat and gristle, sucking the bones with a horrible noise. He must, I thought, be very poor indeed.

"I suppose they have told you snide stories about me," he said, then waved his hand as I rushed to deny it. "You needn't bother," he went on. "I know what they say."

"It doesn't seem to concern you much," I said cautiously.

"Of course it does. Does not every man wish to be held in high regard by his fellows?"

"I have heard many worse things said of others."

Wood grunted, and attended to Lower's plate; as the method of cooking had completely killed my appetite, I passed him my own, which was still laden with food.

"Kind of you," he said. "Very kind."

"You may consider Lower a false friend," I said, "but I may say that he spoke very highly of your skills in the historical way. Which tempts me to ask what it is that you do."

He grunted once more, and I was afraid that the nourishment might render him too talkative. "You are the Venetian physician I have heard of?" he said by way of reply.

"Venetian, but not a real physician," I said.

"Papist?"

"Yes," I said cautiously, but he did not appear about to launch into offensive denunciations.

"You think heretics should burn, then?"

"Pardon?" I said in some surprise at the gaucheness of his conversation.

"If someone is tempted out of the fold of the true church—your own or any other—do you think he should burn?"

"Not necessarily," I said, trying to marshal an argument at short notice. It seemed best to try to keep him on generalities, rather than prying into my private affairs. I detest gossip of all sorts. "He may deserve to lose his life, if you follow the argument of Aquinas, who asked why the counterfeiters of coin should be killed, but not counterfeiters of faith. But that is rare now, I think, whatever you Protestants may hear."

"I meant burn in hell."

"Oh."

"If I am baptized by a heretic priest, are the sins of Adam remitted?" he said thoughtfully. "If I am married by one, are my children bastards? Cyprian said the quality of the sacrament existed *ex opere operantis,* I think, so that a heretic baptism would be no baptism at all."

"But Pope Stephen countered that, and said it existed *ex opere operato,* through the merit of the action, not the standing of the actor," I said. "So you would be in no great danger if it was done on both sides by men of good intent."

He sniffed and wiped his mouth.

"Why do you ask?"

"You believe in mortal sin, you papists," he continued absently. "A gloomy doctrine, I think."

"Less so than your predestination. I believe God can forgive anything, even mortal sin, if he chooses. You say men gain or lose their immortal souls before they are even born and God cannot change it. What sort of poor thing is that for a God?"

He grunted yet again at this, and seem disinclined to engage any further, which struck me as odd considering that he had begun the dispute in the first place.

"Do you have a desire to become a Catholic, perhaps?" I asked, wondering if his sally had been prompted by something other than awkwardness and unfamiliarity with decent conversation. "Is this why you ask? I think you will have to find someone more learned than myself for that. I am a poor churchman."

Wood laughed, and I sensed that I had finally chiseled him out of his morbid introspection—a fine triumph, I think, for there is nothing more persistent than a Protestant in a state of melancholy. "You are indeed, sir. Did I not see you going into a heretic church with Mr. Lower only last Sunday?"

"I went to a service with him at St. Mary's, that is true. But I did not take communion. Although I must say I would have had no trouble doing so."

"You astonish me. How can that be?"

"The Corinthians saw no harm in eating meat offered in sacrifice to pagan idols, as they knew the gods not to exist," I said. "And however mistaken they were on other questions, I am in agreement with them on that. The act is harmless, it is willful false belief which is heresy."

"If we are presented with the truth, and refuse to accept the evidence of our eyes and ears?"

"Obviously a sin, surely?"

"Even if it goes against all accepted opinion?"

"Believing in Christ went against all accepted opinion once. Discerning the truth, however, is not so easy. Which is why we must not be too hasty to reject beliefs hallowed by tradition, even though we may criticize in private."

Wood grunted. "That sounds Jesuitical to me. You would

have no objection to my attending a service in one of your churches?''

"I would welcome you. Not that I have any right either to welcome or exclude.''

"You are very easygoing, I must say. But how do you know that the Anglican church is heretical?''

"For the reasons I give. And because it has been condemned as such by the pope.''

"Oh, I see. So if a proposition was plainly heretical, but had not been condemned? Would I—or you—have liberty to countenance it?''

"I suppose it would depend on the proposition,'' I said, desperately seeking some way out of the conversation, which had suddenly swung back to despondency again. But he was a tenacious man, and did so obviously want company, poor soul, that I could not be cruel. "If you like, I will give you an example. Several years ago, I came across a history of heretical movements in the early church. You know, of course, of the Phrygian Montanus, and his assertion that new prophets in every generation would add to the words of Our Lord.''

"Condemned by Hippolytus.''

"But supported by Tertullian, and commented on favorably by Epiphanius. And not my point, for this history I mentioned talked of a woman follower of Montanus called Prisca, and her sayings have never been condemned, as far as I am aware, as almost no one knows of them.''

"And what did she say?''

"That redemption is a perpetual process, and in each generation the Messiah would be reborn, would be betrayed, would die, and be resurrected, until mankind turns away from evil, and sins no more. And, I may say, very much more of the same sort of thing.''

"A doctrine which has passed from the sight of man, you say,'' Wood replied, strangely more interested in my example than in anything else I had said since I handed him my food. "Not surprisingly. It is surely just an unsubtle version of Origen, who held that Christ is crucified again each time we sin. It is a metaphor taken literally.''

"My point is, that despite the fact that no formal condemnation has ever been made, there can be no doubt that Catholics are obliged to reject it, as they are obliged to reject any heathen religion. Doctrine and liturgy are laid down quite clearly, and we must assume that what is not permitted is by definition excluded.''

Wood grunted. ''You never rebel against what you are told to believe?''

''Frequently,'' I said cheerfully. ''But not on doctrine. There is no need to do so, since it is plainly correct in all particulars. Your Mr. Boyle believes that when science and religion are in conflict, then there is a mistake in the science. That is little different from saying that when the individual mind and the church are at odds, it is the duty of the individual to learn wherein lies his error.''

I could see that Wood was getting far more interested in this conversation than I was, and that he was on the brink of suggesting that we go somewhere to drink and continue our most fascinating discourse. I could think of nothing I wanted less, and so before I was put in the position of having to rebuff him, I stood up hastily.

''You must forgive me, Mr. Wood, but I have a appointment with Lower. I am late already.''

His face fell with disappointment, and I felt sorry for the fellow. It is hard to mean so well, and try so hard, and be kept at arm's length nonetheless. I would have been more congenial had I the time, despite my distaste for his scholarly earnestness and blockish discourse. But, fortunately, I did not have to lie to avoid him: more important matters really did await. I left him sitting there finishing my dinner, all alone, and the only silent person in a room full of merriment and good company.

THIS MAN PETER STAHL WHOM LOWER WISHED TO CONsult was a German, and known to be something of a magician, having a fine knowledge of alchemy. When in drink he could talk fascinatingly about the philosopher's stone, eternal life and how to turn base elements into gold. For myself, I always think that talk is very fine, but not as good as demonstration, and Stahl, for all his claims and obscure phrases, never conferred eternal life on even a spider. As he was not noticeably rich, I assume that he never succeeded in turning anything into gold either. However, as he once said, the simple fact that something has not been done, is no proof that it cannot be; he would accept that such things were impossible only when convinced that matter was immutably imprinted with unique form. All the evidence so far, he said, suggested that it was possible to change base materials into primary elements. If you could change acqua fortis into salt—a simple enough proposition—by what reason did someone like myself scoff at the proposition that, given the right method, it was possible to turn stone into gold? Similarly, all medicine aimed at fending off illness and age and decay; some medicines even worked. Could I then swear—and give reasons for my belief—that there was no ultimate potion which might fend off illness forever? After all, the best minds of antiquity believed it, and there was even Biblical testimony. Did not Adam live for 930 years and Seth 912 years and Methuselah 969 years, as Genesis said?

Lower had warned me that he was a difficult character and that only Boyle could keep him under control. His abilities were matched by equal vices, as he was a sodomite of the most flagrant variety, who delighted in disgusting those who conversed with him. He was in his forties at this period, and showed the signs of decrepitude that vice brings in its train, with heavy lines around a tight mouth full of foully decayed teeth, and a hunched-over deportment indicating the suspicion and distaste in which he held all the world. He was one of those who considered everybody to be his inferior, no matter what their station, attainments or quality. No monarch was as adept as he at ruling kingdoms, no bishop as well versed in theology, no lawyer as subtle at preparing a case. Oddly, the one area where his arrogance did not rule was the one where it might have been justifiable, which was in his skill at chemical experimentation.

The other curiosity about him was that, although he treated everybody with scorn, he gave tirelessly of his time and effort once his curiosity was engaged. Human beings he could not deal with, but set him a problem and he would work to exhaustion. Although he should have aroused little but disgust, I nonetheless developed a cautious regard for the man.

It was hard to persuade him to assist, even though he knew that Lower was an intimate of Boyle, who was at that time paying his wages. As we explained the situation, he sprawled in a chair and looked contemptuously at us.

"So? He is dead," he said in his thick accented Latin, which he pronounced with the old-fashioned weighting and value, quite discredited amongst the *cognoscenti* of Italy, although the English and others (I understand) still become passionately heated on the subject. "Does it matter what happened precisely?"

"Of course," Lower replied.

"Why?"

"Because it is always important to establish the truth."

"And you think that can be done, do you?"

"Yes."

Stahl snorted. "Then you are more optimistic than I am."

"What do you spend your time doing, then?" I asked.

"I amuse my masters," he replied in a disagreeable tone. "They want to find out what happens if you mix verdigris with oil of niter, so I mix it for them. What happens if you heat it, so I heat it."

"And then try to work out why it happens."

He waved his hand airily. "Pfaf. No. We try to work out how it happens. Not why."

"There is a difference?"

"Of course. A dangerous difference. The gap between how and why troubles me greatly, as it should you. It is a difference that will bring the world down on our heads." He blew his nose and looked at me with distaste. "Look," he continued, "I am a busy man. You have come here with a problem. It must be a problem of chemistry, otherwise you wouldn't have demeaned yourself by asking me a favor. Correct?"

"I have a very high opinion of your abilities," Lower protested. "I've given you evidence enough of that, surely. I have been paying you for lessons for long enough."

"Yes, yes. But I haven't been overburdened by social calls. Not that I mind, as I have better things to do than talk.

So if you want a favor of me, tell me what it is, then go away.''

Lower seemed quite used to this performance. I probably would have walked out by this stage, but he very placidly took the brandy bottle out of his satchel, and put it on the table. Stahl peered at it closely—I could see that he was short-sighted, and probably could have done with a pair of spectacles.

''So? What's this?''

''It's a bottle of brandy, with a strange slurry at the bottom, which you can see as well as I can, despite your pretense of being blind. We want to know what it is.''

''Aha. Was Dr. Grove killed by Spirits or by spirits? That's the problem, is it? Is their wine the poison of dragons and the cruel venom of asps?''

Lower sighed. ''Deuteronomy 32:33,'' he responded. ''Just so.'' And then stood patiently as Stahl went through an elaborate display of apparent thought.

''So, how do we test this substance, even though it is corrupted by the liquid?'' The German thought some more. ''Why don't you offer that tease of a servant of yours a glass of this brandy one evening, eh? Solve two problems in one go?''

Lower said he didn't think this was a very good idea. It would, after all, be hard to repeat the experiment even if it were successful. ''Now, will you help us, or not?''

Stahl grinned, showing a range of blackened, yellowing stumps that passed for teeth and which might well have accounted for his ugly temper. ''Of course,'' he said. ''This is a fascinating problem. We need a series of tests that can be repeated, and be sufficiently numerous so that it will identify this sediment. But first I have to extract this sediment in a usable form.'' He pointed at the bottle. ''I suggest you go away and come back in a few days. I will not be rushed.''

''Perhaps we might start, though?''

Stahl sighed, then shrugged and stood up. ''Oh, very well. If it will rid me of your company.'' He went over to a shelf and selected a flexible tube with a piece of thin glass on the end, and inserted this into the open end of the bottle, which he placed on the table. Then, crouching down, he sucked on the other end of the tubing, and stood back as the liquid ran swiftly into a receptacle which he had placed underneath.

"An interesting and useful exercise," he observed. "Common enough, of course, but fascinating nonetheless. As long as the second part of the tube is longer than the first, the liquid will continue to flow out, because the liquid falling downward weighs more than the liquid being required to flow upward. If it didn't, a vacuum would form in the tube, which is impossible to sustain. Now, the really interesting question is, what happens if . . ."

"You don't want to suck all the sediment out as well, do you?" Lower interrupted anxiously as the level of brandy fell toward the bottom of the bottle.

"I saw it, I saw it." And Stahl quickly whipped the glass tube out.

"And now?"

"And now I remove the sediment, which must be washed and dried. This will take time, and there is no reason at all for you to be here."

"Just tell us what you plan."

"Simple enough. This is a mixture of brandy and sediment. I shall heat it gently to evaporate the liquid, then wash it in fresh rainwater, allow it to settle once more, again decant the liquid off and wash and dry it a second time. It should be fairly pure by then. Three days, if you please. Not a moment earlier, and if you do turn up before then, I won't talk to you."

AND SO I FOLLOWED LOWER BACK TO NEW COLLEGE, and the warden's lodgings, a large pile which occupied much of the western wall of the quadrangle. We were taken by the servant into the room in which Warden Woodward received guests, and found Locke already there, stretched out in conversation by the fire, as easy as if he owned the place. There was, I thought, something about the man which could always inveigle his way into the good graces of the powerful. How it was I do not know; he was neither easy of manner nor particularly good company, and yet the assiduity of his attention to those he considered worthy of him was so great that it was irresistible. And, of course, he carefully crafted his reputation for being a man of the utmost brilliance, so that these people ended up patronizing him and feeling grateful for it. In later years he went on to write books which pass for philosophy, although a cursory reading suggests that they do little but carry his bent for flattery onto the metaphysical plane, justifying why those who patronize him should have all power in their hands. I did not like Mr. Locke.

His ease and self-assurance in the presence of Warden Woodward contrasted with the manner of my friend Lower, who fell into despondency when required to produce the mixture of deference and politeness required for dealing with those greater than he. Poor man; he desperately wanted favor, but had not the ability to pretend, and his awkwardness was all too frequently viewed as rudeness. Within five minutes the fact that Lower had been asked to examine Grove's body with Locke there merely to observe had been all but forgotten; all the conversation passed between the lengthy philosopher and the warden, while Lower sat uncomfortably by the side, his humor sinking as he listened in awkward silence.

For myself, I was gladly quiet, as I did not wish to incur Woodward's displeasure again, and it was Locke—to give him credit—who rescued me.

"Mr. Cola here was dismayed at your censure of him earlier in the day, Warden," he said. "You must remember he is a stranger in our society and knows nothing of our affairs. Whatever he said was perfectly innocent, you know."

Woodward nodded, and looked at me. "Please accept my apologies, sir," he said. "But I was distraught and did not mind my words as I should have done. But I had received a complaint the previous evening, and misconstrued your meaning."

"What sort of complaint?"

"Dr. Grove was being considered for a living and was likely to be given the place, but a complaint was lodged only yesterday evening which alleged he was of a lewd way of life, and should not be appointed."

"This was the Blundy girl, was it not?" Locke asked in a wordly, disinterested fashion.

"How do you know that?"

Locke shrugged. "Common knowledge in the taverns, sir. Not that that fact makes it true, of course. Might I ask where this complaint came from?"

"It came from within the Fellowship," Woodward said.

"And more particularly?"

"More particularly it is a college matter alone."

"Did your complainant give any evidence for the accusation?"

"He said that the girl in question was in Dr. Grove's room yesterday evening, and he had seen her go in. He complained lest others see her and bring its reputation into question."

"And was that true?"

"I had planned to ask Dr. Grove this morning."

"So, she was there last night, and Grove was dead this morning," Locke said. "Well, well . . ."

"Are you suggesting she extinguished his life?"

"Heavens, no," Locke replied. "But extreme physical exertion, you know, may in certain circumstances bring on a seizure, as Mr. Cola here so innocently pointed out this morning. That is by far the most likely explanation. If so, then a careful examination will certainly help us. And anything more sinister seems unlikely, as Mr. Lower says the girl seemed genuinely upset when she was informed of Grove's death."

The warden grunted. "Thank you for the information. Perhaps we had better proceed? I have had his body placed in the library. Where do you want to examine it?"

"We need a large table," Lower said gruffly. "The kitchen would be best, if there are no servants around."

Woodward went off to dismiss the kitchen staff, and we went into the next room to examine the body. When the house was deserted, we carried him across the hallway and into the domestic offices. Fortunately Grove had already been laid out and washed, so we were not delayed by that less than agreeable business.

"I suppose we'd better begin, don't you think?" Lower asked, clearing the dinner plates off the kitchen table. We took off Grove's clothes and, in the state in which God had created him, lifted him up. Then Lower got his saws, sharpened his knife and rolled up his sleeves. Woodward decided that he did not want to observe, and so left us to it. "I'll get my pen if you would be so good as to shave his head," Lower said.

Which I willingly did, paying a visit to the closet where one of the servants kept his toiletries and fetching a razor.

"A barber as well as a surgeon," Lower said as he drew the head—for his own interest only, I suspected. Then he put down the paper, stood back and thought for a moment. When fully prepared, he picked up knife, hammer and saw and we all paused a moment in the prayers appropriate for those about to violate and enter God's finest work.

"Skin isn't blackened, I note," Locke said conversationally when the moment of piety was over and Lower began carving his way through the layers of yellow fat to the rib cage. "Are you going to try the heart test?"

Lower nodded. "It will be a useful experiment. I'm not convinced by the argument that the heart of a poisoning victim cannot be consumed by fire, but we should see." A slight ripping sound as the layers were finally severed. "I do hate cutting up fat people."

He paused awhile as he opened up the midriff and held open the thick heavy flaps of fat by nailing each corner to the kitchen table.

"The trouble is," he continued once this was done and he had a clear view inside, "the book I consulted did not specify whether you were meant to dry the heart out first. But you see Locke's point about the lack of blackening on the skin, do you, Cola? A sign against poisoning. On the other hand, it is livid in patches. You see? On the back and thighs? Maybe that counts. I think we must call it inconclusive. Did he throw up before he died?"

"Very much so. Why?"

"A pity. But I'll have his stomach, just in case. Pass that bottle, will you?"

And he decanted in a very expert fashion a slimy, bloody, stinking froth from the stomach into a bottle. "Open the window, will you, Cola?" he said. "We don't want to make the warden's lodging uninhabitable."

"People poisoned commonly do vomit," I said, recalling

a case in which my teacher in Padua had been allowed to poison a criminal to see the effect. The poor unfortunate had died rather unhappily; but as he had been due to have his limbs cut off and his entrails burned before him while he was still alive, he remained until the end pathetically grateful to my master for his consideration. "But I believe they rarely manage to expel all of the stomach's contents."

Conversation ceased at this point as Lower busied himself transferring stomach, spleen, kidney and liver to his glass bottles, passing comment on all of them as he held each individual organ up for me to see before popping it into its bottle.

"The cawl is yellower than usual," he said brightly, as the work slowly restored him to good humor. "Stomach and intestines are an odd brownish color on the exterior. The lungs have black spots on them. Liver and spleen much discolored and the liver looks—what would you say?"

I peered inside at the odd-shaped organ. "I don't know. It rather looks as though it had been boiled to me."

Lower chuckled. "So it does. So it does. Now, the bile; very fluid. Runs all over the place and a sort of dirty yellow color. Most abnormal. Duodenum inflamed and excoriated but with no traces of natural decay. Same applies to stomach."

Then I saw him eyeing the corpse reflectively, as he wiped his bloody hands on his apron.

"No more," I said firmly.

"I beg your pardon?"

"I do not know you well, sir, but already I recognize that look. If you are thinking of opening his skull and removing his brain, then I must beg you to desist. We are, after all, trying to establish the cause of his death; it would be quite illegitimate to go chopping bits off to perform dissections on them."

"And he will be on public view before the funeral, remember," Locke added. "It would be hard to disguise the fact that you had cut his skull in two. It will be bad enough making sure no one sees that his head has been shaved."

Lower clearly considered disputing this, but eventually shrugged. "Keepers of my conscience," he said. "Very well, although medical knowledge may well suffer for your moral stand."

"Not permanently, I feel sure. Besides, we should be putting him back together again."

And so we set to work, stuffing his cavities with strips of linen to present a good appearance, sewing him up, then bandaging the wounds in case any fluids should emerge to stain his funeral garb.

"Never looked better, in my opinion," Lower said when Grove was finally dressed in his best and placed comfortably on a chair in the corner, with the bottles containing his organs lined up on the floor. Lower, I saw, was determined to have those at least. "Now, the final test."

He took the man's heart, put it in a small earthenware dish on top of the stove and poured a quarter pint of brandy over it. Then he took a splinter of wood and lit it at the stove and thrust it into the bowl.

"A bit like plum pudding, really," he said tastelessly as the brandy exploded into flames. We stood around and watched, as the liquid burned, and then eventually spluttered out, leaving an exceptionally unpleasant odor in the air.

"What do you think?"

I examined Dr. Grove's heart with care, then shrugged. "A bit charred over the surface membrane," I said. "But no one could say that it had been consumed, even partly."

"My conclusions as well," Lower said with satisfaction. "The first real evidence in favor of poisoning. That's interesting."

"Has anybody ever tried this test on someone who has indubitably not died of poisoning?" I asked.

Lower shook his head. "Not that I know of. Next time I have a corpse I'll give it a try. Now, you see, had young Prestcott not been so selfish we could have had a comparison." He glanced around the kitchen. "I suppose we had better clear up a bit; otherwise the servants will bolt when they come in tomorrow morning."

He set to work himself with a cloth and water; Locke, I noted, did not assist.

"There," he said after many minutes' silence in which I had tidied, he had washed and Locke had puffed on his pipe.

"If you would call the warden, we can put Grove back. But before we do, what is our opinion?"

"The man is dead," Locke said dryly.

"How?"

"I do not think there is enough evidence to say."

"Sticking your neck out as usual. Cola?"

"I am disinclined on the evidence so far to think his death anything but natural."

"And you, Lower?" Locke asked.

"I would suggest that we reserve judgment until such time as further evidence is forthcoming."

With a careful warning that we were not to inform anyone of the evening's activity, lest too much scandal be excited, Warden Woodward thanked us for our help after we had presented our puny conclusions. The relief on his face—for Lower had not told him about Stahl and he clearly thought the matter was now closed—was self-evident.

chapter thirteen

IT IS THE CUSTOM OF THE ENGLISH TO BURY THEIR
dead with as much speed as they hang them. Under normal
circumstances, Dr. Grove would have been interred in the
cloister of New College already, but the warden had used
some pretext to delay the ceremony for a full two days.
Lower used the time granted him to urge Stahl to speed,
while I was left at liberty due to Mr. Boyle's absence in
London, which town had a greater attraction for him since
his beloved sister moved there.

Most of the day I used up in attending to my patient and
my experiment, and the moment I arrived, I saw with joy
that both were progressing well. Mrs. Blundy was not only
awake and alert, she had even eaten a little thin soup. Her
fever was gone, her piss had a healthy bitterness and, even
more extraordinarily, there were the first signs of improvement in her wound. Little enough, to be sure, but for the first
time I saw that her condition had not deteriorated.

I was delighted, and beamed at her with all the triumphant
affection a physician can have for an obedient patient. "My
dear woman," I said when I had finished my examination,
applied some more salve and sat down on the rickety stool,
"I do believe we may yet snatch you from the jaws of death.
How do you feel?"

"A little better, thank you, praise be to God," she said.
"Not ready to go back to work yet, I fear. It is a great

concern to me. Dr. Lower and yourself have been more than generous, but we cannot survive without my earning money.''

''Your daughter does not earn enough?''

''Not to keep us out of debt, no. She has trouble with her work, for she has a reputation for being fiery and disobedient. It is so unfair; a better girl no mother ever had.''

''She is sometimes more outspoken than a girl in her position has a right to be.''

''No, sir. She is more outspoken than a girl in her position is allowed to be.''

There was a sudden defiance in her weak voice as she said this, although what exactly she meant was not immediately clear to me.

''Is there a difference?'' I asked.

''Sarah was brought up in a society of the most perfect equality between men and women; she finds it hard to accept that there are things forbidden her.''

It was difficult to resist a smirk, but I remembered she was my patient, and so humored her; besides, I had undertaken my travels to learn, and even though this was far from being useful experience, I was broad-minded enough then to tolerate it.

''I am sure a good husband would teach her all she needs to know on that subject,'' I said. ''If one can be found for her.''

''It will be difficult to find anyone she would accept.''

This time I did laugh out loud. ''I think she should take anyone willing to have her, should she not? She has little enough to offer in return.''

''Only herself, but that is much. I think sometimes we did not do right by her,'' she replied. ''It has not ended as we expected. Now she is all on her own, and her parents are a burden rather than a support.''

''Your husband is alive, then?''

''No, sir. But the calumnies that were heaped on him bear down on her as well. I see from your face that you have heard of him.''

''Very little, and I have learned never to believe what I hear when it is bad.''

"In that case you are a rare man," she said gravely. "Ned was the most loving of husbands and the best of fathers who devoted his life to winning justice in a cruel world. But he is dead, and I will soon be so as well."

"She has no resources whatsoever? No people apart from yourself?"

"None. Ned's family was from Lincolnshire, mine from Kent. All my people are dead, and his were dispersed when the fens were drained and they were thrown off their lands without a penny. So Sarah is quite without connections. What prospects she had were taken by slander, and she has spent the small sums she saved for her dowry on me in my illnesses. The only thing she will have from me when I die is her freedom."

"She'll manage," I said cheerfully. "She is young and healthy, and in any case, you do me a great disservice. I am, after all, doing my very best to keep you alive. With some success, I must say."

"You must be very pleased that your treatment worked. It is strange how much I wish to live."

"I am pleased to gratify you. I think that we may have stumbled on a remedy of unparalleled importance. It was a shame that Sarah was all that we had available. If we'd had a bit more time, we might have been able to recruit a blacksmith. Just think, if we had given you the blood of a really strong man, you might be up and about by now. But I'm afraid the spirit contained in a woman's blood will not allow your leg to mend as rapidly. Perhaps in a week or so we could repeat the treatment . . ."

She smiled, and said that she would submit to whatever I thought necessary. And so I left, in a high state of good humor and self-regard.

I met Sarah herself, trudging through the muddy slush of the lane outside, carrying more sticks and logs for the fire. Even when I greeted with good cheer and, to my surprise, she responded warmly.

"Your mother is doing well," I told her. "I am delighted with her."

She smiled easily, the first time I had seen such an expression on her face. "God has smiled on us through you, doctor," she replied. "I am very grateful."

"Think nothing of it," I replied, warmed by the response. "It was fascinating. Besides, she is not fully cured yet, you know. She is still weak; weaker than she herself knows. And I think further treatment might be useful. You must make sure she does nothing that might endanger that. I suspect you will find it difficult."

"I will indeed. She is much used to activity."

Although the thaw was beginning, and the country was slowly emerging from the long dark of winter, it was still ferociously cold when the wind got up, and I shivered in the gusts of bitter air. "I must talk to you about these matters," I said. "Is there anywhere we could go?"

She told me there was a drinking house around the corner which had a fire and I should go there. For herself, she would build up the fire and ensure her mother was comfortable, then join me.

The place she indicated was not at all like the spacious, elegant coffee house kept by the Tillyards, nor even like the grand inns that had grown up to service the coaches; rather it was a place for the mob, and had only the fire to commend it. It was owned by an old woman who sold the ale she brewed to local customers who would come in to warm themselves. There was no one there but myself, and it was obvious it was not a room ever graced by the presence of gentlemen; I was regarded with a curiosity which was not friendly when I opened the door and walked in. Nonetheless I sat myself by the fire and waited.

Sarah arrived a few minutes later and greeted the crone with familiarity: she was welcomed while I was not. "She was an army woman," she said.

This, apparently, was meant to be explanation enough; and I asked no more.

"How are you?" I enquired, as I was anxious to note the effect of the procedure on the donor of the blood as well as the recipient.

"I am tired," she said. "But that is more than made up for by seeing my mother improve."

"She is also concerned about you," I replied. "That is

not good for her. You must present a cheerful countenance.''

"I do as I can,'' she said. "Although sometimes that is not easy. Your generosity, and Dr. Lower's, have been a great boon in recent days."

"Do you have employment?''

"Some. I am working again for the Wood family most days, and in the evenings there is occasionally some work at a glove maker's. I stitch well, although it is hard sewing leather.''

"Why were you so upset about Dr. Grove?''

Instantly I could see the caution come over her face, and I feared was about to be subjected to another one of her outbursts. So I held up my hand to prevent it.

"Please do not think me malicious. I ask for a good reason. I must tell you that there is some cause for concern about his death, and it has been said that you were seen in the college that same evening.''

She still looked stonily at me, so I continued, half wondering why I was taking such trouble. "It may well be that someone else will ask you the same questions.''

"What do you mean about concern?''

"I mean that there is a small possibility that he died of poison.''

Her faced turned pale as I spoke, and she looked down in thought for a few seconds before staring blankly into my eyes. "Is that so?''

"As I understand it, he had discharged you from his employ recently?''

"True. And for no good reason.''

"And you resented it?''

"Very much. Of course. Who would not? I had worked hard and well for him, and never for a moment deserved any reproach.''

"And you approached him in the coffee house? Why?''

"I thought he would have had a good enough heart to help my mother. I wanted to borrow money from him.'' She looked at me angrily, daring me either to pity or criticize.

"And he turned you away.''

"You saw that for yourself.''

"Did you go to his room the night he died?''

"Does someone say I did?"

"Yes."

"Who says this?"

"I don't know. Answer the question, please. It is important. Where were you?"

"That is none of your concern."

We had reached an impasse, I could see. If I kept on pressing, she would walk out, and yet she was very far from satisfying my curiosity. And what possible reason could she have for not being frank? Nothing was so important that it was worth encouraging suspicion in any form, and she must have known by now that I meant her well. I tried one last time, but again she blocked my enquiry.

"Was there any truth in these stories?"

"I know of no stories. Tell me, doctor. Is someone saying Dr. Grove was murdered?"

I shook my head. "I don't think so. There is no reason to think so at the moment and he is to be buried this evening. Once that has taken place, the matter will be closed. Certainly the warden genuinely believes, I think, that there is nothing suspicious about the occurrence at all."

"And you? What do you believe?"

I shrugged again. "I have heard of many men of Grove's age and appetites dying suddenly of a fit, and apart from that it is of little concern to me. My main concern is your mother, and the treatment I have given her. Has she passed any stools?" She shook her head. "Make sure you collect them if she does," I continued. "They will be of great importance to me. Do not let her up, and make sure she does not wash. Above all, keep her warm. And if her condition changes at all, let me know instantly."

chapter fourteen

THE FUNERAL SERVICE FOR GROVE WAS A SOLEMN and dignified affair which began shortly after darkness had fallen. All through the day, I imagined, the preparations were made: the college gardener excavated a space in the cloister next to the chapel, the choir of boys practiced, and Woodward prepared the eulogy. I decided to attend once Lower told me he thought there would be no objection; Grove was, after all, one of the few people I had known in the town. But I insisted on his coming as well; there are few things more distressing than being in a religious ceremony and not knowing what to do next.

He grumbled about it, but eventually agreed. The regime in New College, I gathered, was not greatly to his liking. When it began—the chapel full, the attendant priests in vestments—I could see why, from his point of view. "You will have to explain," I said in a whisper during a lull in the proceedings, "what the difference between your church and mine is. I must say I can discern very little."

Lower scowled. "There is none here. Why they are not open and pronounce their obedience to the whore of Babylon—apologies, Cola—I do not know. They all want to, the scoundrels."

There were, I guessed, about half a dozen or more of Lower's persuasion, and not all were as well behaved as he. Thomas Ken, the man who had disputed with Grove over dinner, sat ostentatiously through the whole service and talked loudly during the requiem. Dr. Wallis, who had been so rude to me, sat cross-armed and with the disapproving quietude of the professional cleric. A few more even laughed at the most solemn moments, earning them ill-tempered looks from others. If the ceremony concluded without degenerating into an open fight, I thought at one stage, then we would be fortunate.

Somehow, though, it came to an end without scandal, and I thought that I could almost feel the relief in the air as Woodward pronounced the final blessing and led the way, white stick in hand, out of the chapel and around the cloister to the open grave. The body was moved over the gaping hole and held up by four of the Fellows; Woodward was preparing the final prayer when there was a scuffling from the back.

I looked at Lower: both of us were sure that tempers had finally boiled over and Grove's last moments above the earth were to be tarnished by doctrinal dispute. A few of the fellows were scandalized and turned round with angry looks; a murmur ran through the congregation as their numbers were forced aside to let through a portly man with gray whiskers, a thick cloak and a look of acute embarrassment.

"What is this about?" Woodward said, turning away from the grave to face the interloper.

"This burial must stop," the man said.

I nudged Lower and whispered in his ear. "Who's that? What's going on?" Lower dragged his attention away and whispered, "Sir John Fulgrove. Magistrate," then bade me keep silent.

"You have no authority in this place," Woodward continued.

"In matters of violence, I do."

"There has been no violence."

"Perhaps not. But I am obligated by my position to satisfy myself. I have received an official notice that murder may have been done, and I am bound to investigate. You know that as well as I do, Warden."

A loud murmur went up once the word murder was mentioned. Woodward stood stock still in front of the grave, as though protecting the body from the magistrate. In fact, he was protecting his college.

"There is no question of murder. I am quite satisfied."

The magistrate was uncomfortable, but determined to stand his ground. "You know that once a complaint is received, then it must be properly investigated. The fact that this death occurred inside the college is of no importance. Your privileges do not extend that far. You cannot exclude me on such a matter, nor can you dispute my writ. I order that this funeral cease until I am satisfied."

With the eyes of the college, and a good part of the university, upon him, Woodward swayed to and fro as he considered how best to respond to this open challenge. He was not, ordinarily, a man to hesitate for a moment but on this occasion he took his time.

"I will not cede to your authority, sir," he said eventually. "I do not accept you have any right to enter this place without my consent, nor to interfere with college business. I am satisfied there is no cause for your presence, and that I could in law order you out."

The audience looked pleased at this statement, and Sir John bridled with indignation. Having thus satisfied the proprieties and made sure he conceded no ground on matters of principle, Woodward submitted, after a fashion. "Yet perhaps you have testimony of which I do not know. If violence has been done, it is the duty of the college to know the truth. I will hear what you have to say and postpone the interment until I have done so. If I find your complaint to be without justification, it will continue, whether you agree or not."

There was a murmur of appreciation at what Lower later told me was a masterly defensive retreat from an untenable position and, while it continued, Woodward ordered the body to be taken back to the chapel. Then he escorted the magistrate out of the cloisters and to his lodgings.

"Well, well," Lower said softly as the two men vanished through the narrow archway which led to the main quadrangle beyond. "I wonder who is behind this."

"What do you mean?"

"A magistrate can only act if someone complains to him that a crime has been committed. Then he must investigate to see whether the complaint is justified. So, who went to see him? It cannot have been Woodward, and who else had an interest? As far as I know the man had no family.''

I shivered. "We are not going to find out standing here," I pointed out.

"You are right. How about a bottle in my rooms at Christ Church? Then we can see if we can figure it out?"

WE MADE LITTLE PROGRESS; DESPITE MUCH TALK AND more wine, the question of who went to see the magistrate was as unresolved when we awoke the next morning as it was when we left New College. The only thing I learned was that the Canary wine the English prefer leaves a wicked remembrance the next morning.

I slept with Lower, being too shaky to return to my own bed by the end of the conversation—which soon left the topic of Grove and ranged widely over the whole field of curiosity. In particular he returned again to the idea of spirit, and whether it was susceptible to investigation—a notion which was of importance for the theory underlying my blood transfusion.

"I suppose," he said reflectively, "we may posit the existence of your life spirit in the blood from the existence of ghosts, for what are they but the spirit released from the body? And I cannot bring myself to doubt these manifestations, for I have myself seen one."

"Really? When?" I replied.

"Only a few months ago," he said. "I was in this very room, and heard a noise outside the door. I opened it up, as I was expecting a visitor, and there was this young man. Very curiously dressed, in velvet, with long, fair hair, and carrying a silken rope. I said hello, and he turned and looked at me. He didn't reply, but smiled sadly, then walked down the stairs. I didn't think much of it, but went back inside. My guest arrived a minute or so later. I asked him whether he had seen the strange youth—he could hardly have failed to do so—but he said no, there had been no one on the stairs at all. Later, the dean told me that a young man had killed himself in 1560. He'd left his room on my staircase, walked to a cellar on the other side of the college, and hanged himself with a silken rope.''

''Hmm.''

''Hmm, indeed. I merely point out that this is one of the rare occasions when the best theories of science and practical observation coincide very well. It is why I do not dismiss your *a priori* notions out of hand. Although I do not rule out the possibility that another explanation might account for Widow Blundy's improvement.''

''To dismiss an explanation you have in favor of one you do not have seems foolish,'' I said. ''But I must point out that you are assuming that the spirit which maintains life is the same as that which survives it.''

He sighed. ''I suppose I am. Although even Boyle has not yet thought up an experiment to discover what that spirit is, assuming it has some physical existence.''

''It would get him into a great deal of trouble with the theologians,'' I said. ''And he seems concerned to maintain the best relations with them.''

''Sooner or later that will come,'' my friend replied. ''Unless we scientists are to confine ourselves solely to material things, and what would be the point of that? But you are right; Boyle is unlikely to take such a risk. I cannot but think it a fault in him. But then your Mr. Galileo has shown the risks of annoying men of the church. What do you think of him?''

Of course, Lower had heard of this celebrated case, and it was much discussed at Padua when I was there, for Galileo had been in the pay of Venice until tempted away to the court of Florence by Medici pomp; he made many enemies thereby, which stood him in no good stead when he came into trouble for saying the earth went round the sun. Even though his fall had occurred almost before I was born, it had frightened many of the curious, and made them think carefully before they spoke. But it annoyed me that Lower should refer to it, for I knew what his opinion would be and that he would twist the facts to attack my church.

''I have the highest respect for him, of course,'' I said, ''and the episode grieves me. I am a man of science, and count myself a true son of the church. I believe firmly with

Mr. Boyle that science can never contradict true religion, and that if they seem at variance, then that is due to our faulty understanding of one or the other. God gave us the Bible and he gave us nature to show his creation; it is absurd to think he might contradict himself. It is man who fails.''

''Someone is wrong in this case, then,'' Lower said.

''Clearly,'' I replied, ''and no one seriously believes the pope's advisors were anything but misguided. But Signor Galileo was at fault as well, possibly more than they. He was a difficult and arrogant man and erred greatly in neglecting to show how his ideas were in conformity with doctrine. In truth I do not believe there was any contradiction. There was a failure to understand, and that had the direst consequences.''

''Not the intolerance of your church, then?''

''I think not, and would say it is proved that the Catholic church is more open to science than the Protestant. Every significant man of science yet has been raised in the Catholic church. Think of Copernicus, Vesalius, Torricelli, Pascal, Descartes . . .''

''Our Mr. Harvey was a good Anglican,'' Lower objected, a little stiffly, I thought.

''He was. But he had to come to Padua for his training, and there formulated his ideas.''

Lower grunted, and raised his glass in salute at my reply. ''You'll make cardinal yet,'' he said. ''A judicious and political response. You believe science is obliged to prove itself?''

''I do. Otherwise it sets itself up as an equal to religion, not its servant, and the consequences of that are too awful to contemplate.''

''You are beginning to sound like Dr. Grove.''

''No,'' I replied after a moment's thought. ''He thought us frauds and doubted the usefulness of experiment. I fear its power and ambition, and concern myself lest its power should make men arrogant.''

I could have grown angry at his remarks, but I felt disinclined to argue and Lower himself was not really trying to provoke. ''Anyway,'' he continued, ''with men like Grove in our church, who are we to condemn? They have less power to cause trouble than your cardinals, but they would do so if they could.'' He waved his hand to dismiss a topic he had tired of. ''Tell me, how is your patient? Is she truly living up to the theories you have heaped upon her shoulders?''

I smiled contentedly. ''She is bearing them marvelously well,'' I said. ''There are very distinct signs of improvement in her, and she tells me she feels better than she has since she fell.''

''In that case, I drink to Monsieur Descartes,'' Lower said, raising his glass, ''and to his disciple, the eminent Dr. da Cola.''

''Thank you,'' I said. ''And I must say that I suspect you of having more regard for his notions than you say.''

Lower raised his finger to his lips. ''Shh!'' he said. ''I have read him with interest and profit. But I would as soon own to being a papist as a Cartesian.''

An odd way of finishing a conversation, but that was how it ended; without even a yawn Lower rolled over—taking the one thin blanket with him and leaving me shivering—and fell fast asleep. I thought aimlessly for some time, and did not even notice when I similarly succumbed to the embrace of Lethe.

NEITHER OF US HAD WOKEN WHEN THE MESSENGER came from Stahl to say that his preparations were complete and if we wished to attend on him at our earliest convenience we could witness his experiment. I cannot say that I felt up to a meeting with the irascible German in my drugged and shaky state, but Lower reluctantly concluded that it was our duty to do our best.

''God knows I don't feel like it,'' he said as he washed his mouth out and straightened his clothes before attacking a piece of bread and a glass of wine for his breakfast. ''But if this has become a magistrate's matter, then we will need to present our findings properly. Not that he is likely to pay us much attention.''

''Why not?'' I asked with some curiosity. ''In Venice physicians are regularly called to give their opinion.''

"In England as well. 'Your honor, in my opinion this man is dead. The presence of a knife in his back indicates an unnatural death.' As long as it is kept simple, there is no problem. Shall we go?" He stuffed more bread in his coat pocket and held open the door. "I'm sure you do not really want to miss it."

Much to my surprise, Stahl seemed almost happy to see us when we dragged ourselves up his stairs and walked into his cramped and smelly lodging off Turl Street a quarter of an hour later. The prospect of demonstrating his ingenuity and skill to an appreciative audience was too much to resist, although he did his best to be churlish. Everything was ready: candles, bowls, bottles of various liquids, six little piles of powder—the stuff which he had extracted from the bottle—and chemicals Lower had purchased and sent round to him.

"Now, I hope you're going to behave yourself, and not waste my time prattling." He glared at us while Lower assured him that we would observe as quietly as possible—a statement which neither he nor Stahl believed for a moment.

The preliminaries done, Stahl settled down to work. As an example of chemical technique, it was fascinating to watch; and while he talked, I found my distaste slipping away in admiration at his ingenuity and methodical approach. The problem, he said, waving at the piles of powder, was perfectly simple. How do we determine what this sediment drawn from the brandy bottle is? We can look at it, but that demonstrates nothing, as many substances are white and can be reduced to powder. We can weigh it, but considering the amount of impurities present, that would prove little. We can taste it, and compare the taste to other things, but that operation—quite apart from the fact that it might be dangerous—would help little unless it had a unique and recognizable taste. From mere visual evidence we cannot say more than that the sediment is a whitish powder.

So, he said, warming to his theme, we must test it a little further: if, for example, we dissolved it in a little sal ammoniack, the mixture might respond in several ways: it might change color, or it might give off heat, or it might effervesce. The powder might dissolve, or float, or sink, still solid, to the bottom of the liquid. If we repeated the experiment with another substance, and it reacted in a similar fashion, could we then say that the two were the same?

I was about to reply in the affirmative, when he waved his finger at us. No, he said. Of course not. If they reacted differently, then indeed we might conclude that the two substances were not identical. But if they reacted in the same fashion, all we could say was that they were two substances which, when mixed with sal ammoniack, responded in the same way.

He paused while we digested this, then resumed once more. Now, you are thinking, he said, how can we possibly ascertain what this material is? And the answer is simple: we cannot. I told you this last week. Whatever you may think there can be no certainty. We can only say that accumulated evidence indicates the strong likelihood that it is such and such a substance.

I had not yet had much experience of law courts in England, but I knew that, if someone like Stahl went into a Venetian trial and spoke like that, the side he was supporting might as well abandon all hope.

"So, how do we do this?" he was asking rhetorically, waving his finger in the air. "We repeat the experimentation again and again and if, after every repeated experiment, the two substances match in their reaction, then we can conclude that the chances of their not being the same shrink to the point where to maintain they are different is unreasonable. Are you with me?"

I nodded. Lower didn't bother.

"Good," he said. "Now, I have in the last few days performed my experiments on a dozen or more substances, and have reached my conclusions. I am prepared here only to demonstrate them: I have not the time to go through the whole process with you. I have here glasses containing five different substances, and we will add our powder one by one to all five, then begin the process of comparison. Now, the first is a little spirit of sal ammoniack,"—he poured a small amount of powder in as he spoke—"the second contains lixivium of tartar, then spirit of vitriol, spirit of salt and lastly, syrup of violets. I also have here a piece of hot iron. I hope you see the logic of this, Dr. Lower?"

Lower nodded.

"Perhaps, then, you would explain to our friend, here?"

Lower sighed. "This isn't a lesson, you know."

"I like people to understand the experimental method. Too many doctors do not; they merely prescribe potions without the slightest reason to think they might work."

Lower groaned, then gave way. "What he is doing," he said, "is subjecting the powders to all variants of matter. As you know, the essential principles of natural things are salt and earth, which are passive, and water, spirit and oil, which are active. The combination of ingredients he has chosen consequently covers all of these, and should provide an overall picture of every variety of matter. He is also testing heat, which is quite illogical of him, as he does not believe that fire is a natural element."

Stahl grinned. "No, I do not. The idea that all matter contains a quantity of fire which can be released on heating I find unlikely. However, this is quite enough chatter. If your friend has got that into his pretty little head, we might begin."

He peered at us closely to see he had our attention, then rubbed his hands together and picked up the first bowl, holding it to the light so we could see clearly.

"The sal ammoniack first of all. You see it has produced particles of a pale sediment with no other apparent movement. Hmm?"

He handed it over for our inspection and we agreed that the other substance he was showing us produced the same result.

"Now, lixivium of tartar. A white cloud in the middle of the liquid, suspended equidistantly between the surface and the bottom."

Again, the other substance behaved in the same fashion.

"Vitriol. A precipitation producing hard crystals forming on the side of the glass. A matching result again."

"Salt." He paused and examined the bowl carefully. "A slight creamy precipitation, but so slight you might miss it entirely.

"Violets. How pretty. A tincture of pale green. Most attractive. Two of them, in fact, as my chosen substance has produced the same result. I hope you are beginning to be convinced.''

He grunted at us in a satisfied fashion, then picked up a pinch of each powder and threw them separately onto the red-hot iron. We watched as they hissed, and gave off thick white fumes. Stahl sniffed at them, then grunted again. ''No flame in either case. Slight smell of—what would you say?—garlic.''

He poured some water on the iron to cool it down, then casually tossed it out of the window, so it could lie on the ground and not poison us. ''And there we are. We needn't waste any more time. We have now run a total of six separate tests, and in each case the material you brought me in the brandy bottle reacts in the same way as this substance here. As an experimentalist of chemistry, gentlemen, I offer you my opinion that the material in the bottle is indeed unlikely not to be the same.''

''Yes, yes,'' said Lower, finally losing patience. ''But what is this other substance of yours?''

''Ah,'' said Stahl. ''The crucial point. My apologies for my little piece of drama. It is called white arsenic. Formerly used as a face powder by the more foolish and vanitous of women, and quite deadly in large quantities. I can prove that as well, for I did one other test.

''I have notes on all this, by the way,'' he said, as he opened up two paper packages. ''Two cats,'' he said, picking the creatures up by the tails. ''One white, one black. Both perfectly healthy last night when I caught them. I fed one two grains of the powder from the bottle, and the other the same amount of arsenic, both dissolved in a little milk. Both beasts are, as you see, quite dead.

''You'd better take both of them,'' Stahl continued. ''As you appear to have been delving into Dr. Grove's intestines, you may want to have a look at theirs as well. You never know.''

We thanked him profusely for his kindness and Lower, gripping a tail in each hand, wandered off to the laboratory to anatomize the beasts.

''And what is your opinion of that?'' he asked as we strolled along the High Street in the direction of Christ

Church once more. Having established that the substance in the bottle was indeed arsenic—or, to be correct, that it consistently behaved like arsenic and never behaved unlike arsenic, so that it could reasonably be said to be arsenic-like—and, moreover, that a cat, when fed the substance, died in a manner very similar to the way that a cat fed with arsenic died, we were but one step away from an alarming conclusion.

"Fascinating," I said. "Ingenious, and thoroughly satisfying in both method and execution. But I must reserve my final opinion until we have seen inside those cats. The syllogism you obviously have in mind is as yet incomplete."

"Arsenic in the bottle, and Grove dead. But did arsenic kill Grove? You are quite right. But you suspect as well as I what conclusions the cats' intestines will indicate."

I nodded.

"We have everything to suggest Grove was murdered except for the one necessary factor."

"Which is?" I asked as we trailed through the unfinished and unworthy entrance to the college and walked through the vast but equally unfinished quadrangle.

"We don't have a reason, and that is the most important thing. It is Stahl's problem with the why and the how, if you like. There is no point working out how it was done if we cannot say why. Fact of crime, and motive for committing it, are all that is needed: the rest is unimportant detail. *Cui prodest scelus, is fecit.* He who profits by villainy, has perpetrated it."

"Ovid?"

"Seneca."

"I believe," I said a little impatiently, "that you are trying to say something."

"I am. Just as Stahl can work out how chemicals mix with each other but has no idea why, so it is with us. We now know how Grove died, but we do not know why. Who might possibly have wanted to take so much trouble to kill him?"

"*Causa latet, vis est notissima,*" I quoted back, and was pleased for once to have foxed him.

" 'The cause is hidden . . .'? Suetonius?"

" 'But the effect is clear.' Ovid again. You should know

that one. We have at least established fact—if the cats are as we suspect. The rest is not in our field."

He nodded. "Considering your method of reasoning about your blood, I find that strange. You have completely reversed yourself. In one case, you had a hypothesis and saw no need for prior evidence. In this case, you have the evidence and see no need for a hypothesis."

"I could just as easily say that you have done the same. Besides, I do not dismiss the need for explanation. I merely say that it is not our job to formulate it."

"That is true," he conceded, "and maybe my discontent is vanity. But I feel that unless our philosophy can also answer the important questions as well, it is unlikely to change much. Both why and how. If science confines itself to how, then I doubt it will ever be taken seriously. Do you wish to attend the cats?"

I shook my head. "I would love to. But I should go and see my patient."

"Very well. Perhaps you will join me at Boyle's when you have finished? And this evening I have a great treat. We must not allow ourselves to become overburdened by experiment. Diversion is also necessary, I think. By the way, I wish to ask you something."

"And that is?"

"Periodically, I make a circuit of the countryside; Boyle mentioned it when you arrived, if you remember. As I can't practice in the town, I have to go outside to earn a little money, and I am very short at the moment. It is a Christian charity, and quite profitable, which is a fine combination. I set up a room on market days, hang out a sign and wait for the pennies to roll in. I was going to leave tomorrow. There is to be a hanging out Aylesbury way, and I want to bid for the corpse. Would you like to come? There will be more than enough work for both of us. You can rent a horse for a week, see the country. Can you pull teeth?"

I bridled at the idea. "Certainly not," I said.

"No? It's easy. I'll be taking some pliers, and you can practice if you wish."

"That's not what I meant. I mean that I am not a barber. Forgive me for saying so, but I risk my father's wrath in acting the doctor, and there are depths to which I will not sink."

For once Lower was not offended. "You're not going to be much use, then," he said cheerfully. "Listen, I am going to towns of a few hundred souls at most. Villagers come from miles around, and they want full treatment. They want to be bled, purged, lanced, have their piles rubbed and their teeth out. This isn't Venice, where you can send them to the barbershop next door. You'll be the only properly trained person they will see for another year, unless some wandering charlatan passes through. So if you come with me, you leave your dignity behind, as I will. No one will see, and I promise not to tell your father. They want a tooth out, you reach for the pliers. You'll enjoy it; you'll never have such appreciative patients again."

"What about my patient? I really don't want to come back to find her dead."

Lower frowned. "I hadn't thought of that. But she doesn't need any attention, does she? I mean, you can't do much except wait and see whether she lives. And if you gave her more treatment that would spoil the experiment."

"That's true."

"I could ask Locke to look in on her. I noticed you didn't take to him much, but he's a fine fellow really, and a good physician. We'll only be away five or six days."

I was doubtful, and did not want someone like Locke informed of my work, although as I knew Lower had a high regard for the man I refrained from saying so. "Let me think about it," I said. "And I'll tell you this evening."

"Fine. Now, these cats await me. And then I suppose we ought to see the magistrate to tell him what we have discovered. Not, I suspect, that he will be very interested."

THUS, THREE HOURS LATER, WE KNOCKED ON THE DOOR of the magistrate's house in Holywell to inform him that, as far as the opinion of two doctors was concerned, Dr. Robert Grove had died of arsenic poisoning. The stomachs and entrails of the cats were quite definite on this point; there was absolutely no difference between them and, in addition, the excoriation closely matched that which we had noted in Grove's own. The conclusion was inescapable by any theoretical approach, whether it be that of Monsieur Descartes or Lord Bacon.

Sir John Fulgrove saw us after only a very short delay; we were ushered into the room he used as his study and as an impromptu courtroom for deciding minor matters. He seemed a worried man, which was no great surprise. Someone like Woodward could make life very unpleasant for any lay official, even a magistrate, who incurred his wrath. Investigating a death was tantamount to alleging murder; Sir John now had to come up with a convincing case to lay before the coroner's court; and for that he needed someone to accuse.

When we told him of our investigations and conclusions, he leaned forward in his chair straining to understand what we were saying. I felt quite sorry for him; the matter was, after all, exceptionally delicate. To his credit, he questioned us closely both as to our methods and the logic of our conclusions, and made us explain several times the more complicated procedures until he understood them properly.

"It is your belief, then, that Dr. Grove died as a result of drinking arsenic dissolved in the bottle of brandy. Is that the case?"

Lower—who did all of the talking—nodded. "It is."

"Yet you will not speculate as to how the arsenic came to be in the bottle? Could he have put it there himself?"

"Doubtful. He had been warned only that evening of its dangers, and said he would never use it again. As for the bottle, Mr. Cola here might be able to assist on that point."

So I explained how I had seen Grove pick up the bottle at the foot of the stairs as he escorted me to the gate. I added, however, that I was not certain it was the same bottle, and naturally I did not know whether the poison was already in it.

"Yet is this poison used medicinally? You were treating him, Mr. Cole?"

"Cola."

Lower explained how it was sometimes used, but never in such quantities, and I said how I had done little more than wash away the medicine he was using, so that the eye might heal itself.

"You were treating him, you dined with him that evening, and you were probably the last person to see him before he died?"

I agreed evenly that this might well be the case. The magistrate grunted. "This arsenic," he continued. "What is it, exactly?"

"It is a powder," Lower said. "Derived from a mineral composed of sulphur and caustic salts. It is both expensive and often quite difficult to find. It comes from silver mines in Germany. Or it can be made by subliming orpiment with salts. In other words . . ."

"Thank you," the magistrate said, holding up his hands to fend off one of Lower's lectures. "Thank you. What I mean is, where is it obtained? Do apothecaries sell it, for example? Is it part of the *materia medica* of physicians?"

"Oh, I see. On the whole, I think, physicians do not keep it about them. It is used only rarely, and as I say, it is expensive. Ordinarily they would apply to an apothecary when it was needed."

"Thank you, indeed." The magistrate's brow furrowed in thought as he considered what we had just told him. "I do not see how your information, valuable though it might be, could possibly be of use should this ever come to a trial. I understand its value, of course, but I doubt that a jury would. You know, Lower, what these men are like, often enough. If a case depended on such flimsy stuff, they would be certain to acquit whomever we charged."

Lower looked displeased, but admitted that Sir John was correct.

"Tell me, Mister Cole . . ."

"Cola."

"Cola. You are Italian, I believe?"

I said I was.

"A doctor yourself?"

I replied that I had studied physic but was not qualified, and had no intention of practicing for a living. My father, I continued, did not want . . .

"You are familiar with arsenic, then?"

I did not for one moment suspect where this line of questioning was leading, and I answered cheerfully enough that I was indeed.

"And you admit you were possibly the last person to see Dr. Grove alive?"

"Possibly."

"So—please forgive me for speculating—so if, for example, you put the poison in yourself, and gave it to him when you arrived for dinner, there would be no one to query your account?"

"Sir John, surely you are forgetting something?" Lower said mildly. "Which is unless you can advance a reason for a deed, you cannot attribute it. And logic rules out the existence of that reason. Mr. Cola has only been in Oxford, only in this country, in fact, for a few weeks. He had only met Grove once before that night. And, I must say, I am willing to vouch absolutely for his good character as, I am sure, would the Honorable Robert Boyle, were he here."

This reminded the man of the absurdity of his line of questioning, I am glad to say, although it did not restore him to my esteem. "My apologies, sir. I did not mean to cause offense. But it is my duty to investigate, and naturally, I must ask questions of those near the events."

"That is quite understandable. No apologies are needed, I assure you," I replied with little sincerity of spirit. His remarks had alarmed me considerably, so much so that I came close to pointing out the fault in his logic—which was that I was not necessarily the last person to have seen Grove alive, for someone had seen Sarah Blundy, it appeared, going into his room after I had left him at the gate.

I was aware, however, that if an Italian and a papist would have been the ideal candidate for a murderer, then the daughter of a sectary, of loose morals and a fiery temper, would have been an adequate replacement. I had no desire to extricate myself from suspicion by pointing an accusing finger at her. She was, I thought, capable of such a thing, but apart from gossip, there was little to suggest any involvement. I felt quite justified in remaining silent until that situation changed.

Eventually, the magistrate gave up trying to say more, and

levered himself out of his chair. "You must excuse me. I have to see the coroner and alert him. Then interview some other people, as well as placating Warden Woodward. Perhaps, Dr. Lower, you would be kind enough to tell him what you told me? I would be happier were he convinced I was not acting out of malice toward the university."

Lower nodded, reluctantly, and went off to discharge his obligation, leaving me free to do as I pleased for the rest of the day.

I WAS MINDFUL THAT, DESPITE SUCH EXCITEMENTS AS the death of Dr. Grove, it was merely a distraction from my proper business, which was above all to see to my family affairs. Although I have dwelt little on it in this narrative, I had been hard at work, and Mr. Boyle had kindly done even more for me. The news, however, was dispiriting and I had little or nothing to show for my labors. Boyle had, as he promised, consulted a lawyer friend of his in London, and he had advised that I would be wasting my time in pursuing the matter. Without concrete proof of my father's ownership of half the business, there was no chance of persuading a court to grant title to half the property. I was best advised to write off whatever assets had been lost, rather than using up more capital in a hopeless quest.

So I immediately wrote to my father and told him that, unless he had some relevant documents in Venice, it seemed the money was lost forever, and that I might as well return home. The letters written, sealed and dispatched in the king's post (I did not care if they were read by the government, so decided against the extra expense of sending them privately), I returned to Mr. Crosse's shop to pass the time in conversation, and prepare a bag of medicines in case I should decide to accompany Lower, although I was already minded not to do so.

"I don't want to go. But if you could have them ready for tomorrow morning, just in case . . ."

Crosse took my list and opened his ledger at the page listing my previous purchases. "I will look them out for you," he said. "There is nothing particularly rare or valuable, so it is no great labor for me."

He looked up at me curiously for an instant, as though he was about to say something, then thought better of it and consulted the ledger once again.

"Do not concern yourself about payment," I said. "I'm sure Lower, or even Mr. Boyle, will vouch for my credit."

"Of course. Of course. There is no question of that."

"Something else concerns you? Pray tell me."

He thought some more, and busied himself arranging vials of liquid on the counter for a few seconds before making up his mind. "I was talking to Lower earlier," he began. "About his experiments over Dr. Grove's death."

"Ah, yes," I said, thinking that he wanted more gossip from those in a position to offer interesting tittle-tattle. "A fascinating man, that Mr. Stahl, if a little difficult."

"Are his conclusions sound, do you think?"

"I can see no fault in his method," I replied, "and his reputation speaks for itself. Why do you ask?"

"Arsenic, then? That is what caused his death?"

"I can see no reason to doubt it at all. Do you disagree?"

"No. Not at all. But I was wondering, Mr. Cola . . ."

Here he hesitated once more. "Come on, man, out with it," I cried cheerfully. "Something is clouding your spirit. Tell me what it is."

He was about to speak, then changed his mind and shook his head. "Oh, it's nothing," he replied. "Nothing of any consequence. I was simply wondering where the arsenic might have come from. I would hate to think it came from my shop."

"I doubt we will ever know," I replied. "Besides, it is the job of the magistrate to find out what he can, so I am told, and no one would blame you, in any case. I would not worry yourself about it."

He nodded. "You are right. Quite right."

Then the door swung open and Lower, accompanied, I was sad to see, by Locke, swept into the shop. Both were dressed up in their finest coats, and Lower was again daring to wear his wig. I bowed to both of them.

"I have not seen two finer gentlemen since I left Paris," I said.

Lower grinned and bowed back, an awkward movement as he was still unsure enough to hold his wig in place with his hand as he did so.

"The play, Mr. Cola, the play!"

"What play?"

"The one I told you about. Or did I forget? The entertainment I promised. Are you ready? Are you not excited? The whole town will be there. Come along. It starts in an hour, and unless we hurry, we won't get the best seats."

His good humor and air of urgency swept all other matters from my mind instantly, and without so much as a further thought about Mr. Crosse and his air of vague concern, I bade him good afternoon, and accompanied my friend out into the street.

GOING TO A PLAY IN ENGLAND, FOR ANY PERSON OF SENsibility who has been exposed to the refinements of Italian and French theater, is something of a shock and more than anything else reminds one how very recently this race of islanders has emerged from barbarism.

It is not so much their behavior, although the vulgar in the audience were perpetually noisy, and, it must be said, some of the better-born were far from quiet. This was due to the wild enthusiasm that the troupe of players generated. It was only a few years since such events had been allowed once more, and the joy of having some novelty to witness had sent the entire town into a frenzy. The very students, it seemed, had been selling their books and blankets to buy tickets, which were outrageously expensive.

Nor was the production so dreadful, although it was fearfully rustic, reminiscent more of Carnival burlesque than the theater proper. Rather, it is the type of play which the English admire that reveals what a crude and violent people they really are. It was written by a man who had lived not far from Oxford, who, alas, had clearly neither traveled nor studied the best authors, for he had no technique, no sense of plot and certainly no decorum.

Thus, the unities which Aristotle rightly taught us ensure that a play remains coherent were jettisoned almost from the first scene. Far from taking place in one location, it began in a castle (I think), then moved to some moor, then to a battlefield or two, and ended up with the author seeing if he could place a scene in every town in the country. He compounded his error by jettisoning the unity of time—between one scene and another, a minute, an hour, a month or (as far as I could see) fifteen years could pass, without the audience being informed. Also missing was the unity of subject, as the main plot was forgotten for long periods and subsidiary tales taken up, rather as though the author had taken pages from half a dozen plays, tossed them into the air, then stitched them together in whatever order they fell to earth.

The language was worse; some I missed as the actors had no sense of declamation, but instead talked as though they were in a room of friends or in a tavern. Of course, the true actor's way, standing still, facing the audience and seducing them with the power of beautiful rhetoric, was scarcely appropriate, as there was little beauty to deliver. Instead what they had on offer was language of breathtaking foulness. At one scene in particular, where the son of some nobleman pretends to be mad and frolics on an open heath in the rain, then meets the king who has also gone mad and has put flowers in his hair (believe me, I am not joking), I quite expected the ladies to be hustled out by protective husbands. Instead, they sat there with all signs of enjoyment, and the only thing which caused a *frisson* of shock was the presence of actresses on stage, which no one had seen before.

Finally there was the violence. God only knows how many were killed; in my opinion it quite explains why the English are notoriously so violent, for how could they be otherwise, when such disgusting events are presented as entertainment? For example, a nobleman has his eyes put out, on the stage, in full view of the audience, and in a fashion which leaves nothing to the imagination. What possible purpose could be served by this gross and unnecessary coarseness except to insult and shock?

In fact, the only real interest in the proceedings—which dragged on so long that the final scenes were played out in blessed darkness—was that it presented me with a panoramic view of local society, as virtually no one was able to resist the temptation to dabble their fingers in the muck that was on offer. Mr. Wood the gossip was there, as were Warden Woodward and the severe, cold Dr. Wallis. Thomas Ken was there, as were Crosse, Locke, Stahl and many others I had seen in Mother Jean's.

And there were many more, not even mentioning the students, whom I had never seen but who were well known to my friend. During one of the frequent interruptions in the proceedings, for example, I saw a thin, haggard man try to talk to Dr. Wallis. That gentleman looked angry and embarrassed, then turned abruptly away.

"Oho," said Lower, watching with interest. "How times do change."

I begged an explanation.

"Hmm? Oh, I suppose you don't know," he said, his eyes still riveted on the scene being played out before him. "How could you? Tell me, what do you think of that little man? Do you think it is possible to read character from physiognomy?"

"I believe so," I said. "If it is not, then a large number of face painters are wasting their time and telling us lies."

"Interpret away, then. We can experiment to see the usefulness of the doctrine. Or the level of your skill."

"Well," I said, carefully studying the man once more as he walked humbly back to his place and without complaint took his seat. "I am no artist and am not trained in the matter, but he is a man in his late forties, with the air of one born to serve and obey. Not a man who has ever held authority or power. Not favored by fortune, although not poor. A gentleman, but of a lowly sort."

"A good start," Lower commented. "Continue."

"Not a man used to imposing himself. With none of the manner or standing of one who might cut a dash in the world. Rather the opposite: his demeanor suggests someone who will always be overlooked and ignored."

"Aha. Any more?"

"One of nature's supplicants," I said, warming to my theme now. "You can see from the way he approached, and the way he suffered his rebuff. Clearly, he is accustomed to such treatment.''

Lower nodded. ''Excellent,'' he said. ''A truly useful experiment.''

''Was I correct?''

''Let us say it was an interesting set of observations. Ah. The play is beginning again. Splendid.''

I groaned inwardly: he was right, and the players were coming on once more, fortunately for the denouement. I could have done better myself: rather than a morally pleasing resolution, the king and his daughter die just at the moment that any reasonable playwright would see that they must live for there to be any moral instruction in the play at all. But, of course, by then everyone else is dead as well and the stage a virtual charnel house, so I suppose they just decided to follow suit, for want of anyone to talk to.

I emerged rather dazed, not having seen so much blood since we anatomized Dr. Grove. Fortunately, Lower suggested an inn immediately afterward. As I needed a stiff drink to recover, I did not even demur when Locke and Wood decided to join us: not my idea of ideal company, but after such a performance I would have taken a drink with Calvin himself, had it been necessary.

By the time we'd walked across town and settled down in the Fleur-de-Lys, Lower had told Locke of my comments about the man's demeanor, which produced nothing more than a sneering smile.

''If I'm wrong, you should tell me how,'' I said a little heatedly, not liking at all to be used for sport in this fashion. ''Who was this man?''

''Go on, Wood. You are the repository of all human gossip. You tell him.''

Clearly pleased to be included in our company and relishing his moment of attention, Wood took a sip of his drink, and called over to the serving hatch for a pipe to be brought. Lower added his call for one as well, but I declined. Not that I object to a little tobacco in the evening, especially when my bowels are tight, but sometimes pipes which have been overused by the general clientele of taverns do have a taste of sour spittle. Most do not mind, I know, but I find it unpleasant and only smoke from my own.

"Well," Wood began in his pedantic fashion when he was refilled with ale and safely alight, "this little man who is so much one of life's failures, so much a natural servant, so much a supplicant, is in fact John Thurloe."

He stopped here for dramatic effect, rather as though I should be impressed. I asked him a bit more sharply than was strictly necessary who, exactly, was John Thurloe?

"Never heard of him?" he said with an air of amazement. "Many in Venice have. And almost everywhere else in Europe. For near ten years that man murdered, stole, bribed and tortured his way across this land and others. He once—and not so very long ago—held the fate of kingdoms in his hand, and played with monarchs and statesmen as though they were mere puppets."

He paused again, and finally realized that he wasn't being clear. "He was Cromwell's Secretary of State," he explained, as though talking to a child. Truly, the man irritated me. "His spy master. Responsible for keeping the Commonwealth secure and Cromwell alive, a task he accomplished with great success, for Cromwell died in his bed. While John Thurloe was there, no assassin ever got close. He had spies everywhere: if ever there was a conspiracy by the king's men, John Thurloe knew about it before they did themselves. He even planned some of their plots himself, I am told, just for the pleasure of destroying them. As long as he had Cromwell's confidence, there were no controls on what he could do at all. None at all. It was Thurloe, they say, who lured Jack Prestcott's father into betraying the king."

"That little man?" I said in astonishment. "But if that's true, what is he doing walking around and going to plays? Surely any sensible government would have hanged him as quickly as possible."

Wood shrugged, unwilling to admit to not knowing something. "A mystery of state. But he lives quietly, a few miles from here. By all accounts he sees no one, and has made his peace with the government. Naturally, all those who swarmed around him when he had power no longer even remember his name."

"Including John Wallis, evidently."

"Ah, yes," Wood said, his eyes twinkling, "including him. Dr. Wallis is a man with an instinct for power. He can smell it. I am sure the first inkling a man of state has of his downfall is when John Wallis stops paying court."

Everybody likes tales of dark and obscure happenings, and I was no different. Wood's tale of Thurloe gave an insight into the kingdom. Either the returned king was so secure that he could allow such people their freedom without fear, or he was so weak he could not bring them to justice. It would have been different in Venice: Thurloe would long ago have been devoured by the Adriatic fishes.

"And this man Wallis? He intrigues me . . ."

But I found out no more, as a young man I recognized as the magistrate's servant came to our table and stood there stiffly until Lower put him out of his misery by asking him his business.

"I am looking for Mr. Cola and Dr. Lower, sir."

We acknowledged ourselves. "And what do you want?"

"Sir John requires your immediate presence at his house in Holywell."

"Now?" asked Lower. "Both of us? It is past nine, and we have not even eaten."

"I believe it cannot wait. It is a matter of the utmost urgency," the lad replied.

"Never keep a man waiting if he has the power to hang you," Locke said encouragingly. "You'd better go."

THE HOUSE ON HOLYWELL SEEMED WARM AND INVITING as we arrived and waited in the hallway before being ushered in to the interview room once more. The fire blazed in the open hearth, and I warmed myself before it, conscious again of how cold the country was in winter, and how underheated were my own lodgings. I was also, I realized, formidably hungry.

The magistrate was decidedly stiffer than he had been only that morning. Once the formalities were over, he led us into the little room, and sat us both down.

"You work very late, Sir John," Lower said amiably.

"Not through choice, doctor," he replied. "But this is a matter which cannot wait."

"It must be serious, then."

"It is indeed. It concerns Mr. Crosse. He came to see me this afternoon and I wish to check his credentials as he is not a gentleman, although, no doubt, eminently trustworthy in all respects."

"Examine away, then. What about old Crosse? He is as good a man as I know, and gives false weight only rarely, and then only to customers he does not know."

"He brought his ledger of sales from his shop," the magistrate said, "which shows quite clearly that a substantial quantity of arsenic was bought four months ago by Sarah Blundy, a serving girl of this town."

"I see."

"Blundy was discharged by Grove for ill-behavior on that same day," the magistrate continued. "She comes from a violent family."

"Forgive me for interrupting," Lower said, "but have you asked the girl? Perhaps she has a perfectly straightforward explanation?"

"I have. After I talked to Mr. Crosse, I went straight there. She said she bought the powder on Dr. Grove's instructions."

"Which may be true. It would be difficult to contradict."

"It may be so. I intend to see if Dr. Grove kept a ledger. The cost of the powder was near a shilling, and an item that expensive might well have been noted. You can vouch for Crosse? He is of good character, and unlikely to bear false witness out of malice?"

"Oh, no. In that respect he is utterly trustworthy. If he says the girl bought arsenic, then the girl bought arsenic," Lower said.

"Did you accuse the girl directly?"

"No," Sir John replied. "It is too early for that."

"You think it a possibility?"

"Maybe so. Might I ask why neither of you mentioned to me the report that she had been seen entering Dr. Grove's room that night?"

"It is not my job to report tittle-tattle," Lower said sternly. "Nor yours to repeat it, sir."

"It is not that," Sir John replied. "Warden Woodward told me, and brought Mr. Ken to repeat his accusation."

"Ken?" I asked. "Are you sure he was telling the truth?"

"I have no reason to doubt him. I am aware he and Dr. Grove were at odds, but I cannot believe he would lie on such an important matter."

"And what did the girl say?"

"She denied it, of course. But she also would not say where she was."

I remembered that she would not tell me either, and my heart filled with foreboding for the first time. Even the most terrible immorality, after all, would be worthwhile owning if it diverted suspicions such as these. So what could the girl have been doing, assuming, that is, she was not lying to cover her guilt?

"In which case it will be her word against Ken's," Lower said.

"His word will naturally carry the more weight," the magistrate pointed out. "And, from the gossip I have heard, it seems the girl had a reason, however perverted, for such a deed. Do I understand that you are treating the mother, Mr. Cole?"

I nodded.

"I recommend that this cease instantly. You should have as little contact with her as possible."

"You are making an assumption about her culpability," I said, alarmed at the turn the conversation was taking.

"I believe I can see the beginnings of a case. But culpability is not my task, I am glad to say."

"The mother still needs a doctor," I said. I did not add that my experiment required constant attention as well.

"I'm sure some other physician will do. I cannot prohibit you, but I beg you to think of the awkwardness. The subject of Dr. Grove will undoubtedly be raised should you encounter the girl—if she is responsible she is bound to want to know how the investigation is progressing, and whether you suspect what was done. You would then be placed in the position either of dissimulating, which is undignified, or giving away information which might cause her to flee.''

I could see the sense of that, at least. ''But if I suddenly stop attending, that might arouse her suspicions also.''

''In that case,'' Lower said cheerfully, ''you will have to come with me on my tour. It will get you out of the way, and the girl will not suspect your absence.''

''As long as you come back. Mr. Lower, will you stand surety for your friend? Ensure his return to Oxford?''

Lower agreed readily, and by the time we left the house, the matter had been settled between them without my being consulted in any way. The next day, it seemed, I would leave on tour, and Lower would persuade Locke to attend to my patient and take whatever notes were required on her condition. This inevitably meant telling him what we had done, which made me uneasy, but there was no alternative. He went off to find his friend, and I returned, heavy at heart and alarmed by the turn of events, to my lodgings.

chapter fifteen

DESPITE ITS INAUSPICIOUS BEGINNINGS, THE MEDI-
cal journey of the next week initially proved to be of great
value to my troubled state of mind. I discovered that, in only
a brief space of time, the atmosphere of Oxford had settled
on me, rendering me as melancholic as most of its inhabitants. There is something about the place; a dampness which
is oppressive to the spirits, which bears down most powerfully on the soul. I have for long had a theory about the
weather which, if God spares me, I would like to develop
one day. I do believe that the wetness and grayness of the
climate will forever preclude the English from making much
of a stir in the world, unless they abandon their island for
more sunny climes. Transport them to the Americas or the
Indies, and their character is such that they could rule the
world; leave them where they are, and they are doomed to
sink in lassitude. I have personal experience of this in the
way in which my normally cheerful temperament became
dampened by the experience of residing there.

Nonetheless, finding myself astride a horse on what
seemed like the first day of spring after a long hard winter,
in the open countryside that begins the moment you cross
the old, dangerous-looking bridge after the college of St.
Mary Magdalen, was a wonderful tonic. Moreover, the wind
had finally shifted from the north to the west, removing the
ill effects of this most deadening of airs. I must add that the

prospect of having nothing to do with Sarah Blundy or the corpse of Robert Grove for a few days also helped.

Lower had organized the expedition well in advance and rushed me off that first morning, pushing the horses hard until we arrived in late afternoon at Aylesbury, in the next county. We put up in an inn, where we rested ourselves until the execution the next morning. I did not attend, taking little pleasure in such spectacles, but Lower did: the girl, he said, made a wretched speech and quite lost the sympathy of the crowd. It had been a complicated case and the town was by no means convinced of her guilt. She had killed a man whom she said had raped her, but the jury judged this a lie because she had fallen pregnant, which cannot occur without the woman taking pleasure in the act. Normally her condition would have spared her the gallows, but she had lost the child and also any defense against the hangman. An unfortunate outcome, which those who believed in her guilt considered divine providence.

Lower assured me his attendance was necessary; a hanging is a detestable sight, but one of his many fascinations was when exactly the moment of death occurs. This related directly to our experiments with the dove in the air pump. Most of those hanged asphyxiate slowly at the end of the rope and it was a matter of some considerable interest to him—and to physick in general—how long it takes for the soul to depart. He was, he assured me, a considerable expert in the matter. For this reason, he positioned himself next to the tree to take notes.

He also got his corpse, once he had tipped the officials and paid a pound to the family. He had it carried to an apothecary of his acquaintance and, after he prayed in his fashion and I in mine, we began work. Some anatomization we performed there—I took the heart while he cracked open the skull and drew some delightful sketches of the brain—then we jointed the rest and placed the portions in several large vats of spirit which the apothecary undertook to deliver to Crosse's shop. He also wrote a letter to Boyle telling them the vats were on their way and should on no account be opened.

"I don't know that he will be so very pleased," he said,

once he had washed his hands and we had retired to the inn for food and drink. "But where else could I send them? My college refuses to have corpses on the premises for any length of time, and if I sent it to anyone else they might well practice on it before I returned. Some people have no shame in these matters."

As for the rest of our trip, there is little point in going into details. The patients came in thick and fast once we had established ourselves in the various inns on our route and I returned ten days later sixty-five shillings the richer. The average fee was four pence, nobody ever paid more than one and sixpence, and when I was paid in kind I had to sell the various geese and ducks and hens at a discount to local traders (we ate one goose, but I could hardly return to Oxford with a farmyard menagerie trailing behind me). All this should give an idea of how many patients I treated.

I will retell the events of one day, because they were of significance. This was in Great Milton, a small settlement to the east of Oxford, to which we had repaired because a distant branch of Boyle's family owned a property there, assuring us a comfortable bed for the night and a chance of ridding ourselves of the lice which we had acquired over the previous days. We arrived about seven in the morning, and went straight to our separate rooms at the nearby inn, while the innkeeper sent a messenger around the village announcing our presence. We had barely prepared ourselves when the first patient arrived, and by the time he had been dealt with (Lower lanced a boil in his fundament, to which treatment he responded with rare good humor) there was a queue forming at the door.

That morning I extracted four teeth, drained several gallons of blood (fancy notions about therapeutic efficacy get you nowhere in the country; they wanted their blood let and that was what they were determined to have), bound wounds, tasted piss, applied salves and took in seven shillings. A brief pause for lunch and then we were off again; lancing sores, wiping pus, setting joints and taking in eleven shillings and eight pence. Throughout, all of Lower's grand theories about the new medicine were abandoned. The patients were not interested in the benefits of iatrochemical potions and were disdainful of innovation. So, instead of prescribing careful concoctions of mercury and antimony, we rebalanced humors like the most hidebound of Galenists, and consulted the stars with a fervor worthy of Paracelsus himself. Anything which might work, for we had not the leisure to consider novel approaches, nor the reputation to apply them.

Both of us were exhausted by the end and even so we had to skulk out the back of the inn to avoid still more patients waiting their turn. The old couple in charge of the house had promised us a hot bath when we introduced ourselves at midday and I was eager to take up the offer: I had not immersed since the previous autumn and felt that not only could my constitution stand it, my morale would be immeasurably lifted. I went first, taking the brandy bottle with me so as to save time, and felt very much better when I emerged. Lower was less carefree about bathing, but the itching in his skin from the lice was such that even he decided to take the risk.

I stretched out in a chair while Lower took his turn in the tub, and was almost asleep when Mrs. Fenton, the servant, told me that there was a message for me. Brought by a servant from the nearby priory.

I groaned. This sort of thing happened all the time; the gentry and families of higher quality would want to avail themselves of the services of a passing physician, but naturally found it beneath them to wait with the rabble. So they would send a message desiring our presence. We attended on them rather than the other way around, and charged heftily for the privilege. Lower invariably took most of this trade, he being English and wanting to make connections for the future, and I was happy to allow him that task.

This time, however, he was in the bath and, in any case, the servant said quite pointedly that my services in particular were desired. I was flattered, yet again amazed at the speed with which news travels in the countryside, and quickly fetched my bag. I left a message for Lower that I would return in due course.

"Who is your master?" I asked, wanting to make polite conversation as we walked back up to the main street of the village, then down a smaller road to the left. My teachers had often recommended this course: by careful questioning of servants, it is often possible to reach a full diagnosis even before you see the patient, thus earning a wondrous reputation.

This time the technique was of little use, as the servant, an old but powerfully built man, did not reply at all. Indeed, he said not a single word until we had walked all the way up to a medium-sized house on the outskirts of the village, gone through the large door and I had been shown into what the English call a parlor, a public room for the reception of guests. Here he broke silence, asked me to sit, and disappeared.

And so I did, waiting patiently, until the door opened and I found myself in the presence of Europe's foremost murderer, if Mr. Wood's tales were to be believed.

"Good evening, doctor," John Thurloe said to me in a quiet, melodious voice as he came into the room. "It was kind of you to come."

Although I could study him properly for the first time, nonetheless I stood by my original assessment. Even knowing his reputation, he still did not at all look like any sort of evil tyrant. He had watery eyes that blinked as if unused to the light, and the meek expression of one who wished desperately to be treated with kindness. If pushed, I would have placed him as a gentle prelate, eking out a quiet but worthy existence in a poor parish, forgotten by his betters.

But Wood's description had penetrated my mind, and I found myself gaping, almost awestruck.

"You are Dr. Cola, are you not?" he went on as I said nothing. I eventually managed to reply that I was, and ask him what was his trouble.

"Ah, not a problem of the body," Thurloe said with a faint smile. "More a problem of the soul, you might say."

I ventured that this was hardly my area of expertise.

"Indeed not. But you may be able to render some assistance. May I be frank with you, doctor?"

I spread my hands as if to say, well, why not?

"Good. You see, I have a guest, who is sorely troubled. I cannot say that he is welcome, but you know how it is with hospitality. He is cut off from the society of his fellow men, and finds my company insufficient. I cannot blame him for this, as I am not an interesting conversationalist. Do you know who I am, by the way?''

"I am told you are Mr. Thurloe, Lord Cromwell's Secretary of State.''

"That is correct. Anyway, this guest of mine needs information which I cannot provide, and he tells me that you might be able to help.''

He had completely lost me, of course. So I said I would willingly oblige. But surely, I continued, Great Milton was not so very cut off from civilization? Thurloe did not reply directly.

"I understand you knew a gentleman by the name of Robert Grove. A fellow of New College, recently deceased. Is that correct?''

That Thurloe should have heard of this amazed me; but I said that, yes, I did.

"I hear there is a question mark over the matter of his death. Would you care to tell me the circumstances?''

I could see no reason why I should not, so I summarized everything that had taken place, from Lower's investigations to Sarah Blundy's conversation with me and the magistrate. Thurloe sat impassively in the chair as I talked, hardly moving at all, an air of the most complete tranquillity upon him; I could barely tell whether he was listening or was even still awake.

"I see," he said when I had concluded. "So if I understand you correctly, when you left Oxford, the magistrate had questioned this Blundy girl, but no more?''

I nodded.

"Does it come as a surprise to learn that she was charged with the willful murder of Dr. Grove two days ago? And is now in prison awaiting the assizes?''

"It would astonish me,'' I replied. "I did not know the English law worked so swiftly.''

"Do you believe the girl is guilty?''

What a question. One which I had asked myself on many occasions during my journey.

"I do not know. That is a matter for law, not reason.''

He smiled at this, as though I had made some cutting remark. Lower told me later that he had been for many years a lawyer, before the rebellion had swept him into office.

"In reason, then. Tell me what you think."

"The hypothesis is that Sarah Blundy killed Dr. Grove. What evidence is there? There is a motive, in that he discharged her from his employ, although many servants are discharged and fortunately few take such revenge. She acquired arsenic on the day she was discharged. She was in New College on the evening of Dr. Grove's death and was reluctant to own it. Certainly, the evidence supports the hypothesis proposed."

"Your method has a weakness, though. You do not mention all the evidence. Only that which supports the hypothesis. As I understand it, other facts support an alternative, which is that you could have killed him, as you were the last person to see him alive, and also had access to the poison had you wanted to kill him."

"I could have, but I know I did not, and I had no reason to do so. Any more than Dr. Wallis had, or Lower or Boyle."

He accepted this point—although why I was telling him I did not know—and nodded. "So it is the combination of different qualities of facts which you believe important. And you conclude that she is indeed guilty."

"No," I replied. "I am very reluctant to do so."

Thurloe affected to look surprised. "But surely that goes against the scientific method? You must accept it, until you have an alternative hypothesis."

"I accept it as a possibility, but would be reluctant to act on it unless it was more secure."

He stood up slowly, in the way the old are forced to do by the stiffness of their joints. "Please help yourself to a glass of wine, doctor. I will return to discuss this matter further in a short while."

I revised my estimate of him as I poured myself a glass. An order is an order, however mildly it is given: Thurloe, I decided, was gentle because he had never needed to be other. It never occurred to me to say that Lower was expecting me, that I was hungry, or that I saw no reason to kick my heels waiting on his pleasure. I stayed where I was, for half an hour or more, until he returned.

With him, when he finally came back, was Jack Prestcott,

his jail cell and shackles now a mere memory, grinning with embarrassment as he followed Thurloe into the room.

"Ah," he said brightly, as I stared at him in outright astonishment, for he was the very last person I ever expected to see again, let alone in such circumstances. "The Italian anatomist. How do, good doctor?"

Thurloe smiled sadly at both of us, then bowed. "I will leave you both to a discussion," he said. "Please do not hesitate to call me if required."

And he left the room, leaving me to gape idiotically. Prestcott, a burlier man than I remembered and certainly more cheerful than he had been on our last meeting, rubbed his hands, poured himself a glass of ale from a jug on the sideboard and sat down in front of me, scrutinizing my face to see if there were any danger signals.

"You are surprised to see me. Good. I'm glad to hear it. You must admit, this is a pretty good hiding place, don't you think? Who'd think of looking for me here, eh?"

He certainly seemed to be in good spirits, very much like someone who had not a care in the world, rather than a man faced with the prospect of imminent hanging. And what, I wondered, was he doing in the house of a man like Thurloe?

"Simple enough," he said. "My father and he were acquainted, after a fashion. I threw myself on his mercy. We outcasts must stick together, you know."

"So what do you want? You are taking a risk announcing your presence to me, are you not?"

"We shall see. Thurloe told me what you said, but would you mind going through the matter again?"

"Which matter?"

"About Dr. Grove. He was good to me, and the only person in Oxford I had an affection for. I was sorely grieved when I heard what had happened."

"Considering how ill you would have used him had he visited you the evening of your escape, I find that difficult to credit."

"Oh, that," he said contemptuously. "I didn't hurt Wallis by tying him up, and I wouldn't have hurt old Grove. But what is a man to do? Die on the scaffold to avoid being

uncivil? I had to escape and this was my only opportunity.
What would you have done?''

"I would not have attacked someone to start with," I replied.

He brushed the point aside. "Now think a minute. Thurloe
tells me that the magistrate hovered ominously around you
for a moment. What if he had clapped you in irons—as he
might have done, you know, for a papist would be a popular
choice. What would you do? Sit tight and hope the jury was
sensible? Or decide they are likely to be a bunch of drunken
good-for-nothings who would hang you for the pleasure of
it? I may be a fugitive, but at least I am alive. Except that
Grove's death concerns me, and I would help if it were possible, for he was kind to me once and I revere his memory.
So tell me, what has been going on?''

Again I went through the story. Prestcott proved a more
appreciative audience, twisting about in his chair, getting up
to refill his glass, punctuating my remarks with loud excla-
mations of approval or dissent. Eventually, I concluded my
tale for the second time.

"And now, Mr. Prestcott," I said sternly, "you must tell
me what this is about."

"What it is about," he said, "is that I now understand a
good deal more than I did a few moments ago. The question
is, what am I to do about it?''

"I cannot advise you until I know what you mean."

Prestcott took a deep sigh, then looked me straight in the
eye. "You know the Blundy girl was his strumpet?''

I said I had heard the story, but added that the girl did not
admit it.

"Of course not. But it's true. I know because we went
together briefly last year before I knew what she was. Then
she moved onto Grove, and seduced him, poor old man, into
her clutches. It was simply done; he had an eye for prettiness,
and she can be very compliant when she puts her mind to it.
She was furious when he dismissed her. I came across her
just afterward, and believe me, I have never seen such a
terrifying countenance in my life. She looked like a devil,
and was snarling and spitting like an animal. He would pay
for it, she said. And pay dearly.''

"Meaning?"

He shrugged. "I thought it just womanly excess at the time. Anyway, shortly after I had my regrettable experience and ended up in jail, so I lost contact with the outside world. Until I escaped. When I walked out of the castle, I had not a clue what to do next. I had no money, no proper clothes, nothing. And I thought I'd better hide lest the alarm was raised. So I went to the Blundys' cottage. I had been there before, and knew it."

He had slipped quietly up the muddy alleyway to Sarah's door, and peered through the window. It was quite dark inside, and he assumed that no one was there. He rummaged around to see if there was any food he could take, and was eating a crust of bread when Sarah returned.

"She had an exhilaration which frightened me," he confessed. "She was surprised to see me, of course, but when I told her I wouldn't hurt her and didn't intend to stay long, she relaxed. She had a small bag with her and, as I thought it might have some more food in it, I took it from her."

"She let you have it?"

"Not exactly. I had to force it from her."

"And I take it there was no food there?"

"No. There was money. And a ring. Grove's signet ring," he said, then paused to rummage in his pocket. He took out a small packet of crumpled paper, which he unwrapped carefully. Inside was a ring with a carved blue stone in the center.

"I remember it well," he continued once I had taken it to examine. "I've seen it on his finger on innumerable occasions. As he never took it off, I was curious how Sarah Blundy came by it. She refused to answer, so I beat her until she snarled that it was none of my business and in any case, Grove wouldn't need it any more."

"She said that? 'Grove wouldn't need it any more?'"

"Yes," Prescott said. "I had other things on my mind so didn't pay that much attention at the time. Now, of course, it all seems quite important. The question is, what to do? I can hardly offer my testimony, as the magistrate will thank me kindly, then hang me as well. So I was wondering if you would take this ring and my story. Once you have gone back and spoken to Sir John Fulgrove I will be long gone, with luck.''

I thought hard, clutching the ring in my hand, and astonished by how much I did not want to believe what I was hearing. "You give me your word that what you are telling me is true?"

"Absolutely," he replied promptly and frankly.

"I would have more sympathy if you were not also of a violent disposition yourself."

"I am not," he said, coloring slightly and raising his voice. "And I resent the remark. Everything I have done was to protect my own and my family's name. There is no similarity between my case, which is an affair of honor, and hers, which is lust and theft. Sarah Blundy will do this again, believe me, doctor. She acknowledges no laws and no restraints. You do not know her, or her sort, as I do."

"She is wild," I admitted. "But I have also seen her polite and dutiful."

"When she wishes," he said dismissively. "But she is entirely without a sense of duty to her betters. That you must have discovered for yourself."

I nodded. It was certainly true. And I thought once more of my hypothesis. I wanted further evidence of unimpeachable veracity, and now I believed I had it. Prestcott had little to gain in coming forward; indeed he potentially had much to lose. It was difficult not to believe him, and he spoke with such an intensity that it was hard to imagine he was not telling me the truth.

"I will talk to the magistrate," I suggested. "I would not say where you are, but merely recount the story. He is a trustworthy man, I think, and keen to conclude this matter swiftly. Many in the university resent his interference, and your witness would be of great use to him. It may be that he will look kindly on you. You must take Mr. Thurloe's advice on this, of course, but I would advise against precipitate flight."

Prestcott considered this. "Maybe. But you must promise me that you will be careful. I am terribly afraid. If someone like Lower knows where I am, he will give me up. He is obliged to do so."

I promised him this with great reluctance and, if I did not keep my word for reasons I will explain, at least I can say that it did Prestcott no harm.

MY ATTEMPT TO KEEP QUIET, HOWEVER, LED TO A SAD deterioration in my relations with Lower, as my absence with what he assumed was a valuable and lucrative client led him once more into jealous despondency. I have met people who would turn so to some degree but I have never met anyone like Lower, whose humor would change on the instant, without warning or good reason.

Twice now he had lashed out and vented his temper on me and I had endured it out of friendship; the third time was worst and the last. Like all the English, he drank prodigious amounts, and had thus occupied himself in my absence, so was violent in mood when I returned. When I entered the house, he was sitting by the fire, clutching himself as though to keep warm, and staring blackly at me. When he spoke he spat his words as though I was his worst enemy.

"Where in God's name have you been?"

Tempted though I was to recount everything, I replied that I had been to see a patient, who had summoned me.

"You have reneged on our agreement, that I was to have such patients."

"We had no agreement," I said, astounded. "Although I am happy for you to have them. But you were bathing."

"I would have dried myself."

"And the patient would have been no use to you."

"That is for me to decide."

"Then decide now. It was John Thurloe, and as far as I could see, he is in perfect health."

Lower snorted derisively. "You don't even lie well. Dear God, how I am sick of your company, with your foreign ways and mincing speech. When do you go back home? I shall be glad to see the back of you."

"Lower, what is the matter?"

"Don't pretend you are concerned about me. The only thing you are interested in is yourself. I have shown you real friendship; took you in when you arrived, introduced you to the best people, shared my ideas with you, and see how you repay me.''

"And I am grateful," I said, beginning to grow angry now. "Truly grateful. And have done my best to earn what I have been given. Have I not also shared my ideas with you?"

"Your ideas!" he said with total contempt. "Those aren't ideas. Those are fancies, idle nonsense with no foundations, dreamed up merely to amuse yourself.''

"That is completely unfair. You know it. I have done nothing at all to earn your anger.''

But my protests were of no use at all. As with the last time, what I said was of no importance; when the storm burst it had to blow itself out and I could do no more to calm it than a tree caught in a tempest. This time, however, I grew angry and resentful and, rather than seeking to mollify him, I felt more keenly his unfairness and fought against his rage.

I will not repeat what was said, except to say that it was too much. Lower grew angrier and I, still unable to fathom the cause, became equally heated. All I know is that this time I was set on resisting him, and this determination drove him to more extravagant fits of fury. I was, he said, a thief, a charlatan, a fop, a papist, a liar, untrustworthy and deceitful. Like all foreigners I preferred the knife in the back to the way of honesty. I was planning to set up in London as a physician, he said, and my strenuous insistence that I fully intended to leave England as swiftly as possible only made him more furious.

Under any other circumstances, honor would have demanded that I call him out, and I suggested this, earning myself more sneers. Eventually I withdrew, exhausted and hungry, for we did not stop to eat while we battled. I went to bed deeply saddened, for I had liked him, and realized now that friendship was forever impossible. His society had brought me advantage, that is certainly true; but the cost I was forced to pay was too great. I was certain that my father, when he received my letters, would give me permission to leave and I decided that perhaps it would be best to anticipate that grant. I was, however, determined to complete the experiment I had undertaken with Mrs. Blundy; if the woman survived and I could demonstrate its efficacy, then at least I would reap something more than bitterness from the sojourn.

chapter sixteen

THE FOLLOWING MORNING LOWER WAS, OF COURSE, all contrition and apology, but this time it was of no use. Our friendship was breached beyond repair: *Fides unde abiit, eo nunquam redit,* as Publius Syrus put it. Now that I had determined to leave, I was less inclined to make the accommodations that such a reconciliation required and, though I accepted his apologies in form, I could not do so in my heart.

I believe he realized this, and our journey back to Oxford was full of silence and uncomfortable conversation. I missed our ease greatly, but could do nothing to retrieve our comradeship; Lower, I think, felt ashamed of himself, for he knew that he had acted unpardonably. As a result, he showed me constant little kindnesses to win his way back into my favor and fell into melancholy when his efforts went unrewarded.

One thing, though, I was obliged in honor to do, for even though I had given my word to Prestcott, I considered my obligation to Lower the greater. I knew little of the law, but I knew that I had to inform him of what had transpired at Mr. Thurloe's house, as it would have been improper for him to hear it from the magistrate or tavern gossip. He listened gravely as I recounted the tale.

"And you didn't tell me? Do you realize what you've done?"

"What?"

"You have made yourself as guilty as them. You may hang now, if Prestcott is ever caught. Did that never occur to you?"

"No. But what was I to do?"

He thought. "I don't know. But if the magistrate decides he wants Prestcott, and he has fled, then you will be in trouble. Do you believe him?"

"I can't imagine why not. He had nothing to gain. It is not as if I would have discovered him had he not summoned me. Besides, there is Dr. Grove's ring. Sarah Blundy will have to explain how she came by that."

"You are sure it is his?"

"No. But if it is, someone will be able to identify it. What do you think?"

Lower considered. "I think," he said after a while, "that if the ring is his, and if some way can be found for Prestcott to say his testimony, then it will hang the girl."

"Do you believe she is guilty?"

"I would be happier to have seen her in his room, pouring arsenic into the bottle. Or to hear it from her own lips. As Mr. Stahl tells us, there is no such thing as certainty, but I am coming to think it probable she was responsible."

Both of us hesitated then, as we realized at the same moment that we were slipping back into intimacy, and instantly an awkwardness intervened. At that moment, my mind was made up, for I realized I could never talk to him with ease, lest he explode once more. Lower knew well what was going through my mind, and fell glumly silent as the horse clopped along the muddy road. I am sure he felt he could do no more: he had apologized for his past words, and could see no need to excuse those he had not yet spoken.

I HAVE ALREADY MENTIONED THAT MY OPINION OF THE theater in England was not high, the tale tedious, the acting dreadful, the declamation poor. Not so with the courts, which supplied all the pomp and drama that the theater lacked, being also better produced and more convincingly expressed.

The spectacle of an assize is not to be matched anywhere on the continent; not even the French, who love the grandiose, have such an awful display in their justice. The essence of the grandeur lies in the fact that justice is mobile; while small crimes are dealt with by magistrates, more important cases are dealt with by the king's representatives sent out from London at regular intervals. These patrol the country in circuit, and their arrival is attended by much circumstance. The mayor awaits the procession at the borders of the town, the local landowners send carriages to drive behind, and the people line the streets as the carriages wend their way to the courthouse, where convoluted proclamations are read out which give the judges authority to hang as many lawbreakers as they please.

Perhaps I ought to explain here the way the English deal with such matters, their method being as singular as many other proceedings in that country. One would have thought that a learned judge would have been sufficient as it is everywhere else, but this is not the case. For, having appointed such a person, they give all his power to a group of twelve men, chosen at random and utterly ignorant of all law. What is more, they are inordinately proud of this most bizarre system and hold this jury in awe as the bedrock of their liberties. These men listen to the arguments in court and vote about the verdict. The case is normally presented by the person who brings the prosecution or, in the case of murder, by family or by a magistrate who acts on behalf of the king. In this case, Grove having no family, the magistrate was bound to prepare the suit at the public expense.

The preparations for the assizes are many and the cost considerable, which is why the High Street was all but clogged with people when we returned. I was fascinated by the spectacle, but it merely put Lower into an ill humor. It was late in the day, neither of us had eaten and we were in two minds whether to stop for nourishment or to proceed straight to Sir John Fulgrove's house in Holywell. We decided on the latter, not least because I was also anxious about Mrs. Blundy: whatever her daughter had done, she was still my patient and my hope of fame. And I was anxious to be free of Lower's company.

Sir John saw me promptly—an aspect of the English law I greatly admire. I have had little to do with our Venetian magistrates, but I know that they believe the grandeur of the law is served by making everything as inconvenient as possible. He also listened to my story with interest, though little gratitude. His demeanor, indeed, had changed greatly in the period I had been away, and he demonstrated none of that agreeable condescension which I had received before.

"It was your duty to report this matter immediately to those in authority," he said. "Thurloe is a traitor and should have been hanged years ago. And you now tell me he is harboring fugitives? Why, the man thinks he is above the law entirely."

"From what I hear," I said quietly, "he is."

Sir John scowled. "It is intolerable that this should continue. He is in open rebellion against the king's government, and yet it does nothing."

"I do not wish to defend him," I said, "as if half of what I have heard is true then he should be hanged forthwith. But in this case, I do not think he believes Mr. Prestcott truly guilty of the crimes of which he is accused. And by keeping him close by, he has surely done a service, if the man has important testimony about Dr. Grove."

The magistrate grunted.

"Do you think this tale unimportant?" I asked.

"No, of course not."

"The girl is going to stand trial?"

"She is. She will answer the case on the last day of the assizes."

"On what charge?"

"Petty treason."

"What is that?"

"Grove was her master; it matters not that she was discharged, because it was as her master that he was killed. That is treason, because a master is as a father to his children, or the king to his people. It is the worst of all crimes; far more serious than murder. And carries a far harsher punishment. When she is found guilty, she will burn."

"You are in no doubt about her guilt?"

"None. My investigations have uncovered a character so foul, so sordid, that it is a wonder she was not unmasked before."

"Has she confessed?"

"Not she. She denies it all."

"And what will you do with my information?"

"I intend," he said, "to take some soldiers and ride straight out to Milton. Where I will clap both Mr. Prestcott and his protector in irons and drag them both back to jail. We will see if Mr. Thurloe can evade the law this time. You must excuse me. I am in a hurry."

THAT ALARMING DUTY DONE, I RETURNED TO THE HIGH street to be told that Mr. Boyle had fallen ill at his sister's house in London and intended to stay there for a few days yet. Then I went to Tillyard's, to fill my stomach and catch up on the news. Locke was there, and seemed mightily glad to see me; I was not so content to see him.

"Next time you have a patient, Mr. Cola," he said once I was settled, "pray keep her to yourself. I have had the devil of a run with her. She has deteriorated since you left."

"I'm sorry to hear it. Why, exactly?"

He shrugged. "I have no idea at all. But she is weakened a little. It began the day that daughter of hers was arrested."

He willingly told me all the details, as he had been attending the woman when it occurred. It appeared that the bailiff had come for Sarah at her house, and had shackled her and dragged her away in full view of the mother. Sarah had not gone quietly; she had screamed and scratched and bitten until she was forced to the floor and bound; even then she continued screaming and had to be gagged as well. The mother had attempted to rise from her bed and it had required Locke's full strength to force her back.

"All the time the poor woman screamed that her daughter had not done anything, and they should leave her alone. I must say, when I saw the girl's performance I could quite believe that she had killed someone. I've never seen such a transformation in a human being before. All quiet and gentle one moment, the next a screaming, raging monster. Quite a horrible performance. And the strength she had! Do you know, it took three full-grown men to pin her down while the chains were put on?"

I grunted. "Her mother?"

"She curled up on the bed and began to cry, of course, and afterward became weak and fretful." He paused and looked at me frankly. "I did what I could but it had no effect; please accept my assurances on that."

"I will have to go and see her," I said. "This is something which has concerned me ever since I heard of the arrest. I greatly fear the mother's condition is bound to get worse, unless we do something drastic."

"Why is that?"

"The transfusion, Mr. Locke. The transfusion. Think of it. I didn't know for sure, but I wondered whether the state of the girl might affect that of the mother, now their spirits are so intermingled in her body. Sarah, no doubt, can withstand the effects; her mother is so much older and weaker, I have no doubt this is what has caused her decline."

Locke leaned back in his chair, his eyebrows raised in what seemed like supercilious disdain but which I now believed was his habitual appearance when deep in thought. "Fascinating," he said eventually. "This experiment of yours has all sorts of consequences. So what do you intend?"

I shook my head sorrowfully. "I do not know. I have no ideas at all. You must excuse me. I should go and see her immediately."

And so I did, the visit confirming the very worst of my fears. The woman was indeed weaker, whatever progress her wound had made had stopped and the stench of sickness hung in the dank little room. I could have wept to see the sight. But she was conscious, and had not yet deteriorated too far. Close questioning discovered that she had not eaten now in near two days; the girl Lower had hired to watch over her had abandoned her post when Sarah was taken, refusing to stay in the house of a murderess. Naturally, she did not refund the money.

It seemed to me that part of the trouble was that the woman was hungry; she needed to eat well and regularly to have any chance at all, so the first thing I did was march straight to a cook house and demand some bread and broth for her. This I fed to her myself, spoonful by spoonful, before I examined and redressed the wound. It was not as bad as I feared. Locke had done a decent job in that respect, at least.

But she still should not have been that ill. Hunger and the dismay of seeing her daughter taken no doubt made her despondent, but I was sure—indeed my entire theory depended on it—of a communication between her and the daughterly blood now commingled in her veins. And if being cast into a rat-infested prison could have this effect, then clearly worse was to come.

"I beg you, kind doctor," she said when I had finished, "how is my Sarah, do you know?"

I shook my head. "I have only just returned from the country, and know less than you do. All I have heard is that she is to go on trial. Have you not had any messages?"

"No. I cannot go there, and she cannot come here. And there is no one who will take a message for me. I hesitate to impose on your goodness . . ."

My heart sank. I knew what she was going to say, and I dreaded the request.

". . . but you know her a little. You know she could not do anything like this. She has never harmed anyone in her entire life, quite the opposite in fact; she is known—even Mr. Boyle knows her—for her willingness and ability to heal. I know you cannot do anything for her but would you go and see her, tell her that I am well and she is not to worry on my behalf?"

I desperately wanted to refuse, to say that I wished to have nothing further to do with the girl. But I could not bring myself to say the harsh words; it would have weakened the poor woman still further and, if my theory was correct, then the more content the girl, the greater the mother's chances as well. So I agreed to the request. I would visit the jail, assuming I was allowed in, and would convey the message.

I HOPE I HAVE LED A GOOD LIFE, AND THAT THE LORD recognizes my efforts to conform to his laws so that I am spared the miseries of eternal torment, for if Hell is half as diabolical as the cells of an English jail on the day before an assize, it is a terrible place indeed. The small forecourt in front of the castle was far more crowded than on the previous occasion I visited it, alive with the bustle of men and women come to succor prisoners, or drawn merely by the possibility of watching new ones arrive. The unfortunate wretches are brought in from far and wide when the judges come to town, that they may stand their turn and hear their fate. The jail, virtually empty last time I was there, was now bursting, the stench of human bodies overwhelming and the noise of the sick, the cold and the desperate deeply affecting. However much many of the creatures deserved to be so lodged, I could not but feel sorry for them, and even had a momentary burst of panic that I might be confused for a prisoner and refused permission to leave again once my task was done.

Men and women are separated, of course, and the poorer sort make do in two large rooms. There is no furniture of any type except straw pallets for them to lie on, and the sounds of the heavy iron chains clanking as the prisoners tossed and turned in a futile attempt to find comfort sang loudly in the background as I picked my way through the mass of bodies. It was bitterly cold, as the room was near the waterline of the old moat, and centuries of damp clung to the walls. The only light came from a few windows, so high up that only a bird could have reached them. It occurred to me that it was just as well the assizes met soon, otherwise an underfed, underclothed girl like Sarah Blundy would die of jail fever long before the hangman had his turn.

It took some time to find her, for she was leaning against the clammy wall, arms around her legs and her head bowed down so that only her long brown hair could be seen. She was singing softly to herself, a mournful sound in that dreadful place, the plaintive lament of a caged bird, singing in memory of its freedom. When I greeted her it was some moments before she lifted her head up. Oddly, I was most saddened and alarmed to see how her normal demeanor had vanished. Instead of the insolent haughtiness, she was quiet and passive, as though as deprived of the air she needed as the dove in Boyle's pump. She didn't even reply when I asked her how she did: merely shrugged her shoulders and hugged herself as if to try and keep warm.

"I'm sorry I have brought you nothing," I said. "Had I known, I would have got some blankets and food."

"That is kind," she replied. "As to the food, you need not bother: the university has a charitable fund and Mrs. Wood, my employer, has kindly offered to bring me meals every day. But I would welcome some warm clothes. How is my mother?"

I scratched my head. "That is the main reason why I have come. She asked me to tell you must not worry about her. To which I can only add my own exhortations. Your concern does her no good, and may do her harm."

She looked at me steadily, seeing straight through my words to the concern on my face. "She is not well, is she?" she said flatly. "Tell me the truth, doctor."

"No," I replied frankly, "she is not as good as I had hoped. I am concerned for her." To my horror, she buried her head in her hands once more and I saw her body shaking, and heard her sobbing in sheer misery.

"Come, now," I said. "It is not as bad as that. She has had a setback, that is all. She is still alive, she still has myself and Lower and now Mr. Locke as well, all desperate to make her better. You must not concern yourself. It is not at all kind to those who are trying so hard for her."

Eventually, after more such encouragement, I talked her round and she lifted up her head, eyes red with crying, and wiped her nose on her bare arm.

"I came to reassure you," I said, "not to make you fret the more. You look to yourself and your trial; that is quite enough to keep you busy. Leave your mother to us. In your current circumstances, there is nothing you can do anyway."

"And afterward?"

"After what?"

"After I am hanged."

"There, now, that is jumping ahead a little!" I cried with very much more cheer than I felt. "You do not have the noose around your neck yet." I did not tell her that her fate might well be much worse than a mere hanging.

"Everyone has already decided," she said quietly. "The magistrate told me when he asked me to confess. The jurors are bound to find me guilty, and the judge is bound to hang me. Who would believe someone like me when I cannot prove my innocence? And what will become of my mother

then? How will she live? Who will look after her? We have
no family, no means of support at all.''

"*When* she recovers," I said heavily, "she will undoubtedly find some suitable employment.''

"The wife of a fanatic and the mother of a murderer? Who
would give her work? And you know as well as I do that
she will be unable to work for many weeks.''

I could not say that this was a false problem, as the
chances were high that she would be dead within a week.
And, God forgive me, I could think of no other comfort to
give.

"Mr. Cola, sir, I must ask you a question. How much does
Dr. Lower pay?''

I took a moment before I understood what she was talking
about. "You mean . . . ?''

"I understand he buys bodies," she said, frighteningly
calm now. "How much does he pay? Because I am willing
for him to have mine if he will undertake to look after my
mother. Please do not look so uncomfortable. It is the only
thing I have left to sell, and I will not be needing it,'' she
concluded simply.

"I—I—I do not know. It depends on the condition of—
ah . . .''

"Will you ask him for me? I am thought to have sold my
body while alive, so it will hardly be a scandal if I sell it
again when I am dead.''

Even Lower, I think, would have had trouble with such a
conversation; I found it quite beyond my powers. Could I
say that, after the pyre, even Lower would not want what
remained? I stammered that I would mention it to him, but
was desperately keen to change the subject.

"You must not abandon hope," I said. "Are you planning
what you will say?''

"How can I?" she asked. "I barely know what I am
charged with; I cannot know who is to give evidence against
me. I have no one on my side, unless someone like yourself,
doctor, will attest to my good character.''

A fraction of a second's hesitation was enough for her.
"There you are," she said softly. "You see? Who is to help
me?''

She looked intently at me as she waited my reply. I did not want to respond; it had not been my intention of coming, but somehow I could not resist her. "I do not know," I said eventually. "I would have liked to, but I cannot explain Dr. Grove's ring."

"What ring?"

"The one stolen from his body, and discovered by Jack Prestcott. He told me all about it."

The moment my answer registered I knew, beyond any shadow of a doubt, that my suspicions were true, and that the magistrate had done his job well. She had murdered Grove. She turned pale when the import of my words hit home. She could have explained almost everything else in one way or another, but she could find no answer to this charge.

"Well, Sarah?" I said when she kept silent.

"It seems there is no escape for me, then. I think it time you went away." It was a resigned, pathetic statement, very much the words of one who realized her deeds were finally proved beyond doubt.

"Are you not going to answer? You will have to answer the court if you do not answer me. So how do you defend yourself against the charge that you killed Grove for revenge, and stole from his body as it lay on the floor?"

The whirlwind which hit me then was one of the greatest shocks in my life. Suddenly transformed from submission, the true features of the girl were suddenly revealed as, snarling with hatred and frustration, she lunged at me, tearing at my face with her nails, eyes wild with madness. Fortunately the chains around her wrist and ankle restrained her, or I swear she would have had my eyes out. As it was I fell backward onto a foul-smelling old woman who instantly reached inside my coat for my purse. I cried out in alarm, and within a few seconds a jailer came in to rescue me, kicking the prisoners, and clubbing Sarah to calm her down. She fell back onto the pallet, screaming and crying harder than I have ever heard any person cry before.

I stared appalled at the monster before me, then collected myself enough to assure the anxious jailer that I was unhurt, apart from a scratch down my cheek, and stood at a safe distance, gulping the foul air to get my breath back.

"If I ever had any doubts about you," I said, "they are gone now. For your mother's sake I will speak to Lower. But do not expect anything further from me."

And I left, so glad to escape the hellish place and the demons within it, that I went straight to the nearest tavern to recover myself. My hands were still shaking half an hour later.

ALTHOUGH MY MIND WAS NOW AT REST ABOUT THE girl's guilt, I cannot say that I was contented in any other way. On the contrary; to be in the presence of such evil is profoundly disturbing, and the manifestation I had witnessed was not forgotten so easily. When I left the tavern, I was much in need of company, to have my mind taken off the sights and the sounds I had encountered. Had my relations with Lower been easier, his natural manner would have restored me. But I had no desire to see him and did not do so until I remembered the girl's request; for my patient's sake, and because I had given her my word, I felt obliged to deliver the message, however futile it might be.

Lower, however, was not to be found in any of his usual haunts, nor was he in his rooms at Christ Church. I asked, and eventually someone told me that he had seen him with Locke and the mathematician Christopher Wren an hour or so previously. As Wren still maintained rooms at Wadham, I should perhaps try there.

I was keen to meet this young man in any case, as I had heard much about him during my stay, and so I went there, asking at the gate where he was and whether he had company. He was with friends, I was told, and had asked not to be disturbed. Porters always say this, of course, so I ignored the advice and walked swiftly up the stairs to the gatehouse room where Wren lived, knocked and went in.

The shock upon entering was considerable. Wren, a short, neat man with flowing locks and a not unpleasing countenance, looked annoyed as I walked into the room and stopped, staring, at the sight which I beheld. Locke had a kind of smirk on his face, like a child caught in some prank, glad to have his naughtiness known to the world. My friend, my very good friend, Richard Lower, at least had the goodness to be discountenanced and embarrassed to have his deceit so exposed that there was no possibility of any doubt about what was taking place.

For on a wide deal table in the middle of the room, a dog was strapped, whining piteously, and rolling its eyes in distress as it struggled to free itself. Next to it was another, more resigned to the torture it was being forced to endure. A long thin tube ran from the neck of one to that of the other, and blood from the incisions made in the necks of each had splattered onto Locke's apron and onto the floor.

They were transfusing blood. Repeating my experiment in secret. Concealing their deeds from me, the person who had best right to be informed of what they were doing. I could not believe I had been so betrayed.

Lower recovered first. "Excuse me, gentlemen," he said without even having the courtesy to present me to Wren. "I must absent myself for a while."

He took off his apron, and threw it onto the floor, then asked me to accompany him into the garden. I dragged my eyes from the scene that so assaulted my spirits, and followed angrily down the stairs.

We walked around the gardens, criss-crossing the box hedges and patches of grass at random for several moments while I kept silent, waiting for him to explain himself.

"Not my fault, Cola," he said after a very long while had passed. "Please accept my apologies. It was unforgivable of me to behave in such a way."

The shock had still not passed, and I could find no words.

"Locke, you see, told Wren of the experiment we—you—had devised for Mrs. Blundy, and he was so excited that he insisted on repeating it. It detracts not a whit from your own achievement, you know. We merely plod along in your footsteps, emulating the master."

He grinned sheepishly, and turned to see how his apology was being received. I was resolved to remain cold.

"The barest courtesy demanded that you inform me, even if you could not bring yourself to invite my attendance."

A grimace replaced the smile. "True," he said. "And I

am properly sorry for it. I did look for you, but didn't know where you were. And Wren wants to go back to London this afternoon, you see . . ."

"So you betray one friend to accommodate another," I interrupted coldly.

This justified comment disconcerted him considerably, and he pretended to become angry. "What betrayal? Once an idea is conceived, it does not remain the property of the person who imagined it first. We do not deny your achievement, nor did we plan to keep it a secret from you. You were not there; that is all there is to the matter. I did not know that Wren was so keen to try it out until I encountered him this morning."

His tone was so insistent that I felt my doubts ebbing away. I so very much wanted to believe him, and to think of him as my friend still, that I could not hold on to my conviction that I was betrayed. But then I remembered the look of shocked exposure on his face as I walked into that room, a more sure confession of guilt than anything I had seen on the face of Sarah Blundy.

"We do not intend to publish this to the world without your knowledge and permission," he continued when he saw he had still not breached my defenses. "And you must admit, it is a better way of doing it. If we—you—make an account of your discovery in a fashion which admits the transfusion was first attempted on a woman, you will be dismissed as reckless and dangerous. If, however, you preface it with accounts of transfusion between dogs, then the disapprobation will be greatly lessened."

"And that is what you were doing?"

"Of course it was," he said, encouraged by the soothing of my anger. "I have told you of my fears if this becomes generally known too quickly. It has to be done in this fashion, and the sooner the better. I am sorry—truly sorry—that you were not there. Please accept my most humble apologies. And, on their behalf, I offer those of Locke and Wren as well, as they never intended any discourtesy."

He bowed low and, as he had no hat on, swept off his wig as he did so. My face cracked with a faint smile at the absurdity, but I was determined this time not to give way because of such a device.

"Come now," he said, discouraged by my reaction. "Do you forgive me?"

I nodded. "Very well," I said flatly, although it was one of the biggest lies I have ever told. But I still needed his good offices and had no alternative, beggar in friendship as I now was, to maintaining at least the appearance of cordiality. "Let us talk no more on this matter, otherwise we will quarrel once again."

"Where were you, anyway?" he asked. "We really did look."

"With Mrs. Blundy, who is sick and getting sicker. And with her daughter."

"In the castle?"

I nodded. "I did not wish to go, but the mother begged me. And it reassured me greatly. If ever a soul was capable of murder, it is that girl. I have no doubts, even though I suspect she will deny the deed, and I would be easier still if she confessed to it freely. But it seems clear to me now that she asked Grove for money to aid her mother that morning in Tillyard's and was rejected. So she took it anyway, murdering him and stealing from his room. It is dreadful that duty to a parent can be so corrupted and twisted."

Lower nodded. "She told you this?"

"Not she," I said. "She will not admit anything. But she does want to do one good deed still, perhaps out of remorse, because I can think of no other reason for it."

Quickly, I told Lower of the offer of her corpse, in return for his agreeing to treat and care for the mother. Lower looked surprised, and—I hate to say it—positively eager that he should benefit in this fashion.

"How does the mother?"

"I doubt you will find her a lengthy burden on your pocket," I said. "That is something else I need to talk to you about. She is failing, and if the girl dies, I believe that the extinction of the spirit in one will have fatal results on the other."

He looked thoughtful as I told him of my fears, and of the only remedy I believed might salvage the situation. "She must have more blood, Lower,'' I said. ''And from a different person, one strong enough and healthy enough to counteract the girl's spirit. Quickly, as well. If Sarah is tried tomorrow, she will die the day after. There is little time.''

''You are convinced of this?''

''Totally. She has already declined along with the girl's spirits, the signs are obvious to see. There can be no other cause that I can imagine.''

He grunted. ''You mean you want to do it today.''

''Yes. For her sake, and for that of our friendship, I would beg a final assistance from you.''

We walked around the garden again in a similitude of friendship as he pondered my reasoning.

''You might be right,'' he said at last. ''Unless there is something we do not know.''

''If we do not know it, we cannot take account of it,'' I pointed out.

Another grunt, then he took one of those deep breaths which indicated he had taken a decision. ''Very well,'' he said. ''This evening. I will bring one of the gardeners from the college who can be relied on to keep quiet.''

''Why not this afternoon?''

''Because I want to see the girl. If I am to have her, I will need a properly signed and witnessed letter to that effect. It will take time, and must be done before the trial begins. You know she will burn?''

''The magistrate told me.''

''The chances of her being much use are small, unless I can persuade Sir John to intervene with the judge.'' He bowed. ''But don't worry. We'll get it done in time. Meet me at the Angel after dinner. Then we'll take care of the mother.''

I PASSED THE REST OF THE DAY IN CORRESPONDENCE and melancholy. Now I had decided to leave as soon as my obligations permitted, I was anxious to depart as swiftly as possible. Only Widow Blundy kept me there, as I had already seen what happened when I did not attend her myself. I took no joy in Sarah Blundy's fate, had little optimism about her mother and my confidence in my friend was at an end. I wanted to accept his assurances about his fidelity, and indeed I had done so; but the seeds of doubt were sown, and had disturbed my soul.

I am not prideful, but I am jealous of my honor and fidelity. And Lower had placed both of those in jeopardy by acceding to Wren's request above my right. Even though he owned to the fault, it did not erase the hurt he had caused me, and completed the distrust which his violent temper had already generated.

I was, in other words, in a gray humor by the time Lower marched into the Angel trailing behind him a cadaverous and sickly looking wretch whom he introduced as one of the undergardeners at his college. For a shilling he would give his blood to Mrs. Blundy.

"But he's no good!" I cried. "Look at him. I wouldn't be surprised if he was in worse health than Mrs. Blundy. It would be better to transfer her blood into him. I wanted someone strong and full of vitality."

"He's enormously strong. Aren't you?" he said, addressing the man for the first time. This latter, noticing Lower had turned in his direction, gave a gap-toothed smile, and whinnied like a horse.

"His great virtue," Lower said as the man drank a quart pot of ale eagerly, "is that he is deaf and dumb. Dr. Wallis tried to teach him to speak, but to no avail. He can't write either. It means, you see, that his discretion is assured. Which, you must admit, is important. That family is held in enough disapprobation already and if it became commonly known that the mother was being kept alive by such means I wouldn't be surprised if she was burned along with the daughter. Here, fellow. Have another."

He signaled for another quart, which was soon set in front of the poor wretch. "Best if he has a little," he said. "I don't want him running away when he sees what we intend."

I was not happy, although I saw the justice of the point. But it says something about how my attitude had changed that I distrusted the motive behind the use of someone who could not testify to what had occurred.

"Did you visit the jail?"

He rolled his eyes. "Lord, yes," he said. "And what a day I have had."

"Had she changed her mind?"

"Not at all. We wrote out a suitable letter—did you know she could read and write as well as you and I? I was astonished—and had it witnessed. That was no trouble. It was the magistrate."

"He opposed the idea? Why?"

"Because I could not persuade him that he was under any obligation to the girl. A damnable nuisance, if I may say so."

"So that's it? No body?"

He looked despairingly at me. "Even if I got her, I'd have to give her over to the pyre when I was finished. The magistrate would only allow me temporary possession. But even that would have been better than nothing. I'm going back to him later to see if there is some way of persuading him."

He glanced at the gardener, who was now well into the third quart of ale. "Oh, come on. Let's get on with it before he's insensible. Do you know," he said as we pulled the wretch up, "I am getting heartily sick of this family? The sooner they are both dead, the better. Oh, damnation! Oh, Cola, I am sorry."

Both his explanation and his apology were justified. For the half-wit must have been drinking even before Lower brought him in, and the three quarts he drank while we talked were too much. With a foolish smile on his face turning to a look of alarm, he slid to the floor, then vomited on Lower's shoes. Lower jumped out of the way and looked at the sight with distaste, then kicked the wretch to confirm his insensibility.

"What do we do now?"

"I'm not going to use him," I said. "We'd have to carry him there ourselves. It's difficult enough with someone who is cooperative."

"He seemed sober enough when we left the college."

I shook my head sadly. "This is your fault, Lower. You knew how important this was, and you have failed me."

"I have apologized."

"That serves me nothing. We'll have to postpone the treatment until tomorrow. And hope she survives that long. The delay may kill her.''

"I think your treatment will accomplish that in any case," he said coldly.

"I did not hear you saying that before."

"You never asked."

I opened my mouth to reply, but gave up. What was the point? For reasons I could not fathom, almost everything we said to each other was taken as a slight or an insult. As he would not explain his behavior, and I could truly find no fault in my own, there was nothing I could do.

"I will not argue with you," I said. "You have undertaken to supply me with some blood, and I hold you to that promise. Then our association can end, as you clearly wish. Will you bring him tomorrow, after the trial?"

He bowed stiffly, and he promised he would not fail me again. Once the trial was over, I should go to Mrs. Blundy's cottage and await him. He would come with the gardener, and we would perform the treatment. There was enough time.

chapter seventeen

At ONE O'CLOCK THE FOLLOWING AFTERNOON, THE trial of Sarah Blundy for the murder of Dr. Robert Grove began in the assize court of Oxford. The crowd was eager; not only did the trial promise much scandalous entertainment, the previous day had seen not a single hanging verdict, and ended not with the judge wearing a black cap, but being presented with the traditional pair of white gloves to show that his hands were clean of blood. But such mercy was considered dangerous, for the awful majesty of the law needs sacrifice. One maiden session (as they are called) was merciful, two in a row would seem weak. What was more, Wood, an assiduous attender of trials who spoke to me briefly before the pushing of the crowd separated us, told me that the judge realized this: someone, that day, would hang. We both knew, I think, who it would be.

There was a murmur of anticipation as Sarah, terribly pale, was led before the court, to stand facing the crowd and listen to the sonorous charges against her. That she, Sarah Blundy, not having the fear of God before her eyes, but being moved and seduced by the instigation of the devil, in the fifteenth year of our sovereign Lord the King, at New College in the City of Oxford, did make an assault upon the Reverend Robert Grove, fellow of that place and formerly her master, feloniously, willfully and traitorously. And the said Sarah Blundy did feloniously, willfully, traitorously and out of malice, did place arsenic in a bottle and cause the said Robert Grove to drink it, of which poisoning the said Robert Grove died. So that the said Sarah Blundy in manner and form aforesaid, feloniously, willfully, traitorously and of malice aforethought, didst kill and murder, against the peace of our sovereign Lord, his crown and dignity.

Mutterings of approval, which caused the judge to look up with warning in his eye, erupted from the mob as they heard this accusation read; it took some time for order to be restored—not that there is ever very much in an English court. Then the judge, who did not strike me as very fearsome in aspect, turned to Sarah and asked her to plead.

She did not reply, but stood with head bowed.

"Come, girl," the judge said, "You must plead, you know. Guilty or not guilty, it is all the same to me. But you must say something, or it will go ill with you."

Still she said nothing, and an expectant hush fell on the audience, as they looked at her standing there, head bowed to hide her terror and shame. I felt a wave of sympathy for her, for who would not be silenced by facing, all alone, the formidable power of justice?

"I'll tell you what," the judge said, a look of concern on his face that the proceedings were about to be disrupted. "We'll run through the charges and the evidence against you. See if that'll make up your mind about your chances of escaping justice. How about that? Sir? Are you ready?"

The prosecutor, a cheerful soul retained by the magistrate to do such business, bounded to his feet and bowed obsequiously. "Your lordship's reputation for kindness is well deserved," he said, and the mob burst into applause to echo the sentiment.

The man next to me, squeezed against me so tightly I could feel every breath he took, turned to me and whispered in my ear that this was no more than the truth; by rights, the law is most harsh on those who flout its authority by refusing to plead, shackling them with weights until either they give in, or die from the pressure upon their chests. Nobody liked this proceeding, but it is the only solution for recalcitrance. By giving the girl a second chance, so to speak, the judge was indeed exceptionally merciful. My neighbor—evidently a regular at trials—said he had never heard of such kindness before.

The prosecutor then began to explain his case: he said that, although he was not the victim of the crime, in matters of murder the victim could obviously not appear for himself; hence his presence. It was not an onerous task, for it was simple enough to see who had committed this foul deed.

In his opinion, he said, the jury would have no trouble at all in bringing in the right verdict. For it was obvious to all— and the town knew well enough already, without having to remind them of it—that Sarah Blundy was a whore of intemperate and violent parentage. So far was she from knowing her correct place, so badly trained, and so unknowing of all morality and decency, that the idea of murder did not shock her in the slightest, such are the monsters produced when parents turn their face from God, and the country from its rightful king.

The judge—clearly not a cruel man, and scrupulously fair—interrupted to thank the prosecutor and wondered if he might proceed. Fine speechifying could take place at the end, if they got that far.

"Certainly, certainly. Now, as to her being a whore; it is well attested that she had seduced poor Dr. Grove and lured him into her power. We have a witness to this, one Mary Fullerton" (here a young girl in the audience smiled broadly and preened herself) "who will swear that one day she delivered some food to Dr. Grove's room and he, mistaking her for Blundy, grabbed her and started fondling her in a lascivious fashion as though she was well used to it."

Sarah looked up at this point and stared sullenly at Mary Fullerton, whose smile disappeared when she felt the gaze upon her.

"Secondly, we have testimony that Dr. Grove, when these accusations were made known, discharged the girl from her employ, so that he might take himself away from temptation and return to a virtuous life. And that she most bitterly resented this.

"Thirdly, we have the testimony of Mr. Crosse, an apothecary, that on the same day as she was discharged Sarah

Blundy bought arsenic from his shop. She has said Dr. Grove asked her to do so, but no one has found any record of such an expenditure in Dr. Grove's papers.

"Fourthly, we have the testimony of Signor Marco da Cola, an Italian gentleman of impeccable integrity, who will tell you that he warned of the dangers of this powder, and heard Dr. Grove say that he would never use it again—a few hours before he died of it."

All eyes, including Sarah's, were on me at this point, and I looked down to avoid the sadness in her eyes. It was true, every word of it; but I wished fervently at that moment that it was not.

"Next, we have the testimony of Mr. Thomas Ken, a divine, that the girl was seen in New College that very evening, and it will be shown that, although she denies this, she refuses absolutely to say where she was, nor has anyone else come forward to say where she was."

"Finally, we have proof of an unimpeachable nature, for we have a witness, Mr. John Prestcott, a young gentleman at the university, who will testify that she confessed to him that very evening of her deed, and showed him a ring which she had ripped from the corpse. A ring which has been identified as Dr. Grove's own signet ring."

The whole room, it seemed, sucked in its breath at this point, as all knew that the testimony of a gentleman on such a matter was unlikely to be gainsaid. Sarah knew it too; for her head sank lower on her chest at the words, and her shoulders slumped in what seemed like the abandonment of all hope.

"Sir," the lawyer resumed, "the considerations against the accused of motive, character and station are as strong as the particular evidence. This is why I have no doubt that, whatever the girl pleads—indeed, whether she pleads or not—the outcome will be the same."

The prosecutor beamed around him to acknowledge the applause from the room, waved his hand in a stately fashion, then sat down. The judge waited until some silence had returned and then turned his attention to Sarah.

"Well, child? What have you to say? You know, I believe, the consequences of what you may utter."

Sarah looked very much as though she might collapse and, though I had little sympathy for her any more, I did feel that it would have been a kindness to have given her a seat.

"Come on, girl," someone cried from the audience. "Speak up. Struck dumb, are you?"

"Silence," thundered the judge. "Well?"

Sarah lifted her head, and I could see properly for the first time what a sad state she was in. Her eyes were red from crying, her face pale, her hair lank and dirty from the jail. A large bruise on her cheek had turned blue from the beating the jailer had given her when she assaulted me. Her mouth trembled as she tried to speak.

"What? What?" the judge said, leaning forward and cupping his hand to his ear. "You'll have to speak louder than that, you know."

"Guilty," she whispered, then slid to the floor in a faint as the audience erupted into catcalls and whistles of disappointment at being denied their fun. I tried to walk over to her, but was prevented from moving by the press of bodies.

"Silence," the judge shouted out. "All of you. Be quiet."

Eventually, they once more calmed down, and the judge looked around him. "The girl has pleaded guilty," he announced. "Which is a great blessing, as we can now proceed quickly. Members of the jury, any disagreement from you?"

The jury members all shook their heads somberly.

"Does anyone else have anything to say here?"

There was a rustle from the crowd as all turned to see if anyone would speak. Then I saw that Wood had stood up, red-faced with embarrassment at his temerity, and at the catcalls which greeted him.

"Quiet, now," said the judge. "Let us not rush. Please sir, say your piece."

Poor Wood; he was no advocate, and had none of the assurance of even a man like Lower, let alone someone like Locke. And yet he was the only person who stood up for the girl, and tried to say something in her favor. It was doomed to fail, even Demosthenes himself could scarcely have succeeded in the task, and I am sure Wood proceeded from generosity of spirit, rather than true faith in his cause. And he did the girl no good at all, for he was so overcome by the sudden light of public attention that he froze into incoherence, and did little more than stand there, babbling in a half-voice that hardly anyone could hear. The crowd put a stop to it; the booing began at the back, then whistling, until even the greatest orator could not have been heard. It was Locke, I think, who ended the misery, and with surprising gentleness, pulled him down. I could see the look of abject failure and dejection on the poor man's face, and grieved for his shame as much as I rejoiced that the moment was over.

"Thank you for your eloquence," said the judge, playing shamelessly to the crowd and unable to resist piling on further humiliation. "And I will take your words into account."

Then he pulled out the black felt cap and put it on his head; as he did so, there was an expectant rustling from the crowd, whose mood had changed from sympathy to the greatest malice. "Hang her," cried one voice from the back.

"Quiet," said the judge, but it was too late. Thus encouraged, more of the crowd joined in, then more, and within seconds, the whole room was full of the sound of that lust for blood which comes over soldiers in battle, or huntsmen as they near their quarry. "Hang her, kill her"; again and again in a rhythmic chanting, with much stamping of feet and whistling. It took the judge several minutes before he successfully restored order.

"I will have no more of this," he said sternly. "Now, is she recovered? Can she hear me?" he asked the court clerk, who had given up his seat that she might be placed on it.

"I believe so, my lord," the clerk said, even though he was bodily holding her upright and had slapped her several times to bring her round.

"Good. Sarah Blundy, listen to me carefully now. You have committed a most horrendous crime, and the sentence the law insists upon for a woman who murders so treasonably is unavoidable. You will be taken to a pyre and burned."

He paused to look around at the courtroom to see how this went down. It was not well received; necessary though it seemed to be, the English did not derive much satisfaction from the pyre, and a subdued mood settled over the room.

"However," the judge continued, "as you have pleaded

guilty, and spared the court a great deal of trouble, we intend to be merciful. You will be given the grace of being hanged before your body is consumed, to lessen the suffering you will have to endure. That is your sentence, and may God have mercy on your soul.''

He stood up and dismissed the court, grateful for having had such a short and satisfactory afternoon. The audience sighed as though it was waking from an exciting dream, shook itself and began to leave while two bailiffs carried the now insensible Sarah out of the room and back to the castle. The whole trial had lasted less than an hour.

chapter eighteen

MY MOOD OF DESPONDENCY INCREASED MARKEDLY
when I saw Mrs. Blundy a few hours later, for the battle was
being waged and lost as I watched.

"I'm so sorry, doctor." Her voice was fainter even than
before, almost a whimper, so sharply did the pain cut into
her. But she was brave, and did her best not to let it show,
lest it be taken as a criticism of my efforts.

"It is I who should apologize," I said, once I had examined her and realized how bad it all was. "You should never
have been left alone for so long."

"How is Sarah?" she asked, and it was the question I was
dreading. I had decided in advance to avoid telling her the
truth that not only had she been found guilty, but that she
had admitted the deed as well.

"She is well," I said. "As well as can be expected."

"And when is the trial?"

I breathed a sigh of relief at that; she had lost her sense
of time and had forgotten what day it was; it made my task
a good deal easier.

"Soon," I said. "I am sure that it will go well. Concentrate on your own troubles; that is the best help you can give
her, because she must be free of distractions if she is to keep
her wits about her."

She was content with that, at least, and I felt for the first
time in my life that sometimes it is better to lie than to tell

the truth. Like all people, I suppose, I had had it beaten into me from an early age that respect for the truth was the most basic attribute of the gentleman; but it is not correct. Sometimes it is our duty to lie, whatever the consequences for ourselves. My falsehood contented her; truth would have made her last hours the purest anguish. I am proud that I spared her.

As no one else was around, I had to do everything myself; I simply hoped as I worked that Lower would come soon, so we could perform the task ahead of us. He was already late, and I was concerned. Grim and miserable work it is, cleaning and wiping and feeding, knowing that it is all for show, to give comfort while the inevitable beckons. The daughter's spirit, a stronger force in all ways, was dragging the mother down with her. Her face was livid, she had pains in her joints, as well as acute gripes in the guts; she trembled, and flushed hot and cold rapidly.

When I had finished, a shivering fit came over her, and she curled up in the bed, her teeth chattering, even though I had built a fire and it was, for the first time, almost warm in the room.

What was I to do? I tried to leave to search for Lower and remind him of his obligations, but this produced the first real movement in her since I had arrived. She grabbed my wrist in a surprisingly strong grip, and refused to let go.

"Please don't go," she whispered through the shivers, "I'm frightened. I don't want to die alone."

I didn't have the heart to leave, although I had no enthusiasm for staying, and my presence would make not one jot of difference without Lower there. However good my experiment, whatever hope it held for the future, he and the daughter had ruined it, and she was now going to bear the responsibility for one more life.

And so I stayed, fighting back the thought, growing now into certainty, that Lower was going to fail me when his aid was most needed. I built up the fire once more, burning more wood in a night than the Blundys had used in the previous six months, and sat wrapped in my cloak on the floor, as she slowly drifted in and out of a delirium.

And what madness she talked when she was sensible,

about her husband and her daughter. Reminiscence, blasphemy, piety and lies were all mixed together so I could scarcely tell one from the other. I tried not to listen, and did my best to avoid condemning her words, for I knew that at times like these the devils which attend all of us in our lives see their chance, and speak with our mouths, uttering words we would never own to were we in full control of ourselves. This is why we give the last rites, to cleanse the soul of those demons so that it leaves the body pure, and this is why the Protestant religion is so cruel, that it denies man that final kindness.

And I still could not understand mother or daughter, as such sweetness and perversity I had never met in combination before or since. Nor could I understand it still when, exhausted by her ravings, first the old woman, and then myself, fell asleep in the hot, airless room. I dreamed of my friend, and occasionally in the night a sound or noise disturbed me, and I awoke thinking that he had come. But each time I realized it was only an owl, or some animal, or the cracking of a log as it burst in the fire.

IT WAS STILL DARK WHEN I AWOKE; I GUESSED ABOUT SIX, certainly not later. The fire had all but gone out, and the room was chilly once more. I rekindled it as best I could and the exercise helped loosen my joints, which were stiff from sleep. Only then did I examine my patient. She seemed little changed, perhaps even slightly better, but I knew she was in no state to withstand any new strain.

Even though my trust for him had diminished, I wished Lower was there to help and advise. But even I could no longer disguise the fact that he had failed me: I was on my own, and had little time to act. I don't know how long I stood there in indecision, hoping that my one alternative would not prove necessary. I hesitated too long; my mind cannot have been working properly, because I stared blankly at my patient until I was brought back by a distant murmur of sound coming from the outside. I shook myself into action when I realized what it was. The sound of voices, massed voices, growing in volume.

Even before I flung open the door to make certain, I knew the sound came from the castle. The crowd was assembling, and I saw the first thin fingers of dawn in the sky. There was not long, and I had no choices left, nor could I delay a second longer.

I prepared my instruments before I woke Mrs. Blundy up, laying out the quills and the ribbons and the long silver tube, so that I could manipulate them with one hand. I stripped off my coat, and rolled up my sleeve, and positioned the stool in the best position.

Then I woke her. "Now, madam," I said, "we must proceed. Can you hear me?"

She stared at the ceiling, then nodded. "I hear you, doctor, and I am in your hands. Is your friend come? I cannot see him."

"We must proceed without him. It will make no difference. You must have blood, and soon; it matters not where it comes from. Now, give me your arm."

It was very much more difficult than the first time; her emaciated state made it fiendishly hard to find a suitable vessel, and I wasted time probing, then withdrawing the quill some half dozen times before I was satisfied. She bore it patiently, as though hardly aware of what was going on, and impervious to the sharp pain I inflicted on her in my haste. Then I prepared myself, cutting into my flesh and jabbing the quill in as quickly as possible while her blood dribbled down her arm.

When the flow of blood from my arm was free and easy, I moved into a better position, then picked up the silver tube and inserted it into the end. The blood swiftly ran through and spurted out in a hot red jet, splashing over the bedclothes as I maneuvered the tube to bring it into line with the quill in her arm.

Then it was done, the conjunction was made and when I saw there were no obstructions I started counting. Ten minutes, I thought, as I managed a smile at the old woman. "Nearly done," I said. "You'll be fine now."

She did not smile back, so I counted, feeling the blood pulsing out of me and myself growing dizzy as I struggled to keep still. In the background the noise from the castle was slowly growing in intensity as the seconds passed. After I had counted near ten minutes, an enormous roar erupted, then died away to complete silence as I pulled the quills out of our arms and bound up the wounds to staunch the flow of blood. It was difficult; in my case I had incised into a large vessel, and I lost more blood before I could close the wound with a bandage. Still the blood soaked through and created a wide stain before I was sure I succeeded.

Then I was finished and all I could do was over. I took a deep breath to steady my spinning head while I packed the instruments away in the bag, hoping only that I was in time. Then the noise from the castle began again, and I turned round to look at my patient. There was a bluish tinge on her lips, I saw, and as the drums rolled in the distance, I picked up her hand and saw that the fingers had discolored as well. The drums picked up in intensity as she began to shake, and cry out in the most excruciating pain and gulp desperately for breath. Then, as the roar of the crowd mounted and became almost deafening, she arched her back and cried out in a strong, clear voice, clear of all sound of agony: "Sarah! My God! Have mercy upon me."

Then silence. The noise from the castle stopped, the rattling, choking sound from the woman's thin throat ceased and I knew I was holding the hand of a corpse. Only a sudden monstrous clap of thunder outside and the noise of heavy rain suddenly beginning to pound on the roof now kept me company.

I was too late. The ripping of the daughter's spirit from her body had been too powerful and violent for such a weakened body to resist; it had torn the life out of the mother through its departure. There was not enough time for my blood to give her the strength she needed. My indecision, and Lower's failure, had made all my efforts worthless.

I do not know how long I sat there, holding her hand, hoping that I had made a mistake and that she had simply fallen into a fit. I was vaguely aware of more tumult from the castle, but paid it little attention. Then I closed her eyes, and combed her hair, and arranged the mean bedclothes as best I could. Finally, though she was not of my religion and might well have scorned me for my efforts, I knelt by the bed to pray for the souls of them both. I believe I was praying for myself as well.

I SUPPOSE I LEFT THAT MISERABLE PLACE FOR THE LAST time about an hour later. I was in no mood to reprimand Lower; instead, I felt a ferocious and overwhelming hunger mingling with my despair, so I went to a tavern to eat for the first time in more than a day. Dimly, as I sat there lost in my misery and thoughts, I listened to the conversation going on all around me; festive and cheerful, and so completely at odds with my spirits that I felt more a stranger than ever before.

At that moment, I hated the English for their heresy, the way they turned a hanging into a festival, timed for market day to profit the traders. I loathed their bigotry and certainty of their own correctness; I hated Lower for his temper and the way he had scorned and betrayed and abandoned me. And I decided, then and there, that I would leave forthwith this terrible little town and this grim, cruel country. There was nothing more for me to do. I had my patient, and she was dead. I had my task from my father but that was futile. I had my friends, but they, it was now clear, were hardly friends of mine. So it was time to be gone.

The resolution made me feel better. I could pack and leave within the day, if need be, but first I realized I would have to inform someone of Mrs. Blundy's death. I did not know what, exactly, was to be done with her body but I was resolved she would not be buried as a pauper. I would ask Lower to perform me this one last service, to take some of my money and see that she was interred with proper solemnity.

The decision brought me back to myself, or maybe it was the food and drink that did it. I picked up my head and noticed, for the first time, all that was going on around me. And realized they were talking of the hanging.

I could not make out exactly what had happened, but it was clear some scandal had attended the event; so, when I saw Mr. Wood in a far corner, I asked him how he was, and whether he knew what had happened.

We had met only a few times in the past, and it was no doubt impolite of me to approach him, but I was desperate to know, and Wood was more than keen to tell me the story.

His eyes bright with the pleasure of scandal, and with a most inappropriate air of suppressed excitement, he asked me to sit by him so that he might tell me in full.

"It is done?" I asked.

I thought maybe he had been drinking, early though it was, for he laughed immoderately at my question. "Oh, yes," he said. "Done it is. She has died."

"I am sorry for you," I said. "Did she not work for your family? It must have been distressing."

He nodded. "It was. Especially for my poor mother. But justice must be served, and it has been." He laughed again, and I felt like striking him for his heartlessness.

"Did she die well? Please tell me," I asked. "I am upset, because the girl's mother has just died as well, and I attended her in her last moments."

Oddly, this upset him a great deal, far more than the hanging of his own servant. "That is very sad indeed," he said quietly, sober all of a sudden. "I knew her, and found her both interesting and gentle."

"Please," I repeated, "tell me what happened."

So Wood began. However much embroidered already, it was a dreadful tale, which reflected badly on all concerned, except for Sarah Blundy herself who, alone, had behaved with dignity and correctness. Everyone else, in Wood's account, disgraced themselves.

He said he had assembled at the castle forecourt just after four to be sure of a good vantage point. He was not the first by any means, and had he delayed even another half hour, he would have missed most of what occurred. Long before the ceremony began, the courtyard was crowded with a sober, somber crowd, all facing the tree which already had the rope dangling from a strong branch, and a ladder propped up against it. A few dozen yards away, the jail officials kept watchers away from the pyre which was to consume the girl's body after she was dead. Some people took logs for mementoes, others to warm themselves at home, and on several occasions in the past a punishment had been postponed because too much wood had been taken to permit the body's consumption.

Then, exactly as the first light dawned, a little door opened, and Sarah Blundy, heavily chained and shivering in a thin cotton shift, her hair pulled back, was brought out. The crowd, he said, grew very quiet at the sight, for she was a pretty girl, and it was hard to believe anyone of her delicate appearance could possibly deserve such a punishment.

Then Lower pushed himself forward and muttered a few words to the hangman, and bowed ceremoniously to the girl as she was led forward.

"Did she say anything?" I asked. "Did she admit her guilt once more?" Strangely, it was important to me at that moment to hear that she was truly guilty. Her admission in the courtroom had reassured me greatly, for it was the final information I required: no one confesses to a crime of that magnitude unless they are certainly guilty, for to do so is to abandon hope of life. It is no less than suicide, the greatest of sins.

"I do not think so," he said. "But I couldn't hear it all. She spoke very softly, and even though I was close by, I missed much of it. But she owned herself one of the worst sinners in the world, and said that she prayed for forgiveness, even though she knew she did not deserve it. It was a short speech, and was very well received. Then a minister offered to pray with her, and she turned him down, saying she needed no prayers from him. He is one of the new men put in by the king, and very far from the views of Sarah and her sort. That, of course, caused more of a stir. Some of the crowd looked displeased, but a fair number—mainly the rougher folk—approved of her courage."

This, he told me, was nothing too much out of the ordinary. It was the task of the church to impose itself at such moments and it was naturally open to the condemned—who had little to lose, after all—to make a last gesture of defiance, if they felt so inclined. Sarah prayed alone, on her knees in the mud and with a quietness and decorum that elicited a sympathetic murmur from the crowd. Then she stood up, and nodded to the hangman. Her hands were bound, and she was helped up the ladder until her neck was level with the rope.

There the hangman stopped her, and began tying the noose.

She moved her head to make herself as comfortable as possible, and then all was ready. She had refused to have her head bound or covered in any way, and the crowd fell silent as they saw her eyes close and her lips move so the name of God would be the last sound to pass her lips. The drummers began their roll, and at the end, the hangman leaned forward, and simply pushed her off the ladder.

Then the thunderstorm started, and within minutes all was awash with muddy water, the torrents so heavy it was hard even to see what was going on.

Wood paused here to take another drink. "I hate hangings," he said, wiping his mouth on his sleeve. "I go and see them, of course, but I do hate them. I don't know anybody who thinks otherwise, or could do once they have seen one. The way the face contorts and the tongue protrudes is so hideous that you understand why normally they insist on the head being covered. And the smell as well, and the way the arms and legs twist and jerk." He shuddered. "Let me talk of that no more. For it didn't last long, and when it was done Lower staked his claim. Did you know he'd bought the body, and come to some sort of arrangement with the judge so that he might have it, and not the professor?"

I nodded. I thought he must have done so.

"It was done in the worst possible way, because the university had heard and the Regius professor thought his prerogatives were being infringed. So he came along as well, to claim his right. There was a brawl in the mud. Can you believe it? Two proctors fighting for the body, held off by half a dozen friends of Lower, who got Locke to help him pick it up and carry it out of the yard. I don't think many knew exactly what was going on, but those who realized were furious and began throwing stones. There was very nearly a riot, and would have been had not the rain persuaded many to leave."

I think this was the last straw for my friendship with Lower. I know what he would say, that a body is a body, but there was a callousness about his action which distressed me greatly. I believe it was because he had abandoned me in order to advance his own career, that given a choice between assisting me in treating the mother, and gaining the daughter for dissection, he had chosen the latter. He would now have his book on the brain, I thought grimly. Much may it profit him.

"So Lower has his way?"

"Not exactly. He took the body to Boyle's and is virtually under siege there. The proctors complained to the magistrate and said that if they can't have the corpse, no one should have it. So the magistrate has now changed his mind, and is demanding it back. Lower, so far, has refused to give it up."

"Why?"

"I suppose because he is doing as much work on the corpse as he can in the time allowed."

"And what about Mr. Boyle?"

"Fortunately, he is in London. He would be appalled to be involuntarily dragged into such an affair." He stood up. "I am going home. If you will excuse me . . ."

I wrapped myself up as well as I could and braved the rainfall to walk along the High Street to the apothecary's. I found Mr. Crosse along with the boy he employed to mix ingredients guarding the door, firmly making sure that no one entered unless Lower gave permission. Including myself. I could not believe it when he held his hand against my chest and shook his head. "I'm truly sorry, Mr. Cola," he said. "But Lower is adamant. Neither you, nor any of these other gentlemen here, are to be allowed to interrupt him while he is working."

"That is absurd," I cried. "What is going on?"

Crosse shrugged. "I believe that Mr. Lower has agreed to hand the body back to the hangman, so that it can be burned as ordered. Until that gentleman comes, he sees no reason why he should not conduct such investigations as he sees fit. He has little enough time, hence his insistence on not being disturbed. I'm sure he would be glad of your participation under ordinary circumstances." He added that he was saddened by what he had heard of our argument, and counted himself still my friend. It was kindly done.

And so, like any common citizen, I had to stand and wait for Lower's pleasure, although Crosse at least did me the favor of allowing me to wait indoors, rather than having to stamp my feet outside, until the hangman arrived to claim his booty.

Then Lower came down, looking tired and worn, his hands and apron still bloody from his labors. The sight of him inside the building caused a small tremor to run through the crowd.

"Are you prepared to submit to the magistrate's orders?" the hangman asked.

Lower nodded, then caught the hangman by the sleeve as he was preparing to take his assistants upstairs.

"I have taken the liberty of ordering a box for the body," he said. "It would not do for her to be carried out as she now is. It will be here shortly, and it would be best to wait."

The hangman assured him that he had seen many gruesome sights in his time, and this would not bother him. "I was thinking of the crowd," Lower said as he disappeared up the stairs. He followed, and, as there was no one to stop me, I followed Lower.

One glance, and the hangman changed his mind; indeed, he turned ashen white at the sight. For Lower had abandoned the delicate workmanship which normally characterized his dissections. In his haste to take the organs he wanted for his work, he had quartered the body, and ripped it open with savagery; removed the head, and sawn it open to take the brain, tearing off the face in his haste, and then tossed the pieces on an oilcloth on the floor. Those fine, beautiful eyes, which had so captivated me the first time I saw her, had been torn from their sockets; tendons and muscles hung from the arms as though savaged by a wild beast. Bloody knives and saws lay all around, along with the piles of the long, dark, lustrous hair which he had hacked off to attack the skull. There was blood everywhere, and the stink of blood filled the room. A large bucketful which he had drained from her stood in another corner, next to glass jars full of his trophies. And the smell was indescribable. In a corner, in a small pile, was the cotton shift she had worn, stained and soiled from her last ordeal.

"Dear God," the hangman exclaimed, looking at Lower with horror, "I should take this out and show it to the crowd.

Then you would join her on the pyre, which is no more than you deserve.''

Lower shrugged with exhaustion and unconcern. ''It is for the common good,'' he said. ''I feel no need to apologize, to you or anyone else. It is you, and that ignorant magistrate, who should apologize. Not me. If I had had more time . . .''

I stood in the corner and felt the tears welling up in me, so tired and sad to see all my hopes and faith shattered. I could not believe that this man whom I had called my friend could act in such a callous way to me, show such a side of himself that previously had been so well hidden. I have no sentimental notions about the body once the soul has departed; I believe it is fitting and honorable to use them for the purposes of science. But it must be done with humility, in honor of something which was made in God's image. To advance himself, Lower had descended to the level of a butcher.

''Well,'' he said, looking at me for the first time. ''What are you doing here?''

''The mother is dead,'' I said.

''I am grieved to hear it.''

''So you should be, as it was your doing. Where were you last night? Why did you not come?''

''It would not have done any good.''

''It would have,'' I said, ''if she'd enough spirit to dilute the daughter's. She died the moment her child was hanged.''

''Nonsense. Pure, unscientific superstitious nonsense,'' he said, rattled by my willingness to confront him with what he had done. ''I know it is.''

''You do not. It is the only explanation. You are responsible for her death and I cannot forgive you.''

''Then do not,'' he said brusquely. ''Hold to your explanation, and to my responsibility if you wish. But do not trouble me at the moment.''

''I demand to know your reasons.''

''Go away,'' he said. ''I will give you no reasons, and no explanations. You are no longer welcome here, sir. Go away, I say. Mr. Crosse. Will you escort this foreign gentleman out?''

. . .

THE EXCHANGE WENT ON A LITTLE LONGER THAN THIS, but in essence those were the last words he ever spoke to me. Since then, I have heard nothing from him at all, and so I still am unable to explain why his friendliness turned to malice and his generosity to the most extreme cruelty. Was the prize so great? Was his feeling of disgust with his deeds turned on me so that he could avoid owning his own fault? But one thing I soon became certain of. His failure to help me with Mrs. Blundy was deliberate. He wanted my experiment to fail, because I could not then claim success.

I am fairly certain now that he already knew what he was going to do. Perhaps he had already started writing that communication which, a year later, appeared in the Transactions of the Royal Society. *An account of the Transfusion of the Blood* by Richard Lower, detailing his experiments on dogs conducted with Wren, and followed up with another which described transfusion between two individuals. So generous he was in acknowledging Wren's help. So open in admitting his debt to Locke. Such a gentleman.

But not a word about myself, and I am sure now that Lower had already determined that I would have no acknowledgment. All he had said in the past about others beating him to recognition, about foreigners and his distaste for all of them came back to me and I realized that anyone less naïve than myself would have been on his guard long before.

But I am still shocked by how far he was prepared to go to steal my fame, for, in order to make sure my claims were not entertained, he spread wicked stories about me among his friends, saying I was a charlatan, a thief and worse. He had narrowly, it was believed, stopped me from stealing *his* idea, rather than the other way around, and only good fortune exposed my duplicity at the last moment.

I left Oxford that same day, traveled to London and, after a week, took ship on an English merchantman headed for Antwerp, then found another to take me to Livorno. I was back in my home by June. I have never left my country again, and have long since abandoned philosophy for the more respectable activities of the gentleman; it pains me to return, even in memory, to those dark, sad days.

One last thing I did before I left, however. I could not ask Lower, so I went to see Wood, who was still willing to receive me. He told me that Sarah's remains had burned that same afternoon, as I was packing my bags, and that all was finally over. There was no one but himself and the hangman at the pyre, and it had burned ferociously. It grieved him to attend, but he felt he had owed her that last attendance.

I gave him a pound, and asked him to see to Mrs. Blundy's funeral, so that she might avoid a pauper's grave.

He agreed to take care of it for me. I do not know whether he kept his word.

The Great Trust

Ideas of the Cavern are the Ideas of every Man in particular; we every one of us have our peculiar Den, which refracts and corrupts the Light of Nature, because of the differences of Impressions as they happen in a Mind prejudiced or prepossessed.

—FRANCIS BACON,
NOVUM ORGANUM SCIENTARUM,
SECTION II, APHORISM V.

chapter one

IT IS SOMETHING OF A SURPRISE, AND EVEN AN EM-
barrassment, to have scarce remembered faces and facts summoned from the gloom of antiquity like so many ghosts. This
has been my experience while perusing the manuscript written by that strange little Venetian, Marco da Cola, lately sent
to me by Richard Lower. I never imagined he had such a
formidable, if selective, memory. Perhaps he took notes as
he went along, expecting to entertain his countrymen on his
return. Such travelers' memoirs are popular enough here; it
is possible the same is true in Venice, although I am told the
inhabitants are a narrow-minded people, convinced nothing
is worthwhile if it lies more than ten leagues from their city.

As I say, the manuscript was a surprise; its arrival as much
as its contents, for I had not heard from Lower for some
time. We were somewhat in company, he and I, when we
were both making our way in London; but then our paths
diverged. I married well, to a woman who brought me a good
addition to my estate, and began to associate with men of
the very highest rank. Whereas Lower somehow missed, failing to endear himself to those most able to do him good. I
do not know why this was. He did, certainly, have an irritability about him which never sits well in a doctor, and was
perhaps too mindful of his philosophy and not enough of his
pocket to make a mark in the world. But my loyalty and

forbearance mean that at least he still numbers the Prestcott family among his few patients.

I gather that he has already sent Cola's words to Wallis, old and blind though he now is, and daily expects to hear his opinion. I can imagine what that will be: Wallis *triumphans,* or a variation thereof. It is only to set the matter aright that I bother to put down a true version of events. It will be a disjointed account, as I am often interrupted by business, but I will do my best.

I should start by saying that I quite liked Cola; he cut an ungainly figure, but pictured himself a *gallant* and made something of an entertainment during his brief stay in Oxford by the gaudiness of his clothes and the air of perfume that he left behind him. He was constantly pirouetting and bowing and paying bizarre compliments, quite unlike the majority of Venetians, who I understand normally pride themselves on their gravity and look askance at English exuberance. His dispute with Lower I do not pretend to understand; how men could come to blows over such trivialities escapes me. There is, surely, something undignified in two gentlemen fighting over the right to be seen the more artisanal: Lower has never mentioned anything of the matter to me and I cannot judge whether or no he has anything to be ashamed of. That acrimonious and foolish business aside, however, the Venetian had much to commend him, and it was unfortunate I did not encounter him in easier circumstances. I wish I could talk to him now, for there is much to ask. Above all, I do not understand why—it is the most glaring of his omissions—he never mentions in his memoir that he had known my father. It is strange, for we talked much of him on the occasions we met, and Cola spoke of him warmly.

Thus my opinion of the Venetian, from what I knew of him. I suspect that Dr. Wallis will paint a different portrait. I never quite understood why that worthy divine so took against the man, but I am fairly certain that he had no real reason to do so. Wallis had some strange obsessions and, of course, a profound dislike of all papists, but often would be just plain wrong: this was one of those occasions.

It is generally known that, until Mr. Newton eclipsed him, Dr. Wallis was considered the finest mathematician this country has ever produced, and this reputation has obscured his occult activities for the government and the malice of his character. Frankly, I have never been entirely certain what either of them do that is so wonderful: I can add up and subtract to get the estate accounts in order, and I can place a bet on a horse and calculate my winnings, and I cannot see why anybody should need to know more. Someone once tried to explain Mr. Newton's notions, but they made little sense. Something about proving that things fall. As I had taken a bad drop from my horse only the previous day, I replied that I had all the proof I needed on my backside. As for why, it was obvious that things fall because God has made them heavy.

However clever he was in matters such as these, though, Wallis was no judge of character, and made fearful mistakes; Cola, I think, was one of them. Because the poor man was a papist and desperately trying to ingratiate himself, Wallis assumed there was some sinister motive behind it all. Personally, I take people as I find them, and Cola never did me any harm. And as for being a papist, that is not my concern; if he chooses to burn in Hell there is nothing I can do to save him.

Despite his amiability, though, it was clear to me at least that Cola was a fool in many respects, an example of the difference between learning and wisdom. I have a theory that too much learning unbalances the mind. So much effort goes into squeezing in knowledge that there isn't enough room left over for common sense. Lower, for example, was a desperately clever man but got nowhere; whereas I, with no education to speak of, have great position, am a Justice of the Peace and also a Member of Parliament. I live in this vast house, built especially for me, and am surrounded by servants, some of whom even do my bidding. A fine achievement, I submit, for someone who was born, through no personal fault, with less than nothing and who once narrowly escaped Sarah Blundy's fate.

That young woman, you see, was a harlot and witch, despite the prettiness and the strangeness of manner which so captivated Cola. Now, in my mature years and having come closer to God, I am astonished at my carelessness in placing my soul in peril by consorting with her. However, as I am a just man, I must state the absolute truth: whatever her other crimes and however much she had to die, Sarah Blundy did not kill Dr. Robert Grove. I know this for a fact, for I also know who did kill him. Had Cola been more mindful of the Bible, he would have realized that the proof lay in those notebooks he carried to jot down the words of others. He reports that at the dinner in New College, Grove had a dispute with Thomas Ken, who stormed out, muttering the words "Romans, 8:13." Cola remembered the reference, wrote it down and entirely missed its significance; indeed, he missed the significance of the whole occasion, failing even to understand why he was invited in the first place. For what is this passage? Unlike him, I took the trouble to find out, and it confirmed the belief I have held all these years: "For if ye live after the flesh, ye shall die." My friend Thomas was convinced Grove did indeed live for fleshly pleasure, and a few hours later he died. Had I not known better, I would have called that a remarkable prophecy.

I accept readily that Thomas was tormented beyond endurance before he acted, for I knew well Grove's qualities and defects. I had suffered much from his barbs as a child myself, when he had taught me as part of his duties in Sir William Compton's household and, although I knew him well enough to see the good that lay therein (once I was large enough not to be beaten by him, for he was formidably strong in his arms) I knew how hurtful his wit could be. Thomas—poor, slow, honest Thomas—was too easy a target for his sallies. So much and so mercilessly did he taunt my friend I might even claim that Grove brought his fate upon himself.

And myself? I have to relate my journeys, not one, but several, all undertaken at the same time in my quest for prosperity and (dare I say it) salvation. Some of what I will say is public knowledge already. Some is known only to myself and will cause great consternation amongst the atheists and the scoffers. I doubt not that what I say will be scorned by the erudite, who will laugh at my presentation and ignore the truth that lies within. That is their concern, for the truth I will tell, whether they like it or not.

chapter two

It is my desire to set out clearly my account of events, and not bother with the sillinesses indulged in by so-called authors trying to earn spurious fame. God forbid that I should ever suffer the shame of publishing a book for money, or of having one of my family so demean themselves. How can one tell who might read it? No worthy book has ever been written for gain, I think; occasionally I am forced to listen to someone reading to while away time in the evening and, on the whole, I find it all quite absurd. All those elaborate conceits and hidden meanings. Say what you mean to say, then be silent, is my motto, and books would be better—and a lot shorter—if more people listened to my advice. There is more wisdom in a decent volume on husbandry or fishing than in the most cunning of these philosophers. If I had my way, I'd mount them all on a horse at dawn, and make them gallop through the countryside for an hour. That might blow some of the nonsense out of their fuddled minds.

So I will explain myself simply and directly, and I have no shame in saying that my narrative will reflect my character. I was at Oxford intended for the law; and I was intended for the law because, though the eldest and only son of my family, I was going to have to earn my living, so low had we sunk in misfortune. The Prestcotts were a very old family but had suffered considerably during the wars. My father, Sir James Prestcott, had joined the king when that noble gentleman raised his standard at Nottingham in 1642, and he fought courageously throughout the Civil War. The expense was enormous, as he maintained a whole troop of horse at his own charge, and he was shortly reduced to mortgaging his land to raise money, confident that this was a wise investment for the future. No one, in those early days, seriously considered that the fighting would end in anything other than triumph. But my father, and many others, reckoned without the king's rigidity and the growing influence of the fanatics in Parliament. The war went on, the country suffered, and my father got poorer.

Disaster occurred when Lincolnshire—where much of the family property was—fell wholly into the hands of the Roundheads; my mother was briefly imprisoned, and much of our revenue confiscated. Even this did not shake my father's resolution, but when the king was captured in 1647, he realized that the cause was lost and so made such peace as he could with the new rulers of the land. In his opinion Charles I had thrown away his kingdom through his folly and mistakes, and no more could be done. Father was reduced to virtual poverty, but at least retired from the fray rich in honor, content to resume his life.

Until the execution. I was only seven on that terrible winter's day in 1649, and yet I recall the news of it still. I think every man alive then can remember exactly what they were doing when they heard that the king had been beheaded in front of a cheering mob. There is now nothing which more brings home to me the passage of the years than to meet a grown man who does not recall, as his strongest memory, the horror that the news produced. Never in the history of the universe had such a crime been committed, and I remember vividly how the sky turned dark and the earth rocked as the anger of heaven was loosed on the land. It rained for days afterward, the sky itself weeping for the sinfulness of mankind.

Like everyone else, my father had not believed it would happen. He was wrong. He always had too good an opinion of his fellows: perhaps that was his downfall. Murder, perhaps: such things happen. But a trial? To execute in the name of justice the man who was its very fount? To lead God's anointed onto a scaffold like a criminal? Such blasphemous, sacrilegious mockery had not been seen since Christ himself suffered on the Cross. England had sunk low: never in their worst nightmares did anyone suspect it could sink so very far down into the sulphur. My father gave his loyalty entire to the young Charles II at that very moment and vowed to dedicate his life to achieving his restoration.

This was shortly before my father's first exile, and before I was sent away from my family for instruction. I was called formally to his room, and went with some trepidation as I assumed that I must have misbehaved, since he was not a man who gave himself much to his children, being too occupied with more important matters. But he greeted me kindly and even permitted me to sit, then told me of what had happened in the world.

"I will have to leave the country for a while, to mend our fortunes," he said. "And your mother has decided that you will go to my friend, Sir William Compton, and receive instruction from tutors while she returns to her own people.

"You must remember one thing, Jack. God made this country a monarchy, and if we stray from that, we stray from His will. To serve the king, the new king, is to serve your country and God in equal part. To give your life for that is nothing, to give your fortune less still. But never give your honor, for that is not yours to give. It is like your place in the world, a gift from the Lord which I hold in trust for you, and which you must guard for your children."

Though I was seven at the time, he had never talked to me with such seriousness before, and I adopted such gravity as a childish face can manage, and swore that he would have cause to be proud of me. I managed not to cry as well, although I remember the effort most strongly. That was strange; I had seen little of him or of my mother in my life, and yet I thought of his imminent departure with great despondency. Three days later, both he and I left our house, never to return as its owners. Perhaps those guardian angels we are told watch over us knew this, and played melancholy music and saddened my listening soul.

For the next eight years, there was little for my father to do. The great cause was lost, and he was in any case too poor to participate. Such was his distress that he was forced to leave the country and seek his living fighting as a soldier, as did so many other Royalist gentlemen. He went first to the Netherlands, then served Venice, fighting on Crete against the Turks in the long, miserable siege of Candia. But when he came back to England in 1657 he immediately became a central member of that group of patriots, later known as the Sealed Knot, which worked incessantly to bring Charles back from exile. He endangered his life, but did so joyfully. They might take his life, he said, but even his worst enemy would acknowledge him to be an upright, honest man.

Alas, my good father was wrong, for he was later accused of the most base treachery, which malevolent lie he never shook off. He never knew who accused him, or even what the charges were, so could not defend himself and refute the allegations. Eventually he left England once more, forced out of his own country by the malicious hiss of the gossip mongers, and died of grief before his name was cleared. I once saw a horse on my estate, a handsome, grand beast, driven to distraction by the incessant viciousness of flies which buzzed all around it. It ran to escape its tormentors, not knowing where they were; when it flicked its tail to drive one off, ten more came to replace it. It ran across an open meadow, fell and broke its leg, and I watched the saddened stablehand dispatch it for its own good. So are the great and noble destroyed by the petty and mean.

I was just eighteen when my father died in his lonely exile and it marked me for life. The day I received the letter that told me he had been buried in a pauper's grave, I broke down in sorrow before a violent anger gripped my soul. A pauper's grave! Dear Heaven, even now the very words make a coldness seep through my body. That this courageous soldier, this best of Englishmen, should end in such a way, shunned by his friends, abandoned by a family which would not even pay for his funeral, treated with contempt by those for whom he had sacrificed everything, was more than I could bear. I did what I could eventually: I never found where he had been buried, and could do nothing for his body, but I built him the finest memorial in the whole county in my church, and I take everyone who comes to see it and meditate on his fate.

It cost me a considerable fortune, but I do not begrudge one penny of the expense.

While I knew my family had been greatly reduced, I was not yet aware of how much we had suffered, for I understood that, on my twenty-first birthday, I would obtain full title to the estates which had been supposedly protected from the government by an assortment of legal devices. I knew of course that these lands would come burdened with so much debt that it would take me years to reestablish myself as a person of moment in the county, but this was a task I relished. I was even prepared to endure several years at the bar, if necessary, to accumulate those riches which lawyers find so easy to come by. At least my father's name would be perpetuated. The ending of a man's life is but death, and that comes to us all in the fullness of time, and we know we have the blessing that our name and honor continue. But the demise of an estate is true extinction, for a family without land is nothing.

Youth is simple, and assumes that all will be well; part of the estate of manhood consists in learning that God's Providence is not so easily understood. The consequences of my father's fall did not appear to me until I left the seclusion of a home where, although I was not happy, I was at least protected from the buffeting of the outside world. Then I was sent to Trinity College, Oxford, for, although my father had been a man of Cambridge, my uncle (who had charge of me when I left Sir William's house) decided I would not be welcome there. The decision spared me no grief, as I was as rejected and despised for my parentage in the one university as I would have been in the other. I had no friends as none could resist cruelty, and I could not tolerate insult. Nor was I able to mix with my own, for although enrolled as a gentleman-commoner, my sniveling, mean uncle allowed me scarce enough money to live as a servitor. Moreover, he allowed me no freedom; alone of my rank, my small money was given over entire to my tutor and I had to beg even for that; I was subjected to the discipline of a commoner and could not leave town without permission; I was even forced to attend lessons, although gentlemen are exempt from instruction.

I believe that many men see my manner now and consider me a rustic, yet I am far from such; those years taught me to hide my desires and my hatreds. I learned swiftly that I would have to endure several years of humiliation and solitude, and that there was little I could do to alter that. It is not my way to rage uselessly against a situation I cannot change. But I noted those who were heartless, and promised myself that, in due course, they would regret their coarseness. Many of them have done so.

I do not even know that I greatly missed the temptations of society, in any case. My attentions have always been focused on my own people, and my childhood prepared me little for more promiscuous intercourse. Such reputation as I had was of a surly, ill-tempered fellow, and the more this grew, the more I was left in a solitude which was broken only by my forays among the townsfolk. I became an adept at disguise, leaving my gown behind me and walking the streets like a citizen with such confidence that I was never once challenged by the proctors for improper dress.

But even these excursions were limited, for once I shrugged off my gown, I also shrugged off my credit and had to pay ready money for my pleasures. Fortunately, the urge for diversion came on me only infrequently. For the most part, I engaged my mind with my studies and consoled myself by conducting such investigations as I could into greater matters. I was gravely disappointed in my expectation that I would soon learn enough to proceed with the getting of money, however, for in all the time I was at the university I learned nothing of the law whatsoever, and was somewhat derided by my fellows for having any such expectation. Jurisprudence there was aplenty; I was swamped in canon law and the principles of Aquinas and Aristotle; I came to have a nodding acquaintance with the Justinianic code, and acquired something of the art of disputation. But I looked in vain for instruction on how to launch a suit in Chancery, to contest a will or query the provisions of an executor.

And while my legal education proceeded, I also decided that I would take the more direct revenge that my father had not been able to exact, for not only did his soul demand it, I considered it by far the quickest way of solving my family's

material problems: once persuaded of the innocence of the
father, I was certain His Majesty would recompense the son.
Initially, I thought the task would be easy: before he fled,
my father's judgment was that Cromwell's Secretary of State,
John Thurloe, had seeded the calumnies against him to
spread dissent in the royalist ranks, and I never doubted that
he was correct. It had all the hallmarks of that dark and
sinister man, who ever preferred a knife in the back to an
upright, honorable combat. But I was too young to do much
and, besides, I assumed that sooner or later Thurloe would
be tried, and the truth known. Again, youth is naïve, and
faith is blind.

For Thurloe was not brought to trial, did not have to flee
the country, had not one penny of his ill-gotten gains taken
from him. The comparison between the fruits of treachery
and the reward for loyalty was stark indeed. On the day near
the end of 1662 that I heard it confirmed there would be no
trial, I realized that any revenge would have to come from
my own hands. Cromwell's evil genius might escape the law,
I thought, but he would not escape justice. I would show all
the world that some people, in this debased and corrupted
country, still knew the meaning of honor. With the purity of
youth it is possible to think in such noble and simple terms.
It is a clarity that experience strips from us, and we are all
poorer for the loss.

chapter three

FROM THAT DAY I DATE THE BEGINNINGS OF THE
campaign that totally occupied me for the next nine months
and which ended in the most complete vindication. I had
virtually no assistance; instead I criss-crossed the country,
seeking out the evidence I required until I finally understood
what had happened and was in a position to act. I was abused
and humiliated by those who did not believe me, or else had
good reason to deflect me from my task. And yet I continued,
buoyed by my duty and by the love of the best father a man
could ever have. I witnessed the depths of turpitude in those
who seek power and understood that, once the principle of
birth is undermined, the disinterest that alone can assure good
government is fatally compromised. If anyone can achieve
power, then all will try, and government becomes a mere
battle in which principle is sacrificed for interest. The lowest
will impose themselves, for the best will shun the gutter. All
I managed was to achieve a small victory in a war which
was already lost.

Such thoughts were far beyond me in those days, as I
walked the streets, sat in lesson and prayer, and lay awake
at night in bed, listening to the snoring and snuffling of the
other three students who shared the same room with my tutor.
One resolution alone stayed in my mind; that I would, in due
course, take John Thurloe by the scruff of the neck and slit
his throat. But I felt strongly that more than mere vengeance

was needed; perhaps those lessons in the law had seeped into me, or perhaps I had imbibed my father's high sense of principle without realizing it. What would he have done? What would he have wanted? This was my ever-present concern. To strike without proof would be false revenge, for I was sure he would not have wanted his only son to be hanged like a common criminal, bringing further stain onto the family. Thurloe was too powerful still for a direct assault. I would need to circle round him, like a huntsman stalking a wily deer, before I could inflict the fatal, final blow.

To set my thoughts in order, I regularly talked over my problems with Thomas Ken. He was one of my few friends—perhaps even my only friend—at the time, and I trusted him absolutely. He could be tedious company, but each of us needed the other and supplied a lack. We knew one another through a family connection, before he was sent to Winchester and thence to New College for a career in the church. His father had been a lawyer consulted on many occasions by my own father when he set himself to oppose those rapacious interlopers who had swept down from London to drain the fens before the war. My father wished both to protect his own interests and also the rights of those families who had grazed the land since time immemorial. But it was hard work, for the bloodsucking thieves who wished to steal other men's land acted under the umbrella of the law. My father knew that the only thing that can oppose a lawyer was another lawyer and so this Henry Ken advised him on many occasions, always honestly and effectively. The diligence of one, and the skill of the other, combined with the unstinting resistance of the farmers and graziers whose livelihoods were threatened, meant that progress in the draining was slow, the expenses bigger, and the profits much smaller than expected.

And so Thomas and I had a natural amity, for it is known that the loyalty and gratitude of Lincolnshire men, once forged, can never be broken. It must be said, however, that we made an odd pair. He was of a severe and clerical disposition, rarely drinking, always praying and constantly looking out for souls to save. He made a religion of forgiveness and, though now a firm Anglican who maintains he was ever so, I know that in those days he inclined to dissent. Naturally, that made him suspect then, where hatred was mistaken for fortitude, and smallness of mind was a sign of loyalty. I confess with some shame now that I took great delight in causing him to become discountenanced, since the more he prayed, the more I laughed, and the more he studied, the more bottles I opened to make him blush. In truth, Thomas would have loved to wine and wench, just as I had to struggle hard to keep out feelings of pious dread which, in the dead of night, would creep upon me. And occasionally, in a sudden burst of anger, or a flash of cruelty in his words, the careful observer could see that his kindness and gentle nature were not natural gifts from God, but were wrenched in a hard-fought battle with a darkness deep in his soul. As I say, it was Grove's misfortune to torment him so much that, one night, the battle was temporarily lost.

For all that, I always found Thomas patient and understanding, and we were useful to one another in the way that people of opposite character can sometimes be. I would give advice about his theological ditherings—soundly, I may say, as he is now a bishop. And he would listen with enormous patience when I would describe, for the fiftieth time, how I would take John Thurloe and slit his throat.

I could hear him let out his breath as he prepared to argue with me again. "I must remind you that forgiveness is one of the gifts of God, and that charity is strength, not weakness," he said.

"Piffle," I said. "I do not intend to forgive anybody, nor do I feel in the slightest bit charitable. The only reason he is still alive is because I do not have the proof I need to avoid a charge of murder." Then I went on to tell him the entire story again.

"The trouble is," I concluded, "I don't know what to do. What do you think?"

"You want my considered opinion?"

"Of course."

"Accept the will of God, get on with your studies and become a lawyer."

"That's not what I meant. I meant, how do I find this proof? If you are a friend, please put aside your nit-picking theology for a while and help."

"I know what you meant. You want me to give you bad advice, that can only imperil your soul."

"Exactly. That's just what I want."

Thomas sighed. "And supposing you find your evidence? What then? Will you go ahead and commit murder?"

"That depends on the evidence. But, ideally, yes. I will kill Thurloe, as he killed my father."

"No one killed your father."

"You know what I mean."

"You maintain that your father was betrayed and falsely disgraced. Justice was not done. Would it not be better to right that wrong by making sure it was, this time?"

"You know as well as I do how much it costs to prosecute someone. How am I meant to pay for it?"

"I merely mention it as a possibility. Will you give me your word that, if it is possible, then you will do it rather than taking matters into your own hands?"

"If it is possible, which I doubt, then I will."

"Good," he said with relief. "In that case we can begin to plan your campaign. Unless, of course, you have one already. Tell me, Jack, I have never asked, since your countenance always discourages such questions. But in what was your father's treachery supposed to consist?"

"I don't know," I said. "It sounds foolish, but I have never been able to discover. My guardian, Sir William Compton, has not spoken to me since; my uncle refuses even to mention my father's name; my mother shakes her head in sorrow and will not answer even the most direct questions."

Thomas's eyes narrowed at my blunt statement. "You have your criminal, but do not yet know with any precision what the crime was? That is an unusual position for a man of law to find himself in, is it not?"

"Perhaps. But these are unusual times. I assume my father was innocent. Do you deny that I must do so? And that, in religion as in law, I have no choice in this matter? Quite apart from the fact that I know my father was quite incapable of acting in so base a fashion."

"I grant it is a necessary starting point."

"And you grant also that John Thurloe, as Secretary of State, was responsible for all that pertained to the destruction of anyone who challenged Cromwell's position?''

"Yes."

"Then Thurloe must be guilty," I concluded simply.

"So why do you need proof, if your legal logic is so fine?"

"Because we live in distempered times, when the law has become the cat's paw of the powerful, who tangle it in rules so that they may escape punishment. That is why. And because my father's character has been so abused that it is impossible to make people see what is obvious."

Thomas grunted at this, for he knew nothing of the law and believed it to have something to do with justice. As I had once done myself, until I studied it.

"If I am to triumph at law," I continued, "I must establish that my father's character was such that he could not have betrayed anyone. At present he is cast as the betrayer; I must discover who put this story about and for what purpose. Only then will a law court listen."

"And how do you intend to do this? Who could tell you?"

"Not many people, and most of those will be found at court. Already a problem, as I cannot possibly afford to go there."

Thomas, dear soul that he was, nodded in sympathy. "It would be a pleasure if you would let me assist you."

"Don't be absurd," I said. "Why, you are even poorer than I am. God knows I'm grateful, but I'm afraid my requirements far exceed your resources."

He shook his head, and scratched his chin in the way he always did before launching into a confidence.

"My dear friend, please don't concern yourself. My prospects are good and getting better. The parish of Easton Parva is coming up in the gift of my Lord Maynard in nine months' time. He has asked the warden and thirteen senior Fellows to recommend a candidate, and the warden has already hinted that he thinks I would be more than suitable, as long as I can make clear my full adherence to doctrine. It will be a struggle, but I will grit my teeth, and then eighty pounds a year will be mine. If, that is, I can fight off Dr. Grove."

"Who?" I asked in astonishment.

"Dr. Robert Grove. Do you know him?"

"Very well. And I still have some tender spots to prove it. He was the curate at Sir William Compton's when I was sent to that family. He acted as my tutor for many years. Such as I know, he put there. What has he got to do with this?"

"He is now back in his place as a Fellow of New College, and he wants my living," Thomas explained, "even though he has no claim to preferment except that he has not received any. Frankly, I am very much better suited. A parish needs a young and sound minister. Grove is an old fool who only gets excited when he thinks about the wrongs done to him in the past."

I laughed. "I would hate to be between Dr. Grove and something he wants."

"I have no great objection to him," Thomas said, as though I needed to be reassured on this point. "I would be happy for him to be pastured out to a comfortable living, if there were two of them. But there is one only, so what can I do? I need that living more than he. Jack, can I tell you a secret?"

"I will not stop you."

"I wish to marry."

"Oh," I said. "That's it, is it? And how much has the lady?"

"Seventy-five a year, and a manor in Derbyshire."

"Very nice," I said. "But you need a living to persuade the father. I see the problem."

"Not only that," he said in some obvious distress. "I am obviously not allowed to marry as long as I am a Fellow of the college, and I cannot cease being a Fellow until I have a living. What is worse," he concluded ruefully, "I like the girl."

"How unfortunate. Who is she?"

"The daughter of my aunt's cousin. A woolen draper in Bromwich. A soundly based man in all respects. And the girl is obedient, meek, hard-working and plump."

"Everything a wife should be. With her teeth as well, I hope."

"Most of them, yes. Nor has she had smallpox. We would do well, I feel, and her father has not dissuaded me. But he has made it clear that he would not countenance the alliance if I cannot match her portion. Which means a living and, as I have no other connections, one that comes from New College or through its influence. And Easton Parva is the only one likely to come vacant in the next three years."

"I see," I said. "These are serious times. Have you been on campaign?"

"As much as possible. I have talked to all the Fellows, and find myself well received. In fact, many have given me to understand I have their support. I am confident of the outcome. And the fact that the gold men will advance me funds now indicates my confidence is not ill-placed."

"And the decision is taken when?"

"Next March or April."

"Then I suggest you start living in the chapel, just in case. Recite the Thirty-Nine Articles in your sleep. Praise the Archbishop of Canterbury and the king every time you take a drink of wine. Let not a breath of dissent escape your lips."

He sighed. "It will be hard, my friend. I can only do it for the good of the country and the church."

I applauded his sense of duty. Do not think me selfish, but I was very keen for Thomas to win his place or, at least, to be the favored candidate for as long as possible. If it was noised that he would not get the living, the moneylenders would shut their coffers with a snap, and that would spell disaster for me as well as for him.

"I wish you the very best of good luck, then," I said. "And I counsel you once more to be cautious. You are prone to saying what you think, and there can be no more dangerous habit in one wanting preferment in the Church."

Thomas nodded, and reached inside his pocket. "Here, my good friend. Take this."

It was a purse, containing three pounds. How can I put this? I was overcome, as much with gratitude for his generosity as I was by disappointment over his limited means. Ten times that much would have been a start; thirty times could have been spent with ease. And yet, sweet man that he was, he gave me all he had and risked his own future in the gift. You see how much I owed him? Remember this; it is important. I take my debts as seriously as my injuries.

"I cannot thank you enough. Not only for the money, but because you are the only person who believes in me."

Thomas courteously shrugged it aside. "I wish I could do more. Let us turn to business now. Who might you approach to tell you about what happened to your father?"

"There is only a handful who might know something. Sir John Russell was one, Edward Villiers another. And there was Lord Mordaunt, who did so well from helping the king back onto his throne that he gained a barony and a lucrative sinecure at Windsor as part of his reward. Then, of course, there is whatever I might one day persuade Sir William Compton to tell me."

"Windsor is not far from here," Thomas pointed out. "Scarcely a day's journey, and only a couple if you walk. If Lord Mordaunt is to be found there, then it would be the most economical place to start."

"What if he will not see me?"

"You can only ask. I recommend that you do not write in advance. It is discourteous, but avoids the possibility that he might be forewarned of your arrival. Go and see him. Then we can decide what to do next."

We. As I say, underneath that clerical exterior, there was a man yearning for the sort of excitement that a little bit of bread and wine could never provide.

chapter four

WELL AND GOOD; BUT BEFORE I WENT, I MADE THE acquaintanceship of the Blundys, mother and daughter, who play such a large role in Cola's story. In doing so, I set in train events which gained me the most terrible enemy, whom it demanded all my ingenuity and strength to defeat.

I do not know who will read this scribbling of mine; possibly no one except Lower, but I realize that in these pages I will be recording some acts in which I can take little pride. Some I feel no need to apologize for; some cannot be rectified now; some can at least be explained. My dealings with Sarah Blundy were due to my innocence and youthful, trusting nature: by no other means could she have entrapped me, and come close to destroying me entirely. For this I must blame my early upbringing. Before the age of six I was raised for a while by a great-aunt on my mother's side; a pleasant lady, but very much the country woman, forever brewing and planting and serving physick to the entire area. She had a marvelous book, vellum-bound and gray with ages of fingering, handed down from her own grandmother, of herbal receipts which she would make herself and dispense to all and sundry, highborn or low. She was a powerful believer in magic, and despised those modern preachers (such she called them, for she was born when the great Elizabeth was still thought beautiful) who scorned what she believed to be self-evident. Crumpled bits of paper, and cloud reading and divination by key and Bible were part of my upbringing.

Despite the prelates, I must say I have yet to find any man who really disbelieves in spirits, or doubts that they have the most profound influence on our lives. Any man who has lain awake at night has heard the ghosts of the air as they pass by, all men have been tempted by evil, and many have been saved by good inhabitants of that ethereal space which surrounds this world and joins us to Heaven. Even by their own standards, the sour-faced prelates are wrong, for they hold fast to Scripture, and that states clearly that such creatures exist. Does not St. Paul talk of a voluntary worshipping of angels? (Colossians 2:18.) What do they think Christ drove into the Gadarene swine?

Naturally, it is hard to tell angels from evil spirits, for the latter are adept at disguise, and often beguile men (and more frequently women) into believing they are other than they truly are. The greatest caution is required when making contact with such beings, for we put ourselves in their hands, by creating a debt of obligation to them, and just as a lord or master remembers his debts, so do these creatures, good or evil. By going to old Blundy I took risks that, in the maturity of age's wisdom, I would now shun. Then I was too carefree and too impatient to be cautious.

Old Blundy was a washerwoman, and by reputation a cunning woman, some said even a witch. This I doubt; I smelled no whiff of sulphur in her presence. I had once encountered what was supposed to be a real witch, who was burned nearby in 1654, and a smelly old hag she was. I now believe this poor woman was probably innocent of the charges which brought her to the stake; the devil is too cunning to make his servants so easily identifiable. He makes them young, and beautiful and alluring, so gracious they might never be detected by the eye of man. Like Sarah Blundy, in fact.

Nonetheless, the mother was a strange old crone, Cola's description of her is wildly off the mark. Of course, she was not at her best when he encountered her, but I never saw any sign of that sympathetic understanding of which he speaks, nor of gentleness and kindness. And constantly asking questions. It was simple enough what I wanted, I told her eventually. Who betrayed my father? Could she help or not?

It all depended, she said. Did I have suspicions? It made a difference to what she did. And to what she would not do.

I asked her to explain. She said that really difficult problems involved conjuring up particularly powerful spirits; it could be done, but it was dangerous. Although I said I would take the risk, she said she did not mean spiritual dangers; she was afraid of being arrested and charged with necromancy. After all, she did not know who I was. How did she know whether I was sent by a magistrate to trap her?

I protested my innocence, but she would not be moved, and repeated instead her question. Did I or did I not know the identity of my target? Even vaguely? I said I did not.

"In that case we cannot roll names in water. We will have to gaze instead."

"A crystal ball?" I sneered, for I had heard of such baubles, and was on my guard to avoid being duped.

"No," she replied seriously. "That is just nonsense used by charlatans. There is no virtue in balls of glass. A bowl of water will suffice just as well. Do you want to go ahead?"

I nodded tersely. She shuffled off to get a saucer of water from the well outside, and I put my money on the table, feeling the skin of my palms beginning to prick with sweat.

She did not bother with any of the mummery that some practitioners adopt: no darkened rooms, no incantations or burning herbs. Just put the bowl on the table, asked me to sit in front of it, and close my eyes. I heard her pour the water in, and heard her pray to Peter and Paul: papist words which sounded strange from her lips.

"Now, young man," she hissed in my ear when she had finished, "open your eyes and gaze at the truth. Be forthright and be fearless, as the chance may not come again. Look into the bowl and see."

Sweating profusely, I slowly opened my eyes and bent forward, staring intently at the still and placid water on the tabletop. It shimmered slightly, as though some movement had disturbed it, but there was none; then I saw it grow darker and change in its texture, rather as though it was a curtain or hanging of cloth. And I began to see something emerging from behind this cloth. It was a young man with fair hair, whom I had never seen before in my life though he seemed familiar somehow. He was there only for an instant, and then passed from view. But it was enough; his features were embedded in my mind forever.

Then the curtain shimmered again and another figure came into view. An old man, this time, gray with age and worry, bent over from the years and so sad it made your heart break to see it. I couldn't see the face clearly; there was a hand over it, almost as though the apparition was rubbing its face in utter despair. I held my breath, desperate to see more. And bit by bit I did; the hand slowly came away, and I saw that the despairing old man was my father.

I cried out in anguish at the sight, then swept the bowl from the table in rage, making it spin across the room and shatter against the damp wall. Then I jumped up, spat an insult at the old woman and ran out of that disgusting hovel as fast as I could go.

It took another three days, and the careful ministrations of Thomas and the bottle, before I was myself again.

I HOPE I WILL NOT BE CONSIDERED CREDULOUS IF I SAY that this strange encounter was the last time I saw my father; I am convinced that his soul was there, and that the disturbance I caused played a great part in the events that came after. I do not remember him well; after the age of about six I met him only a few times as the war meant I was sent first to live with the great-aunt I have mentioned, then to the household of Sir William Compton in Warwickshire, where I spent those years under the tutelage of Dr. Grove.

My father tried to come and assure himself of my progress, although his duties ensured that this was rare. On one occasion only did I spend more than a day in his company, and that was shortly before he was forced into his second and last exile. He was everything a child could hope for in a father; stern, disciplined and wholly conscious of the obligations which exist between a man and his heir. He taught me little directly; but I knew that if I could be half the subject he was, then the king (should he ever return) would count me as one of his best and most faithful servants.

He was not one of these effeminate apologies for gentry

whom we see strutting and mincing their way through the court these days. He eschewed fine clothes (although he was fine looking when he chose) and was disdainful of books. Nor was he a great conversationalist, idling away his hours in talk when practical things were to be done. A soldier, in short, and no man was ever grander in leading a charge. He was lost in the welter of backstabbing and conspiracy that the courtier must master; too honest to dissimulate, too frank ever to win favor. It marked him out, and if it was a fatal flaw, I cannot consider he was diminished by it. His fidelity to his wife was as pure as a poet could imagine, and his courage a byword in the army. He was at his happiest at Harland House, our main seat in Lincolnshire, and when he left it he was as grieved as if his wife had died. And rightly so, for the land at Harland Wyte had been in our family for generations; it was our family, you might say, and he knew and loved every square inch of it.

The sight of his soul in such distress rekindled my enthusiasm for my task, as it was clear it was tormented by the injustice he still suffered. So, when I had sufficiently recovered my strength, I concocted a story about the illness of an aunt from whom I had expectations to gain my tutor's permission to leave town, and set off one bright morning for Windsor. I coached as far as Reading, as the university has no monopoly on the route and prices are affordable, and then walked the remaining fifteen miles. I slept in a field, as it was still just warm enough and I did not wish to spend unnecessarily, but breakfasted in a tavern in the town, so I could brush myself down and wipe my face and present a reasonably proper appearance. I also learned from the keeper that Lord Mordaunt—whom I discovered was bitterly detested in the town for his lack of extravagance—was indeed in residence as warden of the castle, having returned only three days before from Tunbridge Wells.

There was no point in dallying; having come so far, it would have been foolish indeed to hesitate. As Thomas had said, a refusal was the worst I could suffer. So I marched boldly to the castle, then spent the next three hours sitting in an anteroom while my request for an audience was conveyed through an army of lackeys.

I was grateful for my breakfast, as it was well past dinnertime before I received any response. In the interval I marched up and down, awaiting the condescension of the mighty, vowing that I would never behave in such a way to those seeking my patronage when my fortune turned. A promise, I must say, I broke the moment I had the opportunity to do so, as by then I understood the purpose of all this attending: it establishes the proper boundaries, creates a due deference amongst those seeking favors and (most practically) discourages all but the most serious. And eventually my reward came when a servant, more cordial now than before, opened the door with ceremony, bowed and said that Lord Mordaunt would grant me an interview. If I would come this way . . .

I had hoped that simple curiosity, at least, would prompt just such a response and was glad that my guess had proven correct. It was not often, I imagine, that anyone had the presumption to present himself on the noble gentleman's doorstep in such a fashion.

I knew little of the man whom I had traveled to see, except that all expected him to become a figure of great consequence in the government, a Secretary of State at the very least, and soon to improve his barony to a full earldom because of his favor with Lord Clarendon, the Lord Chancellor and the most powerful man in the land. He was a brave plotter on the king's behalf, a man of great fortune from one of the highest families in the land, with a notably virtuous wife and the sort of good looks that makes any man a place. His devotion to the king's service was all the more remarkable since his family had kept out of the struggle as much as possible, and were masters at not committing themselves and emerging with their fortunes intact. Mordaunt himself was said to be cautious in advice, but bold when needful, and disinclined to faction and petty squabbling. This was the surface appearance of the man, at least. His only weakness was impatience and an abrupt way of dealing with those he considered incompetent: but that was a great flaw, for there were many such at court, and even more who wished ill on any friend of Clarendon.

I approached through a series of rooms until eventually I

was led into his presence: a grand and, in my mind, unnecessarily pompous proceeding. At least the final room was small and commodious enough, a bureau stacked with piles of paper and shelves of books. I made my bow and waited for him to address me first.

"I gather you are the son of Sir James Prestcott, is that correct?"

I nodded. Lord Mordaunt was a man of medium height, with a well-formed face spoiled only by a nose disproportionately small. His figure was fine, especially in the legs, his movements gracious and, however grand the ceremony of introduction, he cast that aside the moment that the interview began, and engaged in the most amiable conversation which gave the lie to rumors of his pride and haughtiness. I came away admiring the man for his sagacity; he seemed a worthy comrade in arms for my father, and I believed that each had been equally honored by the trust and love of the other. The contrast with a man like Thurloe could not be greater, I thought: the one tall, fair and open, like a Roman of old in bearing and manner, the other certainly wizened and twisted, operating in the dark, never doing anything in the open, always using the instruments of deceit.

"An unusual approach, verging on the discourteous," he commented severely. "I imagine you must have a good reason."

"The very best, my lord," I said. "I greatly regret troubling you, but I have no one else to turn to. You alone can help me, if you will. I can offer nothing in return, but my needs are small. I want a little of your time; that is all."

"You cannot be so foolish as to expect preferment. I could not help you in that regard."

"I came to talk to people who knew my father. To clear his honor of stain."

He considered this remark fully, digesting all the implications it contained, before he replied, gently but cautiously. "That is commendable in a son, and understandable in a child whose fortune depends on it. But I think you will have an uphill struggle."

In the past, my tendency when faced with such remarks was to erupt into a burning rage, during which I would voice all manner of angry ripostes; as a youth I returned home with many a black eye and bloody nose. But I knew such behavior would not help here: I wanted help, and that could only be obtained through politeness and deference. So I choked back my anger, and maintained a serene countenance.

"It is a struggle I must undertake. I believe my father was innocent of all wrong, but I do not even know what he was accused of doing. It is my right to know, and my duty to repudiate the accusations."

"Your family, surely . . ."

"They know little, and tell less. Forgive me for interrupting, sir. But I need to know at first hand what transpired. As you were one of the key figures in His Majesty's great trust, and are reputed for your fairness, I thought to approach you first of all."

A little delicate flattery often oils the wheels of converse, I find; even when it is recognized for what it is, such comments show a recognition of indebtedness. The only requirement is that the compliments be not too coarse, and do not jar on the ear too loudly.

"Do you think my father was guilty?"

Mordaunt considered the question, still with a faint air of surprise on his face that the discussion was taking place at all. He made me wait a long time so that the kindness he did me was fully appreciated before he sat down, then indicated he would permit me to sit also.

"Do I think your father was guilty?" he repeated thoughtfully. "I'm afraid I do, young man. I tried hard to believe in his innocence. Such belief was earned by a brave comrade, even though we rarely saw eye to eye. You see, I never had any direct indication myself that he was a traitor. Do you understand how we operated then? Did he tell you?"

I told him that I was working more or less in the dark; I had rarely encountered my father once I had come to an age at which such matters were understandable to me, and then he had been as discreet with his family as, I am convinced, he had been with everyone else. There was always the possibility that the soldiers would come for us, and he wanted us to know as little as possible for our sake and his own.

Mordaunt nodded, and thought awhile. "You must understand," he said quietly, "that I—very reluctantly—concluded that your father was indeed a traitor." I moved to protest here, but he held up his hand to quieten me. "Please. Hear me out. That does not mean that I would not be happy to be proven wrong. He always struck me as a good man, and it shocked me to think that was a sham. It is said that the face mirrors a man's soul, and that we can read there whatever is written on his heart. Not with him. With your father, I read wrongly. So if you can prove this was not the case, then I will be in your debt."

I thanked him for his openness—the first time, indeed, I had come across such an even devotion to justice. I thought to myself that if I could persuade this man, then I would have a case; he would not judge unfairly.

"Now," he went on. "How exactly do you plan to proceed?"

I do not remember exactly what I said, but I fear that it was of a touching naïveté. Something about finding the true traitor and forcing him to confess. I added that I was already certain John Thurloe was the man behind it all, and that I intended to kill him when I had the evidence. However I phrased it, my remarks brought a small sigh from Mordaunt.

"And how do you intend to avoid hanging yourself?"

"I suppose I must discredit the evidence against my father."

"Which evidence are you talking about?"

I bowed my head as the depths of my ignorance forced my confession. "I do not know."

Lord Mordaunt looked at me carefully awhile, although whether it was with pity or contempt I could not make out. "Perhaps," he said after a while, "it might help you if I told you something of those days, and what I know of the events. I do not speak because I believe you are correct, but you do have a right to know what was said."

"Thank you, sir," I said simply, and my gratitude to him then was whole and unfeigned.

"You are too young to remember much, and were certainly too young to understand," he began, "but until the very last moment His Majesty's cause in this country seemed doomed to extinction. A few people continued to fight against Cromwell's tyranny, but only because they thought it right to do so, not because there was any anticipation of success. The number of people sick of despotism increased year by year, but they were too cowed to act without a lead. The task of giving that lead was taken on by a handful of loyal subjects, of whom one was your father. They were given the name of the Sealed Knot, because they bound each to the other so tightly through their love of each other and their king.

"They accomplished nothing, except to keep hope alive in men's hearts. Certainly they were active; scarcely a month went by without some scheme or another—a rising here, an assassination there. If these had come to fruition, Cromwell would have been dead a dozen times long before he died in his bed. But nothing of substance took place, and Cromwell's army was always there, a vast block against anyone who wanted change. Unless that army could be defeated, the road to the Restoration would be forever closed, and you do not defeat the most effective army in the world with hope and pinpricks."

I suppose I must have frowned at his criticism of these heroic, lonely men and their struggle, and he noticed it and smiled regretfully. "I do not disparage," he said softly, "I state the truth. If you are serious you need all the information, good and bad."

"I apologize. You are right, of course."

"The Sealed Knot had no money, because the king had no money. Gold can buy loyalty, but loyalty, on its own, cannot buy weapons. The French and the Spanish kept His Majesty on a shoestring, allowing him enough to live in his exile, but not giving enough to do anything. But we were ever hopeful, and I was entrusted with the task of organizing the king's men in England so they might act should our circumstances change. I should have been unknown to Thurloe's office, as I'd been too young to fight in the war and passed those years in Savoy for my education instead. Nonetheless, who I was became known very swiftly: I was betrayed, and could only have been betrayed by a member of the Knot, who knew what I was doing. Thurloe's men swept me up, along with many of my associates, at the very moment when they knew we had incriminating documents on us.''

"Excuse me," I said, foolishly risking a second interruption, even though I could see the first had displeased him. "But when was this?"

"In 1658," he said. "I will not bother you with the details, but my friends, and chiefly my beloved wife, beggared themselves in bribes and so confused the panel of judges who examined me that I was released, and escaped before they realized the size of their error. No such good fortune was with the others. They were tortured and hanged. More importantly, it meant all my efforts in the king's cause were in vain: the new organization I had labored to construct was destroyed before it even began its work.''

He paused, and courteously requested a servant to bring me some cakes and wine, then asked me whether I had heard this story before. I had not, and told him so. I felt like telling him also that I found it thrilling to hear such details of danger and bravado, and that I wished I had been older, that I could have met the dangers with him. I am glad I did not; he would have found the remarks childish, as indeed they were. Instead I concentrated on the gravity of the events he was describing, and asked a few questions about his suspicions.

"I had none. I thought merely I was cursed with the greatest ill fortune. It never occurred to me then that my peril might have been deliberately caused. In any case my meditations on the matter were swept away a few months later, when we heard the glorious news that Cromwell was dead. You remember that, I'm sure?"

I smiled. "Oh, indeed. Who could not? I think it was the happiest day of my life, and I was full of hope for the country."

Mordaunt nodded. "As were we all. It was a gift from God, and we felt at last that Providence was with us. Our spirits rose immediately, and all energies were rekindled, even though his son Richard was declared Protector in Cromwell's stead. And from that hope a new plan emerged, without it even being commanded, a way at least to rattle the régime. There was to be a rising in several parts of the country at once, by forces too big to be ignored. The Commonwealth army would have to split to deal with them and that, it was hoped, would open the way for a swift landing in Kent by the king's forces and a rapid march on London.

"Would it have succeeded? Possibly not, but I do know that every man involved did the best he could. Arms that had been stockpiled for years against such a day were brought out of hiding; men of all sorts declared in secret their readiness to march. Great and small mortgaged their land and melted their plate to provide us with money. The sense of excitement and anticipation was so great even the most dubious were swept up in the enthusiasm and thought that, at last, the hour of deliverance had come.

"And again, we were betrayed. Suddenly, everywhere that men were to rise, troops appeared. They knew as if by magic where arms were stored, and where money was hidden. They knew who had been appointed officers, and who had the plans and lists of the forces. The entire venture, which had taken the better part of a year to bring to fruition, was dashed to the ground and trampled on in less than a week. Only one part of the country reacted swiftly enough; Sir George Booth in Cheshire brought out his troops and did his duty. But he was all alone, and had to face the onslaught of the entire army, led by a general second only to Cromwell himself. It was a massacre; as complete in its destruction as its ruthlessness."

There was a silence in the room as he finished speaking, and I sat there transfixed by his tale. Truly, I had not imagined anything so shocking. The failure of Sir George's rising I knew about, of course, but I never dreamed that his collapse had been caused by treachery. Nor did I suspect this was the crime of which my father was accused. Had he been responsible, then I would have hanged him myself. But I had not yet heard anything to suggest that he was guilty.

"We did not rush to accuse anyone," Mordaunt continued when I put this to him. "And your father led the campaign to uncover the man responsible. His indignation and outrage were terrifying to behold. And yet it appeared this was duplicity; eventually we received documents from within the government which indicated without a shadow of doubt that the traitor was your father. When he was confronted with the evidence in early 1660, he fled abroad.''

"The matter was never resolved, then?" I said. "He did not have the chance of rebutting the charges properly."

"He would have had every chance, had he stayed in England," Mordaunt replied, frowning at the hint of skepticism in my voice. "But the documents, I think, were unanswerable. There was letter after letter in a cipher only he used; notes of meetings with high officials in the government in which conversations were recorded, and containing information he alone could have possessed. Notes of payment . . ."

"No!" I all but shouted. "That I will not believe. You tell me, you dare to say, that my father sold his friends for money?"

"I tell you what is there, plain to see," Mordaunt said severely, and I knew that I had overstepped the bounds of propriety. His favor now hung on the thinnest of threads, and I made haste to apologize for my incivility.

"But the main accusation against him came from the government? You believed that?"

"Government papers, but not from the government. John Thurloe was not the only person to have spies."

"It never occurred to you the papers might have come to you deliberately? To point the finger of accusation at the wrong person and sow dissent?"

"Of course it did," he said tartly, and I could see that I was beginning to weary him. "We were extremely cautious. And if you do not believe me, you should also go and see other associates of his, and they will tell you honestly what they know as well."

"I will do so. Where would I find these people?"

Lord Mordaunt looked at me disapprovingly. "You do need help. London, boy. Or rather, considering the time of year, Tunbridge Wells. Where they are jockeying for position like everyone else."

"And can I come and see you again?"

"No. What is more, I do not want it known that you have been here. I suggest that you conduct yourself with discretion and be careful with whom you talk; this is still a delicate matter, which men remember with bitterness. I do not wish it known that I have helped you in picking at old wounds best forgotten. It is only because of my memory of what I thought your father was, that I have even talked to you today. And I want something in return.''

''Anything in my power.''

''I believe your father was guilty of a monstrous crime. If you find any evidence suggesting I am wrong, you will tell me of it instantly, and I will do everything in my power to help.''

I nodded.

''And if you agree that my conclusions were correct, you will tell me of that as well. Then I can rest peacefully. I am haunted by the possibility that a good man may have been unjustly accused. If you can be persuaded of his guilt, then I will accept it. If not . . .''

''What?''

''Then a good man has suffered, and a guilty one has gone free. That is an evil, which must be corrected.''

chapter five

THE JOURNEY TO TUNBRIDGE WELLS TOOK ME FOUR days as I skirted round London rather than go through it, and I did not begrudge a moment of the time even though I was keen to make swift progress. The nights were still warm, and the solitude filled my heart with a tranquillity that I had scarcely known before. I thought a great deal of what Mordaunt had said, and realized that I had made progress: I knew what my father was accused of doing, and I knew how the accusations were put abroad. Forged papers, coming from within Thurloe's office; finding them would now be part of my quest. More than this, however, I knew that a traitor, well-placed and well-informed, had indeed existed; if it was not my father, the number of people it might be was small— only a handful of trusted men could have betrayed the rising of 1659 so very comprehensively. I had seen his face in old Blundy's saucer of water; now I had to discover his name. I knew how it was done and why; with good fortune I would also discover who.

I could have fallen into company, as many people were on the move, but I shunned all attempts to draw me into companionship, sleeping alone in woods at night wrapped in my blanket and buying such food as I wanted in the villages and small towns I passed through. That solitary mood passed only when I came to the outskirts of Tunbridge Wells itself, and noted the bustle of coaches and carriages, the never-

ending trails of wagons taking produce in to keep the courtiers supplied with their needs, the growing numbers of
itinerant peddlers, musicians and servants, heading there in
the hope of squeezing some money for themselves by selling
their wares. In the last two days I did have a companion
despite myself, as a young whore called Kitty attached herself to me, offering her services in exchange for protection.
She was coming from London and had been attacked the day
before, and did not want the experience repeated. She had
been lucky that first time, as no visible damage was done
beyond some bruises, but she was frightened. Had she lost
her tooth, or broken a nose, her earnings would have suffered
badly, and she had no other trade to fall back on.

I agreed to protect her because the creature had a strange
fascination; for a country boy like myself, such a phantasm
of city corruption had never come into view before. She was
not what the lurid tales had led me to expect; indeed she was
very much more correct than many fine ladies I met in later
life and, I suspect, no less virtuous. She was about the same
age as me, a soldier's bastard abandoned by the mother for
fear of chastisement. How she'd been brought up I do not
know, but she was wiser and more cunning for it. She had
no notion of honesty whatsoever, and all her morality lay in
her obligations—help her and hers and she would owe. Hurt,
and she would hurt back. That was her entire moral universe
and what it lacked in Christianity, it more than made up in
practicality. It was at least a code she could keep to, simple
as it was.

I should say that I did not partake of what she had to offer
the night before we arrived in Tunbridge Wells; fear of the
clap and a heaviness of mind about what I was to do the
next day took away my appetites; but we fed, talked and
later fell asleep under the same blanket and, though she made
fun of me, I think she was quite happy that it was so. We
parted on good terms outside the town, with me hanging back
for fear of being seen in her company.

Like my father, I have never been a man for courts or
courtly ways; indeed, I have always avoided the taint of corruption that goes along with such association. Although I am
no Puritan, there is a level of decency which a gentleman

should maintain, and the court in those days had quickly abandoned any pretense at the sturdy values which make any country fit to live in. Tunbridge Wells shocked me beyond measure. I was quite prepared (for rumors were spreading thick and fast by then) to find the ladies of the court unmasked in public and even sporting wigs and perfume and makeup; I was appalled to discover that the Horseguards were wearing them as well.

But such things hardly concerned me; I was not there to cut a dash, to duel, to lacerate with razor-sharp wit or to worm my way into a position. Nor did I have the resources to do so. To gain a post worth £50 a year, a friend of mine had to lay out near £750 in bribes, all borrowed at interest, and consequently must defraud the government of more than £200 per year to live decently and pay his debts. I scarcely had enough to buy the post of His Majesty's ratcatcher, let alone one worthy of my standing in society. And, given the fact that I was my father's son, all the money in the world would not have won me even that lowly post.

I could not stay in town when I arrived as it was too expensive; the place knew its vogue would not last long and the court would soon turn its fickle attention elsewhere. It was an ugly little settlement with no attractions but the waters, which were *à la mode* that year. All the fops and fools were there, prattling on about how much better they felt for drinking the foul-tasting muck when all the time they jostled to be close to men of influence. Around them, the tradesmen gathered like flies trying to suck what money they could from their purses. I do not know which side was worse: both made me sick at the stomach. Prices were outrageous but, even so, all the rooms were let easily to courtiers willing to pay handsomely to be near His Majesty; many were even in tents on the common nearby. In my brief time there, I never even came within eyeshot of the king. I was too ashamed of my dress to go to a levee, and too concerned of an insult should my name become known. I had a task to accomplish, and did not want my life cut short by some fop's sword. If publicly insulted, I would have to call and I was wise enough to know that I would almost certainly lose.

So, avoiding all the fashionable resorts and those who populated them, I confined myself to the lesser taverns on the outskirts of the town, where the footmen and lackeys would come once their duties were done, to gamble and drink and swap tales of the high and mighty. I saw my traveling companion the once, but she was too obliging to acknowledge me publicly, although she did give me an insolent wink as she passed on the arm of a grand gentleman, who was not ashamed to display his lechery in public.

From the servants I learned very quickly that I had wasted my trip as far as talking to my guardian Sir William Compton was concerned, for he was not there. His advancement had been utterly blasted by a dispute with Lord Chancellor Clarendon over hunting rights in Wychwood Forest, which they both claimed, and as long as Clarendon held the strings of government, Compton could whistle for preferment. He knew this well, it seemed, so had decided to save his money and stay on his estate, not even bothering to come to court.

Two others of the magic circle were indeed present, however: but I soon learned that although Edward Villiers and Sir John Russell had been staunch comrades in adversity, the blessings of success had divided them more than Thurloe's schemes had ever managed. Villiers was in my Lord Clarendon's party, into which he was drawn by Lord Mordaunt, while Sir John, a member of the Duke of Bedford's great family, had attached himself to the opposition, whose only unity came from a detestation of Clarendon. Such is power, that good men, loyal, generous and courageous in the field, squabble like infants when they become courtiers.

Nonetheless, I had two people whom I could approach and I felt that the evening passed gathering gossip in the tavern had been well spent. I was tempted to approach Villiers, as he most clearly had the ear of men in power, but after some consideration I decided to start with easier meat and so set off the next morning to pay my respects to Sir John Russell. I wish I had not done so. I would prefer to pass over this incident in silence, as it reflects badly on one born a gentleman, but I am in the mood to tell everything, "warts and all," as Cromwell said. Sir John refused to talk to me. Would that this were all; but he rebuffed me in a way calculated to humiliate, even though I had never done him or his any wrong. It was some months before I discovered why my name caused him to act in such a way.

What happened was this: I arrived at seven in the morning, and entered the lower part of Russell's inn, asking the landlord to send his manservant so that I might request an audience. Not correct form, I know, but anyone who has ever waited on a court on the move knows that formality is at a discount. All around me were a few dozen or more people, some waiting on favors, some merely eating before going out to attend the audiences of others. The room was abuzz with lesser courtiers trying to take their first step on the long and slippery ladder to preferment and office. I was such a person myself, in a way, and so like them I sat patiently and waited. In this lonely position—for no one is more lonely than a supplicant in a roomful of supplicants—I sat for half an hour, waiting a response. Then an hour, then another half hour. At past ten, two men came down the stairs and advanced on me. The chatter in the room stopped: everyone assumed that I had successfully negotiated the first stage of my suit and wanted to watch the occasion from a mixture of curiosity and envy.

The room was perfectly quiet, so everyone heard the message delivered: indeed, the servant spoke in a sufficiently loud voice to make sure of this.

"You are Jack Prestcott?"

I nodded, and began to rise.

"The son of James Prestcott, the murderer and traitor?"

I could feel my stomach contracting as I sat down again, winded by the shock, and knowing that there was more to come and nothing I could do to avoid the blow.

"Sir John Russell presents his compliments and asks me to tell you that the son of a dog is a dog. He has instructed me to ask you respectfully to take your traitorous presence away from this building, and never have the insolence to approach him again. If you do so, he will have you thrashed. Leave this place, or be thrown into the gutter, as your foul father should have been."

There was total silence. I could feel thirty pairs of eyes boring through me as I gripped my hat and stumbled for the door, aware of nothing at all, just some fleeting impressions.

A sorrowful, almost sympathetic look on the face of the first servant, and the hardness of the other, who rejoiced in humbling me. The look of malicious triumph in some suppliants, the eager interest of others as they thought how they would tell and retell this tale over the next few weeks. And the blood, pounding in my head as the rage and hatred poured into my soul, and feeling as though the force within my skull would split it open. I was sensible of nothing else by the time I reached the door, and do not even recall how I got back to the anonymous misery of my cot above the stables in the tavern.

How long I lay there I am not sure, but it must have been some considerable time: I assume (I was sharing the place with half a dozen others) that there must have been some coming and going, to which I was entirely insensible. All I know is that when I recovered my senses, my beard had grown to a stubble, my limbs were weak and I had to shave before I could show my face to the world once more. The water from the well was freezing cold, but I presented a reasonably civilized appearance when I went down to the inn across the courtyard. I had half forgotten what had transpired, but it came back to me in a flash when I walked through the door. Dead silence, followed by a snicker. I walked up to ask for some beer, and the man beside me turned his back, in the cruel way that comes so naturally to the coarse— although considering the example they had been set by their betters, perhaps it was not so surprising.

IT IS HARD TO RELIVE SUCH HUMILIATIONS, AND EVEN now I find my hand shakes as I dip my pen in the ink and write these words down. So many years have passed, with such grace and goodness in them, yet that moment still cuts deep and the anger returns. I have been told that the heart of a gentleman is the more open to such wounds than those of ordinary people because his honor is the greater, and it may be so. I would have continued had it been likely to serve any purpose, but I knew that the incident had ruined my expedition; there was no way now that I could approach Edward Villiers with any hope of a polite reception, and I would not expose myself to another rebuff. There was no alternative but to leave as swiftly as possible, although I was determined that, before I did so, I would gaze on the face of Sir John Russell, to see whether it matched the vision I had seen in Mrs. Blundy's saucer of water. Mordaunt's visage had not, of which I was heartily glad, and I already knew that Villiers was also different. I confess I hoped that Sir John, who had already done enough to earn my lifelong enmity, would compound his sin and make my quest more simple.

Alas, it was not to be; I spent many hours lurking outside the inn, and (as quietly as possible, so as not to be recognized) outside the fashionable gatherings, listening with gloom to the sounds of revelry within, getting myself soaked to the skin by the first rains of autumn as I stood, doggedly and patiently. Eventually I was rewarded, after a fashion. I had tipped a stall-keeper to point out Sir John when he emerged, and as I was almost giving up hope, he nudged me in my ribs and hissed in my ear:

"'Ere he is, in all his finery."

I looked, half-expecting to see an almost familiar face coming down the steps. "Where?" I said.

"There. That's him," said the trader, pointing out a roly-poly, fat man with a pink face and a straggly, old-fashioned mustache. I watched with the greatest disappointment as this creature (who looked neither deceitful nor familiar) got into a waiting coach. He was not the man that the Blundy woman had shown me.

"Go on then," said the man, "go and present your letter."

"My what?" I said, having forgotten entirely that this was my supposed reason for wanting to know who he was. "Oh, that. Later, maybe."

"Nervous, eh? I know. But let me tell you, young sir, you'll not get anywhere with this bunch unless you go ahead with your plans."

I decided to take this unsought, but probably good, advice by packing my bags and leaving the town. It did not contain what I was looking for.

chapter six

IT IS MID-AFTERNOON AND I AM TOLD (YOU NOTE how it is these days—I am told) that we are setting off for my country seat in the morning; I have little time to continue my narrative. I have already had my head shaved for that damn fool wig, the tailor has been to see me, all is busy with activity. So many things there are to prepare and to get ready, and I care nothing for any of them. These tedious little details are hardly germane to my story, but I notice this tendency in me; it comes more frequently now. My dotage, I suppose it is; I find that I can remember what happened all those years ago more easily than I recall what I was doing the day before yesterday.

To return to my story, I arrived back in Oxford with a deep resentment in my heart and an ever greater determination to defeat my hidden enemies. I had been away more than two weeks, and in that time the town had filled with students and was no longer the quiet, rustic place it is much of the year. Fortunately, this also meant that all those whose help I needed were now in residence. One was Thomas, of course, whose logic-chopping skills, honed in the theological and logical arts which he taught with surprising skill to students, were vital: he could whip through a pile and tease out a meaning faster than anyone I knew. The other was an odd little fellow he brought to see me one day. His name was Anthony Wood.

"Here," Thomas said, presenting Wood to me in his room, "is the answer to all of your problems. Mr. Wood is a great scholar and keen to help you in your search."

Cola describes him briefly and it is one of the few occasions when I can find only small fault with his penmanship; I have never met a more ridiculous creature than Anthony Wood. He was a deal older than myself, perhaps thirty or thereabouts, and already had the bowed back and sunken cheeks of the bookworm. His clothes were monstrous—so old and patched it was hard to see how out of fashion they were—his stockings were darned, and he had the habit of throwing his head back and whinnying like a horse when he was amused. An unpleasant, grating sound which made all in his company suddenly grave, lest they say something witty and be rewarded with his laughter. This, combined with the general inelegance of his movements—all jerks and twitches, so that he could barely sit still for more than a few seconds—began to irritate me the moment I set eyes on him, and it was hard indeed for me to keep my patience.

But Thomas said he would be useful, so I forbore to make fun of him. Unfortunately, the connection, once begun, proved hard to break. Like all scholars, Wood is poor and constantly in search of patronage: they all seem to think that others should pay for their diversion. He has never had any from me, but has never despaired either. He still comes to pay court, in the hope that a coin might slip from my pocket into his ink-stained hands, and never ceases to remind me of the services he rendered all those years ago. He was here a few days back, in fact, which is why he is so fresh in my memory, but said nothing of consequence. He is writing a book, but what is there in that? He has been writing the same one since ever I knew him, and it seems no nearer its conclusion. And he is one of those wiry little men who never seem to age at all, beyond stooping a little more, and acquiring a few more lines on his face. When he comes into a room, it is as though half my life has not happened, and is only a dream. It is only my own aches that remind me.

"Mr. Wood is a great friend of mine," Thomas explained when he saw the look of disgust on my face as I regarded the fellow. "We play music together every week. He is a monstrous student of history and over the last few years has accumulated a great deal of information about the wars.''

"Fascinating," I said dryly. "But I fail to see how he can help."

Wood now spoke, in that high-pitched, fluting voice of his: such precise, mincing enunciation, as neat as a notebook, and scarcely more interesting.

"I have had the honor of encountering many people," he said, "distinguished in war and in public affairs. I have a substantial knowledge of this country's tragic course, which I would be happy to place at your disposal to establish what became of your father."

I swear, he talked like that all the while, all his sentences as perfectly formed as he was grotesque himself. I was not sure what to make of this offer but Thomas told me I must certainly accept, as Mr. Wood was already known for the niceness of his judgment and the voluminous nature of his knowledge. If I needed to know anything about any event or any personality, then I must certainly ask Wood first of all: it would save me a great deal of time.

"Very well," I said. "But I wish to make it clear that you will tell no one of my search. There are many people who would be my enemies if they knew what I am doing. I wish to take them by stealth."

Wood agreed reluctantly, and I told him that I would lay all the facts and information before him in due course, so that he might supplement my findings with information of his own. Then Thomas considerately bundled him out of the room, and I gave my friend a wry and reproachful look.

"Thomas, I know I am in need of all the help I can get . . ."

"You are wrong, my friend. Mr. Wood's knowledge may be crucial to you one day. Do not dismiss him because of his appearance. I have also thought of another useful person for you."

I groaned. "Who might this be, then?"

"Dr. John Wallis."

"Who?"

"He is the Savilian Professor of Geometry, and was deep in the confidence of the Commonwealth by virtue of his skill with codes. Many a secret letter of the king's did he reveal to Thurloe's office, so they say.''

"Should have been hanged, then . . .''

"And now he performs the same service for His Majesty's government, it is rumored. Lord Mordaunt told you the documents incriminating your father used a cipher: if so, then Dr. Wallis might know something of the matter. If you can persuade him to help . . .''

I nodded. Perhaps for once one of Thomas's ideas was going to be useful.

BEFORE EITHER MR. WOOD OR DR. WALLIS COULD DO much to help me, I had an opportunity to repay some of my debt to Thomas by rescuing him from one of the most absurd pieces of ill-judgment. The circumstances were highly amusing, if a little worrying. Everyone knew that Old Tidmarsh the Quaker held some grotesque conventicle in his little house down by the river. Illegal, of course, and considering the trouble such lunatics had already caused, they should have been crushed mercilessly. But no; every now and then a few were locked up, then they were let out again, free to resume their loathsome ways. In fact, they seemed to take pride in it, and blasphemously likened their own sufferings to those of Our Lord Himself. Some (I heard) even claimed to be the Lord in their arrogance, and ran around, shaking their heads and pretending to cure people. The world was full of such madmen in those days. Imprisonment is not the way to deal with such people; half measures merely feed their pride. Leave 'em alone or hang 'em, in my opinion. Or better still, pack them off to the Americas, and let them starve.

Anyway, I was walking down by the castle a few evenings later when I heard a lot of noise and the sound of running feet. For once, it seemed the magistrate had decided to do something. There were sectaries everywhere, jumping out of windows, running this way and that, like ants bestirred in their nest. Never let these people tell you, incidentally, that they sit still and sing psalms when arrested. They are as frightened as anyone.

I stood and watched the sport with merriment until I saw, with great surprise, my friend Thomas all but falling out of the window of Tidmarsh's house, and running up an alleyway.

Instantly, as any friend would, I gave chase. Of all the stupid people, I thought, he was perhaps the stupidest. Here he was, risking his future by indulging his ridiculous piety at the very moment when absolute and total conformity was required.

He was no sportsman, and I caught up with him without any trouble. He almost fainted, poor soul, when I grabbed him by the shoulder and brought him to a halt.

"What in God's name do you think you're doing?"

"Jack!" he said with the most profound relief. "Thank God. I thought it was the watch."

"And so it should be. You must be mad."

"No. I . . ."

The explanation for his absurdity was cut short, however, for two men of the watch now hove into view. We were in an alley, and running would not get us out of trouble. "Keep quiet, lean on my shoulder and leave it to me," I whispered as they approached.

"Good evening, sirs," I cried, slurring my words like one very much drunker than I was.

"And what are you two doing?"

"Ah," I said. "Missed the curfew again, have we?"

"Students, are you? Colleges, please?" He peered at Thomas, whose impression of being drunk was sadly lacking. Had he just a little experience of inebriation he might have done better.

"Where have you been for the last two hours?"

"In the tavern with me," I said.

"I don't believe you."

"How dare you doubt my word?" I replied stoutly. "Where do you think we were?"

"Attending an illegal assembly."

"You must be joking," I said with a fine demonstration of merriment at the absurdity of the idea. "Do I look like a fanatic? We may be drunk, but it is not with the word of God, I'm glad to say."

"I meant him." He pointed at an ever-paler Thomas.

"Him?" I cried. "Oh, dear me no. Ecstasy has been his tonight, but very far from divine. I'm sure the lady concerned would vouch for his devotion, though. Don't let the clerical air fool you."

Thomas blushed at my words, and fortunately this was interpreted as shame.

"I, for my part, have been playing cards, with some considerable success."

"Really."

"Yes. And I am in a splendid mood; I wish to share my good fortune with all the world. Here, sir. Have this shilling and drink my health."

He took the coin, looked at it for a fraction of a second, and then greed overcame duty. "And if you are chasing Quakers," I continued happily once it was tucked away in his pocket, "I saw two gloomy types running up the street over there not three minutes ago."

He looked at me and grinned, showing his gaping gums. "Thank you, young sir. But the curfew is on. If you're still here when I get back . . ."

"Have no fear. Now run quickly, or you will miss them."

I breathed an enormous sigh of relief as they ran off, then turned to Thomas, who showed distinct signs of being sick.

"That's a shilling you owe me," I said. "Now, let's get out of here."

We walked back in silence to New College; I needed to talk to him but could not possibly do so in my own lodging, crammed in as I was with my tutor—who, I imagined, was already in bed. Thomas, however, being now a senior member of a wealthy college, had the freedom to come and go without bothering about the curfews which plagued my life. Small and poky though his room was, he did not have to share it with his students—a luxurious innovation which caused much comment when introduced.

"You must be out of your mind, my friend," I said vehemently when the door was closed. "What on earth were you doing? Indulge your sentiments in private if you must; but to advertise them and risk jail when you are trying to secure yourself a living and a wife is madness."

"I was not . . ."

"No, of course not. You just happened to be amongst that band of Quakers not knowing who they were, and climbed out of the window and ran away for the exercise."

"No," he said, "I was there deliberately. But for a good reason."

"No reason is good enough for that."

"I went to talk to someone. Win their confidence."

"Why?"

"Because I fear I may not get my parish after all."

"You certainly won't if you behave like this."

"Will you listen to me?" he pleaded. "Grove is pressing his case and is winning over several members of the fellowship whom I assumed were on my side. And now he is talking to the warden."

"What can he say?"

"Simple. That he is old and a bachelor, while I will undoubtedly marry and have a family. His needs, in contrast, are simple, and he will hand over a third of the annual revenue from the living to the college."

"Can he do that?"

"If he gets it, he can do whatever he wants; it's his money. He is calculating that it is better to have two thirds of eighty pounds a year than none of it. And Woodward is very mindful of college funds."

"And you can't match the offer?"

"Of course I can't," he said with bitterness. "I wish to marry. The girl's father is only just willing to support the match if I have the full amount. What would your reaction be if I went along and said I'd given a third away?"

"Find another wife," I suggested.

"Jack, I like her. She is a good match, and that living is mine."

"I see your problem. But not what it has to do with climbing out of windows."

"Grove is unsuitable to be in charge of a flock. He will bring scandal onto the church, and drag its good name in the dirt. I know this well, but as long as he was kept away from a living it was not my affair."

"I'm still not following you."

"He is a lecher. I'm sure of it. He engages in illicit concourse with that servant of his, to the shame of the college and the church. It is a disgrace. If his perfidy is proven, then the college will not risk its reputation by giving him a parish. I was trying to discover the truth."

"At a meeting of Quakers?" I said incredulously. The story was getting worse and worse.

"This servant attends sometimes, and is said to be important to them, in fact," he said. "She has a great reputation amongst them for reasons I do not understand. I thought if I attended, I could win her confidence . . ."

I'm afraid that here I burst out laughing. "Oh, Thomas, my dear friend. Only you could try and seduce a girl on your knees."

He blushed scarlet. "I was not trying to do anything of the sort."

"No, of course not. Who is this creature, anyway?"

"A girl called Blundy. Sarah Blundy."

"I know her," I said. "I thought she was quite a good girl."

"That merely demonstrates the limits of your observation. The father was shot for mutiny or something, the mother is a witch, and the girl lived in a hellish society, giving herself freely to anyone who wanted her from the age of ten. I've heard of these people and the sort of things they got up to. I tell you, I shudder even at the thought of talking to her."

"I'm sure having you chant psalms and pray for deliverance would do wonders in winning her over," I said. "Are you sure of this? I have met the girl, and the mother. For a witch's daughter she is very pretty, and for a devilish slut unusually civil."

"I make no mistake."

"Did you talk to her?"

"I had no chance. They are very peculiar, these meetings. We all sat around in a circle, with this Blundy girl in the center."

"And?"

"And nothing. It seemed as though all were waiting for her to say something, but she just sat there. This went on for about an hour. Then we heard shouting from outside, and everyone ran in panic.''

''I see. Even if this belief of yours is true, you are hardly going to get her to tell you,'' I said. ''Why should she? It obviously doesn't bother her and she must need the money. Why should she risk her position to do you a favor?''

''I believe she must secretly despise him. I thought that if I gave her a promise that there would be no consequences, she would see her duty.''

''I think a few coins might sway her better. Thomas, are you sure this is not a mistake? Dr. Grove was my tutor, you remember, and I detected no sign of lustfulness about him in all of four years.''

I am persuaded that Thomas was convinced of the self-lessness of his actions. He genuinely wished the parishioners of Easton Parva to have the very best minister possible and was certain that he was that person. Naturally, he wanted the stipend, and the wife and dowry that went with it, but that merely to make him a better servant of his flock. He was motivated by righteousness, not greed. That was why matters fell out so badly in the end. Simple selfishness causes less harm than desperate virtue.

For my part, I freely confess the selfishness of my own actions. I needed a supply of money, and for that I needed Thomas to have some. Besides, he was my only friend at the time, and I felt beholden to him. For my sake as much as his, I decided that he needed the sort of assistance only I could provide.

''Listen, my friend, go back to your studies, and abandon this meddling because you are not at all suited to it. I will deal with the Blundy girl for you and will soon have her singing like a canary.''

''And how will you do that?''

''I will not tell you. But if you pray for the forgiveness of my sins, then you will be working hard in the next few weeks.''

As usual, he looked shocked at my irreverence, which was just as I hoped. It was so easy to upset him in that way. Laughing happily, I left him to sleep, went back to my college, climbed over the wall undetected and crept softly into the room of my snoring tutor.

chapter seven

I WENT TO SEE JOHN WALLIS, MATHEMATICIAN AND man of God, as Thomas had urged; at this stage I knew little of that grand divine except that he was not well liked, although this I put down to the fact that he had been foisted on Oxford by Cromwell. Much of his unpopularity was due to the fact that, at the general purge of Puritans when the king came back, Wallis had not only kept his position but had even received signs of official favor. Many of those who had suffered for the king and had not been so rewarded resented this bitterly.

Rather presumptuously, I visited him at his home, for he was a rich man and kept rooms in his college, a substantial house in Merton Street and also, I gathered, a place in London. His manservant assumed I was a student wanting instruction and it was only with some difficulty that I gained an audience.

Wallis saw me immediately, for which favor I was impressed; lesser lights in the university had, in the past, kept me waiting for hours for no reason. Consequently, I went into his presence with some rising hope in my heart.

I suppose everybody has in their mind now an idea of what these people look like. The cleric, rosy-cheeked from too much high living; the natural philosopher, absent-minded, a little unkempt with the buttons of his tunic done up in the wrong order and his wig all askew. If there are such people, then the Reverend Dr. John Wallis was not one of them, for he was a man who, I believe, never missed or forgot anything in his entire life. He was one of the coldest, most frightening people I ever encountered. He sat perfectly still and watched me as I came in, indicating only by a slight nod of the head that I should sit down. Now I think more about it, there is something about quietude which is very eloquent. Thurloe, for example, sat very still as well, but the contrast could not have been greater. It may sound strange for me of all people to say it, but Thurloe's stillness had a humility about it. Wallis had the immobility of a serpent as it eyes its prey.

"Well, sir?" he said in an icily soft voice after a while. I noticed that he had a slight lisp, which made the impression of the serpent even stronger. "You want to see me, not the other way around."

"I have come to ask you a favor, sir. On a personal matter."

"I hope you don't want instruction."

"Oh, Lord no."

"Do not blaspheme in my presence."

"My apologies, sir. But I'm not certain how to start. I was told you might be able to help."

"By whom?"

"By Mr. Ken, an MA of this university and . . ."

"I am aware of Mr. Ken," Wallis said. "A dissenting priest, is he not?"

"He is trying desperately to be obedient."

"I wish him well. He no doubt realizes we cannot afford less than total compliance in these days."

"Yes, sir." I noticed that "we." It was only a short while, after all, since Wallis had been a dissenting priest himself, and done handsomely out of it.

Wallis still sat impassively, helping me not at all.

"My father was Sir James Prestcott . . ."

"I have heard of him."

"In which case you also know that he was accused of dreadful deeds, which I know he did not commit. I am convinced that his fall was a plot organized by John Thurloe to hide the identity of a real traitor, and I intend to prove it."

Again, Wallis made no move, either of encouragement or

disapproval; rather he sat there, staring at me with his un-
blinking eyes until I felt a hot flush of foolishness come over
me, and I began to sweat and stammer in my embarrassment.

"How do you intend to prove it?" he said after a while.

"Somebody must know the truth," I said. "I had hoped,
that as you were connected with Mr. Thurloe's office . . ."

Here Wallis held up his hand. "Say no more, sir. You
have an overblown notion of my importance, I think. I deciphered letters for the Commonwealth when I could not
avoid doing so, and when I was sure my natural loyalty to
His Majesty's cause would not in any way be compromised."

"Of course," I muttered, almost admiring the smooth way
the blatant lie dripped from his thin lips. "So my information
was wrong, and you cannot help me?"

"I did not say that," he continued. "I know little, but
perhaps can find out much, if I wish. What papers do you
have of your father's from that period?"

"None," I said. "And I do not think my mother has any
either. Why do you want them?"

"No box? No books? No letters? You must find out where
he was at all times. For if it was said he was in London,
communicating with Thurloe, and in fact you can prove he
was elsewhere, then your cause is advanced greatly. Did you
not think of such a thing?"

I hung my head like a recalcitrant schoolboy, and confessed I had not. Wallis continued to press me, asking me
the most absurd questions about particular books, although I
do not recall the details. My way was the more direct one of
confrontation, not nit-picking through letters and documents.
Perhaps, I thought, Mr. Wood's skills would turn out to be
useful after all.

Dr. Wallis nodded in satisfaction. "Write to your people,
and find out what they have. Bring it all to me, and I will
examine it. Then perhaps I will be able to connect it with
things I know."

"That is kind of you."

He shook his head. "It is not. If there is a traitor at court
it is best to know of it. But rest assured, Mr. Prestcott, I will

not help you unless you can provide proof that you are correct.''

IN MY MIND TIME WAS PRESSING, AND MY TASK DAILY bore in on me, the memory of my father urging me to action. So I began to prepare my travels, and from then on voyaged almost without a break for the next few months, until all was resolved. I was on the move through one of the worst winters I can recall and out again into spring, driven by my duty and my desire for the truth. I traveled on my own, with little more than my cloak and a pack, walking for the most part, trudging up road and tracks, skirting the huge puddles that swamp all byways at that time of year, finding rest where I could in villages and towns or under trees and hedges when there was no alternative. It was a time of the greatest anxiety and fear; until the last I often doubted I could be successful and was concerned that my many enemies would prove impossible to defeat. And yet, I also remember that time fondly, although that is perhaps merely the rosy glow that age always puts on the memory of youth.

Before I set out, I had to honor my promise to help Thomas. Coming across Sarah Blundy was easy, although engaging her in conversation was more difficult. She would leave her lodging at six in the morning to go to the Woods' in Merton Street, where she worked as a servant every day except Monday, which was devoted to Dr. Grove. Here she stayed until seven in the evening. She was given four hours off every Sunday, and one day every six weeks to herself. Most particularly, on Wednesdays she went to do the marketing for the family at Gloucester Green, a wasteland on the outskirts of town where farmers were allowed to sell their produce. She would buy whatever the family needed and (as Mrs. Wood was a notorious miser) had to carry it back herself as she was not given the money for a hired hand.

This, I decided, would be my best opportunity. I followed her at a discreet distance to the market, waited while she made her purchases, then made sure I encountered her at the very moment she was struggling past with two enormously heavy baskets of goods.

"Miss Blundy, is it not?" I said with a look of pleasure on my face. "You don't remember me, no doubt. I had the good fortune to consult your mother some months ago."

She tossed the hair out of her face and looked at me quizzically, then nodded slowly. "That's right," she said eventually. "You did. I trust you found the money well spent."

"It was very helpful, thank you. Most helpful. I'm afraid I did not behave as well as I should have done. I was very concerned and upset at the time, and this no doubt came through in my lapse of manners."

"That's right," she said. "It did."

"Please," I said. "Let me make some small amends. Allow me to carry your baskets. They are far too heavy for you."

Without any pretense of protest, she instantly handed over both of them. "That is kind," she said with a sigh of relief. "It is the part of the week I like the least. As long as I am not taking you out of your way."

"Not at all."

"How do you know where we are going?"

"It doesn't matter," I said hastily to cover my mistake. "I have nothing at all to do, and I would willingly carry these all the way up Heddington Hill for the pleasure of your company."

She tossed her head back and laughed. "Then you certainly don't have much to do. Fortunately I will not impose on your good offices so much. I am heading only for Merton Street."

They were formidably heavy, and I half-resented the girl for being so willing to hand them both over. One would have been more than sufficient. What was worse, she looked at me with scarcely concealed amusement as I struggled with what she carried as a matter of course.

"Are you treated well there?" I asked as we walked—I panting along, and she walking with a light and easy step.

"Mrs. Wood is a good mistress," she replied. "I have nothing to complain about. Why? Were you about to offer me a position?"

"Oh, no. I cannot afford a servant."

"You are a student, is that right?"

I nodded. Considering that my gown was flapping in the sharp wind, and my cap in constant danger of being blown into the gutter, it was not a greatly perceptive remark.

"You aim at the church?"

I laughed. "Dear me, no."

"Do you disapprove of the church? Am I talking to a secret Catholic, perhaps?"

I flushed with anger at the remark, but remembered in time that I was not passing the morning for my own amusement.

"Far from it," I said. "Sinner I may be, but not to that extent. My nonconformity comes from a different direction entirely. Although in action I am blameless."

"I congratulate you."

I heaved a sigh. "I do not congratulate myself. There is a group of God-fearing people I would like to associate with, but they wouldn't even consider accepting me. And I cannot say that I blame them."

"And who is that?"

"I had best not say," I said.

"At least you could risk telling me why you are so unwelcome."

"Someone like me?" I said. "Who would have such a person, so steeped in every monstrosity? I know it, I sincerely repent it, but I cannot erase what I have been."

"I always thought that many groups of people welcomed sinners. There hardly seems much point in only welcoming the pure. They are already saved."

"That's the idea they put about, of course," I said with a great show of bitterness. "In truth they turn from the people who really need them."

"They told you this?"

"They didn't need to. I certainly would not accept someone like myself. And if they did I have no doubt they would constantly fear I would disrupt them."

"Has your life been so wicked? It is difficult to imagine, as you can be little older than myself."

"You were no doubt brought up in a righteous and pious family, though," I pointed out. "I, unfortunately, did not have such good fortune."

"It is true I was blessed in my parents," she said. "But

you can be certain that any group which would turn you away would not be worth belonging to. Come, sir. Tell me whom you have in mind. I might be able to find out something for you. Ask whether you would be welcome, if you are too timid to approach them yourself.''

I looked at her with gratitude and delight. ''Would you? I hardly dare ask. It is a man called Tidmarsh. I have heard he is a saintly preacher, and that he has gathered around him the few people left in Oxford who are not corrupted.''

She stopped and stared at me. ''But he is a *Quaker*,'' she said quietly. ''Are you aware of what you are doing?''

''What do you mean?''

''God's people they may be, but He is giving them sore trials. If you become associated with them, you will lose whatever protection your birth gives you. You will be jailed, and beaten, and spat on in the street. You may even have to give your life. Even if you are spared, your friends and family will shun you and you will be held in contempt by the world.''

''You will not help me.''

''You must be certain you know what you are doing.''

''Are you one?''

A momentary suspicion passed across her face, then she shook her head. ''No,'' she said. ''I am not. I was not brought up to invite troubles. I think that as prideful as gaudy dress.''

I shook my head at the remark. ''I do not pretend to understand you. But I am sorely in need of help.''

''Find it elsewhere,'' she said. ''If God commands it, you must obey. But make sure you know what He wants first. You are a young gentleman, with all the advantages that brings. Don't throw them away on a whim. Think and pray hard first. Theirs is not the only route to salvation.''

We had been walking awhile down St. Aldates, then along Merton Street, and had paused outside the door of her mistress's house while she delivered this last injunction. I imagine she was merely trying to shield herself, but even so, her advice struck me as wise. If I had been some impetuous youth on the brink of making a grave mistake, she would have given me pause for thought.

I walked away slightly discomfited, which now I understand. I was deceiving her, and she gave kindness in return. It made me very confused, until I later learned how much greater her trickery was than mine.

chapter eight

IT WAS NOT DIFFICULT TO CONTRIVE SEVERAL chance meetings with her in the few weeks that followed, and I slowly won her friendship. I told her that I had decided to take her advice but my soul was still tormented. All the sermons in the world could not reconcile me to the established church. I had learned that her father had been an extremist of the worst sort, so busy advocating the murder of property owners and the establishment of a republic that he had no time for Christ. Accordingly, I had to modify my approach.

"When I think of the hopes that existed in the world only a few years ago," I said, "it makes me grieve. What were common aspirations are now cast out and despised, and the world is given over to greed and selfishness."

She stared at me solemnly as though I had uttered a profound truth and nodded. We were walking down St. Giles, I having managed to meet her as she was coming back from a cookshop with the Woods' dinner that evening. It smelled delicious, hot and tasty, and the odors made the juices turn in my stomach. I could see that she also was hungry.

"What do you do after you have delivered this?"

"Then I am finished for the day," she said. It was already dark, and cold in the air.

"Come with me. Let us eat together. I can see you are as hungry as I am, and you would do me a favor to keep me company."

She shook her head. "That is kind, Jack. But you should not be seen with me. Neither of our reputations will be improved by it."

"What is your reputation? I know nothing of it. I see only a pretty woman with an empty stomach. But if it concerns you, we can go to a place I know where the clientele make both of us seem like saints."

"And how do you know such places?"

"I told you I was a sinner."

She smiled. "I cannot afford it."

I waved my hand. "We can discuss that at a later stage, once your stomach is filled."

Still she hesitated. I leaned over the bowl of food she was carrying and sniffed deeply. "Ah, the smell of that gravy, running over the lumps of meat," I said longingly. "Can't you just imagine a plate of it before you, with a fresh, crusty loaf and a tankard? A plate piled high, the steam rising into the air, the juices . . ."

"Stop!" she cried, laughing out loud. "All right. I'll come, if only you'll stop talking about food."

"Good," I said. "So deliver your meal, and come with me."

We went to a small place on the very outskirts of the town, past Magdalen College and over the river. No one from the university, not even students, ever ate there, it being too far away in distance, and too low in reputation. The food was execrable as well; Mother Roberts was as bad a cook as she was disgusting a person, and the food was like the woman: larded with fat and giving off a foul smell. Sarah looked uneasy in the little room where she served up the gruel, but ate with the appetite of one who rarely gets enough. The main virtue of Mother Roberts was that the ale she served was strong and cheap, and I regret the passing of those days. Now that men of business make beer and are trying to stop women selling the ale they brew, I believe the great days of this country are over.

The best quality of the brew was that by the time Sarah had drunk a quart of it, she'd become talkative, and susceptible to my questions. As much as I remember it, I set the conversation down here. On my prompting, she told me that she not only worked for the Wood family, but had also found work with Dr. Grove. She did little for him, except clean his room, prepare his fire and a bath once every quarter—for he was fastidiously clean about his person—and he paid generously. The only trouble, she said, was his desire to bring her within the Established Church.

I said that this Grove must be something of a hypocrite to speak so, as he had a reputation for being a hidden papist. If I thought this would draw her out, I was wrong, for she frowned and shook her head fervently. If he was such, she said, she had never seen the slightest sign of it, neither in his room nor in his manner.

"And he works you hard?"

On the contrary, she insisted. He had treated her with the utmost kindness at all times, even though she had seen him be extremely unpleasant with others. Her main concern was that he would get a living out in the country soon. He had told her only a few days before it was a near certainty.

This upset me mightily; I already knew Grove to be blameless in his adherence—in fact he was probably more in conformity with the church than Thomas himself—and it seemed unlikely that my friend's suspicions about his morals had any substance. Nor could the girl be persuaded to denounce him falsely for money. She had an honest air to her.

"He surely can't have much skill at running a parish," I said. "No doubt because he has been in the university for so long. Otherwise he would be wary of having a pretty young woman to clean his rooms. There is bound to be talk."

"There is nothing to talk about, so why should anyone trouble?"

"I do not know, but lack of substance has never dissuaded a gossip yet, I think. Tell me about this reputation of yours that I should be so wary of," I said, thinking that if I could prove Grove was willingly taking a sectary to his bosom, this might do just as well. So she told me a little about her father's career in the wars, and described what to my ears seemed as black a monster as ever lived, a mutineer, atheist and rabble-rouser. Even through her description I perceived that the only thing to be said in his favor was his evident courage. She did not even know where he was buried, as he was too foul even to be allowed a consecrated grave. We shared that misfortune, at least.

She was already casting her spell over me, I think, for I found myself strangely drawn to her despite a freedom about her talk which should have been a warning. We had a strange amount in common; she worked for Grove, I had been in his charge. Both of our fathers had evil reputations, and although that of my own was unjustified, I knew what it was to be cursed in this fashion. And unlike many sectaries, she did not have the burning eyes and humorless demeanor of the fanatic. Nor was she ugly like most of them, their souls drawn to Jesus because no mortal man wants their bodies. She ate with surprising and natural delicacy, and when in drink she behaved well. I had talked little with women in my life, as they were either too protected or too low for proper conversation, and my experience with the whore outside Tunbridge Wells and the way she had laughed at me had begun to rankle.

I was beginning to want her as we left the table, and naturally thought that her willingness to dine alone with me in such a place, and her open conversation, meant she was equally inclined to me. I knew of people such as her, in any case, and had heard tales of their laxity. I was all the more keen because she was of no use: there was no truth in Thomas's thoughts about Grove, and she would tell no tales. Fool that I was to think in such a fashion, for her trap was about to shut its jaws as it had done, no doubt, many times before. I thought I was being charming and seductive, favoring her with my condescension; instead she was exploiting my youth and trusting nature, leading me into that sin she fully intended to use for her own devilish ends.

It was well past eight when we left, and already dark, so I told her we had best travel back across Christ Church meadow to avoid the patrols. "I was caught a few weeks back by the curfew," I said. "I cannot afford to be caught again. Come with me; you will be safer."

She accepted without demur, and we cut past the botanical gardens and into the meadow, at which point I slipped my arm around her waist. She stiffened slightly, but did not protest. When we were in the middle of the field, and I was certain there was no one close by, I stopped, took her in my arms and tried to kiss her. Instantly she began struggling, so I squeezed her tightly to show that, while some resistance was to be expected, she should not overact her part. But she kept on struggling and averting her face, then started hitting me with the flat of her hands, pulling at my hair and making me lose patience. I tripped her up and pushed her to the ground. Still she struggled so, perfectly furious at her behavior, I was forced to slap her.

"How dare you?" I exclaimed indignantly once the struggling had momentarily stopped. "A meal isn't a high enough price for you? You expect something for nothing? What do you think you are? Do you plan to pay me back some other way?"

She started struggling again, so I pinned her to the cold, damp ground, pulled up her thin skirt and prepared myself. I was hot in blood by now, as her refusal had both angered and excited me, and I gave no quarter. I may have hurt her, I do not know, but if I did it was her own fault. When I had finished I was content, and she was subdued. She rolled away from me and made no more protest, lying on the cold grass.

"There," I told her. "So what was that noise about? It cannot have been a surprise to someone like you. Or did you think I wanted to feed you for your conversation? Come now, if I had wanted talk I would have gone out with one of my fellows, not a serving girl whose company has to be hidden."

I shook her playfully, in good humor again. "Don't make such a fuss. Here's an extra tuppence. Don't take it amiss. You're not some virgin who has lost something of value."

Then the harpy rolled over and slapped me, full in the face, then scrabbled at my face with her claws and pulled at my hair so hard some of it even came out in her hand. I have never been treated in such a fashion in my life, and the shock took my breath away. She had to be taught a lesson, of course, and I did so, although with little pleasure. I have never liked beating people, not even servants, however deserving. It is one of my greatest weaknesses, and I fear it leads them to hold me in less respect than they ought.

"There," I said when she was crouching on the grass, her head in her hands. "Next time, I won't want any of this nonsense.'' I had to bend down and talk into her ear to make sure she would hear me. I noticed she was not crying. "You will treat me with proper respect in future. Now, to show there are no hard feelings, take this money, and let's forget all about it.''

As she didn't want to get up, I left her to show I wasn't susceptible to such wheedling behavior. The evening had not been as useful as I had imagined, in that the problem of Dr. Grove was not yet solved, but it had had an agreeable ending. I even noticed, out of the corner of my eye, that she had a strange expression, almost a smile, I thought, on her face as I turned to go. That smile stuck in my mind for a long while afterward.

chapter nine

I WOULD HAVE LEFT THE MATTER THERE, HAD NOT a dream that very same night disturbed me greatly. I was climbing a staircase and there was a large oak door at the top, which was firmly closed. It frightened me but I summoned all my strength and pushed it open. It should have been the bedroom, but instead I found myself in a gloomy and humid cellar.

The sight inside was a fearful one; my father was lying on a bed, as naked as Noah, and covered in blood. Sarah Blundy, dressed all in white and wearing that same smile, stood over him, knife in hand. As I entered, she turned placidly toward me. "Thus dies a man of honor," she said in a whisper.

I shook my head, and pointed accusingly at her. "You have murdered him," I said.

"Oh no." And she nodded at me. I looked down, and in my hand was the bloody dagger she had been holding herself only a moment before. I tried to let it go, but it would not leave my hand. "You see? You are forever stained now," she said.

That was the end of the dream, or, if there was more, I cannot recall it. I woke up frightened, and it took some effort to rid my spirit of the pall that it cast over me, which was strange considering that I had never before paid much attention to such phantasms and, indeed, had always laughed at those who placed such store by them.

I asked Thomas what he thought when I encountered him and we went for a drink in a tavern, and he, of course, treated the matter with gravity, as he did everything. Their meaning, he informed me, depended on my constitution. What was the dream exactly?

Naturally, I left out the background to it; he was exceptionally condemnatory of fornication, and I did not wish to dispute with him over trifles.

"Tell me, do you tend to a dominance of the choleric humor?" he asked when I had done.

"No," I said. "Melancholia, rather."

"I take it you don't know much about dreams?"

I admitted the fact.

"You should study them," he said. "Personally, I find them superstitious nonsense, but there is no doubt that the vulgar believe all sorts of stuff can be read from them. One day, such foolishness may be condemned; certainly no reputable priest should pay any attention to such drivel. However, that age has not yet come, so we must beware.

"You see," he said warming to his theme and shifting his thin backside in his seat in the way he did when he was settling down for a long discourse, "dreams come from various sources all acting in conjunction. Generally there is a dominant source, and it is that which we must isolate to identify the true nature of the apparition. One source is vapors rising from the stomach to the brain, causing it to overheat; such an occurrence happens when you have overindulged in food or drink. Did you do that before the dreams?"

"Far from it," I told him, thinking back to my meal at Mother Roberts's.

"The next is an imbalance of your humoral constitution, but as you tell me that melancholia is dominant in you, we must rule that out as well; this is obviously a dream in which the choleric exerts its influence, the choler tending to produce black dreams, because of its color.

"So that leaves the spiritual influence; a vision, in other words, either inspired by angels as a warning, or by the devil as a torment and temptation. Either way, the dream does not look well; the girl is strongly associated with the death of a man, a father. A dream of murder is a terrible sign; it foretells hardship and imprisonment. Tell me again, what else was there?''

''The knife, the girl, the bed, my father.''

''Again, the knife bodes ill. Was it bright and sharp?''

''Must have been.''

''A knife indicates that many people of ill will are ranged against you.''

''I know that already.''

''It also foretells that if you have a lawsuit pending, you are likely to lose it.''

''The bed?'' I asked, becoming more and more miserable at the prospect he was laying out before me.

''Beds, of course, are about your marriage prospects. And for it to be occupied by the corpse of your father again does not signify well at all. As long as he is there, you will not marry; his body prevents it.''

''Which means that no woman of quality would touch the son of a traitor like myself,'' I exclaimed. ''Again, I hardly need a divine messenger to tell me that.''

Thomas looked forward into his tankard. ''And then there is the girl,'' he said, ''whose presence puzzles me. Because the dream says plain that she is your misfortune and your judge. And that cannot be. Why, you scarcely know her, and I can see no possibility that your current difficulties can be laid at her door. Can you explain this to me?''

Even though I knew more than I could comfortably tell Thomas, I could not explain it. I can do so now, for I have pondered long and hard on the matter. It is clear to me that my initial visitation to Widow Blundy created an imbalance amongst the spirits, a dependency in which I was embroiled, and that by taking my pleasure with the daughter I allowed myself foolishly to fall into a trap. That I was prompted by the urgings of a devil and was seduced into her power is now equally obvious.

The message of the dream was in fact simple, had I only the wit to understand. For it showed clearly that the girl's entrapment was aimed at deflecting me from my quest, with the result that failing to clear my father's name would be a form of murder. Once I understood that, I was fortified, and encouraged in my resolve.

Of course, such insight did not come instantly, for I have never claimed to be a cunning thinker in such matters. I learned, as all men must, by experience and from the application of common sense, so that ultimately only one explanation is left which answers all. At that time, my only thought was that the girl might lay some piddling complaint against me to the proctors of the university, who took a poor view of students consorting with the town's whores, and that the investigation might force me to remain in town. A defense was needed and attack is the best form of it.

When I left Thomas and walked up Carfax, I came on an exceedingly ingenious solution; in brief, I tipped Mary Fullerton, a vegetable girl in the market and one of the most dishonest and scurrilous wretches I knew, to confirm the story by telling how she had gone one day to deliver some fruit to Dr. Grove and been mistaken for Sarah. The moment she got in the room (I instructed her to say), Grove had come up behind her and started fondling her breasts. When she protested (here she claimed to be a virtuous girl, which certainly was not the case), Grove said "What, girl? You do not want what you were so eager to have yesterday?" Better still, I sought out Wood and told him a story about Dr. Grove and his rutting ways with his servant. It was guaranteed that, within a day or so, the story would spread and soon get back to the Fellows of New College, such was Wood's ability as a gossip.

So let the slut complain if she will, I thought. No one will believe her and she will do nothing but bring scandal and shame on her own head. Looking back now, I am less sanguine. My cunning did not deliver the living into Thomas's hands and, though it might have fended off Sarah Blundy's worldly revenge, it enraged her to ever greater heights of malice.

I KNEW NOTHING OF THAT WHEN I LEFT OXFORD A FEW days later—a blessed release, for I always detested the town, and have not revisited it for more than ten years now—and believed rather that I had enjoyed the girl, protected myself and helped my friend at one and the same time. Such contentment did not last long after I crossed the border into Warwickshire and made my way to my mother, although again I ignored the first sign that anything was amiss. I spent money on a carriage to Warwick, planned to walk the last fifteen miles to save money, and set off in good heart, pausing after an hour or so for some water and a bite of bread. It was a lonely spot on the road, and I sat down on a grassy verge to rest. After a while, I heard a rustling in the bushes and got up to investigate; I had scarcely walked four paces into the undergrowth than, with a hellish squalling, a polecat sprang up and scratched my hand, causing a deep gash which bled profusely.

I started back in alarm and fright and tripped over a root, but the animal did not press home its advantage. It vanished immediately as though into thin air and, had it not been for the blood dripping from my hand, I would have sworn I'd imagined it. I told myself, of course, that it was my own fault, that I had probably got too near its brood and paid the price. Only later did it occur to me that, in my many years' acquaintance with that part of the world, I had never heard anyone mention such creatures living there.

Later, of course, I knew better the origins of the beast but then I merely blamed myself, bound up my hand and got on with the journey, arriving after three days' travel at my mother's people. Our destitution had left her no choice but to throw herself on their charity and they had taken her back, but not as family ought. My mother had disobliged them mightily by marrying as she pleased, and they did not let her forget for an instant that, in their opinion, her sorrow was punishment for her disobedience.

Accordingly, they made her live little better than a servant. True, she was allowed to eat at the main table—they maintained the old custom, now almost forgotten, of eating with the entire household—but they always made sure she sat at the end and subjected her to almost daily insult. They were the very model of what have since come to be known as Trimmers—they would have got on well with Dr. Wallis, had they ever met. Under Cromwell, the family sang their psalms and praised the Lord. Under Charles they bought the family curate his vestments and read the Book of Common Prayer every evening. The only thing beneath them, I think, was popery, for they were the most fervent haters of Rome and constantly on the lookout for the malign touch of priest-craft.

I always loved the house, but I believe it has been remodeled now, reconstructed along modern lines by one of Sir Christopher's innumerable imitators. Now the rooms are regular and well-proportioned and the light no doubt floods in through the modern sashes, the chimneys draw properly and the drafts are kept to a minimum. For my part I regret this enthusiastic conformity to whatever men of fashion in Europe tell us is elegant. There is something false about all that symmetry. It used to be that a gentleman's house was the history of his family, and you could see in its lines when they had been in funds and expansive, or when times were hard. Those curling chimney stacks, and corridors and eaves stacked one next to the other, provided the comfort of a sweet disorder. One would have thought, after Cromwell's attempts to impose uniformity on us all through his armies, that no more was needed. But I am out of harmony with the times, as usual. The old houses are being destroyed one by one, and replaced by gimcrack structures which will probably last no longer than the grasping, arrogant new families who construct them. Built so fast, they can be swept away as quickly, along with all the people they contain.

"How do you stand for such humiliation, madam?" I asked my mother when I visited her in her room one evening. I had been there for some weeks and could stand the mean piety, the arrogant self-importance of these people no more. "To have to endure their superiority every day would try the patience of a saint. Not to mention their insufferable reproaches, and pained kindnesses."

She shrugged as she looked up from her embroidery. It was her habit to pass time in this way in the evening, making cloths which, she would tell me, would be mine once I had found a wife and an income. "You should not be unfair to them," she said. "They are more than generous to me. They were under no obligation, after all."

"Your own brother?" I cried. "Of course he is under an obligation. As your husband would have been had the positions been reversed."

She did not answer for a while, and concentrated on her labor while I stared once more into the big log fire. "You are wrong, Jack," she said eventually. "Your father behaved very badly toward my brother."

"I am sure it was all my uncle's fault," I said.

"No. You know how I revered your father, but he could be hot-tempered and rash. This was one of those occasions. He was entirely at fault, but refused either to admit it or make amends."

"I cannot credit it," I said.

"You do not know what I am talking about," she said, still patient. "I will give you a small example. During the war, before your father left to fight abroad, the king sent round collectors to levy an impost on all the great families. The demands on my brother were harsh and unfair. Naturally, he wrote to my husband, asking him to intercede and get the amount reduced. He wrote back a very offensive letter, saying that with so many people giving their lives, he did not intend to help my brother avoid giving his silver. It would have been a small enough service to do for his family. And when Parliament in turn made its levy, my brother had to sell a large parcel of land, he was now so impoverished. He never forgave your father."

"I would have arrived with a troop of horse to take the money myself," I said. "The needs of the king's cause outweighed all others. Had more people seen that, Parliament would have been defeated."

"The king was fighting to preserve the law, not merely to keep himself on the throne. What point was there in success if everything he was battling for was destroyed thereby? Without the families of the realm, the king was nothing; preserving our fortune and our influence did as much for his cause as fighting for him."

"How convenient," I scoffed.

"Yes," she said. "And when this king returned, your uncle was there to take up his position as magistrate and reestablish order. Without my brother, who would have controlled this part of the world, made sure our people welcomed the king back? Your father was penniless and without influence.''

''I would rather have a penniless hero for a father than a rich coward,'' I said.

''Unfortunately you now claim descent from a penniless traitor, and live on the kindness of the rich coward.''

''He was no traitor. You, of all people, cannot believe that.''

''All I know is that he brought ruin on his family, and made his wife a beggar.''

''The king gave him life and honor. What else could he do?''

''Spare me your childishness,'' she snapped. ''War is not a tale of chivalry. The king took more than he gave. He was a fool and your father was a greater fool for sustaining him. For years I had to juggle with creditors, bribe soldiers and sell our lands, just so he could be the man of honor. I watched our funds dwindle to nothing so he could cut a figure as an equal with noblemen on ten times the income. I watched him reject a settlement with Parliament because the man sent to negotiate with him was not a gentleman. That particular show of honor cost us dear, believe me. And when we were reduced to penury, I had to come with nothing but the clothes on my back to throw myself on my brother's mercy. He took me in, fed me and housed me while your father dissipated what remained of our fortune. He pays for your education so you can live, and he has promised to set you up in London when you are ready. In return, he gets nothing from you but contempt and childish remarks. You compare his honor with your father's. Tell me, Jack, where is the honor in a pauper's grave?''

I sat back, stunned by her vehemence and grievously disappointed. My poor father, betrayed even by the one person who owed him all obedience. My uncle had even managed to subvert her. I did not blame her; how could a woman resist such pressures, when they were constantly applied? It was my uncle I blamed, using my father's absence to blacken him to the person who should have defended his name to the last.

"You talk as though you are going to say he was a traitor after all," I said eventually, when my head had stopped spinning. "I cannot believe that."

"I do not know," she said. "And so I try to believe the best. In the year or so before he fled I hardly saw him; I do not know what he was doing."

"You do not care who betrayed him? It does not disturb you that John Thurloe is free though guilty, while your own husband lies dead through betrayal? You do not want revenge for this?"

"No, I do not; it is done and cannot be changed."

"You must tell me what you know, however little it is. When did you last see him?"

She stared long at the fire that was fading in the grate and letting the cold wrap itself around our bodies; it was always an icy house, and even in the summer you needed a heavy coat if you went out of the main rooms. Now winter was coming in, the leaves falling and the winds beginning to blow, the chill was taking over the house once more.

It took some urging before she answered my questions about papers and letters and documents which might show what took place, for Wallis's request was still in my mind and I wished to oblige him if I could. Several times she refused, changing the subject and trying to divert me into other matters, but each time I insisted. Eventually she gave way, realizing it would be easier than to resist. But her unwillingness was obvious and I never entirely forgave her for it. I told her that I had above all to know everything possible about what had happened around January of 1660, just before my father fled, and when the plot against him was reaching its climax. Where was he? What had he done or said? Had she even seen him in that period?

She said she had; indeed, it was the last time she had ever seen him. "I received a message through a trusted friend that your father needed me," she began. "Then he came here unannounced and at night. He had no dealings with your uncle and spent only one night here, then left again."

"How was he?"

"Very grave, and preoccupied, but in good spirits."

"And he had a troop with him?"

She shook her head. "Just one man."

"Which man?"

She waved my question aside. "He stayed the night as I say, but didn't sleep; just fed himself and his comrade, then came to talk to me. He was very secretive, making sure that no one heard, and making me promise not to reveal a word to my brother. And before you ask, I have not done so."

I knew at the bottom of my heart that I was on the verge of receiving a message of unparalleled importance, that my father had meant me to hear this, otherwise he would have sworn my mother to complete silence. "Go on," I said.

"He talked to me very intently. He said he had discovered the worst treason imaginable, which had shocked him so greatly he had initially refused to believe the evidence of his own eyes. But now he was convinced, and he was going to act."

I all but cried out in frustration at this. "What treason? What act? What discoveries?"

My mother shook her head. "He said it was too much to confide in a woman. You must understand that he never told me any secrets, or gave me any confidences at all. You should be surprised he said so much, not that he said so little."

"And that was all?"

"He said he would uncover and destroy men of the greatest evil; it was dangerous, but he was confident of success. Then he pointed to the man who had been sitting in the corner all the while."

"His name, madam? What was his name?" At least, I thought, I might have something. But again she shook her head. She did not know.

"He may have been called Ned; I do not know. I think I had met him before, before the war. Your father told me that, ultimately, only your own people were to be trusted, and that this man was such a person. If anything should not take place as planned, then this man would come and give me a packet, which contained everything he knew. I was to guard it well, and use it only when I was sure it was safe to do so."

"And what else?"

"Nothing," she said simply. "Shortly after they left, and

I never saw him again. I received a message from Deal a few weeks later saying he was having to leave the country for a short while, but would be back. He never did come back, as you know.''

"And this man? This Ned?''

She shook her head. ''He never came, and I never received any package.''

HOWEVER DISAPPOINTING IT WAS THAT MY MOTHER had nothing to help Dr. Wallis, the information she gave me was an unexpected bonus. I had not expected her to have such knowledge, and had applied to her only as an afterthought. Sad though it is for a son to acknowledge, I found it increasingly hard to maintain my civility with her, so much was she being drawn back to her own family, which had only ever approved of my father while he possessed a good estate.

No; my purpose in going into Warwickshire was quite different, for I wanted to consult the papers concerning my Lincolnshire estate, so that I might know when I could expect to take possession. I knew that the matter had been complicated; my father had told me so on many occasions. By the time the fighting became serious and his confidence in the king began to slacken, he was aware that far more than his own life was at risk, and that the entire family might well be destroyed. Consequently, he drew up a settlement designed to protect it.

In brief, and following the latest practice in the country, he devised the real estate on a trust, for the use of himself and, on his death, of myself. A will drawn up at the same time made my uncle his executor and Sir William Compton my guardian, charged with the proper disposal of both the personal and real estate. It sounds complicated, but nowadays any man of property will understand it all perfectly well, it has become such an ordinary means of protecting a family from danger. Back then, however, such complexities were all but unheard of: there is nothing like civil strife to make men ingenious and lawyers rich.

I could not ask to see the papers, as they were in the

keeping of my uncle and it was scarcely likely he would agree to the demand. Nor did I want to warn him of my interest, lest he take steps to destroy them, or alter anything in his own favor. I had no intention of allowing my uncle to cheat me, an activity which came as second nature to him.

So that night, when I was sure everyone was asleep, I made my search. My uncle's study, where he conducted the estate business and held meetings with his agents, was unchanged from the days when he used to summon me to give me lectures about God-fearing good conduct, and I crept quietly in, remembering without even thinking about it that the door had a squeak that could easily rouse the entire household. Holding up my candle, I could make out the stout oak table where the accounts were laid every Michaelmas, and the iron-banded chests in which the vouchers and accounts were kept.

"Formidably difficult, are they not? Do not worry, when they are your responsibility you will understand them. Just remember the golden rules of property: never trust your managers, and never bear too hard on your tenants. You will lose in the end." Thus I remember my father talking to me, I suppose when I was five, maybe less. I'd come into his own office at Harland House because the door was open, even though I knew it was forbidden. My father was alone with reams of paper all around, the sand shaker by his elbow, the wax heated for affixing the seals to the documents, the candle smoking in the wind. I half expected to be beaten, but instead he looked up and smiled at me, then gathered me onto his lap and showed me the papers. When he had more time, he would begin my education, he said, for a gentleman had much to learn if he was to prosper.

That day never came, and the thought made my eyes smart with tears as I remembered that room at my own home, the home I might have lost forever and which I had not even seen for more than a decade. Even so, the smell of it came back to me, strong and sure, a mixture of leather and oil, and I stood for some time in sadness before coming to and remembering my task, and the urgency of getting on with it.

My uncle used to keep the keys to the strongbox in the sword cupboard, and it was here that I immediately looked when I recovered myself. Fortunately, his habits had not changed and the big iron key was in the usual place. Opening the box took no time at all, and then I sat down at the big desk, positioned the candle, and began to go through the documents which I took out, one by one.

I was there for several hours before the candle failed. It was tiresome work, for most of the bundles were of no interest, and were discarded the moment they were opened. But eventually, I found the details of the settlement. I also found twenty pounds which, after some hesitation, I took. Not that I wanted to rely on such tainted money, but I reasoned that by rights it was mine in any case, so I should have no qualms about using it.

Words cannot express the full horror of what I discovered, for the documents provided a complete and dispassionate outline of the most despicable and complete fraud. I will put it simply, for no amount of ornamentation will increase the effect: my entire estate was sold by Sir William Compton, the man appointed to guard my interest, to my uncle, the man supposedly entrusted with maintaining the integrity of the land. This foul piece of trickery had been accomplished the moment my poor father was laid into his pauper's grave, for the final deed of sale was signed and dated not two months after his death.

I had, in short, been utterly, and entirely, dispossessed.

I had never liked my uncle, and had always detested his conceit and his arrogant ways. But I had never suspected he might be capable of such a monstrous betrayal. For him to take advantage of his family's disarray and turn it to his own profit; to make use of my father's death and my minority to pursue such a grubby scheme; to coerce my own mother into connivance with the destruction of her son's interest—all this was far worse than I could ever have imagined. He assumed that my age and lack of funds would prevent me from fighting back. I determined, then and there, that he would shortly learn how very wrong he was.

What I could not understand were the actions of Sir William Compton, my guardian and a man who had always treated me with the greatest of kindness. If he, too, had conspired against me then I was truly alone; but despite the clear evidence I could not believe that a man of whom my father always spoke in the highest terms, to whom, indeed, he was prepared to consign his heir, could have acted with duplicity. A bluff, hearty man, the very backbone of the nation in robust honesty, described even by Cromwell himself as that "godly cavalier," he must also have been duped to act in this fashion. If I could find out how, then again my cause would advance. I knew I would soon have to question him as well, but recoiled from the task until I could present him with more evidence. For I had been dispatched from his house of Compton Wynyates the moment my father fled: I did not know what reception I would receive, and, I admit, was afraid of his scorn.

I knew, as I closed the casket and locked it, then slipped quietly back to my room, that my task had grown enormously in complexity, and that I was now more alone than I ever dreamed. For I was betrayed in one way or another by everyone, even those closest to me, and had no resources but my own determination. Every step I took, it seemed, my labors grew greater and more difficult, for now I not only had to find the man who betrayed my father, I also had to confound those who so swiftly moved to profit from his disgrace.

It had not yet occurred to me that the two quests might be one and the same, nor even that, in comparison to the other struggle that was about to burst upon me in full flood, these problems were almost trivial.

I soon received some indication of what lay ahead for, about two hours before dawn, I slept. I wish I had not; I should have left the house immediately and been on my way, had I done so I would have avoided the most fearsome experience of a night that was already harrowing. I do not know how long I was asleep, but it was still dark when a voice awoke me. I drew the bed curtain back and saw, in the casement of the window, the clear figure of a woman leaning in, as though standing outside, though it was on the second floor. Although I could not make out the face, the flowing dark hair instantly confirmed my suspicions. It was the Blundy girl. "Boy," she hissed, time and again, "you will fail. I will ensure it." Then, with a sigh more like wind than breath, she vanished.

I sat, shivering with cold, for an hour or more until I had convinced myself that what had occurred was no more than the fever of a disordered and tired mind. I told myself that the dream was nothing, just as the earlier one had been nothing. I reminded myself of all the worthy priests who had said that to pay credence to such imaginings was presumptuous. But they were wrong; while I have no doubt that many so-called prophets who interpret their dreams as divine messages are ignorant and hare-brained, mistaking vapors for angels and humors for the Lord, some dreams are indeed spirituous in origin. And not all come from God. As I tried to lie back in the bed and sleep once more, the wind rattling against the window kept me awake and I remembered that I had not opened it before I went to bed. Yet there it was, opened and fixed open, although not by my hand.

I changed my plan when I went down the next morning and left as swiftly as was decent. I said no farewells to my mother, and certainly none to my uncle. I could not bear the sight of them, and was afraid I might let slip some remark and reveal that I had uncovered their plot.

chapter ten

I WILL NOT DESCRIBE MY TURBULENT EMOTIONS AS I made my way to the border which divides the counties of Warwickshire and Oxfordshire; that my soul burned with the desire for revenge must be obvious, and I do not feel the need to put down on paper what any man in my position must have experienced. It is my task to describe what I did, not what I felt on the matter: the transience of emotions makes them a sorry waste of time. In the history of man, it is glorious action which provides all matter of significance, and all lessons for posterity. Do we need to know how Augustus felt when he heard the news that Actium had extended his dominion over the entire globe? Would it magnify the glory of Cato to have a record of his sentiments as the knife plunged into his breast? Emotions are but the tricks of the devil, sent to tempt us into doubt and hesitation, and obscure the deeds committed, whether good or ill. No man of sense, I think, will ever pay them much attention, for they are a distraction, a surrender to womanish sentiment that should be concealed from the world if they cannot be suppressed in the heart. It is our task to overcome the passions, not digress on their intensity.

So I will say merely I was troubled that as fast as I made progress in one sphere, I was assaulted in the other. The more I stalked John Thurloe, the more demons stalked me, for I had not shaken off the concern generated by the succession of dreams and visitations, and my brain was so befuddled that their obvious cause was hidden. Instead, I fruitlessly pondered this disharmony as I trudged southward through the heartland of the wars, taking in, almost every mile, the continued record of destruction that had been meted out to the land. So many buildings, so many fine dwellings were still in disarray, their owners, like my own father, no longer having the money to rebuild. Manor houses burned out or dismantled for their stone, fields still abandoned and overgrown with weeds, for the tenants will not work without a firm hand to keep them in their place. I stopped in Southam in the midst of a fit of that melancholy which has always plagued me, and spent some money on a bleed in the hope that I might be rebalanced and fortified. Then, weakened by the experience, I spent more money on a bed for the night.

It was providential that I did, for I heard at the table that a great magus had passed through that same day, wise in healing and all matters of the spirit. The man who told me— who joked but was frightened within—said he was an Irishman, who had a guardian angel that extended protection over him, that he might never come to harm. He was one of the *adepti,* who could cure merely by passing his hands over the afflicted spot, and was in constant converse with spirits of all forms, which he could see as ordinary men see each other.

I heard, also, that this man was heading south, intending to make his way to London, for he was intent on offering his services to the king himself. This venture, I understand, came to nothing; his ability to cure by touch (and it was a real skill; I saw it myself, and many others attested to it) was considered presumptuous, for he said he could cure scrofula by this means, knowing full well that this is the prerogative of kings, and has been since time immemorial. Being Irish as well, he was naturally seen as subversive, and was constrained to leave London after only a short stay.

So, the next morning I set off, confident that my youthful legs, and early start, would soon allow me to catch up with this Valentine Greatorex and consult him about my problems. At least I knew I would not have to beg, since the money from my uncle's chest was still in my belt, and I could afford, for once, whatever was asked of me.

I caught up with him within a few hours at a village just on the Oxfordshire side of the border; he was staying at an inn and once I learned this I hired a room myself, then sent up word of my desire for an interview. I was summoned immediately.

I went to the meeting with some trepidation for, although I might have met a wizard before, I had never encountered an Irishman. I knew, of course, that they were terrible people, wild and disobedient, with a monstrous cruelty. The stories of the massacres they perpetrated on poor Protestants in late years were still fresh in my mind, and the way they continued to battle despite the chastisement meted out to them by Cromwell at Drogheda and other places proved that they were scarcely human in their bloody viciousness. I do believe that the only time Cromwell enjoyed the full and unrestrained support of the English was when he set out to subdue these murderous creatures.

Mr. Greatorex, however, satisfied neither my notion of what a wizard nor of what an Irishman should be like. I imagined him old, stooped, flame-haired and with wild, staring eyes. He was in fact scarcely a dozen years senior to myself, with a gentlemanly bearing, neat and precise movements and a solemnity of expression that would have done credit to a bishop. Until he spoke, he could have passed for a prosperous trader in any small town in the country.

His voice, however, was extraordinary, and I had never heard the like before, although I now know that the softness of expression and musicality of tone is characteristic of these people, who use words of honey to disguise their natures. As he plied me with questions, his words swept gently over me and I relaxed until I was aware of nothing in the room at all except his voice, and the gentleness of expression in his eyes. I understood, I think, how a rabbit must feel when it is frozen by the look of the snake, and how Eve must have felt also, willing to do anything at all to please the serpent, and earn more words of comfort from it.

Who was I? Where had I come from? How had I heard of him? About what did I wish to consult him? All these were necessary questions, and similar to the ones Widow Blundy had put to me to assure herself I was not sent to trap her. I answered fully until we came to my encounter with Sarah Blundy. Then Greatorex leaned forward in his chair.

"Let me tell you, sir," he said softly, "that it is a very great mistake to tell me lies. I do not take kindly to being deceived. I am not interested in how badly you behaved, although I can see you abused this girl shamefully."

"I did nothing of the sort," I protested. "She was willing; she must have been so, and put on the pretense afterwards in order to extract more money from me."

"Which you did not give her."

"I was generous enough."

"And now you fear you are cursed. Tell me your dreams."

I told him, and about the polecat. He listened quietly as I recounted each piece of evidence.

"It did not occur to you that the daughter of the cunning woman might be able to encompass such attacks?" I said it had not, but the moment he suggested the idea that Sarah Blundy was responsible, I realized that it was obvious and knew also that my inability to see was itself part of the enchantment she had laid on me.

"And have you spoken to her since?" Greatorex continued. "It may offend your dignity, but often the surest way of dealing with such matters is to make amends. If she accepts your apology, she must then remove any curse she has placed on you."

"And if she does not?"

"Then other measures will be required. But it is the best first step."

"I believe you are frightened of her. You do not think you can contend with her."

"I know nothing of the matter. If she truly has such power, then it would indeed be difficult. I see no shame in admitting it. Darkness is strong. But I have contested such people before, and, I think, have had as many victories as defeats. Now, tell me. What does she have of yours?"

I told him I did not understand the question but when he explained, I described the way she had scratched at my face with her nails and pulled some of my hair from my head. I had hardly spoken before he walked across to me. Before I could react in any way, he drew out a knife and grabbed me by the hair, dragging the knife across the back of my hand in one swift movement. Then he simply tore a lock from my head.

I jumped up cursing him with all my strength and inventiveness, the magic of his voice gone in an instant from my mind. Greatorex, however, merely resumed his seat as though nothing of importance had passed, and sat waiting for me to control myself.

"My apologies," he said when I had calmed. "But I needed blood and hair in the same circumstances in which she took it. The more painful the taking, the more powerful the relic. I believe that may be why such power is attributed to the relics of saints, and why the remains of martyrs who died in great agony are considered the most potent."

I clutched my head with my bloody hand and glared at him. "Papist nonsense," I growled. "What now?"

"Now? Now you go away for a few hours. To be certain that you are indeed bewitched, rather than merely believing so, and to discover what are the forces ranged against you, I need to cast your horoscope. It is the surest, indeed it is the only, way of penetrating the darkness. If only the courts would make more use of people like myself, then the process of the law would be that much the surer. But in this foolish age, it is frowned on. So much the worse for the age."

"I was told no witch has ever been caught by the law. Do you believe that?"

"Some have no doubt been punished by accident. But can the law apprehend such people if they do not wish it? No. I cannot credit it."

"So these women who have burned of late? They were falsely accused?"

"For the most part. Not deliberately, I am sure. There is too much evidence of the devil's presence among us for their existence to be gainsaid. Any sensible man must conclude that the powers of evil have been trying to seduce Christian women, taking advantage of the troubles that have so stirred the souls of men. Once authority is broken, Satan sees his chance. Besides, the only sensible argument against witchcraft is that women do not have souls, and therefore have nothing to trade with the devil. But this is flatly contradicted by all authority.''

"Nothing can be done, you think? Such people cannot be stopped?"

"Not by you lawyers."

"How do you know I am a lawyer?"

He smiled, but ignored the question. "The whole of existence is a contest between light and dark. All the battles that are important for mankind have been waged without most people even knowing they were taking place. God has given special powers to his servants on earth, the magi, white witches, adepti, call them what you will. They are men of secret knowledge charged with contending with Satan from generation to generation."

"You mean alchemists, people like that?"

He looked scornful. "Once, maybe, I meant such people. But their skill and power is waning. They seek now to explain what is, not to explore its power. Alchemy is now a mechanical trade, full of brews and potions which will be able to explain how things are made, but loses sight of the greater questions, of what they are for.''

"You are an alchemist?"

He shook his head. "No. I am an astrologer and, if you will, a necromancer. I have studied the enemy, and I know his powers. My skills are limited, but I know what I can do. If I can help you, I will. If not, I will tell you so.''

He stood up. "Now, you must give me the information I require, then leave me in peace for a few hours. I need the exact time of your birth, and the place of it. I need the time and place of your conjunction with this girl, and the times of your dreams and encounters with the animals.''

I gave him all that he required, and he dismissed me to walk around the village, which I was quite happy to do, for I knew it had been the scene of one of the battles of the war, in which my father had played a distinguished and noble role by advising the king so well that the day ended with the capture of all the enemy's cannon and the death of much of his force. Had the king kept my father close to him, rather than relying on the advice of better-born but less experienced men, the result might have been different. But the king came increasingly to rely on cowardly pen-pushers like Clarendon, who wanted merely to surrender, not to fight.

It is low-lying, lush land around the northern part of Oxfordshire, fine countryside for crop and cavalry, and its richness could be seen even when all was dead, the fields brown and still and the trees stripped of their leaves for winter. The hills give some concealment to troops, but do not greatly impede their movement, and the woods are small in scale and easily skirted. I walked out of the village and up the river, imagining in my mind how the two armies had slowly edged their way upstream, the king on one side, General Waller and the rebels on the other, watching each other like cocks in a ring for a slip which would give the slightest advantage. It was my father who gave the advice which turned the day, encouraging the king to move the van forward, and advance the rear at a slower pace, opening up a gap in the middle which he knew a man like Waller would not be able to resist. Sure enough, Waller sent a good portion of his horse and all his cannon over the little bridge at Cropredy, and they were still in disarray from breaking ranks to cross when the good Earl of Cleveland, warned of the tactic, fell upon them and cut them to ribbons.

It must have been a wonderful sight to have beheld; to have seen the cavalry, so far from their current perfumed dissolution, charging in perfect order, their sabers glistening in the sun, for I remember my father saying that it had been a warm, cloudless day of midsummer.

"Tell me," I asked of a laborer who passed me by, giving me the downcast look of sullen suspicion which all villagers adopt with foreigners. "Where is the tree the king dined under the day of the battle?"

He scowled at me, and made to sidle past me, but I grabbed him by the arm and insisted. He nodded in the direction of a small lane. "There is an oak tree in the field at the end of that track," he said. "That is where the tyrant ate."

I struck him, full in the face, for his impudence. "Mind your tongue," I warned him. "You will not talk like that in my presence."

He shrugged, as if my reproof was of no importance to

him at all. "I speak the truth," he said, "as is my duty and right."

"You have no rights and your sole duty is to obey," I replied incredulously. "The king was fighting to save us all."

"And on that day all my crops were trampled, my son killed and my house ransacked by his troops. What cause do I have to love him?"

I moved to hit him again, but he guessed my intention and shrank back like a dog that has been beaten too often, and so I waved the miserable creature to be out of my sight. But he had spoiled my mood; my plan of standing where the king had stood, so I could breathe in the atmosphere of the time, seemed less appealing now, and after a moment's hesitation, I turned back to the inn in the hope that Greatorex had finished his task.

He had not, and he made me wait a good hour before he came down the stairs bearing the sheets of paper which, supposedly, bore all my past and future on them in his little squiggles. His attitude and mood had changed, no doubt to frighten me and thus put up his fee; whereas before he had been relaxed and, I think, treated my tale with less than complete seriousness, now he had a heavy frown, and an air of the greatest concern.

I had never troubled before, and have troubled little since, with astrology. I care not to know what the future brings for, by and large, I already know. I have my place and in the fullness of time, tomorrow or thirty years hence, I shall die, as God wills. Astrology is of use only to those who do not know their position, or what it will be; its popularity is a mark of a people in distress and a society in torment. No doubt that is why such people as Greatorex were so much in demand during the troubles, for then a man could be a grandee one moment and less than nothing the next. I have no doubt that if the leveling principle prevails amongst us, and more men claim advancement merely for merit, then the fortunetellers will profit the more. Certainly, that was why I needed him then, and why I dismissed such people when I needed them no longer. No man who truly accepts the will of God can attend to astrology, I now think, for whatever happens is the goodness of Providence; if we accept that, we should not want to know more.

"Well?" I asked when he had composed his papers before me. "What is the answer?"

"It is disconcerting and worrying," he said, with a theatrical sigh. "And I hardly know what to make of it. We live in the strangest of times, and the heavens themselves bear witness to great prodigies. I myself know this; there is a great teacher, far greater than I can ever be, who might explain it to me if I can find him; I have traveled from Ireland for that express purpose, but so far with little success."

"Times are hard indeed," I said dryly. "But what about my chart?"

"It disturbs me greatly," he said, peering at me as though I was newly introduced to him, "and I scarcely know how to advise you. It seems you were born for a great purpose."

Perhaps this is the currency of all soothsayers, I do not know, but I felt that he was saying the truth, and I felt that it was so; what greater purpose was there, after all, than the one I had taken on myself? Greatorex's confirmation of it bolstered my strength greatly.

"You were born on the day the battle of Edgehill was fought," he continued, "a strange and frightening day; the skies were in disarray, and portents abounded."

I did not point out that you hardly needed to be an adept to see that.

"And you were born not greatly distant from the battle," he continued. "Which means your chart was affected by the events which went on around you. You know, of course, that the chart of the querent intersects with that of the country in which he is born?"

I nodded.

"So, you were born a Scorpio, with your ascendant in Libra. Now, as far as the question you pose is concerned, you asked it at exactly two o'clock, and it was for that time that I prepared the horoscope. The best sign of witchcraft is if the lord of the twelfth house be in the sixth, or if one planet be lord of the ascendant and the twelfth, which may happen when the proper ascendant may be intercepted, then it may be witchcraft. If the converse applies, however, and the lord of the ascendant be in the twelfth or sixth, then it shows that the querent occasioned his problems by his own willfulness.''

I sighed heavily, beginning to regret having placed myself in the hands of a canting magician. Evidently Greatorex perceived my disdain.

''Do not dismiss this, sir,'' he said. ''You think this is magic, yet it is not. It is the purest of science, the only way man has to penetrate the secrets of the soul and of time itself. Everything is performed through the finest of calculations, and if it is the case that the lowest is joined to the highest, as all Christians must believe, then it is obvious that the study of the one must reveal the truth of the other. Did not the Lord say, 'Let there be lights in the firmament of heaven to divide the day from the night; and let them be for signs'? Genesis 1:14. That is all astrology is; reading the signs that God in his providence has given us to guide our way if we will only take notice of them. Simple in theory, though hard in practice.''

''I do not for a moment doubt the truth of it,'' I said. ''But the details weary me. It is the answers that give me greatest concern. Am I bewitched or not?''

''You must let me answer in full, for a partial answer is no response at all. It is the conjunction of your birth chart with the transitional chart which is of the greatest concern to me; for they are strangely at odds. Indeed, I have never seen the like before.''

''So?''

''The transitional chart indicates clearly that some form of enchantment is present, for Venus, which rules your twelfth house, is most firmly in the sixth.''

''So the answer is yes.''

''Please; be patient. Your birth chart also places the ascendant in the twelfth, which indicates that you are inclined to be the author of your own misfortunes. The opposition of Jupiter and Venus makes you prone to magnify your problems without justification, and the conjunction of the moon in the ninth house and in Pisces means you are liable to fantastical notions that lead you into rash acts.

''Which indicates the need for caution in this matter, and

the most cautious move you can make is to acknowledge your fault. For you are at fault, and her anger has the force of justice behind it, whatever she might be. The easiest solution is not to fight it, but to ask forgiveness.''

''And if she refuses?''

''She will not if your contrition is genuine. I will make it the more plain. The indicator of the enchantment is in exact opposition to the conjunction of your troubles caused by Mars in the second house.''

''And what does that mean?''

''That means the two aspects of your life are one and the same. Your fear of bewitchment and what you tell me of your other troubles are intimately connected, so much so that the one is the other.''

I stared at him in astonishment, for he had said the same of my chart as Thomas had said of my dream. ''But how can that possibly be? She never knew my father, nor could she possibly have known him. Surely her power is not such that she can intervene in affairs of that importance.''

He shook his head. ''I state the situation, I cannot offer an explanation. But I do urge you to take my advice. This girl—this witch as you call her—is more powerful than any I have ever encountered.''

''More than you.''

''Far more than me,'' he said solemnly. ''And I am not ashamed to admit it. I would no more go against her than I would jump off the tallest cliff. And nor should you, for any victories will be illusory, and defeat will be total. Any counter-magic I can offer is unlikely to be of use, even if it has a temporary effect.''

''Give it to me anyway, so I know what to do.''

He thought for a moment, as if doubting my sudden enthusiasm. ''Do you give me your solemn word that you will take my advice and approach the girl first?''

''Of course, whatever you say,'' I said hastily. ''What is the spell? Give it to me.''

''You have to do it yourself.'' He handed me a phial containing the hair and the blood he had so violently taken from me. ''This is silver, which is the moon's metal. It contains a simulacrum of what she has of you. You must either get your own back from her and destroy it, to remove the object of her spells, or failing that, you must take this phial and fill it with her urine or her blood. Bury it when the moon is waning; as long as it is undiscovered, she will have no power over you.''

I took the phial and put it carefully in my bag. ''Thank you, sir. I am grateful. Now, what do I owe?''

''I am not finished. There is a matter far more grave.''

''I think I have heard enough, thank you. I have my potion, and want no more of you.''

''Listen, my friend, you are rash and foolish, and you do not listen well to those wiser than yourself. Please do so now, as a great deal is at stake.''

''Oh, very well. Tell me.''

''I repeat again, that the girl who is the focus of your attention is no ordinary witch, if she is one at all. You asked earlier whether I was afraid to contest witches, and the answer is no; generally speaking I am not. But in this case I am indeed very frightened. Do not engage with this creature, I beg you. And there is one other thing as well.''

''And what is that?''

''Others might take your fortune and livelihood, even your life. But your greatest enemy is yourself, for only you have the power to destroy your own soul. Tread carefully. Some people are fated from the moment of their birth, but I hold that nothing is absolutely preordained, and we can choose a different path if we will. I tell you what may be, not what must be.''

''Now you are talking nonsense, to frighten me and get more money.''

''Listen to me,'' he said, leaning forward and staring at me intently, using all his powers to bend me to his will. ''The conjunction of your birth is strange and frightening, and you should beware. I have seen it only once before. I do not wish to see it again.''

''And that was?''

''In a book I was allowed to see only once. It belonged to Placidus de Tito, and he had it by descent from Julius Maternus himself, the greatest magus of them all, perhaps. In it, there were many horoscopes, drawn from many periods.

It had the birth charts of Augustus and Constantine, of Augustine and many, many popes. There were soldiers and churchmen and politicians and doctors and saints. But only one did I see which was like yours and you must take warning from it, if you can and if you will. I tell you again that if you do not heed my warnings, then far more than your life is at risk.''

''And whose horoscope was it?''

He looked at me gravely, as though afraid to speak. ''It belonged to Iscariot,'' he said softly.

I AM QUITE PREPARED TO ADMIT THAT I LEFT THAT MAN shaken to the depths of my soul, terrified at what he told me and perfectly under his spell. I will even say that it took some considerable time before I recovered my balance, and was able to dismiss most of what he said as a tissue of nonsensical babblings. I give him full credit for his skill, for he had mixed a little knowledge with a great deal of impudence to forge a weapon of great power, able to command him large sums of money from the credulous. After a while, I was even able to laugh at the way he had imposed himself upon me, for I had quite believed him; he had sensed my fear and concern, and had exploited my worries to enrich himself.

How he did this, how all these people act, is clear after a little thought; his questioning taught him all he needed to know, and he then wrapped up in his magical words what I had already said, mixing it in with the sort of common advice my mother might well have given me. Add all this to obscure references to occult texts, and you have the perfect fraud—it is easy to succumb, and requires great effort of character to resist.

But resist I did, although I considered that there were a few nuggets among the dross I had received. To begin with, the very idea of begging that girl's pardon disgusted me, but wiser counsels prevailed as I lurched my way back to Oxford. What was my purpose, after all, but to remove the stain on my family and recover what was mine? If this girl was in some way bound up in that, then the sooner her malign influence was removed the better. I had, in fact, little faith in the man's magic; he had told me little that was remarkable, and much which was clearly wrong. I might have to resort to his spells, but I had little confidence in them and decided that, painful though it might be, an approach to the girl was the most likely, and the most direct, way of removing the problem.

Nonetheless, I decided first to discuss my investigations with Thomas and went to see him immediately on my return to see how his campaign was faring. I did not get around to my own problems for some time, so deep was he in misery. I learned then that my stratagem for helping him had not been as effective as I had desired, for Dr. Grove had dismissed Sarah Blundy when the rumors about his morals began to spread, and his action was seen as a sign of resolute sacrifice rather than an admission of guilt.

"Already they are saying that he is likely to get the living," Thomas said gloomily. "Of the thirteen senior Fellows, five have already offered their support to him, and some of those I counted on do not look me in the eye anymore. Jack, how could this have happened? You know what he is like, more than most people. I asked the warden for reassurance only this morning, but he was stiff and unfriendly to me."

"It is the changing times," I said. "Remember, many of Grove's old friends are in positions of influence close to the government. Even Warden Woodward must beware of displeasing the powerful at such a time. He was put in by Parliament and must give regular signs of conformity himself, lest he be put out again by the king.

"But don't despair," I said heartily, for his long face and heavy sighs were beginning to grate upon me, "the battle is not yet lost. You have a few weeks yet. You must keep cheerful, as there is nothing people like less than seeing reproach in a face at every meal. It will harden their hearts against you even more."

Another heavy sigh greeted these words of wisdom. "You are right, of course," he said. "I will do my best to look as though poverty was nothing to me, and seeing the lesser man win gave me the greatest of pleasure."

"Exactly. Just what you must do."

"So distract me," he said. "Tell me your progress. I trust you paid my respects to your mother?"

"I did indeed," I replied, even though I had forgotten, "and although I was not best pleased to see her, I learned much of interest from the trip. I have discovered, for example, that my own guardian, Sir William Compton, was persuaded to connive with my uncle to defraud me."

I said it with as much levity as I could manage, although bitterness gripped my heart as I explained the situation to him. Typically, he chose to search for a kindly explanation.

"Perhaps he thought it for the best? If, as you say, the estate was indebted, there was a risk you would be thrown into a debtors' prison the moment you reached your majority, then it was surely a kindness on his part."

I shook my head vehemently. "There is more to it, I know it," I said. "Why was he was so willing to believe that my father, his best friend, was guilty of such a crime? What had he been told? Who had told him?"

"Perhaps you should ask him."

"I intend to do just that, when I am ready. But first I have some other matters to attend to."

I FOUND SARAH BLUNDY LATE THAT EVENING AFTER A long wait; I had thought of going to her abode, but decided that I could not face mother and daughter together, and so stood at the end of the alley for upward of an hour before she emerged.

I do not mind admitting that my heart was beating fast as I approached, and that the wait had put me in a foul temper. "Miss Blundy," I said as I walked up behind her.

She spun round quickly and took a few steps backward, her eyes instantly blazing with the most vicious hatred. "Keep away from me," she spat, her mouth curled up in an ugly snarl.

"I must talk with you."

"I have nothing to say to you, nor you to me. Now leave me in peace."

"I cannot. I must talk to you. Please, I beg you, hear me out."

She shook her head and made to turn away and continue her journey. Much as I hated to do so, I ran round in front of her to block her path, and assumed the most supplicatory of expressions.

"Miss Blundy, I beseech you. Listen to me."

Perhaps my expression was more convincing than I thought, for she stopped and, assuming a look of defiance— mingled, I was glad to see, with some fear—waited.

"Well? I am listening. Speak, then leave me in peace."

I took a deep breath before I could bring myself to utter the words. "I have come to beg your pardon."

"What?"

"I have come to beg your pardon," I repeated. "I apologize."

Still she said nothing.

"Do you accept my apology?"

"Should I do so?"

"You must. I insist upon it."

"And if I refuse?"

"You will not refuse. You cannot refuse."

"I can easily do so."

"Why?" I cried. "How dare you talk to me in this way? I have come here as a gentleman, though I had no need to do so, and abased myself to acknowledge my fault, and yet you dare to refuse me?"

"You may have been born a gentleman; that is your misfortune. But your actions are those of one far lower than any man I have ever known. You violated me, although I gave you no cause to do so. You then spread foul and malicious rumors about me, so I am dismissed from my place, and jeered at in the streets, and called whore. You have taken my good name, and all you offer in return is your apology, said with no meaning and less sincerity. If you felt it in your soul, I could accept easily, but you do not."

"How do you know?"

"I see your soul," she said, her voice suddenly dropping to a whisper which chilled my blood. "I know what it is and what is its shape. I can feel it hiss in the night and taste its coldness in the day. I hear it burning, and I touch its hate."

Did I, or anyone else, need a franker confession? The calm

way she confessed to her power frightened me mightily, and I did my best to summon the contrition she wanted. But she was right on one score: I felt little; her devils made her see true.

"You are making me suffer," I said in desperation. "It must stop."

"Whatever you suffer is less than you deserve until you have a change of heart."

She smiled, and my breath caught in my throat as I saw the look on her face, for it confirmed everything I had feared. It was the clearest admission of guilt that any court of law ever heard, and I was only sorry that there was no one else around to witness that moment. The girl saw that I had understood, for she pitched up her face and let out a peal of laughter.

"Leave me be, Jack Prestcott, lest worse befall you. You cannot undo what has been done; it is too late for that, but the good Lord punishes those who transgress and will not repent."

"You dare speak of the Lord? How can you even utter His name?" I shouted in horror at the blasphemy. "What are you to do with Him? Talk of your own master, you fornicating witch."

Straightaway, her eyes flashed with the darkest anger, and she stepped forward and struck me on the face, grabbing my wrist and pulling my face to her own. "Never," she hissed in a dark voice which seemed more like that of a familiar than her own, "never talk to me like that again."

Then she pushed me away, her breast heaving with emotion, while I too was winded by the shock of the assault. Then, lifting her finger at me in a warning, she walked off, leaving me trembling in the middle of the empty street.

Less than an hour later, I was seized by a powerful griping of the guts which left me curled up on the floor, vomiting out my stomach so violently I could not even cry out in pain. She had renewed her attack.

I COULD NOT TALK TO THOMAS ABOUT THIS MATTER; HE could not give me any help at all. I doubt that he even believed in spirits; certainly he was of the opinion that the only proper response was prayer. But I knew that this would be insufficient; I needed a powerful counter-magic fast, and there was no means of getting it. What was I to do, run after Blundy and ask her if she wouldn't mind pissing in the bottle Greatorex had given me? Unlikely to be successful; nor did I feel like breaking into her cottage and ransacking it for the charm the Irishman said she must be using against me.

I must point out one thing here, which is that my account of my talk with Blundy is accurate in every single detail; it could hardly be other, for her words were engraved on my mind for years after. I say this, because it contained confirmation of everything I knew, and justification of everything that occurred thereafter. There is no room for doubt or misinterpretation: she threatened me with worse and she could hardly do me harm in any other way except through her magic. I do not need to persuade or assert on this matter: she admitted it quite freely when she had no need to do so, and it was only a matter of time before she made good on her promise. From that moment I knew that I was engaged in a battle which would end in the destruction of one or the other. I say this plainly, for it must be understood that I had no choice in what I did: I was desperate.

Instead of Thomas, I went to see Dr. Grove, for I knew that he still believed in the power of exorcism. He had once lectured us about this, when he had heard of an affair of sorcery in nearby Kineton when I was about fifteen. He warned sternly about dabbling with the devil and that evening, most strangely and generously, led us in prayer for the souls of those suspected of compacting with darkness. He told us that the invincibility of the Lord can so easily turn back Satan's powers, if it is genuinely desired by those who have delivered themselves into His arms, and it was one of his major contentions with the Puritans that, by disparaging the rite of exorcism, they not only lowered the priesthood in the eyes of the population (who continued to believe in spirits whatever their ministers said) but also removed a potent weapon in the never-ending battle.

Apart from catching a glimpse in the distance when once I was walking down the High Street a few months earlier, I hadn't cast eyes on him for nearly three years and I was surprised when I entered his presence once more. Fate had been kind to him. Whereas I remembered a man barely enough fed, with threadbare clothes a size too big for him and a mournful expression on his face, now here before me was a roly-poly character evidently too eager to make up for lost time in the matter of food and drink. I liked Thomas and wanted only the best for him but I felt then he was wrong in thinking Grove unqualified for the parish of Easton Parva. I could see him already, rolling down to the church after a good dinner and bottle of wine, to lecture his parishioners on the virtues of moderation. How they would love him, as well, for everyone likes a character to fit the part life has allotted him. The parish, I felt, would be a happier place with Grove as its leader than with Thomas, even if it would be less mindful of the awesome fear of the Lord's chastisement.

"I am glad I find you well, doctor," I said as he allowed me into his room, as packed with books and as littered with paper as I recall the quarters allotted to him at Compton Wynyates.

"You do indeed, Jack, you do indeed," he cried, "for I no longer have to teach snotty-nosed youths like yourself. And, if God's will be so, will shortly no longer have to teach anyone at all."

"I congratulate you on your escape from servitude," I replied as he gestured me to move a pile of books and sit down. "You must relish your improved estate. From being a family priest to being a Fellow of New College is a grand recovery for you. Not that we were not all extremely grateful for your earlier misfortune. For how else would we have had such a learned tutor?"

Grove grunted, pleased at the compliment, but half suspecting I was joking at his expense.

"It is indeed a great improvement," he said. "Although I was grateful to Sir William for his kindness, for if he had not taken me into his household, I would have starved. It was not a happy time for me, I'm sure you realize that. But then, it turned out to be an unhappy period for you as well. I hope that life as an undergraduate is more to your taste."

"Well enough, thank you. Or at least it was. At present, I am in grave trouble, and I need to beg you for help."

Grove seemed concerned at this bald statement and earnestly asked what was the matter. So I told him everything.

"And who is this witch?"

"A woman called Sarah Blundy. I see you know the name."

Grove looked dark and angry at the mere mention, and I thought that perhaps it might have been better had I not said, but in fact I did well.

"She has caused me great grief recently. Very great grief."

"Ah, yes," I said vaguely. "I did hear some slanderous talk."

"Did you indeed? Might I ask from whom?"

"It was nothing, merely tavern gossip. I had it from a man called Wood. I straightaway told him his words were shameful. I came close to boxing his ears, I must say."

Grove grunted once more, then thanked me for my kindness. "Not many people would have had such an honorable response," he said curtly.

"But you see," I continued, pressing my advantage, "she is a dangerous character, in one way or another. Everything she does causes trouble."

"The witchcraft is confirmed by astrology?"

I nodded. "I do not trust this Greatorex absolutely, but he was adamant that I was bewitched and that she was formidably powerful. And there can be no other source of it. As far as I am aware, no one else has cause to resent me in any way."

"And you have been attacked in your head and your guts, is that right? By animals, and visited in dreams."

"On several occasions, yes."

"But if I remember, you had such headaches when you were a child as well, is that not the case, or is my memory playing false?"

"All people have headaches," I said. "I was not aware that mine were of any greater intensity."

Grove nodded. "I feel you are a troubled soul, Jack," he continued in a kindly fashion. "Which distresses me, for you were a happy child, even though wild and untameable. Tell me, what concerns you, that your face is become set in such an angry expression?''

''I am under a curse.''

''Apart from that. You know there is more than this.''

''Do I need to tell you? Surely you know the disasters that have afflicted my family. You must; you were in Sir William Compton's family long enough.''

''Your father, you mean?''

''Of course. What distresses me most is that my family, my mother in particular, wishes to forget the whole matter. There is my father, his memory weighed down by this accusation, and no one except myself seems concerned to defend him.''

I had misjudged Grove, I think, for I had a childish apprehension of seeing him, half expecting that the passing of years would be as nothing and he would again pull out his rod; it was as well that he was more able to treat me as an adult than I was to think as one. Rather than telling me what to do, or lecturing me, or giving advice I did not wish to hear, he instead said very little, but listened to me as we sat there in his darkening room, without even getting up to light a candle when the evening lengthened. Indeed, until I spoke of my troubles that evening in New College, I had not realized I had so very many of them.

Perhaps it was Grove's way of religion that made him so quiet, for although no papist, yet he believed in the confessional, and would give absolution in secret for those who truly desired it, and whom he trusted to keep their mouths shut. In fact, it occurred to me that, if I so wished, I could at that very moment blight his chances forever and secure Thomas's place. All I had to do was beg him to hear me, and then report him to the authorities as a hidden Catholic. Then he would be too dangerous for preferment.

I did not do so, and perhaps it was a mistake. I thought Thomas was young, and another parish would come along in due course. It is natural (so I now know) for youth to be in a hurry, but ambition must be tempered by resignation; enthusiasm by deference. I did not think so then, of course, but I like to believe there was more than simple self-interest in my decision to spare Grove from the disgrace I could have visited upon him so easily.

Self-interest there was, as I shall reveal; in fact I later wondered at the mystery of Providence which led me to him, for my distress led me to my salvation, and turned the curse under which I labored into the agent of my success. It is remarkable how the Lord can take evil and turn it into good, can use a creature like Blundy to reveal a hidden purpose quite the opposite to the intended hurt. In such things, I believe, are the true miracles of the world, now that the age of prodigies is past.

For Grove was teaching me again, in the best disputational fashion, and I never had a better lesson. Had my real tutors been so skilled, I might even have taken to my legal studies with more of a will, for in his hands I understood, if only fleetingly, the heady brew that argument can be; in the past he had confined his instruction to fact, and drilled us ceaselessly in the rules of grammar and suchlike. Now that I was a man and entered into that age when rational thought is possible (a sublime state, given to man alone, and denied by God's will to children, animals and women), he treated me as such in matter of education. Wisely, he used the dialectic of the rhetor to examine the argument; he ignored the facts, which were too tender in my mind, and concentrated on my presentation to make me think anew.

He pointed out (his arguments were too close for me to remember the precise stages of his reasoning, so I present here only an outline of what he said) that I had presented an *argumentum in tres partes;* formally correct, he said, but lacking the necessary resolution and thus incomplete in evolution and hence in logic. (As I write this, I realize I must have paid more attention to my lessons than I knew, for the nomenclature of the scholar comes back to me surprisingly easily.) Thus the *primum partum* was my father's disgrace. The *secundum* was my penury through being disinherited. The *tertium* was the curse I had fallen under. The task of the logician, he pointed out, was to resolve the problem, and unify the parts into a single proposal, which could then be advanced and subjected to examination.

So, he said, consider afresh. Take the first and the second

parts of your argument. What are the common threads which link them together?

"There is my father," I said. "Who is accused and who lost his land."

Grove nodded, pleased that I could remember the basics of logic, at least, and was prepared to lay out the elements in the correct fashion.

"There is myself, who suffers as a son. There is Sir William Compton, who was executor of the estate and comrade of my father in the Sealed Knot. That is all I can think of at present."

Grove inclined his head. "Good enough," he said. "But you must take it further, for you maintained that without the accusation, the first part, your land would not have been lost, the second part. Is that not the case?"

"Yes."

"Now, was this an indirect, or a direct causation?"

"I don't know that I understand."

"You posit a minor accident; that the second was an indirect consequence of the first, without examining the possibility that perhaps the link was the inverse. You cannot argue, of course, that the loss of your land caused your father's disgrace, for that would be temporally impossible and thus absurd. But you might perhaps argue that the *prospect* of losing the land led to the accusation, and that in turn led to the actual loss; the *idea* of alienation generated the *reality* through the *medium* of accusation."

I stared at him in bewilderment as the words hit home, for he had spoken the suspicion that had nagged at me ever since that night I spent in my uncle's office. Could this possibly be the case? Could the accusation that destroyed my father have been prompted by nothing more than greed?

"Are you saying . . . ?"

"I am not saying anything at all," Dr. Grove said. "Except to suggest that you think through your arguments with greater care."

"You are deceiving me," I said. "Because you know something of this matter which I do not. You would not direct me to think in this direction if you had not good reason to do so. I know you well, doctor. And your way of argument would also suggest that I must consider the other obvious form of accident.''

"Which is?"

"Which is that the link connecting the two states of accusation and alienation is the fact that my father was indeed guilty.''

Grove beamed. ''Excellent, young man. I am pleased with you indeed; you are thinking with the detachment of the true logician. Now, can you see any other? We may, I think, leave out random misfortune, which is the argument of the atheist.''

I thought long and hard, as I was pleased that I had pleased, and wished to win more praise; I had rarely done so in lessons and I found it a strange and warming experience.

"No,'' I said eventually. "Those are the two main categories which must be considered. Everything else must be a sub-class of the two alternative propositions.'' I paused for a moment. "I do not wish to diminish this conversation, but even the best of arguments requires some matter of fact to give it ballast. And I have no doubt that at some stage you will indicate that in crucial areas this is lacking.''

"You are beginning to talk like a lawyer, sir,'' Grove said. "Not like a philosopher.''

"This is surely a question where law is applicable. Logic can only advance you so far. There must be some way of distinguishing between the two propositions, which are either that my father is guilty or that he is not. And that cannot be accomplished by metaphysics alone. So tell me. You know something of the circumstances.''

"Oh, no,'' he said. "There I must disabuse you entirely. I only met your father the once, and while I found him a handsome, robust man I can hardly offer any judgment or even assessment of him. And I heard of his disgrace only incidentally when I overheard—quite by chance—Sir William telling his wife that he felt obliged to tell what he knew.''

"What?'' I said, lurching forward in my seat with such violence that I believe I frightened the man. "You heard what?''

Grove queried me with an air of genuine bafflement. "But you must know this, surely?" he said. "That Sir William was the person who made public the accusations? You were in the house at the time. Surely you heard something of what was happening?"

"Not a word. When was this?"

He shook his head. "Early in 1660, I believe. I cannot really remember with any exactness."

"What happened?"

"I was in the library, searching out a volume, for Sir William gave me free run of his books for as long as I was there. It is not the best of libraries, but it was a small oasis in the desert for me, and I drank there frequently. You remember the room, no doubt; it faces east for the most part, but turns a corner toward the end, and off there is the office in which Sir William conducted all the domestic business of the estate. I never disturbed him in it, because he always got into a fearsome temper when he had anything to do with money; it brought home his reduced state too painfully. Everyone knew to steer clear of him for many hours afterward.

"On this occasion his wife did not, and that is why I know to tell you this. I saw little, and did not hear all, but through a crack in the door as it stood ajar, I saw that good lady on her knees before her husband, imploring him to think carefully about what he was to do.

"My mind is decided," he said, not unkindly, even though he was unused to having his actions queried. "My trust has been betrayed, and my life sold. That a man could act in such a way is difficult to imagine, that a friend could do so intolerable. It cannot go unpunished."

"But are you sure?" my lady asked him. "To level such an accusation against a man like Sir James, who has been your friend twenty years, and whose son you have brought up almost as your own, cannot be done in error. And you must bear in mind that he will—he must—challenge you. And such a contest you would lose."

"I will not fight him," Sir William replied, more kindly this time, for he could see that his wife was concerned. "I acknowledge my inferiority in arms. Nor do I have the least doubt that my accusations are the absolute truth. Sir John

Russell's warning leaves no doubt of that at all. The letters, the documents, the notes of the meetings he had from Morland; I can confirm many of them from my own knowledge. I know his handwriting and I know his cipher.''

''Then the door shut, and I heard no more; but my lady spent the next few days in great distress, and Sir William was more than usually preoccupied. He left for London at the end of the week, in a most secret departure, and I imagined there communicated his suspicions and evidence to others in the king's circle.''

I almost laughed as I heard this tale, for I remembered those times well. Sir William Compton had indeed left the house and galloped away one morning. The household had been somber indeed the previous few days, as though the body was taking a sickness from the head which rules it, and I remember again Sir William talking to me before he left and telling me that I must soon leave. It was time he said, to return to my own people, as I was old enough to attend to my duties. My childhood was now over.

Three days later, the day after Sir William rode away at dawn, I was put on a cart with all my belongings and sent to my uncle. I had not known anything of the storm that had been brewing under my very nose.

BUT THE WAY I LEFT COMPTON WYNYATES IS FAR FROM my story, and I must tell more of my meeting with Dr. Grove. On the matter I had called on him for, he refused to help. He would not perform an exorcism, for Blundy had reached into his soul ahead of me, and made his selfishness such that he was afraid to open himself to criticism at this most delicate moment of his career. Try as I might, I could not persuade him; all he would say was that, if I could provide him with better demonstration of the enchantment, then he would reconsider the matter. Until then, he would only offer that we might pray together. I did not wish to offend him, but I demurred at the prospect of spending an evening on my knees; besides, the news he had given me had galvanized my senses, and I was willing, for a while, to put all superlunary matters aside.

The important thing was that I now had a further connection in my chain of deceit, and I questioned the doctor closely on the matter. *Documents he had off Morland via Sir John Russell.* Which meant that Sir John had merely forwarded these materials from someone else. He was happy to spread the rumor, it seemed, but had not initiated it. Was that a fair inference? Dr. Grove said it sounded so, although he was sure that Russell had acted in good faith. But he could not help me further about the source. It was infuriating; one word from Russell would have saved me much trouble but I knew, from the way he had behaved in Tunbridge, that I would never hear that word from his lips. As I left Grove's room in New College, I decided it was time to visit Mr. Wood.

In my haste and excitement, I had forgotten one important detail, and as the heavy studded door of Wood's house in Merton Street was dragged open I remembered that Sarah Blundy was employed by the family. To my great relief, however, it was not the girl who opened, but Wood's mother, who looked not at all pleased to see me, even though it was not late.

"Jack Prestcott's compliments to Mr. Wood, and he would beg the indulgence of an interview," I said. I could see she was half-minded to tell me to go away, and return only when an appointment was made, but she relented and instead gestured for me to enter. Wood came down to meet me a few moments later, also looking not best pleased. "Mr. Prestcott," he said when all the bowing was done, "I am surprised to see you. I wish I could have had more time to prepare for the honor."

I ignored the rebuke, and told him that it was a matter of urgency. I was in town only for a short while. Wood grumbled like the fusspot he was, pretended that he had so many matters of import to deal with, then gave way and led me to his room.

"I am surprised not to see that Blundy girl here," I said as we climbed back up the stairs. "She does work as a maid for you, does she not?"

Wood looked uncomfortable. "We discussed the matter,"

he said, "and decided it would be best to dismiss her. Probably a sensible decision, and certainly the best for my family's reputation. But I am not content with it, nonetheless. My mother was very partial to her. Remarkably so, in fact; I could never account for it."

"Perhaps she was bewitched," I said as lightly as possible. Wood gave me a look which indicated something of the same had passed through his mind.

"Perhaps," he replied slowly. "Strange how we all end in thrall to our servants."

"Some servants," I said. "Some masters."

A suspicious, furtive look showed he had seen the criticism but wished to deflect it. "You are not here to talk about the difficulty of hiring reliable maids, I think," he said.

I told him of my problem, and something of my interview with Dr. Grove. "I know this evidence, presumably the same material Lord Mordaunt told me about, was made known to the world by Sir William. I now know he had them via Sir John Russell from someone called Morland. Now, who is Morland?"

"That, I think," he said as he scurried around the room like a lost mole, searching through one pile of papers after another until he came onto the pile he needed, "that, I think is not a great mystery. I think this must be Samuel Morland."

"And he is . . . ?"

"He is now, I understand, Sir Samuel. Which is in itself quite remarkable, and gives much food for thought. He must have rendered a very signal service to be so favored, considering his past. Unmasking a traitor in the king's ranks might well qualify."

"Or passing forged documents which purported to do so."

"Oh, indeed," Wood said, nodding his head and snuffling. "Indeed, for Morland was noted for what you might call his penmanship. He worked in Thurloe's office for some time, I believe, and even tried to succeed him when Thurloe was thrown out in the last days of the Protectorate, if I remember the story properly. Then, I think, he threw in his lot with the Royalists. His timing was impeccable."

"So the idea of forged documents does not strike you as being absurd."

Wood shook his head. "Either your father was guilty, or he was not. If he was not then some device must have been employed to create the illusion of culpability. But the only way you will find out, I think, is to tackle Morland himself. He lives somewhere in London, I imagine. I was told by Mr. Boyle that he concerns himself with hydraulic engines for drainage schemes and suchlike. They are said to be most ingenious."

I almost fell on my knees to thank the silly little man for the information, and had the grace to admit that Thomas had been correct in recommending him to me. As quickly as was decent, I left that house. The next morning, after a night made sleepless by my fevered excitement, I coached to London.

chapter eleven

I HAD NEVER BEEN IN A LARGE METROPOLIS BEFORE; Oxford was by far the grandest town I had ever entered. Most of my life had been spent either on country estates where the largest habitation was a village of a few hundred souls, or small market towns, such as Boston or Warwick, with populations of only a few thousand. London (so I am told, although I do not believe anyone knows for certain) contained then some half million people. It sprawled over the landscape like a vast, bleeding pustule on the face of the earth, sickening the land, and poisoning all who lived in it. I was at first fascinated, as I pulled up the leather to peer out of the coach window, but this amazement turned to disgust as I perceived the shocking meanness of life in such a place. I am not (as must be clear by now) much of a bookman, but there is a line in a poem which I was forced to construe by Dr. Grove in my youth, which has stuck with me. I do not recall the poet, but he was obviously a wise and sober man, for he said, "I cannot live in the city, for I have not learned to lie." So it always will be; the honesty of the country man is at a disadvantage in the town, where duplicity is prized, and straightforwardness scorned, where all men look after only themselves, and generosity occasions only laughter.

Before I made enquiries for Sir Samuel Morland, I decided I needed as much to collect myself and prepare myself for the interview which lay ahead. So I took my pack and walked across the great thoroughfare which links London with Westminster (although there is so much construction it will soon be completely impossible to discern where one city ends and the other begins) and took myself northward to find a place which sold something to eat and drink. I soon came to a *Piazza* (as it is called, though *square* should be good enough for any Englishman) which I am told can stand equal with any in Europe. It did not seem so grand to me; the buildings were ruined by the squalor all around, of women selling vegetables, and dirt and waste trampled underfoot. There were eating houses there, but the prices were such that I removed myself in horror at the audacity of the owners. Round the corner was another street which seemed much calmer, although again I was deceived, for this Drury Lane was accounted one of the most vile and dangerous in the city, full of bawds and cutthroats. All I saw was the theater, shortly to open, and witnessed the actors in the uniforms which won them protection from the law, and mighty ridiculous they looked.

From Covent Garden, I walked to London, diverting only up a squalid alley near St. Paul's Cathedral to leave my possessions in a dingy little tavern I had been told was both cheap and honest. It was so, but unfortunately did not accompany these virtues by being quiet and clean as well. The blankets were crawling with lice, and such evidence as there was indicated that my future bedmates were less than genteel. But I had lice in my hair anyway, so decided there was little point in spending my money on better. Then I began to make enquiries about Sir Samuel Morland. It did not take long to find his address.

It was an old house in an ancient street near Bow Church and, I don't doubt, was one of those burned to the ground a few years later in the fire, for it was an ancient construction of wood and thatch which would have been the more attractive had any care been taken on its upkeep. That, of course, is another problem with city life, as when owners are not the same as inhabitants, then no care is taken of buildings, and they molder and decay, casting a distemper on the streets and becoming a breeding ground for vermin. The lane itself was narrow and dark from the overhanging storys above, and a riot of noise from the traders who plied their wares up and down its length. I looked for the sign of an ox as instructed, but it was so discolored that I walked up and down twice before I realized that the tattered and broken piece of wood above one door had once carried such an image on it.

When the door opened, I was not even asked my business but was invited in with no ceremony at all.

"Is your master at home?" I asked the man at the door, who was as disgraceful looking a servant as ever I had come across, covered in dirt and dressed in the foulest of clothes.

"I have no master," said this creature in surprise.

"Forgive me. I must be at the wrong house. I am looking for Sir Samuel Morland."

"I am he," he replied, so that it was now my turn to look astonished. "Who are you?"

"My name is . . . ah . . . Grove," I said.

"I am delighted to make your acquaintance, Mr. Grove."

"And I yours, sir. I am sent by my father. We own some marshland in Dorset, and have heard reports of your ingenuity in drainage . . ."

I could not even finish my lie, for Morland grabbed me by the hand and pumped it up and down. "Excellent," he said, "Excellent indeed. And you wish to see my engines, do you not? Use them to drain your land?"

"Well . . ."

"If they work, eh? I see your mind perfectly, young man. What if this inventor is a fraud? Best to spy out the land, so to speak, before committing funds. You are tempted, because you know of the ingenuity of the Dutch, and how they have increased the yield of their land an hundredfold, and turned marsh into the richest pasture, but you do not fully believe it. You have heard of the fen drainage, and the use of pumps there, but do not know if they would be appropriate for you. That is the case, is it not? Do not bother to deny it. It is well for you that I am not a suspicious man, and freely show my designs to all who desire to see them. Come," he said cheerfully, grabbing my arm once more and pulling me to a door, "come this way."

In some bemusement at this behavior, I was dragged from the small entrance hall into a large room beyond. I guessed it had once been the house of a woolen merchant, and had been used for storing bales. Certainly it was very much larger than the frontage of the house suggested (these merchants always play poor, and hide their wealth from public view) and sweet and fresh from the wide-open doors at the end, which gave in so much light despite the time of year that I was briefly dazzled.

"What do you think? Impressive, eh?" he said, mistaking the hesitation this caused for astonishment. When I could see clearly again, though, I was indeed astonished, for I had never seen such a collection of bric-a-brac in my life. A dozen desks, and each one overflowing with strange instruments and bottles and casks and tools. Bits of wood and metal were stacked up against the walls, and the floors were covered in shavings and pools of greasy liquid and cuttings of leather. Two or three servants, probably those artisans able to make up engines to his designs, were at work at benches, filing metal and planing wood.

"Extraordinary," I replied, as he clearly wanted me to express some approbation.

"Look," he said enthusiastically, again removing the obligation to speak. "What do you think of this?"

We were standing in front of a finely carved oak table, which was empty save for an extraordinary little device, scarcely bigger than a man's hand, of beautifully wrought and engraved brass. On top were eleven small wheels, each one carved with numbers. Below, in the body of the machine, was a long plate which evidently concealed other dials, for small holes cut in the surface revealed yet more numbers.

"Beautiful," I said. "But what is it?"

He laughed in delight at my ignorance. "It is a calculating machine," he said proudly, "the finest in the world. Not, alas, unique, as some little Frenchman has one, but" (he lowered his tone to a confidential whisper) "his doesn't work very well. Not like mine."

"What do you do with it?"

"You calculate, of course. The principle is the same as Napier's bones, but far more ingenious. The two sets of wheelwork registers numbers from one to ten thousands, or from halfpennies up, if you wish it for finance. The handle engages this by a series of cogs, so that they turn over in the correct proportion. Clockwise for addition, anti-clockwise for subtraction. My next machine, which is not yet perfected, will be able to calculate square roots and cubes and even perform trigonometry.''

''Very useful,'' I said.

''Indeed. Every counting-house in the world will shortly have one, if I can find a way of telling them of it. It will make me a rich man, and experimental science will advance in leaps and bounds when it is no longer confined to adepts in mathematical calculation. I sent one some time ago to Dr. Wallis at Oxford, as he is the best man in that business this country has.''

''You know Dr. Wallis?'' I asked. ''I am acquainted with him myself.''

''Oh yes, although I have not seen him of late.'' He paused and smiled inwardly to himself. ''You might say we were by way of being in business together once.''

''I will send your salutations, if you so wish.''

''I do not know that he would greatly welcome them. My thanks for the offer, nonetheless. But it is not what you are here for, I know. Come into the garden.''

So we left his arithmetical engines, thank heavens, and I followed him out into the open air, where he paused in front of what seemed to be a large barrel with a tall tube coming out of the top. This he regarded with a sad, wistful look on his face, then shook his head heavily and sighed.

''Is this what you wished to show me?''

''No,'' he said regretfully. ''This I have reluctantly abandoned.''

''Why is that? Does it not work?''

''Far from it. It works too well. It was an attempt to harness the power of gunpowder to the problem of pumping. You see, it is a great problem in mining. The distance below the earth of mines these days—sometimes four hundred feet or more—means that the effort required to extract water, which means raising it by an equivalent distance, is formidable. Do you know the weight of a tube of water four hundred feet high? Of course not. If you did, you would be astounded at the audacity of man in even thinking of the idea.

Now you see, my conception was to get a sealed container above earth filled with air which descended into the water below ground, with another linked tube coming up into the open.''

I nodded, although he had largely lost me already. ''In the container, you explode a small measure of gunpowder, which causes a great rise in tension within. This rushes down the one tube, and forces the water up the other. Repeated often enough, you would get a constant flow of water upward.''

''Sounds splendid.''

''It does. Unfortunately, I have not yet thought of a way of ensuring explosions of the right quality and consistency. Either the tube bursts, which is dangerous, or you get a single plume of water fifty feet high which then stops. I have a patent on the idea, so I am in no danger of being overtaken by rivals, but unless I figure out the solution a very good idea may well be wasted. I have considered using heated water, because water turned into vapors demands a much larger space—some two thousand times, did you realize that?—and acquires irresistible strength in the process. Now, if some way could be made to force the vapor down the tube, or into some pumping mechanism, then the strength required to lift the water would be there.''

''And the problem?''

''The problem is making the hot vapors go in the direction required, rather than in any other.''

I understood scarce a word, but his animation and enthusiasm were such that I could imagine no way of shutting off the flow of words from his mouth. Besides, my willingness to listen seemed to endear me to him, and thus rendered him more likely to give me the information I required. So I plied him with questions, and affected the gravest of interest in all those matters which normally would have excited nothing but my contempt.

''So you do not have a pump which works, is that what you are telling me?'' I asked eventually.

''Pumps? Of course. Pumps aplenty. All sorts of pumps. Chain pumps and suction pumps and cylinder pumps. I do not yet have an *efficient* pump, an *elegant* pump, which will perform its allotted task with simplicity and grace.''

"So what about these fens? What is used there?"

"Oh, that," he said almost scornfully. "That is a different matter entirely. Of little interest at all in matter of technique." He glanced at me, and remembered, again, why I was there. "But, of course, all the better an investment for that, as it requires no novelty. The problem is a simple one, you see, and simple problems should best have simple solutions. Do you not agree?"

I agreed.

"Many areas of fenland," he said, "lie beneath the level of the sea, and properly should actually be underneath the sea, very much as the greater part of the Low Countries should be, because, if not, they would have to change their name."

He chuckled at his little joke awhile, and I joined in politely. "You know this, of course. Now, it is easy enough to prevent more water from entering by building dikes; the Hollanders have been doing this for centuries, so it cannot be very difficult. The problem is to evacuate the water that is already there. How is this to be done?"

I confessed my ignorance, which pleased him.

"Rivers are the simplest; you cut a new river, and the water flows away. Pipes are another. Wooden pipes underground which collect the water and allow it to flow off. The problem with that is that it is both expensive and slow. What is more, the land around (you remember) is higher, as is the sea. So where is this water to go?"

I shook my head again. "Nowhere," he said with vehemence. "It cannot go anywhere, for water will not flow uphill. Everyone knows that. This is why much of the fenland has not been completely drained. With my pumps, you see, the problem can be overcome and in the contest between man's wishes and nature's desires, nature can be made to yield a victory. For water will indeed flow uphill, and be carried off, leaving the land useful."

"Excellent," I said. "And very profitable."

"Oh, indeed. Those gentlemen who have formed a company for the drainage of their lands will become prosperous indeed. And I hope to turn a profit myself, for I have some land there, in Harland Wyte. Sir? Are you all right?"

I felt almost as though I had been struck a heavy blow in my stomach, for the mention of Harland Wyte, my family land, the heart of my father's entire estate, was so unexpected that it left me breathless, and I fear must almost have given myself away by the way I turned pale and gulped for air.

"Forgive me, Sir Samuel," I said, "I am prone to this momentary light-headedness. It will pass." I smiled reassuringly, and pretended to be recovered. "Harland Wyte, you say? I do not know it. Have you owned it long?"

He smirked cunningly. "Only a few years. It was a great bargain, for it was going cheap and I saw its value better than those selling it."

"I'm sure you did. Who was the seller?"

But he brushed my question aside and would not be drawn, preferring to expand on his cleverness than on his turpitude. "Now I will complete the drainage, then sell it on, and pocket a handsome profit. His Grace the Duke of Bedford has already agreed to purchase it, since he already owns most of the land all around."

"I congratulate you on your good fortune," I said, giving up the line of enquiry and trying another approach. "Tell me, sir, how you know Dr. Wallis? I ask as he has tutored me on occasion. Does he consult you on his experimentations and mathematics?"

"Good heavens, no," Morland replied with sudden modesty. "Although I am a mathematician myself I freely admit that he is my superior in all respects. Our connection was very much more worldly, for we both at one stage were employed by John Thurloe. Of course, I was a secret supporter of His Majesty's cause, whereas Dr. Wallis was a great man for Cromwell in those days."

"You surprise me," I said. "He seems a loyal subject now. Besides, what services could a priest and mathematician provide for someone like Thurloe?"

"Many and varied," Morland said with a smile at my innocence. "Dr. Wallis was the finest maker and breaker of codes in the land. He was never beaten, I think; never yielded to a stronger in cryptographical technique. For years Thurloe used his services; bundles of letters in code would be sent to him in Oxford, and the translations would come back on the next coach. Remarkable. We almost felt like telling the king's men that they really should not waste their time putting letters into code at all, for if we captured them, Wallis could always read them. If he is your tutor, you should ask to see some; I'm sure he has them still, although he naturally does not advertise such records of his past activities.''

''And you knew Thurloe as well? That must have been extraordinary.''

He was flattered by the compliment, and this goaded him to try and impress me the more. ''Indeed. I was almost his right-hand man for three years.''

''You are a family connection of his?''

''Oh, dear me no. I was sent as an envoy to Savoy to plead on behalf of the persecuted Protestants. I was there for several years, and kept my eye on exiles there as well. So I was useful, and became trusted and was offered the post when I returned. Which I kept until I fled when discovered passing intelligence to His Majesty.''

''His Majesty is lucky in his servants, then,'' I said, despising the man suddenly for his self-satisfaction.

''Not all of them, by any means. For every loyal man like myself, there was another who would have sold him for a bag of sovereigns. I unmasked the worst of them by making sure that some of the documents Wallis produced were seen by the king.''

I was so close, I knew it. If I could only keep calm so that his suspicions were not aroused, I knew I could tease unheard-of treasures from him.

''You hint that Dr. Wallis and yourself are no longer on good terms. Is it because of what happened in those days?''

He shrugged. ''It no longer matters. It is all past now.''

''Tell me,'' I said, insisting, and I knew the moment the words were out of my mouth that I had pushed too far. Morland's eyes narrowed, and the air of eccentric good humor drained out of him like sour wine from a bottle.

''Perhaps you have acquired more interests at Oxford than in your studies, young man,'' he said quietly. ''I would advise you to go back to your Dorset estate, and concern yourself with that, if indeed any such estate exists. It is a dangerous business for any man to occupy himself with matters that are none of his affair.''

He took me by the elbow and tried to guide me to the front door. I shook my arm free scornfully, and turned to confront him. "No," I said, confident that he would be no match for me, and that I could shake the information out of him if I so wished. "I wish to know . . ."

The sentence went uncompleted. Morland clapped his hands, and instantly a door opened, and a rough-looking man came into the room, a dagger thrust obtrusively in his belt. He said nothing, but stood awaiting orders.

I do not know whether I could have defeated such a man; it is possible, but it was just as possible that I would not. He had the air of the old soldier about him, and was certainly far more experienced in swordplay than I was myself.

"You must excuse my conduct, Sir Samuel," I said, controlling myself as best I could. "But your stories are fascinating. It is true I have heard many tales at Oxford, and they interest me greatly, as they must all young men. You must forgive the enthusiasm and curiosity of youth."

My words did not conciliate him. His suspicion, once aroused, could not be laid to rest. In his years of deceit and duplicity he had no doubt learned the value of silence, and he was not to be tempted into taking any risk. "Show this gentleman out," he said to the servant. Then he bowed to me politely, and withdrew. I was back on the noisy street outside a few moments later, cursing myself for my stupidity.

IT WAS OBVIOUS BY THIS STAGE THAT I NEEDED TO GET back to Oxford. My quest was nearing its end and the answer to my remaining questions lay in that county. But it was too late to leave, as the next coach did not go until the following day. Had I been less exhausted, the constant scratching of the fleas in the straw pallet that was my communal bed would have irritated, and the noise of my companions disgusted, my senses. As it was, they occasioned no dismay at all, once I had securely bound my money bag to my waist, and ostentatiously placed my dagger under my pillow so that all could see that they were to beware of taking advantage of my sleep.

The following morning I dawdled like a true gentleman of leisure, slowly drinking a pint of ale with my bread, and only leaving the place when the sun was well up.

As I had nothing better to do, I played the viewer of sights, visiting St. Paul's Cathedral—a scandalously run-down pile of stone, quite reduced from its former glory by the depredations of the Puritans, and yet more glorious in its decrepitude than the ill-formed conceit which is now being built to replace it. I watched the booksellers and hawkers of pamphlets who congregated in St. Paul's yard, and listened to the criers and constables reciting the list of crimes and deceits which had been the previous night's crop of malice. So many thefts, assaults, riots, it seemed the whole town must have been up all night to have committed them. Then I walked to Westminster and saw the palace and gazed in awe at the very window from which King Charles stepped to his bloody martyrdom, covered now in black crepe to commemorate that evil deed, and reflected awhile on the punishments the nation had endured because of that sinful act.

Such entertainments tired me quickly, though, so I bought myself some more bread from a street seller, and walked back through Covent Garden, which was no more agreeable to my senses now than it had been the previous day. I was hungry, and trying to decide whether to spend the vast quantity of money needed for a pint of wine in that place, when I felt a light touch on my arm.

I was not such a bumpkin that I did not realize what was probably about to take place, and I spun round and reached for my knife, then hesitated when I saw a finely dressed young woman standing beside me. She had a good face, but it was so covered in wig and beauty spots and rouge and whitening that God's gifts to her could scarcely be discerned. Most noticeable of all, I remember, was the stink of perfume which so covered her natural aromas that it was like being in a flowershop.

"Madam?" I said coldly as she raised an eyebrow and smiled at my alarm.

"Jack!" cried the creature. "Do not say you have forgotten me?"

"You have the advantage."

"Well, you may have forgotten me, but I cannot forget the gallant way you protected me under the stars near Tunbridge," said she.

Then I remembered: the young whore. But how changed she was, and though her fortunes had obviously improved, in my eyes she had not changed for the better.

"Kitty," I said, remembering her name at last. "What a fine lady you have become. You must forgive me for not knowing you, but the transformation is so great you cannot blame me too much."

"No, indeed," she said, waving a fan in front of her face in an affected manner. "Although no one calls me lady who knows me truly. Whore I was, and now I am raised a mistress."

"My congratulations," I said, for evidently she thought this was in order.

"Thank you. He is a fine man, well connected and extremely generous. Nor is he too repulsive; I am a lucky woman indeed. With fortune, he will give me enough to buy myself a husband before he tires of me. But tell me, what are you doing here, gaping like a yokel in the middle of this street? It is not the place for you."

"I was looking for some food."

"There is plenty here."

"I cannot—will not—afford that."

She laughed merrily. "But I can and will."

And with a brazenness which took my breath away, she linked her arm in mine and led me back to the Piazza and a coffee shop called Will's, where she demanded a room to herself, and for food and drink to be brought. Far from being affronted at such a request, the servant obliged with obsequiousness as though she was indeed a lady of consequence, and a few minutes later we were in a commodious room on the second floor, overlooking the bustle below.

"No one will object?" I asked anxiously, concerned that her lord might send some bravoes around in a fit of jealousy. It took her some moments to work out what I meant by this, but then she laughed again.

"Oh no," she said. "He knows me too well to think me capable of ruining my prospects by such an indiscretion."

"May I know the name of your benefactor?"

"Of course. Everyone else does. He is my Lord of Bristol, an entertaining and well-placed favorite of the king's, if rather old. I caught him at Tunbridge, so you see I have great reason to be grateful to you. I was there scarcely a day before I received a message asking to meet me. I pleased him as best I could, and kept him entertained, and thought that was that. The next thing I know, he wants my company back in London, and offers a handsome incentive."

"Is he in love with you?"

"Goodness, no. But he is hot-blooded where his wife is an old prune, and he is mortally afraid of disease. It was all her idea; she spotted me in the street first of all and drew his attention to me."

She wagged her finger at me. "You look about to launch into a sermon, Jack Prestcott. Do desist, I pray you, or you will vex me. You are too virtuous to do anything but disapprove strongly, but what would you have me do? I sell my body for my little bit of wealth and comfort. All around there are priests and ministers who sell their souls for theirs. I am in good company, and one more sinner among such a throng will hardly be noticed. I tell you, Jack, virtue is a lonely state in this age."

I hardly knew what to say to this frank expression of depravity. I could not approve of her, but I was disinclined to condemn, for that would have meant an end to our acquaintance and, despite everything, her company pleased me. All the more so because, to show off her good fortune, she ordered the best food and wine, and insisted I eat as much as my stomach could hold and my head endure. All the while she talked to me of town gossip, and of her lover's inexorable rise at court so that (she said) he was a serious rival to Lord Clarendon in the king's favor.

"Of course, Clarendon is powerful," she said, affecting to know all the secret dealings of the government. "But all the world knows that his ponderous gravity drives the king to distraction, while the gayness of Lord Bristol keeps His Majesty amused. And this is a king who always sacrifices on the altar of amusement. So Lord Clarendon is vulnerable; it will not take much to eject him, and then I will be the second whore in the kingdom, after Lady Castlemaine. It's a pity my lord is a papist, as that is a great hindrance to him, but even that can be overcome, perhaps.''

''You think any of this might happen?'' I asked, fascinated despite myself. It is odd how gossip of the high and mighty exercises such interest.

''Oh, yes. I hope so. For Lord Clarendon's sake as much as anything.''

''I hardly think he will thank you for your solicitude.''

''He should,'' she said, seriously for a moment. ''Truly he should. For I have heard worrying tales. He has annoyed many powerful people and some are less peaceable and generous than my lord. If he does not fall from power, I fear worse may befall him one day.''

''Nonsense,'' I said. ''Fall he will, but he is an old man and that is only natural. But he will always be rich and mighty and favored. Such people as he, who never raise a sword nor put their courage to the test, always survive and prosper while better men fall by the wayside.''

''Oho,'' she said. ''Spoken from the heart, I would say. Is this why you are in London?''

I had forgotten I had told her of my quest, and nodded. ''I was here to enquire after a man called Sir Samuel Morland. Have you ever heard of him?''

''I believe I have. Is he not a man who concerns himself with mechanical devices? He often approaches people at court trying to beg influence for some scheme.''

''Does he have any strong patrons?'' I asked. It is always well to know what you are dealing with; it would be alarming to discover that the man you wish to attack is defended by someone far more powerful.

''Not that I know of. I believe he is associated in some way with schemes for draining fenland, so he may know the Duke of Bedford, but more than that I could not say. Do you want me to find out? It would be easy enough to do, and a pleasure to oblige.''

''I would be deeply grateful.''

''Then that is all the encouragement I need. It shall be done. Would you care to come to my lodging this evening? I attend my Lady Castlemaine in the morning, and my lord in the afternoon, but the evenings are my own, and I am free to receive whomever I like. That is our understanding, and I must invite people, if only to show that I am keeping him to our agreement.''

"It would be a pleasure."

"And now, I hope you are refreshed and prepared, as I must leave you."

I stood up and bowed deeply to thank her for her kindness, and was bold enough to kiss her hand. She laughed with merriment. "Stop, sir," she said. "You are being deceived by appearances."

"Not at all," I said. "You are more a lady than many I have met."

She blushed and made fun of me to cover her pleasure at the compliment. Then she swept out of the room, accompanied by the little black servant given to her as a present and who had been there throughout our interview. Her lord was easygoing and gracious, she said, but there was no need to risk his displeasure unnecessarily.

IT WAS ALREADY DARKENING, AND COLD, SO I PASSED the hours in a coffee shop near St. Paul's, reading the journals and listening to the conversation of others, which filled me anew with disgust for the city and its inhabitants. So much bravado, so much bragging, so much time wasted in idle, foolish talk designed for nothing but to impress their fellows and impose on their betters by pretense. Gossip in the town is a commodity, to be bought and sold; if it is not possessed, then it is fabricated, like coiners make specie out of dross. I was at least undisturbed, for no man there sought my company and I was truly glad it was so; while others now habitually frequent these shops, and lower themselves in what they call good company, I shun the vulgar and public places.

The time passed, if only slowly, and eventually the hour of my appointment came. I was apprehensive of the meeting, despite our differing stations in life which should have ensured my comfortable superiority. But London is corrosive to deference. Who you are is less important than what you seem; a fraudster of no family can impose himself on a gentleman from an ancient line simply by being better dressed and having a winning manner. For my part, I would reestablish the rules the great Queen insisted upon; no merchant should be allowed to dress as a gentleman, and should pay the price for any impudent imitation, for it is fraud and should be punished as such, just as it is fraud for whores to disguise their nature.

Vice had brought great rewards in Kitty's case and, though I was loath to admit that good can come from bad, she lived in a fashion which showed a great deal of what we are now taught to call *gout*. I am glad, I must say, that we English are still robust enough to need to borrow words from the French for such nonsense. While many of her fellow laborers for Venus would have flaunted the spoils of conquest, she lived simply, with solid oak furniture, rather than the gilded stuff of the foreigner; simple arras on the walls to keep in the warmth, not some gaudy tapestry. The only piece of gross vanity was a portrait of herself on one wall, impudently matched to one of her lord on the opposite, as though they were husband and wife. That, I felt, was insulting, but she assured me when she saw my disapproval, that it was a gift and she could do no other.

"Jack," she said when we had greeted each other and sat down, "I must talk to you seriously for a moment."

"By all means."

"I must ask you for a great courtesy, if you please, in return for giving you the information you require."

"A courtesy is yours for the asking," I said, slightly ruffled, "without the need to bargain for it."

"Thank you. I wish you to promise never to reveal where we met."

"Of course," I said.

"It never happened. You may have met a young whore on the road in Kent, but that was not me. I now come from a good, but poor family in Herefordshire, and was brought to London by my lord as a distant relative of his wife's family. Who I was, and what I was, is unknown, and must remain so."

"It does not seem to have done you a great deal of harm."

"No. But it would, when his protection is withdrawn."

"You think of him so?"

"Of course. He will not be cruel, I think. He will settle an annuity on me and already I have saved a good amount of money. By the time I am too old, I will have the means to support myself. But what then? I must marry, I suppose; but I will not get a good bargain if my past is known."

I frowned at this. "You propose to marry? Do you have a suitor?"

"Oh, plenty," she said with a pretty laugh. "Although none has dared to come forward; that would be far too audacious. But a woman of some property, as I will be, who can offer a connection to one of the most influential men in the kingdom? I am a prize, unless someone destroys my chances through careless talk. I cannot say marriage appeals, however."

"For most women it is a dream."

"To hand over my hard-earned fortune to my husband? Be unable to do anything without his permission? Risk being disinherited of my own money when he dies? Oh, yes. A wonderful dream."

"You are making fun of me," I said gravely.

She laughed again. "I suppose. But my position in my future husband's household will be stronger if I am Katherine Hannay, daughter of John Hannay, esquire of Hereford, than formerly Kitty the whore."

I must have looked despondent, for it was not easy to comply. Suppose I heard that she was to marry a gentleman, even if not of my acquaintance? Was it not my duty to warn him? Could I stand by as a man put his name at risk, and lived forever under the threat of exposure?

"I do not ask your approbation, nor your patronage. Merely your silence," she said softly.

"Well," I said, "it seems we live in an age where whores become ladies, and ladies play the whore. Family counts for nothing, and appearance is all. I cannot say you would not make as good a wife as many a real lady. And so I give you my word, Miss Hannay of Hereford."

I gave her a lot with those words, and she appreciated it, and it was with a heavy heart indeed that I felt obliged to go back on them in later years, when I heard that she was to marry Sir John Marshall, a gentleman of some fortune in Hampstead. I anguished greatly over what to do, and with the very greatest of reluctance concluded that my duty could not avoid the necessity of writing to the man and telling him what I knew of the woman who threatened to impose herself on his name.

That, fortunately, was all in the future; for then she was deeply grateful to me, and would not have assisted me otherwise.

"I hope my little discoveries can repay this second kindness you have given me. I doubt it very much, but I will tell you what I have found out, and later I will introduce you to Mr. George Collop, who has agreed to come and take some refreshment."

"Who is he?"

"He is the receiver-general of the Duke of Bedford. A powerful man, as he has direction of one of the greatest fortunes in the land."

"I hope he is honest, then."

"He is. And loyal to a fault. And able as well. Which is why he is paid near a hundred pounds a year in hand, with all his costs and living on top of that."

I was impressed. My father had always done his own administration, and in any case could not have afforded to pay anything like that to a single servant.

"For all that, there are many people who would willingly pay him double, for he has made the duke even richer than he once was. It is said that His Grace will scarcely buy a new pair of hose without asking Mr. Collop's opinion first."

"What is his connection with Sir Samuel Morland?"

"Fens," she said. "He is in charge of the duke's involvement in draining the fenland. He knows more about it than anyone, and so knows a great deal about Sir Samuel."

"I see. What else have you discovered for me?"

"Not so very much. This Morland has acquired some pensions and sinecures since His Majesty returned, but boasted of many more which were not given him. It seems he considered that he did such a service that no reward would be great enough. However, my lord does not think much of this assessment."

"You must be clearer with me, Kitty," I said. "This is, or may be, a legal matter. I cannot leave anything bound up in the obscurity of dark words."

"I had this from my lord this afternoon," she said. "You know, I am sure, that he was one of the king's most loyal followers, and endured years in penury and exile for his sake. He does not look favorably on those who switched their allegiance at the last moment. He says that he knows for sure that Morland encountered Lord Mordaunt when both were in Savoy. He was involved in the arrest of Mordaunt and other conspirators and took part in the trial at which Mordaunt was acquitted. My lord also mentioned to me that of Morland's rewards and pensions, nearly all have been won at the specific request of Lord Mordaunt. A strange courtesy to extend to a man who supposedly tried to hang you. More, indeed, something you would do for a man to whom you were connected by long friendship. So my lord said."

I looked at her long and hard as she said this, and she nodded seriously at me. "You must draw your own conclusions," she said. "I questioned my lord, but he would give no direct answer, saying merely that what is obvious is usually also true."

"What did he mean?"

"He said he could not help more plainly, for it would be seen as an attack on Clarendon if he leveled accusations against Mordaunt: the two are so closely attached criticism on one is an assault on the other. But he wishes you well, and begs you take his advice. If you look hard enough, you will find proof of what he says. Jack, whatever is the matter?"

The relief I felt at those words was so great that I had to lean forward in my chair and hug myself, so near did I feel to exploding from sheerest joy. At last, I had someone who would credit what I always knew to be the truth, and at last I had the pointer I needed. Odd it was indeed to have it from such a source; that the solution, or the near solution, to my troubles should fall from the mouth of a harlot. But thus it transpired, for the angels of the Lord can take as many strange forms as the servants of the devil.

I now knew who had trumped up accusations against my father; I knew who the traitor really was, and now I needed to discover why my father was chosen out of all the possible candidates for such treatment. I was close to the point of being able to confront Thurloe with his own turpitude, and justify his death. I fell to my knee and kissed her hand, again and again and again, until she burst out laughing and pulled it away.

"Come now," she said merrily, "what have I said that produces such adulation?"

"You have ended years of anguish, and restored the name of my family. With luck you will also have restored my fortune and prospects as well," I said. "If anything deserves adulation, it is surely that."

"Thank you, kind sir," she said. "Although I cannot consider I have done anything of such merit. All I have done is repeat my lord's words to you."

"In which case I thank him through you. He must be the kindest and best master a man—or woman—could have. It may be impertinent on my part, but if the opportunity arises when it can be done without embarrassment, please convey my gratitude, and make sure he is aware that, should he require a service, I will perform it willingly."

"I will be sure to do so. Are you staying in London long?"

"I must leave tomorrow."

"A pity. I would like to present you to him. Next time, write to me in advance, and I will make certain you are publicly acknowledged by him as a friend."

"A friend is too much, I think," I said. "But I would be grateful to be seen as in his interest."

"It shall be done. And here," she said as she heard a heavy clumping of boots up the stairs, "is undoubtedly Mr. George Collop."

He was a man of low extraction; that was clear from the moment he walked through the door and bowed deeply to what he thought was the lady who greeted him. His movements were awkward, his speech coarse and with a heavy

Dorset accent. It seemed he was the son of a tenant farmer, and had forced his way into His Grace's attention by his skill. All well and good, but the price was heavy, for having to listen to that rolling burr must have been tiresome indeed. It said much for his qualities as a comptroller of finance, for he had none other to recommend him.

Many years in the intimate presence of gentility had done little to soften his manners or refine his talk; he was one of the low who glory in their roughness. It is one thing to despise the effeminacy of city and court; quite another to set your face against the basic qualities of breeding. In the way he collapsed in a chair with enough force to make the legs bend, then pulled out a cloth to wipe his face from the walk up the stairs—for he was a heavy, thickset man with a red face and mottled nose—Collop made it clear he cared naught for politeness.

"This gentleman, Mr, ah, Grove," Kitty began, with a smile toward me, "is fascinated by the fen project," she said. "And so I asked you to meet him, as there is no one who knows more of it than you, as you oversee His Grace's works there."

"That's right," he said, and said no more, thinking it sufficient contribution.

"His father has a very boggy piece of land, and was considering whether the engines of Sir Samuel Morland would be of use. He has heard much of them but cannot tell bombast from true report."

"Well," he said, then stopped again, lost in consideration of such a weighty matter.

"My father," I put in, anxious to relieve Kitty of some of the onerous conversational duty, "is concerned that the machines will involve great expense and might prove to be money put out to waste. He is extremely keen to discover the truth of the matter, but finds Sir Samuel himself less straightforward."

Collop heaved with a brief, private amusement for a moment. "That he is," he said eventually. "And I cannot help you, as we do not use his machines."

"I rather gained the impression he was crucial to the project."

"He is the sort of man to give himself airs of importance he does not deserve. In fact, he is an investor only. Sir Samuel has some three hundred acres at Harland Wyte, which will be worth ten times its purchase when the land is drained. Of course, it is insignificant compared to His Grace's interest, which is ninety thousand acres."

I gasped in astonishment, which Collop observed with satisfaction.

"Yes, it is a mighty undertaking. Some three hundred and sixty thousand acres in all. Barren land, which by the ingenuity of man and the grace of God will yield plenty. Already doing so, in fact."

"Not so barren, surely? What about the inhabitants already there? There are very many of those, I think."

He shrugged. "Some, who scratch a living. But they are removed when necessary."

"It must be hugely expensive."

"That it is. And many men have put money into the venture, although the reward is so certain it presents little risk, except where villagers or landowners delay the work."

"So it is not certain, then?"

"All problems can be overcome. If squatters object, they are ejected; if landowners refuse to cooperate, then ways are found round their objections. Some straightforward, others"—here his eyes twinkled with amusement—"others less straightforward."

"But surely no landowner objects?"

"You'd be surprised. For all sorts of mean and ignorant reasons, people have put obstacles in our way for upward of thirty years. But most are seen to now the Prestcott problem has been solved."

My heart quickened at the words, and I was hard put not to let out some exclamation. Fortunately, Collop was not an observant man and Kitty, seeing my shock, diverted him for full ten minutes with inconsequential court gossip.

"But I interrupted you, dear sir," she said brightly after a while. "You were telling us about your battles. Who was the man you mentioned, Prestwick? Was that it?"

"Prestcott," Collop corrected her. "Sir James Prestcott. A thorn in our side for years."

"He did not see the advantages of being rich, did he? Strange how some people require some convincing."

Collop chuckled. "Oh, no. He knew the advantage of wealth. It was his jealousy that was the problem."

Kitty looked enquiringly, and Collop was more than happy to oblige, little aware of how he was condemning himself and others with every filthy word he uttered.

"He did not benefit as much from the division of land and feared the arrival of greater men than he in an area his family had dominated for generations. So he incited the local inhabitants to damage our works. We built dikes, the rabble came out at night and drove holes in them, flooding the land again. We brought cases against them and he, as a magistrate, found them all not guilty. It went on for years.

"Then came all the troubles, and this Sir James went into exile. But the war also made the money dry up, and in any case, part of his land cut straight across the line of a river we needed to dig, and he would not sell it to us. Without it, an entire river would have to be diverted, or some fifteen thousand acres abandoned."

"Surely then it would have been wise to offer more?"

"He would not take it," Collop wagged his finger with a smirk on his face. "But then the goodness of the Lord shows itself," he said. "For what do we eventually discover when we are on the point of despair? That all the while good Sir James is in fact a traitor. My lord's cousin, Sir John Russell, had it from Sir Samuel Morland himself, and he provided all the information we needed to make Prestcott flee abroad once more. The trustee of his property was forced to sell up to avoid bankruptcy, and we had our river dug just where we wanted it."

I could not bear even to look at his gross, smug face any longer, and was seriously afraid that, if I heard much more, I would run him through on the spot. A red haze spread over my eyes and my head spun with dizziness as I walked to the window. I could barely think, so powerful was the pain that gripped my head, and I felt the beads of sweat running down my forehead and onto my clothes as I fought for breath. To be forced to listen as this dirty man of no name encompassed the downfall of my father to gain a profit made my soul revolt. I had no appetite to exult in the fact that I was so much closer to my goal, for to find motives so mean and tawdry made me tremble with sorrow. Now, at least, I knew why Sir John Russell had refused even to cast eyes on me at Tunbridge Wells; he could not have borne the shame and lived.

"Are you not well, sir?" I distantly heard Kitty anxiously enquiring, as she must have seen my face pale as I stood by the window trying to control myself. It was as if she spoke from a great distance; she had to repeat the words several times before I could attend to them.

"Yes, thank you. It is a migraine, to which I am prone. I think it must be the city air, and the heat in your apartment. I am not used to it."

Collop at least had the grace to offer instantly to withdraw. I heard the ceremonious and courteous way in which she thanked him for calling, and summoned the servant to show him out. It was some considerable time, I think—it could have been minutes but just as easily hours—before I was able to leave that window. She had, by then, produced a cold compress which she placed on my forehead, and a glass of chilled wine to restore my senses. She was, in fact, a naturally kind woman, one of the kindest I have known.

"I must offer you my apologies," I said eventually. "I fear I must have caused you grave embarrassment."

"Not at all," she replied. "You lie there until you feel able to move. I did not understand the import of the words entirely, but I could see they were a grave shock to you."

"That they were," I said. "Worse than I imagined. I should have known, of course, that something this mean was behind everything, but I have looked so long that its discovery took me entirely by surprise. I am not, it seems, a man for a real crisis."

"Would you like to tell me?" she said as she bathed my forehead once more. She was close to me, and her perfume no longer repelled me, but had the precise opposite effect; the warmth of her bosom against my arm similarly excited hidden feelings deep inside me. I held her hand as it rested on my chest and drew it close, but before I could make my desires known further, she stood up and walked back to her seat, giving me a sad, and I think regretful, smile.

"You have had a shock," she said. "It would be best not to follow it up with a mistake. I think you have more than enough powerful enemies already without seeking to make new ones."

She was right, of course, although I could have answered that with so many, one more would make little difference. But she was not willing; that would have made no difference with the Kitty I originally knew, but I was as under the spell of the times as much as anyone. Despite everything, I could not but treat her as a woman of standing, and so desisted, even though to continue would have brought much needed release.

"So? Are you going to explain why you turned so pale?"

I hesitated, then shook my head. "No," I said. "This goes too deep. It is not that I do not wish to confide in you, but I am anxious lest anything be known of my progress. I do not wish to forewarn anyone. But please tell your lord of my gratitude, and my intention to act on his words speedily."

She agreed to this, and reined in her curiosity with dignity. For my part, my business was done, and I prepared to leave. Again and again, I thanked her for her kindness and her usefulness, and wished her well in her fortune. She kissed me lightly on the cheek on our parting, the first time, I believe, a woman had ever done such a thing to me, for my mother never touched me at all.

chapter twelve

THE JOURNEY BACK TO OXFORD GAVE ME TIME TO consider everything I had heard and learned, although the malevolence which had dogged me for so long continued to swirl all around. The horses slipped their harness and had to be recovered by the coachman; a sudden and unlikely storm suddenly blew up out of nowhere and turned the road into a sea of mud; most frightening of all, a huge crow flew into the carriage when one of the passengers lifted the blind, and fluttered around in panic, pecking and beating its wings against us—myself most of all—before being strangled and its corpse hurled out again. It was not only myself who saw these mishaps as more than mere accident; a minister also traveling to Oxford was similarly concerned, and even remarked how the ancients viewed such birds as evil portents, and the emissaries of malevolent spirits. I did not tell him he was nearer the truth than he knew.

This reminder of the darkness to which I was returning weighed on my mind, but I put it from me enough to turn over again and again the catalogue of misdeeds that my enquiries had brought to light. By the time I arrived in Oxford, it was all laid out and the case was as clear and lucid as any presented in a court of law. A fine speech, it would have been, although I never had cause to deliver it. I fear that I caused some consternation in the coach as we lumbered toward Oxford, for I became so involved in my thoughts that

I must have talked aloud on several occasions, and made dramatic gestures with my arms to emphasize the points I was making to myself.

But for all the bravado of my mind, I knew that I was not yet finished. A perfect argument, flawless in its conception and its development, leading toward a conclusion that is unavoidable in its logical progression, is all very well in disputation where power of structure will carry all before it. It is of less use in the courtroom, whatever the rhetoricians say of their art. No; I needed testimony as well and, what was more, I needed it from someone who would match the standing of those gentlemen I would be accusing. I could hardly, after all, rely on Morland or Lord Mordaunt to speak truth, and Sir John Russell had made his partialities perfectly clear. Thurloe would not speak for me, and Dr. Grove could do me little good.

Which meant I had to see Sir William Compton. He, I was still sure, was as upright and honest a man as could be, and the thought that my suspicions about him were certainly wrong came as the greatest relief. It would have been impossible to persuade him to act dishonorably, and I was certain he consented to the sale of my lands only when he was convinced my father's sin was so great that no further consideration need be given my family. To consider yourself betrayed by a man you called friend, this would have been a bitter blow indeed. And if he believed my father, his closest comrade, a traitor, then others would as well: that, surely, was why he was chosen to disseminate the information.

I could not go to see him directly as the weather was so bad the roads were all but impassable and, in any case, my obligations at the university were pressing. I had missed much of the term, and was forced to make amends like a sniveling schoolboy before I could go off once more. Not much was required other than my presence, but there was little I could do about it. And a week or two of quiet reflection was no bad thing, I think, even though at the time my fiery temperament naturally wanted to bring the matter to an end as soon as possible.

My few friends, by this stage, were abandoning me, so preoccupied were they by their own petty affairs. It grieved me greatly, and saddest of all was the distraction of Thomas who, when I called on him, neither asked me how I was nor how my quest was progressing. I was barely in the room before he launched into bitter complaints, revealing such a violence of soul that the ultimate outcome should not have surprised me as much as it did.

In short, it was becoming clear to him that his claims on the living were to be shunted aside in favor of Dr. Grove. The times were changing faster than he had reckoned. The new laws on conformity which the government had introduced made almost any deviation from the steady orthodoxy of the Anglican church punishable. Independents, Presbyterians, everyone but virtual Catholics (in my friend's opinion) were to be crushed and starved, denied any possibility of preferment.

Personally, I welcomed such legislation as long overdue. The sectaries had done well under Cromwell and I could see no reason why they should be allowed to continue in prosperity now. For twenty years or more we had endured these arrogant presumptives, who had expelled and tormented those who disagreed with them while they had the power to do so; why should they now complain when such power was turned with just vengeance on themselves?

Thomas did not see the matter in such a way, of course. In his opinion, the health of the land depended on his gaining eighty pounds a year and the state of marital bliss this would bring in its train. He could not see the danger he posed, and the more it seemed his ambition would be denied him, the more it fed his antagonism for Dr. Grove, subtly metamorphosing it from disagreement to dislike and, ultimately, to a burning and violent hatred.

"It is the college," he said. "And in particular the warden. They are so cautious; so determined not to give offense or attract the least degree of criticism from anyone that they are prepared to subsume the interests of the parish and install a man such as Grove."

"Are you sure of this?" I asked. "Has the warden actually said so to you?"

"He does not need to," Thomas said in disgust. "Indeed, he is too crafty a man ever to say anything directly at all."

"Perhaps the matter is beyond his control," I suggested. "The living is not in the warden's gift."

"His influence will be decisive. Lord Maynard has asked the college's opinion before he bestows the parish on someone, and that opinion will be communicated through the warden," Thomas said. "Lord Maynard is coming to the college soon and we must all dine together, then the senior Fellows will give their verdict. Jack," he said desperately, "I do not know what to do. I have no other possible patron. I am not like Grove who could count on the favor of many a great family, if he would but ask."

"Now, now," I said cheerfully, although I was becoming irritated with him for his selfishness. "It is not as bad as that. You are still a Fellow of this college, and a man of learning and probity must always find a place for himself in the world. You must cultivate the mighty with the same enthusiasm that you apply to your studies, for the one is useless without the other. You know as well as I that association with those who can advance you is the sole means that men of worth have of gaining a place in the world. And you, if I may say so, have too much neglected this world in favor of the other."

I meant no criticism, although perhaps it was there. Certainly Thomas bridled at my words, so delicate was his spirit and so tender to just reproach.

"Are you saying it is my own fault that I am to be defrauded in this manner? It is my responsibility that my warden advances another at my expense?"

"No," I replied. "Not at all. Though more elegance of address might have persuaded more fellows to support your cause. What I am saying is that you have made no effort whatever to cultivate others. You must frequently hear of those with livings in their gift. Have you written to them? Taken up opportunities to give their sons tuition when they come to this town? Have you published any of your sermons and offered the dedication of them to any men of influence? Have you made the gifts and performed the attentions that create an obligation? No. You have not. In your pride you have studied and thought that enough."

"It should be. I should not have to bow and scrape. I am a minister of the Lord, not a courtier."

"And that is your arrogance and conceit. Why should you be so different from everyone else? Do you think your qualities so great, your virtue so large, and your learning so extensive that you can scorn to beg like ordinary men? And if your purity and loftiness do not come from unreasoning pride, be assured that that is how they must appear to others."

It was a harsh reply, but it was necessary and, if I was aware of injuring him, I did it with the best of intentions. Thomas was a good man but not a worldly one, and therefore quite unsuited for the Church of England. I do not say this in jest; for the church is the best reflection of God's intentions on earth, and it was He who ordered man according to His will. Thomas was obliged to apply to others for support, as those beneath him must apply to him in turn. How else can any civil society continue to work, without a constant flow of gratuity from one to the other, high to low? Did he think that the mighty would apply for the honor of giving him patronage? His refusal not only indicated his lack of humility; it was, at bottom, Godless.

Perhaps I was in error in saying what I did; certainly I was wrong to continue to drive the point home, for I am sure that it helped Thomas on to the catastrophe which played such a part in Mr. Cola's narrative. But it is often the way with conversation, that people, having caused a hurt, try to reassure themselves by making it worse.

"Thomas," I said kindly, because I thought that the sooner he was aware of the truth the better, "Grove is older than you and has a superior claim. The thirteen men who run this college have known him for years, while you are a relative newcomer. He has taken care to be pleasant to Lord Maynard, while you have not. And he has offered the college a proportion of the living, which you cannot do. I wish it were otherwise, but you must face the fact: you will not get this place as long as Grove is alive and wants it for himself."

Had I known the outcome, of course I would not have spoken, but his mildness of manner was such that I never for a moment considered that the realization might drive him into such evil action. Moreover, had I remained in close association with him, I do not believe Dr. Grove would have died.

It is known that a resentment unexpressed grows in the soul; I certainly had experienced such a malady myself. With my counsel and restraint, Thomas's breast would not have filled with so immoderate a hatred that he took the steps he did. Or at least, I might have discerned his mind and stopped him.

But I was in prison at the time, and could do nothing to stay his hand.

I SEE THAT I HAVE SCARCELY MENTIONED DR. WALLIS since I recounted my visit to his house in Merton Street, and I must do so briefly now to indicate the man's bad faith. For according to Morland he had known at least something about the plot against my father, and therefore he had lied outright to me on the subject. He asked me to find him documents in my father's possession, when he had all he needed already in his desk. I determined to confront him with this duplicity, and so wrote him a polite letter, presenting my compliments and enquiring delicately for an interview. I received a dismissive reply. So, a few days later, I decided to pay him a visit.

He was, at that stage, lodged in New College, for building works had encumbered his house and his own college had no accommodation which would match his rank. His wife had been dispatched to London, to which city Wallis intended to fly as soon as the end of term permitted. I noted with some amusement that he was now a close neighbor of Dr. Grove, as I could not imagine two gentlemen less likely to be on civil terms.

Wallis was in an ill humor, as he was a man who clearly did not relish any form of inconvenience. Being turfed out of his own lodging, virtually deprived of his servants and forced into unwanted society through having to eat in college when he could not prevail on the kitchen to send his meals up had no good effect on his mood. This I could see the moment I entered the door, and I was accordingly prepared to be maltreated at his hands. He was brutally unkind, offensive and threatening by turns, so much so that I regretted approaching him in the first place.

In brief, he upbraided me for writing to him and told me

I had no claim on him at all. That he had undertaken reluctantly to oblige if I would provide him with the necessary materials, but resented mightily being harried in such a way.

"I have already told you I have nothing," I said. "Whatever my father may have had was lost. It seems, in fact, that you possess more papers than I do, as I am told that you deciphered the documents which incriminated my father."

"I?" he said in mock surprise. "What makes you think that?"

"Sir Samuel Morland took some letters you worked on, and passed them on to the king. They supposedly demonstrated my father was a traitor. I believe that those coded letters were forged on Thurloe's instructions. I would like to see them so I can demonstrate this."

"Samuel told you all this?"

"He told me a pack of lies. It is a truth I discovered on my own."

"In that case I congratulate you," he said, suddenly friendly. "It seems you have been cleverer than myself, for I never suspected that I was in any way duped by either Thurloe or Samuel."

"Will you give them to me?"

"Alas, I cannot, young man. I don't have them."

"You must. Morland said . . ."

"Samuel is a great romancer. It is possible that what you say is true and that Samuel imposed himself on me in this fashion. But I have none of the originals."

"So where would they be?"

He shrugged, and I knew from the way he moved and the way his eyes would not meet mine that he was lying. "If they still exist, I imagine Mr. Thurloe would have them. If you can find sufficient patience, I will make discreet enquiries for you . . ."

With great expressions of thanks on my part, and an equally hypocritical expression of admiration on his side, I left his room soon after, as convinced as I could be that Dr. Wallis had those letters close by him somewhere.

•   •   •

I WAS LAID LOW IN MY BED FOR SEVERAL DAYS AFTER this meeting, which distressed me. However, I knew the cause of the infirmity, and also knew well that summoning a physician would be throwing good money after bad, so I lay and suffered until the worst of the affliction was passed and my head had cleared enough for me to move. Much of the time I spent in prayer, and I found that blessed exercise a great comfort to me, calming my soul and filling me with a strange and powerful strength, enough to complete the task my father had set me.

It was the second day of March before I set out for Compton Wynyates, slipping from my tutor's bed before dawn, dressing on the landing so as not to disturb the other students slumbering within, and wrapping myself up with the thickest and warmest clothes I had. I took one of my fellow students' pair of boots, having tried them on in secret a few days before. My need was very great. The cold was dreadful, worse than anything for many years, and without stout high leather my suffering would have been intolerable. Then I prevailed on a tradesman heading north with a consignment of gloves and other goods for Yorkshire to let me sit in the back of his wagon until Banbury, in exchange for which I pushed when the cart bogged down in the road, and took a turn driving the horses when he wearied.

From Banbury I walked, and arrived at Compton Wynyates late in the evening, well after darkness had fallen. I clapped my hands as I walked through the great front door to summon the servant that my arrival could be announced. I did so with bravado, but I was highly nervous, for I had no idea whether I would be well received. In the back of my mind all the time was the reception I had received from Sir John Russell; I could not bear to be so rejected by Sir William also.

But I was swiftly reassured, for he soon descended to greet me himself, and made a great show of welcoming me to the house. Whatever resentment he may have harbored for my name did not rise to the surface.

"I am astonished to see you, Jack," he said cordially. "What brings you here? Surely term is on at the university and you are still a student? I am surprised you were given permission to leave the town. Such laxity never existed in my day.''

''This was a special dispensation, and I have an indulgent tutor,'' I said.

''Well, I am pleased you are here,'' he said. ''It has been too long. We have a fine fire in the parlor, so come and warm yourself immediately. This hall is as cold as charity itself.''

I was dumbfounded with relief by this reception, and upbraided myself for doubting his kindness. Amiability was Sir William's natural demeanor and he was very much the country gentleman in that regard. Thickset, and with a florid complexion, he had a simple directness that made him devotedly loyal to such causes and people as he clasped to his heart.

I was too cold and tired to pursue that question at that moment; rather, I allowed him to lead me through to the great fire, and sit me down within the aura of its warmth, which made such a delightful contrast with the chill of the room beyond the flames' influence. There I was served hot wine and food by a servant, and left alone in peace until I had finished my meal. Sir William excused himself, saying he had small business that would not wait, but that he would be back in a half hour.

I was almost asleep when he returned; not that he took such a long time, but the heat and the drink drugged my mind and made me realize how dreadfully weary I was. I was also saddened as I sat there, so warm and comfortable. Not long ago, this had been my home and I found that, despite everything that had happened, I still felt it to be such. I had spent more time in the company of his family than I had in that of my own; this house I knew better than that abode which was no longer mine even in name. In a conflict of slumbering emotions I sat quietly by the fire drinking my wine, pondering such strangeness until the return of Sir William forced me back into some semblance of alertness.

It is at this point that I must return to one essential purpose of my narrative, or at least to that matter which caused me to reach for pen and paper to start with. I must discuss my dealings with Signor Marco da Cola and the worth of his narrative. As I said much earlier in this account, I find his memory a strange one indeed, for he discourses at length on the trivial, and ignores studiously matters of much greater import. I do not know and, at this great distance, I care less, why this is; my only concern here is to correct his account in those passages where I am directly concerned.

The first was that evening at Sir William's house, for by his side when he returned to the fire was Marco da Cola.

I must assume that he had some good reason for falsifying the story of his arrival in England, for I can attest that it is erroneous. He cannot have arrived as he said; he did not come to London, then proceed more or less directly to Oxford. He was in this country many days beforehand. A strange little fellow I found him, too; his clothes, all lavender and purple with the strangest of cuts, were such as would draw attention in such a place, and the aroma of perfume that entered the room long before he did was quite unforgettable. Later, when he saw me in prison in the company of Lower, I could almost tell who my visitor was long before the jailer opened the cell door, so strong was the smell he gave off.

But I took to him, odd though he was, and only later discerned that there was more to him than instant appraisal suggested. To meet, he was short and stout, with merry eyes and an easy laugh. Everything amused him, and everything attracted his interest. He said little, not being greatly proficient in English (though much better than I at first imagined) but sat quietly, bobbing his head and chuckling with appreciation at our conversation, as though he was hearing the best jokes in the world, and the wittiest of conversations.

Only once, during that first encounter, did I even have half a suspicion there might be more to him; when Sir William and I were talking, I saw a flash in his eyes, and the most fleeting glimpse of cunning passed across that chubby, harmless-looking face. But who pays attention to such details, when all else indicates the opposite? It was a trick of the light only; a reflection of the flames in the dimness of the room, and nothing more.

As he was unwilling, or unable, to play any manful part in the conversation, Sir William and I talked instead, and gradually almost forgot the presence of the foreigner in our midst. Sir William introduced him as a man with whom he had dealings in trade, for as Master of the Ordnance (his paltry reward for his labors on behalf of the king) he was thrown in contact with many foreign traders, and Cola's father was, it seemed, a man of great power in such matters. Moreover, said Sir William, he and his family had been good friends to the great cause over the years, and now naturally wanted to supply some of those goods His Majesty needed.

I wished them well, and hoped they would both profit from the association for, if Sir William's position gave him little standing, it held out instead the probability of considerable wealth. A dedicated Master of the Ordnance, taking what bribes and profits came his way, could amass a considerable fortune in a short time by controlling the army's supplies, and Sir William was not wholly discontented with his position. He had, it must be said, greater need of money than honor at that time.

I suppose I can see why the presence of such a man would need to be kept discreetly quiet, although Cola's delicacy in hiding such matters so long after the event strikes me as being excessively fine. For Sir William (as I have mentioned) was in dispute with my Lord Clarendon, and any man who angered the Lord Chancellor had to tread very carefully in the execution of his office. It mattered not that Clarendon had so joyously looted the treasury himself since the moment the king returned; his enemies had to beware, for what was encouraged in Clarendon's friends was used to tear down his enemies. The more isolated he became, the more the attacks on those who wished to be rid of him grew in violence. The most ordinary behavior could be turned into a weapon, for Clarendon was not a lawyer for nothing. Taking the fruits of office could, in a twinkling of an eye, become bribery and corruption, and such matters have swept many an honest person from office.

"And now, Jack," said Sir William after we had talked awhile, "you must allow me to say something in all seriousness. And do please listen until I have finished."

I nodded.

"You are, no doubt, all too aware of the great matter that passed between your father and myself. I would like to make it as clear that I in no wise associate you with those events, even though you are his son. You will always be welcome in this house and my acquaintance."

Partisan of my father though I was, I was aware of the deep goodness of that statement, if it came from true sincerity. I was inclined to believe that it did, for he had not the guile to dissimulate well, nor the hardness of heart to toy so cruelly with another. This made him a loyal friend, and a bad conspirator. The simplicity of his own soul made him unsuspecting of base motives in others, and so made him the perfect instrument for those wishing to bend the truth to their own ends.

"I thank you for those words," I replied. "I did not expect such a welcome from you. I was afraid that circumstances had engendered some bitterness between us."

"So they had," he replied seriously. "But that was an error on my part. I wanted you out of my sight, because I could not stand the reminder your presence brought me. I now see this was cruel. You have never done me harm, and have suffered more than anyone."

His statement brought a tear of gratitude to my eyes, as it had been a long time since anyone had talked to me with such kindness. I knew the limits of his generosity, for he believed absolutely in my father's guilt, and, oddly, found I honored him the more for it. It is no easy business to embrace the child of a man who you think has done you such injury.

"That is certainly true," I replied. "And I think I have been imposed on far more than was just. This is the cause of my visit. You were the trustee of my inheritance, and yet I have no inheritance. My lands are now in other hands, and my position is ruined. You may have considered that all bonds of loyalty between you and my father were dissolved, but your trust continued in that matter. So how is it that I am penniless now? I see from your face that this question disturbs you, and I do not in any way wish to level an accusation, but you must admit it is a fair question to ask."

He nodded soberly. "It is, although my wonder is not that you ask, but that you do not know the answer already."

"It is my understanding that I have been left with nothing at all. Is that correct?"

"Your fortune has been much diminished, it is true, but it

has not been extinguished entirely. There is enough for you to rebuild, if you are industrious. And there is no place better for making a name than the Inns of Court, and no profession more suited for amassing wealth than the law. My Lord Clarendon,'' he said with a smile of contempt, ''has demonstrated that beyond contention.''

''But the estate was sold, even though entailed. How could that be?''

''Because your father insisted on assigning it as guarantee for his debts.''

''He could not do that.''

''No. But I could.''

I stared at him as he admitted this, and he looked uncomfortable at feeling my gaze rest on him.

''I had no choice. Your father came to me and begged. He said it was my duty as a friend and a comrade to help him. Having tied up his lands so they could not be confiscated if he should come into misfortune, he discovered that he could not use them to raise money either. He absolutely insisted that I act on his behalf, and authorize the loan. All I was required to do was sign the papers.''

''And you did.''

''I did. And later discovered he had not played absolutely fair with me. Or with his creditors, for he had raised several loans at the same time, pledging the estate many times over. After the debacle, I found myself liable for the debts as trustee. Had I been a rich man myself, I perhaps could have assisted, but you know, I think, something of my situation. And, I must be frank, I was not in the humor to be generous at that time.''

''So the estate was dissolved.''

''No. Even so we did our best to keep it in your family. Your uncle bought it and I insisted on a clause that, should you ever be in a position to pay cash down, he would sell the land back to you. We also reached a settlement with the creditors; a generous settlement, I must say, for they accepted much less than they were owed; only some land was sold out of the family entire.''

''Including Harland Wyte, which will be the most valuable of all the land when it is drained. How come that was sold to the man who accused my father in the first place?''

Sir William looked surprised at the depth of my knowledge, and paused before he spoke again. ''No,'' he said after a short while. ''Sir Samuel did not act with great generosity of spirit, I must say, but we had little choice. You must remember that the revelations about your father were initially known to only a very few people and it was imperative to keep it so. The moment his creditors heard a whiff of the matter, they would have swooped immediately. We needed time, and needed Morland to keep quiet. I regret to say that his consent was expensive. The sale of Harland Wyte at an advantageous price to him bought us eight weeks in which to act.''

I bowed my head in the greatest of sadness, for I did not doubt that he was telling me the absolute truth as he saw it. I was heartily glad of it; I had encountered so much duplicity in the past few months that I no longer expected to meet an honest man and, I fear, was overinclined to harbor suspicions. In his way Sir William was betrayed every bit as much as my father had been, for his goodness had been perverted to evil ends. I knew that sooner or later I would have to tell him so, lay bare the whole scandalous history and confront him with what he had done in all innocence and with the very best of intentions. It concerned me, for I was afraid it would break his heart. And I also knew that I, as much as those evil men, would have to stoke up the fires of his wrath so that he would fight to correct the injustices in which he had participated.

IT WAS NOT TO MY ADVANTAGE TO PURSUE THE CONversation much further that night; I did not wish to seem overanxious and, in any case, I was desperately tired. Shortly after, then, I put on my cloak, picked up a candle and made my way from the warmth of the fire to the chamber I had always used. Presumably Sir William had roused out a servant when I arrived, for the room was already prepared for me; there was even a small fire burning in the grate, although it gave out more consolation than warmth. I shivered in that cramped little room, but nonetheless gave thanks as I knelt down to pray that I was not in one of the great, cavernous chambers more honored guests received. The Italian gentleman, I thought, would be suffering mightily that night. My devotions finished, and in that calm frame of mind which habitually comes over men of faith when they give thanks in true humility, I was in half a mind to wrap myself up as much as I could and get straight into the bed. But I was grimy from the journey and reluctantly decided to wipe my face first. A bowl of water had been placed on the chest by the great window and, after I had shuttered the casements tight, I cracked the thin layer of ice, then plunged my face into the bitterly cold water.

Then I received a rude reminder of the hydra-headed nature of my woes. Even after so many years I cannot bring myself to write down the obscene images that were conjured up in that bowl of water, illuminated solely by the flickering candle on the chest. The lubricious and foul torments presented to me were such that only the most devoted slave of Lucifer could have imagined them; to send them forth to anguish the soul of a Christian after prayer was an act of the most profound evil. The noises that reverberated through my head as I found myself leaning heavily over that bowl, desperate to tear away my eyes yet unable to move a single muscle, made me cry out with horror and terror. And yet (I confess) I was fascinated by the scenes I witnessed. Even the spirits of the pure and innocent were subjected to most violent depravity, and made to enjoy the abuse. I saw the image of my father—not he indeed, but a devil in his guise— stretched out as Sarah Blundy pleasured him in the most disgusting fashion imaginable. All sorts of demons cavorted lewdly in my sight, sure I was watching and relishing the torture they imposed. I could not speak, and could not move to take myself away from the foulness, because I was not prepared for it any more. I had grown weak, and believed that perhaps the assault was over, that perhaps the Blundy girl had relented, or given up her revenge. I now had all the evidence I needed that she had been merely preparing an ever more vicious attack. Nor, it seemed, did it involve only myself, if her diabolical master's reach could torment those who should be beyond harm and impervious to pain.

It took the mightiest of efforts to tear myself away from that monstrous sight, to cast the bowl onto the floor and fling myself into the corner of the room, where I lay panting, unable to believe that it was all over. I lay there much of the night, I think, cowering in sheer terror lest it start again, and remained motionless until my limbs were stiff and my body icy with the cold. When I could stand it no more, and the pain overwhelmed my fear, I rose from my hiding place and spent some considerable time checking that the windows were firmly closed, and pulling the chest across the room so that the door was barred so tightly even the devil himself would have trouble gaining entry. Then I tried to sleep, afraid of the moment when the candle would finally gutter out. I had never been afraid of the dark before then. That night it terrified me.

chapter thirteen

I WAS STILL SHAKY FROM FEAR AND LACK OF SLEEP when Marco da Cola engaged me in conversation the next morning. I was not greatly responsive, as I was very much preoccupied with the attack on me, but his persistent efforts eventually forced me to be as civil as possible. Looking at me with his twinkling eyes and smiling quite vacuously, he began by saying he understood that my father was Sir James Prestcott.

I fully expected that he was going to examine me on my father's fall, so answered in the coldest manner I could. But, rather than adopting a grave and distressed face, typical of those who intend to patronize with their commiseration, he brightened considerably at my response.

"That is excellent, indeed," he said in an accent so thick he was barely comprehensible. "Truly excellent."

He beamed with pleasure at me.

"Might I enquire why you say so? It is not a response I have been used to, of late."

"Because I knew your most admirable father well, a few years ago. I was greatly saddened to hear of his misfortunes. You must allow me to offer you my most sincere condolences on the loss of a man who must have been a perfect father."

"That he was, and I thank you," I said. I had taken a dislike to the foppish little foreigner, for such people are highly distasteful to me in ordinary circumstances. In this case, I was aware that my opinion needed revision. There were few people kind enough even to acknowledge an acquaintance with my father, let alone to praise him.

"You must tell me how you met him," I said. "I know nothing of that time when he was out of the country, except that he was forced to sell his services as a soldier."

"He sold them to Venice," Cola replied, "which was grateful for them, for he was a brave man. If more people were like him then the Ottoman would not be threatening the very heart of Europe."

"So he was valued by your state? I am glad of it."

"Highly. And he was as popular with the officers as he was with the men; he was gallant but never foolhardy. When he decided to return to his home those of us who wished your king well consoled ourselves that our loss would be your sovereign's gain. I find it difficult to believe that the man I knew could act meanly in any way."

"You must not believe all the information you hear," I assured him. "I am persuaded that my father was the victim of an abominable crime. With luck, I will soon have the proof of it."

"I am glad," Cola said. "Truly glad. Nothing would give me greater pleasure."

"You were a soldier yourself?"

He hesitated a moment before replying to my question. "I have trained in medicine in recent years, among other things," he said. "A most unmilitary occupation. And I occupy myself mainly with questions of curiosity. I admired your father greatly, but have never had much affection for his profession."

And the little man walked off, leaving me to give thanks that my father's character was such that it invariably left a favorable impression on those who encountered him, when they were unaffected by the poison of rumor.

Sir William had already left the house; he was an assiduous governor of his estate, believing firmly that it was his obligation to see to such matters himself. Besides, he always enjoyed it and would have been the happier had he devoted himself entirely to country pursuits. The profits of the court, however, could not be resisted, and at least four times a year he had to go to London to oversee his office. But the rest of the time he was in Warwickshire and nearly every day, whatever the weather, he would collect one or two of his favorite hounds and leave the house early in the morning, to pay calls, give advice and issue orders. Around noon he would return, red-faced from the exercise, radiating contentment and satisfaction before eating and taking a nap. In the evening he would see to the paperwork which any estate of size generates, and check his wife's governance of the household. This routine he repeated without variation every day, and I believe that every day he went to bed and slept soundly, confident of having blamelessly fulfilled all his many obligations. His life was, in my opinion, most completely admirable and content, as long as no unwelcome intrusion disturbed its placid rhythm.

Because of this I was unable to engage him in further conversation until that evening, when, his business done, he became once more the genial host. It was Cola, once Lady Compton had withdrawn, who brought up the subject of my father's innocence. Sir William instantly looked very distressed indeed at the remark.

"I beg you, Jack," he said sadly, "put this matter behind you. You should know that it was I who received the evidence of your father's guilt, and I can assure you on my life that I would not have acted had I not been totally convinced. It was the worst day of my life; I would have been a happier man had I died before I discovered that secret."

Again, I felt no anger rising in my breast as I had on so many previous occasions. I knew that this kind man spoke with the most complete sincerity. I also knew that he had been an innocent dupe, as betrayed as my father, for he had been tricked into plunging the knife into his best comrade. It was with the greatest regret, therefore, that I replied to his words.

"I fear, sir, that I will shortly require you to bear yet more distress. Because I am within a whisker of proving what I say. I am convinced that the evidence which convinced you was forged and had been concocted by Samuel Morland to protect the true traitor. It was given to you because your honesty was so unquestioned that an accusation from your lips would be the more easily believed.''

Sir William turned deathly somber at these words, and the silence in that room when I had finished was total.

"You have proof?" he asked incredulously. "I cannot believe it; to accept that a man could so coldly plot such a thing is incredible."

"At the moment my proof is incomplete. But I am certain that when it is presented properly I will induce John Thurloe to confirm it. And if that happens I do not doubt that Morland will sell his partner in deceit to save his own neck. But I will also need you to confirm some parts of the story. I believe my father was chosen as the victim so the Russell family could remove my father's objection to their profiteering. You are the only one who can say the information came from Sir John Russell to begin with, and that he had it from Morland. Will you say that?"

"With all my heart," he said vehemently. "And more. If what you say is true, I will kill them both with my own hands. But please do not think badly of Sir John unless you must. I saw his face when he told me of the news, and the distress was obvious."

"He is a good actor, then."

"And he also pledged himself, through his family, with your father's creditors for a while, so the estate could be sold at the best possible price. Had he not done so, you would now be in very dire straits indeed."

That, of all things, made me angry; the idea that I was meant to be grateful to such a man was infuriating, and the cunning way he had hidden his depredations under the appearance of selfless virtue and kindness sickened me beyond belief. It was desperately hard for me to resist jumping up there and then, denouncing all the Russell family, and upbraiding Sir William himself for his foolishly trusting blindness.

But I succeeded, although I let Cola converse with him for upward of half an hour before I was confident enough to speak again. Then I merely told him that I was sure, absolutely sure, that what I said was correct. And that in due course I would prove it to him.

"What evidence do you have so far?" he asked.

"Some," I said, unwilling to go into further details and dismay him by the fact that my case was not yet complete. "But not enough. I do not have the forged letters; when I have them I will be able to confront Thurloe directly."

"And where are they?"

I shook my head.

"You do not trust me?"

"I trust you completely. You are the nearest thing I have on this earth to a father, now that my own is no more. I honor and reverence you for all you have done for me. And I would not for the world burden you with the knowledge I possess. I am proud to place myself in danger of assault from these men, for they know that I am on their trail. I will not place others in danger without good reason."

This pleased him, and he told me that if my father was as guiltless as I believed, then I was a worthy son to him. Then the conversation diverted onto other paths with the Italian, a man most eager to learn about foreign lands, earnestly plying Sir William and myself with questions about the country and the way it was governed. Sir William told him much and I learned a great deal also, for although I knew that he did not like Lord Clarendon, I had thought that their dislike was mainly personal. Instead, I received my first great lesson in the politics of the land, for he told me how Clarendon, a man of little background, was so extending himself from his country estate nearby, that he was pushing his interest deep into the land usually controlled by the Compton family, up through Oxfordshire and across Warwickshire.

"He had the presumption to insist, absolutely insist, that one of the Warwick county Members of Parliament at the last election be one of his men, because he said it was vital there should be sympathetic men in the Commons to do the king's business. As if my family does not know, has not always known, where its duties lie. He has reached an understanding with the Lord Lieutenant of Oxfordshire, and is now handing out bribes to the gentlemen of Warwickshire."

"I understand he is in ill health," Cola said. "If so, he cannot remain in his position for long."

"I can only hope not," replied my guardian. "He is out to destroy my family."

"That is not surprising," I said sadly. "His friends have already destroyed mine."

We talked no more of this, as Sir William showed signs of distress at the thought, and Cola kindly began to ask about the late wars. Sir William reminisced about the battles and the heroic deeds he had seen; Marco da Cola talked of his country's war on Crete, and its brave resistance to the brutality of the Turk. I, having no stories of daring to contribute, listened to their tales, basking in their acceptance of my presence and feeling myself a man among equals. If only, I thought, it could always be like this. Then I would be happy, and want for nothing. A fire, a glass and amiable companionship is all any man needs for true contentment. I have them all now, and the future I glimpsed that evening is every bit as good as I imagined.

I COULD HAVE STAYED IN THAT HOUSE FOR A LONG TIME, and I was most reluctant to tear myself away; the tasks that lay before me were daunting and the prospect of renewing the struggle brought no pleasure. But I resolved that the sooner I began the better so, when Cola had retired to his chamber and Sir William went back to his office to attend to business, I slipped softly down the stairs and out of the great door.

It was entirely dark, with no moon and not even a star visible in the sky as I walked; it was only because I knew the house so well that I managed to find the track which led to the road; the small torch I had brought with me from the fire scarcely gave enough light to see more than a few yards ahead of me. It was cold as well, and my feet crunched on the frost that lay thick on the frozen ground. All around the night-birds fluttered, and the animals patrolled their nocturnal domain, searching for their prey, or trying to escape their fate.

I was not frightened, nor was I even apprehensive. I am told that this is unusual, for often we are given to know of impending danger, and our necks prickle or our scalp itches as the peril approaches. Not so in my case; I was concerned merely with finding the gate and the road to Banbury, and I had to concentrate so much to keep my feet on the path, and avoid the ditches which I remembered on either side, that I had no thought for anything else.

It was only the noise which broke that caution, and even then I did not react immediately, thinking—if I thought at all—that it was some fox or badger crossing in front of me, just out of reach of my torch's light. Only at the very last moment did all my senses scream out that I was in mortal peril, and force me to leap bodily out of the way of the hideous fiend which rose up out of the earth and blocked my path.

It had taken the form of a man, but such apparitions are never perfect, and the careful eye can always see where the imitation fails. In this case it was the movement, all jerky and irregular, that betrayed the fact that here was a monster, not a human being. It had tried to take the form of an old gentleman, but it was covered in rancid pustules and hideous deformities, with bent back and irregular gait. And its eyes—strange this, and I never understood how it could be—were dark as pitch, but burned brightly in the dark, and I could see the flames of hell itself deep within. The noise it made as it wheedled and cajoled and tried to fascinate me into its trust was the most revolting of all. Indeed, I believe it did not speak; rather, I heard its entreaties like the hissing of a snake and the squeaking of a bat as they sounded in my head, but not in my ears. "No, Jack," it hissed, "you must not leave yet. Please stay with me. Come with me."

I remembered the visions I had seen the previous night, and shuddered at the implication of the words, and willed myself to ignore its importuning. I tried crossing my fingers and holding them up to its face, but this symbol of Our Lord's suffering occasioned no more than a snigger of dismissal. I began to recite the Lord's Prayer, but my dry mouth and parched lips allowed no sound to escape.

And so, in blind terror, I retreated back up the path, keeping my eyes on the beast stalking me and fearing that it might at any moment grab hold of me and tear my soul out of my body.

I told it to leave me in peace, but there was no response except a hideous laugh and a sucking sound like that of a bog pulling a sheep under the surface, and I felt a cold, clammy sensation on my arm as it reached out a skinny hand to grip me. I leaped back, and swung my dagger round, more in the hope of indicating my intention of resisting than with any expectation of mounting an adequate defense. But my stout-heartedness and immunity to the creature's blandishments seemed to have an effect, for the devil relies on willing submission, and cannot easily force those who genuinely repudiate his blandishments. The monster fell back, gurgling with surprise at my forthright movement, leaving an opening. Using the same hand to push it farther away from me—an error, for it had a foul, putrid smell which was hard to wash off—I ran past, up the path to the gate.

I do not know where I ran, I was simply concerned with putting as much distance between myself and the hideous deformity as I could. Eventually, I came to the river that runs nearby, and walked down to the water's edge to bathe my hand and clean it of the smell that still filled my nostrils. I was panting hard from terror and the running, and must have stayed there, crouched down and huddled against a boat drawn up on the shore for the night, looking at the water for upward of an hour or more. Then, eventually, I roused myself, convinced that the danger must surely be past, and began to walk once more, calm but on the alert for more attacks.

I heard the dogs some half an hour later. They caught up with me shortly after that and, after I was manhandled to the ground, kicked and abused, I was informed to my absolute astonishment and disbelief that Sir William Compton had been brutally attacked, and that I was being held responsible for the deed.

chapter fourteen

I NEED NOT, I THINK, DWELL TOO MUCH ON THESE events. My treatment was abominable, and the accusations leveled against me a disgrace. While it is necessary and reasonable that criminals be treated in such a fashion, to incarcerate and humiliate gentlemen in such a brutal manner is beyond comprehension. The period I spent awaiting trial was one of the deepest distress and, in my weakened state, the Blundy girl sensed her opportunity, and I was driven near mad by the constant pains and visions that she sent to me, night and day.

I had been ready for the witch to launch another attack, but did not realize she had such strength and evil purpose. It took some thought to grasp the full cunning of what had happened, and once understood the explanation is straightforward. It cannot be doubted that Sir William heard me leave the house and came to investigate, and at that moment his form was taken over by a demon so effectively that my eyes could not penetrate the disguise; after I stabbed it with my dagger, the spell dissolved and the fiendish cloak evaporated. It was a devilishly evil attack, for the witch must have realized by then that she could not destroy me. So she thought instead to have others act for her: having me hanged would accomplish the task perfectly.

When I was thrown into the jail cell, and shackled with chains to its wall, I quickly came to realize that, without extraordinary fortune, she would succeed. For I had indeed stabbed Sir William and brought him near to death and, what was more, he had survived and would undoubtedly say that I attacked without warning. My defense was no defense at all, for who would believe me if I told the truth?

And for many days, I could do little but sit in my loathsome cell and wait. I was not without visitors and messages, but they were of little comfort. My dear uncle wrote to say that he washed his hands of me entirely, and would not help my cause in any way. Thomas tried his best, although I could see his disapproval very clearly on his face. But he tried, at least, when he could tear his mind off the fact that the final contest with Grove for the living was nearing, and would take place when Lord Maynard came to dine in the college.

Then came Lower, accompanied by Marco da Cola.

I will not repeat a description of Lower's impudent (and premature) demands for my corpse; Cola's account is accurate enough. On that first occasion, the Italian did not acknowledge me, and I pretended also not to know him as he clearly wished it. But he returned, alone, that same afternoon on the pretext of bringing me some wine, and we had a conversation in which he told me of what had transpired that terrible night.

For himself, he said, he spoke from hearsay alone; he had heard and seen nothing of importance. It was only the sudden commotion, of people shouting, women wailing and dogs barking that aroused him and brought him from his bed to investigate. From then on his whole occupation was with Sir William and his wound, for he had labored hard throughout the night and was alone responsible for the fact that he had not died. He assured me that Sir William would recover, and had already made so much progress that he felt free to leave him in the care of his wife.

I told him my heart was glad. Although I knew it would not yet be welcome, I begged him to deliver a message assuring Sir William of my joy at his safety, telling him of my total innocence, and asking whether he was conscious of the fraud perpetrated on his body. This he undertook to do, and then (having formed my plan for escape) I urgently repeated my request that Dr. Grove come to see me as soon as possible.

I was astonished when Wallis turned up in his stead the next evening, but my mind quickly saw that this happy chance presented fresh opportunities. He questioned me about Sir William, and asked a huge raft of inane and pointless questions about Marco da Cola which were so imbecilic I will not trouble to record them here. Naturally, I told him as little as possible, but subtly kept the conversation going with little hints and suggestions until I was sure the jailer would be too drunk to pay much attention. Then I overpowered him, trussed him up—I confess I tied the knots tighter than I would have done for Grove—and left. He was so surprised and indignant, I almost burst out laughing with pleasure. It was so very simple, I could scarcely believe my good fortune.

Knowing that Wallis was safe and sound gave me an opportunity I could scarcely dared have hoped for, as I knew that his room would be open to my attentions. So I crossed the town to New College, and used his key to get through the main gate. Again, the simplicity of the task made me believe that I was under special protection: the door to his room was unlocked, the bureau was easily opened, and the folio of documents—even labeled "Sr Ja: Prestcott"—was in the second drawer; half a dozen sheets of papers all so incomprehensible I assumed they must be the coded missives I sought. These I stuffed under my shirt for safekeeping, and prepared to leave, delighted with my success.

I heard the low but horrible scream when I was on the landing about to descend. Instantly I froze, convinced first that the devils had come for me once again and, when I was reassured on that point, worried that my luck had changed, and that the noise would draw attention and lead to my discovery. Hardly daring to move, I held my breath and waited; but the quadrangle remained as quiet and deserted as it had been before.

I was also perplexed; it was a noise of great pain, and clearly came from Dr. Grove's room immediately opposite Wallis's. With some trepidation, I knocked on the inner door—the great outer door was not closed—then quietly pushed it open and peered inside.

Grove was still alive, but only barely so, and the sight tore at my heart and drew anguished protest from my mouth. His face was contorted with the most excruciating pain, his limbs twitching and fluttering, as he thrashed about on the floor like a madman in the throes of an attack. He looked at me as I lit a candle in the grate and held it over him, but I do not think he recognized me. Rather, with an unsteady hand he indicated something on the table in the corner, then, with froth and spittle gurgling from his gaping mouth, he fell back on the floor and expired.

I had never witnessed such an agony, and pray with fervor that such a sight should never again assault my eyes. I was petrified by the sight, and dared not move, half afraid he was dead, and half that he would come back to life again. It was only with the greatest of effort that I stirred myself and looked to see what he had pointed at in that last, pathetic gesture. The bottle and glass on the table still contained a great deal of liquid. I sniffed cautiously and it gave no hint of mortal danger, but it seemed at the very least likely that poison lay behind what I had just witnessed.

Then I heard the footsteps coming up the stairs, and terror gripped my heart as tightly as my hand gripped a knife I saw on Grove's desk.

Louder and louder they grew, up one pair, pausing on the landing, then the other. It could not be Wallis, surely, I thought. He could not have escaped. And I knew that if any man came into this room, I would have to kill him.

The steps grew louder, and stopped on the landing, and there was a long pause before the thunderous knocking came on the door to Grove's room. Perhaps it was not; perhaps it was simply the lightest of tapping, but it seemed to me loud enough to waken the dead from their graves. I stood there in darkness, and prayed desperately that the visitor would think that Grove was not there, and go away. But in my nervousness and efforts to be quiet I accomplished the opposite, for I brushed against a book on his table, and sent it crashing to the ground.

All my prayers and wishes were of no avail then; there

was a pause, and then I heard the latch of the door moving, the unmistakable sound of the door itself creaking open, then a footfall on one of the loose and creaking oak floorplanks.

When I saw that the visitor had a lantern, and would soon see both myself and Grove's body, I knew I could hide no longer, so I reached forward and grabbed him by the neck, and pushed him backward out of the room.

My antagonist had little strength, and put up almost no resistance to me in his surprise and terror. It took scarce a second or two to wrestle him to the ground on the landing, stop the lantern from setting fire to the entire building, and then see who he was.

"Thomas!" I cried in the greatest surprise when the feeble light played across his ashen, frightened face.

"Jack?" he whispered hoarsely with even greater astonishment. "What are you doing here?"

I released him quickly, and brushed him down, and apologized for manhandling him. "What I am doing is very simple," I said. "I am escaping. But I think maybe you have some explaining to do."

His head fell when I said that, and he looked as though he was about to burst into tears. It was very strange, all this conversation: a priest and a fugitive, huddled close together on the landing, talking in whispers while in the next-door room only feet away there lay a still-warm corpse.

The look on his face, I may say, would have hanged him in any courtroom in the land even had the jury not known the long and bitter story which had led up to this event. "Oh, dear God, help me," he cried. "What am I to do? You know what I have done?"

"Keep your voice down," I said testily. "I have not gone to all the trouble of escaping just to be caught by the sound of your wails. What's done is done. You have been stupid beyond belief, but there is no going back. You cannot undo it now."

"Why did I do it? I saw the warden standing there, and even before I knew it, I had accosted him, and told him a complete pack of lies about that servant of his."

"What? Thomas, what are you talking about?"

"Blundy. That girl. I told the warden that Grove had gone

back on his word, and that I'd seen her sneaking into his room tonight. Then I realized . . ."

"Yes, yes. Let's not get into that. What did you come here for, anyway?"

"I wanted to see him before it was too late."

"It is too late."

"But surely, there must be something I can do?"

"Stop being childish," I snapped back at him. "Of course there isn't. Neither of us have any choice. I must run; you must go back to your room and sleep."

Still he sat there on the floor, clutching his knees. "Thomas, do as I say," I commanded. "Leave it to me."

"It was his fault," he moaned. "I couldn't stand it any more. The way he treated me . . ."

"He'll not make that mistake again," I replied. "And if you keep calm, we'll both survive to see you with a bishop's miter. But not if you panic, and not unless you learn how to keep your mouth shut."

I could not bear to remain there any longer, so I pulled him to his feet. Together we crept down the stairs and at the bottom I pointed him in the direction of his room.

"You go back to your room and sleep as best you can, my friend. Give me your word you will say nothing and do nothing without discussing it with me first."

Again, the wretch just hung his head like a schoolboy.

"Thomas? Are you listening?"

"Yes," he said, finally raising his eyes to look at me.

"Repeat after me, and swear you will never mention anything of this evening. Or you will hang us both."

"I swear," he said in a dull voice. "But Jack . . ."

"Enough. Leave everything to me. I know exactly how to deal with this. Do you believe me?"

He nodded.

"You will do as I say?"

Another nod.

"Good. Go away, then. Good-bye, my friend."

And I pushed him in the back to get him walking, and waited until he was halfway across the quad. Then I went back up to Grove's room, where I took his key, so I could lock the door, and his signet ring.

The plan that had leaped, fully formed, into my mind was so simple and complete that it must have been due to some inspiration, for I must modestly admit that I could hardly have devised such a perfect solution unaided. What had happened was perfectly clear, and Cola's document confirms it. For that was the day Lord Maynard had dined, and the great contest for his favor had taken place between Grove and Thomas. As might be expected, Thomas was outwitted, outthought and humiliated. He had never been one for public dispute, but had prepared himself so much, and worked himself into such a fit of anxiety about the encounter, that he was barely capable of speech. Grove, instead, was ready, for he had encountered Cola and knew that the Italian would be the perfect foil for demonstrating his orthodoxy and robust defense of the church.

So the Italian sat there, thinking he was engaged in a conversation about philosophy, while all the time Grove was showing his fitness for a parish by disagreeing with everything he said. Easily enough done, since Grove removed Thomas from the contest by ignoring him and battering him with insults until Thomas despaired at being constantly interrupted and walked out, I suspect so that no man might see his tears. I believe he went mad from despair, and denounced Grove to the warden shortly after in some half-thought-out act of desperation. Then he realized that it would soon be exposed as a lie, and a malicious one at that, so he went one, fatal, step further.

Not a goodness for a man of God, and yet I knew that Thomas had much good in him; he had shown me that time and again. And even had that not been the case, I was bound to him and owed him my assistance, for he was not only a friend, he was quite incapable of looking after himself. The loyalties of Lincolnshire I have mentioned before.

It was the possibility of aiding myself at the same time which indicated that some guardian angel must be about, whispering into my mind.

I should return to my narrative, however, and say that by the time I left Grove's room with his signet in my pocket it was nine o'clock by St. Mary's, and I knew that I had eight hours before the jailer would come to my cell in the castle and discover my escape. My movements were unconstrained and I was at total liberty to do whatever I wished. What I wished to do at that moment was kill Sarah Blundy, as it had long been clear to me that only through the death of one or the other of us would this diabolical contest be brought to an end.

I knew, of course, that this was impossible. I could no more kill her with my own hands than she could kill me. Others had to do that and, just as she had laid a trap for me, that I should be hanged, so I could do the same to her.

It was slightly before midnight, I think, that I made my way through the fortifications that still surrounded the town and avoided the night watch. Certainly I heard the great bells of the city making their mournful toll as I walked swiftly across the fields parallel to the London road, which I dared not use until I was past Heddington Village. Dawn was beginning to come over the horizon by the time I approached the village of Great Milton.

chapter fifteen

I WAITED UNTIL THE MORNING WAS WELL AD-
vanced, spending my time observing the house unseen to see
how many people there were and what might be my best
means of escape should that be necessary. Then, my heart
thudding in my chest, I prepared myself, walked up to the
door and knocked. It was pleasantly warm in the hallway,
which was surprisingly far from opulent. I knew, of course,
that Thurloe had made himself as rich as Croesus during his
years of power as Cromwell's henchman and was disconcerted to see him in such modest accommodation. I only saw
one servant in all the time I was there, and although the house
was comfortable, it was not of the size and splendor I expected. But I assumed that this was another example of the
arrogant humility of the Puritans, who make such a show of
their piety and disdain for worldly possessions. Personally, I
always detested them for that, grabbing with one hand and
praying with the other. It is the duty of men of rank to live
in a suitable state, even if they have no inclination.

The servant, an old fellow who blinked like an owl
brought suddenly into the light, told me that his master was
busy at his books, and that I should wait in the main parlor.
Mr. Thurloe would be glad of a visitor to divert him, he said.
Not this one, I thought to myself as I followed his instructions and walked in the commodious, warm room at the eastern end of the house. Not this one.

He came in a few minutes later, a gaunt man with long, thin hair around a high-domed forehead. His skin was pale, almost translucent and, apart from heavy lines around his eyes, he seemed younger than I knew he must be. Now I knew what had transpired, and how he had manipulated men, good and bad, to his will, I was half minded simply to run him through then and there, without wasting further time. He'd find out who his assailant was soon enough, I thought, when the flames began to lick around his soul.

I was determined, but felt my resolution ebb with every step he took toward me. For months now, lying awake at night, I had imagined myself whipping out my father's sword and thrusting it into his heart, intoning some suitable words as he expired with a look of cowardly terror on his face, crying for mercy, slobbering with fear, while I stood implacable over him. I had no sword, but Grove's knife would do as well.

Easy to imagine, harder to accomplish. Killing a man in battle when the blood is hot is one thing; dispatching one in a peaceful parlor, with the fire crackling comfortably in the grate and the smell of burning apple logs in the air, is quite another. Doubt assailed me for the first time: Would killing a man unable to defend himself not suddenly lower me to his level? Would not my great act be demeaned if it was performed in an unseemly manner?

I suspect I would not be so bothered now, although as it is unlikely that I will ever be in such a situation again (the Lord having smiled on me) it is easy to say and difficult to prove. Perhaps, indeed, it was my doubt and my hesitation which earned me that divine forbearance.

"Good morning, sir, you are welcome," he said quietly, examining me curiously all the while. "I see you are cold; pray let me get you some refreshment."

I wanted to spit at him, and say I would not drink with a man like him. But the words stuck in my throat, and in my weakness and confusion I stood there mute while he clapped his hands and asked the servant to bring some ale.

"Do sit, sir," he said, after another long silence when he had again examined me carefully, for I had, with my normal politeness, jumped up to bow to him when he entered. "And please be careful you do not impale yourself on your dagger.''

All this he said with a wry smile, and I blushed and stammered like a schoolchild caught throwing things in class.

"What is your name? I believe I know your face, although I see so few people now that I trick myself into recognizing total strangers." He had a soft, gentle and educated voice, quite unlike anything I had expected.

"You do not know me. My name is Prestcott."

"Ah. And you have come to kill me, is that right?"

"It is," I said stiffly, feeling more and more confused.

There was another long pause, as Thurloe sat, marked the page in his book, closed it and laid it neatly on the table. Then he placed his hands in his lap and looked at me once more.

"Well? Go ahead. I would hate to detain you unnecessarily."

"Don't you want to know why?"

He seemed almost puzzled at the question, and shook his head. "Only if you wish to tell me. As far as I am concerned, compared with meeting the Lord and His standing in judgment of me, of what importance is the why or the wherefore of men? Do take some ale," he added, pouring out a glass from the broad earthenware pot the servant had brought.

I shrugged the glass aside. "It's very important," I said petulantly, realizing as I spoke that I was drifting further and further away from my imagined behavior.

"In that case I am listening," he said. "Although I cannot understand what injury I may have done you. You are surely too young to be my enemy?"

"You killed my father."

He looked worried at the statement. "Did I? I don't recall it."

At last he was talking in a way which angered me, which I knew was necessary if I was going to accomplish my aim.

"You damnable liar. Of course you do. Sir James Prestcott, my father."

"Oh," he said quietly. "Yes. Of course I remember him. But I thought you must have meant someone else: I never harmed your father. I tried to at one stage, of course; he was one of the handful of the king's servants who was not a fool."

"That was why you destroyed him. You couldn't catch him, or do battle with him, so you poisoned men's minds against him with lies and clawed him down that way."

"You hold me responsible?"

"You were."

"Very well, then. If you say so," he said calmly, and lapsed into silence.

Again he had wrong-footed me. I don't know what I expected: either a vehement denial or an outrageous justification of his deeds. I certainly did not anticipate him not seeming to care one way or the other.

"Defend yourself," I said hotly.

"With what? I do not have your knife or your strength, so if you want to kill me, you will not find it a difficult task."

"I mean defend what you did."

"Why? You have already decided that I am guilty, so I fear that my feeble replies will not sway you."

"That's not fair," I cried, realizing as I spoke that this was the sort of childish remark a man like my father would never have made.

"Few things are," he said.

"My father was no traitor," I said.

"That may be the case."

"Are you saying you didn't destroy him? You expect me to believe that?"

"I haven't said anything. But since you ask, no. I did not. Of course, I have little influence over whether you believe me."

Later in life—too late to be of use to me then—I understood how John Thurloe had risen to such an eminence that he was the one person in the land who dared contradict Cromwell. You punched, Thurloe rose up again, sweetly reasonable and soft-voiced. You kept on punching, he kept on getting up, always gentle and never losing his temper, until you felt ashamed of yourself and listened to him instead. Then, when you were off balance, he simply persuaded you around to his point of view. He never thrust himself forward, never forced his opinions on you but, sooner or later, the anger and opposition exhausted themselves by dashing against his persistence.

"You did it to others, and you expect me to believe that you didn't to my father?"

"Which others?"

"You didn't say he was innocent. You had the chance."

"It was not my job to ensure that my enemies were strong and unified. Besides, who would have believed me? Do you think a certificate of honesty from me would have cleared his reputation? If the king's party wished to tear into themselves and chase ghosts, what was that to me? The weaker they were, the better."

"So weak that the king is on his throne and you are here in obscurity," I sneered, conscious not only that his arguments were good, but also that I had never even considered them before, so clear and obvious had his guilt appeared to me.

"Only because the Protector died, and he thought . . . Well, no matter," he said softly. "There was a vacuum, and nature abhors a vacuum. Charles didn't win his throne back; he was sucked back by forces far greater than he could have mustered on his own. And it remains to be seen whether he is strong enough to keep his seat."

"You must have been delighted," I said with heavy sarcasm.

"Delighted?" he repeated thoughtfully. "No; of course not. I had worked for ten years to make England stable and free from tyranny and it was no pleasure to see that blown away on the winds. But I was not as upset as you might imagine. The armies were on the march, and the factions only Cromwell could have controlled were forming again. It was the king or war. I did not oppose Charles. And I could have done so, you know. Had I so wished, Charles would have been in his grave for years by now."

He said it in such a calm and matter-of-fact way that for a moment I didn't grasp the full horror of what he was saying. Then I gasped. This little man had gravely decided, as a matter of policy, whether his rightful monarch, anointed by God, would live or die. Charles, by grace of Thurloe, King of England. And I knew that he was saying nothing more than the truth: I was sure that he and the Protector had considered such a course. If they had rejected it, it was not because they recoiled from such a crime—they had committed so many already—but because it was not to their convenience.

"But you didn't."

"No. The Commonwealth acted within the law; and suffered gravely as a result. How much easier it would have been if the elder Charles had succumbed to a mysterious illness and died, with our hands clean in public, however shamefully we had behaved in secret. But we tried him, and executed him . . ."

"Murdered him, you mean."

". . . and *executed* him in full public view, never once seeking to hide what we were doing. The same goes with the other traitors—loyal patriots, I suppose they now are—who were caught. Name me one who was murdered in secret, without being publicly tried."

Everyone knew there had been thousands; but as they had been done away with secretly, naturally I did not know their names, and I told him so.

"I see. So I killed countless people, but you cannot name a single one. Are you intended for the law, Mr. Prestcott?"

I said that, due to the family misfortunes, I was indeed.

"I wondered. I was a lawyer myself, you know, before I took to public service. I very much hope your family fortunes mend, as I do not think you will be a great adornment to the profession. You do not present a very good case."

"We are not in a court of law here."

"No," he agreed. "You are in my parlor. But if you wish, you may turn it into a courtroom, and you may make your first speech. I will answer, and you can then make up your mind. Come now; it is a handsome offer. You get to be prosecution, judge, jury and (if you win your case) executioner. Such an opportunity comes very infrequently to a man of your age."

For some reason, I didn't even question him anymore. It was too late now for the bold action I had originally intended. I now wanted him to acknowledge I was right, and hear him admit that he deserved my punishment. That was why I fell in with him—and why I still think that he was wrong. I would have made a good lawyer, even though I am profoundly grateful I was not reduced to such a state.

"Well," I began, "the thing is . . ."

"No, no, no," he interrupted me gently. "We are in a court, sir. Your presentation is a disgrace. Never begin a speech with, 'Well, the thing is . . .' Do they not teach rhetoric in the university anymore? Now, begin properly, always making sure you address the judge respectfully—even when he's an old fool—and the jury as though you are sure they are a benchful of Solomons, even if you've spent the morning bribing them. Start again. And don't be shy; you can't be shy if you want to win."

"My lord, members of the jury," I began. Even after all these years, I am still amazed by the way I meekly did as instructed.

"Much better," he said. "Go on. But try to pitch your voice a little more effectively."

"My lord, members of the jury," I said heavily and with some irony, for I did not wish it thought that I gave way to this play-acting without some resentment. "You sit here to judge one of the most evil crimes in the history of mankind; for the defendant before you is charged not with simple theft or the murder of a man committed in hot blood, but with the cold and calculating destruction of a gentleman, too good and too honorable to be harmed in any other way.

"This gentleman, Sir James Prestcott, cannot speak to tell you of the injuries done to him. His family must do that for him in the traditional manner, so that his cries for justice from beyond the grave can be assuaged, and his soul can sleep in peace."

"Very good," said Thurloe. "A handsome start."

"As the judge, I must request the defendant to keep his silence. If this is a law court, the proper forms must be maintained."

"My apologies."

"I do not ask you to condemn this man without laying out the full facts of the case; that is all I need to do to make you to realize, without a shadow of a doubt, that this man is guilty. I shall state the case and stop: no high-flown rhetorical persuasion is needed.

"The goodness, the loyalty and the courage of Sir James Prestcott were such that he gave everything in the king's cause, and was prepared to give still more. When most had given up, he returned from exile to work for the blessed Restoration which we now all enjoy. Some joined him in this struggle, but few as wholeheartedly, and some did so merely out of consideration for their own gain. Some betrayed their friends and their cause for their own advancement, and whenever John Thurloe came across such people, he used them, then protected them by ensuring the blame for the damage they caused fell on the shoulders of others. His main informant, and the man who should have been punished for the deeds which destroyed my father, was John Mordaunt.''

I paused here to see whether revealing the depths of my knowledge so suddenly shocked him. It did not; rather he merely sat there, entirely without movement and with no sign even of interest.

"Let me explain. Mordaunt was the youngest son of a noble family, which was keen not to take sides in the war and instead wished to profit whoever might triumph. Mordaunt was supposedly inclined to the king but was too young to take an active part in the fighting and so was sent away, like many others, to travel abroad where he could be safe. In particular he went to Savoy, and there he met Samuel Morland, a man already in the service of the Commonwealth.

"Mordaunt was already linked to the king's cause, Morland to Cromwell's. When exactly the two of them entered into a partnership to advance themselves is uncertain, but I think that in all essentials it was a done deed by the time Sir Samuel returned to England in 1656. Mordaunt also returned and began to gain a reputation among the Royalists, his skill, intelligence and reputation for acumen considerably aided, I believe, by the constant information which Morland gave him. But the price the Royalists paid for his reputation was high indeed, for Mordaunt bought it by betraying every single plot the king's men developed.

"At one stage, the traitors made a bad mistake and in 1658 Mordaunt was arrested in a general roundup of Royalist sympathizers. It is inconceivable that a man as ruthless as John Thurloe would let someone so important escape had he truly been in the king's cause. But was he led to the gallows like his associates? Was he tied to a chair and tortured to discover his valuable hidden knowledge? Was he at the very least kept in close custody? Not at all. He was released within six weeks, it was said because the jury was bribed by his wife.

"It would, I believe, have taken a very large bribe indeed to persuade a juror to run the risk of releasing the most dangerous man in England, and incurring Thurloe's wrath. But, in fact, no bribe was needed; the jurors were instructed how to vote, and followed those instructions without payment. Mordaunt returned to the fray, his fame for audacity and courage enhanced, and his position unquestioned.

"By this stage it was clear to the Royalists that a traitor did exist, and must be unmasked. Thurloe, accordingly, began to hatch a plan to deflect attention onto others and protect his source of information. So he had a series of documents concocted to protect the true traitor. They used a cipher my father used, contained information he would have known. But why pick on him, rather than any of the other Royalists, who would have served just as well?

"Perhaps Mr. Thurloe can be acquitted in this respect, for I believe that Samuel Morland's greed played a part here, as he profited hugely from my father's disgrace, knowing that the family of his associate John Russell would reward him well if he helped them sweep aside obstacles to their plans for the fenlands. So Morland approached that family, and told them that Sir James Prestcott could be removed if it was made worth his while. Sir John Russell leaped on the information Morland provided and began to disseminate it widely, and his passionate advocacy deceived Sir William Compton into denouncing and destroying his closest friend.

"Thus, the second aspect of the plan, which joined the destruction of my father's reputation to that of his estate, was brought into being. I do not know whether he ever imagined that so many powerful people desired, indeed required, his fall. Thurloe, protecting the government; Mordaunt and Morland, whose future rested on his shouldering the blame for their deeds; and the might of the Russell family, which gained the freedom it needed to exploit the fenlands. Everybody profited handsomely from the arrangement, and the cost was small. Only the life and honor of a single man needed to be sacrificed.

"It is impossible to counter accusations made in such a way; there were no charges, so how could they be refuted? No evidence was produced, so how could it be shown to be forged? My father withdrew with a dignity that was mistaken for cowardice. He fled to avoid calumny, false imprisonment and even the assassin's knife, and this was mistaken for guilt. And all along Thurloe, the author of his misfortunes and the one man who could have cleansed his honor, said not a word. Who else could have conceived of such a scheme? And who else had the means to put it into operation? Only John Thurloe, who knew everything, saw everything, and was the moving force behind all occult activities.

"And I, members of the jury, am reduced to the sorry state which you behold. I have no resources, no connections and no influence except that of argument and my unquenching belief in the justice of my case, and the goodness of this court. I am sure it will be more than enough."

Is this what I said, word for word? No; of course it is not; I am sure that my youth tripped my tongue and that the speech was not half as assured as I like to remember it. My friends who read books tell me this is the way of history. Even great historians write down what the actors should say, rather than what they did. So it is with myself, and if I have improved and polished over the years, then I do not apologize for it. I remember the occasion, though, as if I did speak in this way, restrained but passionate, zealous but controlled, standing before him, fixed upon his countenance, strangely concerned to convince him that what I said was true but realizing that I was as concerned to convince myself

He did not reply at once, that I remember clearly. Rather, he continued to sit impassively, his book folded on his lap, nodding quietly. After a short while, when there was no sound but the crackling and hissing of the logs in the grate, he began to reply, still maintaining the fiction of the drama.

"I will not condescend to my learned prosecutor by complimenting him on a fine speech, sincerely delivered as only a son could manage. The honesty of the words I do not doubt; the courage and zeal for justice is also beyond question, and it is honorable in one so young to take such a weighty task on his shoulders unsupported.

"But this is a court of law, and cannot admit of sentiment. So, I must point out that the case for my guilt is thin, and the proof offered is insubstantial. The word of a father carries weight with a son, but not with a court. If you are to translate your own convictions into accepted fact, you must rest your case on much more than the protestations of a man under accusation. That I destroyed an innocent is a grave charge, and cannot be allowed to stand by mere assertion.

"Sir James Prescott was accused of treachery, and he was destroyed: I admit I am the obvious person to suspect. For long years I was responsible for the safety of the government, and I do not deny that the methods I used were many and various. This was necessary, for there were indeed plots against us; so numerous that I can no longer recall them all. Time and again agitators tried to return the country to the horrors of war and civil strife. It was my job to prevent this, and I performed the task to the best of my abilities.

"Was there an informer, a traitor, in the ranks of the king's men? Of course; not one, but very many. There are always people willing to sell their friends for money, but often I did not need the wares they tried to peddle. The Royalists were always the most foolish of conspirators. The proposed risings involved so many people with loose tongues that we would have been deaf indeed not to have heard of them. The satanic skill attributed to me was flattering, but wrong: for the most part my success was due solely to the stupidity of those who pitted themselves against me.

"As for Samuel Morland, he was not without ability, but his greed and faithlessness made him less than useful and I had long wanted to dismiss him from my office. I could not do so, because he held in his hands our most useful informer on the doings of the king's men, whom he called Mr. Barrett.

"Of all the government's sources of information, this Mr. Barrett was by far the best. We merely had to ask and Mr. Barrett provided the answer through Samuel. And Samuel refused to say who this man was. If I disposed of Samuel's services, I also lost Mr. Barrett, and Samuel was clever enough to realize this was the only reason I tolerated his presence. I often wondered whether he was passing information as well as receiving it, and took care that he knew as little as possible about our office's operations. As long as this trade did not become too disadvantageous, I did not discourage it.

"Who was Mr. Barrett? You are quite right; I also concluded it was John Mordaunt, and had him arrested so I could interview him personally and try to establish a direct connection that would eliminate the need for Samuel. But Mordaunt denied everything; either he suspected a trap, or he was indeed innocent, or his loyalty to Samuel was too great. Either way, I got nothing from him.

"It was a mistake on my part, for my action made clear my enmity to Samuel, and when his opportunity came he conspired against me, and caused my temporary ejection from office. When I recovered my position, he then went over to the king's party for fear of my revenge and denounced your father to win acceptance.

"So you see I do not wish here to dispute your case, that the traitor was John Mordaunt and that your father was sacrificed to protect him, although I would dispute some details if there was leisure to do so.

"I dispute one assertion only, however, and do so because your case against me rests entirely on it, and I can prove it wrong. You say I caused your father's disgrace, that I organized the forgeries and their dissemination, and I say plainly that not only did I not do so, I could not have done so, for when this happened I no longer had any place or influence in the government.

"I was dismissed from the Republic's service late in 1659, when Richard Cromwell decided he could no longer survive as Protector and gave up the struggle. A pity; he was not without ability. I fell from power with him, and was without influence for many months. It was in this period that the material relating to your father was created and it was passed to Sir John Russell, and thence to Sir William Compton. This is a matter of simple fact. I said there was a grave flaw in your reasoning, and this is that flaw. However true your general case might be, I cannot have been responsible for it.''

Such a simple mistake I made, and it hit me as a hammer blow. With all my earnest inquisition, I had never stopped for a single moment to consider the chaos that attended the dying days of the Commonwealth, the incessant struggling for position and treachery amongst old partners as they strove to save themselves and their corrupt edifice from destruction. Cromwell died, his son took over, fell from power and was replaced by cabals of fanatics in Parliament. And in all this, Thurloe lost his grip, for a while. I knew that, and had not considered it important; had not checked the facts and the dates. And from the moment I had started talking, Thurloe had sat there calmly waiting for all my eloquence to end, knowing that with a simple puff he could blow over my entire case against him.

''You are telling me that Morland alone brought about the destruction of my father?''

''That would be one interpretation,'' Thurloe said gravely. ''Indeed, from the evidence you have presented it would be the obvious one.''

''What am I to do?''

''I thought you had come here to kill me, not to ask my advice.''

He knew he had escaped. In effect he had told me that, on two occasions, when I had seen Mordaunt and later Morland, I had had the guilty ones in my grasp. One I had left with my thanks and best wishes. The other I had considered a mere instrument, a greedy little wretch perhaps, but essentially a source of information and nothing more. I felt a fool, and was ashamed that this man should see my stupidity, and lay it out so calmly.

''It is time to draw this to an end,'' Thurloe resumed. ''Do you find me guilty, or not. I have said you have the decision. I will abide by your verdict.''

I shook my head, tears of frustration and shame welling up in my eyes.

''Not good enough, sir,'' he pressed. ''You must pronounce.''

''Not guilty,'' I mumbled.

''Pardon? I am afraid I did not hear.''

"Not guilty," I shouted at him. "Not guilty, not guilty, not guilty. Do you hear now?"

"Perfectly, thank you. Now, as you have shown your devotion to justice—and I appreciate how much it has cost you—I will show mine. If you want my advice, I will give it. Tell me everything you have done, read, said, thought and seen. Then I will see if there is any way I can help you."

He clapped his hands again, and again the servant appeared, this time to be asked for some food, and more fuel for the fire. And then I began to talk and explain, starting at the very beginning and leaving out only the help and assistance given to me by Lord Bristol. I had promised to say nothing, and did not wish to anger a future patron by going back on my word. I even told him of my enchantment by Sarah Blundy and my determination to bring our contest to an end once and for all. But this topic I dropped; it was none of his business and I could see from his face that he did not believe in such matters.

"You have a gift to offer in your ability to accuse Mordaunt, for many people dislike him, and he is closely associated with Lord Clarendon. You must sell your goods to the right people, and you will get a high price."

"To whom?"

"Sir William Compton, I imagine, will be understandably anxious to prosecute you for your attack. As he also detests Lord Clarendon, he might consider it worthwhile waiving his suit if you contributed to the downfall of his greater enemy. And if Clarendon's friend Mordaunt is weakened, then Clarendon will be gravely weakened. More people than Sir William Compton would thank you generously for that. You must approach them, and see what they offer in return."

"That is all very well," I said, scarcely daring to hope for so much after so many frustrations. "But I am a fugitive. I cannot go to London, nor even to Oxford, without being arrested. How can I approach anyone?"

The majesty of the king's justice, however, he shrugged off. People like Thurloe, I was learning, did not consider the law a matter of great importance. If his enemies wished to destroy him, innocence at law would not save his life; if he had sufficient strength, no amount of guilt would bring him into danger. The law was an instrument of power, no more. And he offered me a dangerous bargain, a terrible choice. I wanted justice, but Thurloe told me there was no such thing, that all motion was the conflict of power. If I wanted to reestablish myself, I had to drag down the enemies of others in the same way they had dragged down my father. I could achieve my aim, but only by abandoning the purpose of it. It took many days of thought and prayer before I accepted.

When I had done so, Thurloe made the journey into Oxford during which he discussed the matter with Dr. Wallis after their encounter at the play. Although I had strong misgivings, he told me that Wallis was by far the easiest way of communicating with those men in government who might assist. Despite the way I had abused him in the jail, Thurloe did not seem to think it would be hard to win Wallis's cooperation, although he never troubled to explain to me why this should be so.

"Well?" I asked eagerly when at last I was summoned on Thurloe's return. "Will Wallis help?"

Thurloe smiled. "Perhaps if there is an exchange of information. You mentioned an Italian gentleman at Sir William Compton's."

"Da Cola, yes. A most civil man, for a foreigner."

"Yes. Cola. Dr. Wallis is most interested in your opinion of him."

"I know that. He has asked me before, although I have no idea why he was so fascinated."

"That need not concern you in the slightest. Will you say on oath what you know of this man? And answer any other questions he might pose, freely and frankly?"

"If he will help me, then of course I will. It is harmless enough. What do I get in return?"

"Dr. Wallis is able, I understand, to give you crucial information about the package your father had intended to send to your mother. That package contained everything he knew of Mordaunt and his activities. Whom he saw, what he said, and all the consequences. With that in your possession, your case will be easily won."

"He knew this all along? And did not say so?"

"He does not have it himself, and he is a dark and deep

man. He never gives something for nothing. Fortunately you now have something to offer. But he can tell you whom you must approach to obtain it. Now, do you agree to this bargain?''

''Yes,'' I said enthusiastically. ''Of course. With all my heart. Particularly if he only wants information in return. For a prize like that he could have my life, and willingly too.''

''Good,'' Thurloe said, smiling with pleasure. ''That is settled. Now we have to remove the threat of the law, and renew your freedom of movement. I mentioned your concern about this woman Sarah Blundy, and of the ring that you have from Dr. Grove's body. The woman has now been placed under arrest for his murder.''

''I am glad to hear it,'' I said, more exultation gripping my heart. ''I have told you how I know she killed him.''

''You will testify against her, your sense of justice will be noted and the charges against you dropped. Do you give me your word that this girl actually killed Grove?''

''I do.'' It was a lie, I know, and even as I spoke I resented bitterly the need to speak it.

''In that case all will be well. But only, I repeat, if you answer all questions Dr. Wallis poses.''

My heart was close to bursting with delight as I contemplated how I was triumphing in every single sphere. Truly, I thought, I was blessed, that so much should be given to me so swiftly. I was all enthusiasm for a moment, but then my spirit deflated. ''It is a trap,'' I said. ''Wallis will not help me. It is just a lure to get me to go back to Oxford. I will be thrown back into jail and hanged.''

''That is a risk, but Wallis is after bigger game than yourself, I think.''

I snorted. It was easy, I thought, to be calm and detached at the thought of someone's else's neck being stretched. I would have liked to see how he contemplated a march to the hanging tree himself.

THE NEXT MOVE CAME A FEW DAYS LATER. I HAD RE-luctantly come to accept that I would have to take the risk and place myself in Wallis's hands, but my courage had failed me, and I was in this state of indecision when Thurloe came softly into the room where I was spending my time, and announced that I had a visitor.

"A Signor Marco da Cola," he said with a faint smile. "It is strange how that man shows up in the most unexpected places."

"He is here?" I said, standing up with astonishment. "Why?"

"Because I invited him. He is staying nearby and when I was told, I thought I really must meet the gentleman. He is most charming."

I insisted on seeing Cola, for I wanted to hear everything. It was Thurloe who suggested that he might prove ideal as the intermediary for approaching the magistrate in Oxford, for I think even he did not trust Wallis as much as he said.

I do not need to justify, I hope, what I told him. I have given enough evidence to show how I had to escape the curse upon me and how limited my resources were. I had begged for release from Sarah Blundy's curse, but had been rebuffed. She had tricked me into attacking my own guardian; the efforts of magicians, priests and wise men to repulse her had all failed, and—though I have not mentioned it in my story as much as I could have done—almost daily I was assaulted by strange happenings, and my nights were a torment of fervid visitations, so that I had no peaceful sleep. She attacked me mercilessly, perhaps with the hope that I would be sent insane. I now had the possibility of striking back, once and for all. I could not possibly afford to let that chance slip through my fingers. And I also had my loyalty to Thomas.

So I told Cola that I had visited her cottage on my escape, and had seen her as she came in, wild and excited. I told him that I had found Grove's ring in her dress, and how I had instantly recognized it and taken it from her. How she had turned pale when I demanded how she had come by it. And how I would testify to all of this at her trial. I almost believed it myself by the time I had finished.

Cola agreed to relay this to the magistrate, and even reassured me by saying he was sure that my willingness to come forward in the name of justice, even though I was placing myself at risk, would stand me in good stead for the future.

I thanked him and, indeed, felt so warmly toward him that I could not forbear from giving him some information of my own.

"Tell me," I said, "why is it that Dr. Wallis concerns himself with you? Are you friends?"

"No, indeed," he said. "I have only met him once and he was very uncivil."

"He wishes to talk to me about you. I do not know why."

Cola repeated he had no understanding of it, then brushed the matter aside and asked me when I proposed to come to Oxford.

"I think it would be best to wait until just before the trial. I hope the magistrate will grant me bail, but I am in a mood not to be overtrusting."

"So you will see Dr. Wallis then?"

"Almost certainly."

"Good. I would like to offer you hospitality afterward, to celebrate your good fortune."

And he went. I mention it only to demonstrate that there was much which Cola does not include even when he gives an account of conversations. Much of the rest of what he says is more or less correct, however. The magistrate arrived in high dudgeon and was all for arresting both Thurloe and myself until he heard of my evidence against Blundy; then he was all sweetness and accommodation—although I suspect Dr. Wallis may have already intervened and told him of the probability that Sir William would withdraw his suit, as indeed he did a few days later. Then I waited until word came that the trial was to begin and journeyed back into Oxford.

I did not have to give evidence, as it turned out, as the woman confessed to the crime—a surprising thing for, as I say, on this she was innocent. But the evidence against her was strong, and perhaps she realized that it was all over. I did not care; I was merely glad that she was to die, and that I did not have to perjure myself.

She hanged the next day, and instantly I felt her malign presence lifting from my spirit, like the first breath of cool, clear wind after a thunderstorm has removed the oppression from the air. It was only then that I realized how much she had tormented me, and how constant had been the drain on my soul.

IN EFFECT, THERE ENDS MY STORY AS WELL, FOR THE rest is outside the scope of Cola's account, and much of my own triumph is already well enough known. I never saw Cola again, for he left Oxford shortly afterward, but Wallis was highly satisfied with what I told him and gave me all the information I required. Within a month my name was restored and, although it was considered impolitic to proceed directly against Mordaunt, his rise was forever blocked. The man who, at one stage, was going to be the most powerful politician in the country ended his days in grubby obscurity, shunned by his old friends, enough of whom knew the truth about him. The favor of many men in high places, in contrast, won me the rewards my birth and position merited, and I exploited my good fortune so successfully I was soon able to begin rebuilding my estates. And, in the fullness of time I built my mansion just outside London, where my detested uncle comes to pay court to me, in the futile hope that I will pass some goodness on to him. Needless to say, he goes away empty-handed.

I have done much in my life which I regret and, if I had the opportunity, there is much I would now do differently. But my task was all important, and I feel reassured that I am acquitted of any serious offense. The Lord has been good, and though no man deserves it, my salvation has been no injustice. I would not have so much, and such a tranquillity of mind, had I not been blessed by His merciful providence. In Him I place all my trust, and have endeavored only to serve as best I can. My vindication is my assurance of His favor.

The Character of Compliance

The Idols of the Theatre have got into the human Mind from the different Tenets of Philosophers and the perverted Laws of Demonstration. All Philosophies hitherto have been so many Stage Plays, having shewn nothing but fictitious and theatrical Worlds.

—FRANCIS BACON,
NOVUM ORGANUM SCIENTARUM,
SECTION II, APHORISM VII.

chapter one

HAVING BEEN SENT THE COLLECTED NOTES OF THE papist Marco da Cola, I feel it necessary to comment, lest others also come across his outrageous scribblings and believe what he says. So let me state it plainly that this Cola is a pernicious, deceitful and arrogant liar. The wide-eyed naïveté, the youthful enthusiasm, the openness he presents in his narration are nothing but the most monstrous of frauds. Satan is a master of deception, who has taught his servants his tricks. ''Ye are of your father the devil . . . for he is a liar, and the father of it'' (John 8:44). I intend to expose the full extent of the duplicity he reveals in this memoir of his, this true account (as he has it) of a voyage to England. This Cola was the worst of men, the most savage of murderers, and the greatest of deceivers. It was only by the grace of Providence that I escaped that night when he tried to poison me, and it was the greatest misfortune that Grove took the bottle for himself and died in my place. I had half expected some attempt once he arrived in Oxford, but had thought more in terms of a knife in the back: I never conceived of such a cowardly assault, and was not prepared for it. As for the girl, Sarah Blundy, I would have spared her had that been possible, but could not do so. An innocent died, one more of Cola's many victims, but many more would have done so had I not kept my counsel. It was a hard decision to take, but still I try to acquit myself of wrong. The danger was great, and my own sufferings were hardly less.

I say this calmly and with consideration, but it has cost me much to do so, for the arrival of the manuscript came as the greatest shock. Lower, indeed, had not intended to send it to me even though he sent one to that man Prestcott; it was only when I heard of its existence that I demanded to see it and made it clear I would brook no refusal. My intention was to expose the manuscript as a piece of imposition as I could not believe it genuine, but now I have read it I know my initial assumption was wrong. Contrary to my belief, and the assurances of those I had reason to trust, it is clear that Marco da Cola really is still alive.

I do not know how this can be and I most certainly wish it were not so, since I did my best to ensure his death and was certain I had succeeded; I was told that he had been taken to the edge of the boat, and there pushed into the North Sea, that his deeds might be punished and his lips forever sealed. The captain himself told me the boat had hove to for many minutes until the man sank beneath the waves. The knowledge had given me some solace over the years, and it is cruel to have that consolation so rudely ripped away, for that manuscript shows plain that those I trusted lied to me and my triumph ended in fraud. I do not know why, but it is now too late to discover the truth. Too many of those who might know the answer have died, and I now serve new masters.

I feel I should explain myself; I do not say, you note, justify myself, as I believe that throughout my career I have been consistent. I know that my enemies do not accept this, and I suppose that the reasonableness of my actions in the course of my public career (if such you can call it) has not been absolutely clear to uninformed minds. How is it, they say, that a man can be Anglican, Presbyterian, loyal to the martyr Charles, then become chief cryptographer to Oliver Cromwell, deciphering the most secret letters of the king to aid the parliamentary cause, then return to the established church and, finally, use his skills to defend the monarchy once more when it was restored? Is that not hypocrisy? Is that not self-serving? So say the ignorant.

To which I reply, no. It is not, and anyone who may sneer

at my actions knows very little about the difficulties of re-balancing the humors of a polity once it has become subject to disease. Some say that I changed sides from day to day, and always for my own advantage. But do you really believe that I needed to settle merely for the professorship of geometry at the University of Oxford? Had I been truly ambitious, I would have aimed at a bishopric at the very least. And do not imagine I could not have had it: it was not my aim. I have not been governed by selfish ambition and have studied more to be serviceable than great. I endeavored at all times to act by moderate principles in compliance with the powers in being. Since my earliest days when I discovered the secret patterns of mathematics and dedicated myself to their exploration, I have had a passion for order, for in order lies the fulfillment of God's plan for us all. The joy of a mathematical problem solved with elegance and the pain of seeing the natural harmony of man disrupted are two sides of the same coin; in both cases I believe I allied myself to the cause of righteousness.

Nor did I desire fame and reputation for myself as a reward; indeed, I shunned these as vanity and was content for others to take the great positions of church and state, knowing rather that my secret influence was of far greater weight than theirs. Let others talk; it was my task to act and I did so to the best of my ability; I served Cromwell because his iron fist could bring order to the land and stop the bickering of faction when no one else could, and I served the king when that God-ordained role passed to him on Cromwell's death. And I served each well; not for their sake certainly, but because by doing so I served my God, as I have tried to do in all things.

My desire for myself was merely to be left in peace to approach the divine through the mysteries of mathematics. But, as I am a servant of God and of the realm as I am of philosophy, I have frequently been constrained to put such selfishness aside. Now there is another who will surpass me, as David surpassed Saul, or as Alexander surpassed Philip, I can do so easily: then it was a real hardship. Mr. Newton says he sees so far because he stands on the shoulders of giants. I hope it will not seem vanitous if I say that my shoulders are among the strongest to support his glory, and I am ever mindful (though too modest to repeat in public) of that saying of Didacus Stella, a dwarf standing on the shoulders of a giant may see farther than a giant himself. More than this, I could have seen farther myself, and taken some of his great fame, had my duty not called me to other things so insistently.

Now that it is so many years ago, many people assume that the restoration of the kingdom was a simple matter. Cromwell died and in due course the king returned. Would that it had been that straightforward: the secret history of that momentous event is known only to a few. At the beginning I thought that, at best, the king might last six months, a year if he was lucky, before the passion of faction erupted once more. It seemed to me that he would have to fight for his inheritance, sooner or later. The country had been in turmoil for near twenty years; there had been war and strife, property had been trampled on, the rightful rulers of the country killed and expelled, all stations of men upturned. "I have seen the wicked in great power, and spreading himself like a green bay tree" (Psalms 37:35). Were people who had become used to authority and riches simply going to renounce these baubles? Was it really to be expected that the army, unpaid and discarded, would quietly accept the king's return and the defeat of everything they had striven to establish? And could it be hoped that the king's supporters would remain united, when the opportunities for dissent presented to them were so great? Only men without power do not desire it; those who have felt its touch crave ever more of its embrace.

England was a country on the edge, surrounded by enemies within and without: the least spark could have rekindled the flames. And in this powder keg the most powerful men in the kingdom were engaged in a struggle for the king's favor which only one person could win. Clarendon, Bristol, Bennet; the Duke of Buckingham, Lords Cavendish, Coventry, Ormonde, Southampton: there was not room for all in His Majesty's favor and only one person could run his government for him, for none would tolerate partners. The battle was fought in the dark, but its consequences sucked many men in; I was one, and took upon myself the task of damping the flames before all was consumed. I flatter myself that I succeeded well, despite the efforts of Marco da Cola. He says at the start of his manuscript that he will leave out much, but nothing of significance. That is his first great lie. He puts in nothing which is of significance; I will have to do that to expose his perfidy.

My INVOLVEMENT IN THE MATTER WHICH THIS COLA tries to hide began near two years before he arrived on these shores, when I traveled to London to attend a meeting of like-minded natural philosophers at Gresham College. This organization, which later became our Royal Society, is not now what it was, despite the presence of luminaries like Mr. Newton. Then it was a ferment of knowledge, and only someone who attended could know what a buzz of excitement and endeavor attended those early meetings. That spirit has gone now, and I fear it will never return. Who now can match that band—Wren, Hooke, Boyle, Ward, Wilkins, Petty, Goddard and so many more names which will live forever? Now its members are like a bunch of ants, forever collecting their tawdry rocks and bugs, always accumulating, never thinking, and turning away from God. No wonder they come to be despised.

But then all was joyful optimism; the king was back on his throne, the country was peaceful once more, and the whole world of experimental philosophy was there to be explored. We felt, I think, like Cabot's crew when they first caught sight of the New World, and the excitement of anticipation was intoxicating. The meeting itself was very fine, as befitted the occasion; the king himself attended, and graciously presented a mace to signify his royal condescension in supporting our endeavors, and many of his most powerful ministers came too—some of whom were subsequently elected to our ranks when the Royal Society was officially formed, although, it must be said, they contributed little but luster.

Afterward, once His Majesty had made a pretty speech and we were all given the opportunity of bowing personally to him, and Mr. Hooke had demonstrated one of his more ingenious (and showy) machines to entrap the royal imagination, I was approached by a man of middling stature, with quick, dark eyes and a supercilious manner. He wore an oblong black patch over the bridge of his nose, which covered (so they say) a sword wound received when he was fighting for the late king. Personally I am not so sure; no one ever saw this famed injury, and that patch drew attention to his loyalty more than it covered a wound. Then he was known as Henry Bennet, although the world later knew him as the Earl of Arlington and he had just returned from the embassy of Madrid (though this was not yet common knowledge). I had heard vague reports that he was charging himself with maintaining the stability of the kingdom, and I was swiftly to receive full confirmation that this was, indeed, the case. In brief, he asked me to attend on him the following morning at his house on the Strand, as he wished to make my acquaintance.

The next day, accordingly, I presented myself, half expecting to be hurled into the midst of a formal levee, surrounded by petitioners and claimants all wanting the attention of a man close to the court. There were indeed a few people there, but not many and they were ignored. I concluded from this that Mr. Bennet's star had not yet risen too far or, for reasons of his own, he was keeping his connections, and even his presence in London, fairly quiet.

I cannot say that he was pleasant; indeed, he had a formality of manner which verged on the grotesque, so keen was he to observe all the niceties of protocol, and maintain rankings in a clear form. It came, I believe, from spending too long in Spain, which is notoriously prone to such excesses. He took the trouble to explain to me that he had provided a chair with a padded seat, as befitted my dignity as a doctor of the university; others, it seemed, had to make do with a hard seat or remain standing, depending on their station. It would have been unwise of me to hint that I considered such punctiliousness absurd: I did not know what he wanted and the government was about to send a visitation to the university to eject members inserted by the Commonwealth. As I had been so inserted, Mr. Bennet was not a man to annoy. I wanted to keep my position.

"How do you consider the state of His Majesty's kingdom?" he said abruptly, not being a man to waste too much time putting his guests at ease or winning their confidence. It is a trick often played by men in power, I find.

I replied that all His Majesty's subjects were naturally delighted at his safe return to his rightful throne. Bennet snorted.

"So how do you account for the fact that we have just had to hang another half dozen fanatics for plotting against the government?"

" 'This is an evil generation,' " I said. (Luke 11:29.)

He tossed a sheaf of papers over to me. "What do you think of those?"

I looked at them carefully, then sniffed dismissively. "Letters in cipher," I said.

"Can you read them?"

"Not at the moment, no."

"Could you read them? Tease out their meanings?"

"Unless there is some particular difficulty, yes. I have had some considerable experience in such matters."

"I know that. For Mr. Thurloe, was it not?"

"I provided no information which might have injured the king's party, even though it was in my power to do it considerable harm."

"Are you now prepared to do it any good?"

"Of course. I am His Majesty's loyal servant. I trust you remember that I took great risks with my fortune in protesting against the murder of the late king."

"You satisfied your conscience in the matter, but not to the point of leaving office, or turning down preferment when it was offered, I recall," he replied coldly, and in a manner which gave me little optimism about winning his favor. "No matter. You will be pleased at the opportunity of demonstrating how great your loyalties are. Bring me those letters deciphered tomorrow morning."

And so I was dismissed, not knowing whether to bless my luck or curse my misfortune. I went back to the inn where I habitually stayed in London—this was before I acquired my house in Bow Street on the death of my wife's father—and settled down to work. It took all day, and most of the night,

to get the letters done. The art of decipherment is a complicated one, and was getting more so. Frequently it is simply
a matter of figuring out how one letter or group of letters
was replaced by another: you work out by substitution that
(for example) "a" stands for "the," 4 stands for king, d=l,
f=d, h=on, g=i, v=s, c=n; and it is simple enough to decide that a4gvgcdhfh means that the king is in London. You
will note that while the method (much favored by the Royalists in the war, as they were, I'm afraid to say, rather
straightforward souls) of substituting one letter for another is
simple, the method of making a letter occasionally substitute
for a letter, and occasionally for a syllable or a word, is more
difficult. Nonetheless, it still presents few problems. What is
more difficult is when the value attached to the letters constantly changes—a method first proposed in England by Lord
Bacon but, I understand, in fact invented by a Florentine over
a hundred years ago and now claimed by the French, an
insolent nation which cannot abide that anything should not
come from their land. They steal that which is not theirs; I
suffered myself when a wretched little clerk called Fermat
dared to say my work on indivisibles was his own.

I will try to explain. The essence of this method is that
both sender and recipient must have the same text. The message begins with a group of numbers which reads (say) 124,
5: meaning that the key begins on page 124, word five, of
this text. Let us suppose that this page begins: "So Hatach
went forth to Mordecai unto the street of the city, which was
before the king's gate." (Esther 4:6, a puzzling text on which
I have given an elucidatory sermon, shortly to be published.)
The fifth word, "to," is your starting point, and you substitute "t" for "a," thus getting an alphabet:

abcdefghijklmnopqrstuvwxyz
tuvwxyzabcdefghijklmnopqrs

so that your message, "The king is in London," now reads
"maxdbgzblbgehgwhg." The important thing is that, after a
given number of letters, normally twenty-five, you move to
the next word, in this case Mordecai, and start again, so that
m=a, n=b and so on. Variations on this method exist, of

course. But the point is to ensure that the value of letters changes sufficiently frequently for it to be all but impossible to make the code out unless you have the text on which it is based. I will explain why this was important later on.

I was worried that the scripts given me might be of this type; I could possibly have deciphered them eventually, but not in the time allowed. If I am vain about my abilities, it is with some justice; only one text has ever defeated me, and that was in special—though important—circumstances which I will deal with later. But every time I am handed a coded letter, I know that bitter experience of failure might be mine once more, for I am not infallible and the possible variant combinations are virtually infinite. I myself have constructed codes which are unreadable without the right texts for decipherment, so it was perfectly possible that others could do so as well; indeed I am surprised that I have not been defeated more often, as it is easier to construct an impregnable code than it is to breach its walls. Fortunately, in the case of Mr. Bennet's letters I was again lucky: the authors were as simple-minded in their approach as were the Royalist conspirators in their day. Few people, I find, are prepared to learn from experience. Each epistle had a different code, but they were simple ones and each was long enough to allow me to fix the meanings. At seven the next morning, accordingly, I presented myself once more to Mr. Bennet, and handed over my labors.

He took them, and glanced over the fair copy I had prepared. "Would you summarize them for me, doctor?"

"They appear to be a group of letters to one individual, probably in London," I said. "All specifying a date, January twelfth. There are references in two of them to weapons, but not in the others. One mentions the kingdom of God, which I imagine rules out papists, and indicates that the authors are Fifth Monarchists or groups associated with them. Internal evidence suggests two of the letters come from Abingdon, which also indicates a seditious origin to the letters."

He nodded. "And your conclusions?"

"That the matter should be looked into."

"Is that all? That seems very casual."

"The letters themselves prove nothing. Had I written

them, and been arrested, my defense would be that they were all to do with my cousin's wedding.''

Mr. Bennet snorted.

''Far be it from me to give you advice, sir, but precipitate haste might be troublesome. I assume that you obtained these letters by occult means?''

''We have an informant, that is correct.''

''So if you swoop, your informant will be of no further use to you, as it will be obvious you knew where to look. Look, sir, it is more than likely that these letters indicate that a rising of some sort will happen, and that it will be in several parts of the country, led from the capital.''

''That is what concerns me,'' he said.

''Use your informant to find out where the provincial risings are to be, and on January eleventh, move troops there. I take it the king does have troops he can count on?''

''No more than a few thousand can be trusted absolutely.''

''Use them. As for London, sit back and watch; find out who is involved and how many, and have troops ready. Make sure the court is guarded. Then let the rising happen. Cut off from any support it will be easy to put down, and you will have solid evidence of treason. You may then act as you please. And collect such praise as will be your due for your prompt action.''

Bennet leaned back in his seat and watched me coldly. ''My aim is to guard the king, not to gather praise.''

''Of course.''

''For a cleric you seem to have a remarkable grasp of these matters. It may be that you were in deeper with Mr. Thurloe than I suspected.''

I shrugged. ''You asked my advice, and I gave it. You do not have to take it.''

He had not dismissed me, so I sat there while he stared out of the window before pretending to notice me again.

''Go away, sir,'' he said tartly. ''Leave me in peace.''

I did as ordered, and left thinking that I had not succeeded in disarming a man who could do me very considerable harm, and that my tenure at the university would be short-lived. I resigned myself to this as best I could; I was wealthy enough through my mother's side and had no fear of starvation or penury but, nonetheless, I liked my position and the stipend it brought, and had no desire to relinquish it.

I had played my cards as well as I could. The great virtue of deciphering letters is that it is profoundly difficult for anyone else to say whether you have done it correctly. In this case the interpretation (allied to a certain knowledge of my own) enabled me to demonstrate my potential usefulness at no great cost. For the letters clearly indicated that the uprising which so exercised Mr. Bennet was, in fact, going to be little more than the screaming and yelling of a few dozen fanatics and could in no way threaten the king. This band might believe that, with God's help, they could take London, the country and perhaps even the entire world; I saw fairly clearly that their so-called rising would be farcical.

But, with a little prodding from Bennet, as I later learned, the government took it seriously, and began having nightmares about the bitter and unpaid remnants of Cromwell's army rising all over the country. In late January (such is the length of time it takes to get information from London to Oxford in winter) news began to come through that Thomas Venner's band of Fifth Monarchist maniacs had fallen into the trap so skillfully set for them and been arrested after creating a stir that had lasted for all of five hours. More, a sudden decision had led the government to station a squadron of cavalry at Abingdon and in half a dozen other places a few days before, and to this wise move was attributed the fact that the old soldiers there had remained quiescent. In my opinion they had never considered doing anything at all, but no matter; the effect was made.

Five days after I heard of all this, I received a letter summoning me to London. I went there the following week and was instructed to visit Mr. Bennet, who had now been permitted to move into accommodations in Whitehall where he was so much closer to the king's ear.

"I imagine you have heard of the monstrous treason which the government successfully repressed last month?" he said. I nodded.

"The court was mightily alarmed," he went on. "And it has shaken the confidence of many. Including His Majesty, who can no longer hold on to the illusion that he is universally beloved.''

"I am distressed to hear that."

"I am not. There is treason everywhere in this country, and it is my job to stamp it out. At least now there is a chance that someone might listen to me when I give warnings."

I sat silently.

"When we met last, you gave me certain advice. His Majesty was impressed by the speed with which the rising was put down, and I was pleased to have talked over my policy with you."

Which, roughly translated, meant that he had taken all the credit and that I should bear in mind that he was my sole conduit to royal favor. It was kind of him to spell it out so clearly. I nodded.

"I am glad to be of service. To you and His Majesty," I said.

"Here," he said, and handed me a piece of paper. It contained a document confirming the king's trusty and well-beloved servant John Wallis in his post as Professor of Geometry at the University of Oxford, and another, appointing the same trusty and well-beloved John Wallis as Royal Chaplain to the king, at a salary of two hundred pounds a year.

"I am deeply grateful and trust I will be able to repay such favor," I said.

Bennet smiled, a thin and unpleasant smile. "That you will, doctor. And please do not think we expect you to deliver many sermons. We have decided to take no action against the radical rump at Abingdon, or at Burford or Northampton. It is our wish that they should be left at liberty. We know where they are, and a bird in the hand . . ."

"Just so," I said. "But that is of little purpose unless you are constantly informed of what they are doing."

"Precisely. I am convinced they will try again. Such is the nature of these people; they cannot stop, for to stop would be to commit sin. They regard it as their duty to continue agitation."

"Some as their right, sir," I murmured.

"I do not wish to engage in dispute. Rights and duties. It

is all treason, wherever it comes from. Do you agree or not?"

"I believe the king has a right to his place and it is our duty to keep him there."

"So will you see to it?"

"I?"

"You. You do not fool me, sir. That air of the philosopher does not deceive. I know exactly what tasks you performed for Thurloe."

"I'm sure you have heard an exaggerated report," I said. "I acted as cryptographer, not as an intelligencer. But that is of no matter. If you want me to see to it, as you put it, I am content to serve you. But I will need money."

"You will have what you require. Within reason, of course."

"And I beg to remind you that communication with London is not so very rapid."

"You will have a warrant giving you leave to act as you see fit."

"And does that include use of the garrisons nearby?"

He frowned, then said, very reluctantly, "In an emergency, if need be."

"And how will I stand with the Lords Lieutenant of the counties?"

"You will not stand with them at all. You will communicate only with me. No one else, not even in the government. Is that understood?"

I nodded. "Very well."

Bennet smiled again, and stood up. "Good. I am very pleased, sir, that you agree to serve your sovereign in this fashion. The kingdom is far from secure, and all honest men must labor to prevent the spite of dissent from emerging once more. I tell you, doctor, I do not know whether we will succeed. At the moment our enemies are dispirited and fragmented. But if we ever loosen our grip, who knows what might happen?"

For once I could agree with him wholeheartedly.

I WILL NOT HAVE IT THOUGHT THAT I ENTERED INTO my role with enthusiasm or without thought. I was not going to tie my fortunes to a man who might drag me down with him should he prove to have only an unsteady purchase on power and position. I knew little enough about this Mr. Bennet and so, the moment I had registered my appointment as Royal Chaplain with the appropriate offices, and dispatched the confirmation of my university position back to Oxford to confound my enemies there, I set myself to find out a little more about him.

He certainly had given ample evidence of his loyalty to the king, as he had shared exile with him and been entrusted with diplomatic missions of some importance. More to the point, he was a skillful courtier—too skillful, indeed, for Lord Clarendon; the king's first minister had spotted his abilities and, rather than enlisting his support, had instantly seen him as a threat. The enmity grew, and Bennet grew close to other of Clarendon's rivals while he waited his chance. He also attracted a circle of young men, all of whom went around praising each other's brilliance. He was spoken of as a man who would rise to the very top—and nothing ensures success at court as an expectation that success will be forthcoming. To sum up, he had supporters below him, and supporters above him; but as long as Clarendon enjoyed the king's favor, Mr. Bennet would rise but slowly. It was uncertain how long his patience would last.

Until it was clear whether he would continue to rise, or fall in the attempt, I had as much interest as Mr. Bennet in making sure my connection to him remained unknown. Besides, he concerned me in other respects as well: his love of Spain was well known, and the idea of helping a man with such sympathies distressed me somewhat. On the other hand, I desired to be of service, and Bennet was the only conduit by which my skills and abilities could be put to use. Nor did I consider the maneuverings of the great to be my affair. Who reigned supreme at court, who had the ear of the king, made little immediate difference; the kingdom's safety (strange days that we lived in) depended far more on the activities of those lower folk who were to win my attentions. I have mentioned the discontented radicals, soldiers and sectaries who formed such a large well of opposition to the government. From the moment the king returned, there was constant turmoil from these people, who were never as meekly accepting of the manifest will of God as their professions suggested they should be. Venner's rising was a mere squib of no great import, badly organized, funded and led, but there was no reason to think it would be the last, and constant vigilance was of the utmost importance.

The enemies of the kingdom had men of discipline and ability in their ranks: anyone who had witnessed (as I had) the triumphs of Cromwell's armies knew that. Moreover, they were fanatics, ready to die for their delusions. They had tasted power, and in their mouths it was as sweet as honey. (Revelation 10:9.) Even more dangerous was the fact that outsiders were ready to manipulate them and urge them on. My dealings with Cola (which I intend to narrate here) were more dangerous and more hidden still. A trust in God is very fine, but God also expects you to look to yourself. My greatest concern was that those in power would become complacent and underestimate their enemies. Although I cannot say I liked Bennet, we agreed that there was a real danger which needed to be confronted.

And so I returned to Oxford, resumed my mathematical enquiry, and began weaving a web in which to catch the king's enemies. Mr. Bennet's perspicacity in choosing me was considerable: not only had I some small skill in the matter already, I sat in the middle of the kingdom and, of course, had a network of contacts throughout Europe which could readily be exploited. The Republic of Learning knows no boundaries and few things were more natural than to write to colleagues in all countries to seek their views on mathematics, philosophy—and anything else. Piece by piece, and at very moderate expense, I began to have a better picture than anyone of what was going on. I did not, of course, rise to the level of Mr. Thurloe, but although never entirely trusted by my masters, I pursued their enemies and largely succeeded in heaping mischief upon them, and spending mine arrows among them. (Deuteronomy 32:23.)

chapter two

I FIRST HEARD OF MARCO DA COLA, GENTLEMAN (SO-called) of Venice, in a letter from a correspondent in the Low Countries, to whom the government paid a moderate competence to observe the activities of English radicals in exile. Particularly, this fellow was requested to watch keenly for the slightest contact between them and anybody close to the Dutch government, and to note any absences or unusual visitors. This man wrote to me in the October of 1662 (more to justify his gold than for any other reason, I suspect) and said nothing at all except that a Venetian, one Cola, had arrived in Leiden and had spent some time in the exiles' company.

That was all; certainly there was no reason at that time to imagine that this man was anything other than a wandering student. I gave the matter little attention beyond writing to a merchant, then traveling to Italy to acquire paintings for Englishmen with more money than sense, asking him to identify this man. I might mention in passing that picture dealers (now more common since it became legal to bring such works into the country) make excellent investigators, as they come and go as they please without causing suspicion. Their trade brings them into contact with men of influence, but they are so lowly and absurd in their pretensions to gentility and education that few ever take them seriously.

I received no reply until the beginning of 1663, my correspondent's laxity and the winter posts both conspiring to cause delay. Even then, his response produced little of interest and, lest anybody think I was careless, I append here Mr. Jackson's letter:

Reverend and learned sir,

In response to your request, while in Venice to acquire works of beauty for my Lord Sunderland and others, I had leisure to put in hand those enquiries which you requested. This Cola is, it seems, the son of a merchant, who studied at the University of Padua for several years. He is near thirty years of age, of middling height and well-built. I have found out little about him for he left the Veneto so long ago several thought him dead. He is, however, reputed to be an excellent shot and fine swordsman. Reports have it that the father's agent in London, Giovanni di Pietro, acts as observer on English affairs for the Venetian ambassador in Paris, while his elder son Andrea is a priest and confessor to Cardinal Flavio Chigi, nephew to Pope Alexander . . . Should you wish me to enquire further, I would be more than happy . . .

The letter then concluded with hopeful remarks saying that if I wanted to acquire any paintings, Thomas Jackson Esquire (not that he had any right to call himself such, being a mere painter) would be most grateful for the privilege of obliging.

When I received this letter, I naturally wrote to Mr. Bennet about this man Giovanni di Pietro—if the Venetians did have a correspondent in London, I felt the government should know who he was. Somewhat to my surprise, I received a curt note back: This di Pietro was already known to them, was of no danger to the government and Mr. Bennet was sure I had much more profitable areas of enquiry. He reminded me that my task was the repression of sectaries; other questions were none of my concern.

I was too occupied to be other than thankful for this as there were definite signs that the sectaries were indeed rumbling again and I had more than enough to keep me busy. Reports reached me of consignments of arms flitting about the country, of little conventicles of radicals meeting, then dispersing. Most dangerous of all, a solid report came that Edmund Ludlow, the most dangerous and able of the old generals still at liberty, had been receiving an unusually large number of visitors in his exile in Switzerland. The beast was stirring, but still it was like trying to measure the waters in the hollow of your hand (Isaiah 40:12). In several parts of the country I knew that trouble was brewing: I did not know why, or who was behind it all.

It should not be thought that my activities took place only in Oxford: I was, naturally, bound to be there during some of the term but much of the year I was at liberty, and spent a good part of my time in London, for not only did this give me access to the Secretary of State (Mr. Bennet received his reward that November), much of learned society was migrating there as well and I naturally wished to spend time in their company. The great venture of the Royal Society was under way, and it was vital that it was constructed along good lines, only admitting proper people and keeping out those who wished to pervert it to ungodly ends: papists at one extreme, atheists at the other.

Shortly after a meeting of the Society, Matthew, my servant, though far more than that, came to me. I will dwell much on this young man in my narrative, for he was as dear to me as a son; dearer, in fact. When I consider my own sons, doltish buffoons with whom no man of sense can converse, I despair of my misfortune. "A foolish son is the calamity of his father" (Proverbs 19:13); how much have I meditated on the truth of this saying, for I have two such fools. I tried once to teach the elder the secrets of decipherment, but might as well have attempted to instruct a baboon in the theories of Mr. Newton. They were left to my wife when young, since I was too busy on government business and in the university to attend to them, and she brought them up in her image. She is a good woman, everything a wife should be, and brought me an estate, yet I wish I had never been constrained to marry. The services a woman provides in no manner compensate for the inadequacy of her company, and the liberties she curtails.

I have been greatly occupied at times of my life with the

problems of educating the young; I have worked on the most unpromising material, persuading the dumb to speak and trying, from that, to arrive at general principles about the malleability of the infant mind. I would have young boys entirely removed from the company of women, especially that of their mothers, from about the age of six so that their minds might be occupied with lofty conversation and noble ideas. Their reading, their education and even their play should be directed by a man of sense—and by that I do not mean those wretches who habitually pass themselves off as schoolteachers—so that they might be excited to emulate what is great, and shun what is ignoble.

Had a boy such as Matthew come into my company but a few years earlier, then I believe I could have made a great man of him. The moment I saw him, I was struck with an inexpressible regret, for in his carriage and in his eyes I saw the son and companion I had prayed God to give me. Scarcely educated, and even less well trained, he was more a man than those children of mine who had every care expended on their puny minds, and whose ambition nonetheless extended no further than a desire to secure their own comfort. Matthew was tall and fair, and had such an expression of the most perfect compliance in his manner that he compelled the favor of all who encountered him.

I first met him when he was questioned by Thurloe's office about a group thought to be too radical for the country's peace; he was perhaps sixteen at the time. I merely attended, rather than conducted the interview (a business for which I never had much patience) and was immediately struck by the forthright honesty in his responses, which showed a maturity beyond both his station and years. He was, in fact, entirely innocent of any wrongdoing and was never suspected of such; but he was acquainted with many dangerous people, even though he did not share their opinions in any way. He was reluctant to give information about his friends and I found this innate sense of loyalty an admirable trait and thought that, could it but be redirected to more worthy ends, this ignorant child might yet be turned into a man of worth.

His interrogation was kept secret lest he lose credit with his friends, and I offered afterward to engage him as a ser-

vant at a decent wage; he was so astonished by his good
fortune that he accepted with alacrity. Already he had some
small learning, for he was the orphan of a printer in the city,
and could read well and write with accuracy. And as I
tempted him with knowledge, he responded with an enthusiasm I have never met, before or since, in any pupil.

Those who know me may find this incredible, for I know
I have a reputation for impatience. I willingly admit that my
tolerance for the idle, the stupid or the willfully ignorant is
swiftly exhausted. But give me a real pupil, one burning with
the desire to learn, who needs only a touch of sweet water
to yearn for the whole river of knowledge, and my care is
all but infinite. To take such a boy as Matthew, to form him
and see his comprehension expand and his wisdom develop,
is the richest of experiences, if also the most difficult and
calling for unrelenting effort. The getting of children is the
vulgar work of nature; fools can do it, peasants can do it and
women can do it. Framing those moving lumps into wise and
good adults is a task fit only for men and only they can
properly savor the result.

"Train up a child in the way he should go: and when he
is old, he will not depart from it"(Proverbs 22:6). I had no
extravagant hopes but I thought that, in time, I would establish him in some position in the government and ultimately
teach him my skills in cryptography, that he might be useful
and make his way to position. My hopes were more than
satisfied, for however fast Matthew learned, yet I knew he
could go faster. But I confess this merely excited my own
desires for him still further and I often lost my temper when
he misconstrued a phrase, or bungled a simple proposition in
mathematics. But I always thought that he knew my anger
came from love and selfless ambition for him, and he seemed
to try at all times to earn my approbation.

I knew this, knew his devotion to me was so great he
would sometimes labor too much, and still I pushed him even
when my desire was to tell him to rest and sleep, or give
him some token of my affection. Once I got up and found
him sprawled at my desk. All my papers were disorganized,
candle fat had spilled over my notes and a glass of water had
tipped on a letter I was writing. I was furious, as I am nat-

urally fastidious in matters of organization, and straightway pulled him to the ground and beat him. He made not one word of protest, said nothing in his own defense, but submitted patiently to my punishment. Only later (and not from him) did I learn that he had been up all night, trying to master a problem I had set him, and had finally fallen asleep through simple exhaustion. It was the hardest thing not to beg his pardon, to resist giving way to sentiment. He never suspected, I think, that I regretted my deed, for once a perfect submission is undermined and questioned, then all authority dissolves, and the weaker are the greatest losers. We see this everywhere we look.

I was aware, of course, of Matthew's connections with men of dubious loyalty and opinion, and could not forbear to use him on occasion to run errands and listen to gossip. In this often distasteful and dishonorable business he was invaluable, for he was both observant and intelligent in his manner. Unlike many of those I was forced to rely on—cutthroats, thieves and madmen for the most part, whose word could never be taken on trust—Matthew soon won my complete confidence. I called him in to me when I was in London, and wrote to him every second day while in Oxford, for I delighted in his company and missed it badly when we were apart as, I hope, he missed mine.

By the time he came to me that morning in 1663, he had been my servant for several years and had grown in stature to the point that I knew I would soon have to find him a permanent position of his own. Already I had delayed too long, for he was rising twenty, and outgrowing his tutelage. I could see him straining, and knew that if he was not soon released, he would come to resent my authority. But I held him to me still, unable to let go. I blame myself for this greatly, and think that his desire to leave me may have made him incautious.

When he told me he was to deliver a package to the private mails on behalf of a group of radicals, I immediately took notice. He did not know what this package was but had undertaken to take it to a merchant who delivered mails on his ships. It was common enough—especially amongst those who did not wish their letters to be read. The unusual occurrence was that someone like Matthew was to perform a task more suited for a child. It was not certain, but he had a feeling that the package might be of significance, especially as the destination was the Low Countries.

For many months now, there had been rumblings all over the country, with shadowy figures flitting about and mutterings of discontent. But there was no form or unity to the collection of reports which allowed me to discern the shape of their plans. Left to themselves, these radicals presented no serious threat to anyone, so great were their divisions and despair; but, should a man of authority and skill organize and fund them properly they could easily become so. Matthew had, I thought, provided the first beginnings of that external correspondence I had long been looking for. As it turned out, he was wrong, but it was the best mistake he ever made.

"Excellent," I said. "Bring me the package. I will have it opened, examine the contents and send you on your way."

He shook his head. "Not so simple, I'm afraid, sir. We— they—have learned caution of late. I know I am not suspected in any way but I am to be accompanied from the moment it is put into my hands to the moment I hand it over. It will be impossible for you to have access to it in such a fashion. Not for the time you will need to copy it."

"And you are sure it is worth the effort?"

"I don't know. But you asked me to mention any communication with the exiles . . ."

"You did very well indeed. Now, your suggestions? You know I value your opinion."

He smiled with pleasure at this small token of regard. "I assume it will stay in the merchant's house until it is placed on board one of his ships. But not for long; they want it on its way as quickly as possible. That, perhaps, will be the only opportunity for obtaining it in secret."

"Ah. And what is the name of this merchant?"

"Di Pietro. He is a Venetian and has a house near the Tower."

I thanked him profusely for his work, and gave him some small money as a reward, then dismissed him to consider what he had said. It troubled me a little, even though it made no obvious sense. For what was a Venetian doing helping sectaries? In all probability he was merely carrying mail for a fee, uninterested in either senders or recipients, but I was mindful that this was the second time the name of di Pietro had arisen. That fact alone made me more determined to examine those letters.

I had some leisure to ponder the problem, but not much: Matthew was due to deliver the package the following evening. Bennet had told me to leave di Pietro alone; but he had also told me to find out about the king's enemies in England. He had not told me what to do when these two commands were in contradiction.

So I went to Tom Lloyd's coffee shop, where men of trade were wont to gather to exchange news and organize themselves into better profits. I knew some people in this world, as I would occasionally venture capital in this fashion, and had learned who was to be trusted and who deserved only to be shunned. Particularly, I knew a man called Williams who spent a considerable amount of time gathering up individuals with money to risk, and putting them in contact with traders who needed finance. Through him, I had placed to advantage some small part of my surplus funds in the East Indies, and also with a gentleman who captured Africans for the Americas. This latter was by far the finest investment I ever made, the more so because (the captain of the vessel assured me) the slaves were instructed vigorously in the virtues of Christianity on their voyage across the ocean and thus had their souls saved at the same time as they produced valuable labor for others.

I told Williams, when I ran him to earth, that I was interested in putting some funds into the activities of an Italian house called Cola, and wondered whether this man was sound and trustworthy. He looked at me a little strangely, and replied cautiously that, as far as he knew, the house of Cola was funded entirely on its own resources. He would be very surprised indeed to discover that he was bringing in outsiders. I shrugged, and said this was what I had been told.

"Thank you for the intelligence, then," he said. "Your news confirms what I have suspected."

"Which is?"

"That the house of Cola must be in considerable trouble.

Venice's war against the Turks has devastated his business, which has always been in the Levant. He lost two ships last year with full cargoes, and Venice still cannot prise open markets controlled by the Spaniards and Portuguese. He is a fine trader; but he has fewer and fewer people with whom he can trade.''

''Is this why he set up here?''

''Undoubtedly. I believe that without the goods England takes from him, he would not float for long. What, exactly, is this venture?''

I said I wasn't sure, but had been assured it was of the greatest potential.

''Probably to do with printed silks. Very profitable, if you know what you are doing, but a disaster if you do not. Sea water and silk do not mix very well.''

''Does he have his own ships?''

''Oh, yes. And very well-found vessels they are.''

''He has an agent in London, I believe. Called di Pietro. What is he like?''

''I know him only a little. He keeps himself to himself. He doesn't mix much with others in the trading world, although he is well in with the Jews of Amsterdam. Again a warning for you, for if we go to war with the Dutch, that connection will be worse than useless. The house of Cola will have to choose which side it is on, and will inevitably lose yet more business.''

''How old is di Pietro?''

''Oh, old enough to know what he is doing. In his fifties, I believe. He talks occasionally of going back home and living an easier life, but says his employer has too many children who need to be provided for.''

''How many children?''

''Five, I believe, but three are daughters, poor man.''

I grimaced in sympathy, even though the man might well turn out to be an enemy. I knew enough to be aware that for a trader, whose lifeblood depended on keeping his capital close by, three daughters could be a killing burden. Fortunately, even though my two sons were both fools, they were presentable enough to be married to women of fortune.

''Indeed, a grave disappointment,'' Williams continued.

"Especially as neither of the sons is minded to follow him. One is a priest and—begging your pardon, doctor—useful only for consuming money rather than creating it. I believe the other plays the soldier; he did so, at least. I have not heard news of him for some time."

"A soldier?" I said with astonishment, for this quite important fact had been entirely missed by the picture dealer, and I made a note to reprove him for his laxity.

"So I understand. Perhaps he never showed any inclination to trade and the father was too wise to force him. That was why Cola married the eldest daughter to a cousin in the Levant business."

"Are you sure he's a soldier? How do you know this?" I said, returning to the question and, I could see, arousing Williams's suspicions.

"Doctor, I do not know any more," he replied patiently. "All I know is what I hear around the coffee shops."

"Tell me what you hear, then."

"Knowing about the son will reassure you about investing in his business?"

"I am a cautious man, and believe in knowing everything I can. Wayward children, you must admit, can be a ferocious drain. What if the son is in debt, and his creditors make a claim on the father while he has my money?"

Williams grunted, not believing me but willing not to press.

"I was told by a fellow merchant who tried to open trade in the Mediterranean," he explained eventually. "By the time the pirates and the Genoese had finished with him, he realized it was hardly worth the trouble. But he spent some time there a few years back, cruising around, and once landed a cargo on Crete for the garrison at Candia."

I raised an eyebrow. It was a brave, or a very desperate, man indeed who would try to run a cargo through the Turks to supply that particular market.

"As I say," Williams said, "he had taken losses and was desperate, so he took a chance. A successful throw, it seems, as he not only sold his entire cargo but was allowed to take a cargo of Venetian glass back to England by way of reward."

I nodded.

"Anyway, there he met a man called Cola, who said his father was a merchant in the luxury trade of Venice. Now, perhaps there are two Colas who are merchants in Venice. I do not know."

"Go on."

He shook his head. "There you have my entire fund of knowledge on the subject. The doings of the merchant's children are not my concern. I have more immediate matters to worry about. What is more, doctor, so do you. So why don't you tell me what it is?"

I smiled and stood up. "Nothing," I said. "Certainly I know nothing which might help you to a profit."

"In that case, I am not in the slightest bit interested. But if ever . . ."

I nodded. A bargain is a bargain. I am pleased to say that I discharged my debt in due course as, through me, Mr. Williams was one of the first to know about the plans to reequip the fleet the following year. I gave him enough forewarning to allow him to buy up every mast pole in the country, so he could sell them to the navy at the price he named. Between us, we profited handsomely, God be praised.

THE MERCHANT HE MENTIONED, ANDREW BUSHROD, I tracked down in the Fleet prison, where he had been for several months: his creditors had tired of him when a ship carrying most of his capital had gone down and his family had refused to come to his rescue. This, apparently, was his own fault: when prosperous, he had declined to contribute to a cousin's marriage portion. Naturally, they felt no obligation to him when hard times came.

So, he was not only in the Fleet, he was also at my mercy as I had sufficient influence to have him released if he did not cooperate; then his sanctuary would be lost, and his creditors would pounce. It took some effort to sift out the dross from what he told me and his accuracy in point of detail was dubious: it is enough merely to contrast his description of Cola with the plump, perfumed dandy I later encountered, to see that, even though his wounds then perhaps affected his appearance. Briefly stated, Bushrod's account was that he had taken a ship into the Mediterranean and to Leghorn to sell a cargo of woolen goods there. The price he gained—he was no businessman—just about paid the cost of the voyage, and he was casting around for goods to bring back to England. At this point he chanced upon a Venetian, who told of a hugely profitable voyage he had just made to Crete, running food and weapons into Candia harbor under the noses of the Turks.

The town and its defenders were so short of everything they would pay virtually any price. For his part, however, he would not go back again. Why not? asked Bushrod. Because he wanted to live into his old age, the man replied. Although the Turkish fleet was incompetent, the pirates were much more effective. Too many of his friends had been caught and a lifetime in the galleys was the best you could expect if you were. The man then pointed out a beggar in the street outside, whom he said was once a sailor in a Candia ship. He had no hands, no eyes, no ears and no tongue.

Bushrod was not brave, and was little interested in saving Crete for Christendom or for Venice. But he was out of funds, his crew had not been paid and his creditors would be waiting for him when he returned home. So he contacted the Venetian consul in Leghorn, who told him what sort of goods would be required, and then took a fat contract to bring out any wounded who were fit to travel—four ducats for a gentleman, one for a soldier, half for a woman.

They hugged the Italian coast as far as Messina, where they offloaded some pottery, then headed as quickly and directly as possible for Crete. Candia, he said, was the worst experience of his life. To be in a town of several thousand people all of whom expected to die shortly, abandoned by all Christendom, aware that their mother country was tiring of them, and persecuted endlessly by foes on sea and land, was almost too much to bear. Everything was coarsened and brutal after the longest siege in the history of the world. There was an air of desperation and violence which terrified him into lowering his prices, afraid that the townspeople would otherwise set on him and take everything he had for nothing. He still made a big enough profit to make the voyage more than worthwhile, and then set about preparing for the return journey by advertising for passengers. One of the people who took up his offer was named Cola.

"Name?" I said. "Be more precise, man. What was his name?"

Marco, he said. That was it. Marco. Anyway, this Cola was in a bad way, gaunt and thin, gloomy of attitude, dirty and unkempt, and half delirious from pain and the huge amounts of alcohol he took as his only medicine. It was difficult to believe that he could ever have been much of an advantage to the Venetian defenses, but Bushrod soon learned that he was wrong. The young man was treated with respect by officers many years his senior and held almost in awe by the common foot soldiers. Cola was, it seemed, the best scout in Candia, adept at slipping past Ottoman outposts, carrying messages to outlying fortifications, and causing all sorts of light disruption. On many occasions, he had deliberately and successfully set traps for high-ranking Turks and killed them, gaining a reputation for bloodcurdling ferocity and ruthlessness. He was skilled at striking in silence and escaping undetected and was, it seemed, something of a zealot for the Christian cause, despite all appearances to the contrary.

Curious about his passenger, Bushrod tried to engage him in conversation on several occasions during the voyage back to Venice—which this time passed without incident. But Cola was reticent, hiding behind a gruff and melancholy silence. Only on one occasion did he reveal himself, and that was when Bushrod asked if he was married. Cola's face darkened and he said that his fiancée had been taken into slavery by the Turks. He had been sent out to Crete to examine the girl, who came from a good family, and had agreed to the match. She had been dispatched ahead of him to Venice, and the ship was captured. Not a word had ever been heard of her again, and he very much hoped she was dead. Against his father's wishes, the young man had stayed in Candia to exact such revenge as he could.

And now?

And now he no longer cared. He was badly injured and he knew that Candia would soon fall. There was neither the determination nor the money nor the faith to defend it. He was undecided whether to return or not; perhaps his skills could be better employed elsewhere.

Then Marco da Cola had reached for a bottle, and spent nearly the entire voyage sitting on deck, uttering not another word, drunk or sober, until the ship docked in Venice.

So MUCH FOR THAT; ZEAL AGAINST THE HEATHEN WAS hardly something of which I could disapprove, and yet it was curious. We had a soldier (or ex-soldier) consorting with republicans in the Low Countries; the father's agent a Venetian observer sending regular messages to his masters abroad and transporting messages from malcontents in England. Lots of little pieces, none of which added up. Yet there was something which needed to be unraveled, and the obvious starting point was that package which, despite Mr. Bennet's strictures, I decided was within my competence.

Lest anyone think that I could call on an army of assistants in the fashion of Thurloe, I must hasten to state the true facts. Although I had a number of people who passed me information, I had precisely five in the entire country who could be relied on to act for me and two of these, I must confess, frightened even me. Nor was this matter my only, or even my main, occupation. I have mentioned the rising which I knew was being planned, and that naturally was my greatest concern. But there were also countless other irritations, most nonsensical although each with dangerous potential. The garrison at Abingdon had been purged, but was still less than satisfactorily quiescent. Sectaries and conventicles grew up like so many mushrooms across the landscape, giving scope for malcontents to meet and draw courage from each other. There were persistent reports that (yet again) the Messiah had returned to usher in the Millennium, and was traveling the country in some guise, preaching and teaching and sowing sedition. How many of these characters had there been in the past few years? Dozens at least, and I had hoped that quieter times had put an end to them, but it was not apparently, the case. Finally, in the middle of the affair I intend to relate, a drunken Irish magus called Greatorex turned up in Oxford and held court at the Mitre Inn to milk the gullible of their coins, so I had to divert much time to persuading him to move on his way. I had enough on my plate, in other words, and though I worked without stint I must say that neither then nor later were my efforts ever fully recognized or rewarded.

For the particular task of getting hold of these letters, I had to call on the services of one John Cooth, whose loyalty to the king was due solely to my having intervened when he nearly killed his wife in a drunken frenzy, then slit a man's throat for (he said) trying to put a pair of horns on him. He was in no wise intelligent but was skilled at housebreaking and was thoroughly in my debt. I thought he would serve, especially as I gave him a strict lecture about what he was to do, and how he was to do it. In particular I told him there was to be absolutely no violence, and I labored the point so much even a man of his diminished wits must understand.

Or so I thought. When Matthew told me that the package had been delivered to di Pietro's house and was to go aboard one of his ships the next morning, I told Cooth to bring it to me as rapidly as possible. Cooth dutifully returned a few hours later and gave me a package which contained all the mail being sent, including the letters delivered by Matthew. I copied them, and he took it back. And the next morning Matthew came with the news that Signor di Pietro had been murdered.

I was appalled by this, and prayed to the Lord for forgiveness for my foolishness. It was fairly obvious to me, despite Cooth's denials, what had happened: he had gone into the house and, instead of just taking the package, had decided to help himself to the contents of the treasury as well. Di Pietro was roused, came to investigate and Cooth had cold-bloodedly cut open his throat so badly the head was almost severed from the body.

Eventually I wrung a confession out of him: what was it to me, he said, whether he'd killed the man or not? I'd wanted the package, I'd got the package. I lost patience, and cut him off. He was going back to jail, I said, and if he so much as breathed a word of this, he'd hang. Even he understood my seriousness and the matter went no further; I soon learned that Cola had an English partner who wanted the entire business, and was unconcerned about discovering the author of a deed which had served him so profitably. It took many days but, after much effort, I felt I could relax, relatively certain that Mr. Bennet would not hear of the affair.

chapter three

THIS UNFORTUNATE BUSINESS AT LEAST PROVIDED me with di Pietro's mailbag, which turned out to be far more interesting than even I had hoped. For not only did it include the letters being sent to the radicals, it also contained another, unmarked in any way, which came from a different and unknown source. I only looked at it because I remembered the habits that Thurloe had inculcated into his office, one of which was that when examining a mailbag for suspicious correspondence, check everything else it contains as well. There were twelve letters in all, one from the radicals, ten entirely innocuous and concerned only with trading matters, and this one. Its lack of address alone would have alerted my attention, the fact that the seal on the back was entirely blank merely added to my determination. I only wished that little Samuel Morland had been there by my side, for no man was ever swifter at removing a seal, nor better at putting it back unnoticed. My own efforts were more laborious, and I cursed mightily as I wrestled with that most delicate task. But I did it, and did a fine job, so that once it was battered a little by transporting, I felt sure no one would see my handiwork.

And it was worth the effort. Inside was as fine a piece of coding as I had ever seen—a very long letter of about twelve thousand characters, in the complicated random cipher I described earlier. I felt a tingling of excitement as I contemplated it, for I knew it to be a challenge worthy of my skill.

But at the back of my mind was a more worrying thought, for ciphers are like music and have their own rhythms and cadences. This one, as I scanned it, sounded in my mind as being familiar, like a tune heard once before. But I could not yet place the melody.

Many times have men asked me why I took up the art of decipherment, for it seems to them to be a vulgar occupation, not in keeping with my position and dignity. I have many reasons, and the fact that I enjoy it is but the least of them. Men like Boyle are absorbed by teasing out the secrets of nature, in which I also take the greatest pleasure. But how wonderful it is also to penetrate the secrets of men's minds, to turn the chaos of human endeavor into order and bring the darkest deeds from night into daylight. A cipher is only a collection of letters on a page; this I grant. But to take that confusion and turn it into meaning through the exercise of pure reason provides a satisfaction which I have never managed to communicate to others. I can only say that it is not unlike prayer. Not vulgar prayer, in which men chant words while their minds are elsewhere, but true prayer, so complete and profound that you feel the touch of God's grace on your spirit. And I have often thought that my success shows His favor, a sign that what I do is pleasing to Him.

The letter sent by the sectaries was pathetically easy to unravel, and scarcely interesting; had I known what it contained I would never have bothered as it was not worth di Pietro's life or the trouble his murder caused me. It spoke of preparations in that pompous language so beloved of sectaries, and referred elliptically to a place I confidently identified as Northampton. But there was little meat, nothing which justified the risk I had taken. If that lay anywhere, it was in the last, mysterious letter; I was determined to read it, and knew I must have the key.

Matthew came to me as I sat at my desk, the unreadable letter in front of me in all its defiance, and asked whether he had done well.

"Very well," I told him. "Very well indeed, although largely by chance: your letter is uninteresting; it is this other one which fascinates me." I held it up for him to examine, which he did with his habitual neatness and care.

"You know this already? You have unraveled it all?"

I laughed at his faith in me. "A different letter, a different source and, no doubt, a different addressee. But I know nothing and have unravelled less. I cannot read this letter. The code is based on a book, which determines the sequence of the cipher."

"Which book?"

"That I do not know, and unless I can find out, I will understand nothing. But I am sure it is important. This sort of code is rare; I have come across it only a few times, and then written by men of the highest intelligence. It is too complex for fools."

"You will succeed," he said with a smile. "I am sure of that."

"I love you for your confidence, my boy. But this time you are wrong. Without the key, the door will remain locked."

"So how do we find this key?"

"Only the person who wrote it, and the person who will read it, will know what it is and have a copy."

"So we must ask them."

I thought he was joking and began to reprove him for his levity, but I saw in his face that he was quite serious.

"Let me return to Smithfield. I will tell them that there was an attempt to steal the letter which failed. And I will offer to go myself on the boat, to guard it and ensure it comes to no harm. Then I will discover to whom this one is sent, and what is the key."

The mind of youth sees in such a simple and direct way that I could hardly conceal my amusement.

"Why do you laugh, doctor?" he asked, his brow furrowing. "What I say is right. There is no other way of discovering what you need to know, and you have no one else to send."

"Matthew, your innocence is charming. You would go, you would be discovered and all would be lost, even if you escaped unharmed. Do not bother me with such foolishness."

"You treat me always like a child," he said, saddened by my remark. "But I can see no reason for it. How else can you discover what this book is, and who it is sent to? And if you cannot trust me, who else can you send?''

I took him by the shoulders and looked into his angry eyes. ''Do not be upset,'' I said, more gently. ''I spoke as I did not out of contempt, but concern. You are young, and these are dangerous people. I do not wish you to come to harm.''

''I thank you for it. But I desire nothing more than to do something of value for you. I know my debt to you and how little I have repaid it. So please, sir, give your permission. And you must decide fast; the letters must be returned, and the boat leaves tomorrow morning.''

I paused, and studied his fair face, its perfection spoiled by his resentment, and knew from the sight more than from his words that I would have to loosen the bonds, or lose him forever. Still, I tried one more time.

'' 'If I be bereaved of my children, I am bereaved' '' (Genesis 43:14).

He looked at me gently, and with such kindness; I remember it still.

'' 'Provoke not your children to anger, lest they be discouraged' '' (Colossians 3:21).

I bowed to that, and let him go, embracing him as he left, and watching from my window as he walked down the street outside, until he was lost from sight in the crowds. I saw the spring in his step, and the joy in his walk that came from his freedom, and I grieved over my loss. I spent the afternoon in prayer for his safety.

I DID NOT HEAR FROM HIM FOR A WHOLE FORTNIGHT, and was tormented by distress and fear every day, lest the boat had sunk, or he had been discovered. But he acquitted himself better than I had expected and showed more skill than many an intelligencer properly waged by the government. When I received his first letter I wept with both relief and pride.

''*Most reverend sir,*'' the letter began,

Following your instructions, I shipped aboard the bark Colombo and made my way to the Hague. The crossing was terribly bad, and at one stage I was sure the mission would fail because it seemed certain the ship would sink with all hands. Fortunately the master was an experienced man and brought us through safely, if very ill.

By the time we docked, I had thoroughly ingratiated myself with this man and learned that he did not wish to spend much time in port. He was distressed about the death of di Pietro, concerned for his job and wanted to head back for London as swiftly as possible. So I offered to deliver the letters to their destination on his behalf, saying I would be glad of the chance to spend some time in this part of the world. As he had no notion there was anything special about any of them, he agreed readily and says he will bring me back to London when he comes over with his next load of goods.

We went through the list as properly as any post officer, and checked the addresses of each envelope against the list he had in his hand.

"This one has no address," I told him, picking up the letter which interests you so much.

"Nor it has. But no matter, it is here on my list."

And he pointed out for me to see that he had instructions, in di Pietro's own handwriting, that this particular letter was to be delivered to a man called Cola, in Guldenstraat.

Sir, I must tell you that the house concerned is that of the Ambassador of Spain, and that this Cola is well known there. I have not yet delivered it, for I was told he would not be there until tomorrow, so I refused to hand it over, saying I was under strict instructions to give it into his hands alone. In the meantime, I have prevailed on the English in this place to give me lodging, which they agreed to with great friendliness, for they feel cut off and anxious for any news of home.

When I return I will of course call upon you to offer such further news as I have found. Please be assured, dearest and kindest sir, etc. etc. . . .

Even though the affection of my dear boy's salutation warmed me, I fear I might have forgotten myself sufficiently

as to box his ears with frustration had he been present. I
realized that he had done a fine job; but nonetheless he had
not succeeded as completely as I needed. I still did not have
the name of the book that formed the key, and without that
I was not greatly advanced. But, however much he had failed
in this, I realized he more than made up for it elsewhere. For
I knew that the Ambassador of Spain, Esteban de Gamarra,
was an implacable, dangerous foe of England. That one piece
of information alone justified everything I had done so far.
For this Cola, I had been told months earlier, was associating
with radicals, and now here he was with an address at the
Spanish embassy. It was a fascinating puzzle.

The information placed me in a quandary, because if I had
disobeyed by pursuing di Pietro, interfering in this matter
was even more grave. Mr. Bennet was still my sole protector
and I could not afford to lose his good will if I could not
replace him with someone better. However, any form of link
between the Spanish and the radicals was of the utmost seriousness. The prospect of an alliance between the upholder
of Catholicism and the most fervent fanatics of Protestantism
was hardly to be countenanced, but nonetheless I held in my
hand the first faint glimmerings of such a connection, and I
could not allow what seemed unlikely in abstract to overawe
the most direct and compelling evidence.

This has ever been my lodestone, in philosophy as in governance; the mind of man is weak, and often cannot grasp
patterns that appear to be against all reason. The codes I have
spent so much of my life in deciphering are a simple example
of this, for who could understand (if they did not know) how
a jumble of meaningless letters could inform the reader of
the thoughts of the greatest in the land, or the most dangerous
in the field. It is against common sense, and yet it is so.
Reason beyond ordinary human understanding is often to be
met with in God's creation, so much so that I have had occasion to laugh at Mr. Locke, who makes so much of common sense in his philosophy. ''Great things doeth he, which
we cannot comprehend'' (Job 37:5). In all things, we forget
this at our cost.

Reason said Spaniards would not pay to put Republican
sectaries in power, nor would these self-same sectaries will-

ingly subordinate their desires to Spanish policy. Yet the evidence was beginning to hint at precisely some such understanding between them. I could, at that stage, make nothing of it and so declined to elaborate fantastic theories; but at the same time I refused to reject evidence simply because it did not immediately coincide with reason.

I was certain to be ridiculed if I presented my information to Mr. Bennet, who prided himself on his understanding of the Spanish and was convinced of their friendship. Nor could I take any action against the sectaries, for as yet they had done nothing ill. So I could do nothing: once I had deciphered the letter, discovered who had written it, and amassed more evidence, then perhaps I could present a stronger case, but until then I had to keep my suspicions to myself. I very much hoped that Matthew would remember my instructions that getting the key to the letter was vital, as it was extremely difficult to communicate with him in any way. In the meantime I wrote a report to Mr. Bennet informing him (in general terms) that something was stirring among the radicals, and assuring him of my best service.

A WEEK LATER, MATTHEW REPAID MY TRUST IN HIM, and I received another letter which contained something of the information I required. He offered four possibilities, apologizing for being able to do no better. He had delivered the letter once more, and this time had been shown into a small room, which appeared to be an office. He found it disgusting, for it was lined with crucifixes and stank with the odor of idolatry, but while waiting for Cola himself to appear, he saw four volumes on the desk and swiftly noted down their titles. I was pleased by this, as it vindicated my faith in him: to act so was intelligent and courageous, and he would have been in great danger if anyone had come through the door while he was writing. Unfortunately, the finer points of the cryptographer's art were lost on him: he did not realize (perhaps this was my fault for not having instructed him properly) that each edition of a book differs and that the wrong edition made my message as unintelligible as the wrong book. All I had to go on was the following, which he had copied out, letter by letter, in total ignorance of its import:

> *Titi liuii ex rec heins lugd II polyd hist nouo corol*
> *duaci thom Vtop rob alsop eucl oct*

Almost as importantly, and very much more dangerously, he encountered Cola himself, and gave me an early indication of the man's powers of deception. I have the letter still. Of course, I keep every remembrance of Matthew—every letter, every little exercise book he once filled is in a silver box, lined in silk and bound with the lock of hair I stole one night while he lay asleep. My eyesight is fading now and soon I will be able to read his words no longer; I will burn them for I could not bear to have anyone else read them to me, or snigger at my weakness. My last contact with him will be lost when the light flickers out. Even now I do not open that box up very often, as I find the sadness difficult to bear.

Cola at once began to exercise his charm, trapping the lad—too young and naïve to realize the difference between kindness and its simulacrum—into acquaintanceship, then the appearance of friendship.

> *He is a chubby man with bright eyes, and when he ap-*
> *peared and I gave him the letter, he chuckled with*
> *thanks, clapped me on the back and gave me a silver*
> *guilder. Then he questioned me closely about all things,*
> *showing great interest in my replies, and even begged*
> *me to return that he might question me further.*
>
> *I must say, sir, that he gave no sign of any concern*
> *with matters political, nor did he ever mention anything*
> *the slightest bit improper. Rather, he showed himself the*
> *perfect gentleman, courteous in manner, and easy to*
> *approach and talk to in all things.*

So easy it is to delude the trusting! This Cola began to steal his way into Matthew's affections, no doubt conversing with the facility of the passing acquaintance, never approaching the care that I had devoted to the lad over so many years. It is easy to entertain and fascinate, harder to educate and love; Matthew, alas, was not yet old or discriminating enough to tell the difference, and was easy prey to the ruthlessness of the Italian, who beguiled with his words until he needed to strike.

The letter disturbed me, for my main concern was that Matthew's natural amiability might permit some ill-chosen words to slip out and alert Cola to my awareness of him. I forced my mind to concentrate on problems more easy to resolve, and took up once more the question of the coded letter and its key.

Only one of the books Matthew mentioned could be the one I needed, the problem was to determine which one. The easiest solution was denied me: for I knew that Euclid had only been printed in octavo but once, in Paris in 1621, and I had that edition in my own library. It was simple enough, therefore, to discover it was not the one I wanted. That left the remaining three. Accordingly, the moment I arrived back in Oxford I summoned a strange young man of my acquaintance, Mr. Anthony Wood, whom I knew to be an expert squirreler in such matters. I had rendered him many favors in those days, earning his gratitude for allowing him access to manuscripts in my care, and he was pathetically eager to repay my kindnesses to him, although as a price I had to listen to interminable discussions about this press and that press, one edition after another and so on. I suppose he thought I was interested in the minutiae of ancient learning and attempted to curry favor by drawing me into scholarly conversation.

It took him some considerable time before he returned to my room one evening (building works at my house having forced me, meanwhile, to rent space at New College—a regrettable fact which I will discuss later on) and reported that in all probability he had worked out which books were meant, although personally he believed that, in the case of the Thomas More and the Polydore Vergil, better editions existed at a more modest cost.

I detested having to play such silly games, but I patiently explained, nonetheless, that I had set my heart on these particular versions. I wished, I said, to experiment with making comparisons between the various editions, so as to prepare a complete version, without faults, for the world. He admired greatly my devotion, and said he understood perfectly. The *Utopia* of Thomas More, he said, was a quarto, and undoubtedly the translation by Robinson which Alsop had published in 1624: he could tell that because Alsop only produced one edition before changing times meant that publishing the works of Catholic saints became a risky occupation. A copy, he said, was in the Bodleian library. The History of Polydore Vergil was also simple: there were not many new editions of this fine author published in Douai, after all. It had to be the idiosyncratic edition of George Lily, an octavo printed in 1603. Copies were not hard to come by and, indeed, he had seen a version only the other day at Mr. Heath's, the bookseller, at a price of one shilling and sixpence. He was sure he could bargain the man down—as if I cared about two pence.

"And the fourth?"

"That is a problem," he said. "I think I know which edition you refer to here. It is the 'Heins' which gives it away, of course. This refers to the handsome edition of Livy's histories by Daniel Heinsius, issued in Leiden in 1634. A triumph of skill and learning which, alas, never received the approbation it deserved. I assume this refers to volume two of the edition, which was a duodecimo, in three volumes. Few were printed and I have never seen one. I know it only by reputation—others have shamelessly used his insights without ever crediting their true author. Which is a burden true scholars must constantly bear."

"Make enquiries for me," I told him with heavy patience. "I will pay a good price for it, if it is to be had. You must know booksellers and antiquarians and collectors of libraries and the like. If there is one, someone like you will be able to find it, of that I feel sure."

The silly man looked modestly down his nose at the compliment. "I will do my best for you," he said. "And I can assure you, that if I cannot find a copy, no one else will be able to."

"That is all I ask," I replied, and ushered him out as quickly as was possible.

chapter four

I HAVE READ OF LATE A SCURRILOUS PAMPHLET
which (without naming me directly) said that the crisis with
which I was dealing at this stage was a fabrication, whipped
up by a government to foment fear of sectaries and that it
did not, in fact, exist. Nothing could be further from the truth.
I hope I have already made my good intentions and my honesty clear. What I did, I admit: I freely own that I over-
emphasized the danger of the rising which led to my
employment by Mr. Bennet, and claim for myself the mistake
which led to the regrettable death of Signor di Pietro. I hope
there is no doubt about the sincerity of my remorse, but the
fact remains that the man was carrying subversive and conspiratorial material, and it was necessary for the security of
the kingdom to have it.

I feel as though I ought to set out some of my thinking,
lest it be thought that my punctiliousness over letters and
obscure books makes me seem fussy and obsessive. For it
had struck me as obvious that these books which Matthew
had told me about were most unusual. Everybody knows
about the sectaries and their pathetic claims to learning. Self-
taught scrabblers in the dust, most of them, seduced by
second-rate reading into the delusion that they are educated.
Educated? A Bible whose sublime subtlety and symbolic
beauty they cannot even begin to understand, and a few
screeching pamphlets by that handful of dissenters whose

arrogance exceeds their shame, is all they have by way of education. No Latin, no Greek, and certainly no Hebrew; unable to read any language but their own, and assaulted by the ravings of false prophets and self-appointed Messiahs even in English. Of course they are not educated; knowledge is the province of the gentleman. I do not say that artisans cannot know, but it is obvious that they cannot assess, as they possess neither the leisure nor the training to consider free from prejudice. Plato said so, and I know of no serious person who has denied him.

And the writer of this letter to Cola was using one of these fine texts for his code? Livy, Polydore, More. Initially it made me shudder to think of such hands even touching these works, but then I reconsidered: some scruffy pamphlet I would have accepted, but these? Where did they get their hands on books which belong only in the library of a gentleman?

By the time Wood reappeared, sniffing and twitching like a little mouse, I had established that neither the More nor the Polydore Vergil was the book I required. The answer therefore lay in the Livy: find it, find who possessed it, and my investigation would advance in a great leap. Wood told me that a long-dead London bookseller had brought half a dozen copies into the country in 1643, as part of a general shipment for scholars. What had happened to them after that, alas, was unclear, as the man had been a supporter of the king, and all his stock was confiscated in fines when Parliament secured its hold on London. Wood assumed these books were dispersed then.

"So you mean to tell me, after all that, that you cannot get me a copy?"

He looked a bit surprised by my sharpness of tone, but shook his head. "Oh, no, sir," he said. "I thought you might be interested, that is all. But they are rare, and I have identified only one person who definitely had one, which he brought in himself from abroad. I know of it because my friend Mr. Aubrey wrote to a bookseller in Italy on some other matter . . ."

"Mr. Wood, I beg you," I said, my patience very near to expiring. "I do not wish to know every single detail. I merely need the name of the owner so I might write to him.''

"Ah, you see, he is dead.''

I sighed heavily.

"But do not despair, sir, for by the greatest good fortune, his son is a student here, and would no doubt know whether the book remains in the family. His name is Prestcott. His father was Sir James Prestcott.''

THUS MY STORY AND COLA'S TALES (AS FICTIONAL AS boccaccio and as unlikely as the rhymes of Tasso, though less finely hewn) begin to intersect through the medium of poor deluded Prestcott, and I must lay out the details as best I can, although I fully admit that I am not entirely clear about some of the circumstances.

The lad had come to my attention several months previously, when I heard of his visit to Lord Mordaunt. Mordaunt had properly communicated with Mr. Bennet, and news of the event was passed on to me as a matter of course; students, and sons of traitors, seeing fit to interrogate members of the court was no usual occurrence, and Mr. Bennet thought that an eye should be kept on the young man.

I knew few of the details but had heard enough to be certain that Prestcott's belief in the innocence of his father was as ludicrous as it was touching. I was uncertain what the precise nature of his betrayal was, for I had left the government's employ by then, but the noise he created signified something of great importance. I knew something of it because, as my skills were indispensable, in early 1660 I was requested to work on a letter with the greatest urgency. I have mentioned it before, for it was my one failure and the moment I saw it, I knew that there was little chance of success. As much to preserve my reputation as my position (the fall of the Commonwealth was becoming increasingly certain, and I had no wish to prolong my association with it) I declined the task.

The suasion placed upon me was great, however. Even Thurloe himself wrote to me, using a mixture of flattery and threat to win compliance, but still I refused. All communications were brought by Samuel Morland himself, a man whose weaselly words and concern for self-advancement I detested, and his presence alone made me obdurate.

"You cannot do it, can you, doctor?" he said in his sneering way, on the surface so amiable, but still barely hiding his cocky contempt for all others. "That is why you refuse."

"I refuse because I am doubtful why I am asked. I know you too well, Samuel; everything you touch is corrupt and deceitful."

He laughed merrily at this, and nodded in agreement. "Perhaps so. But this time I have noble company."

I looked at the letter once more. "Very well," I said. "I will try. Where is the key?"

"What do you mean?"

"Samuel, do not treat me like a fool. You know very well what I mean. Who wrote this?"

"A Royalist soldier, called Prestcott."

"Ask him for the key, then. It must be a book, or a pamphlet. I must know what the code is based on."

"We don't have him," Samuel replied. "He fled. The letter was found on one of our soldiers."

"Why so?"

"A very good question indeed," Samuel said. "That is why we want this letter deciphered."

"Ask this soldier, then, if you cannot lay your hands on Sir James Prestcott."

Samuel looked apologetic. "He died a few days ago."

"And there was nothing else on him either? No other paper, no book, no piece of writing with it?"

Morland looked discountenanced for once, a fact which gave me some pleasure, for he usually adopted such a self-satisfied air that it was satisfying indeed to see him uncertain and nervous. "This was all we found. We had been expecting more."

I tossed the letter onto my desk. "No key, no solution," I said. "Nothing I can do, and nothing I will try to do. I do not intend to work myself to death because of your foolish incompetence. Find Sir James Prestcott, find the key, and I will assist you. Not until then."

Rumors that had swept through government and army in the previous few weeks gave some clue of course; I had heard of fighting down in Kent, also of a frenzied investigation, conducted with the greatest secrecy and ferocity. Later I heard of the flight of Sir James Prescott abroad, and of his being accused of betraying the 1659 rising against the Commonwealth. That, in itself, struck me as highly unlikely: I knew something of the man and considered him about as supple as a large piece of oak planking, with an absolute conviction in his own beliefs. Men had sinned, men must be punished and revenge taken: that was the alpha and omega of his politics, and this limited vision was strengthened by his own privations in the war. It made him useless as a conspirator but, in my opinion, also made him unlikely to conceive of anything so subtle as betrayal: he was too upright, too honorable, and far too stupid.

On the other hand he clearly had done something which made both Royalists and Thurloe earnestly desire his death and his silence, and I did not know what that was. I assumed the answer lay in the letter which made little Samuel sweat so, and when he had gone I naturally tried my hand to make it out. I made no progress at all, for the skill of its author was great, far beyond anything I would have expected from a military dolt like Prescott.

I mention this because the words which Wood spoke to me so innocently brought me to a realization I should have had some time before. Mentioning it now, when it actually occurred to me, risks making me seem foolish; all I can say is that I will not accept judgment from those with inferior skills to mine. Recognizing a form of code is like recognizing a style in composition or poetry; it is impossible to say what triggers the realization, and I doubt there is another man alive who would have seen that the letter I had found in di Pietro's mailbag, sent to this Marco da Cola, was written in the same code, had the same form, the same *feel* as that letter of Sir James Prescott's, brought to me some three years earlier by Samuel Morland. Once I had grasped the form, I could examine the structure: two days' hard work on both of them led me to the inevitable and clear conclusion that both were constructed with the same book. A copy of Livy, I knew, had been used to encode the letter to Cola, and so now I knew that the same Livy had been used for the Prestcott letter.

Had I been more sure of my ground, I would have summoned young Prestcott, told him the position and asked for the Livy. However, I clearly could not do this without telling him of its significance and as I knew of his obsessions, I did not want to be responsible for reopening a matter so obviously sensitive: many people had worked hard to keep those events hidden, whatever they were, and I would receive no thanks for drawing attention to them once again. So, I had to approach him in a more subtle fashion and therefore decided to make use of Thomas Ken.

This Ken was a desperately ambitious young man who had the utmost clarity about his desires. For Ken, God's interests and his own were indistinguishably mingled, so much so that one might have thought the whole of salvation itself depended on his getting £80 a year. He once had the presumption to ask me for my favor in securing a living in the gift of Lord Maynard and disposable by New College. Not being a member of that society, I naturally had little say in the matter and it was obvious that Dr. Robert Grove—more learned and balanced, and certainly more deserving—would carry the day whatever I said. But it was an inexpensive way of securing his devotion, and I gave him the expression of my support, for what that was worth.

In return, I insisted that he help me when I required his services and, in due course, recommended that he persuade Mr. Prestcott to seek my assistance. Prestcott duly came, and I questioned him closely about his father's possessions. Alas, he knew nothing of any book by Livy, nor indeed of any documents at all, although later on he did confirm what Morland had said: it appeared his mother had been expecting a package from his father which never arrived. It was exceptionally frustrating: I needed only a little good fortune and I could not only unravel the secret correspondence of this Marco da Cola, I could also take to myself one of the closest secrets of the realm.

But that fool Samuel had allowed the only man who might tell me the answer to die.

chapter five

MY DUTIES IN THIS PERIOD ENFORCED A STRANGE rhythm of life upon me, for I was forced to exist like some nocturnal creature, which hunts while others sleep, and rests from its labors while most of creation is active. When all people of rank left London for their estates, or to follow the court from one place of idle amusement to the other, so I left the country to take up residence in London. When the court returned to Westminster, I removed myself back to Oxford.

I did not find this displeasing. The obligations of the courtier are time-consuming and largely fruitless unless you are chasing the prizes of fame and position. If you are merely concerned with the safety of the kingdom, and the smooth running of the government, then maintaining a presence there is pointless. In the entire country, fewer than half a dozen people have true power. The rest are governed, in one way or another, and I had more than sufficient contact with those who were truly of significance.

Among these, I found few natural allies and many who, either deliberately or because of the limits of their comprehension, worked against the interests of their own country. Such a state, I may say, was to be found everywhere in those days, even amongst the philosophers who thought they were merely teasing out the secrets of nature. Having no care for thought, they did not consider what they did, and allowed themselves to be led down the road to the most dangerous of all positions.

As the years have gone by, the parallels have become ever more clear to me, for it is easy, out of greed or generosity, to fall into traps set by others. A few weeks ago, for example, I prevailed in a controversy which, until I pointed out the dangers, seemed the most minor of matters, a question that could excite only the most abstruse minds. The Secretary of State (no longer Mr. Bennet) wrote to me to ask whether this land should join with the rest of the continent and adopt the Gregorian calendar. I believe my opinion was solicited merely to gain approval for something which had already been agreed: it was surely absurd for this country, alone in Europe, to have a different calendar and be forever seventeen days behind everyone else.

They changed their minds swiftly when I pointed out the implications of such a seemingly harmless move. For it struck at the heart of church and state, encouraging papists, and dismaying those who fight to keep foreign dominance at bay. Do our armies contest the arrogant might of France, merely for our independence to be given away under more peaceable guise? To accept this calendar is to accept the authority of Rome; not merely (as the unsubtle say) because it was a reform that the Jesuits devised, but because to bow our heads means also to accept the right of the Bishop of Rome to determine when our church celebrates Easter; to say when all major festivals and holy days fall. Once conceded in principle, all else follows naturally; to bow to Rome in one thing will lead to obedience in others as well. It is the obligation of all Englishmen to resist the blandishments of those siren voices who say that such small matters will bring benefits with no disadvantages. It is not true, and if we must stand alone, then so be it. England's glory has ever been to resist the pretensions of continental powers, which seduce into slavery, and wheedle into subjection. Honoring God is more important than the unity of Christendom. Thus my response, and I am glad that it prevailed; the argument has been settled once and for all.

So it was after the Restoration and the stakes were then even higher. Many men were open or concealed Catholics and had insinuated themselves into places of high influence at court. There were those (I do them credit and say it was for reasons genuinely held) who believed that the best interests of the state lay in binding it closely to France; others wished to obstruct the ambitions of the Bourbons by making common cause with the Spanish.

Week by week, and month by month, the factions contested with each other, and foreign bribes flowed in. Not a minister, nor officeholder, failed to enrich himself from this battle, for that is what it was. At one moment the Spanish faction held the upper hand, as Mr. Bennet and others consolidated their positions and took more power into their hands. At another the French struck back, subsidizing the dowry paid for the king's new wife. And the Dutch looked anxiously from one great enemy to another, knowing that if they allied with one, they would be attacked by the other. The interests of justice and religion were lost sight of in their entirety as the battles at court played out in miniature the greater battles that were yet to come on the seas and fields of Europe.

And there were two great enigmas: the king, who would have allied with anyone who paid enough to subsidize his pleasure, and Lord Clarendon, who opposed any foreign entanglements, believing His Majesty's position at home to be so insecure that the least trembling from abroad would shake his throne irrecoverably. His views prevailed in 1662, but others, such as Lord Bristol, held the opposite view, thinking either that fine victories abroad would strengthen the crown, or secretly hoping for the opportunities that defeat would offer. For many wanted to bring about Clarendon's fall, and worked tirelessly to accomplish his ruin. A defeat in arms would destroy his career more surely than anything else, and I do not doubt that many loyal servants of the king lay awake at night, hoping that one would come to pass.

For the moment, though, the greatest weapon the opponents of Clarendon had was the scandalous behavior of his daughter, which had convulsed the court scarcely six months before, and severely weakened the chancellor's position. For the wretched woman had married the king's brother, the Duke of York, without troubling to gain permission first.

That his daughter was well pregnant by the time of the nuptials, that Clarendon loathed the Duke of York deeply, that he was as deceived as the king, none of this was of any consequence. Royal authority had been held to ridicule, and the king had lost a valuable card in the diplomatic game: the duke's hand in marriage would have been a fine inducement to seal an alliance. It was said Clarendon himself would not have the subject raised in his presence, and was said to pray daily that the queen would give birth to an heir, so that he could be acquitted of conniving to put his own daughter on the throne, which would surely happen should the king die without legitimate issue. It was not a matter easily forgiven, and his enemies, above all Lord Bristol, who had the finest wit of them all, made sure it could not be forgotten either.

Such maneuverings among the mighty and the puffed-up did not attract my attention overmuch; foolishly so, perhaps, as more attention to the details of such petty squabbles would have helped me greatly. I was, as yet, far from understanding that these intrigues were fundamental to my own enquiries, and without them I would have had no grounds for concern over anything. This, however, is a matter which will become clear in its proper place. At that time, I saw myself in all modesty as a servant—one of importance, perhaps, but nonetheless with no interest in courtly battles nor even with a concern for influencing the policy of the realm. My task was to tell my masters the secret history of the kingdom, so they might reach their decisions with knowledge, if they wished to do so. In this, my importance was crucial, for good intelligence is the mother of prevention, and the measures of suppression being taken were far from complete. Town walls were being razed, but not fast enough; sectaries of all sorts were being arrested and fined, but there were always more, and the more cunning kept themselves in concealment.

ANYBODY READING THIS ACCOUNT MAY WONDER WHY I was prepared to give such attention to the question of Marco da Cola, since I have as yet described little to justify my effort. In fact, he was still only of passing interest to me, one of those lines of enquiry which are pursued for the sake of

thoroughness: there was nothing solid on which I could concentrate, and little more than curiosity to keep my attention
focused. I had, it was true, established a possible link between the exiles and the Spanish, and he and his family
formed that link. I had an incomprehensible letter and an
intriguing connection with another document written three
years previously. Finally, I had the enigma of Cola himself,
for it struck me as unusual that he could spend many months
in the Low Countries without his profession of soldier being
commonly known. Nor could I understand why his father, a
man of known ability, was prepared to release his only effective son from his family obligations. Yet, not only was
the younger Cola apparently entirely unengaged in trade, he
was not even married.

Such were my thoughts, and I mentioned the puzzle to Mr.
Williams, my merchant friend, when I met him the day after
I arrived in London in early 1663.

"Let me pose you a problem as an adventurer," I said.
"Let us say that you lose your main markets and trading
partners through ports being closed by war. You have three
daughters, one of whom is married, and two are rapidly approaching marriageable age. You have only one useful son.
What tactics do you adopt to defend and expand your business?"

"Once I have stopped panicking, and praying for a turn
of good fortune?" he said with a smile. "I can think of worse
situations to be in, but not many."

"Let us say you are a naturally calm man. What do you
do?"

"Let us see. Much depends on the reserves I have at my
disposal, and the relations I have with my family, of course.
Will they step forward and help? That might fend off an
urgent crisis and give me time to recover. But it gains me
room to maneuver, it does not solve the problem. Obviously,
the need is to find new markets, but to break into a new port
requires money, as it is often necessary to sell at a loss for
some time to establish oneself. Now, the easiest solution is
to establish an alliance with another house. You marry a son
if you have one and if your position is strong, a daughter if
it be weak. The situation you describe indicates the need to

marry a son to advantage, for that brings money into the business, rather than putting it out. However, you are also at a disadvantage, of course, for you need markets, and that suggests that marrying a daughter will be required.''

"And where do you find the money for that? Any possible ally will be aware of the problem and drive a hard bargain, will they not?''

Mr. Williams nodded in agreement. ''That is precisely the case. In my position, I think I would have to consider a marriage of the son out of business to a lady of as much fortune as I could find, and immediately use the dowry to marry a daughter to trade. With good fortune my family might end up with a small surplus, without luck I might have to borrow at interest to fund the difference. But that would be no problem if my trade recovered. It is not a strategy that is guaranteed to bring success, but it offers by far the best chance of it. Why do we have sons except for such purposes?''

"So if I said this trader not only seemed to have no plans to marry his son, but had even let him go wandering Europe, where he is out of reach and consuming substantial amounts of money?''

"Then I would be strongly adverse to venturing money in any enterprise with which he is concerned. Am I right in thinking that you are still occupying yourself with the house of Cola?''

I nodded, with great reluctance. I had no desire to take Mr. Williams into my confidence in any way, but he was too intelligent to be fooled and an honest admission, I considered, might be enough to bind him to obligations of silence.

"Do not think that such matters have not come into our minds as well,'' he said.

"Our?''

"We traders. We are jealously eager to hear news of our competitors and, sad though it is, rejoice too much to hear of a rival's downfall. The better of us are always reminded that such a fate can easily befall anyone, of course. It takes very little ill fortune to turn riches into dust. One storm, or a war unforeseen, can be a catastrophe.''

"You may rest easy on that score," I reassured him. "I

cannot predict the weather, but no war will catch you unawares if I am able to assist you.''

"I am grateful for that. I have a large cargo bound for Hamburg next week. I would like it to arrive.''

"As far as I am aware, the prospect of Dutch pirates being allowed free run of the North Sea does not appear imminent. But it would still be wise to guard against the unscrupulous anticipating matters.''

"Believe me, I have taken every precaution possible. I am proof against the single privateer.''

"Good. Now, if I may return to Cola, what does the community of traders say?''

"That the father's affairs are bad and getting worse, in a word. He has long suffered his eastern markets to be whittled away by the Turks; Crete is now all but lost; he made a brave venture to open up a new business in London, but that has been crippled by the death of his manager here, and the audacity of his English partner who has taken the business for his own. And there are rumors he has been selling ships to raise money. Three years ago he had a fleet of more than thirty ships; now it is down to almost twenty. And he has warehouses in Venice full of goods, which is money moldering to no purpose. If he does not move them he cannot meet his creditors. If he does not do that, he is finished.''

"He is held in good credit?''

"Everyone is held in good credit until they stop paying their bills.''

"So how do you explain the father's actions? Or the son's?''

"I cannot. He has an excellent reputation, so I must assume there is very much more to the situation than is accessible to a coffee-house gossip like myself. I cannot imagine what that might be. Be assured that if I hear anything I will let you know instantly.''

I thanked him and left. My interpretation of the situation was correct, and for that I was glad; but I was no closer to fathoming the problem than I was before.

• • •

THE NEXT PIECE OF INFORMATION WHICH ADVANCED my enquiry came from my involvement in the Royal Society, and took another ten days to fall into my lap, more by the grace of God than my own efforts. Fortunately, there was much to occupy my mind in that period, or I would have become very ill-tempered. It is a great failing and one I have long labored to overcome. "Blessed is he that waiteth" (Daniel 12:12): the text I know by heart, but do not find it easy to follow.

I have mentioned this august organization already, and hinted how communications developing with men of curiosity all over the world aided my work. I had initially taken on the task of secretary for correspondence myself, but found my other duties burdensome, and gradually relinquished the task to Mr. Henry Oldenburg, a man of no experimental bent but with a pleasing ability to encourage others. He called one morning to summarize recent correspondence with me, because I knew well that notice of experiments and discoveries properly communicated was of the greatest importance to prevent foreigners claiming credit which was not theirs. The reputation of the society was the honor of the country, and the prompt establishment of priority was vital.

I may say here that this process gives the lie to Cola's complaints over the matter of blood transfusion, as it was established (and not by us) that public knowledge of discoveries gives precedence. Lower did this, Cola did not; what is more, he is unable to provide any evidence whatsoever of his claims, while Lower can not only produce letters announcing his discovery, but can also call on men of unimpeachable integrity, like Sir Christopher Wren, to vouch for him. To demonstrate I am not partial in this matter, I can also cite Mr. Leibniz when he laid claim to a new method for interpolation by contrasting series of differences. When told that Regnauld had already communicated a similar proposition to Mersenne, Leibniz immediately withdrew any claim to priority: he accepted that making the matter known was decisive. Similarly, it is clear that Cola's complaints are quite without foundation, for who did what first is unimportant. Not only did he fail to publish, his initial experiment was conducted in secret, and ended with the patient's death.

In contrast, Lower not only performed before witnesses, he eventually gave a demonstration before the whole society, long before any squeak of protest was heard from Venice.

During my discourse with Oldenburg, we discussed many questions of membership and regulation with great amiability before passing onto more liberal matters. Then I received the greatest shock.

"I have heard, by the way, of a most interesting young man, who might be considered at some stage as a corresponding member in Venice. We lack, as you know, any useful contacts with the curious of that Republic."

I was genuinely delighted, and not at all suspicious at this, for Oldenburg was always keen to search out new ways of binding philosophers of all lands together, and make the enterprise of one known to others.

"I am delighted to hear of it," I said. "Who is this young man?"

"I heard of him from Dr. Sylvius," he replied, "for he has been sitting at that great man's knee and is highly thought of for his skill. His name is Cola, and he is a wealthy young man from a good family of well established traders."

I expressed the greatest of interest.

"Better still, he is to come to England shortly, so we will have an opportunity to talk to him and find out his qualities for ourselves."

"Sylvius says this? He is coming to England?"

"Apparently so. He intends to come next month, I believe. I was about to write him a letter, expressing our desire to welcome him on his arrival."

"No," I said. "Do not do that. I greatly admire Sylvius for his knowledge, but not for his judgment of his fellows. If you extend an invitation to this young man, and he turns out to be of no great ability, we may find it difficult to avoid a snub by not electing him. We will find him soon enough when he arrives, and can examine him at our leisure."

Oldenburg agreed to this without demur, and as an extra precaution I took the letter from Sylvius to study more carefully. There was little more in it, although I noted that what he said was that Cola was due to come to England on a matter of "urgent business." Now what could that be? He had no interest in trade, and coming to tour this part of the world could hardly be described as a matter of urgency. So why was this former soldier coming here?

The next day, I thought I could guess.

chapter six

MOST REVEREND DOCTOR AND REVERED MASTER,
the letter from Matthew began,

*I write in the greatest haste, for I have news which may
be of some considerable importance to you. I have ingratiated myself most thoroughly in the servants' quarters of the Spanish embassy and pride myself that I have
learned many secrets. Should I be discovered, my life
will be at an end, but the value is such that I must take
the risk.*

*I do not know what is planned with any exactitude,
for I pick up only gossip. But servants always know far
more than they should, or than their masters suspect,
and it is noised here that a great coup is being planned
for April against our country. Señor de Gamarra has,
it seems, been planning this for some time with men of
high rank in England itself, and his scheming is near to
fruition. More than this I cannot discover, for there are
limits to the knowledge even of chambermaids, but it
may be that I will know more later.*

*I must tell you, sir, that I believe your suspicions of
Marco da Cola to be erroneous, for he is a gentleman
of the greatest friendliness and I have detected no military aspect to him at all; quite the opposite in fact, he*

seems made for gayness and amusement, and his generosity (as I can myself attest) is great indeed. A kinder, less secretive, gentleman I have rarely met. Moreover, it appears he is to leave shortly, and in a few days time is to give a farewell feast, with music and dancing, to which he has invited me as his particular guest, so great has been my success at winning his favor. He pays me a great compliment in keeping me by his side, and I am sure you will agree it is the best place for me to be if I am to determine whether or no he means us ill.

I am sorry, sir, that I cannot say more at present; I fear my enquiries will arouse suspicions if I ask too much.

My anger and dismay at this piece of youthful folly knew no bounds, although I did not know whether I was more angry at Matthew for his stupidity, or at this Cola for the way he had so filthily wormed his way into his affections. I had never permitted him such entertainments, for they are both sinful and spoil a child's education faster than any other mistake in their upbringing. Rather, I had attended to his soul, knowing that, hard though it is because of the natural frivolity of youth, work and the inculcation of duty were both more proper and rewarding. That this Cola should use such tricks to turn him away from righteousness—and, I feared, away from me—caused great anger, as I knew how easy it was to do as well as I knew the difficulty of remaining unyielding when all my desire was to see a smile of pleasure on his face. Unlike Cola, though, I would not buy his affection.

Even more, the way such devices were used to befuddle his senses concerned me, as even at a distance, I could see that Matthew's assurances about Cola were wrong: I knew already he was coming to England, for Oldenburg had told me so. And the coup being planned was set for just after the time when he would arrive on our shores. It was easy to forge the connection between the two, and I realized that the time I had at my disposal was very much less than I anticipated. I felt as though I was a novice playing a game of chess, and that my opponent's pieces were slowly moving across the board, setting up an assault which, when it came, would be as irresistible as it was sudden. On every occasion I thought that, if only I had more information, I could make sense of the whole business; but every time that extra intelligence came into my hands, it again proved insufficient. I knew there was some plot, and I knew approximately when it was to take place. But although I knew its agent, I did not know its object or its sponsors.

I may say that I found myself very lonely in my thoughts, for I was being forced to consider great matters, without the advice of others to temper my mind and hone my argument. Ultimately, I decided I would have to present my case to someone else, and thought carefully about whom I might choose. I could not, of course, talk frankly to Mr. Bennet as yet, nor could I countenance an approach to another member of Thurloe's old intelligencing organization, as their loyalties were entirely suspect. Indeed, I felt entirely alone in a suspicious and dangerous world, for there were few who were not, potentially at least, sympathetic to one side or the other.

Accordingly, I made an approach to Robert Boyle, too abstracted of mind to be concerned with politics, too noble of purpose to be seduced by faction, and a man of the most notorious discretion in all matters. I had, and have still, a high opinion of his ingenuity and piety, although I must say I do not believe his achievement as great as his fame. Yet he was the best possible advocate of the new learning for, faced with his ascetic nature, his cautious endeavor and his profound devotion, it was difficult for any man to accuse our Society of harboring subversive or impious notions. Mr. Boyle (who disguised, I think a certain naïveté under the cloak of gravity) believed that the new science would aid religion, and that the fundamental truths of the Bible would be confirmed by rational means. I felt, in contrast, that this would hand a weapon of unparalleled power to the atheists, since they would soon insist that God submit to the proofs of the scientist, and if He could not be pinned to a theorem, they would say they had proved He did not exist.

Boyle was wrong, but I admit it was with the best of reasons, and this dispute between us never produced a breach in our friendship which, if never warm, was of great duration.

He was of the best family, and had a balanced (though weak) constitution and sound education; all these produced an excellent judgment which was never swayed by considerations of gain. When I discovered him at his sister's house in London, I asked him to visit and gave him a fine meal of oysters, lamb, partridge and pudding and then persuaded him to treat the conversation in the utmost confidence.

He listened silently as I laid out—in greater detail than I originally planned—the whole pattern of hint and suspicion which concerned me so greatly.

"I am greatly flattered," he said when I had done, "that you choose me for such confidence; but I am not certain what you want of me."

"I want your opinion," I said. "I have certain evidence, and I have a partial hypothesis which is in no way contradicted by any of it. Yet it is not confirmed either. Can you think of an alternative which fits as well, if not better?"

"Let me be clear. You know this Italian gentleman is connected both to radicals and to the Spanish; you know that he is coming to our shores next month; those are your essential, though not your only, facts. You believe that he is coming here to cause us harm; that is your hypothesis. You do not know what that harm might be."

I nodded.

"So let us see if indeed there is an alternative which might supplant your main hypothesis. Let us start by proposing that Cola is what he says: a young gentleman touring the world, with no interest in politics. He falls in with English radicals because he meets them by chance. He knows high Spaniards because he is a gentleman of quality from a wealthy Venetian family. He plans to come to England because he wishes to gain some knowledge of us. He is, in fact, entirely harmless."

"You leave out the secondary facts," I said, "which bolster one proposal but weaken the other. Cola is the senior son of a trader in considerable difficulties, his first obligation should be his family, yet he is in the Low Countries spending money in idle amusements. You need a good reason for such behavior, which my thesis can absorb, while yours cannot. He had little or no reputation for curiosity until the moment he arrived in Leiden, but was known for his courage and bravado with arms. In your thesis we must account for a remarkable change in character; in mine we do not. And you do not take account of the central matter, which is that he was the recipient of a letter disguised in a code previously used by a traitor against the king. Innocent tourists of curiosity, I think, rarely receive such missives.''

Boyle nodded, and accepted the counter-argument. ''Very well,'' he said, ''I concede your hypothesis is the stronger, and must take priority. So I will attack your conclusion; we grant that Cola is in potential an imminent danger; does that lead inevitably to the conclusion that this danger will be realized? If I understand it rightly, you have no idea or notion of what this man might do when he comes here. What could one solitary individual accomplish that would pose such a danger?''

''He can say something, do something or be a means of transmission,'' I replied. ''These are the only types of action which are possible. Any danger he poses must be contained in one of these three categories. By transmission, I mean he could bring a message, or money, or take either of these away; I cannot think this is the case, both the radicals and the Spaniards have more than enough means of transporting anything they choose without making use of a man such as he. Similarly, I cannot see what he might say that could pose any form of threat, and which would require his presence in this country. So that leaves deeds. I ask you, sir, what deed can a single, solitary man accomplish that would pose a danger to this kingdom if, as seems reasonable, his profession is of significance in determining his movements?''

Boyle looked at me, but did not venture an answer.

''You know as well as I,'' I continued, ''that the one thing a soldier does which others do not do is kill people. And one man cannot kill many. The fewer who die, the more important they must be to make an impact.''

I lay out this conversation—in abridged form, for we talked many hours on the matter—to demonstrate that my fears were not the product of a mind suspicious of everyone and seeing dangers in mere shadows. No other hypothesis fitted the case as exactly, and so no other should be considered until it was discredited. This is the rule of experiment, and applies to politics as much as it does to mathematics or medicine. I presented my argument to Boyle and not only did he fail to come up with an alternative explanation, he was forced to concede that my own hypothesis was by far the one which best fitted the available facts. I did not believe I had reached certainty; only a scholastic would claim such prowess. But I could claim a probability more than strong enough to justify my concern.

Strike at the body, and the wound soon heals even though it may be a great gash. Strike only one small blow at the heart, and the effect is catastrophic. And the living, breathing heart of the kingdom was the king. One man, indeed, could bring all to ruin where an entire army would be ineffective.

Lest this seem incredible, and my fears fantastic, I beg you consider the number of such murders in recent history. Only half a century before, that great man Henry IV of France was stabbed to death, as were the Prince of Orange and Henry II before him. Under forty years ago the Duke of Buckingham was murdered by his own servant; judicial murder had ended the lives of the Earl of Strafford, Archbishop Laud and the blessed martyr Charles. I myself had encountered many plots to murder Cromwell, and even the Lord Chancellor in exile condoned the murder of the Commonwealth's ambassadors at The Hague and Madrid. Public life was steeped in blood, and the murder of a king aroused no more repugnance in the breasts of many than did the slaughter of a domestic beast. We had become inured to the most horrendous of sins, and thought of them as instruments of policy.

I knew now that this plot I had detected was not the work of the fanatics, whose role, I suspected, would be merely to take the blame for any atrocity committed for the benefit of others. Those others had to be the Spanish, and the ultimate aim would be to detach England from its freedoms and bring our country back into Romish subjection. Kill the king, and his brother, an avowed Catholic, succeeds to the throne. His first act is to swear vengeance on the assassins of his beloved Charles. He blames the fanatics and swears to extirpate them all. Moderation is thrown to the winds, and the men of extremes take power once more. The result would be war, of course, in which Englishman would be pitted against Englishman once more. This time, though, it would be more terrible still, for the Catholics would call on their Spanish masters for aid, and the French would be bound to intervene. The nightmare of all princes since Elizabeth, that this land should become the cockpit of Europe, was fearsomely close.

For this last speculation I had no direct evidence, yet it was a reasonable projection from the evidence to hand; for logic allows us to see the future, or at least its likely development. Just as in mathematics when we can imagine a line, and then imagine it projected out farther, even to infinity, through the exercise of rational thought, so in politics we can consider actions and calculate consequences. If my fundamental hypothesis was granted—and it stood up to Boyle's criticism as well as to my own dispassionate querying—then certain results would follow. I have laid out those possibilities to ensure my fears are understood. I admit that I was wrong in detail and will, at the appropriate moment, lay out my errors pitilessly; but nonetheless I claim the overall structure of my hypothesis was sound, in that it was capable of accepting modification without having to be abandoned.

Matthew would not, I was sure, make any more progress in The Hague. He had become foolish through Cola's attentions and could not see the evidence which, I knew, was in front of his eyes. More, I was concerned about him, for he risked placing himself in peril and I desired him away from Cola as swiftly as possible. Nor was this concern misplaced, for the Lord granted me the most frightening of dreams which proved my worries had foundation. On the whole I do not greatly attend to such things, and indeed I dream only rarely; but this one was so clearly spiritual in origin, and so clearly foresaw the future, that even I resolved to take note.

Though I had not yet received Matthew's letter about the feast, yet it was in my vision and I, later discovered, that was the very night the feast took place. For it was on Olympus, and Matthew was servant to the gods, who plied him with all manner of food and wine until he was drunk and silly. Then one man at the table, whom I knew to be this Cola though I did not know his face, crept up and took him from behind, plunging a sharp sword into his belly again and again, until Matthew cried out with the greatest of pain. And I was in another room, seeing it all but unable to move, telling Matthew to get away. But he would not do so.

I woke up in great fear, knowing that the greatest danger threatened; I hoped Matthew was safe, and worried without end until I knew he was unharmed. I thought Cola was on the way to England, but could do little to discover his whereabouts, so meagre were my resources. I also had to decide whether I should pass a warning to His Majesty, but decided against because I knew it would not be taken seriously. He was a courageous, not to say foolhardy, man and had lived so long in the expectation of sudden murder that it no longer swerved him from his devotion to pleasure. And what was I to say? ''Highness, a plot exists to kill you so your own brother might take your place''? Without proof, such a statement would at the very least mean a swift end to my pensions and places. I do not accept that the diagonal of a square is incommensurable with its sides because someone tells me; I accept it because it can be demonstrated to be so and, in this matter, while I could advance a theory better than any other, I could not yet demonstrate it.

A WEEK LATER, MATTHEW RETURNED TO ENGLAND AND told me that Marco Da Cola had indeed left the Low Countries, and that he did not know where he had gone. What was more, the man had near a ten day start, for Matthew had been unable to find a boat which would take him to England for some days after this farewell feast of his and (I suspect) had so convinced himself of the man's harmlessness he had not hurried to return to my side.

Disappointed and concerned though I was, Matthew's very presence in the room lifted my heart. The intelligent gaze which gave his face such beauty rekindled the warmth in me which was extinguished in his absence; it was no surprise to me that Cola had taken to him, and kept him by his side. I thanked God for his safe return, and prayed that all my fears had been merely phantasms of a disordered and worried mind, with no substance to them.

But I was swiftly disabused of that, for when I chastised

him for his laxness, and told him he was most certainly in error about the Italian, for the first time in our acquaintanceship he refused to bow to my superiority, and told me frankly I was wrong.

"What do you know?" he asked. "You who have never met the man, who have no proof but only suspicion? I tell you, I do know him, have spent very many hours in the most pleasant conversation, and he is no danger to you or any other man."

"You are deceived, Matthew," I replied. "You do not know what I know."

"So tell me."

"I will not. These are high matters of state, which are no concern of yours. It is your duty to accept my word, without question, and not be deceived into thinking a man harmless because he pays you compliments and gives you presents."

"You think he bought my affections? You think me such a fool? Is that it? Because you never say a word to me except to criticize, and whose only gift has been to beat me when I make a mistake."

"I think you are young and inexperienced," I said, certain now that my worst fears had indeed been realized. "You must remember that I know what is best for you. But I forgive you for your words."

"I do not want your forgiveness. I have done everything you asked of me, and more. It is you, who accuse all men falsely, who should ask forgiveness."

I was tempted to hit him, but held myself back and instead made an attempt to end a discussion which was as foolish as it was inappropriate.

"I will not justify myself to you, except to say that when I can tell you everything I will do so, and you will understand how wrong you are. Now, come, Matthew, my boy. You are just arrived and we are fighting. This is no way to begin. Come and take a drink, and tell me of your adventures. I truly wish to hear it all."

Eventually he was calmed and reassured, and sat beside me and bit by bit we resumed our habitual relation, spending the next few hours in solitary and pleasant company. He told me of his travels, delighting me with his skill at observing, and his ability to go to the heart of the matter without diversion, although he said nothing of Cola's farewell, and I found that I did not ask him. In return, I told him how I had passed the time in his absence, of the books I had read, explaining to him the importance of controversies and disputes in a way which (I confess) I had not done before. He left me that evening, and I thanked God in prayer for such a companion, for without him my life was empty indeed. But my heart was uneasy, as for the first time I had failed to command him, and had had to ask for his friendship. He had given it, but I did not know whether I could count on it forever. I knew that before very long I would have to reimpose the correct order, and remind him of his subservience, lest he become arrogant. The thought deadened my mood, and then, when I considered what he had told me, I became more somber still.

I was sure that, if not actually in England already, then Cola was on his way and was likely to arrive before I could pick up his trail again. Whatever the Italian intended, I hoped very much that he would not act swiftly. The next morning I sent Matthew back to his friends in East Smithfield in the hope that they would have heard some news. I did not expect much from this, and was not greatly disappointed when he reported that they knew nothing, but it was an obvious step to take, and one of the few that I could take with ease.

Then I went amongst my trader friends, enquiring with as much subtlety as urgency allowed whether they knew of any boat which had brought a lone passenger to these shores. Italian, Spanish or French; Cola might well have passed himself off as any of these, and many sailors would not have cared to tell the difference. Again, my hopes were not high, and again I learned nothing of interest. It was not certain, but I thought it likely he would have arrived by one of the lesser ports of East Anglia and, if he had Spanish money at his disposal, could well have come in a boat hired for the purpose.

At this point, the resources I had at my disposal were exhausted. I could, of course, write to every portmaster in East Anglia, although not without making my interest generally known. Receiving the replies could take up to a month, and even then I would be unable to judge the usefulness of any information received, not being personally acquainted with my correspondents. What was I to do otherwise? Walk the streets of London, in the hope of recognizing a man I had never seen and who was known to no one in this country? Sit in my study and hope that he made himself known to me before he executed his task?

Neither option seemed sensible and, with the very greatest reluctance, I decided I would have to provoke some sort of reaction that would bring him to light, or frighten him off. It was a finely judged experiment, which would only be successful if it produced a single result. I was like an experimentalist who has his theory, and conducts an experiment to confirm it; I had not the luxury of the true philosopher, who can perform his operations and construct his theory from the evidence of his eyes.

I pondered this matter for a day before concluding that I had no alternative and, as the opportunity offered, I decided to throw hesitation aside. The Society was to hold a meeting, at which many matters were to be discussed, and the evening concluded by the public vivisection of a dog. These are always popular, and I fear that several operators conducted their experiments more to excite the pleasure of the audience than for any utility.

But many always wished to come, guests were encouraged to spread the fame of our work, and the company afterward was always merry and free. I straightaway asked Mr. Oldenburg if he would do me the favor of inviting Señor de Moledi as a guest of honor, impressing on that gentleman that his presence would be warmly appreciated.

This de Moledi was Spain's representative in England, and a close associate of Caracena, the governor of the Spanish Netherlands and a man with a great hatred of all things English. It was inconceivable he would be ignorant of any attempt on the king, even though he would have been wise not to know too many details. Consequently, if I was to stir the pot a little, he was by far the best person to approach. If my intervention worked and produced some practical response, I might at last have the solid evidence I needed, and would be finally in a position to lay out my suspicions with some hope of being believed.

The meeting that evening was a crowded one, although the communications read out by Mr. Oldenburg in his dull monotone scarcely deserved much attention. One paper on the geometry of the parabola was as absurd as it was incomprehensible, and my opinion was crucial in having it, and its author, rejected out of hand. Another by Mr. Wren on the sundial was, as usual with that fine man, a model of lucidity and elegance but scarcely of major significance. Correspondence from abroad produced its usual crop of interest, mixed in with bombast and faulty thinking. The only matter of moment I recall (and consulting the minutes of the meeting I see my memory serves me well) was an excellent reading by Mr. Hooke on his work with a microscope of his own devising. However detestable that man was as an individual, he was one of the finest artisans of our little group, close in observation, meticulous in recording. His revelations of the entire worlds to be found in a simple drop of water astonished us all, and produced an almost tearful commentary from Mr. Goddard, who praised the Lord mightily for His creation, and for His goodness in allowing His creatures to comprehend ever more of His works. Then, prayers ended the formal session, and those who had a mind to watched the experiment with the dog.

I could see from his expression that de Moledi had as little taste for the howlings of a tormented beast as I, and so I approached him and said that no one would take it as an insult to the gathering if he did not attend; for my part I also intended to absent myself, and if he wished to take a glass of wine with me, I would be honored by his company.

To this he assented and, having already arranged the matter beforehand, I led him through to the room Wren maintained at Gresham College, where a good Canary wine awaited us.

"I hope, sir, you did not find the occupations of we men of curiosity distasteful. I know that it must seem a strange interest, and that some consider it impious."

We spoke in Latin, and I was pleased to find that his own fluency in that blessed tongue was no less than mine. He seemed the most courteous of men and, if most Spaniards were like him, I could see how a man like Mr. Bennet, who placed such store in the niceties of address, might be seduced into loving the nation. For my part, I was safe from being deceived by such matters, for I knew all too well what lay behind the fine manners.

"On the contrary; I found it eminently diverting, and I very much hope that men of good curiosity from all over Christendom will join together in free discourse. There are many in Spain, as well, who are interested in these matters and I would willingly introduce them to your Society, if you find that agreeable."

I accepted with pleasure, and made certain I would remember to warn Oldenburg of the danger. Spain is a country which had ruthlessly subjected all enquiry to persecution, and for such a place as this to desire communication with us would have been laughable had it not been so cruel.

"I must say I am glad to make your acquaintance, Dr. Wallis, and even more pleased to have the opportunity of talking to you in private. I have, of course, heard much of you."

"You surprise me, Your Excellency. I do not know how my name has come to your ears; I did not realize you took an interest in mathematics."

"I take very little; excellent pursuit though it no doubt is, I have no head for figures at all."

"That is a pity. I have long believed the purity of mathematical reasoning is the finest training a man might have."

"In which case, I must own to my deficiencies, for my great interest is canon law. But I did not hear of you for your expertise in algebra. Rather for your skill in the comprehension of codes."

"I am sure whatever you heard was greatly exaggerated. I have few abilities in that line of work."

"So great is your reputation as the finest man in the world, that I was wondering whether you might share your knowledge."

"With whom?"

"With all men of good will, who wish to bring the darkness into light, and ensure the peace of all Christendom."

"You mean I should write a book about it?"

"Maybe you should," he said with a smile. "But that would be a long operation, and bring you little reward. More, I wondered whether you might travel to Brussels, and give instruction to some young men of my acquaintance, who would prove, I am sure, to be some of the finest pupils you have ever had. Naturally, this labor would be well rewarded."

The audacity of the man was astonishing; he slipped so easily and readily into the suggestion, it fell from his lips so normally, that I did not even feel resentment at the proposal. There was, of course, not the slightest chance of my even considering the offer; perhaps he knew that. In my life I have had many such proposals; I have turned them all down. Even good Protestant states I have declined to aid in any way at all, most recently rejecting a hint that I should instruct Mr. Leibniz in my art. I have always been determined that my skill should be my country's alone, and should not be available to any who might become an antagonist.

"Your offer is as generous as my worth is small," I replied. "But I fear my university duties are such that I would never be allowed leave to travel."

"A great pity," he replied, with no trace at all of surprise or disappointment. "If your circumstances ever change, the offer will undoubtedly be renewed."

"As you have done me a great honor, I feel obliged to repay your kindness instantly," I said. "For I must tell you that a plot is afoot by your enemies to besmirch your reputation, by spreading the most scurrilous rumors."

"And this comes from your work, does it?"

"It comes from different places. I know many people of high standing, and converse frequently with them. Let me tell you frankly, sir, that I feel strongly you should be allowed to defend yourself against idle tittle-tattle. You have not been in this country long enough to understand the power of gossip in a country so ill-used to the discipline of strong and firm government."

"I am grateful for your concern. Tell me, then. What is this gossip I should concern myself with?"

"It is said that you are no friends of our monarch, and

that should misfortune befall him, people would not have to look far to find the source of his troubles.''

De Moledi nodded at these words. "Slander indeed," he said. "For it is known that our love for your king is complete. Did we not aid him in his exile, when he was cast out and penniless? Provide him and his friends with a home, and money? Risk war with Cromwell because we would not abandon our obligations to him?"

"Few people," I replied, "remember past goodness. It is in the nature of mankind to think the worst of their fellows."

"And does a man such as yourself harbor such suspicions?"

"I cannot believe that any man of honor could intend harm to a man so manifestly loved by God," I said.

"That is true. The great difficulty with lies is that they are hard to contradict, especially when others spread them with malicious intent."

"They must be contradicted," I said. "If I may speak plainly?"

He gave his assent.

"Your interest at court, and your friends there, will be hurt by these stories if they are allowed to go unchecked."

"And you wish to assist me? Forgive me for saying so, but I did not expect such a kindness from a man such as you, whose opinions are well known."

"I freely admit I have no great love for your country. Many men within it I honor deeply, but your interests and ours must ever be in conflict. I can say the same for France, however. The well-being of England must always lie in ensuring that no foreign country ever attains a predominant position amongst us. That has been the policy of the wisest of our princes for generations, and must continue. When France is strong, we must look to the Habsburgs; when the Habsburgs are strong, we should bolster France."

"And do you speak for Mr. Bennet as well?"

"I speak for no man but myself. I am a mathematician, a priest, and an Englishman. But I am sure you know the admiration Mr. Bennet has for your country. His position, also, will not be aided by such talk."

De Moledi stood up, and bowed graciously. "I understand

well that you are the sort of man to whom thanks should only be offered in words, and so in words alone do I offer them. I will say only that a different man would go from this room very much the richer for his kindness.''

I WRAPPED UP MY WARNING TO DE MOLEDI IN NO BAD advice and, as was my continual habit before my failing eyes made the practice impossible, I wrote down a short account of my meeting with him to aid my memory. I have the note still, and I see that the counsel I gave was practical and wise. I had little expectation that it would be taken, however. The state is like a large ship with a numerous crew; once set on a course, it is difficult to change tack with any speed, even when such an alteration is manifestly sensible.

De Moledi's response to my conversation was swift, however; far faster and more determined than I had anticipated. The following evening, one of Mr. Bennet's men came to my house and handed me a letter which informed me that my presence was urgently required.

His standing had increased grandly since our previous meeting, and he wished all to know of his power as Secretary of State for the South. It is unwise even now to compare any man unfavorably with Cromwell, but there was a simplicity about that great bad man which was far more impressive for being totally unpracticed and unfeigned. For Cromwell truly was a great man, the greatest, I believe, this country has ever known. His clarity of mind, his strength and certainty were such that, born to a gentleman's estate, he made himself a kingdom; had he been born to a kingdom, he would have made himself an empire. He reduced three nations, which perfectly hated him, to entire obedience; governed by an army which wished his ruin, and inspired fear across a continent and beyond. He held the country in his palm yet would often greet a visitor himself, and pour wine with his own hands. He had no need of display, for there was no mistaking his authority. I said this once to Lord Clarendon, and he agreed with my account.

Mr. Bennet was a lesser man, with smaller genius; all of his worth could have fitted into Cromwell's thumbnail. And yet, what pomp he had adopted. The progression through the antechambers had increased to positively Spanish proportions, and the obsequious behavior of the servants had grown to such an extent that it was hard for a simple man such as myself to repress a certain sense of disgust at the display. It took a full fifteen minutes to make my way from the entrance to his chambers into his presence; King Louis in all his present magnificence, I think, cannot be more difficult to approach than was Mr. Bennet then.

It was all for show, and in conversation he was as English as he was Spanish in manners. Indeed, his bluntness came close to discourtesy, and he kept me standing throughout the interview.

"What, exactly, do you think you are doing, Dr. Wallis?" he shouted, waving a piece of paper at me, too far away for me to see. "Are you mad that you disobey my express orders?"

I told him I did not understand the question.

"I have here a strongly worded note," he said, breathing heavily that I might feel, see and hear his anger all at the same time, "from a very indignant Spanish ambassador. Is it true that you had the presumption yesterday evening to lecture him on the peace of Christendom, and tell him how his country's foreign policy should be run?"

"It most certainly is not," I replied. My curiosity at this turn of events was overcoming my alarm at the evident anger my patron was demonstrating. I knew Mr. Bennet well enough to know that he lost his temper very rarely, for he believed firmly that such demonstrations were inappropriate in a gentleman. False shows of rage were not tactics he used to overawe his clients, and I came to the conclusion that, on this occasion, he was perfectly sincere and genuinely furious. This, of course, made my own situation the more perilous, since he was not a man whose favor I could afford to lose. But it also made the conversation more interesting, as I could not easily understand the source of his fury.

"How do you explain the offense you have given him then?" Bennet continued.

"I do not know what the offense is. I conversed—I thought most pleasantly—with Señor de Moledi yesterday evening, and we parted with mutual expressions of regard. It may be that I angered him by refusing a large bribe, I do not know; I thought I had turned down the offer with the greatest of tact. Might I ask what is the complaint?''

"He says you all but accused him of fomenting a plot to kill the king. Is that true?''

"It is not. I never mentioned any such thing, nor would I ever have dreamed of doing so.''

"What do you think you said?''

"I merely told him that it was strongly held by many that his country wished England no good. It was not an important part of the conversation.''

"But it was cautiously said," Bennet said. "You say nothing without deliberation. So now I want to know why. Your reports to me in the last few months have been so obviously full of half-truths and evasions that I am beginning to tire of them. Now I command you to tell me the exact truth. And I warn you that if I am not satisfied of your total candor I will be highly displeased.''

Faced with such an ultimatum, I could do no other. And it was the greatest mistake that ever I made. I do not blame Mr. Bennet; I blame myself for my weakness, and I know that the punishment meted out to me for my error was so crushing a burden that I have suffered for it every day of my life since. I am graced in that I come from a hardy, long-living family on both my mother's and my father's sides, and I live in full expectation of continuing in this world for many years yet. On innumerable occasions since that day I have prayed that this blessing be taken from me, so great is the remorse I suffer.

I told Mr. Bennet of my suspicions. In full and, I now believe, in greater detail than I needed provide. I told him of Marco da Cola, and the threads of suspicion that had attached themselves to him. I told him of my understanding that he was, if not already here, then on his way to this country. And I told him of what I believed he planned to do when he arrived.

Bennet listened at first impatiently, then with becoming gravity, to my account. And when I had finished, he got up and stared for many minutes out of the window of the little chamber where he habitually carried on his business.

Eventually he turned to face me, and I could see from his expression that the anger had passed. I was not, however, to escape further reproof.

"I must commend you," he said, "for the diligence your love of His Majesty has produced. I do not doubt for a minute that you have acted with the very best of intentions, and that your desire was simply and wholly the safety of the realm. You are a most excellent servant."

"I thank you."

"But in this matter, you have made a serious error. You must know that in diplomacy nothing is ever as it seems, and what may appear as common sense is often the opposite. We cannot go to war. Who should we fight? The Spanish? The French? The Dutch? All together or in combination? And with what are we meant to pay an army? Parliament will barely provide to keep a roof over the king's head as it is. You know, I am sure, that I am partial to the Spanish, that I regard the French as our greatest enemy. Even so, I will not countenance an alliance with them, any more than I could support a pact against them. For the foreseeable future, at least, we must steer a delicate course between these obstacles, and allow nothing to push the king into the arms of one side or the other."

"But you know as well, sir," I said, "that Spanish agents are operating freely, spending their gold to buy support."

"Of course they are. And so are the French and the Dutch. What of it? As long as all spend with the same enthusiasm, and none gains the upper hand, then no harm is done. Your comments in themselves do little harm, please do not think that. But if your suspicions become generally known, then the French interest will be strengthened. Young Louis has deep coffers. His Majesty is tempted already, even though it would be a disaster. It is imperative that nothing disturbs the balance which those who have the interest of the country at heart have created. Now, tell me, does anyone else know of this suspicion you have?"

"Absolutely not," I said. "I am the only person with a full knowledge of it. My servant Matthew no doubt has some understanding, since he is an intelligent boy, but even he does not know the full story."

"And he is where?"

"He is now back in England. But you need have no fears about him. He is totally bound to me."

"Good. Talk to him and make sure he understands."

"I am happy to obey your wishes in this matter," I continued, "but I must repeat that, as far as I can see, the matter is a serious one nonetheless. With the sanction of the Spanish crown or not, this man is coming to the country, and I believe him to be very dangerous to us. What am I to do about it? Surely you do not think that he should be left in peace."

Bennet smiled. "I do not think you need have any concern on that score, sir," he said. "This is not the only tale of conspiracy, and I have finally persuaded His Majesty to increase the guard around him night and day. I see no chance of even the most desperate of assassins reaching him."

"This is no ordinary soldier, sir," I said. "He had a reputation for daring and ruthless murders against the Turks on Crete. He must not be underestimated."

"I understand your concerns," Bennet replied. "But I must point out that, if you are correct—and I do not accept that you are so—the comments you made to de Moledi will have been noted. He will take the greatest of care to make sure nothing occurs which thrusts us into the arms of his greatest enemy. An alliance with France would surely follow any such event, for this scheme could only work if its true author never became known, and you have ensured that that cannot be."

There the interview ended. I left with my position badly, but not irrevocably, weakened. I had not lost his favor, and certainly had not been threatened with any sanction. Far more important was the fact that my confidence was shaken; I had not anticipated de Moledi's reaction. He had, indeed, behaved as an innocent might well do in the circumstances, with surprise and protest. And what Mr. Bennet said was true; an assassination of the king now made no sense, if its sole achievement was to deliver England into the hands of the French.

I did not realize, although I was beginning to suspect, that my conclusions were based on faulty propositions; this required more and more terrible evidence, before all doubts were swept away.

chapter seven

I NEVER DISCOVERED PRECISELY WHEN MARCO DA
Cola arrived in England, or by what means, although I am
certain he had already stepped ashore before I spoke to the
Spanish ambassador; this belief was later confirmed by Jack
Prestcott when I interrogated him. By the third week of
March, Cola was in London and I assume he was warned
that something of his purpose had become known to me; he
must also have learned that Matthew was my servant, and
that the lad also knew much that was dangerous.

I saw Matthew that morning; he came to my house in the
greatest of hurry, his face flushed with achievement, to say
that he had found Cola in London, and planned to go and
see him. Instantly I knew I had to prevent any such encounter.

"You will not," I said. "I forbid it."

His face fell, then turned dark with anger, an expression I
had never before seen on him. At once, all my fears returned
after I had successfully kept them at bay, hoping that all
would be well once more now he was back by my side.
"Why? What nonsense is this? You look for this man, and
when I find him for you, you forbid me to discover where
exactly he is."

"He is a killer, Matthew. A very dangerous man indeed."

Matthew laughed in the lighthearted way he had, which
had once given me such pleasure but did so no longer. "I

do not think an Italian holds much danger for a child of London," he said. "Certainly not this one."

"Oh, but he does. You know the streets and the alleys, and all the ways across the town far better than he. But do not underrate him. Promise me you will leave him be."

His laughter faded, and I could see I had wounded him once more. "Is that it? Or do you want to deny me a friend who might do me good, who might patronize me freely, without requiring so much in return? Who listens to me, and values my opinions instead of forever criticizing and imposing his own? I tell you, doctor, this man was kind and good to me; he did not beat me and always behaved well."

"Stop it," I cried, anguished that I should be compared to another in such a cruel way, and have this Cola's success thrust at me merely to wound my heart. "It is true what I say. You must not go near him. I cannot bear the thought of him touching you, hurting you in any way. I wish to protect you."

"I can look after myself. And I will show you that I can. I have known thieves and murderers and fanatics since the day I was born. Yet here I am, unscratched and unharmed. And you think nothing of this, and talk to me as though I were a child."

"You owe me a great deal," I said, angry with his anger, and wounded by his words. "And I will have your respect and courtesy."

"But you will not give it, as I also deserve. You never have."

"That is enough. Get out of my room, and come back when you are ready to apologize. I know why you wish to see him. I know what he is and what he wants of you; I see it better than you can. Why else would a man like him keep a boy like you by his side? Do you think it is for your wit? You have little. Your money? You have none. Your learning? You have what I gave you. Your breeding? I picked you up from the gutter. I tell you, if you go to him tonight, I will not have you in this house again. Do you understand?"

I had never threatened him so before, and had not intended to do so then. But he was fast slipping from my grasp. The temptation of dissoluteness was growing on him, encouraged by this man, and it had to be stopped immediately. He had to know I commanded, and was his master. Otherwise he would have been quite lost.

But it was too late; I had delayed too long, and the corruption had already gone too deep. Still, I thought he would have asked my pardon and realized his error, as he had been prepared to do so recently in the past. But he stared at me, not knowing whether I was serious or not, and seeing that gaze I weakened and spoiled all.

"Matthew," I said, "my boy, come to me." For the first time in my life, but God help me, not for the first time in my dreams, I took him in my arms and held him tightly to me, hoping to feel the softness of his response. Instead, Matthew stiffened, then pushed his arms hard against my chest, and broke away, stumbling backward in his haste to part from me.

"Leave me be," he said in a hushed voice. "You cannot command me, nor forbid me anything. It is not me who has done wrong here, and not this Italian who keeps me for impure reasons, I think."

And he walked out, leaving me to bitter anger, and the sadness of regret.

I never saw Matthew alive again. That same evening Marco da Cola cold-bloodedly cut his throat in a dark alley, and left him to bleed to death.

Even now, I can hardly bear to recall the details of the day I learned that no amends would ever be made. My housekeeper's husband (I had allowed the woman to marry the previous year, and had such a regard for her honesty that I did not see fit to throw her out) came himself to Gresham College, where I was dining with Mr. Wren, to tell me of the calamity. He was a big, slow, stupid man, fearful of my wrath but courageous enough to bring the bad news himself.

He trembled as he stood there before me and told me what had happened. With some resource, he had gone to the scene itself when the news came, and asked those who lived nearby what had transpired. It appeared there had been a murderous assault a few hours previously. Matthew had been attacked from behind, his mouth covered and his throat slit with a single cut. There had been no noise, no sound of any shouting, none of the normal commotion that signifies a struggle or a robbery in progress. The culprit was not seen by anyone and Matthew was left to die. It was not a duel, not a fight of honor, he was not given the chance to die in the knowledge at least of having acted as a man should. It was pure and simple murder, carried out in the most despicable manner. My dream had warned me, and I had let it happen nonetheless.

I see from Cola's memoirs he even has the audacity still to indicate his crime, although he pretends it was self-defense. He says he was set on by bravoes, who (he claims) he thought were sent by the former associate of his father. With what nobility and courage did he defend himself against such bloodthirsty rogues! With what modesty does he recount how, all alone, he sent them packing. He does not say, of course, that his assailant was but a boy of nineteen, who never fought a man in his life and who certainly intended him no harm. He does not say that he followed the boy, and deliberately set upon him, leaving him no chance of defending himself. He omits to say that he committed this one crime that he might be free to commit still greater ones later.

And he does not say that he extinguished the light of my life by that deed, cast all into darkness and ended all joy forever. Matthew's death rested on my shoulders, for my mistrust excited him to bravado, and it mattered not that I suffered most from the mistake. Such a glory to God, my Absalom, my clay, which I had fashioned myself into the finest of creation. Would to God I had died for thee, my son, my son. (2 Samuel 18:33.)

His obedience matched his piety, his piety his loyalty, and his loyalty his beauty. I had imagined growing old with him by my side, to comfort me as no woman ever could. He alone made the day bright, and the morning glow with hope. Such love had Saul for David, and I wept at the bitterness of my punishment.

"He that loveth son or daughter more than me is not worthy of me" (Matthew 10:37). How often had I read those words without understanding the burden they lay on all mankind, for I had never loved any man or woman before.

And the lesson was swift and harsh, and I rebelled against

it. I begged the Almighty it should not be, that my servant was wrong, that another had died in his place.

And I knew the cruelty of desiring that another suffer instead of me, that another father should grieve for me. Our Lord had accepted His cross, but even He had prayed the burden might be taken from Him, and so I prayed as well.

And the Lord told me I had loved the boy too much, and made me remember those nights when he had slept in my bed, while I lay awake listening to his breathing, wishing only to reach out and touch him.

And I remember how I begged deliverance from my desires, and also wished them fulfilled.

This was my punishment, so fully deserved. I thought I would die under the pain of it, and never recover from the loss.

And in my heart my anger grew fierce and cold, for I knew also that it was Marco da Cola who had tempted my dearest boy away from me, and seduced him so he would not notice as the knife slipped from its scabbard.

I asked that God should say to me as he had to David, "I will deliver thine enemy into thine hand, that thou mayest do to him as it shall seem good unto thee" (1 Samuel 24:4). I vowed that this Cola's brutality would undo him.

It is written: "Whoso sheddeth man's blood, by man shall his blood be shed" (Genesis 9:6).

I GIVE THANKS THAT I ALLOW NO MAN TO SEE MY EMOtions and that I have ever had a deep sense of duty, for it was only that which forced me to rise and rededicate myself to my purpose. And so I prayed, then forced myself once more to my task; a harder deed I have never done, for I maintained always my habitual demeanor, which men call coldness, while all the time my very heart was bleeding with grief. I will add no more of this matter; it is properly for no man's ears. But I will say that from then on, I had one purpose in mind, one aim and one desire, and that stayed with me in my dreams and every second of my waking day. I abandoned all desire to show my superiority by deciphering that which defeated all others. Books by Livy, letters to Cola now become mere links in my great evidential chain: I knew of them already and did not need to hold the one in my hand, or comprehend the precise meaning of the other. They had served their purpose, and I had a more urgent task before me than the solution of intellectual puzzles.

Matthew had said he did not believe that he was suspected by Cola in the Low Countries; had the Italian done so, the boy would surely have died before ever he set foot on English soil. It was accordingly clear that Cola had discovered this in London, and thus also certain that the information had reached him because I had told Mr. Bennet of my suspicions, and named Matthew as one privy to them. I should have known that there is no such thing as a discreet courtier, nor can any man keep a secret in Whitehall. So I resolved that I would no more inform Mr. Bennet of my progress: not only did I not want loose talk to warn Cola further, I also wished to stay alive myself, and knew that if the Italian had slaughtered Matthew because of the little he knew, then how could he avoid making a similar attempt on my life?

Nonetheless, it was no surprise to me at all when I heard that a young gentleman of curiosity had arrived in Oxford and had expressed the intention of staying some time.

But it was a considerable surprise when virtually his first move was to establish contact with the Blundy family.

chapter eight

HERE I MUST PAUSE AND GIVE AN ACCOUNT OF THAT family, since Cola's own narrative is not to be believed in any particular and it is obvious that, if Prestcott touches on the subject in his scribblings, then he will give nothing but a wildly misguided account. He formed some strange fascination for the girl and was convinced she intended him harm, although how she could have accomplished this feat I do not pretend to understand. Nor was it necessary: since Prestcott seemed intent on doing himself so much harm there was little point in anyone else adding to it.

I knew of Edmund Blundy's reputation as an agitator in the army and heard he had died; equally I was naturally aware that his wife had settled in Oxford along with her daughter. Through my informers I kept watch on them for a while but on the whole let them be: if they kept within the law, then I saw no reason to persecute them, even though their dissent in matters of religion was blatant. As I hope I have made clear, my concern was the good ordering of society, and I had little interest in quibbling as long as an outward show of conformity was maintained. I know that many (some people for whom I have a high regard in other matters, such as Mr. Locke) hold to the doctrine of toleration; I disagree most strongly if that is taken to mean worship outside the body of the Established Church. A state can no more survive without general unity in religion than it can without common purpose in government, for to deny the church is, ultimately, to deny all civil authority. It is for this reason I support the virtuous mediocrity which the Anglican settlement observes between the meretricious gaudiness of Rome, and squalid sluttery of the fanatical conventicles.

With the Blundys, mother and daughter, I was pleased to see that the lesson inflicted on them by the failure of their aspirations was learned. Although I knew that they kept up contact with all manner of radical acquaintance in Oxford and in Abingdon, their personal behavior gave little cause for concern. Once every three months they attended church and, if they sat resolutely and stony-faced at the back, refusing to sing and standing only reluctantly, that did not concern me. They signified their obedience, and their acquiescence was a lesson to all who might have contemplated defiance. For if even the woman who had once directed the fire of soldiers on royalist troops at the great siege of Gloucester no longer had the will to resist, then why should less fiery folk do otherwise?

Few people know of this tale nowadays; I mention it here partly because it illustrates the character of these people and partly because it deserves to be recorded, the sort of anecdote, indeed, in which a man like Mr. Wood takes such delight. Ned Blundy was already in the service of Parliament at that stage, and his wife followed him with all the other soldiers' women, that her man might be fed and clothed in decency on the march. He was part of Edward Massey's troop and was in Gloucester when King Charles laid siege. Many know of that fierce encounter, in which the resolution of one side was met by the determination of the other, and neither lacked anything in courage. The advantage was with the king, for the town's defenses were slight and ill-prepared, but His Majesty, as was usual with a prince ever more noble than wise, failed to move with the necessary speed. The Parliamentarians began to hope that a little more endurance on their part would enable the relieving army to come to their assistance.

Persuading the citizenry and the ordinary soldiers of this was not an easy task, the more so as the officers' bravery depleted their ranks, leaving many platoons and companies headless. On the occasion I refer to, a company of Royalist soldiers attempted to break through one of the weaker sections of the town's defenses, knowing that the soldiers defending it were disheartened and irresolute. Indeed, it seemed initially that the bold assault would be successful, for many gained the walls, and the discouraged defenders began to pull back. Within minutes, the wall would be theirs and the entire besieging army would pour over.

Then the woman of the tale stepped forward, girded her petticoat into her belt and picked up the pistol and sword of a fallen soldier. "Follow or I die alone," she is said to have shouted, and charged into the mob of attackers, hacking and cutting all around. So ashamed were the Parliamentarians at having their cowardice exposed by a mere woman, and so commanding was the tone of their new leader, that they reformed themselves and charged also. They refused to give any further ground, and the ferocity of their assault forced the Royalists back. As the attackers made their way to their lines once more, the woman formed the defenders into a line, and directed fire into their backs until the very last musket ball had been used up.

As I have said, this was Edmund Blundy's woman, Anne, who already had a reputation for bloodcurdling ferocity. I do not necessarily believe that she bared her breasts before charging into the Royalist ranks, so that they would be less able to strike at her through gallantry, but it is certainly possible and would be quite appropriate to the reputation she established for immodesty and violence.

Such was this woman who, I believe, was more violent in temper and deed than was her husband. She laid claim to being a wise woman, saying her mother had such power, and her mother's mother before her. She even intervened to make speeches at soldiers' gatherings, exciting awe and derision in equal part. She it was, I believe, who incited her husband onto ever more dangerous criminal belief, for she utterly scorned all authority unless she chose, willingly, to accept it. A husband, she maintained, should have no more authority over a wife, than a wife over a husband. I have no doubt that she would eventually have claimed that man and donkey should live in equal partnership as well.

And it was certainly true that neither she nor her daughter had renounced such beliefs. While most, grudgingly or with enthusiasm, set aside old opinions when times changed and the king returned, some persisted in error despite the manifest withdrawal of divine favor. These were the people who saw the return of the king as God's test of their belief, a brief hiatus before the coming of King Jesus and the establishment of His thousand-year rule. Or they saw the Restoration as a sign of God's displeasure, and an incentive to become ever more fanatical to win back His approval. Or they spurned God and all His works, bemoaning the turn of events, and sank into the lassitude of greed disappointed.

Anne Blundy's exact beliefs I never fathomed, and indeed had no interest in doing so; all that counted for me was that she remained quiescent and in this she seemed more than willing to oblige. I did, however, once question Mr. Wood on the matter, for I was aware that his mother employed the girl in their house as a general work-all.

"You know of her background, I imagine," I asked him. "Her parentage and her beliefs?"

"Oh, yes," he said. "I know what they were, and I know what they are now. Why do you ask?"

"I have an affection for you, young man, and I would not wish your family, or your mother, to be besmirched."

"I am grateful for the attention, but you need have no fear. The girl is in perfect conformity with all the laws, and is so dutiful that I do not believe I have ever heard her express a single opinion. Except when His Majesty returned, when her eyes filled with tears of perfect joy. You may rest assured that this must be so, for my mother will scarcely have even a Presbyterian in the house."

"And the mother?"

"I have met the woman only a few times, and found her quite unremarkable. She has scraped together enough money for a washing house, and works hard for her living. I think her only concern is to put by enough money for her daughter to have a dowry, and this is Sarah's main concern as well. Again, I know something of her reputation through my researches, but I believe the madness of faction has left her as entirely as it has left the country as a whole."

I did not completely take Mr. Wood's word, since I had my doubts about his ability to see deeply into such matters, but his report settled my mind and I gladly turned to more interesting quarry. Occasionally, I took note that the daughter would travel to Abingdon or Banbury or Burford; that men of doubtful loyalty—such as the Irish magus I mentioned earlier—would visit their little cottage. Nonetheless, I had few worries. They seemed determined to abandon their previous desire to remake England in their own image, and appeared content simply to make as much money as their positions and abilities would allow. To that laudable aim, I could not object, and I paid them little attention until Marco da Cola went straight to their cottage on the pretext of treating the old woman for her injury.

I have, naturally, read his words on this subject with the greatest of care, and am almost admiring at the consummate skill with which he makes all out to be innocent and charitable. His technique, I note, is to tell something of the truth in everything, but wrap each little fragment of veracity in layer upon layer of falsity. It is hard to imagine a man would take such trouble, and if I did not know the truth of the matter I would undoubtedly be convinced of the genuineness of his candor, and the extent of his generosity.

But look at the matter from a wider perspective, with the benefit of more information than Mr. Cola is willing to provide. Conversant with radical circles in the Low Countries, he comes to Oxford and within hours makes the acquaintance of the family who knows more such people than anyone else in the county. Even though they are far outside his social sphere, he visits them three or four times a day, and is more attendant than a real physician would be with even the wealthiest of clients. No man of sense or reason acts in such a way, and it is a tribute to Mr. Cola's tale that, on reading it, such absurd and unlikely behavior seems perfectly comprehensible.

Once Mr. Boyle told me he had also gravitated into the society of the High Street Philosophers, I knew that at last I had some possibility of learning more about the man's movements and thoughts.

"I hope you do not mind that I took him under my wing

in this way," Boyle said when he mentioned it to me, "but your account was so fascinating that when the man himself appeared in the coffee house, I could not resist examining him myself. And I must say I think you are entirely wrong about him."

"You did not dissent from my argument."

"But it was an easy speculation, based on abstraction. Now that I have met him, I do not concur. We must always take character into account, surely, for that is the surest guide to a man's soul and therefore to his intentions and deeds. I see nothing in his character which would coincide with your speculations about his motives. Quite the reverse."

"But he is cunning, and you are trusting. You might as soon say a fox is harmless to a hen because it approaches gently and softly. It is only dangerous when it strikes."

"Men are not foxes, Dr. Wallis, and nor am I a hen."

"You admit the possibility of error, though?"

"Of course." And Boyle smiled in that thin and arrogant way of his which indicated his difficulty in even conceiving of the notion.

"So you see the wisdom nonetheless of keeping an eye on him."

Boyle frowned with displeasure at the idea. "I will do no such thing. I am happy to oblige you in many ways, but I will not play informer. I know you occupy yourself in such a fashion, but I do not wish to be involved in any way. It is a base and shabby trade you profess, Dr. Wallis."

"I greatly respect your delicacy," I said, ruffled at his words, as he rarely expressed himself with such force. "But sometimes the safety of the kingdom cannot afford such a fastidious approach."

"The kingdom cannot afford to be cheapened by squalid activities among men of honor, either. You should take care, doctor. You wish to guard the integrity of good society, yet you use the habits of the gutter to do so."

"I would like to reason men into good behavior," I replied. "But they seem remarkably impervious to such persuasion."

"Just be careful you do not harry men too much, and push

them into unreasonable behavior they would not ordinarily countenance. It is a risk, you know.''

''I would normally agree. But I have told you of Mr. Cola, and you agreed that my fears are reasonable. And I have more than enough wounds of my own now to be sure of the danger this man poses.''

Boyle expressed his sympathies for Matthew's death, and gave me words of comfort; he was the most generous of men, and was willing to risk a rebuff by intimating that he was aware of the magnitude of my loss. I was grateful to him, but could not allow his words on Christian resignation to deflect me from my aim.

''You will pursue this man to the end, but you have no certainty that he did kill your servant.''

''Matthew was following him closely, he is here to commit a crime and is a known killer. You are right; I have no absolute proof, for I did not see the deed, nor did anyone else. I defy you, however, to assert with any reason he is not responsible.''

''Perhaps so,'' replied Boyle, ''but in my case I will not condemn until I have more certainty. Take my warning, doctor. Be sure your anger does not obscure your vision and drag you down to his level. 'Mine eye affecteth mine heart,' it says in Lamentations. Make sure the reverse does not become too true.''

He stood up to go.

''At least, if you will not help, I trust you have no objection to my approaching Mr. Lower,'' I said, angered at the lofty way he could dismiss matters of such importance.

''That is between you and him, although he is careful of his friends, and quick to take offense on their behalf. I doubt he will assist if he knows what you want, as he is greatly taken with the Italian, and prides himself on his good judgment of men.''

Thus forewarned, I asked the doctor to see me the next day. I had some regard for Lower. At that time he affected a frivolous and carefree manner, but even a man less acute than myself could see that he had a burning desire for fame and craved worldly success more than anything else. I knew that staying in Oxford, cutting up his beasts and playing the assistant would not satisfy him forever. He wanted recognition for his work, and a place with the greatest of the experimentalists. And he knew as well as any that to stand a chance in London he would need luck and some very good friends indeed. This was his weak spot, and my opportunity.

I summoned him on the pretext of asking his advice about my health. There was nothing wrong with me then and, apart from a weakness about my eyes, nothing wrong with me now either. Nonetheless, I affected a pain in my arm, and submitted to an examination. He was a good physician: unlike many of those quacks who intone ponderously, come up with some complex diagnosis and prescribe an expensive and fatuous remedy, Lower confessed himself quite bemused and said he didn't think there was really anything the matter with me. He recommended rest—a cheap enough remedy, it must be said, but one which I could not afford, even had it been needed.

"I understand that you have made the acquaintance of a man called Cola, is that right?" I asked him when we had settled down and I had given him a glass of wine for his trouble. "Taken him under your wing, in fact?"

"I have indeed, sir. Signor Cola is a gentleman and a subtle philosopher. Boyle finds him very useful. He is a man of charm and knowledge, and his thoughts on blood are fascinating."

"You greatly relieve me," I said. "For I have a high opinion of your judgment in these matters."

"Why do you need relieving? You don't know him, do you?"

"Not at all. Think nothing more on the subject. I have always taken it as a principle to doubt the word of foreign correspondents; certainly when their opinion is in contestation with that of an Englishman I set them aside with pleasure. I gladly forget the tales I have heard."

Lower frowned. "What tale is this? Sylvius penned a very favorable portrait of him."

"I'm sure, I'm sure," I said. "And no doubt accurate, as far as he could see. We must always take men as we find them, must we not, and assess contradictory reports in the light of our own experience? 'But the tongue can no man tame; it is an unruly evil, full of deadly poison' " (James 3:8).

"Somebody says something evil about him? Come sir, be frank with me. I know you are too good a man to calumnize, but if malicious reports are being spread it is best the subject of them know, so he can defend himself."

"You are right, of course. And my only hesitation is that the report is so weak that it is scarcely worth giving it any attention. I have no doubt in my mind that it is utterly false. Certainly it is difficult to believe that a gentleman could act in such a coarse fashion."

"Which coarse fashion is this?"

"It concerns Signor Cola's days at Padua. A mathematician there with whom I have correspondence mentioned the matter. He is known to Mr. Oldenburg of our Society, and I can vouch for his good faith. He said merely that there had been a duel. It seems that one man had conducted some ingenious experiments on blood and had told all about them to this Cola. Cola then claimed the experiments as his own. When called to acknowledge the true author, he issued a challenge. Fortunately the fight was stopped by the authorities."

"These misunderstandings do happen," Lower said thoughtfully.

"They do, of course," I agreed heartily. "And it may well be that your friend was entirely in the right. As he is your friend, indeed, I expect that he was. Some people are greedy for fame, though. I am glad philosophy is usually so free of such impositions; to suspect one's friends, and mind one's words lest they steal the glory that is rightfully one's own, would be intolerable. Although, as long as the discovery is made, what does it matter who is credited with it? We do not conduct ourselves for fame, after all. We are doing God's work, and He will know the truth of the matter. What should we care, then, for the opinions of others?"

Lower nodded, so firmly that I could see I had successfully put him on his guard.

"Besides," I carried on, "nobody would be so foolish as to enter a dispute with someone like Boyle, for who would believe his claims against the word of such a man? It is only those whose reputation is not well established who are vulnerable. So there is no problem, even if Cola is as my correspondent described.''

My reasoning in talking thus to Lower was entirely honorable, even if it involved a deception. I could not tell him of my real concerns, but it was vital that Cola should not have liberty to practice his deceit by exploiting Lower's trust. ''He that taketh warning shall deliver his soul'' (Ezekiel 33:5). By exciting Lower's concern over Cola's probity, I had made him more likely to discover the man's duplicity where it truly lay. I persuaded him not to mention the matter, for I told him that if the report were true no good would come of it and if it were false it would merely create an enmity where none should exist. He left me a more sober man, more distrustful than he had been when he arrived and that, also, was a goodness. It was unfortunate, however, that his lack of control so nearly frightened Cola away: he was too open to dissemble, and Cola's manuscript shows all too well how easily his doubts and worries bubbled to the surface in anger and harshness.

DURING THE CONVERSATION, LOWER ALSO MENTIONED that Cola had accompanied him to visit Jack Prestcott in his jail cell, that the Italian had willingly provided the boy with wine and, it appeared, returned to deliver it in person, spending a good long while in his cell conversing with him. This was another curiosity which had to be examined with care. Cola was a Venetian and Sir James had served that country, and perhaps he was merely showing consideration for the son of a man who had served his country well. The other link was the copy of Livy, for Sir James had encoded a letter using it in 1660, and Cola had received one disguised with the same book three years later. I could not fathom it at all, so realized I would have to interview young Prestcott again— and this time thought I would get the truth from him, as his current situation left him little scope for being difficult with me.

I may say that I was beginning to have some doubts about my understanding of Cola's aims, for his actions did not correspond with what I assumed he intended to accomplish. I was not (I repeat again) at all dogmatic in my belief; the conclusions I reached derived from fair principles and a reasoned, unprejudiced comprehension. To put it simply, it was borne in on me that if he desired to strike against the king, who now divided his time between Whitehall, Tunbridge and the racecourses at Newbury, then Oxford was a strange place to be living. And yet, here Cola was and showing no signs whatsoever of moving away. It was for this reason that, when Dr. Grove informed me the Italian was to dine in college that day, I overcame my repugnance and concluded that I must be present, so I could see and hear the man for myself.

Perhaps here I should sketch a character of Dr. Grove, for his end was tragic and he was, along with Warden Woodward, the only Fellow of New College for whom I had any regard. That we had nothing in common apart from Holy Orders is certainly true; the merits of the new philosophy had entirely escaped him, and he was also even more severe than I in his belief in the necessity for total conformity in the church. For all that, he was nonetheless a man of kindly disposition, whose ferocity of policy lay oddly with his generosity of spirit; he had no cause to love me, for I represented everything he detested, yet he sought out my acquaintanceship: his principles were of a general nature, and in no way affected his judgment of individuals.

Apart from being a divine, he thought of himself as a private astronomer, although nothing had ever been published and, I am sorry to say, nothing ever was. Even had he lived, I suspect that the fruit of his labors would never have seen the light of the day, for Grove was so modest of his skills, and so unconcerned with public acclaim, that he believed publishing both arrogant and presumptuous. Rather, he was one of that ever-rarer breed of man who honor God and University in modest silence, believing learning to be its own reward.

He had returned to his university when the king had returned to his throne, and he now wished to leave and take up a living of his own in the country when the next one came available. The chances of him doing so were good, for against him was ranged merely the paltry and youthful figure of Thomas Ken, whose claim appealed to some simply because they wished to rid themselves of a dreary presence in the college. In some ways his imminent departure saddened me, for Grove's company I found strangely conducive. I would not say we were friends; that would be going too far, and certainly he had a manner of address that was easily found objectionable by those who did not perceive the goodness within. Grove's weakness was a quick tongue and a barbed wit, which he had never mastered. He was a man of contradiction, and his conversation could never be taken for granted; he could be the kindest of men, or the most waspish. He had, indeed, perfected the technique of being both at the same time.

It was Grove who invited me to lodge at New College when building works made my home uninhabitable. Death and a delayed election to a Fellowship had created a vacancy in a room and the college, as was its practice, had decided to rent the space out until a new Fellow staked a claim. I had never before enjoyed the common life, even as an undergraduate myself, and was more than content to put it behind me when I gained my first preferment. As a professor, of course, I was entitled to marry and keep my own home, and so it was near twenty years since I had lived cheek-by-jowl with others. I found the experience strangely entertaining, and the solitude of my own room suitable for work. I even regretted my youth and wished again for that irresponsibility when all is still to be done, and nothing is certain. But the feeling soon passed, and by this time, the appeal of New College was waning fast. Apart from Grove, all the Fellows were of low quality, many were corrupt and most inattentive to their duties. I withdrew more and more, and spent as little time as possible in their midst.

Grove was my companion on many evenings, for he took to knocking on my door in his desire of discussion. I did my best to discourage him at first, but he was not easily put off, and eventually I found that I almost welcomed the disturbance, for it was impossible to brood overmuch when he was there. And the disputes we had were of high quality, even though we were often sadly mismatched. Grove had trained himself in scholastic disputation, which I had done my best to shake off as constricting the imagination. And, as I endeavored to point out to him, the new philosophy simply cannot be expressed in terms of the definitions and axioms and theorems and antitheses and all the other apparatus of formal Aristotelianism. For Grove this was fraud and deceit, as he held, as a matter of doctrine, that the beauties and subtleties of logic contained all possibilities, and that if a case could not be argued through its forms, then that proved the flaw of the case.

"I am sure you will find Mr. Cola an interesting disputant," I said when he told me that the Italian would sup that same evening. "I gather from Mr. Lower that he is a great enthusiast for experiment. Whether he will understand your sense of humor I cannot predict. I think I will dine in myself, to see what results."

Grove beamed with pleasure, and I remember him wiping his red, inflamed eye with a cloth. "Splendid," he said. "We can make up a threesome, and maybe drink a bottle together afterward and have a real discussion. I will order one. I hope to have great sport with him, as Lord Maynard is dining, and I wish to show my skills in dispute. Lord Maynard will then know what sort of person will be taking his living."

"I hope this Cola does not take offense at being used in such a fashion."

"I'm sure he will not even notice. Besides, he has a charming manner and is perfectly respectful. Quite unlike the reputation of Italians, I must say, since I have always heard it said they are fawning and obsequious."

"I understand he is Venetian," I said. "They are said to be as cold as their canals, and as secretive as the doge's dungeons."

"I did not find him so. Muddle-headed and with all the errors of youth, no doubt, but far from cold or secretive. You may find out for yourself, though." Here he paused and frowned. "But I forget. I have no sooner offered you a bottle than I find I must withdraw my invitation."

"Why is that?"

"Mr. Prestcott. You know of him?"

"I heard the tales."

"He sent a message wishing to see me. Did you know I

was his tutor once? Tiresome boy he was, not intelligent and no head for learning. And very strange indeed, all charm one moment, sulks and tantrums the next. A nasty, violent streak in him as well, and greatly given to superstition. Anyway, he wishes to see me, as it appears the prospect of hanging is making him reconsider his life and his sins. I do not want to go, but I suppose I must.''

And here I took a sudden decision, realizing that, if I was to trade with Prestcott, I had best do it as soon as possible. It may have been mere whim, or perhaps an angel guided my lips as I spoke. It may have been simply that I did not trust a sudden display of piety from Prestcott, who I had been told only the day before was in no repentant frame of mind. It does not matter; I took the fateful decision.

"You certainly must not," I said firmly. "Your eyes look fearfully sore, and I am certain that exposure to a night wind will only weaken them further. I will go in your place. If it is a priest he wants, I suppose I can do that as well as you. And if it is you he particularly desires to see, then you may go at a later date. There is no rush. The assize does not come for more than a fortnight, and waiting will only make the boy more compliant.''

It required few of the arts of persuasion to make him take my advice. Reassured that a needy soul was not being neglected, he thanked me most sincerely for my kindness and confessed that an evening tormenting an experimentalist was very much more to his liking. I even ordered the bottle for him as his eye was so bad; it was delivered by my wine seller, and placed at the foot of the staircase, with my name on. That was the bottle Cola poisoned, and why I know it was intended for myself.

life so carelessly and with such ruthlessness. Everything about his appearance disgusted me, so much so that I felt my throat tightening and thought, for a moment, that nausea would overcome me entirely. His air of amiability merely pointed up the magnitude of his cruelty, his exquisite manners reminded me of his violence, the expense of his dress, the speed and coldness of his deed. God help me, I could not bear the thought of that stinking perfumed body close to Matthew, those fat and manicured hands stroking that perfect young cheek.

I feared then that my expression must have given away something, informed Cola as that I knew who he was and what he was to do, and it may even be that it was the look of horror on my face which prompted him to move faster, and attempt my life that same night. I do not know; both of us behaved as well as we could; neither, I think, gave anything away thereafter and, to all outsiders, the meal must have appeared perfectly normal.

Cola has given his account of that dinner, wherein he mixes insult to his hosts with exaggeration about his own conversation. Oh, those splendid speeches, those reasoned responses, the patient way in which he smoothed ruffled feathers and corrected the egregious errors of his poor seniors! I must apologize, even at this late date, for not having appreciated his wit, his sagacity and his kindliness, for I confess all of these fine qualities completely escaped my notice at the time. Instead, I saw (or thought I saw, for I must have been wrong) an uneasy little man with more mannerisms than manners, dressed like a cockatoo and with an insinuating assumption of gravitas in his address which failed completely to disguise the superficiality of his learning. His affectation of courtly ways, and his scorn of those kind enough to offer him hospitality, was apparent to all who had the misfortune to sit near him. The flourish with which he produced a little scrap of cloth to vent his nostrils excited the ridicule of all, and his pointed remarks—in Venice everyone uses forks; in Venice wine is drunk from glass; in Venice this, in Venice that—aroused only their disgust. Like many who have little to say, he said too much, interrupting without courtesy and favoring with the benefit of his wisdom those who did not desire it.

I felt almost sorry for him as Grove, with a twinkle in his eye, goaded him like a stupid bull, pulling him first one way, then the other, persuading him to make the most ridiculous statements, then forcing him to contemplate his own absurdity. There was no matter under the heavens, as far as I could see, on which the Italian did not have a firm and fixed opinion, and not a single opinion which was in any way correct or thoughtfully arrived at. In truth, he astonished me, for in my mind's eye I had imagined him to be quite other. It was hard to comprehend how such a man could be anything other than a buffoon, incapable of causing harm to any man unless he bored him to death, or asphyxiated him with the wafts of perfume that escaped his body.

Only once did he let down his guard, and only for the most fleeting of instants did I penetrate through that mask to what lay underneath; then all my suspicions returned in full force, and I realized that he had almost succeeded in his aim of disarming all caution. I was unprepared for it, although I should not have been so easy in giving my contempt, for that merchant I had interviewed in the Fleet prison had forewarned me. He had mentioned his astonishment that hardened soldiers on Candia treated the man with the greatest respect, and I allowed myself to be taken in as well.

Until the moment came when, for the only time in the evening, Cola was thrust into the background by the eruption of hostility between Grove and Thomas Ken. For Cola was like one of those actors who strut the stage, preening themselves in the light of the audience's attention. While they have eyes on them, they are the characters they pretend to be, and all present believe that they are indeed seeing King Harry at Agincourt or a Prince of Denmark in his castle. But when another speaks and they are in the background, watch them then; see how the fire in them goes out, and how they become mere actors again, and only put on their disguise once more when their turn to speak comes once more.

Cola resembled such a player. When Ken and Grove exchanged quotations, and Ken walked heavily out, bowed down by the certainty of his defeat—for the election to the living had been set for the next week and Grove's victory was assured—Cola let slip the mask he had worn so well. In the background for the first time, he leaned back to regard the scene being played out before his eyes. I alone watched him; the squabbles of college fellows had no interest for me, as I had witnessed so many already. And I alone saw the flicker of amusement, and the way in which everything said and unsaid in that fight was instantly comprehensible to him. He was playing a game with us all, and was confident of his success, and he was now underestimating his audience as I had underestimated him. He did not realize that I saw, that instant, into his soul and perceived the devilish intent that lay hidden there, coiled and waiting to be unleashed when all around had been lulled into thinking him a fool. I took succor from that flash of understanding, and thanked the Lord for allowing me such a sign; for I knew then what Cola was, just as I knew I could defeat him. He was a man who made mistakes, and his greatest error was overconfidence.

His conversation was tedious even to Grove but good manners dictated that he be invited back to share a drink after the supper was concluded and the final blessing given. I know this to be the case, even though Cola says differently. He says that Grove escorted him directly to the college gate, and there all contact between them ceased. This cannot be, as a man of Grove's natural courtesy would not have acted so. I do not doubt that the refreshment was curtailed, and I do not doubt that Grove lied by saying he had to go and visit Prestcott as a way of getting rid of the man, but it is inconceivable that the evening would have ended as Cola says. It is another deliberate falsehood I have detected in his account, although by this time I believe I have indicated so many that there is scarcely point in continuing the exercise further.

What is certain is that Cola expected me to go to my room, find the bottle of brandy laced with poison at the foot of my stairs—who else might it have been for, since Grove was the only other person on the stairs and he was supposed to be absent that evening?—and expected me to drink it. He then returned late in the night and, though he did not find me dead, ransacked my room and took not only the letter I had intercepted, but also the letter given to me by Samuel in 1660. It was an evil scheme, made all the worse later by his willingness to stand by and let the Blundy girl die in his place, for I have no doubt he procured that arsenic in the Low Countries, then lied outright in saying he had none in his pharmacopoeia. It is monstrous to contemplate, but some men are so wicked and depraved that no deceit is beyond their powers.

What Cola did not anticipate is that the real object of his murderous venom would be so far beyond his reach. For I did go to see Prestcott and, even though I had to suffer the greatest indignation at that wretched boy's hands, at least the affront was matched by useful information. It was a cold evening, and I wrapped myself up as well as I could for the interview; Prestcott at least had enough friends in the world to provide him with blankets and warm clothing, although their generosity did not extend to allowing him a fire in the grate or anything other than candles of the cheapest pig fat, which sputtered and stank as they gave off their feeble light. I had mistakenly omitted to bring any of my own, so the conversation took place in virtual darkness, and to this, as well as my foolish generosity of spirit, do I attribute Prestcott's ability to surprise me in the way he did.

The meeting began with Prestcott's refusal even to listen to me unless I had promised to unshackle him from the thick heavy chains which bound him to the wall—a necessary restraint, as I later learned.

"You must understand, Dr. Wallis, that I have been chained up like this for nearly three weeks, and I am mightily tired of it. My ankles are covered in sores, and the noise of the chains rattling every time I turn over is sending me mad. Does anyone expect that I will escape? Burrow through the four feet of stonework to the outside world, leap down sixty feet into the ditch and run away?"

"I will not unchain you," I said, "until I have some expectation of cooperation."

"And I will not cooperate until I have some expectation of continuing to live beyond the next assizes."

"On that I may be able to offer you something. If I am satisfied by your replies, then I will assure you of a pardon from the king. You will not go free, as the insult to the Compton family would be too great for them to bear, but you will be suffered to go to America, where you can make a new life."

He snorted. "More freedom than I desire," he said. "Freedom to plow the earth like some peasant, wearied to death by the dronings of Puritans and hacked to death by Indians whose methods, I may say, we would do well to imitate here. Some of these people would make any sensible man reach for his hatchet. Thank you, good doctor, for your generosity."

"It is the best I can do," I said, although I am not sure even now whether I intended to do it. But I knew that if I offered him too much he would not believe me. "If you accept, you will surely live, and later on you may win a reprieve and be allowed to return. And it is the only chance you have."

He thought a long while, slumped on his cot and huddled in his blanket. "Very well," he said reluctantly. "I suppose I have no choice. It is better than the offer I received from Mr. Lower."

"I'm glad you at last see reason. Now then, tell me about Mr. Cola."

He looked genuinely surprised at the question. "Why on earth do you want to know about him?"

"You should only be glad that I do. Why did he come and see you here?"

"Because he is a civil and courteous gentleman."

"Do not waste my time, Mr. Prestcott."

"Indeed, I do not know what else to say, sir."

"Did he ask you for anything?"

"What could I give him?"

"Something of your father's, perhaps?"

"Such as?"

"A copy of Livy."

"That again? Tell me, doctor, why is that so important to you?"

"That is not your affair."

"In that case I do not care to answer."

I thought it could do me no harm, as Prestcott did not have

the book in any case. "The book is the key to some work I am doing. If I have it, I can decipher some letters. Now, did Cola ask you about it?"

"No." Here Prescott rolled on his little cot and convulsed with merriment at what he thought was a fine joke at my expense. I began to weary mightily of him.

"Truly, he did not. I am sorry, doctor," he said, wiping his eye. "And to make amends I will tell you what I know. Mr. Cola was recently a guest of my guardian and was staying there when Sir William was attacked. Without his skill, I understand Sir William would have died of his injuries that night, and he is evidently a formidably clever surgeon to patch him up so neatly." He shrugged. "And that is all there is to be said. I can tell you no more."

"What was he doing there?"

"I gathered they had a joint interest in trading matters. Cola's father is a merchant, and Sir William is Master of the Ordnance. One sells goods, the other uses government money to buy them. Both desire to make as much money as possible, and naturally they wished to keep their association quiet, for fear of Lord Clarendon's wrath. That, at least, is how I understand things."

"And why do you understand them so?"

Prescott gave me a look of contempt. "Come now, Dr. Wallis. Even I know how Sir William and Lord Clarendon detest each other. And even I know that if the faintest whiff of corruption attached itself to Sir William's exercise of his office, Clarendon would use it to eject him."

"Apart from your own supposition, do you have any reason to think this fear of Lord Clarendon's wrath is why Cola's association with Sir William was kept hidden?"

"They talked of Clarendon incessantly. Sir William hates him so much, he cannot keep him out of his conversation at times. Mr. Cola was exceptionally courteous, I think, in listening so patiently to his complaints."

"How is that?"

Prescott was so naïve that he did not even begin to comprehend my interest in everything that Cola did or said, and as gently as a lamb I led him through every word and gesture that he had heard the Italian utter, or seen him make.

"On three occasions when I was there, Sir William returned to the subject of Lord Clarendon, and every time he harped on about what a malign influence he was. How he held the king in the palm of his hand, and encouraged His Majesty's licentiousness, so that he might have free run to loot the kingdom. How all good Englishmen wished to oust him, but were unable to summon the resolve or the courage to take decisive action. You know the sort of thing, I am sure."

I nodded to encourage him and to establish that sympathy in conversation which encourages greater openness of discourse.

"Mr. Cola listened patiently, as I say, and made valiant attempts to deflect the conversation into less heated areas, but sooner or later it came back to the Lord Chancellor's perfidy. What particularly incensed Sir William was Clarendon's great house at Cornbury Park."

I believe I must have frowned here, as I could not grasp the meaning of it. The wealth that had been heaped on Clarendon since the Restoration had, indeed, incited great envy, but there seemed no particular reason why this should focus on Cornbury. Prestcott saw my perplexity, and for once was kind enough to enlighten me.

"The Lord Chancellor has acquired large portions of land right up into Chipping Norton, deep into Compton territory. Sir William believes that a concerted assault is being launched on his family's interest in South Warwickshire. As he said, not long ago the Comptons would have known how to deal with such impudence."

I nodded gravely, since my penetration into this great mystery was deepening with every word that dropped from Prestcott's lips. I was beginning to think, even, that I would keep my word to the lad, for his testimony might well prove useful in the future, and I could not have that were he to swing.

"Mr. Cola successfully diverted the talk onto other matters, but nothing was safe. Once he mentioned his experience of English roads; even that brought Sir William back to the topic of Clarendon."

"How so?"

Prestcott paused. "It is a very trivial matter."

"Of course it is," I agreed. "But tell me nonetheless. And when you have done, I will ensure you are unshackled, and remain so for the rest of your short stay in this place."

I have no doubt that, like all people in similar circumstances, he invented where he could not remember; such duplicity is common and was expected. It is the task of the expert interrogator to separate wheat and chaff, and allow the winds to blow away the rubbish from the precious seed.

"They were talking of the road which runs northward from Witney to Chipping Norton, and which Cola had taken on his way to Compton Wynyates. Why he did so I cannot imagine, as it is not the most direct route. But I gather he is one of these curious gentlemen. Nosy, I call them, who peek and pry at all things not their affair, and call it enquiry."

I suppressed a sigh, and smiled at the boy in what I hoped would appear as sympathy. Prestcott, at least, appeared to take it as such.

"It is, apparently, the road which my Lord Clarendon takes on his way to Cornbury, and Cola joked that if Sir William was fortunate, Clarendon might be shaken to death by the journey, or drowned in a water-filled hole, so bad was the condition of the road, and so lax the county at maintaining it. Do you really want to hear this, sir?"

I nodded. "Continue," I said. I could feel the tingle in my blood as I knew I was almost there, and could brook no further delays. "Tell me."

Prestcott shrugged. "Sir William laughed, and tried to match him by saying that maybe he would be shot by a highwayman as well, for it is known he always travels with only a small retinue. Many a man had been murdered of late, with the assailant never apprehended. Then the conversation went on to other things. And that," Prestcott said, "is that. End of the story."

I had it. I knew I had unraveled the layers of the problem and penetrated deep into its heart. It was like one of those conundra, sent out in competition by mathematicians to challenge their rivals. However formidable in appearance, however deliberately designed to perplex and confuse, yet there is always a simplicity at their core, and the art of victory lies in careful thought and a calm working through of the outer reaches until that center is arrived at. Like an army laying siege to a castle, the skill lies not in a wide assault around the perimeter, but a gentle probing of the outworks until the weak spot of the defenses—for there always is one—is revealed. Then all the strength of the attack can be focused on that one point until it gives way. Cola had made the mistake of visiting Prestcott; I had persuaded Prestcott to tell me of their connection.

And now I had nearly the whole plot in my hand, and my earlier error was made clear. Cola was not here to kill the king, as I had thought. He was here to murder the Lord Chancellor of England.

But I still could not credit that this thick-headed gentleman, Sir William Compton, was capable of such subtle deviousness that he might plot with the Spanish for months and sponsor a hired murderer. As I say, I knew him. A challenge, or some such bravado, I could have understood. But not this. I had gone far; but not far enough. Behind Compton, I was sure, lay another. There had to be.

And so I questioned Prestcott further, seeking out every contact he had made, every single name Sir William or Cola had mentioned. He gave some useless answers, but then decided to bargain some more.

"And now, sir," he said, moving his legs so the chains around his ankles rattled and chinked against the floor, "I have talked long enough, and had confidence in your fidelity to give you much with nothing in return. So now unlock these shackles, that I may walk about the little room like a normal man."

God help me, I did as he asked, seeing little harm in it, and wishing to give him encouragement to continue in a cooperative fashion. I summoned the jailer, who unlocked the shackles and presented me with the key, asking me to be so good as to relock them once more when I left. It cost a shilling in bribes.

Then he left the cell, and Prestcott listened in what I thought was mournful silence as the steps echoed down the stone staircase once more.

I will not go into the details of the humiliation I suffered at the hands of that madman once the footsteps had died away. Prestcott had the cunning of the desperate, I the inattention of the concerned, for my mind was on what he had told me. In brief, within minutes of being left alone once more, Prestcott had used violence on me, stopping my mouth, binding my hands and shackling me to the cot so tightly I could neither move nor raise the alarm. I was so outraged I could barely even think correctly, and was suffused with rage when he finally put his face close to mine.

''Not pleasant, eh?'' he hissed in my ear. ''And I have endured many weeks of it. You are lucky; you will be here only for one night. Remember; I could easily have killed you, but I will not.''

That was all. He then sat unconcernedly for some ten minutes or more until he judged the time was right, then put on my heavy cloak and hat, picked up my Bible—my family Bible, given into my hands by my own father—and bowed in a gross parody of courtesy to me.

''Sweet dreams, Dr. Wallis,'' he said. ''I hope we do not meet again.''

After five minutes, I gave up struggling and lay until the morning brought my release.

SUCH IS THE PROVIDENTIAL GOODNESS OF THE LORD, that He is at His most gentle when His judgment seems most harsh, and it is not for man to doubt His wisdom; instead he can only give thanks with the blindest faith that He will not abandon His true servant. The next morning, my complaints were revealed for the petty whinings they were, when the full extent of His goodness was revealed to me. I say now that the Lord is good, and loves all who believe in Him, for by what other means could my life have been preserved that night?

Only an angel of goodness, guided by the hand of the Most High, could have steered me away from the abyss and, by preserving me, allowed the kingdom to escape calamity. For I do not believe that I was so favored for my own worthless life, which is no more significant in His eyes than the least grain of dust. But as He has so constantly shown His favors to His people, so He chose me to be the instrument of their preservation, and in joy and humility, I accepted the responsibility, knowing that by His will I would succeed.

I was released shortly after dawn began, and straightaway went to the magistrate, Sir John Fulgrove, to report what had happened so he could raise the alarm and begin the hunt for the fugitive. I did not, at that stage, report my interest in the boy, although I did urge him to make sure, if possible, that he did not lose his life if caught. Then I ate in an inn, for being a prisoner is hungry work, and I was chilled to the bone.

And only then, deep in thought, did I return to my room in New College, and discover the horrors that had taken place that night, for Grove had died in my place and my room had been ransacked, with my papers gone.

Cola's authorship of this outrage was as clear to me as if I had seen him pour the poison into the bottle with my own eyes, and his calm audacity in coming back to the college to be the very first to discover (with what expressions of shock! with what distress and horror!) the results of his own wickedness appalled me. I was told by Warden Woodward that he it was who attempted, by subtle inference and weasel words, to steer the college toward thinking that Grove had died of a seizure and it was in order to expose this lie that I asked Woodward to have Lower investigate the matter.

Lower was, of course, flattered by the request and willingly obliged. My trust in his skills was not given without reason, either, for one look at Grove's corpse made him pause and look highly perturbed.

"I would hesitate strongly to say this was a seizure," he said doubtfully. "I have never seen any man foam at the mouth so in such a case. The blueness of the lips, and the eyelids, is consistent with such a diagnosis, however, and I have no doubt that my friend fastened onto these signs too speedily."

"Could he have eaten something?" the warden asked.

"He ate in hall, did he not? If it was that, then you should all be dead. I will examine his room, and see what there is to be found there, if you like."

And thus Lower discovered the bottle, the sediment inside it, and returned to the warden's lodgings in great excitement, explaining the experiments which might be devised to show what the substance was. Woodward was not at all interested in these details, although I found them fascinating and, having conversed on many occasions with Mr. Stahl myself, I realized Lower was perfectly correct in proposing to use his services. There was, of course, the question of Cola, for any such move would be bound to alert him. Accordingly, I decided that it would be best to confront the matter head on, and suggested to Lower that he involve the Italian at every stage of the investigations, to see whether his actions or speech gave any hint of his thoughts. I could easily have had him arrested on the spot, but I was also certain that I had not yet fathomed the whole of the mystery. I needed more time, and Cola had to be at his liberty a while longer.

Although I did not make my reasoning plain, Lower caught the inner meaning of my recommendations.

"Surely you do not suspect Mr. Cola of this?" he asked. "I know you have heard ill reports of him, but there can be no reason for him to do such a thing at all."

I reassured him absolutely, but pointed out that, as he was perhaps the last person to see Dr. Grove, naturally some doubt must attach to him. It would be discourteous to a guest to make this known, however, and I begged that no hint of the suspicion come to his attention.

"I would not have him return to his native country speaking ill of us for all the world," I said. "Which is why I think it a good idea if you persuade him to attend the dissection. For you can have him stand alone near the body and touch it, and see whether it accuses him."

"I have no reason to believe that is an accurate test of such matters," he said.

"Nor I. But it is a recommended procedure in such matters, and has been employed for generations. Many of the finest lawyers admit it as a useful part of examination. Should some prodigious eruption of blood occur from the corpse when Cola approaches it, then we will know of it. If not, then his name is half-cleansed of stain already. But do not let him know he has been tested in such a fashion."

chapter ten

It is not my intention to repeat what others have said, nor to retell stories which I did not myself witness. Everything I say comes from my direct encounter, or from the testimony of men of unimpeachable character. As Cola was unaware of the suspicion in which he was already held, he had no reason to distort his account of that evening when he, Lower and Locke cut up Dr. Grove in Warden Woodward's kitchen. For that reason, I understand the account he gives of it is largely truthful.

Lower reported to me that he had arranged for Cola to stand alone by the naked corpse before any incision had been made into the flesh, and seen well that the soul of Grove had not called out for vengeance, nor accused his murderer of the deed. Whether this means such examinations are in fact of no merit, or whether proper prayers must be offered, or whether (as some say) the test must take place on consecrated ground to work, I do not presume to speculate. For a while at least, Lower had the suspicions of the man he thought his friend lifted from his shoulders, and I had the leisure to pursue my thoughts and conduct my first examination of the Blundy girl.

I summoned her to my room the following afternoon on the pretext of wishing to interview her for a post in my household, for the builders, wretched idlers though they were, were at last coming to the end of their labors and there was every prospect I might once again have a home to call my own. Having risen in state somewhat in the previous year, I had decided that I would have four servants, not three as before, and give in to my wife's ceaseless importuning by giving her a girl of her own. The prospect filled me with sadness, for I was having at the same time to consider finding a replacement for Matthew, and the weight of his loss bore the more heavily on me by contemplating the dirty, illiterate, stupid wretches who presented themselves, and who were no more fit to clean his shoes than to fill them.

Not that I would ever have considered Sarah Blundy for any post, although in all matters of outward show I could have done a great deal worse. I am not one of those men who might allow a good Christian wife to have some French strumpet to comb her hair. A sober, hard-working girl of sense and piety is required instead, clean in her habits and unslovenly of behavior. Such girls are hard to find and, with different antecedents and beliefs, Sarah Blundy would have been in all respects admirable.

I had not encountered her directly before, and I noted with interest the dignified subservience of her entry, the modesty of her address and the sense of her words. Even Cola, I recall, comments on these very same qualities. But the impertinence that he also detected was not hidden for long, for the moment I told her frankly that I had no intention of giving her a position, she raised her jaw and her eyes flashed with defiance.

"You have wasted my time in summoning me here, then," she said.

"Your time is there to be wasted, if that is what I choose to do with it. I will have no insolence from you. You will answer my questions, or face serious trouble. I know well who you are, and where you are from."

Her life, I must say here, was no concern of mine. Had she foisted herself off on some unsuspecting man, who was ignorant of what she was, her good fortune would not have grieved me greatly. But I knew no man would willingly take her if her past was known, for to do so would expose him to public contempt. Through this, I could force her to comply.

"You have, I believe, recently acquired the services of an Italian physician for your mother. A man of great standing and high dignity in his profession. Might I ask by what means you pay for this?"

She flushed and hung her head at the accusation.

"Remarkable, is it not, that such generosity should be offered? Few English physicians, I am sure, would be so carefree of their time and skills."

"Mr. Cola is a good, kind gentleman," she said. "Who does not think of payment."

"I'm sure not."

"It is true," she said, with more spirit. "I told him frankly I could not pay him."

"Not in money, anyway. And yet he labors on your mother's behalf."

"I think of him only as a good Christian."

"He is a papist."

"Good Christians can be found everywhere. I know many in the Church of England, sir, more cruel and ungenerous than he."

"Mind your tongue. I do not want your opinions. What is his interest in you? And your mother?"

"I know of none. He wishes to make my mother better. I care to know no more than that. Yesterday he and Dr. Lower conducted a strange and wonderful treatment, which cost them great trouble."

"And has it worked?"

"My mother is still alive, praise be, and I pray she will improve."

"Amen. But to return to my question, and this time do not try to evade. To whom have you delivered messages on his behalf? I know your connections with the garrison at Abingdon, and with the conventicles. To whom have you gone? With messages? Letters? Someone must take his communications, for he sends none in the post."

She shook her head. "No one."

"Do not make me angry."

"I do not wish to. I am telling you the truth."

"You deny you went to Abingdon . . ."—I consulted my notebook—"last Wednesday, the Friday before that, the

Monday before that? That you walked to Burford and stayed there the Tuesday? That you have met Tidmarsh as part of his conventicle even in this town?''

She did not reply; and I could see my knowledge of her was a shock.

''What were you doing? What messages were you delivering? Who did you see?''

''No one.''

''Two weeks ago, an Irishman called Greatorex also visited you. What did he want?''

''Nothing.''

''Do you take me for a fool?''

''I do not take you for anything.''

I hit her for that for, though a tolerant man, I will not accept more than a certain degree of insolence. Once she had wiped the blood from her mouth, she seemed more subdued; but still she gave me nothing.

''I have delivered no messages for Mr. Cola. He has said little to me, and less to my mother,'' she whispered. ''He talked to her a great deal on one occasion; that was when he sent me to buy him drugs from the apothecary. I do not know what they said.''

''You must find out.''

''Why should I so?''

''Because I tell you.'' I paused, and realized that appealing to her better nature was fruitless, so took some coins from my desk, and placed them before her. She looked at them with astonishment and disdain, then pushed them back.

''I have told you. There is nothing.'' But her voice was weak, and her head bowed as she spoke.

''Go away now, and think well on what you say. I know you are lying to me. I will give you one further chance to tell me the truth about this man. Otherwise you will regret your silence. And let me give you a warning. Mr. Cola is a dangerous man. He has killed on many occasions in the past, and will do so again.''

Without further words she left. She did not take the money still in front of her, but gave me a look of burning hatred before she turned away. She was cowed, I knew that. Even so, I was not sure it was enough.

• • •

THINKING ABOUT MY DEEDS ONCE MORE, I CAN SEE ALready that an ignorant would consider me harsh. I can hear the protests already. The necessary courtesies between high and low, and so on. To all of which I agree without reservation; gentlemen are indeed under an obligation to give a daily demonstration that the positions in which God established us all are just and good. As with children, they should be chided with love, corrected with kindness, chastised with a firm regret.

The Blundys, however, were very different. There was no point in treating them with kindness when they had already thrown off any acknowledgment of their superiors. Both husband and wife had scorned the links which bind each to all, and accompanied this revolt against God's manifest will with quotations from the Bible itself. All these Diggers and Levellers and Anabaptists thought they were shedding their chains with God's blessing; they were instead severing the silken cords which kept men in harmony, and would have replaced them by shackles of thickest iron. In their stupidity they did not see what they were doing. I would have treated Sarah Blundy, and anyone, with kindness and respect. If it had been deserved, if it had been reciprocated, if it had not been dangerous so to do.

My frustrations at this stage were gigantic; when talking to Prestcott, I had the whole affair in the palm of my hand, but it had slipped away from me through my own foolishness. I admit also that I was anxious to preserve my own life as well, and was fearful that another attack would be launched against me. It was for this reason that I took the step of informing the magistrate that, in my opinion, Dr. Robert Grove had been murdered.

He was aghast at the news, and perturbed at the implications of what I told him.

"The warden has no suspicions of foul play, and would not thank me for telling you of mine," I continued. "Nonetheless, it is my duty to inform you that in my opinion there is sufficient reason for suspicion. And it is therefore imperative that the body be not buried."

Of course, it mattered not to me what happened to the body; the confrontation with Cola had already taken place and yielded no useful result. I was more concerned that Cola know his deed was being uncovered, bit by bit, and that he felt my opposition to his aims. With luck, I thought he might communicate with his masters to tell them of all that had transpired.

For a brief while I was on the verge of having the man arrested. I changed my mind because of Mr. Thurloe, who traveled into Oxford to see me shortly after. Cola has described the way he approached me at the play in his memoir and I have no intention of repeating it. The shock he noted on my face was well seen: I was astonished, not only because I had not seen Thurloe for near three years, but because I hardly recognized him.

How changed he was from his days of greatness! It was like meeting a total stranger who yet reminds you of a person once known. In appearance there was little obvious alteration, for he was the sort of man who looks old when young, and young when old. But his demeanor bore no trace of that power which he had held so firmly in his hands. While many had bitterly resented the loss of authority, Thurloe seemed like one glad to be rid of the burden, and content in his reduction to insignificance. The set of his head, his face and the expression of deep concern had passed from him so totally that, these small details altered, the whole had changed almost beyond recognition. When he approached me, I paused awhile before making my greeting; he smiled back quietly, as if seeing my confusion, and acknowledging the cause of it.

I do believe he had so firmly placed that period of his life behind him that, even had it been offered, he would have declined to take on any public office. He later told me that he spent his days in prayer and meditation, and counted that as of more worth than all his efforts for his country. He was largely unconcerned with the society of his fellow men and, as he made clear, did not like to be disturbed by those who sought to recall what was now irretrievably past.

"I bring a message from your friend Mr. Prestcott," he murmured in my ear. "Perhaps we might talk?"

Once the play was over I went straight home (I had moved back to my domestic comforts that afternoon) and awaited him. He was not long in coming and sat down with all the calm imperturbability that was his normal mode of conduct.

''I understand your taste for power and influence has not been slaked, Dr. Wallis,'' he said. ''Which does not surprise me in the slightest. I hear you have been questioning this young man, and have enough influence to have him pardoned if you so desire. You are attached to Mr. Bennet now, I believe?''

I nodded.

''What is your interest in Prestcott, and this Italian gentleman you ask him about?'' he asked.

Even the shadow of Thurloe's authority still blinded more than full exposure to the powers of a man like Mr. Bennet, and I say that it never occurred to me not to answer him, nor to point out that he had no right whatsoever to question me.

''I am certain that there is a plot which might return this country to civil war.''

''Of course there is,'' Thurloe said, in that calm way with which he greeted all matters, however serious. ''When at any stage in the past few years has there not been? What is new about this one?''

''What is new is that I believe it to be organized by the Spanish.''

''And what is it to be this time? Massed attack by Fifth Monarchists? A sudden cannonade by rebellious guardsmen?''

''One man. The Venetian gentleman who now passes as a philosopher. He has already killed twice, my servant and Dr. Grove. And he stole letters from me which are of the greatest importance.''

''This is the physician you asked Prestcott about?''

''He is no physician. He is a soldier, a known killer, and is here to murder the Earl of Clarendon.''

Thurloe grunted. For the first time in my life, I saw him surprised.

''You would be best to kill him first, then.''

''Then his paymasters will try again, and swiftly. At least this time I know who he is. Next time I might not be so lucky. I must use this opportunity to uncover the English end of the conspiracy and stop it once and for all.''

Thurloe stood up, took the heavy poker from the hearth and rearranged the logs on the fire so that he sent a shower of sparks up the chimney. He did this for some time; it was always a habit of his to occupy himself with some trivial physical task while he thought.

Eventually he turned to me once more. ''If I were you, I should kill him,'' he repeated. ''If this man is dead, then the plot is at an end. It may be revived, but it may not. If he slips away from you, then you will have blood on your hands.''

''And if I am wrong?''

''Then an Italian traveler dies, ambushed on a road by highwaymen. A great tragedy, no doubt. But all except his family will forget it within weeks.''

''I cannot believe you would take your own advice in these circumstances.''

''You must. When I looked out for Oliver, I always moved immediately when I heard of a plot against his person. Risings, conspiracies, all those minor matters, they could be left to run a little, because they could always be defeated. Assassination is different. One mistake and you are ruined forever. Believe me, Dr. Wallis: do not overreach yourself with subtlety. You are dealing here with men, not geometry; they are less predictable, and more given to causing surprise.''

''I would agree wholeheartedly with you,'' I said, ''were it not for the fact that I have no man I could rely on to do this, and a botched attempt would only make him more cautious. And for suitable help I would have to inform Mr. Bennet more thoroughly. I have told him a little, but very far from all.''

''Ah, yes,'' Thurloe replied thoughtfully. ''That ambitious and pompous gentleman. You consider him less than safe?''

I reluctantly nodded: I still did not know how Cola had found out so quickly about Matthew; it was certainly possible, though dreadful to contemplate, that Bennet himself might have passed on that information and might also be involved in the plot against Clarendon.

Thurloe leaned back in his chair and considered, sitting so

long and quietly that I was half afraid he had fallen asleep in the heat of the fire, that perhaps his mind was no longer what it was, and that he could no longer occupy himself with such matters.

But I was wrong; eventually he opened his eyes and nodded to himself. "I would doubt his involvement, if that is what concerns you," he said.

"Is there something you know that makes you conclude this?"

"No; I know less of the man than you do. I proceed from character, no more. Mr. Bennet is an able man; very able indeed. Everyone knows it, and the king is more aware than most. For all his faults, this is not a prince who surrounds himself with fools; he is not like his father. Mr. Bennet will dominate the government when Clarendon goes, as soon he must. He has power within his grasp; all he has to do is wait for the fruits of office to fall in profusion into his lap. Now, is it likely that a man such as this would suddenly indulge himself in these grandly extravagant actions, which can in no way improve his prospects? Risk all on the throw of dice when patience will soon bring all he wants? That is not his way, I think."

"I am glad you think so."

"But there must be a sponsor in England, this is certainly true. Do you know who this is?"

I shrugged helplessly. "It could be any one of many dozen people. Clarendon has enemies without end, for good reasons and bad. You know that as well as I do. He has been attacked in print and in person, in the House of Commons and in the House of Lords, through his family and his friends. It was only a matter of time, I think, before someone attacked his body. That moment may be soon."

"A rash man, it must be," Thurloe observed, "to act in such desperation, as however good a soldier your Venetian is, the chance of him missing and being captured must always be there. It may be, of course, that he is being held in reserve, that he will be called into action only if other attempts to ruin Lord Clarendon fail."

"Such as?" I asked, feeling that once again, Thurloe was

teaching me as he had an entire generation of servants of the state. "How do you know all this, sir?"

"I keep my ears open, and I listen," Thurloe replied with quiet amusement. "A course I recommend to you, doctor."

"And you have heard of another plot?"

"Maybe so. It seems that enemies of Clarendon are trying to weaken him by associating him with treason. In particular, the treason of John Mordaunt in betraying to me the rising of 1659. In this matter they seek to employ the good offices of Jack Prestcott, the son of the man who took the blame for that regrettable event."

"Mordaunt?" I asked incredulously. "Are you serious?"

"Oh, perfectly serious, thank you. Shortly before Cromwell died," he continued, "I myself attended a meeting alone with him where he mapped out his own death, which he knew could not be greatly delayed. He could barely walk, so much had his final illness gripped him, and so severe were the treatments meted out to him by his physicians. He knew as well as any he had but a little time remaining, and he regarded the prospect unflinchingly, wanting only to ensure that his affairs on earth were settled before the Lord took him.

"He instructed me how to proceed, confident that his orders would be obeyed, even though he was no longer here to enforce them. His protectorate would pass temporarily to his son Richard, he said, and that would buy the time necessary to conclude negotiations with Charles about how best to effect a restoration of the monarchy. The king was to be allowed back only if he was shackled with so many chains limiting his deeds that he would never act as his father had.

"Naturally, the whole affair was to be kept the closest guarded secret; no meeting was to be noted, no letters, and not a word should be spoken outside the small circle on both sides privy to the talks.

"I did as I was told because he was right: only Cromwell kept civil war at bay, and when he went it would resume unless the breach in the nation was healed. And the English are a monarchical people, who love subjection more than freedom. It was desperately difficult, as if the fanatics on either side knew of it, then we would all be cast aside. Even so, they came close to taking power again, and I was thrown out of office for a while. Even then, though, I kept the talks going, with John Mordaunt representing His Majesty. One of the conditions, of course, was that all plans and plots for risings should stop: and if the Royalists themselves could not stop them we were to be given enough information so we might do so. Accordingly, Mordaunt gave us full details of the 1659 rising, which was put down with considerable loss of life.

"Many more would have died had war resumed properly, but that would not save Mordaunt if the details of this transaction were known. The trouble is that this young man Prestcott is trying to prove his father innocent, and must inevitably prove Mordaunt guilty if he is to succeed, for he has been told enough to know who was really responsible. Then it would be assumed that Clarendon gave Mordaunt his orders."

"Did he?"

Thurloe smiled. "No. The king gave them himself. But Clarendon would accept the blame to save His Majesty from criticism. He is a good servant, and better than this king deserves."

"Prestcott knows of all this?"

"Not exactly. He is convinced that Mordaunt was a traitor, acting on his own behalf. I have encouraged him in his belief that Samuel Morland was in league with him."

"This gets ever more bizarre," I commented. "Why did you do that?"

"For the obvious reason that otherwise he would have acted on his belief in my responsibility and slit my throat. You might, incidentally, do me the service of seeing Samuel next time you are in London and warning him that this young man has decided to kill him."

"And you say someone has been helping Prestcott?"

"I believe so," Thurloe replied.

"Who?"

"He is too cunning to say unless the price is right."

"His testimony is worthless in any case," I said, furious that the little wretch dared bargain with me, and on such a matter.

"In a court? Of course it is. But you understand politics better than that, doctor."

"What does he want?"

"Proof of his father's innocence."

"I do not have it."

Thurloe smiled.

I grunted. "I suppose there is no reason why I should not promise him anything he wants. Once I have his testimony, of course . . ."

Thurloe wagged his finger at me. "Indeed. But do not take him for a fool, sir. He has some wit, even though I doubt his sanity. He is not a trusting man, and wants an indication of your good will first. You do something for him, he will reciprocate. He does not trust anyone."

"What does he want?"

"He wants charges against him abandoned."

"I doubt I could accomplish that. My relations with the magistrate are not such that he will readily do me any favor."

"You do not need one. Mr. Prestcott is willing to provide damning evidence that some woman called Blundy murdered this man Grove. I am not certain how he came by it, especially as you tell me this Italian was responsible. But we must use such opportunities as we are given. It should be possible to persuade the magistrate that a certain conviction in a murder case is better than a possible conviction in one of assault. Her trial means his freedom, and cooperation."

I stared at him uncomprehending, before realizing he was perfectly serious. "You want me to connive in judicial murder? I am not an assassin, Mr. Thurloe."

"You do not need to be. All you have to do is talk to the magistrate, then keep your silence."

"You never did such a wicked thing," I said.

"Believe me, I did. And gladly. It is the servant's duty to take sin onto his own shoulder so that his prince may remain safe. Ask Lord Clarendon. It is to safeguard good order."

"That is, no doubt, how Pontius Pilate consoled himself."

He inclined his head. "No doubt he did. But I think the circumstances are different. It is not, in any case, as if you do not have an alternative. This woman does not have to die. But you would not then find out who is sponsoring the Italian. Nor would you have that much chance of bringing him to trial. But I sense you want more than this."

"I want Cola dead, and I want those who brought him here destroyed."

Thurloe's eyes narrowed as I said this, and I knew that the intensity of my reply, the hatred in my voice had let him see too much. "It is unwise," he said, "in matters such as this, to be swayed by sentiment. Or by a desire for revenge. By grasping too much, you may lose everything." He stood up. "And now I must leave you. I have delivered my message, and given my advice. I am sorry that you find it so hard, although I understand your reluctance. If I could persuade Mr. Prestcott to be more reasonable, then I would certainly do so. But he has the pig-headedness of youth, and will not be swayed. You, if I may say so, have some of the same qualities."

chapter eleven

I PRAYED FOR GUIDANCE THAT NIGHT, BUT NO WORD of help or comfort came to me; I was entirely deserted and abandoned to my own indecision. I was not so blind as to forget that Thurloe undoubtedly had his own reasons for intervening, but I did not know what these might be. Certainly, he would not avoid deceiving me if he felt it necessary. He had few powers left, and I fully expected him to use those that remained.

At the very least, I felt I should keep open all possible courses, and a few days later I spoke to the magistrate who immediately placed Sarah Blundy under arrest. As she had already been questioned it was natural that she would be afraid and I did not wish anything to be rendered impossible by her precipitate flight. Had she run, she knew more than enough people to give her refuge, and I would have had little chance of ever finding her again.

By that stage Cola had gone on his medical tour with Lower. I was furious when I heard of this and immediately feared that his expedition might be the culminating point of his conspiracy, but Mr. Boyle reassured me when he informed me in a letter from London that the Lord Chancellor did not intend to leave for his country estate for another few weeks. My nightmare of an imminent ambush on the London road, the coaches ravaged and all blamed on old soldiers turned highwaymen, ebbed away from me, as I realized that

Cola must be merely filling in idle time as he waited. Perhaps, indeed, Thurloe was right, and Cola was in England only for employment if a more peaceable attempt to unseat Clarendon failed.

Moreover, I was glad of the breathing space the knowledge gave me, for I had momentous decisions to make and was about to embark on a course which would either bring me to ruin, or would pull down one of the great men in the land: this is not something anyone does with a light heart.

So in that peaceful week in which Cola traveled the countryside (I understand that his account is again accurate in some details, for Lower told me that he labored with diligence among his patients) I considered all the possibilities which lay before me, went over all the evidence indicating my conclusions about the dangers this man Cola posed were correct. And I could see no fault in them, and defy anyone else to doubt them either: no innocent ever acted in such a guilty fashion. Apart from that, I renewed my assault on Sarah Blundy, for I thought that if I could persuade her to say what interest Cola had in her family, then I might spare myself from the humiliation of having to give in to the wishes of a half-crazed adolescent like Jack Prestcott.

She was brought to me in a small room normally occupied by the castle warden. Incarceration had done little for her appearance and, as I swiftly discovered, had in no way eroded her insolence.

"I trust you have meditated on the matters we talked of before. I am in a position to help you, if you will only allow me to do so."

"I did not kill Dr. Grove."

"I know that. But many people think you did, and you will die unless I help you."

"If you know I am innocent, then surely you must help me anyway? You are a man of God."

"Perhaps that is true. But you are a loyal subject of His Majesty, yet you refused to help me when I asked you for only the slightest assistance."

"I did not refuse. I knew nothing that you wanted to hear."

"For someone who may shortly be hanged you seem remarkably reluctant to avert that terrible fate.''

"If it is God's will that I should die, then I will do so willingly. If it is not, then I shall be spared.''

"God expects us to labor on our own behalf. Listen, girl. What I ask is not so dreadful. You have become involved, no doubt innocently, in the most fiendish scheme imaginable. If you assist me you will not only go free, you will be rewarded well.''

"What scheme?''

"I certainly do not intend to tell you.''

She fell silent.

"You said,'' I prompted, "that your benefactor, Mr. Cola, talked on occasion with your mother. What did they talk about? What did he ask? You said you would find out.''

"She is too sick to be asked. All she has told me is that Mr. Cola always showed her the greatest courtesy, and listened with great patience whenever she felt like talking. He said little himself.''

I shook my head in exasperation. "Listen, you stupid girl,'' I all but shouted at her. "This man is here to commit a horrendous crime. The first thing he did when he got here was contact you. If you are not helping him, what was the purpose of that?''

"I do not know. All I know is that my mother is sick, and he has helped her. No one else offered, and without his generosity she would be dead. More than that I do not know, or care to know.''

She looked at me straight in the eyes as she continued. "You say he is a criminal. No doubt you have good reason for that. But I have never seen or heard him behave in any way except with the utmost civility, more, perhaps, than I properly deserve. Criminal or papist, that is how I judge him.''

I state here that I wished to save her, if I could, if she would only allow me to do so. With all my heart I willed her to break, and say everything she knew. With good fortune she would make Prestcott's testimony unnecessary, and I could then refuse his bargain. I pressed again and again, far longer than I would have done with anyone else, but she would not give way.

"You were not in New College that evening, nor were you at home tending your mother. You were running errands for Cola. Tell me where you were and who you spoke to. Tell me what other errands you have run for him in Abingdon and Bicester and Burford. That you will counter the evidence against you, and win my help at one and the same time."

She lifted her head to me, defiant once more.

"There is nothing I know that can help you in any way. I do not know why Mr. Cola is here; if he was not motivated by Christian charity I do not know why he is helping my mother."

"You have been carrying messages for him."

"I have not."

"You were carrying one for him on the night Grove died."

"I was not."

"Where were you then? I have established you were not tending your mother as your duty required."

"I will not tell you. But as God is my witness, I have done nothing ill."

"God is not testifying at your trial," I said, and sent her back to her cell. I was in a black humor. I knew at that moment that I would trade with Prestcott. May the Lord forgive me, I had given the girl every opportunity of saving herself, but she threw her own life away.

THE NEXT DAY I RECEIVED AN URGENT LETTER FROM MR. Thurloe. I quote it here as direct testimony to events I did not myself witness.

Most honored sir,

It is my duty and pleasure to acquaint you with certain developments which you have a right to know as a matter of urgency, for you must act swiftly, lest the opportunity slip. The Italian gentleman who interests you so much has been to this village and, although he has now left in the company of Mr. Lower once more (I believe

heading back for Oxford) he has greatly frightened Mr.
Prestcott: reports of Cola's ruthlessness have so struck
the young man that he was greatly concerned of his
intentions in coming here.

As much out of curiosity as in any hope of discovering
his design, I spent a good time talking to him, and dis-
covered a young man both highly personable and
charming, although this perception did not deflect me
from taking my normal precautions to guard against
sudden attack. None materialized, however, and I took
the liberty of informing him of the arrest of Sarah
Blundy, so that he might not be afraid of returning to
Oxford, if such concerns motivated him. I trust this
meets with your approval. While Prestcott and Cola
talked, I took it upon myself to see Dr. Lower, and im-
pressed on him the necessity of ensuring that Cola did
not slip away undetected; he was greatly perturbed and
I must say quite angry at the thought that he had been
deceived, but eventually agreed to comply with my
wishes and give no hint of any suspicion. He is too
transparent in his emotions, however, to give me great
confidence that he will manage such a feat.

I spent much of the night in an agony of indecision before
I came to the inevitable conclusion. Prestcott demanded a
high price and his soul would burn in hell for it. But it was
a price I could not bargain down. I needed that testimony
and I needed to know who was behind the conspiracy against
Clarendon. I hope my account here shows how much I tried.
On three occasions at least I had done my best to find a way
around the predicament. For more than a week I had avoided
acting, in the vain hope that an alternative would allow me
to escape the decision, and had risked much in the delay.
With a heavy heart, I concluded I could delay no more.

Sarah Blundy died two days later. On this subject I have
no more to add; my words would serve no purpose.

John Thurloe came to see me that same afternoon. "I do
not know whether to offer congratulations or not, doctor.
You have done a terrible right thing. More important than
you know, even."

"I think I know the significance of my deeds," I said. "And their cost."

"I think not."

Then, with that implacable coolness I knew so well, Thurloe told me the greatest secret of the realm, and for the first time I understood plainly how he and people like Samuel Morland had enjoyed such immunity from any sanction since His Majesty's restoration. And I also learned the true nature of Sir James Prestcott's treachery, a betrayal so dangerous it had to be disguised in a lesser treason that it might never be known.

"I had a man in my office, a soldier," Thurloe said, "who served as a particularly reliable emissary on all sorts of matters. If I wanted a particularly dangerous letter delivered, or prisoner kept safe, then this man could always be relied upon. He was perfectly fanatical in his hatred of monarchy and held a republic to be an essential beginning for God's kingdom on earth. He wanted a parliament elected by vote, including the vote of women and the propertyless, a distribution of land, and perfect toleration of all worship. He was, in addition, highly intelligent, quick-witted and able, if a little too thoughtful for perfection. But I considered him totally loyal to the Commonwealth because all possible alternatives he thought so very much worse.

"Unfortunately I was wrong in my assessment. He was a Lincolnshire man, and years before had formed an attachment to a local landowner who had defended the people of that place from the depredations of the drainers. At a moment of crisis, this loyalty came back to haunt him and overwhelmed all sense and reason. I must say we knew nothing of this until we found the letter Samuel asked you to decipher on his body."

"What is this to do with anything, sir? Please do not tell me riddles, I have enough of my own."

"That landowner, of course, was Sir James Prestcott, and the soldier was Ned Blundy, the husband of Anne, and the father of the woman who died two days ago."

I stared at him in the greatest surprise.

"On my last visit, I told you of the way John Mordaunt informed me of the 1659 rising. Another, smaller plot which he also told me about was a local piece of troublemaking planned for Lincolnshire by Sir James Prestcott. It was not serious, but General Ludlow was going to send off a regiment to deal with the problem before it could cause any trouble. Ned Blundy knew of it, as he was asked to deliver dispatches on the matter, and out of this fenland loyalty of his, passed on a warning which saved Prestcott's life, which would otherwise have most certainly been forfeit.

"The association, once renewed, led to the divulgence of more and more secrets, for both were fanatics and found common cause in hating those who wanted peace. Blundy applied himself to learning all the secrets of the talks about a restoration, which he could do more easily than was proper, for men are never as discreet or careful as they should be. Through him Prestcott learned of them as well. He knew which members of the king's party had been deliberately handed over to the government, which plots had been betrayed in advance so they could do no harm.

"And he became a very angry man, intent on revenge. When he heard that the king himself was coming to England in secret for final talks with me, he could contain himself no longer. He went down to Deal that same February in 1660, when the king was due to arrive, and lay in wait. I do not know how long he was there, but one morning after the talks had been going on, the king went for a walk in the gardens of the house we were using; Sir James came out at him, and tried to kill him with his sword."

I knew nothing of any of these talks, and certainly nothing of any assassination attempt, so well had the matter been hidden by all concerned, and I was astonished both to learn of it and that Thurloe was telling me now.

"Why did it not succeed?"

"It very nearly did. The king received a cut in the arm, which shocked him mightily, and would certainly have died had not another hurled himself in front of him and taken the final, fatal blow in his own heart."

"A brave and good man," I said.

"Perhaps. Certainly a most unusual one, for it was Ned Blundy who sacrificed himself in this fashion, and died for a man he detested, and permitted the restoration of that monarchy he had spent his life opposing."

I stared at him blankly at this extraordinary tale. Thurloe smiled when he saw my incomprehension, and shrugged.

"An honorable man, who believed in justice and saw none in murder, perhaps. I am certain Sir James had not consulted him in any way over what he intended. I can give no greater explanation to you of his motives and think none is probably needed: Blundy was a good soldier and loyal comrade, but I never once heard of him killing unnecessarily or acting with any cruelty to his enemies. I am sure he was happy to save Prestcott's life, but not to assist Prestcott in killing another, even if it was a king."

"And Sir James? Why did you not kill him? It seems to be your preferred solution in such cases."

"He was not an easy man to kill. The meeting took place with the very minimum of people, and almost no guards so pursuit was impossible: we relied on secrecy rather than force for safety. So Sir James escaped with few difficulties after the attack and daily we expected to hear that he had put his knowledge into circulation. On both sides we hunted furiously but to no avail. We could not say what he had done, as that would have involved revealing the depths of our talks, and so our only hope was to discredit him in advance so that if he did speak out, no one would believe him. Samuel did his usual competent job forging letters, and there were enough people amongst the king's men who could be bribed to accept the situation without too much enquiry. Prestcott fled abroad, and died. It is ironic; he was the worst of traitors to his king, but was entirely innocent of the crimes of which he was accused."

"Your problem at least was at an end."

"No. It was not. He would not have acted in such a desperate way on Ned Blundy's word alone. He insisted on seeing evidence, and Ned provided it."

"What sort of evidence?"

"Letters, memoranda, dockets, dates of meetings and the names of people at them. A great deal of material."

"And he did not use it?"

Thurloe smiled sadly. "Indeed not. I was forced to conclude that he did not have it; that Ned Blundy had kept it together with the key to the ciphers which hid their meanings.''

''And this was the man Samuel mentioned?''

''Yes. Shortly before his death, Blundy visited his family for the last time. It was reasonable to conclude he must have left it with them; on such a matter he could rely on no one else, not even the oldest comrade in arms. I had their house searched on several occasions, but discovered nothing. But I am certain that either the girl or her mother knew where it was, and that they were the only ones to know. Blundy was too sensible to trust others with such a secret.''

''And they are dead. They can't tell you where it is now.''

''Precisely. Nor can they tell Jack Prescott.'' Thurloe smiled. ''Which is the greatest relief of all. Because if he had that material, then he could have asked for an earldom and half a county, and the king would have given it to him. And Clarendon would have fallen without a murmur.''

''And this is what you told Prescott I would give him?''

''I said merely you would give him information. Which you can now do, since I have passed it on to you.''

''You know already what Prescott's information is?''

''No. But I must be strictly honest and say that I can guess what it is.''

''And you decided not to tell me, so I would have that girl killed.''

''That is correct. I would have preferred to have those documents of Blundy's so I could destroy them. But as that seemed unlikely to come about, it was best no one else should have them either. They would damage the standing and safety of too many people, including myself.''

''You had me commit murder for your own ends,'' I said flatly, appalled by the man's ruthlessness.

''I told you power is not for the squeamish, doctor,'' he said quietly. ''And what have you lost? You want your revenge on Cola and his patrons, and Prescott will let you have it.''

Then he signaled for Prescott to be brought, and the youth came in, preening himself in satisfaction at his own skill. At least I was sure that would not last long. I had agreed to spare him from trial, but I knew the knowledge he would have from my lips would be a greater punishment. Nor was I in a mood to spare him anything.

He began with lengthy and hypocritical assertions of his great gratitude to me for my kindness and mercy; these I cut short brusquely. I knew what I had done, and I wanted no congratulations. It was necessary, but my hatred and contempt for the man who had forced me to it knew few bounds.

Thurloe, I believe, saw my impatience and anger, and intervened before I became too outraged.

"The question is, Mr. Prestcott, who has guided you to your conclusions? Who gave you the hints and suggestions which have led you to your conviction about Mordaunt's guilt? You have told me much about your enquiries, but you have not told all, and I do not like to be deceived."

He flushed at the accusation, and attempted to pretend he was not frightened of the threat implicit in Thurloe's quiet, gentle voice. Thurloe, who could be more terrifying with less effort than any man I knew, sat out the bluster.

"I say again, you have not told something. By your own account, you had never heard of Sir Samuel Morland, yet found out much about him and his interests quite easily. You had no introduction to Lord Bedford's steward, yet were received by him and found him free with all manner of information. How did you know to do this? Why would such a man have talked to you? This was the critical moment in your quest, was it not? Before that all was dark and obscure, after it everything was clear and lucid. Someone told you Mordaunt was a traitor, someone told you of his connection to Samuel Morland, and encouraged you in your quest. Before then, all was suspicion and half-formed idea."

Prestcott still refused to answer, but hung his head like a schoolboy caught cheating in his work.

"I hope you are not going to tell us you made it all up. Dr. Wallis here has taken substantial risks on your behalf, and has entered into a bargain with you. That contract will be null and void unless you fulfill your side of it."

Eventually he raised his head and stared at Thurloe, a strange and (I would have said) almost maniacal smile on his face. "I had it from a friend."

"A friend. How kind of him. Would you care to share the name of this friend?"

I felt myself leaning forward in anticipation of his reply, for I was sure his next words would answer the question for which I had risked so much.

"Kitty," he said, and I stared at him in total puzzlement. The name meant nothing to me at all.

"Kitty," Thurloe repeated, as imperturbable as ever. "Kitty. And he is . . . ?"

"She. She is, or was, a whore."

"A very well-informed one, it seems."

"She is now very well-placed in her trade. It is extraordinary, is it not, how fortune favors some people? When I first met her she was walking to Tunbridge to ply her trade. Six months later, she is comfortably installed as the mistress of one of the greatest men in the land."

Thurloe smiled encouragingly in that bland way of his.

"She is a girl of great good sense," Prestcott continued. "Before her rise, I was kind to her, and when I encountered her by chance in London she paid me back handsomely, by retelling gossip she had heard."

"By chance?"

"Yes. I was walking around, and she saw me and approached me. She happened to be passing."

"I'm sure she was. Now, this great man who keeps her. His name is . . . ?"

Prestcott drew himself more upright in the chair. "My Lord of Bristol," he said. "But I beg you not to say I told you. I promised my discretion."

I sighed heavily, not only because my case was advanced immeasurably, but also because Prestcott's answer was so obviously true. Just as it was not in Mr. Bennet's character to risk all on a throw, so it was very much in that of Bristol to chance all he had so recklessly. He thought of himself as the king's greatest adviser, although in truth he had no office and little authority. His open Catholicism had debarred him from position, and in all matters he was bested by Clarendon on policy. It rankled, for he was undoubtedly a man of great courage and loyalty, who had been by the king's side as long as any, and shared exile and poverty with him. He was a man of extraordinary qualities, and had as good an education as any man of that age, a graceful and beautiful person, with great eloquence in discourse. He was equal to a good part in any affair, but was the unfittest man alive to conduct it, for, great though his qualities were, his vanity and ambition far exceeded them, and he had a confidence in his capacities which often intoxicated, transported and exposed him. He espoused policies of the smallest prudence and the greatest hazard, but did so with such sweet reason that they seemed the only course to take. It would not be difficult to persuade others that he had attempted Clarendon's murder, for he was perfectly capable of inventing such a foolishness.

"You may rest assured that we will not betray your trust," Thurloe said. "I must thank you, young man. You have been very helpful."

Prestcott looked puzzled. "And that is it? You want no more of me?"

"Later maybe. But not at the moment."

"In that case," he said, turning to me, "you will favor me with one piece of information as well. The evidence of Mordaunt's guilt which Mr. Thurloe tells me undoubtedly exists. Where is it to be found? Who has it?"

Even in my mood of blackness, I felt the ability to pity him then. He was stupid and deluded, cruel and credulous by turns, violent in deed and soul, full of bile and superstition, a monster of perversion. But his one genuine feeling was the reverential love he had for his father, and his faith in his honesty was so direct it had carried him through all his journeys and troubles. That goodness had been so corrupted by rancor it was hard to see the virtuous kernel within, and yet it was there. I took no pleasure in extinguishing it, nor in telling him that his cruelty made him the author of his own, ultimate misfortune.

"There was only one person who knew where it was."

"And the name, sir? I will go there directly." He leaned forward eagerly, a look of unsuspecting anticipation on his youthful countenance.

"Her name is Sarah Blundy. The person you insisted must die. You have stopped her mouth for good, and that proof will now remain hidden forever, for she must have hidden it well. You will now never prove your father's innocence, nor get your estates back. You name will be forever tarnished with the title of traitor. It is a just punishment for your sins. You must live knowing you are the author of your own misfortunes.''

He sat back again with a knowing smile, ''You are making fun of me, sir. It is your way, perhaps, but I must ask you to be more direct with me. Tell me the truth, please.''

I told him again. Adding more details, then still more details until the smirk faded from his face, and his hands began to tremble. I say again, I took no pleasure in it, and though it was just, I took no satisfaction either in the hideous additional punishment that was then meted out to him. For as I told him precisely how his father had betrayed the king, and come close even to murdering him, his voice fell into a growl, and the hideous demonic look that came over his twisted and contorted features frightened even Thurloe, I believe.

It was well that he had not lost his old habits of caution, and had a servant in the background, ready for all eventualities. As I finished, Prestcott launched himself at my throat, and would surely have torn the very life from me had he been granted just a few more seconds before being manhandled to the ground.

As a priest, I necessarily believe in the possession of men by demons, but I think that I had always used the notion in careless, thoughtless ways. I could not have been more wrong, and those skeptics who disbelieve in such things are deluded by their own vanity. There are indeed demons, and they can take over the bodies and souls of men and drive them to frenzies of malice and destruction. Prestcott was all the proof I could ever need to persuade me to put aside skepticism forever, for no human form would be capable of the violent bestiality I saw in that room. The monstrous devil in Prestcott, I believe, had controlled his thoughts and deeds for many months, but in such careful, subtle ways that its presence was unsuspected.

Now it was finally frustrated, its fury and violent activity burst out in hideous extremity, making him roll on the floor, scratching the boards with his fingernails until the blood spurted from them and was dragged in thin red lines down the grain of the wood. It took a great effort to restrain him, and even we were unable to stop him crashing his head, time and again against the furniture, and trying to bite us whenever we incautiously put a hand near him. And he screamed hideous obscenities all the while, although fortunately most of the words could not be made out, and continued thrashing around until he was bound and gagged and taken to the university prison, there to wait the arrival of some member of his family to take him in charge.

chapter twelve

I WOULD HAVE LEFT FOR LONDON IMMEDIATELY even had I not been told, by Mr. Wood of all people, that Cola had fled Oxford after hearing of Sarah Blundy's death. Both she and the mother were now dead, and I felt that, at the very least, some of his plans were frustrated; his ability to communicate with those supposedly assisting him was greatly diminished, enough to make any further sojourn in Oxford useless to him. More importantly, I considered he must have heard of Prestcott's descent into frenzy: if Thurloe was right, and the first attempt on Clarendon was to be through the young lunatic, then he would have realized that the move had failed, and it was now time for him to act. This thought, more than any other, prompted me to leave as speedily as possible.

The journey was as tedious as ever, and I lurched along, conscious that my quarry was but a few hours ahead of me. But no one at Charing Cross recalled someone answering his description when I arrived and asked questions. So I went directly to Whitehall, where Mr. Bennet was most likely to be found, and sent in a message begging the favor of an interview with the utmost urgency.

He saw me within an hour; I resented the delay, but had prepared myself for an even greater one.

"I hope this is indeed important, doctor," he said as I entered his chamber which, I was relieved to see, was empty save for himself. "It is unlike you to cause such a commotion."

"I believe it is, sir."

"So tell me what is on your mind now? Still concerned with plots?"

"Indeed. Before I explain, I must ask a question of the greatest importance. When I informed you of my suspicions a few weeks ago, did you communicate this to anyone? Anyone at all?"

He shrugged, and frowned at the implied criticism. "I may have done."

"It is important. I would not ask otherwise. Less than two days after I spoke to you, Cola murdered my most trusted servant, whose name I gave you. He then came to Oxford and attempted to kill me also. He knew I had a copy of a letter of his, and he stole it, along with another I have kept by me for years. I have since become convinced that the man who has organized his presence here is Lord Bristol. What I must know is whether you informed his lordship of my suspicions."

Mr. Bennet said nothing for a long while, and I could see that his acute and rapid mind was assessing every aspect of what I said, and every implication of my words as well.

"I hope you do not suggest . . ."

"Had I done so, I would hardly have raised the subject with you. But your loyalty to your friends is well known, and you would not expect any man so indebted to the king to act against his interest. And I believe Cola's target is not the king, but the Lord Chancellor."

This surprised him, and I could see that all now began to make sense to his mind in a way it had not before. "The answer to your question is that I believe I did mention it to Lord Bristol, or at least to one of his entourage."

"And his relations with Lord Clarendon are as bad as ever?"

"They are. But not so bad that I can easily consider he would act in such a way. He is given to mad schemes, but I have always considered him too weak to achieve much. Perhaps I underestimated him. You had best tell me exactly why you conclude this."

I did so, and Mr. Bennet listened with the greatest gravity throughout, not even interrupting when I confessed to having been in consultation with John Thurloe. When I finished he again said nothing for a long while.

"Well, well," he said at last. "A string to hang an earl. It is difficult to credit, and yet I must do so. The question is, how to deal with the situation."

"Cola must be stopped, and Bristol punished."

Mr. Bennet looked at me with contempt. "Yes, of course. It is easier said than done, however. Do you know what Cola's plans are?"

"Not in detail."

"How he communicates with Lord Bristol?"

"No."

"Whether there be any letters or hard evidence that he has ever done so?"

"No."

"And you expect me to do what? Charge his Lordship with high treason, perhaps? You forget, perhaps, that just as I am your patron, so he is mine. If I am to break with him then I must justify myself absolutely, or be accused of perfidy. If Lord Bristol falls, half the court falls with him, and there will be few restraints on Clarendon, and even fewer on the king. The economy of the entire government will be disrupted and crippled. I tell you, Dr. Wallis, I find it hard to credit that the man can risk so much."

"He does. He must be stopped and you must take his place."

Bennet looked at me.

"I do not flatter you, or tell you anything you do not feel in your own heart. Your value to His Majesty is well known. Your usefulness in balancing the interests of Lord Clarendon would be equally clear. Lord Bristol's lack of moderation has prevented him from doing that. You can, and can do so the better if you are free of his foolishness. You have to break with him and pull him down yourself. If you do not, you can be certain that he will fall anyway, and you will go down with him."

Still he stared at me, but I was emboldened to continue, for I knew that I was speaking to his soul. "You are bound to him as a man who has brought you up, and advanced you, and I know you have repaid that debt loyally and well. But you are not obliged to aid him in evil, and his attempt at such a thing dissolves all ties.''

Finally he reacted to my words, and rested his head in his hands, his elbows on the desk, the most informal posture I had ever seen him adopt. ''Throw the dice, you think, doctor? And if Clarendon is killed anyway, and Bristol actually succeeds? What mercy for me and mine, then? Have you thought how long you would retain your position?''

''Not many weeks. But I doubt I would live long in any case, so the loss of office would be a minor problem for me.''

''I have long considered what my true degree should be at court. You no doubt think me ambitious, and so I am. But I am also a good servant to His Majesty, and whatever my own beliefs, I have always advised him for the best. I deserve the highest places in the land. Clarendon has always blocked me, as he blocks all who are younger and more agile than he. And you tell me that I have to abandon a man who has always been kind to me, and keep in power one who detests the very air I breathe?''

''I am not saying you should keep him in power. I am merely pointing out that you must not in any way associate yourself with his murder, and to stay silent is such an association.''

Mr. Bennet considered, then gave way, as I knew he would in due course.

''Do you plan to confront Lord Bristol, or inform Lord Clarendon?'' I asked.

''The latter. I have no desire to level accusations. Others can do that. Come, Dr. Wallis. You must come as well.''

I HAD NEVER BEFORE MET THE LORD CHANCELLOR OF England in person although I had, naturally, seen him on numerous occasions. His grotesque corpulence did not surprise me, although the ease with which we gained access to him did. He maintained little formality about his person; no doubt his years in exile, when he lived a hand-to-mouth existence and often even had to do without so much as a servant, had taught him the virtues of simplicity—although I noted that similar deprivation had imparted no such lesson to Mr. Bennet.

As Mr. Thurloe had said, he was a man of the utmost loyalty to his master the king, who had on numerous occasions treated his servant shabbily, and was, in future years, to treat him more shabbily still. Nonetheless, Clarendon stood resolutely by him, steering him away from such follies as he could. He worked tirelessly while in exile for His Majesty's return, and strove mightily to keep him there once this great goal was accomplished. His great weakness was that which attends many older men, for he placed too great store on the wisdom of age. No doubt, deference is a virtue, but to expect it without question is great foolishness, and stirs up only resentment. Mr. Bennet was one whom he had needlessly antagonized, for in their common good sense they were natural allies. But Clarendon blocked Bennet's friends on all occasions, and would rarely allow the spoils of office to go to anyone outside his own circle.

The antagonism between the two men was scarcely discernible, however. Mr. Bennet's punctiliousness and Clarendon's natural gravity meant that anyone less observant or less knowing than myself would have assumed that relations between the two were entirely cordial. But they were far from that, and I also knew that underneath the coolness of his manner, Mr. Bennet was certainly highly anxious of the outcome of this meeting.

When dealing with matters of true importance, Mr. Bennet was not a man to disguise his meaning with elaborate phrases or half-spoken implications. He introduced me as his servant and I bowed, then he announced curtly that I had a matter of the utmost importance to communicate. Clarendon's eyes narrowed as he recalled who I was.

"I am surprised to see you in such company, doctor. You seem able to serve many masters."

"I serve God and the government, sir," I replied, "the former because it is my duty, the latter because I am asked to do so. Were my services not required and requested, I would happily live in pleasant obscurity."

He ignored this reply, and walked heavily about the room

in which we had found him. Mr. Bennet stood silently, a look of barely concealed disquiet on his face. He knew that his future rested entirely on how I conducted myself in the encounter.

"D'ye find me fat, sir?"

The question was obviously addressed to me. The Lord Chancellor of England came to rest in front of me, wheezing with the effort of taking a few steps, his hands resting on his hips as he spoke.

I looked him steadily in the eye. "Of course I do," I said.

He grunted with satisfaction, then hobbled over to his seat and sat down, gesturing to us that we might do the same.

"Many men have looked me straight in the eye as you did, and sworn blind that the resemblance to Adonis was extraordinary," he observed. "Such is the power of high office, it can even distort men's sight, it seems. I throw such men out. Now, Mr. Bennet, tell me what it is that makes you overcome your detestation for me. And why you bring this gentleman with you."

"I will allow Dr. Wallis to speak, if that is agreeable to you. He has all the information at his fingertips, and it will sound better from him."

The chancellor turned to me and I, once more, recited my tale as briefly as possible. Again I must confess all my weaknesses, for this narration is of no use if I behave in an Italian manner and leave out what is not in my interest. I did not tell Lord Clarendon about Sarah Blundy.

I had lived with the facts for so long now that none of it even surprised me anymore; it was instructive to see how more ordinary men (if I may for a moment call the Lord Chancellor such) reacted to accusations I now took for granted. Clarendon's face grew stony and pale as I laid out my investigations and conclusions, his jaw clenched hard in anger, and eventually he was unable even to look at the bearer of such news.

There was a long, a very long, silence when I finished. Mr. Bennet would not speak; the chancellor, it seemed, could not. For my part I considered my role over; I had done my task and reported my findings to those with the power to act. I was aware of the momentous thing I had done, and realized anew the tremendous power of words, which can tumble men from on high in an instant, and accomplish more in a few sentences than entire armies in a year's campaign. For men are held above their fellows by the gossamer of reputation, which is so soft and fragile a breath can blow it away.

Eventually Clarendon spoke, and subjected me to the closest interrogation I have ever endured in my life; he was a lawyer, and like all lawyers loved nothing more than the chance to show off his skills in questioning. My interrogation went on for the better part of an hour, and I answered as best I could, calmly and without resentment. Again I will be open about the matter; for the most part my answers satisfied him; but his skill probed my case mercilessly and whatever weaknesses existed were soon laid out for him to inspect.

"So, Dr. Wallis, your belief in Mr. Cola's military skills . . ."

"Comes from a trader who conveyed him to Venice from Italy," I replied. "He had no reason to lie to me as he did not know of my interest in the man. He was not of any breeding, but I consider him a reliable witness nonetheless. He reported what he saw and heard, my conclusions are in no part based on his opinions."

"And Cola's links with radicals?"

"Well attested by my informants in the Low Countries, and by my own servant. He also formed a strong connection with a notorious family in Oxford."

"With Sir William Compton?"

"He was seen by a reliable witness at Sir William's house, and stayed there for many days. They discussed you on several occasions, the route you planned to take in a few weeks time, and expressed the hope you might be ambushed on the road."

"With my Lord Bristol?"

"Sir William is of Lord Bristol's interest, as I am sure you know . . ."

"So is Mr. Bennet here."

"I told Mr. Bennet of my suspicions before I had any inkling of who Cola's master was. He told Lord Bristol, and within twenty-four hours my servant was murdered by Cola. I was myself the target of an attack a few days later."

"That is insufficient."

"It is, but it is not all. Lord Bristol is known to favor a Spanish alliance, and Cola also has strong connections with the governor of the Netherlands; he is a known Catholic, and hence does not acknowledge the authority of the king, Parliament or the laws of this country. And it is not the first time he has attempted a foolish scheme. Moreover, his hand has guided a young man for many months in an attempt to attack you by destroying the reputation of Lord Mordaunt."

Eventually I had no more. Clarendon would be convinced or not. It is a strange business, trying to persuade a man he is to be killed; and it says much for Lord Clarendon that he wanted good reason before he would own himself satisfied. Many men less than he would have happily leaped at the suspicion, and invented any extra evidence in order to destroy a rival.

"But they have never met? No man has seen them together? There are no letters, no one has overheard any conversation between them?"

I shook my head. "No; but I would doubt if it is likely. Common sense dictates that all contact be through a third party."

Clarendon leaned back in his chair, and I heard the joints creaking from the strain. Mr. Bennet had sat quite impassively throughout, showing no sign of emotion on his face, neither helping me nor hindering me. He was entirely quiet until Clarendon turned to him.

"You are convinced of this, sir?"

"I am convinced you may well be in danger, and that all possible means should be taken to prevent any harm coming to you."

"That is generous from a man who loves me so little."

"No. You are His Majesty's closest minister, and it is the duty of all to protect you as the king himself. If the king chose to dismiss you, I would not exert myself to prevent your fall; you know that, I am sure. But it is as treasonable for anyone else to force His Majesty as it is criminal to kill a man outside the law. If Bristol wishes this, I will have none of him."

"Do you think he does? That is the question, is it not? I

do not intend to sit here and see whether a knife in my back proves Dr. Wallis correct. I cannot charge Lord Bristol with treason, for the case is not strong enough and the king would see any attempt to prosecute as a misuse of my office. And I will not adopt such methods myself.''

''You have in the past,'' Mr. Bennet said.

''Rarely; and I will not in this case. Lord Bristol has been at the king's side, and his father's side before that, for more than twenty years, and I have been with him. We shared exile, despair and deprivation together. I loved him as a brother, and do still. I cannot harm him.''

The discourse which passed between the two men continued in such a way; moderation, subtlety and regret being the only emotions and feelings they expressed. This is the way of the courtier, who talks in a code more deep and impenetrable than any of the petty conspirators who were my daily antagonists. I do not even doubt that they meant everything that they said; but left unsaid, and understood by each other beneath the words, a more pitiless conversation was taking place, with each man bargaining and plotting how to turn the situation I had created to their own advantage.

I do not despise them for this; each man believed, I am sure, that the triumph of him and his was for the general good. Nor do I think such flexibility an error; in the past few years England had suffered greatly at the hands of rigid men of principle, who would not bend and could not change. That Clarendon and Mr. Bennet competed for the king's favor added luster to His Majesty's glory. Forcing that favor, taking away his right to choose, was the sin of Parliament in the past and Lord Bristol in the present. That was why both had to be opposed.

Nor was I surprised that both men wished to comprehend fully the potential damage to themselves of Bristol's fall. For the consequences would be great, as they are whenever a mighty interest collapses. The Digby family, which he headed, had a strong following in the House of Commons and in the West Country; many of his friends and family had been placed at court and in offices of state. Removing Lord Bristol was one thing; rooting out his family was another.

''I hope we may take it that this Italian must be stopped,'' the Chancellor said, with the first glimmerings of a smile I had seen since I had told him my information. "That is the beginning. The more serious problem, if I may put it so, is Lord Bristol. I do not wish to accuse him, let alone bring articles of impeachment against him myself. Will you do so, Mr. Bennet?"

He shook his head. "I cannot. Too many of his people are my people as well. It would tear us apart, and I would not be trusted again. I will not support him, but cannot plunge a knife into his back."

They both fell silent, willing the end, yet shrinking from the deed. Eventually I ventured to speak, somewhat abashed at offering counsel to such people without being asked, but confident that my skills matched theirs.

"Perhaps he can bring about his own fall," I said.

Both men looked at me gravely, wondering whether to upbraid me for having spoken, or encourage me to continue. Eventually Clarendon nodded that I had his permission to speak.

"Lord Bristol is foolhardy, easily wounded in vanity and honor and excessively fond of grand gestures. This he has demonstrated. He must be forced to act in a way which is so intemperate and foolish that even the king becomes exasperated with him."

"And how do you suggest we accomplish this?"

"He has made an attempt, I think, through this young man called Prestcott, which has now failed. Then Cola must also be stopped. Afterward he must be goaded and provoked until he loses all reason. It would take some considerable time to hire another killer, many months, at least. You must whittle away at his position quickly before he can try again."

"For example?"

"There are many things you might do. He is steward of my university; you might suggest he be relieved of the post on the grounds of his Catholicism. Eject some of his supporters from their positions."

"That will not provoke; merely irritate."

"My Lord, may I speak plainly?"

Clarendon nodded.

"Your daughter married the Duke of York against your will and without your knowledge."

Clarendon nodded slowly, ready to anger. Mr. Bennet sat absolutely still, watching me as I spoke the most dangerous words I had ever uttered. Even to mention the notorious match to the chancellor could end a man's career, for it had nearly ended his when it became known. It was rash even to allude to it and even rasher to bring it up as I was about to do. As best I could, I ignored the cold and stony look from the chancellor, and pretended not to notice that Mr. Bennet's support was manifestly absent.

"I hesitate to recommend such a course, but my Lord Bristol must be made to think that Her Majesty the Queen is barren, and that you were well aware of this when you advocated the match."

There was dead, total silence after I uttered the words, and I feared that I would bring his wrath upon me. Again he surprised me; rather than erupting in fury, he merely asked in a cold, frigid voice: "And how would that serve?"

"Lord Bristol is jealous of your ascendancy; if he believes for certain that you connived to place your own daughter on the throne by exploiting the queen's incapacity, he will be consumed with jealousy at your prospects, and could be persuaded to try and impeach you in the House of Commons. If Mr. Bennet refuses to support such a move at the crucial moment, it will fail, and the king will have to deal with a man who has tried publicly to usurp his authority by forcing his chief minister out. He would have to act to preserve the crown's reputation."

"How would this tale be put into circulation?"

"A young colleague of mine at Oxford, Dr. Lower, is greatly desirous of making his way in London. Were you to favor him, I am sure he would allow it to be said that he had been called in secret to examine the queen and found clear evidence of her barrenness. Naturally, if put on oath, Mr. Lower would tell the truth, and deny he had performed any such examination."

"Of course," Mr. Bennet intervened, "you have no choice, if you accept this proposition, but to trust that I will come out in your support at that crucial moment. I am happy to give you my word, but on such a matter as this, do not expect it will be enough.''

''I think, sir, that ways can be found to make it in your interest to keep your word.''

Bennet nodded. ''That is all I ask.''

''You agree to this idea?'' I said in astonishment that it should meet with so little resistance or objection.

''I believe so. I will endeavor to use the fall of Lord Bristol to bolster my position as the king's chief minister; Mr. Bennet will use it to strengthen his so that he might pull me down in due course. That comes afterward, however; for the time being we must consider ourselves allies in a common, and necessary, purpose.''

''And the Italian must not cause any troubles,'' Bennet said. ''He cannot be arrested, nor brought to any account where he can speak. The government cannot afford to be shaken by tales of treason so close in amongst the king's friends.''

''He must be killed,'' I said. ''Lend me some soldiers, and I will ensure it is done.''

And this too was agreed. I left the meeting some time later, confident that my duty was complete, and that now I could concentrate on my personal vengeance.

chapter thirteen

AFTER THIS ENCOUNTER, CLARENDON KEPT TO HIS house surrounded by guards, and put it out that his gout (a real complaint, for he was tormented by the disease mercilessly, and had been for many years past) was upon him again. His visit to Cornbury was canceled and he cowered at home, leaving only to make the short journey from Piccadilly to Whitehall to wait on the king.

And I hunted for Cola, using all the powers I had been given to search out his whereabouts. I had fifty soldiers ready for use, and every informer was pressed into service. All of the radicals I could lay my hands on were arrested, in case the Italian had taken refuge with them; the Spanish ambassador's house was discreetly watched, back and front, and I had people going around nearly every tavern, inn and hostel asking for information. The docks were watched as well, and I asked my merchant friend Mr. Williams to put it abroad that any foreigner asking for a passage was to be reported to me immediately.

The French, I believe, do these things more effectively, as they can call on what they term a police to ensure order in their towns. After the experience of searching for Cola, I came to think that such a body might be of some use in London as well, although there seems no chance of it ever being established. Perhaps with such a force, Cola might have been found more quickly; perhaps he might not have come so close to accomplishing his aim. All I knew was that, for three days of disappointment, I searched in vain. There was not even a whisper of the man, which I considered incredible for one normally so noticeable. That he was in London was certain, there was nowhere else for him to go. But it was as if he had dissolved into the air like a spirit.

I had, of course, to make regular reports to Lord Clarendon and Mr. Bennet about my progress, and I could sense their ebbing confidence as, day after day, I told them of my failure. Mr. Bennet said nothing directly, but I knew him well enough to see that my own position was now at stake as well, and that I had to find the Italian speedily if I was not to lose his support. The visit on the fourth day of my search was the worst, for I had to stand throughout the interview once more and suffer his ever-growing coldness, which bore heavily on me as I walked afterward across the courtyards of the palace to the river.

Then I stopped, for I knew that I had detected something of the utmost importance, but could not instantly place in my mind what it could be. But I had a presentiment of the greatest danger which would not leave me, however much I thought and tried to discover what idea had been raised in my mind. It was a beautiful morning, I remember, and I had decided to revive my spirits by walking from Mr. Bennet's quarters across Cotton Garden, then through a small passageway into St. Stephen's Court to get to Westminster Stairs. It was in this little passageway, enclosed by heavy oak doors at either end, that the worry came upon me first, but I shrugged it off and continued to walk. Only as I stood on the quayside and was about to get into my boat did the understanding come to me, and I immediately made my way as swiftly as possible back to the nearest guards.

"Sound the alarm," I said, once I had established with him my authority. "There is an assassin in the building."

I gave him a swift description of the Italian, then returned to Mr. Bennet, and burst in on him without, this time, waiting for any formalities. "He is here," I said. "He is in the palace."

Mr. Bennet looked skeptical. "You have seen him?"

"No. I smelled him."

"I beg your pardon?"

"I smelled him. In the corridor. He wears a particular perfume, which is quite unmistakable, and which no Englishman would ever use. I smelled it. Believe me, sir, he is here."

Bennet grunted. "And what have you done about it?"

"I have alerted the guards, and they are beginning to search. Where is the king? And the chancellor?"

"The king is at his prayers, and the chancellor is not here."

"You must place extra guards."

Mr. Bennet nodded, and straightaway summoned some officials and began giving orders. For the first time, I think, I understood why His Majesty held him in such high regard, for he acted calmly and without any show of disturbance, but moved with the greatest dispatch. Within minutes, guards were surrounding the king, the prayers were brought to an early conclusion—although not so hastily that any alarm was given to the attending courtiers—and small parties of soldiers fanned out across the palace, with its hundreds of rooms and courtyards and corridors, searching for the intruder.

"I hope you are right, sir," Mr. Bennet said, as we watched a small party of officials being stopped and scrutinized. "If you are not, then you will not have to answer to me."

Then I saw the man I had sought for so many days. Mr. Bennet occupied a set of rooms on the corner, with one pair of windows giving out onto the Thames, the other onto the alleyway leading to Parliament Stairs. And down this, walking calmly from Old Palace Yard past the Prince's Lodgings, I saw a familiar figure. Without any shadow of a doubt, it was Cola, as cool as ever, though dressed less conspicuously, looking for all the world as though he had a perfect right to be there.

"There," I shouted, grabbing Mr. Bennet by the shoulder. It took him a long time to forgive the action. "There he is. Quickly now!"

Without waiting, I ran from the room, down the stairs, shouting for guards to follow me as swiftly as possible. And I stood, like Horatius Cocles himself, barring the way to Parliament Stairs, the waiting boats and Cola's only chance of escape.

I had no notion of what to do next. I was quite unarmed, perfectly alone and without any means of defending myself against a man whose murderous skills were well attested. But my desire and my duty impelled me forward, for I was determined he should not escape me, and the revenge I was bound to seek.

Had Cola pulled his weapon and lunged at me the moment he saw me standing in front of him, his escape would have been certain and my death equally assured. I had only surprise in my armory, and I was quite aware that it was but a feeble weapon.

It worked, nonetheless, for when Cola did see me, he was so astonished that he did not know how to react.

"Dr. Wallis!" he said, and even managed a smile of what could almost have passed as pleasure. "You were the last person I expected to see here."

"I am aware of that. Might I enquire what you are doing?"

"I am seeing the sights, sir," he replied. "Before beginning my journey home, which I plan to do tomorrow."

"I think not," I said with relief, for I could see soldiers approaching over the courtyard. "I think your journey is already at an end."

He turned round to see what I was looking at, then his face frowned with puzzlement and dismay.

"I am betrayed, I see," he said, and I breathed a great sigh of relief.

HE WAS TAKEN, WITH NO FUSS OR DISTURBANCE, TO A room off Fish Yard, and I went with him. Mr. Bennet went to find His Majesty that he might be informed of events and also, I believe, to inform Lord Clarendon that the danger was at an end. For my part, I felt dizzy with my success and gave thanks that I had discovered the man before, rather than after, he had caused any damage. I saw him locked in, then began to question him closely, although for all the information I collected, I might as well have saved my breath.

Cola's bravado amazed me, for he affected to be delighted at the sight of me, despite the circumstances. He was pleased, he said, to see an old face.

"I have felt myself very solitary since I left your fine town, Dr. Wallis," he said. "I do not find the people of London greatly welcoming."

"I cannot imagine why. But you were hardly a popular figure in Oxford when you left, either."

He looked distressed at the comment. "It seems not. Although I am quite unaware of what I did to deserve such churlishness. You have heard of my dispute with Mr. Lower, I imagine? He mistreated me very badly, I do not mind telling you, and I am at a loss to explain why. I shared all my ideas with him, and was sorely treated in return."

"Maybe he learned more about you than your ideas, and was not pleased to be harboring such a person. No man likes to be deceived, and if he was too gentlemanly to challenge you openly, it is not discourteous to indicate annoyance."

A crafty look of caution came over his bland, wide face as he sat down opposite and studied me with what seemed to be vague amusement.

"I suppose I have to thank you for that, do I? Mr. Lower told me you were forever burrowing your nose in other people's business, and occupying yourself with matters that were none of your affair."

"I may claim that honor," I said, determined not to be drawn by his offensive tone. "I act for the good of the country and its legitimate government."

"I'm glad to hear it. So should all men do so. I like to think of myself as equally loyal."

"I believe you are. You proved that in Candia, did you not?"

His eyes narrowed at my demonstration of knowledge. "I was not aware that my fame had spread so far."

"And you knew Sir James Prestcott as well?"

"Oh, I see," he replied, a false understanding dawning. "You had it from that strange son of his. You must not believe everything you hear from that young man. He has the most bizarre of delusions about anything and anyone connected to his honored father. He is quite capable of inventing any tale about me in order to reflect glory on that poor man."

"I can hardly think of Sir James as a poor man."

"Can you not? I met him under different circumstances, when he was reduced to selling his sword for hire, and with scarcely a penny to his name. A sad fall, that, when no one of his fellows would reach out a hand to help him. Can you really condemn him so much? What loyalty did he owe anyone by then? He was the bravest of men, the most courageous of comrades, and I honor his memory as much as I lament his end."

"And so you come to England yourself, and tell no one of your own bravery?"

"A period of my life which is entirely at an end. I do not wish to recall it."

"You associate with the king's enemies wherever you go."

"They are not my enemies. I associate with whomever pleases me, and whom I find good company."

"I want my letters back. The ones you stole from my room."

He paused, then smiled. "I know of no letters, sir. Search me and my belongings if you wish, but I may say I resent the imputation that I am a thief. Such things should not be said lightly by one gentleman to another."

"Tell me about my Lord Bristol."

"I must say I am not acquainted with the gentleman."

His face was entirely passive, and he looked me evenly and unflinchingly in the eye as he came out with this denial.

"Of course not," I said. "Nor have you heard of Lord Clarendon."

"He? Oh indeed. Who could not have heard of the Lord Chancellor? Naturally I have heard of him. Although I do not know what the question signifies."

"Tell me about Sir William Compton."

Cola sighed. "What a lot of questions you ask! Sir William, as you know, was a friend of Sir James. He told me that if I ever came on a tour to England that Sir William would be glad to offer me hospitality. Which he most generously did."

"And was attacked for his pains."

"Not by me, as that seems to be the implication of your statement. I understand young Prescott did that. I merely kept him alive. And no one will deny I did a fine job."

"Sir James Prescott betrayed Sir William Compton, and was detested by him. You expect me to believe he would willingly ask you into his house?"

"He did. As for the detestation, I saw no sign of it. Whatever enmity there was, must have died with him."

"You discussed the murder of the Lord Chancellor with Sir William."

The change in the Italian's demeanor as I made this statement was remarkable. From an easygoing affability, the manner of a man who feels himself in no danger at all, he stiffened; only slightly, but the difference was extreme. From here on, I could sense he watched his words more carefully. At the same time, though, the air of amusement persisted in some fashion, as though he was still confident enough to anticipate no great danger for himself.

"Is that what this is about? We discussed many things."

"Including an ambush on the road to Cornbury."

"English roads, I gather, are full of perils for the unwary."

"Do you deny you placed a bottle with poison in it for me to drink that night in New College?"

Here he began to look exasperated. "Dr. Wallis, you are beginning to weary me greatly. You ask about the attack on Sir William Compton, even though Jack Prescott was charged with the crime and all but owned his authorship by his escape. You ask about the death of Dr. Grove, even though that girl was not only hanged for the offense but even confessed to it quite voluntarily. You ask about discussions on Lord Clarendon's safety, even though I am here, quite openly, in London, and the chancellor is in excellent health. May that happy state continue for him. So what is your purpose?"

"You do not deny, either, that you killed my servant Matthew in London in March?"

Here he affected an air of puzzlement once more. "You lose me again, sir. Who is Matthew?"

My face must have shown the full coldness of my anger, as he looked disconcerted for the first time.

"You know perfectly well who Matthew is. The lad you so generously took under your wing in the Low Countries. The one you took to your feast and debauched. The one you met again in London and murdered so cold-bloodedly, when all he ever wanted from you was friendship and love."

Cola's flippant air had now evaporated, and he twisted and turned like a fish to avoid confronting what even he knew was his duplicity and cowardice.

"I remember a young lad in the Hague," he said, "although his name was not Matthew, or so he told me. The outrageous charge of debauchery I will not even dignify with an answer, for I know not where it originates. As for murder, I merely deny it. I admit that I was set upon by a cutpurse shortly after I arrived in London. I admit I defended myself as best I could, and ran off the moment I could. The identity of my assailant, and his condition when we parted company, I cannot vouch for although I did not think him so badly injured. If someone died, I am sorry for it. If it was this boy, I am sorry for that as well, although I certainly did not recognize him and would not have hurt him if I had, however much he had deceived me. But I would advise you, in future, to pick your servants with more care and not give employment to people who supplement their wages with nighttime thievery."

The cruelty of this statement cut through me like Cola's sword cut Matthew's throat, and I wished at that moment I had a knife of my own, or more freedom to act, or a soul which could encompass taking the life of another. But Cola knew full well that I was under constraint; he must have sensed it the moment I arrived, and he used his knowledge to bait and torment me.

"Be very careful what you say, sir," I said, barely controlling my voice. "I can do you great harm if I wish."

It was, for the time being, an empty threat, and he must have sensed it also, for he laughed easily and with contempt. "You will do what your masters tell you to do, doctor. As do we all."

chapter fourteen

I DRAW NOW TO AN END; ALL ELSE I HEARD OF AT second hand, or saw as an observer, and I do not presume to comment at length on matters better left to others. I was, however, on the quay the next day when Cola was brought to the boat. I watched the carriage roll up and saw the Italian, with a carefree spring in his step, march down the gangplank onto the deck. He even saw me, and smiled, and bowed ironically in my direction before disappearing below. I did not wait to see the boat get under way, but took a carriage back to my house, and left for Oxford only after I had heard from the captain of the vessel himself that Cola, and his luggage, had been tipped into the water some fifteen miles away from the shore and in such heavy weather that he could not have survived for long. Even though my revenge was complete, it brought me little satisfaction and it took many months before anything of my old calm returned. My happiness never did.

Eventually Mr. Bennet, now Lord Arlington, insisted on my services again; my reluctance and distaste proved no defense against his desires. In the months in between much had happened. The alliance of Clarendon's and Bennet's interests held long enough for both to accomplish their aims. Faced with the destruction of his plan of murder, the open rumor that in due course Lord Clarendon's daughter would sit on the throne of England, and the constant harassment of his people, Bristol hazarded all and tried to impeach the chancellor of treason in Parliament. It excited nothing but ridicule and contempt, and Bennet dissociated himself from the move; what assurances of support he had given Bristol in advance to tempt him into action I do not know. His Majesty was so offended by the attempt to force the removal of his minister that he exiled Bristol to the continent. Clarendon's position was strengthened, and Bennet received his reward by adopting as his own many of Bristol's family. More importantly, the prospect of a Spanish alliance received a mortal blow and was never mooted again.

The understanding between the two men could not last long; both of them knew that, and all the world knows how it ended. Lord Clarendon, as good a servant as a king ever had, was eventually forced into exile himself, confronting from his poverty in France the ingratitude of his king, the cruelty of his comrades, and the open avowal of Catholicism by his daughter. Bennet rose to take his place and ultimately he too fell from power, toppled by another, as he had toppled Clarendon. Such is politics, and such are politicians.

But for a while at least my efforts safeguarded the kingdom; the discontented, though well funded from Spain, could achieve nothing when faced by a government undistracted by division. I am still constantly aware, so many years later, of the terrible cost of this triumph.

All was caused by my desire to punish the man who had brought me such sorrow. And now I discover that this man, whom I hated as much as I loved Matthew, eluded my grasp and escaped my wrath. I performed ignoble deeds and even so was frustrated of my revenge. I know in my heart that I was betrayed, as the captain of that vessel who told me plain he had seen Cola drown would not have dared lie to me unless he was frightened of another more powerful still.

But I do not know who took these decisions to spare Cola and hide it from me, nor yet why they were taken. Nor do I have much chance now of discovering: Thurloe, Bristol, Clarendon, they are all dead; Bennet sulks in his gloomy retirement and talks to no man. Lower and Prestcott manifestly do not know, and I cannot imagine Mr. Cola will deign to enlighten me. The only person I have not talked to is that man Wood, but I am certain he knows little except scraps and details of no significance.

I have never disguised what I have done, though I have never advertised my deeds either. I would not have done so now, but for the arrival of this manuscript. What I have done, I own. At least events proved me correct in all substance. Even those who would criticize me must take this into account: had I not acted, Clarendon would have died and the country might well have been consumed once more. That fact, and that alone, more than justifies all I did, the injuries I suffered and those which I imposed on others.

And yet, though I know this to be true, the memory of that girl has begun to haunt me. It was a sin to wash my hands of her and stay quiet while she was condemned to death. I have known it always but never accepted it before now. I was tricked by Thurloe into that dreadful deed, and was motivated solely by my desire for justice and always thought this excuse enough.

All is known to the highest Judge of all and to Him I must entrust my soul, knowing that I have served Him to the best of my ability in all my acts.

But often now, late at night when I lie sleepless in my bed once more, or when I am deep in the frustration of prayers which no longer come, I fear my only hope of salvation is that His mercy will prove greater than was mine.

I no longer believe it will.

An Instance of the Fingerpost

When in a Search of any Nature the Understanding stands suspended, then Instances of the Fingerpost shew the true and inviolable Way in which the Question is to be decided. These Instances afford great Light, so that the Course of the Investigation will sometimes be terminated by them. Sometimes, indeed, these Instances are found amongst that Evidence already set down.

—FRANCIS BACON,
NOVUM ORGANUM SCIENTARUM,
SECTION XXXVI, APHORISM XXI.

chapter one

A FEW WEEKS AGO, MY OLD FRIEND DICK LOWER sent me this huge pile of paper, saying that, as I am a voracious collector of curios and suchlike, perhaps I should have it. For himself, he was tempted to throw it all away, such were the lies and sad contradictions it contained. He said (in a letter, for he has now retired to Dorset, where he lives in considerable ease) that he found the manuscripts wearisome. Two men, it seems, can see the same event, yet both remember it falsely. How, he went on, will we ever reach certainty on anything, even when of good will? He pointed out several instances in which he was a direct participant and said they had occurred in an entirely different fashion. Naturally, one is the extraordinary attempt to decant new blood into Widow Blundy through a goose quill, which Signor Cola claims as his own. Lower (whom I know to be a very honest man) disputes this account entirely.

He mentions two men, you note, Cola and Wallis, though there be three manuscripts. Naturally, he omits entirely that of Jack Prestcott, as he is bound to do. The law cannot punish and indeed takes no note of a man who is insane; if his current actions are beyond reason, how can his memories be trusted? They are merely the babblings of disorder, filtered through the distortions of disease. Prestcott's sad mind has thus transformed Bedlam into his great house; his head is not shaved for his wig as he says, but to allow the application of vinegar to his frenzy; those poor wretches who restrain the lunatics become his servants, and the many visitors he complains of are those characters who pay their penny every Saturday to peer through the iron bars of the cages, and laugh at the madmen in their distress. I have done it myself, on the occasion recently when I went to talk to Prestcott on the matter, but I found no diversion or satisfaction in it.

But several of Prestcott's statements are true. I know it and admit it, even though I have no cause to love him. He went mad, Lower tells me, when he was confronted with proof that his own malice had frustrated all his hopes and efforts, and that the warnings he had received from that Irishman were true after all. Perhaps so; my point is that, up to then, he was more or less sane and so perhaps his recollections are as well, even if the meaning he drags from them is entirely false. It requires intelligence, after all, to present a case as he does: had he kept his wits he might have been a fine advocate after all. Every single person he talked to told him that his father was guilty, and he was. With the greatest of skill he points to evidence of innocence, and ignores all that which suggests the true depths of his father's turpitude. At the end, I almost believed him, even though I knew better than most that it was a tissue of nonsense.

But is the poor soul's account any the less trustworthy than the others, which are also twisted and distorted, albeit by different passions? Prestcott may be mad, but Cola is a liar. Perhaps there is but one lie of commission, in contrast to all the omissions and evasions which might otherwise be discounted. He lies nonetheless, for as Ammian says, *Veritas vel silentio consumpitur vel mendacio*; truth is violated by silence and by falsehood. The falsity is contained in such an innocuous sentence it is not surprising that even Wallis overlooked it. But it distorts every other thing in the manuscript and makes truthful words false because, like a schoolman's argument, it draws conclusions with impeccable logic from a false premise. "*Marco da Cola, gentleman of Venice, respectfully presents his greetings.*" So he begins, and from there on every word must be considered carefully. Even the manuscript's existence must be considered, for why did he write it at all after so many years? On the other hand, to say he is mendacious does not mean that the motives and deeds attributed to him by Wallis are correct. The Venetian was not at all what he seemed, nor what he claims now to be, but he certainly never had designs on the safety of the kingdom or the life of Lord Clarendon. And Wallis himself was so used to living in the dark and sinister world of his own devising that he could no longer tell truth from invention, or honesty from falsehood.

But how can I tell which assertion to believe, and which to reject? I cannot repeat the same events time and again with subtle variations as Stahl did with his chemicals to demonstrate how Dr. Grove had died. Even if I could, the infallible philosophical method seems inadequate when it comes to problems in which motion derives from people rather than dead matter. I once attended a class on chemistry given by Mr. Stahl and must say I emerged none the wiser. Lower's own experiments on blood transfusion first produced the belief that this was the greatest cure for all ills, and later (when many people in France had died) the *savants* decided that no, on the contrary, this was a fatal and inadmissible procedure. It cannot be both, gentlemen of philosophy. If you are right now, how were you so wrong before? How is it that when a man of God shifts his opinion it proves the weakness of his views, and when a man of science does so it demonstrates the value of his method? How is a mere chronicler such as myself to transmute the lead of inaccuracy in these papers into the gold of truth?

MY MAIN QUALIFICATION FOR COMMENTING ON THESE bundles is the disinterested state which is (we are told) the *primum mobile* of a balanced understanding: little of this has anything to do with me. Second, I think I can with justice claim a certain knowledge: I have lived my entire life in Oxford and know the city (as even my detractors admit) better than anyone else has ever done. Finally, of course, I knew all the actors in this drama; Lower was then my constant companion, as we ate together at least once a week at Mother Jean's; through him I met all the men of philosophy, including Signor Cola. I worked with Dr. Wallis for many years when he was the keeper of the university archives and I was their most assiduous frequenter. I even had the honor of discoursing with Mr. Boyle and once attended a levee in the presence of my Lord Arlington although, I regret to say, I did not have the opportunity of making my addresses to him.

More than this, I knew Sarah Blundy before her misfortune and (not being a man given to puzzles and conundrums) I will reveal my secret immediately. For I knew her after it as well, hanged, dissected and burned though she was. More, I think I am the only person who can give a proper accounting of those days, and show all the goodness which prompted such cruelty, and the providential grace that brought out such malice. On certain matters, I can appeal to Lower, for we share many secrets; but the crucial knowledge is mine alone, and I must convince on my own authority and by the dexterity of my words. Curiously, the less I am believed, the more certain I will be that I am correct. Mr. Milton set out in his great poem to justify the ways of God to men, as he says. He has not considered one question, however: perhaps God has forbidden men to know His ways, for if they did know the full extent of His goodness, and the magnitude of our rejection of it, they would be so disheartened they would abandon all hope of redemption, and die of grief.

I AM AN HISTORIAN, AND TO THIS TITLE I ADHERE DEspite critics who make out that I am what they term an antiquarian. I believe truth can come only from a solid foundation of fact, and I set myself from an early age to begin the task of building such a basis. I intend no grandiose schemes for the history of the world, mind; you cannot build a palace before you have leveled the ground. Rather, just as Mr. Plot has written (very finely) the natural history of our county, so I am engaged in its civil history. And what a deal there is! I thought it would take a few years of my life; now I see I will die an old man and the task will still be unfinished. I began (once an early intention of the priesthood had left me) by wishing to write about our late troubles during the siege, when the Parliament men first took the town, then cleansed the university of those less than perfectly in agreement with them. But I rapidly perceived that there was a nobler task awaiting me, and that the entire history of the university might vanish forever were it not safeguarded. So I abandoned my original work and began the greater one, even though I had amassed considerable material by that stage and publication would, undoubtedly, have gained me both the fame in the world and the patronage of the mighty which have forever eluded my grasp. However, I care not for this: *animus hominis dives, non arca appellari solet*; and if it be considered one of Tully's paradoxes to say that it is a man's mind, not his coffers, which confers richness, then that shows that the age of Rome was just as blind and corrupt as our own.

It was because of this earlier work that I met both Sarah Blundy and her mother, who will figure so much in my account. I had heard of Ned, the old woman's husband, several times in my travels through the documents and, although not a major figure in my tale of the siege, the passions he aroused excited my curiosity. A black-hearted villain, the devil's child, worse than a murderer, a man one shuddered to behold. A latter-day saint, one of the manifest elect, kind, soft-spoken and generous. Two extremes of opinion, and not much in between; they could not both be correct and I wished to resolve the contradiction. I knew that he took part in the mutiny of 1647, left the town when it was put down and, as far as I was concerned, left my story as well: I did not know then whether he was alive or dead. But he had taken a role in a matter which made something of a stir, and it seemed a pity to miss the opportunity of an eyewitness account (even that of a woman if I could not find the man himself) when I discovered, in the summer of 1659, that his family lived nearby.

I was apprehensive of the encounter: Anne Blundy had a reputation for being a wise woman (from those who did not dislike her) or a witch (from those less favorably inclined). Her daughter, Sarah, was known to be wild and strange but had not yet gained that reputation for skill in healing which led Mr. Boyle to wonder if any of her recipes could be used for the poor. I must say, however, that neither the pathetic description offered by Cola, nor the cruel one of Prestcott, do the old woman any justice. Even though she was near fifty, the fire in her eyes (communicated to her daughter as well) spoke of a lively soul. Wise she was perhaps, although not in the way normally meant: no muttering or shambling or obscure incantations. Shrewd, rather, I would say, with an air of amusement which mingled strangely with a deep (although heterodox) piety. Nothing I saw ever gave an indication of the murderous harpy of Wallis's tale, and yet I do believe that on this he speaks the truth. More than most, he has himself shown that we are all capable of the most monstrous evil when convinced we are right, and it was an age when the madness of conviction held all tightly in its grasp.

Gaining her confidence was no easy matter, and I am not convinced I ever won it entirely. Certainly, had I made my approach to her later, when her husband was dead and the king was back on his throne, she would inevitably have assumed I was sent to trap her, especially as I knew Dr. Wallis by then. Such a connection would have made her suspicious, as she had no cause to love the new government, and especial reason to fear Wallis. Understandably so: I learned soon enough to fear him myself.

Then, however, I had not yet had my introduction to the man, Richard Cromwell was still holding on to power by his fingertips and the king was in the Spanish Netherlands, eager for his inheritance but not daring to grasp it. The country was stirring and it seemed that the armies would soon be on the march once more. My own house was searched for arms that spring, as was that of everyone I knew. We had only sporadic news of the world in Oxford and the more I have talked to people over the years, the more I realize that in fact virtually no one knew what was going on. Except for John Thurloe, of course, who knew and saw everything. But even he fell from power, swept away by forces which, for once, he could not control. Take that as proof of how distempered the country was in those days.

There was little point in approaching Anne Blundy politely. I could not, for example, write her a letter introducing myself as I had no reason to assume that she might be able to read. I had little choice but to walk to her lodgings and knock on the door, which was opened by a girl of perhaps seventeen who was, I believe, the prettiest thing I had ever seen in my life: a fine figure (if a little thin), a full set of teeth and a complexion unblemished by illness. Her hair was dark, which was a disadvantage, and although she wore it loose and largely uncovered she still dressed modestly and I do think that, had she been attired in sackcloth, it would have seemed a wonderfully becoming garment in my eyes. Above all, it was her eyes which fascinated, for they were the deepest black, like raven's wings, and it is known that of all colors, black is the most amiable in a woman. "Black eyes as if from Venus," says Hesiod of his Alcmena, while Homer calls Juno ox-eyed, because of her round, black eyes, and Baptista Porta (in his *Physiognomia*) sneers at the gray-eyed English, and joins with Morison in lauding the deep glances of languorous Neapolitan ladies.

I stared awhile, quite forgetting my reason for calling, until she politely but not with servility, distantly but not with impudence, asked me my business. "Please come in, sir," she said, when I told her. "My mother is out at the market; but she should be back any moment. You are welcome to wait, if you wish."

I leave it to others to decide whether I should have taken that as a warning about her character. Had I been with someone better stationed I would naturally have gone away, not wishing to presume on her reputation by being alone with her. But at that moment, the chance of talking to this creature seemed to me the best possible way of passing the time until the mother returned. I am sure I half wished that the woman might be greatly delayed. I sat myself (I fear with something of a swagger, as a man of parts might do when associating with inferiors, God forgive me) on the little stool by the fireplace, which unfortunately was empty, despite the cold.

How do people converse in such situations? I have never succeeded in a matter which others seem to find simple. Perhaps it is the result of too many hours spent in books and manuscripts. Most of the time I had no trouble at all; with my friends over dinner, I could converse with the best of them and I pride myself still that I was not the least interesting. But in some circumstances I was at a loss, and making conversation to a serving girl with beautiful eyes was beyond my powers. I could have tried playing the gallant, chucking her under the chin, sitting her on my knee and pinching her bottom, but that has never been my way, and most obviously was not hers either. I could have ignored her as not worth my attention, except that she was. So I ended up doing neither, staring at her dumbly, and had to leave it to her.

"You have come to consult my mother on some trouble, no doubt," she prompted after she had waited for me to begin a conversation.

"Yes."

"Perhaps you have lost something, and want her to divine where it is? She is good at that. Or maybe you are sick, and are afraid of going to a doctor?"

Eventually, I dragged my eyes away from her face. "Oh, no. Not at all. I have heard of her great skills, of course, but I am most meticulous and never lose anything. A place for everything, you know. That is the only way I can proceed in my work. And my health is as good as man might expect, thanks to God."

Babbling and pompous; I excuse myself by pleading confusion. She assuredly had not the slightest interest in my work; few people have. But it has always been my refuge in times of trouble, and when confused or sad my thoughts fly to it. Toward the end of this affair, I sat up at nights, week after week, transcribing and annotating, as a way of shutting the world out. Locke told me it was for the best. Strange, that: I never liked him, and he never liked me, but I always took his advice, and found it answered.

"Amen," she said. "So why have you come to see my mother? I hope you are not betrayed in love. She does not approve of philters and such nonsense, you know. If you want that sort of foolishness, you can go to a man in Heddington, although personally I think he is a charlatan."

I reassured her that my quest was entirely different, and that I did not wish to consult her mother on any such business. I was beginning to explain when the door opened and the woman returned. Sarah rushed to assist, as her mother collapsed on a trestle stool opposite, wiped her face and got her breath back before she peered at me. She was poorly but cleanly dressed, with gnarled hands strong from years of labor, and a red, round open face. Although age was beginning to gain its inevitable triumph, in her manner she was far from the desolate, broken bird of a woman she later became, and moved with a sprightliness that many others more favored in life do not have at her age.

"Nothing wrong with you," she said forthrightly after gazing at me in a way which seemed to see me entire. Her daughter had the habit as well, I later learned. I think it was that which made people frightened of them, and consider them insolent. "What are you here for?"

"This is Mr. Wood, Mother," Sarah said as she came back from the tiny room next door. "He is an historian, so he has been telling me, and wishes to consult you."

"And what ailments afflict historians, pray?" she said with little interest. "Loss of memory? Crabbed writing hand?"

I smiled. "Both of those, but not in my case, I am pleased to say. No; I am writing a history of the siege, and as you were here during that period . . ."

"So were several thousand other people. Are you going to talk to them all? A strange way of writing history, that."

"I model myself on Thucydides . . ." I began ponderously.

"And he died before he could finish," she interrupted, a comment which surprised me so much I almost fell off my stool. Quite apart from the speed of her riposte, she had evidently not only heard of that greatest of historians, she even knew something about him. I looked at her more curiously, but evidently failed to disguise my astonishment.

"My husband is a great book man, sir, and takes pleasure in reading to me, and getting me to read to him of an evening."

"He is here?"

"No; he is still with the army. I believe he is in London."

I was disappointed, of course, but resolved to make do with what I could discover from the wife until such time as Blundy himself might return.

"Your husband," I began, "was of some significance in the history of the town . . ."

"He tried to combat injustice here."

"Indeed. The trouble is that no one I have come across

seems to agree on what he did and said. This is what I want to know.''

"And you will believe what I tell you?"

"I will set what you tell me against what other people tell me. From that the truth will emerge. I am convinced of it."

"In that case you are a foolish young man, Mr. Wood."

"I think not," I said stiffly.

"What are your religious persuasions, sir? Your loyalties?"

"In religion, I am an historian. In politics, an historian as well."

"Much too slippery for an old woman like me," she said with a slightly mocking tone in her voice. "Are you loyal to the Protector?"

"I took an oath to the government in power."

"And what church do you attend?"

"Several. I have attended services in many places. At present, I attend at Merton, as I am bound to do since it is my college. I must tell you, I suppose, lest you accuse me again of being slippery, that I am of an Episcopal instinct."

Her head bowed in thought as she considered this, her eyes closed, almost as though asleep. I feared very much that she would refuse, thinking that I would twist what she said. Certainly she had no reason to think that I would be in any way sympathetic to a man like her husband; I knew enough of him already to be sure of that. But there was nothing more I could do to persuade her of my honorable intentions. Fortunately, I was not stupid enough to offer her money, as that would inevitably have been my downfall, however much she needed it. I must say here that never once did I discern in her, or her daughter, any of the greed which others claim to have seen so easily, although her poor situation would have been ample cause for it.

"Sarah?" she said after a while, her head lifting from her chest. "What do you think of this angular young man? What is he? A spy? A fool? A knave? Someone come to disinter the past and torment us with it?"

"Perhaps he is what he says, mother. I think you might talk to him. Why not? The Lord knows what happened, and even an historian from the university cannot hide the truth from Him."

"Clever, child: a pity our friend here did not think of it himself. Very well," she said. "We must talk again. But I have a customer soon who has lost the deeds of his house and I must divine their whereabouts. You must come back another day. Tomorrow, if you wish."

I thanked her for her kindness, and promised that I would be there the next day, without fail. I was conscious that I was treating her with unnecessary deference, but something prompted me to act so: her person demanded courtesy, though her station did not. As I was picking my way through the debris and puddles in the street outside, I was stopped by a whistle behind me, and, as I looked around, I saw Sarah running after me.

"A word, Mr. Wood."

"By all means," I said, half noticing my pleasure at the prospect. "Do you object to taverns?" This was a normal enquiry in those days, as many of the more obscure dissenters did so object, and very strongly. It was best to find out who you were dealing with early on, for fear of bringing down a heap of abuse.

"Oh no," she said. "Taverns I like." I would have led her to the Fleur-de-Lys, that belonging to my family and a place where I could have drink cheaply, but I was concerned for my reputation so instead we went to another place, a low hovel scarcely better than her own dwelling. I noticed that she was not treated with friendliness when we entered. Indeed, I had the feeling sharp words might have been exchanged had I not been there. Instead, all the woman gave me, along with the two tankards, was a sneering smile. The words were polite, the sentiment they hid was not, although I could not make it out. Though I had nothing to be ashamed of, I found myself blushing. The girl, alas, noticed and wryly commented on my discomfort.

"Not at all," I said hastily.

"It's all right. I've had worse." She even had the tact to lead the way to the quietest corner of the place, so that no one would see us. I was grateful for this consideration, and warmed to her for it.

"Now, Mr. Historian," the girl said when she had drunk a quarter of her pot, "you must tell me frankly. Do you mean well by us? Because I will not have you causing us more trouble. My mother needs no more. She is tired and has found some peace in the last few years, and I do not want that disturbed."

I tried to reassure her on this point: my object was to describe the long siege, and the effect that the quartering of troops on the city had had on learning. Her father's role in the mutiny, and in stirring up the passions of the parliamentary troops, was of significance, whatever it was, but not critical: all I wanted to know was why the troops had refused their orders then, and what had happened. I hoped to set all that down before it was forgotten.

"But you were here yourself, weren't you?"

"I was, but I was only fourteen at the time and too busy at my studies to notice anything untoward. I remember being mightily displeased when New College school was turned out of its room by the cloister, and I remember thinking that I had never seen a soldier before. I remember standing near the outworks, hoping I could pour boiling oil on someone, hoping to perform deeds of valor and be knighted by a grateful monarch. And I remember how frightened everybody was at the surrender. But all the important facts, I do not know. You cannot write a book based on such paltry material."

"You want facts? Most people are content to make up their own. That's what they did with Father. They said he was turbulent and wicked, and abused him for it. Their judgment does not satisfy you?"

"Maybe it will. Maybe it is even correct. But I ask myself questions, nonetheless. How did such a man come to be trusted by so many of his fellows? If he was so verminous, how was he also courageous? Can the noble (if I may use the term for such a person) coexist with the ignoble? And how did he"—here I made my first ever venture into gallantry—"how did he have such a beautiful daughter?"

If she was pleased by the comment, there was no sign of it, alas. No modest look, no pretty blush, just those black eyes staring intently at me, making me feel more ill at ease.

"I am determined," I continued, covering over my little

essay, "to discover what transpired. You ask whether I mean you ill or well, and I tell you I mean you neither."

"Then you are immoral."

"The truth is always moral, because it is the image of God's Word," I corrected her, feeling, yet again, that I was misspeaking myself and hiding behind solemnity. "I will give your father his say. He will not get it from anyone else, you know. He either speaks through me, or is forever mute."

She finished off her tankard, and shook her head sadly. "Poor man, who talks so beautifully, to be reduced to speaking through you."

I do believe she was entirely unconscious of the insult: but I had no desire at that moment to rebuff her by giving the reprimand she deserved. Instead, I looked at her attentively, thinking that this initial confidence might at least get her to speak well of me to her mother.

"I remember once," she continued after a while, "hearing him addressing his platoon after a prayer meeting. I can't have been more than nine, I suppose, so it would have been around the time of Worcester. They thought they would be fighting soon, and he was encouraging and calming them. It was like music; he had them swaying to and fro as he spoke, and some were in tears. Possibly they would die, or be captured, or end their lives in jail. That was the will of God and it was not for us to presume to guess what that was. He had given us only one lantern to discern His goodness, and that was our sense of justice, the voice of Right which spoke to all men in their souls if they would listen. Those who examined their hearts knew what the Right was, and knew that if they fought for it, they would be fighting for God. It was a battle to lay the foundation of making the earth a common treasury for all, so that everyone born in the land might be fed by the earth, all looking on others, even old, sick or female, as equals in creation. As they slept and ate, and fought and died, they should remember that."

I didn't know what to say. She had spoken softly and gently, her voice caressing me as she spoke the words of her father; so quiet, so kind and, I realized with a start, so profoundly evil. I began, very faintly, to understand how it was done and what the appeal of this Blundy was. If a mere girl could be so seductive, what must the man have been like? The right to eat: no good Christian could object. Until you realize that what this man desired was the overturning of the right of masters to command their employees, the theft of property from its owners, the hacking at the very roots of the harmony which binds each to all. Quietly and kindly, Blundy took these poor ignorants by the hand, and led them into the power of the devil himself. I shuddered. Sarah looked at me with a faint smile.

"The raving of a lunatic, you think, Mr. Wood?"

"How can anyone who is neither a fool nor a monster think otherwise? It is obviously so."

"Coming from a family of lunatics, I see things a little differently," she said. "I suppose you think my father used ordinary people for his own evil ends. Is that it?"

"Something like that," I said stiffly. "That it was devilish was attested by the eating of babies and burning of prisoners."

She laughed. "Eating babies? Burning prisoners? What liar said that?"

"I read it. And many people have said so."

"And so you believed it. I am beginning to doubt you, Mr. Historian. If you read there are beasts in the sea that breathe fire and have a hundred heads, do you believe that too?"

"Not unless I have good reason to."

"And what does a learned man like yourself account a good reason?"

"The proof of my own eyes, or the report of someone whose word can be trusted. But it depends on what you mean. I know that the sun exists, because I can see it; I believe that the earth goes around it because logical calculation concludes that, and it is not contradicted by what I can see. I know that unicorns exist because such a creature is possible in nature and reliable people have seen one, even though I have not myself; it is unlikely that fire-breathing dragons with a hundred heads exist because I cannot see how a natural creature can breathe fire without being consumed. So it all depends, you see."

Such was my answer and I still think it was a good response, presenting complicated ideas in a simple way for her benefit, although I thought it unlikely she would understand. But, far from being grateful for my instruction, she continued to pursue me, leaning forward in her eagerness to dispute like a starving beggar who had been offered a crust.

"Jesus is our Lord. Do you believe that?"

"Yes."

"Why?"

"Because His coming was in conformity to the predictions of the Bible, His miracles proved His divinity and His resurrection proved it still more."

"Many people claim such miracles."

"And in addition I have faith, and hold that to be better than all reason."

"A more earthly question, then. The king is God's anointed. Do you believe that?"

"If you mean, can I prove it, then no," I replied, determined to keep my distance. "That is not a certain belief. But I do believe it, because kings have their position, and when they are thrown off the natural order is disturbed. God's displeasure with England has surely been manifest in past years, in the suffering it has borne. And when the king was murdered, did not enormous floods demonstrate the disruption of nature that had taken place?"

She conceded this obvious point, but added: "But if I said these prodigies were because the king had acted traitorously to his subjects?"

"Then I would disagree with you."

"And how would we decide who was correct?"

"It would depend on the weight of opinion of reasonable men of position and character who heard both propositions. I do not wish to belabor it or give undue reproof, but you cannot be called of position and character. Nor," and here I made another attempt to switch the conversation to a more appropriate topic, "nor could someone so pretty ever be mistaken for a man."

"Oh," she said, dismissing my kindly warning to mind her own business with a toss of her head, "so whether the king is appointed by God, or justly a king at all, depends on the decisions of men? Is there a vote?"

"No," I said, slightly flushed at finding myself apparently unable to halt this increasingly ridiculous encounter, "that's not what I'm saying, you ignorant girl. God alone decides that; men merely decide whether to accept God's will."

"What's the difference if we do not know what God's will is?"

It was time to bring this to an end, so I stood up to give her a physical reminder, so to speak, of our respective positions.

"If you can ask questions like that," I said sternly, "then you are a very foolish and wicked child. You must have had a very perverted upbringing indeed even to think of such things. I am beginning to see that your father is as evil as they say."

Instead of being sobered by my reproof, she leaned back on her stool and let out a peal of laughter. Very angry now at being answered back in such a way, I left her, feeling a little shaken, and took refuge in my books and notes for the rest of the morning. It was merely the first of many occasions when she reduced me to such a display of foolishness. Do I have to say again that I was young? Does that excuse the way her eyes fuddled my thoughts, and the fall of her hair tripped my tongue?

chapter two

I INTEND TO BREAK MY OWN RULE ABOUT PROPRIETY, and talk much of Sarah Blundy: it is necessary. I do not intend to cause distress by libertine discourse on matters of the heart, a subject which, as all but courtiers know, does not belong on the public page. But there is no other way of explaining my interest in the family, my concern over her fate, and my knowledge of her end. I must be regarded as a competent witness where my personal recollection is important, and therefore must provide proof of my knowledge. Words without fact are suspect: so I must provide the facts. They are simply stated.

At that time the Wood family was still in funds, and I lived in a house on Merton Street with my mother and sister, in which I kept the top floor for myself and my books. We needed a servant, as sluttishness had forced my dear mother to discharge the one we had, and I (having discerned the Blundys were in sore straits) suggested Sarah. My mother was far from happy about the idea, knowing something of ithe family's reputation, but I persuaded her that she would be cheap, having resolved that I would make up her wages myself out of my small competence. Besides, I asked, what was so terrible about her? To this she had no specific answer.

Eventually, the thought of saving a ha' penny a week brought my mother around; she consented to interview the girl and (reluctantly) conceded that she did indeed seem properly modest and obedient. But she let it be known that she intended to watch the girl like a hawk, and at the first sniff of blasphemy or sedition or immorality she would be out the door.

And so she and I were brought into close proximity, hindered, naturally, by the necessary distance that must exist between master and servant. Though she was no ordinary servant: indeed, she soon achieved an ascendancy in the house which was all the more remarkable for being largely uncontested. Only once was battle joined, when my mother decided (there being no man in the house except me, and my mother always regarding herself as the head of the household) to give the girl a beating, expecting that the child would submit placidly to her chastisement, as she ought. I do not know what the offense was, probably very little, and my mother's irritability was more likely due to the pain she received from a swollen ankle that had afflicted her for several years.

Sarah did not think this was a good enough reason. Hands on hips, blazing with defiance, she refused to bend. When my mother advanced on her, broom in hand, she made it clear that if my mother so much as laid a finger on her, she would thrash her back. Thrown out the house instantly, you might think? Not a bit of it. I wasn't there at the time, otherwise the incident might never have occurred, but my sister said that within half an hour, Sarah and my mother were both sitting in front of the fire talking, with my mother almost apologizing to the child, a sight never witnessed before or since. Thereafter, my mother said not a word against her and, when Sarah's time of trouble came, it was she who cooked food for her and took it to the prison.

What had happened? What did Sarah say or do which made my mother so charitable and generous for once? I did not know. When I asked, Sarah just smiled, and said that my mother was a good and kind woman who was not as fierce as she seemed. More than that she would not tell, and my mother said nothing either. She always grew secretive when caught out in a kindness, and it may be that it was simply that, shortly after, her ankle stopped giving her pain: it is often the case that simple things like this can bring remarkable changes in demeanor. I often wonder if Dr. Wallis would have been less cruel had he been less afraid of the blindness that began to creep up on him in this time. I myself have been unreasonably offensive to my fellows when blighted by toothache, and it is well known that the mistaken decisions that ultimately led to the fall of Lord Clarendon were taken when that nobleman was wracked with the agonizing pain of the gout.

I mentioned that I occupied two rooms on the top floor, from which other members of my family were excluded. I had books and papers everywhere, and was constantly afraid that someone, in a misguided act of kindness, would tidy them up and set my work back by months. Sarah was the only person I allowed in and even she tidied up only under my supervision. I came to dream of those visits to my scholarly aerie and, more and more, I passed time in conversation with her. My room got dirtier and dirtier, it is true, but I found myself waiting eagerly for the tread of her footsteps on the rickety stair that led to my attic. Initially, I would talk about her mother; but that soon became a pretense to prolong her presence. Even more so, perhaps, because I knew little of the world and less of women.

Perhaps any female would have interested me, but Sarah quickly had me entranced. Slowly the pleasure turned to pain, and the joy to anguish. The devil came to visit me at all hours; at night, while I was at my desk working, in the library, turning my mind from my work and leading me on to foul and lubricious thoughts. My sleep suffered, my work also and, although I prayed mightily for help, there was no answer. I begged the Lord to spare me this temptation, but in His wisdom He would not, but allowed instead ever more demons to come and taunt me with my weakness and hypocrisy. I woke in the morning thinking of Sarah, spent the day thinking of Sarah, and tossed myself to sleep at night, thinking of Sarah. And even when I slept there was no respite, for I dreamed of her eyes and her mouth and the way she laughed.

It was intolerable, of course: no respectable connection was possible, so great was the distance between us. But I thought I knew enough of her to believe she would never consent to be my harlot; she was too virtuous, no matter what her origins. I had never been in love, nor even shown half as much interest in a woman as in the least of the books in the Bodleian library, and I confess that I cursed God in my heart that, when I did fall (and the similarity with the fate of Adam I never felt so strongly), it was with an impossibility, a girl of no fortune or family, scorned even in taverns, and with a villain for a father.

And so I remained tongue-tied and miserable: anguished when she was there, worse when she was not. Would that I had been a robust, thoughtless man like Prestcott, who never bothered with the complexities of affection, or even like Wallis, with a heart so cold that no human being could warm it for long. Sarah, I believe, was not without affection for me either: although always respectful in my presence, I still felt something in her: a warmth, the way she looked and leaned forward as I showed her a book or a manuscript which indicated some regard. I think she liked talking to me; she was used to masculine conversation because of her father, who had instructed her, and she was hard put to confine her mind to topics suitable for women. As I was always ready to talk about my work, and was easily distracted into discussing anything else, she seemed to regard her visits to clean my quarters with as much eagerness as I did myself. I think I was the only man then who spoke to her for some reason other than to give her orders or make lewd remarks; I can find no other explanation. Her childhood, her upbringing and her father, however, remained something of a blank to me; she rarely spoke of them except on those occasions when a chance remark slipped from her lips; when I asked directly she generally changed the subject. I hoarded these occasional comments like a miser hoards his gold, remembering each chance phrase, and turning them over in my mind, adding each to each, like coin in a casket, until I had a good supply.

Initially I thought her reticence due to shame at the degradation to which she had descended; now I think it merely caution, lest it be misunderstood. She was ashamed of little and regretted less, but accepted that the days when people like her might hope of a new world were over: they had tried and failed miserably. I will give one important example of how I garnered my evidence. Shortly after the Restoration of His Majesty was proclaimed in the town, I came back from viewing the preparations for the festivities. Celebrations erupted all over the land that day, both from Parliament towns which felt the need to demonstrate their new loyalty, and from towns like Oxford which were able to rejoice with more genuine feeling. We were promised (by whom I cannot recall) that the fountains and gutters themselves would run with joyous wine that night, as in the days of ancient Rome. I found Sarah, sitting on my stool and weeping her heart out.

"Whatever is the matter, that you sob so on a glorious day like this?" I cried. It was some time before I got an answer.

"Oh, Anthony, it is not glorious for me," she said. (This being our secret intimacy, that I permitted her to address me so in my room). Initially, I had thought that she had one of those mysterious womanly complaints, but quickly realized that grander matters were on her mind. She was never immodest or gross in her talk.

"But what is there to be so sorrowful about? It is a fine morning, we can drink and feed at the university's expense, and the king is coming back to his own."

"And everything has been in vain," she said. "Does so much waste not make you want to weep, even as you celebrate? Near twenty years of fighting trying to build God's kingdom here, and it is all swept away by the will of a few greedy grandees."

Now, to refer thus to those great men whose wise intervention had been crucial to the recall of the king (so we were told and I believed until I read Wallis's manuscript) should have alerted me, but I was in too good a mood.

"God works in mysterious ways," I said cheerfully, "and sometimes chooses strange instruments to work His will."

"God has spat in the face of His servants who worked for Him," she said, her voice falling into a hiss of despair and rage.

"How can it be God's will? How can God will that some men be subject to others? That some live in palaces while others die in the street? That some rule and others obey? How can God will that?"

I shrugged, not knowing what to say or how to begin saying it, just wanting her to stop. I had never seen her like this, clutching at herself and rocking to and fro as she spoke with a passion that was as disgusting as it was fascinating. She frightened me, but I could not walk away from her. "He obviously does," I said eventually.

"In that case He is no God of mine," she said, with a sneer of contempt. "I hate Him, as He must hate me and all of His creation."

I stood up. "I think this has gone far enough," I said, appalled at what she was saying and alarmed that someone downstairs might overhear. "I will not have this sort of talk in my house. Remember who you are, girl."

Thus earning from her a scornful look of contempt, the first time I had so totally and instantly lost her affections. I felt it deeply, being distressed at her blasphemy but even then more pained by my loss.

"Oh, Mr. Wood, I am just beginning to guess," she said and walked straight out, not even doing me the honor of slamming the door. I, my good humor gone and strangely unable to recover my concentration, spent the rest of the afternoon on my knees, praying desperately for relief.

THE LOYAL CELEBRATION THAT EVENING WAS EVERY-thing that good Royalists could have hoped for: town and university vied with each other to be the more zealously loyal. Starting with my habitual friends (I had by that time made the acquaintance of Lower and his circle), we drank our fill of wine at the fountain in Carfax, ate beef at Christ Church, then proceeded to more wine and delicacies at Merton. It was a delightful occasion, or should have been; but Sarah's mood had affected me, and taken away my joy. There was dancing, which I merely watched; singing, where I was without song; speech-making and toast-giving, where I kept my silence. Food for all, and myself without appetite. How could anyone not be happy on a day like this? Above all someone like me, who had hoped for His Majesty's return for so long? I did not understand myself, was desolate, and not good company.

"What is it, old friend?" asked Lower, pounding me merrily on the back as he came back breathless from a dance, already slightly the worse for drink. I pointed at a thin-faced man, dead drunk in the gutter, saliva dripping down his chin.

"See," I said. "Do you remember? For fifteen years one of the elect, persecuting loyalty and applauding fanaticism. And now look. One of the king's most devoted subjects."

"And soon to be thrown out of his places as he deserves. Allow him a bit of oblivion for his troubles."

"You think? I don't. Some people always survive. He is one."

"Oh, you are an old misery, Wood," Lower said with a great grin. "This is the greatest day in history, and you are all sour-faced and glum. Come, have another drink and forget about it. Or someone might think you a secret Anabaptist."

And so I did, and another, and another. Eventually Lower and the others wandered off, and I couldn't be bothered chasing after them; their simple (to my mind) good humor and careless pleasure made me melancholy to tears. I wandered back to Carfax, which was a fateful thing to do. For as I got there, and helped myself all alone to another cup of wine, I heard a cackle of laughter from a side street; normal enough that evening, except this time there was that slight but unmistakable edge of menace which is difficult to describe and impossible to miss. Made curious by the sound, I peered down the alley and saw a group of young oafs gathered in a semicircle against a wall. They were laughing and shouting, and I half expected to find in the center of the crowd some charlatan or raree man whose wares and tricks had failed to please. But instead it was Sarah, her hair astray, her eyes wild, her back against the wall, and they were taunting her mercilessly. Harlot, they said. Traitor's bastard. Witch's daughter.

Bit by bit they were working themselves up, taking a little step further each time, edging toward the point when words ceased and assault began. She saw me, and our eyes met, but there was no entreaty in them; rather she bore it all herself, almost not seeming to notice the foul words hurled at her. Almost as though she wasn't listening, and did not care. She might not want help, but I knew she needed it, and knew no one but myself would lift a finger for her. I worked my way through the crowd, put my arm around her and pulled her out and back toward the main street, so quickly the mob hardly had time to react.

Fortunately it was not far; they did not like the theft of their entertainment and my status as scholar and historian would have served me little had the spot been any more isolated. But there were people drunk, but still civilized, only a few yards away, and I managed to get us close enough to safety before the insults erupted into actual violence. Then I pulled her through the cheerful, good-humored celebrations until, seeing their prey lost, the mob dissolved and went in search of other sport. I was breathing hard, and the fright and the drink made me slow to recover my wits. I'm afraid that physical danger is not something to which I am used; I emerged more shaken than Sarah.

She did not thank me, but just looked at me, with what seemed like resignation, or perhaps sadness. Then she shrugged and walked away. I followed; she walked faster, and so did I. I thought she was walking home, but at the end of Butcher's Row she turned and cut across the fields behind the castle, walking ever faster with myself now maddened by my beating heart, swirling head and confusion.

It was in the place called Paradise Fields, once the most beautiful of orchards and now fallen into a sad and infertile neglect, where she stopped and turned round. As I came up to her, she was laughing but with tears coming down her cheeks. I reached out for her, and she clutched hold of me as though hanging on to the only thing left in the entire world.

And, like Adam, in Paradise I sinned.

WHY ME? I DON'T KNOW. I HAD NOTHING TO OFFER HER, not money nor marriage, and she knew that. Perhaps I was gentler than others; perhaps I comforted her; perhaps she needed some warmth. I do not deceive myself that it was much more, but nor do I lower myself now to think that it was any less: perhaps no virgin, she was no harlot either. Prescott lied cruelly there; she was virtue itself and he was no gentleman to say otherwise. Afterward, when her tears had stopped, she got up, straightened her clothes and walked slowly off. This time I did not follow. The following day, she cleaned my mother's kitchen as though nothing had happened.

And I? Was that the Lord's answer to my entreaties? Was I sated and satisfied, the demons exorcised from my soul? No; my fever was stoked up even further, so that I could hardly bear to see her for fear that my trembling and pallor would give me away. I kept to my room, and alternated between sinful thoughts and atonement through prayer. By the time she came up to my room a few days later, I must have looked like a ghost, and I heard the familiar steps coming up the stairs with a mixture of terror and joy such as I have never experienced before or since. And so, of course, I was rude to her, and she played the servant with me, each settling into our roles like actors in a play, but all the time willing the other to say something.

Or at least I did; I do not know about her. I told her to tidy up better; she obeyed. I instructed her to lay a fire; she dutifully and without a word did as she was told. I told her to go away and leave me in peace; she picked up her bucket of water, and opened the door.

"Come back here," I said and she did that too. But I had nothing else to say to her. Or, rather, I had so much. So I went to embrace her, and she allowed me; standing upright and still, enduring a punishment.

"Please, sit down," I said, letting her go, and again she obeyed me.

"You ask me to stay, and to sit down," she began when I said nothing. "Do you have something to say to me?"

"I love you," I said in a rush. She shook her head.

"No," she said. "You do not. How can you?"

"But two days ago . . . Was that not something? Are you so coarse that it meant nothing to you?"

"Something, yes. But what would you have me do? Wilt in the despair of love? Become your woman, twice a week instead of cleaning? And you? Are you going to offer me your hand? Of course not. So what is there to be done or said?"

It was her practicality which maddened me; I wanted her to suffer as much as I, to rail against the unkindness of fate that so separated us, yet her robust common sense did not allow that.

"So what are you? You have had so many men that one more has no effect on you?"

"Many? Perhaps so, if that is what you want to think. But not as you mean; only ever for affection's sake, when I was given the choice."

I hated her for that frankness; had I taken her virtue, and had she been weeping with remorse at her fall in value, I would have understood and comforted her; I knew the words for that because I had read them somewhere. But to regard her loss as of so little moment, and to discover that it had not been given to me but to someone else was more than I could endure. Later, although I could never condone something so obviously in contradiction to God's word, I accepted it, as much as possible, for she was her own law. However much she might obey my orders, she would never be obedient.

"Anthony," she said gently, seeing my distress, "you are a good man, I think, and you try to be Christian. But I know what you have been doing. You see me as a fitting recipient of your charity. You want me to be good, and virtuous, at the same time that you want to roll with me in Paradise Fields before you go off and marry a woman with as much of an estate as you can find. Then you will convert me into a harlot who tempted you to sin while you were in drink, if that makes your prayers easier and gives your soul comfort."

"You think that of me?"

"I do. You manage easily enough when you are talking to me about your work. Then your eyes light up and you forget what I am, in your pleasure at talking. Then you treat me honestly, without foolishness or awkwardness. Only one person has ever done this before."

"And he was?"

"My father. And I have just learned that he is dead."

I felt a wave of compassion for her as I heard her words, and saw the sadness in her eyes; it was something I understood well, as I had lost my own father when I was scarcely ten, and I knew well how painful it is to be brushed by such grief. I felt even more sad when she told me the details, for she was told (cruelly and falsely, it now seems) that her father had been killed when going back to his old habits of disobedience and troublemaking.

The details were unclear, and likely to remain so; the army was never punctilious about giving details to the families in such cases. But it seemed then that Ned Blundy's agitations had finally become too much: he was arrested, given a military trial, and hanged forthwith, the body cast into an unmarked grave. The courage of his last moments, which Thurloe knew of, and Wallis discovered, was concealed from the family even though they would have taken great solace in it. Even worse, neither Sarah nor her mother were told where he rested, and did not even discover for some months that it had happened.

I sent her home to be with her mother, and told my own that she was not well. She appreciated the kindness, I think, but presented herself again the next morning, and never mentioned the matter again. Her mourning and grief she kept entirely within her and only I, who knew her better than most, caught the occasional glimpse of a distant sadness as she worked.

THUS MY LOVE FOR THE GIRL HAD ITS BIRTH, AND MY misery should be talked of no more. I still waited eagerly for her twice a week so that I could talk to her and, for a while, she went with me on occasion to Paradise Fields. No one ever knew of this, and my discretion was not because I was ashamed to consort with her; it was too precious to be the occasion of laughter in a tavern. I know how other people consider me; the ridicule of my fellows, even those I have helped, is a cross I have borne all my life. Cola, in his manuscript, repeats the remarks of Locke and even Lower, both of whom were pleasant to my face, and whom I still count almost as friends. Prestcott took my help, and laughed behind my back, Wallis did the same. I would not tarnish my affections with the scorn of others, and my regard for that girl would certainly have excited great ridicule.

It was, in any case, only one part of my life; much of my time I continued with my work and, discouraged by my growing doubts about what I was doing, I found myself turning more and more to the collection of facts, no longer daring to say what they meant. My work on the siege languished, and I turned instead to memorials; facts carved in stone and brass, so that I could assemble a list of the most important families of the county back through the ages. It sounds commonplace now, but I was the first even to consider the idea.

And I wandered through all the archives, cataloguing manuscripts that no hand had touched for generations as a way of earning small money and making myself useful. For what are we but our past? If that is lost, we become nothing. Even though I had no immediate intention of making use of the material myself, it was my duty and my pleasure to ensure that others could do so, if they were so minded. All the libraries of Oxford were in a dreadful state, their most precious treasures neglected for decades as men had turned their minds to the passion of faction, and learned to despise the old wisdom because they could not read it afresh. In my small way, I preserved and catalogued, and dipped into the vast ocean of learning that awaited, knowing all the time that the life of one man was insufficient for even the smallest part of the wonders that lay within. It is cruel that we are granted the desire to know, but denied the time to do so properly. We all die frustrated; it is the greatest lesson we have to learn.

It was through work such as this that I met Dr. Wallis, as he was keeper of the university archives when I most needed access to them, even though, as professor, he should never have been allowed the post. Although I grant his methodical mind did impose some order on documents which had been sadly neglected for years, nonetheless I could have done better (doing most of the work, unrecognized) and better deserved the salary of £30 a year.

I had heard rumors, of course, about his occult activities: his abilities as a decipherer of documents were no secret; indeed, he rather boasted of them. But I knew nothing, until I opened his manuscript, of his dark work for the government; had I known the full extent, I think that everything might have become very much simpler. Wallis was defeated (even if he only realized it when he in his turn saw Cola's narrative) by his own cleverness and his obsession with secrecy. He saw enemies everywhere, and trusted no one. Read his words and see the motives he imputes to all who came into contact with him. Does he say anything good about anyone? He lived in a world where everyone was a fool, a liar, a murderer, a cheat or a traitor. He even sneers at Mr. Newton, denigrates Mr. Boyle, exploits the weaknesses of Lower.

All men were there to be twisted to serve his ends. Poor man, to think of his fellows thus; poor church, to have him as minister; poor England, to have him as its defender. He lambastes everyone, but who caused more death and destruction than he? But even Wallis could love, it seems, though when he lost the one person in his life he held dear, his reaction was not to come back to God in prayer and repentance, but to unleash still more cruelty on the world, and find that it served no purpose. I had encountered this Matthew of his on several occasions, and always felt sympathy for him. The obsession was clear to anyone, for Wallis could never be in a room with the lad without constantly looking at him, and making comments in his direction. But nothing gave me greater surprise than to read of Wallis's affection, for he treated the boy abominably and all wondered how the lad endured such cruelty.

I admit that the servant suffered less than the children, whose inadequacies were publicly and frequently acknowledged so vilely that once I saw the eldest break down in tears under the barrage, but nonetheless even Matthew had to put up with constant carping and malice; only with a man like Wallis could this be a way of expressing love. I had nothing but disgust for him. On one occasion when I saw his face twisted and purpled with rage at the lad and told Sarah of it, she chided me gently.

"Do not think badly of him," she said, "he wishes to approach love, but does not know how. He can only adore an idea, and has to castigate the reality when it cannot compare. He wants perfection, but is so blinded in spirit he can only sense it only through his mathematics, and has no place in his heart for people."

"But it is so cruel," I said.

"Yes. But it is also love. Can you not see that?" she replied. "And it is surely his only route to salvation. Do not condemn the one spark in him that was given by God. It is not for you to judge."

Then, however, I cared little for any of this: I wanted access to the archives, and Wallis quite literally had the key to them. So, as the king returned and tried to reestablish himself on the throne, as plots and counterplots swirled over the country like a snow blizzard, I left my room in Merton Street and went to the library, where I unbundled and catalogued and read and annotated until not even candlelight permitted me to work any longer. I worked in the icy cold of winter, when it grew dark in midafternoon, and in the boiling heat of summer, when the sun beat down on the lead roof just above my head and I grew half crazed from thirst. No weather or circumstance deflected me from my task, and I grew oblivious to all that was going on around me. I allowed myself to pause for an hour or so to eat, often in company with Lower or others like him, and in the evening would allow myself the greatest joy and solace of my life, which has always been music. Wine and music rejoice the heart, it can so mollify the mind, and soothe tempestuous affections, says Jason Pratensis, and Lemnius says it soothes also the arteries and the animal spirits, so that (here I cite Mr. Burton) when Orpheus played, the very trees tore up their roots that they might approach to hear better. Agrippa adds that the elephants of Africa are greatly pleased with it, and will dance to a tune. However sad and weary, an hour of the viol with good company nearly always brought me satisfaction and peace, and I would play, alone or with others, every evening an hour before prayer; it is the finest way I know of ensuring good sleep.

There were five of us who used to meet together twice a week and sometimes more frequently to play, and a most delicious harmony it was. We rarely talked, and scarcely even knew each other, but would meet and pass two hours or more in the most perfect friendship. I was neither the best nor the worst of the players, and by dint of practicing hard frequently appeared the superior. We used to meet where we could, and in 1662 settled in a room which we took above a newly opened coffee house next to the Queen's College, further down the High Street and on the opposite side from Mr. Boyle's rooms.

It was here that I first met Thomas Ken, whose companionship led me into the acquaintance of Jack Prestcott. As Prestcott says, Ken is now a bishop, and a very grand man indeed, so full of circumstance that his meager origins would astonish all who did not know him at that time. The thin, pinched cleric anxious for advancement, the ascetic concerned only to commune with Christ, has transformed himself into a portly ecclesiastical grandee, living in his palace with forty servants, dispensing his charity and a loyal devotee of whatever regime happens to hold his income in its grasp. It is a form of principle, I suppose, this willingness to transform the conscience for the common peace, but I do not admire it greatly, despite the comfort it has brought him. I remember with much greater affection the earnest young fellow of New College, whose only leisure was to scrape away at the viols in my company. He was an execrable musician, with little aptitude and no ear, but his enthusiasm was boundless and our group was short of a viol, and so we had little choice. I was truly shocked to learn that he had malevolently invented a tale about Sarah which took her one step closer to the gallows; so many people seemed to desire her death that even then I sensed a malignant fate taking pleasure in her destruction, turning people into her enemies for no reason that I could discern.

It was through my intervention that Sarah began to work for Dr. Grove, as Thomas (quite innocently) asked the assembled musicians one evening whether we knew of any servant wanting employment. Grove, recently returned to his fellowship, needed such a person and Ken was keen to help. He hoped to win the affection and patronage of the man, and initially tried hard to be obliging. Unfortunately, Grove could not countenance people like Ken in his college, and rebuffed all attempts at friendship; Ken's courtesies were wasted, and an enmity grew which did not need a dispute over a parish to become acrimonious.

I said that I knew just the person, and asked Sarah the next time I saw her. One day a week to tidy his rooms, carry up his water and coal, empty his pots and see to his laundry. Sixpence a day.

"I'd be glad of the work," she said. "Who is this man? I won't work for anyone who thinks he can beat me. You know that, I think."

"I don't know him at all, so I cannot vouch for his character. He was ejected long ago and is only just returned."

"A Laudian, then? Am I to work for a stalwart Royalist?"

"I would find you an Anabaptist Fellow if there were any, but people like this Grove are the only ones liable to make an offer these days. Take it or not, as you please. But go and see him: he might not be as bad as you fear. After all, I am a stalwart Royalist myself and you manage to contain your disgust, more or less, when you are around me."

That earned me one of those lovely smiles I still remember so very well. "There are few as kind as you," she said. "More's the pity."

She wasn't eager, but her need for work overcame her scruples, and eventually she went to Grove and took the position. I was pleased for this, and saw what a delight it is to be able to patronize others, even if in a small way. Through me, Sarah had enough work to live and even to save, if she was careful. For the first time in her life she was living a settled, respectable existence, in her place and apparently content. It comforted me greatly, as it seemed a good omen for the future; I was glad for her and thought maybe the rest of the country would prove equally tractable. My optimism was, alas, badly misplaced.

chapter three

I RUN AHEAD OF MYSELF. MY EAGERNESS TO PUT ALL down on paper means that I leave much out which is vital; I should measure out my facts, so that all who read can discern the pattern of events with clarity. This, in my opinion, is what proper history should be. I know what the philosophers say, that the purpose of history should be to illustrate the noblest deeds of the greatest men, to give examples for the present generation of debased inferiors to emulate, but I do believe that great men and noble deeds can look after themselves; few, in any case, stand up to much close examination. The view is not unchallenged anyway, I think, as the theologians wag their fingers and say that truly the whole purpose of history is to reveal the wondrous hand of God as He intervenes in the affairs of man. But I find this a doubtful program as well, at least as it is commonly practiced. Is His plan truly revealed in the laws of kings, the actions of politicians or the words of bishops? Can we easily believe that such liars, brutes and hypocrites are His chosen instruments? I cannot credit it; we do not study the policies of King Herod for lessons, but rather seek out the words of the least of his subjects, who finds no mention in any of the histories. Look through the works of Suetonius and Agricola; study Pliny and Quintilian, Plutarch and Josephus, and you will see that the greatest event of all, the most important happening in the entire history of the world, entirely passed them by despite their wisdom and learning. In the time of Vespasian (as Lord Bacon says) there was a prophecy that one who came out of Judaea should rule the world; this plainly meant our Savior, but Tacitus (in his History) thought only of Vespasian himself.

Besides, my job as an historian is to present the truth, and to tell the tale of these days in the approved fashion—first causes, narrative, summation, moral—would be, surely, to present a strange picture of the time in which it happened. In that year of 1663, after all, the king was nearly toppled from his throne, thousands of dissenters were locked in jail, the rumblings of war were heard over the North Sea and the first portents of the great fire and the greater plague were felt throughout the land, in all manner of strange and frightening events. Are all these to be relegated to second place, or be seen merely as a theater set for Grove's death, as though that was the most important occurrence? Or am I to ignore that poor man's end, and all events which took place in my town, because the maneuverings of courtiers which took us to war the next year, and nearly consumed us in civil strife once more, are so much more important?

A memorialist would do one, an historian the other, but perhaps both are mistaken; historians, like natural philosophers, come to believe reason sufficient for understanding and deceive themselves that they see all, and comprehend everything. In fact their labors ignore the significant and bury it deep under the weight of their wisdom. The mind of man unaided cannot grasp the truth, but only constructs fantasies and fictions which convince until they convince no more, and which are true only until discarded and replaced. The reasonableness of humanity is a puny weapon, blunt and powerless, a child's toy in a baby's hand. Only revelation, which sees past reason and is a gift neither earned nor deserved, says Aquinas, can take us to that place which is illumined with a clarity beyond all intellect.

The ramblings of the mystic, however, would serve me ill in these pages, and I must remember my calling; the historian must work through the proper recitation of facts. So I will go back awhile to the start of 1660, before the Restoration of His Majesty, before ever I knew Paradise Fields, and shortly after Sarah had begun to work in my mother's house. And, instead of windy rhetoric, I will tell how I visited the Blundys' cottage one day to ask a few extra questions about the mutiny. As I approached down the lane, I saw a short man leave the cottage and walk swiftly away from me; on his back he had a pack such as travelers use. I looked at him with some passing curiosity, simply because he had come from Sarah's house. He was not young, not old, but had a determined gait and walked off without glancing back. I only had one look at his face, which was fresh and kindly, though scored deeply with lines and weather-beaten like that of a man who had spent most of his life outside. He was clean-shaven, and had an unruly mop of fair, almost blond, hair which was uncovered by any hat. In build he was slight, and not tall, yet he had an air of wiry strength to him, as though he was used to enduring great privations without flinching.

It was the only sight I ever had of Ned Blundy, and I regret greatly that I had not arrived a few minutes earlier, as I would have dearly liked to question him. Sarah told me, however, that it would have been a waste of my time. He had never been open with strangers and trusted only slowly; she thought it very unlikely he would have been forthcoming even had he not been unusually preoccupied on what turned out to be his last visit.

"I would still have liked to have started an acquaintance," I said, "as perhaps in the future we might meet again. Were you expecting him?"

"No, indeed not. We have seen very little of him in recent years. He has been always on the move and my mother is too old to go with him. He also thought it better if we stay here and make our own lives. Perhaps he is right, but I miss him greatly; he is the dearest man I know. I am worried for him."

"Why so? I did not see him well, but he has the air of a man able to look after himself."

"I hope so. I have never doubted it before. But he was so serious in his leave-taking that he frightened me. He spoke so gravely, and gave such warnings about our safety that I am concerned."

"Surely it is natural for any man to be concerned for his

family when he is not there to protect them?''

''Do you know a man called John Thurloe? Have you heard of him?''

''Of course I know his name. I am surprised you do not. Why do you ask?''

''He is one of the people I am to be wary of.''

''Why?''

''Because my father says he will want this off me if he learns of it.''

She pointed to a large bundle on the floor by the fireside, wrapped in cloth, bound up with thick cord and sealed with wax at every point.

''He did not tell me what it was, but said it would kill me if I opened it, or if anyone ever knew it was here. I am to hide it securely, and never breathe a word to anyone until he comes back to reclaim it.''

''Do you know the story of Pandora?''

She frowned and shook her head, so I told her the tale. Even though preoccupied, she listened, and asked sensible questions.

''I take it as a good warning,'' she said. ''But I intended to obey him in any case.''

''But you promptly tell me, before your father is even past the city walls.''

''There is no place here to hide it where it would not be found within minutes by a determined searcher, and we have few trustworthy friends who would not also be examined. I would like to ask you the greatest favor, Mr. Wood, as I trust you and think you a man of your word. Will you take it and conceal it for me? Promise you will not open it without my permission, and never reveal its existence to anyone?''

''What is in it?''

''I have told you. I do not know. But I can tell you that nothing my father does is base or cruel or means harm. It will only be for a few weeks, then you can give it back to me.''

This conversation—which ended with my agreement—may strike any reader of my words as strange. For it was as foolish for Sarah to trust me as it was for me to hide a package which might have contained any number of horrors to cause me grief. And yet both of us chose wisely; my word once given is sacrosanct and I never even considered violating her trust. I took the package away and concealed it in my room underneath the floorboards, where it remained undisturbed and unsuspected. I did not even think of opening it or going back on my promise in any way. I agreed because I never even considered not doing so; I was already falling under her spell, and willingly conceded any request which bound her to me, and earned her gratitude.

Of course, the package was that bundle of documents which Blundy had shown to Sir James Prestcott, and which Thurloe held to be so dangerous he searched for years to recover it. It was for those papers that, after Blundy died and Sir James Prestcott fled, Thurloe's agents fanned out across the land, given any powers they wanted. It was to discover that bundle that Sarah's house was ransacked, and ransacked again, her mother received the injury which killed her, her friends and acquaintances, those of her father and mother too, questioned closely and brutally. It was for this package that Cola came to Oxford, and it was for the same package that Thurloe steered Jack Prestcott and Dr. Wallis into hanging Sarah, lest she reveal its whereabouts.

And I knew nothing of this, but I kept it safe as I had promised, and no one ever thought to ask me about it.

I AM VERY MUCH AFRAID THAT MY NARRATIVE, SHOULD any have cause to read it, will not please as much as those three on which it is based. I wish that, like them, I could offer a simple, straightforward narrative of events, full of obvious statements and gripped by the adamantine embrace of conviction. But I cannot do so because the truth is not simple, and these three gentlemen present only a simulacrum of verity, as I hope I have already demonstrated. I am sworn not to leave out contradictions and confusions, nor am I so full of my own importance that I have sufficient confidence to leave out all but what I did, saw and said myself, for I do not credit that my own presence was of critical importance. I must set down fragments, all jumbled up and criss-crossing the years.

So now I go forward again, and begin my tale in earnest. Around the middle of 1662, after I had known Sarah Blundy for nearly three years and the kingdom had been at peace for two, I was moderately contented with my lot in life. My routine was as unshakeable as it was rewarding. I had my friends, with whom I associated in the evenings, either at dinner or at music parties. I had my work, which was finally beginning to find the purpose which has occupied me ever since, bringing ever richer rewards in knowledge. My family was well enough established with no member, not even the most distant cousin, bringing anxiety, expense or dishonor to our door. I had secure and unchallenged possession of an annuity which, however small, was more than enough to provide food and lodging and such necessaries as my work required. I suppose that I would have liked more for, if I already realized that I would never take on the expense of marriage, I would happily have spent more on books, and engaged more completely in those acts of charity which illuminate the life of man when properly undertaken.

This was a minor concern, however, since I have never been one of those bitter and envious men who desire to be as rich as their fellows, and define insufficiency as what they themselves possess. All of my friends in those days have become far wealthier than myself. Lower, for example, became the most fashionable doctor in London; John Locke was supported in great style by generous and wealthy patrons and received countless pensions and annuities from the government before the enmity of the powerful forced him into exile. Even Thomas Ken battened on to a fat bishopric. But I would not change my life for theirs, for they constantly have to concern themselves with such matters. They live in a world where, if you do not perpetually rise, then you inevitably fall. Fame and fortune are of the most evanescent quality; I have, and can lose, neither.

Besides, none of the three gentlemen are contented, I know; they are too aware of the price of their money. All three regret the passing of their youth, when they thought they would do as they chose and dreamed of greater things. Without the demands of family—the incessantly open mouths of his own children and those children of his brother—Lower might have remained in Oxford and carved a name for himself deep into the tree of fame. But instead he went to practice as a fashionable physician, and has done no useful work since. Locke detests those who reward him so well, but was too used to good living to abandon the habit which now means he must live in Amsterdam for his own safety. And Ken? What choices he has made! Perhaps one day he will take a stand in public for what he truly believes. Until then he will remain in the torment of his own devising, assuaging the demons of self-criticism by his ever more extravagant works of benevolence.

As long as I have had my labor, I have been contented, and wanted no more. In those days particularly I believed myself to be delightfully set up, and suffered no melancholy longings to distract me. I was, as I say, pleased that I had established Sarah in a good and reliable position with Dr. Grove, and complacent that the comforting drift of my life would continue unabated. This was not to be, for bit by bit the events which are narrated in the three manuscripts I have been reading invaded my little world, and disrupted it entirely. It took a very long time indeed before I was able to reestablish something of the balance that sound scholarship and peaceful existence both require. Indeed, I think that I never did.

The first pinprick at my bubble of contentment came in late autumn. I was in a tavern, where I had paused one evening after a long day breathing in the dust of Bodley's books. I was perfectly quiet and rested, having no thought in my mind at all to distract me, when I overheard part of a conversation between two low and verminous townsmen. I did not want, or intend, to listen but sometimes it cannot be avoided; words force their attention upon the mind, and will not be kept out. And the more I heard, the more I had to hear, because my body stiffened and was made icy cold by their gossip.

"That Leveller whore the Blundy girl." That was, I think, the only phrase which initially my ears discovered amid the general hubbub in the room. Then, word by word, more of the conversation came to me. "Rutting cat." "Every time she cleans his room." "Poor old man, must be bewitched." "Wouldn't mind a chance myself." "And him a priest. They're all the same." "You can tell just by looking, really." "Dr. Grove." "Spread her legs for anybody." "Is there anyone who hasn't?"

I now know these vile and disgusting reports to be absolutely false, although I did not know until I read Prestcott's manuscript that they had originated with him after his cruel rape. Even then I did not instantly believe what I heard, for many lewd and boastful stories are told in drink, and if they were all true then there could scarcely be a virtuous woman in the country. No, it was not until Prestcott himself approached me that my refusal turned to doubt, and the creeping demons in my mind began to gnaw at my soul, making me hateful and suspicious.

Prestcott has recounted our initial meeting, called in as I was by Thomas Ken to assist: Ken hoped that I would do what he could not, and persuade the lad to give up what was liable to be a hopeless quest. Ken had tried, I think, but Prestcott's violent response to all criticism restrained his efforts. He hoped that a cogent detailing of the facts would produce a reasonable response, and that Prestcott would listen to me if I gave such an account.

It took only a short acquaintance, however, before I realized that I neither liked Mr. Prestcott, nor wanted to involve myself in his fantasies in any way. So when he saw me in the street later and hailed me, my heart sank, and I prepared a story about how I had not yet completed my investigation.

"That is of no matter, sir," he said jovially, "since there is nothing I can do with it at the moment. I am shortly off on a tour of the country, to my people and to London. It will wait until I return. No, Mr. Wood, I need to talk to you on a particular matter, for I have a warning to give you. I know you to be of a respectable family, and no member more so than your much admired mother, and I am loath to stand by and let your name be tarnished."

"That is kind of you," I said in astonishment. "I am sure there is nothing we need concern ourselves with. What, exactly, do you mean?"

"You have a servant, do you not? Sarah Blundy?"

I nodded, a feeling of concern creeping over me. "We do. A fine worker, dutiful, humble, and obedient."

"So she no doubt appears. But as you know, appearances can be deceptive. I must tell you that her character is not as good as you like to think."

"It grieves me to hear it."

"And it grieves me to tell you. I am afraid that she is engaged in fornication with another of her employers, a Dr. Grove, of New College. Do you know the man?"

I nodded coldly. "How do you know this?"

"She told me. Boasted of it."

"I find that difficult to believe."

"I did not. She approached me and offered herself to me for money in the grossest and coarsest fashion. Naturally, I spurned the offer, and she as good as said that her qualities could be vouched for by many others. Many, many other satisfied clients, she said with a grin, and added that Dr. Grove was a new man since she had taken to providing him with the sort of satisfaction the church could not offer."

"You grieve me when you say this."

"I apologize for that. But I thought it for the best . . ."

"Of course. It was kind of you to take such trouble."

That was the essence of the conversation; there certainly was not much more to it, but what an effect it had on my mind! My first reaction was to reject absolutely what he had told me, and persuade myself that what I knew of the girl, and my sense of her goodness, were more valuable than the testimony of an outsider. But my suspicions gnawed at me, and would not be tamed, and finally consumed me entire. Could my own sense of her nature be counted more valuable evidence than the actual experience of someone else? I thought of her in one way, it appeared Prestcott knew her to be other. And did my own experience contradict what he said? Had not the girl given herself to me freely? I had not paid her, but what did that say of her moral nature? Surely it was mere vanity on my part to think she had lain with me out of regard? The more I thought, the more I perceived what had to be the truth. She, alone of all women, had allowed me to touch her, and I had become infatuated as a result, instead of seeing that I could have been anyone. The desires of women are stronger than those of mere men; this is well known and I had forgotten it. When in heat they are ravenous, and insatiable, and we poor men think it love.

What is this jealousy, this emotion which can overwhelm and destroy the strongest of men, the most virtuous of creatures? What alchemy of the mind can transmute love into hate, longing into repulsion, desire into disgust, in such a way? Why is it that there is no man alive immune to its hot embrace, that it can banish all sleep, all reason and all kindness in an instant? What hangman, says Jean Bodin, can torture so well as can this fear and suspicion? And not men alone, for Vives says doves are jealous, and can die of it. A swan at Windsor, finding a strange cock with its mate, swam miles in pursuit of the offending beast and killed it, then swam back and killed the mate as well. Some say it is the stars which cause jealousy but Leo Afer blames climate, and Morison says that Germany has not so many drunkards, England tobacconists, France dancers, as Italy has jealous husbands. In Italy itself it is said men of Piacenza are more jealous than the rest.

And it is a changeable disease, shifting its form from one place to the next, for what will drive a man into madness in one place, will not affect another elsewhere. In Friesland, a woman will kiss the man who brings her drink; in Italy the man must die for it. In England young men and maids will dance together, a thing which only Siena abides in Italy. Mendoza, a Spanish legate in England, found it disgusting for men and women to sit together in church, but was told such a occurrence was only disgusting in Spain, where men cannot rid themselves of lascivious thoughts even in holy places.

As I am prone to melancholy, I am more susceptible to jealousy, but I know many choleric or sanguine people just as afflicted; I was young, and youth is jealous although Jerome says the old are more so. But understanding a disease, alas, can never cure it; knowing whence jealousy comes no more attenuates the malady than understanding the source of a fever; less so, for at least in physick a diagnosis can produce a treatment, while for jealousy there is none. It is like the plague, for which there is no cure. You succumb, and are consumed by the hottest of fires and in the end it either burns out, or you die.

I suffered the cloak of jealousy, which burned my soul as the shirt dipped in the blood of Nessus drove Heracles to agony and death, for near a fortnight before I could abide the torment no more. In that time everything I saw and heard confirmed my worst suspicions, and I grasped eagerly the slightest hint or sign of her guilt. Once, I almost brought myself to confront her, and went down to her cottage for that purpose, but as I approached I saw the door open, and a strange man come out, bowing in farewell and paying the most elaborate of respects. Instantly, I was sure this was some client, and that her shame and degradation was now so great she had taken to plying her trade in her own house, for all to see. My anger and shock was so great I turned around and walked away; my fear so consuming I straightaway went to my room and subjected myself to the most intimate of investigations, for the danger of becoming pox-ridden loomed large in my mind. I found nothing but was scarcely reassured, since I did not know anything at all of the malady. So I summoned all my courage and, red-faced with shame, took myself off to see Lower.

"Dick," I said, "I must ask you the greatest favor, and beg for your complete discretion."

We were in his rooms at Christ Church, a commodious apartment in the main quadrangle which he had occupied now for some years. Locke was there when I arrived, and so I forced myself into idle conversation, determined to wait as long as necessary before I got him on his own. Eventually Locke left, and Lower asked what it was that I needed.

"Ask away, and if I can oblige, I will willingly do so. You look in great distress, my friend. Are you ill?"

"I hope not. That is what I want you to determine."

"And what do you think it may be? What symptoms do you have?"

"I have none."

"No symptoms? None at all? Sounds very serious to me. I shall examine you thoroughly, then prescribe the most expensive medicines in my pharmacopoeia, and you will be well instantly. By God, Mr. Wood," he said with a smile, "you are the ideal patient; if I could have a dozen like you, I would be both rich and famous."

"Do not joke, sir. I am deadly serious. I fear I may have caught a shocking disease."

My manner of speaking convinced him I was in earnest and, good doctor and kind friend that he was, he instantly dropped his bantering tone. "You are certainly worried, I can see that. But you must be a little more frank. How can I tell you what your illness is unless you tell me first? I am a doctor, not a soothsayer."

And so, with great reluctance and fearing his mockery, I told him all. Lower grunted. "So you think this slut may have lain with everyone in Oxfordshire?"

"I do not know. But if the reports are correct, then I may be sickening."

"But you say this has been going on for two years or more. I know the diseases of Venus do commonly take some time to show themselves," he conceded, "but rarely this long. You do not notice any signs on her? No sores or pustules? No running pus, or creamy discharges?"

"I did not look," I said, gravely affronted at the idea.

"That is a pity. Myself, I always look very carefully and I would counsel you to do the same in future. It doesn't have to be obvious, you know. You can hide it under a pretense of love with only a little practice."

"Lower, I do not want advice, I want a diagnosis. Am I sick or not?"

He sighed. "Drop your breeches, then. Let's have a look."

With the gravest embarrassment at the humiliation, I did as I was told and Lower subjected me to the most intimate examination, lifting and pulling and peering. Then he put his face close to my private parts and sniffed. "Seems perfectly fine to me," he said. "Pristine condition, I'd say. Scarcely taken out of its wrapping."

I breathed a sigh of relief. "So I am not ill."

"I didn't say that. There are no symptoms, that is all. I would suggest you take remedies in large quantities for a few weeks, just to be on the safe side. If you are too bashful to get them yourself, I will buy some from Mr. Crosse and give them to you tomorrow.''

"Thank you. Thank you so much.''

"Not at all. Now, get dressed. I would suggest, by the way, that you avoid all intimate contact with this girl again. If she is as these reports suggest, then sooner or later she will become dangerous.''

"I fully intend to.''

"And we must make her character generally known, lest others fall into her snare.''

"No," I said. "I cannot permit that. What if these reports are false? I would not calumnize her unnecessarily.''

"Your sense of justice does you credit. But you must not hide behind it. Such people as she are corrosive to any society, and must be known. If you must be fastidious, then confront her directly, and find out. At the very least, we must pass warning to Dr. Grove, so he can act as he sees fit.''

I did not act hastily; I needed more than gossip and the testimony of Jack Prestcott before I was prepared to act. Instead, I kept a more careful watch on her, and (I admit with shame) followed her on occasion when her labors were done. I was greatly distressed to have my worst fears confirmed still more, for on several occasions she did not go home, or did so only briefly. Instead, I saw her leave the town, walking purposely on one occasion in the direction of Abingdon, a town full of soldiers where I knew that trollops were in great demand. I could see no other explanation, and I note with chagrin that Wallis, when he discovered the same information, decided the only explanation was that she was carrying messages to and from radicals. I mention this to indicate the dangers of inadequate and partial evidence, for we were both wrong.

But I did not see this at the time, although I think I was prepared to listen openly and frankly to any explanation she might offer. The next day after a sleepless night during which I wished fervently that I might be spared the encounter, I told Sarah to sit down when she came into my room, and said I wanted to speak to her on a matter of grave importance.

She sat quietly, and waited. I had noticed that in previous days she had not been her usual self, and had worked less hard, and been less cheerful than was her wont. I had not paid a great deal of attention, as all women are prone to these moods, and scarcely noticed that for her it was out of her normal character. I did not know then, and did not discover until I read Jack Prestcott's memoir, that this was due to his cruel violation of her. Naturally, she could not tell any of this—what woman's reputation could endure such shame?—but she would not easily forget an offense once committed. I understand fully why Prestcott submitted to the delusion that she had bewitched him in revenge, however ridiculous the belief. For her hatred of the malice of others was implacable, so much had she been schooled by her upbringing to expect justice.

I had also noticed that she had spurned my affections, and moved out of reach quickly on the one occasion when I had tried to touch her, shrugging her shoulder in what appeared to be disgust at my hand on her shoulder. I was hurt by this initially, then I put it down as more evidence that she was turning away from me for the richer rewards offered by Dr. Grove. Again, I did not know the exact truth until I saw it, scribbled down in Prestcott's hand.

"I must talk to you on a matter of the gravest importance," I said when I had prepared myself properly. I noticed, and remember well, that I had a strange pressure in my breast as I began to talk, and my words came breathlessly, as though I had run a great distance. "I have heard some terrible reports, which must be dealt with instantly."

She sat and looked at me blankly, with scarcely any interest in her face at all. I believe I stuttered and tripped on my words as I forced myself to continue with the interview, and even turned to examine my shelves of books, so I would not have to look her in the face.

"I have received a grave complaint about your behavior. Which is that you offered yourself brazenly and coarsely to a man of the university, and have been fornicating in the most disgusting fashion."

Again, there was a silence of some duration before she replied: "That is true," she said.

That my suspicions and the reports seemed confirmed did not comfort me. I had hoped that she would indignantly refute the charges, allowing me to forgive her, so we might continue as before. Even at that stage, however, I did not jump to conclusions. Evidence must be confirmed independently.

"And who is this man?" I asked.

"A so-called gentleman," she said. "Called Anthony Wood."

"Do not be impudent with me," I cried in anger. "You know perfectly well what I mean."

"Do I?"

"Yes. You have abused my generosity by seducing Dr. Grove, of New College, and not content with that alone, you also threw yourself on an undergraduate, Mr. Prestcott, and tried to get him to satisfy you as well. Do not deny it, for I heard it from his lips."

She turned pale, and I take it as an indication of the foolishness of those who believe character can be read in the face that I assumed this to be shock at the discovery of her wiles. "You heard that?" she said, her face white. "From his lips indeed?"

"I did."

"Then it must be true. For a fine young man like Mr. Prestcott could surely never lie. And he is a gentleman, while I am merely a soldier's daughter."

"Is it true? Is it?"

"Why do you ask me? You think it so. You have known me for what? Near four years now, and you believe it so."

"How can I not? Your behavior is all of a piece. How can I trust you in your denial?"

"I have not denied anything," she said. "I think it none of your affair."

"I am your employer," I said. "In the eyes of the law, your father, responsible for your behavior in all particulars. So tell me: who was that man I saw coming out of your house yesterday?"

She looked puzzled for a moment, then realized who I was referring to. "He was an Irishman, who came to see me. He traveled a long way."

"Why?"

"That is not your affair either."

"It is. It is my duty to myself as much as it is to you to prevent you from bringing shame on this family. What will people say if it becomes common currency that the Woods are employing a whore in their house?"

"Maybe they will say that the master, Mr. Anthony Wood, also lies with the slut whenever he can? That he takes her to Paradise Fields and there fornicates awhile before taking himself off to the library and making speeches about the behavior of others?"

"That is different."

"Why?"

"I am not having an argument with you about abstract matters. This is serious. But if you can act thus with me, you can do so with others. That is obviously the case."

"So how many other sluts do *you* know, Mr. Wood?"

I was red with anger at this time, and blamed her absolutely for what happened next. All I had desired was some sort of frank and open response. I would have liked her to deny everything, so that I might generously exonerate her. Or confess it frankly, and beg my forgiveness, which I would have willingly conferred. But she would do neither, and instead had the insolence to fling my accusations back in my face. Very swiftly, it seemed, we plunged into the darkness of our association, for whatever may have transpired between us, I was still her master. By her words she made it clear she had forgotten this, and was abusing our intimacy. No man of sense could admit there was any similarity between our behaviors, even had the accusation any substance, for she was beholden to me while I was free of any dependency to her. Nor could any man tolerate the foulness of her speech to me; even in the heat of passion I had never addressed her in anything but the most courteous terms and could not tolerate such language.

I stood up in shock and took a step toward her. She fell back against the wall, eyes wide with anger, and pointed at me, arm outstretched from her shoulder, in a strange, frightening gesture.

"Do not take a single step closer to me," she hissed.

I stopped dead in my tracks. I do not know what I intended. Certainly I do not think there was any violence in my mind, for I have never been one to behave in such a way. Even the worst of servants has never received a blow from me, however much it was deserved. I do not claim this as any particular quality; and in the case of Sarah I know I would dearly loved to have beaten her black and blue, to revenge myself for the abuse I had suffered. But I am certain I would never have done more than try to frighten.

That fright, however, was enough for her to abandon all the show of docility. I did not know what she might have done had I taken a further step, but I felt then a tremendous will within her, and I did not feel able to challenge it.

"Get out of this house," I said when she had lowered her arm. "You are dismissed. I will not lay a complaint against you, however much I have a right to do so. But I never want you in here again."

Without another word, but with a glance of the purest contempt, she walked out of the room. A few seconds later, I heard the front door close.

chapter four

HAD I BEEN PRESTCOTT, I MIGHT HAVE CONCLUDED from this encounter that Sarah was evil and possessed; certainly there was something powerful and terrifying in her gesture, and in the flame of her eyes at that moment. This is something I will dwell on properly at the right moment; for now, however, I must say merely that not only did such a thought never occur to me, I can refute absolutely Prestcott's assertions.

It requires no great learning or knowledge to do so; even by his own account, Prestcott's conclusions were wrong and he was let down by his own ignorance and derangement. For example, he says that demons took over the body of Sir William Compton and changed its shape, but this is plainly contradicted by all authority, for the *Malleus Maleficarum* says plain it is not possible; Aristotle says this can be caused only by natural causes, particularly the stars, yet Dionysius says the devil cannot change the stars: God will not allow it. Prestcott never found any evidence of Sarah having cast an enchantment over his hair and blood, and the visions he suffered were due more, I think, to the devils he had himself summoned into his mind than any sent there by others.

Nor did he read those signs aright which he had himself summoned, for in the bowl of water shown him by Anne Blundy, he sought the author of his misfortunes, and she showed him truly: he saw, quite plainly, his own father and a young man: that man, I believe, was none other than himself. These two people brought all the troubles on their own heads through their violence and their disloyalty. Greatorex repeated the warning and again he ignored it. Jack Prestcott had the answer in his hand, Wallis says so plainly and I know it to be true, and yet in his madness he blamed others, and helped destroy Sarah, and put all hope forever out of his reach.

He very nearly put it out of mine as well. I scarcely saw Sarah at all for the next few months, as I took myself back to my manuscripts and my notebooks. When not working, though, my mind incessantly and disobediently returned to her, and my distress grew into resentment, and then into the most bitter hatred. I rejoiced when I heard that Dr. Grove had dismissed her, and that she was without work of any sort; I took satisfaction in the fact that no one else would employ her for fear of comment; and once I saw her in the street red in face with anger and humiliation, subjected to the lewd remarks of students who had also heard the stories. This time I did not intervene as I had once before, but turned away after I was certain she had seen me, so that she would know my contempt continued unabated. *Quos laeserunt et oderunt,* as Seneca has it, those you have injured you also hate, and I believe I felt already that I had been less than just, but did not know how to reverse my harshness.

Shortly after this business, when my spirits were still low and my habits continued unsociable—for I knew my humor did not appeal, and so avoided the company of my fellow men lest they demand to know what ailed me—I was summoned to Dr. Wallis. This was a rare occurrence, for although I was earning him his salary as keeper of the archives, he did not honor me frequently with such attention; any business between us was habitually conducted at chance meetings, in the street or in the library. As everyone who knows Wallis will realize, the summons alarmed me, for his coldness was truly terrifying. This is one of the rare matters on which Prestcott and Cola agree—both found his presence disturbing. It was, I think, the blankness of his countenance which gave such alarm, for it is hard to know a man when the visible indicators of character have been so rigorously suppressed. Wallis never smiled, never frowned, never showed either pleasure or displeasure. There was only his voice—soft, menacing and permanently laced with scarce-hidden nuances of contempt beneath a courtesy which could evaporate as swiftly as a summer dew.

It was at this meeting that Wallis asked me to discover for him the edition of Livy he sought. I will not recount the conversation as it actually took place; stripped of his sneering remarks about my character, the essence of his version is accurate enough. I promised to do my best and did so, leaving no library unexamined and no bookseller unbothered by my enquiries. But he did not tell me why he wanted it: I still knew nothing of Marco da Cola, who arrived several weeks afterward.

I SUPPOSE I MUST NOW CONCENTRATE MORE FULLY ON that gentleman, and approach the heart of the matter. I am aware I have delayed unseasonably; it is something which I find painful to recall, so great was the torment he caused me.

I heard of Cola's existence a few days before I met him; on the evening of his arrival, I think, I ate with Lower at a cookhouse, and he told me of the occurrence. He was quite excited about it; Lower in those days always had a taste for the novel and the exotic and had yearnings to tour the world. There was not the slightest chance that he would do so, for he had neither the money nor the leisure to travel, nor yet the easiness of mind to put aside his career. Absence is the greatest danger of all for the physician, since once out of the mind of the public, it is difficult to fight back into esteem. But it pleased him for some time to talk about how he would one day tour the universities of the continent, meeting the men of science and discovering what they were doing. The arrival of Cola rekindled these notions in his breast, and I am sure he imagined himself arriving in Venice, and being treated to the greatest hospitality by Cola's family to repay the courtesies done in Oxford.

And he liked the man, strange as he found him, for Lower was nothing if not broad in his appreciation of humanity. Indeed, the little Italian was hard not to like, unless one be of a hard and suspicious turn of mind like John Wallis. Short and already tending to a certain roundness in the belly, with bright, sparkling eyes which twinkled readily with amusement, and an engaging manner of leaning forward in his seat which gave the impression of fascinated attention when you spoke, he was a charming companion. He was full of observations on all he saw, and none of these (that I heard) was pejorative; Cola seemed one of those happy few who sees only the best, and prefers not to notice the worst. Even Mr. Boyle, who gave his affections with the greatest difficulty, seemed to grow fond of him, despite Wallis's warnings. This was the most extraordinary of all, perhaps, for Boyle liked peace and quiet; he suffered noise and disturbance almost as physical pain, and even at the height of the most exciting experiment, insisted on an air of moderate calm amongst those who were assisting. No servant was allowed to clatter about with equipment, or talk above a whisper; all had to be done with almost a religious demeanor—for, in his opinion, to study nature was a form of worship.

So the success of the boisterous, noisy Cola—always bursting into peals of laughter, whose flat-footed movements led him to bump noisily, with loud and extravagant oaths, into tables and chairs—was something of a mystery to us all. Lower ascribed it to the Italian's obvious and genuine love of experiment, but personally I put it down to his gentlemanly amiability, and we might say with Menander that his reception was the fruit of his stately manners. Mr. Boyle was excessively sober in his demeanor, yet occasionally I suspected that there was part of him which admired those who were lighthearted and cheerful. Perhaps he would have been himself, had he been less stricken with ill health. I was not aware that, in part, Boyle's attention was prompted by ulterior motives, but even this does not suffice, for he was not a man who could pretend an affection out of duplicity. No; Wallis's intervention with Boyle merely makes that Italian's success the more striking—or makes Wallis's belief the less acceptable. For Boyle was as well acquainted with Cola as any in England, and a fine judge of character. I find it impossible to credit that he would have extended his affection had he discerned anything at all which corresponded with Wallis's fears. Moreover, Boyle had no need to fear Wallis and I believe held him in a certain amount of distaste: more than any, he was capable of making up his own mind, and his opinion should thus be given more weight when reaching any judgment on this matter.

The gradual disenchantment of Lower with Cola, however, did have much to do with Wallis, for he preyed like the serpent before Eve on Lower's fears and hopes, twisting them to his own ends. Wallis knew Lower was desperate for success, for all his family depended on him since it was clear that his elder brother (through the perversions of religious belief) would never be in a position to give much support. And Lower had a large family, for not only were his parents still living, he had several unmarried sisters who needed portions, and innumerable demanding cousins. Merely to satisfy part of their expectations, he would have to be the most successful physician in London. It says much for his sense of duty that he applied himself with the greatest success when he took up the challenge; and it says as much for the weight of this burden on his mind that he, swiftly came to see Cola as a threat to his progress.

Lower had, after all, worked hard with Mr. Boyle and others to deserve and receive their patronage. He had done countless labors and small services for no payment and had proved an assiduous courtier. The rewards were to be Boyle's support for his membership of the Royal Society; his approval when he finally plucked up the courage to advance his cause with the College of Physicians; his patronage when the position of Court Physician came vacant, as well as the huge family of patients that Boyle's approval could bring to him when he began his practice in London. And he deserved all the success and all the support Boyle could provide, for he was a very good physician indeed.

Having worked so hard and being now, at the age of some thirty-two years, on the verge of entering the lists, he was frightened lest some event snatch those greatly desired rewards from him. Cola presented no threat to him, and would not have done even had he been what Lower feared, for Boyle patronized those with merit and did not play favorite with his clients. But Lower's jealousy and worry was inflamed by the words of Dr. Wallis, who played on his ambition by saying that Cola had the reputation for stealing other men's ideas. I do not (though my own path has been so different) condemn moderate ambition, such as drove Themistocles to match the glory of Miltiades, or fired Alexander to seek the trophies of Achilles; rather it is the excess of ambition that becomes pride, drives courtiers to beggar themselves and their families, and makes good men behave with cruelty and recklessness, which all men of sense must condemn; Wallis's purpose was to drive Lower into this great fault and for a while he succeeded, even though Lower battled manfully with his jealousy. The conflict within him, I believe, exacerbated those changes in mood, from exultation to darkness, from excessive friendliness to bitter condemnation, which caused Cola so much grief.

Initially, however, all was very well. Lower bubbled with enthusiasm as he described his new acquaintance and I could see he hoped that a true friendship would develop. Indeed, he was already treating Cola with that consideration and courtesy normally reserved for acquaintances of much longer standing.

"Do you know," he said, leaning forward with an arch look of amusement on his face, "so good a Christian physician is he, he has even undertaken to treat the old Blundy woman? Without any hope of payment or reward, although as he is Italian perhaps he intends to take payment in kind from the girl. Should I warn him, do you think?"

I ignored the remark. "What is wrong with the old woman?" I asked.

"Fell and broke her leg, apparently. A nasty wound by all accounts, and she is unlikely to survive. Cola took her on after the daughter had the gall to approach Dr. Grove in public to ask for money."

"Is this man any good? Does he know anything about such injuries?"

"That I cannot say. All I know is that he has set to work with a great enthusiasm, completely mindless of the disadvantages of such a client. I applaud his kindness, if not his sense."

"You would not treat her yourself."

"With only the greatest reluctance," he said, then hesitated. "No, of course I would. But I am glad I was not asked."

"You have taken a shine to this man."

"Indeed. He is quite delightful and extremely knowledgeable. I look forward to many long conversations during his stay, which may be a long one, as he is out of funds. You must come and meet him; visitors to this town are few and far between these days. We must make what use we can of them."

There the subject of itinerant Italians was dropped, and the conversation passed onto other matters. I left my friend later with a feeling of concern in the back of my mind, for I was distressed to hear of the misfortunes of Sarah's mother. This was, after all, many months since our last encounter and the passage of time had softened my feelings. I am not a man much given to hatred, and find that I cannot sustain a continued resentment, however grave the injury suffered. While I had no desire to resume my acquaintance, I no longer wished to see that family visited by troubles, and still nurtured an affection of sorts for the old woman.

Here again I confess freely, and say I wished to play the part of magnitude. However much she had caused me injury, yet I wished to show myself charitable and forgiving. Perhaps this was the greatest punishment I could bestow, for I would show her the extent of her foolishness, and lord it over her with my condescension.

So, after much thought, the following evening I covered myself in my cloak, put on my warmest hat and gloves (Cola was certainly right about the coldness of the weather; my friend Mr. Plot has meticulously gathered measurements which show it to have been bitterly cold. Although spring came suddenly and brilliantly only a week or so later, winter held the country in its icy grip until the last moment) and walked down to the castle.

I was nervous of being seen, and even more nervous about encountering Sarah, as I had no expectation of being welcomed. But she was not there; I knocked, waited, then walked in with relief in my heart, thinking that I would be able to comfort the mother without the risk of angering the daughter. That woman, however, was asleep, no doubt due to some potion or other, and although I was tempted to wake her so that my kindness might not go unnoticed, yet I refrained from doing so. Her face shocked me, so gaunt and pale that it resembled a death's head; her breathing was harsh and difficult and the smell in the room was oppressive in the extreme. Like all people, I have witnessed death on many occasions; I watched my father, my brothers and sisters, my cousins and my friends all die. Some young, some old, of injury, illness, plague and simple old age. No one, I think, can reach the age of thirty without knowing death intimately, in all its guises. And it was in that room, waiting its chance.

There was nothing I could do at that moment. Anne Blundy did not need any practical help I could give, and any spiritual comfort would not have been pleasing to her. Reluctantly I stood watching her, overcome by that sudden hopelessness that results from wanting to do well but not knowing how, until a footstep at the door roused me from my meditations. Overcome with a fear and a sudden reluctance to confront Sarah herself, I quickly took myself into the little room next to the chamber, since I knew there was a small door through which I could once again gain the street.

But it was not Sarah; the footfalls in the room were far too heavy for that, and so I paused out of curiosity to know who had come into the house. By carefully peering through the door—a deceit I am ashamed to acknowledge, as it is the sort of falseness no gentleman should ever perpetrate—I could see that the man in the next room must be this Cola; no Englishman (in those days at least) would ever have dressed in such a fashion. He was behaving very strangely, however, and his activities caught my attention in such a way that I compounded my ill-behavior by continuing to watch, and continuing to make sure that I was myself unobserved.

First, he came in and established as I had that Widow Blundy was still perfectly asleep, then knelt down beside her, took out his rosary and prayed deeply for a short while. As I say, I had considered doing something of the same myself in a more Protestant way, but knew her better than to think even that would be welcomed. Then he acted most strangely indeed, taking out a small phial which he opened, and spreading some oil on his finger. He applied this finger gently to her forehead, made the sign of the cross and prayed again before putting the bottle back under his coat.

This was odd enough, although might be explained by great personal devotion, which I could admire as much as I condemned his error in doctrine. Thereafter, he bewildered me completely, as he got up abruptly and began searching the room. Not out of idle curiosity, but a thorough and determined search, pulling the small number of books off the shelves and flicking through them one by one before shaking them to see if anything should flutter out. One, I noted, he tucked under his coat so it could not be seen. Then he opened the little chest next to the door which contained all the Blundys' possessions, and went through that as well, meticulously searching for something. Whatever it was he did not find it, for he closed the lid with a heavy sigh, and muttered some imprecation in his native language—I did not understand the words, but the sense of disappointment and frustration was clear enough.

He was standing in the room, clearly wondering what to do next, when Sarah arrived.

"How is she?" I heard her say, and my heart stirred to hear her voice again.

"She is not well at all," said the Italian. He had a thick accent, but spoke clearly and evidently understood the language perfectly. "Can you not attend to her more?"

"I have to work," she replied. "Our position is already grave now my mother cannot earn. Will she recover?"

"It is too soon to say. I am drying out the wound, then I will rebind it. I fear she is developing a fever. It may pass, but I am concerned. You must check every half hour for signs of the fever getting worse. And, strange as it may seem, you must keep her warm."

I see here that my recollection of the conversation matches that of Mr. Cola very well; his memory is sound as to the beginning of the matter, so I will not continue to repeat what he has already said. I will, however, add that I noticed something he does not mention, which is that there was instantly in that room a most palpable tension between the two of them, and, while Sarah behaved perfectly normally, concerned only for her mother, Cola became distinctly and ever more agitated as the conversation proceeded. I thought initially that he was alarmed at the thought that his bizarre behavior might have been spotted, but realized this could not be. I should have left instantly, and slipped away while I had the chance to do so unobserved, but I could not bring myself to go.

"I am fortunate indeed. Forgive me, sir. I mean no insolence. My mother told me how well and generously you acted to her, and we are both deeply grateful for your kindness. We are not used to it, and I am truly sorry I misspoke. I was frightened for her."

"That is quite all right," Cola replied. "As long as you do not expect miracles."

"Will you come again?"

"Tomorrow, if I can. And if she worsens, come and find me at Mr. Boyle's. I will be attending him. Now, about payment," he said.

I reproduce, more or less word for word, the conversation as set down by Mr. Cola, and admit that his account, as far as my own memory serves, is impeccable. I will merely add one thing which, strangely, finds no mention in his description. For as he spoke about payment, he took a step closer to her, and rested his hand on her arm.

"Oh yes, your payment. How could I think you would forget about that. We must deal with that urgently, must we not?"

It was only then that she broke away, and led him into the room where I swiftly concealed myself in the gloom so I might escape observation.

"Very well then, physician, take your payment."

And, as Cola says, again with perfect truth, she lay herself down and pulled up her dress, revealing herself to him with the most obscene of gestures. But Cola does not mention the tone in her voice, the way her words trembled with anger and contempt, and the sneer on her face as she spoke.

Cola hesitated, then took a step backward and crossed himself. "You disgust me." It is all in his account, I merely plagiarize his words. But again I must differ on a point of interpretation, for he says he was angry and I did not detect that. What I saw was a man horrified, almost as though he had seen the devil himself. His eyes were wide, and he all but cried out in despair as he recoiled from her and averted his gaze. It was many days before I learned the reasons for this bizarre behavior.

"Lord forgive me, your servant, for I have sinned," he said in Latin, which I could understand and Sarah could not. I remember it well. He was angry at himself, not at her, for she was nothing to him but a temptation which had to be resisted. Then he ran, stumbling in his hurry out of the room, not slamming the door, it is true, for he left too fast to shut it at all.

Sarah lay there on the straw pallet, breathing deeply. She rolled over and buried her head in her arms, face down into the straw. I thought she was merely going to sleep, until I heard the unmistakable sounds of her weeping her heart out, heavy choking sobs which tore at my soul and rekindled, in an instant, all my affections.

I could not help myself, and paused not even an instant to reflect on what I was doing. She had never cried so before, and the sound of such deep sadness flooded my heart, dissolving all bitterness and rancor, and leaving it pure and clean. I took a step forward, and knelt down beside her.

"Sarah?" I said softly.

She jumped in fright as I spoke, pulling her dress down to cover herself and recoiling from me in terror. "What are you doing here?"

I could have given long explanations, could have made up a story about how I'd just arrived and was anxious about her mother, but the sight of her face made me abandon any thought of pretense. "I have come to ask your forgiveness," I said. "I do not deserve it, but I have wronged you. I am so very sorry."

It was easy to say, and I felt as I spoke that those words had been waiting their chance for months. Instantly I felt better, and relieved of a great weight. What was more, I truly think I did not mind whether she forgave me or not, for I knew she would be quite within her rights not to do so, as long as she accepted that my apology was genuine.

"This is a strange time and place to say such a thing."

"I know. But the loss of your friendship and regard is more than I can bear."

"Did you see what happened just now?"

I hesitated before admitting the truth, then nodded.

She did not instantly reply, then began shaking; I thought that it was with tears once more, but then discerned to my astonishment that it was with laughter.

"You are a strange man indeed, Mr. Wood. I cannot make you out at all. On no evidence at all, you accuse me of the most vile behavior, and when you see a scene such as that, you ask my forgiveness. What am I to make of you?"

"I hardly know what to make of myself, sometimes."

"My mother is going to die," she continued, the laughter ceasing, and her mood changing on the instant.

"Yes," I agreed. "I am afraid she is."

"I must accept it as God's will. But I find it impossible to do so. It is strange."

"Why so? No one has ever said obedience and resignation are easy."

"I am so frightened of losing her. I am ashamed, for I can hardly bear to see her the way she is now."

"How did she break her leg? She fell, Lower told me, but how could that be?"

"She was pushed. She came back here in the evening when she had closed the wash house, and found a man in the house, looking through our chest. You know her well enough to realize she would not run away. He got a black eye, I think, but she was pushed to the ground and kicked. One of the blows broke her leg. She is old and frail and her bones are not strong any more."

"Why did you not say so? Make a complaint?"

"She knew him."

"All the more reason."

"All the less. He is a man who worked once for John Thurloe's office, as did my father. Even now he will never be caught or punished for anything he might do."

"But what . . . ?"

"We have nothing, as you know. Nothing that could interest him, at any rate. Except those papers of my father's, which I gave to you. I said they were dangerous. Do you have them safe still?''

I assured her it would take many hours to find them in my room, even if someone knew they were there.

Then I told her of what I had seen that evening, and said that Cola also had made a thorough search. She shook her head sadly. ''Lord, why dost Thou persecute Thy servant so?''

I wrapped my arms around her and we lay there together, I stroking her hair and giving what comfort I could. It was not much.

''I ought to tell you about Jack Prestcott,'' she began eventually, but I hushed her.

''I do not want, or need, to hear anything,'' I said.

Better that it should be forgotten, whatever it was; I did not want to hear, and she was grateful to be spared the humiliation of having to speak.

''Will you return to work for us?'' I asked. ''It is not much to offer, but if it becomes known in the town that the Woods will admit you into their house, it will begin to mend your reputation, quite apart from giving you money.''

''Will your mother have me?''

''Oh, yes. She was very angry when you left, and has never stopped complaining how much better the housework was done when you were there.''

She smiled at that, for I knew my mother had never once allowed herself to issue even the faintest word of praise in Sarah's hearing, lest it make her grow proud.

''Perhaps I will. Although as it seems I am not to pay for doctors now, then my need for money is the less.''

''That,'' I said, ''is carrying submission to divine will too far. If it can be done, then your mother must have attention. How do you know this is not a test of your love for your mother, and that she is meant to survive? Her death would be punishment for your negligence otherwise. You must have treatment for her.''

''All I can afford is a barber, and even they might refuse. She has refused any treatment I can give her, and I could not help in any case.''

''Why?''

"She is old, and it is her time to die, I think. I can do nothing."

"Perhaps Lower could."

"He can try, if he will, and I would be happy if he succeeded."

"I will ask him. If this Cola will say she is no longer his patient, then he might be prevailed upon. He will not abuse a colleague by doing so without his leave, but it sounds as though there should be no trouble gaining that."

"I cannot pay."

"I will see to that, somehow. Don't you worry."

With the very greatest reluctance I pulled myself up. For all the world, I would have stayed there all night, something I had never done before, and which I found strangely enticing; to hear her heart beat against mine and feel her breath against my cheek were the sweetest sensations. But it would have been an imposition and would also have been noticed the next day. She had a reputation to rebuild, and I had one to preserve. Oxford then was not like the king's court, nor even had it the laxity of the town now. All had ears, and too many were swift to condemn. I was myself.

MY MOTHER PRESENTED ONLY THE MOST CURSORY OF objections when I announced that Sarah had repented of her sins and added that, in any case, they were smaller than common tittle-tattle pronounced. It was a mark of charity to forgive the sinner if regret was genuine, and I concluded that I was sure this was the case.

"And she is a good worker, who might, perhaps, now accept a ha'penny less a week," she said shrewdly. "We'll certainly get none better at that wage."

So it was agreed, with yet another ha'penny earmarked from my pocket to make up the difference, and Sarah was reengaged. There then followed the problem of her mother, and I talked to Lower about it a few days later, when I had the opportunity. He was a difficult man to get hold of then, for he was hard at work on his fine examination of the brain, the dedication of which made him most anxious.

"To whom should I address it?" he asked me with a worried frown before I could speak. "It is a most delicate matter, and by far the most concerning part of the whole enterprise."

"Surely not," I said. "The work itself . . ."

He waved his hand dismissively. "The work is nothing," he said. "Pure labor and applied concentration. The expense of publication is worse than that. Do you know how much a good engraver costs? I must have high-quality illustrations; the whole point is lost if the drawings are botched, and with some of these people you can't tell a human brain from a sheep's once they are done. I need at least twenty, all done by a London engraver." He sighed deeply. "I envy you, Wood. You can produce all the books you want and not pay attention to these questions."

"I would like many engravings," I said. "It is very important that readers see the representation of the people I mention, so they can judge for themselves that my account of their characters is accurate, by comparing deeds and features."

"True, true. My point is that your words can stand on their own if need be. In my case, the book is all but incomprehensible if there are not illustrations of great expense."

"So worry about that, not the dedication."

"The illustrations," he said gravely, resuming the worried look, "are mere money. A nightmare, but a straightforward one. The dedication is my entire future. Am I ambitious, and risk aiming too high? Or modest, aim too low and waste my effort for no gain?"

"The book must be its own reward, I think."

"Spoken like a true scholar," he replied testily. "All very well for you, with no family to provide for, and content to remain here forever."

"I am as jealous of fame as the next man," I said. "But that will come from admiration of the book, not by using it as a weapon to bludgeon your way into the favor of the mighty. To whom do you consider giving it?"

"In my dreams, when I think of glory, I naturally think of giving it to the king. After all, that Galileo man in Italy addressed one piece of work to the Medici, and was given a rich court position for life as a result. I imagine His Majesty being so impressed that he straightaway appoints me royal physician. Except," he said bitterly, "that there is one already, and his gracious Majesty is too hard up for two."

"Why not be more imaginative? There are so many addressed to him already and he cannot be grateful to every author in England; you would merely be lost in the melee."

"Such as?"

"I don't know. Someone who is rich, would appreciate the gesture, and whose name would attract attention. How about the Duchess of Newcastle?"

Lower cackled. "Oh, yes," he said. "Very funny. I might as well dedicate it to the memory of Oliver Cromwell. A fine way, if I may say so, to ensure that the world of curiosity never takes me seriously again. A woman experimentalist, indeed; an embarrassment to her family and her sex. Come now, Wood, be serious."

I grinned. "Lord Clarendon?"

"Too predictable and might fall from power, or die from a seizure, before it came out."

"A rival? The Earl of Bristol?"

"Dedicate a book to a professing Catholic? Do you want me to starve to death?"

"A rising star, then? This Henry Bennet?"

"May well become a falling star."

"A man of learning? Mr. Wren?"

"One of my best friends. But he can no more advance me than I can advance him."

"Mr. Boyle, then."

"I like to think I have his patronage already. It would be a waste of an opportunity."

"There must be someone. I will think on it," I told him. "It's not as if the book is about to go to the printers."

Another groan. "Don't remind me. Unless I get some more brains, it never will. I do wish the courts would hang someone."

"There is that young man in jail at the moment, whose chances are not good. Jack Prestcott. It is likely he will be hanged in a week or so. Heaven knows he deserves it."

And so, you see, it was I who reminded Lower of Prestcott, whose arrest had caused something of a stir in the town some ten days previously, and caused him to go off to solicit his body. And I believe it was true that Lower took Cola along, rather than Cola devising some means of visiting the young man in jail, as Dr. Wallis assumed. Indeed, as I will make clear, Mr. Cola had very good reasons for not having anything to do with Prestcott if he could avoid it. It must have been a considerable shock for him to come across someone whom he had met before.

The mention of Prestcott naturally brought my mind back to Sarah Blundy, and the condition of her mother, and I suggested to Lower he might consider treating her.

"No," he said firmly, "I cannot take the patient of another physician, even if Cola is not one. That is the most appalling manners."

"But Lower," I said, "he will not treat her, and the woman will die."

"If he tells me so, then I will reconsider. But I hear she cannot pay."

I frowned at this, for I knew well that my friend habitually and to his own disadvantage treated many who could not afford his services. Lower saw my reaction and looked very ill at ease.

"It would have been different had I offered knowing the situation, but she imposed on poor Cola quite abominably, not telling him she had no money. We physicians have our pride, you know. Besides, I don't want to treat her. You of all people should know what she's like, and I am amazed at your asking me."

"Perhaps I was wrong. The girl has been slandered, at least in part, I am sure of it. Besides, I am not asking you to treat her, I'm asking you to treat her mother; if need be, I will stand the cost."

He thought a moment, as I knew he would, for he was too good a man—and as a physician too much in need of practice—to turn down an opportunity.

"I will talk to Cola, and see what he says," he said. "I will no doubt see him later. Now, you must excuse me, my friend, for I have a busy day. Boyle is running an experiment I wish to observe, I will have to consider approaching this young man you mention in jail, and in addition to all that I have to go to Dr. Wallis for a consultation."

"Is he ill?"

"I hope so. He would be a fine patient to have, if I can cure him. He is well in at the Royal Society, and if I have both him and Boyle behind me, then my entrance will be assured."

And with high hopes he went off, only to be told, so I see from Wallis's manuscript, that his friend Cola was out to steal his ideas. Poor man; no wonder he was so ill-humored with Cola later that day, although it does him credit that he spoke not a word against the Italian, for Lower tried not to level accusations unless he was sure of his ground. Few, alas, put their principles into action in this way; I have met many a scientist who will intone gravely of Lord Bacon and the virtues of the inductive method, yet will rush to believe the idlest gossip without any thought of contradiction. "It seems reasonable to me," they say, not realizing this is pure nonsense. Reason cannot seem anything; I thought this was the whole point of it. It must be capable of demonstration, and if it merely "seems," then it is not reason.

As is known, Lower did speak to Cola, and I to Sarah, and persuaded her that she had no option but to apologize to the Italian so that he would consent to treat the mother once more. This, I may say, was a hard task to accomplish and, had it been her own death that was in prospect, no words or arguments would have persuaded that proud, strange girl to give way. But it was another's life that was at stake, and she accepted that she must submit. For my part, I was concerned lest the Italian renew his advances and decided to reduce the possibility by offering payment myself. It meant doing without near two months' supply of books, but it was an act of charity that I thought would be well made.

I did not, however, have any money. My income in those days came from an annuity on funds I had lent to my cousin to buy his tavern, and he had undertaken to pay me the sum of £67 every Lady Day. He performed this task dutifully, and I was content that I had placed my small fortune to advantage, for nothing is more secure than one's own family—though even this is not always certain. However, he would not, and could not, pay in advance and I had grossly exceeded my budget recently in buying a new viol. Apart from food, and the money I gave my mother, I was almost without funds for several months, and had to live modestly myself to avoid disaster. The three pounds I needed for Cola was a sum far beyond my resources. I could advance near twenty-four shillings, borrowed another twelve from various friends who held me in good credit, and raised nine shillings by selling some books. That left me with fifteen shillings to find, and it was because of this that I summoned my courage and made an appointment to see Dr. Grove.

chapter five

I HAD NEVER MET THE MAN, AND KNEW ONLY OF HIS reputation, which stated that he was irascible and difficult in character, backward in outlook and with a pronounced tendency to cruelty when he had drunk more than a little. He was nonetheless said to be of great brilliance, but time and misfortune had perverted this, and dedicated his acumen to rancor and bitterness. Wallis, I note, speaks well of him, as does Cola, and I do not doubt that he could display great courtesy when he chose; indeed there was none more charming if he thought you worthy or of a similar rank to himself. But a meeting with Grove was a lottery, and the reception he accorded was in no way influenced by the occasion; instead he would use his interlocutors for his own purposes, as his mood dictated.

I was aware of all this, and went nonetheless, for I could think of no other who might assist: I have never had wealthy friends and at that time most of my acquaintance were poorer even than I. I was certain now that, in the matter of the tales I had heard, Grove had been slandered as badly as had Sarah, and was equally sure that he would be grieved his servant had been so punished by baseless malice. I understood, of course, that he might not wish to offer public assistance for the sake of his reputation, but was confident that an opportunity for private aid would be most welcome to him.

So I went and, as a result, brought about his death. I state the fact baldly, so there should be no mistaking the matter. All in their reports give their conclusions, their thoughts, their reasons and their suspicions about why and how this event took place. Many sorts of evidence have been called into the matter; Cola used confession to conclude Sarah was responsible and believed that personal testimony could not be gainsaid. She admitted the deed, therefore had committed it, and I agree that in most cases this is the strongest evidence there is. Prestcott, in his muddled way, used the procedures of legal reasoning, deciding who best benefited and then, as no other information contradicted this, concluded that Thomas Ken was responsible. Dr. Wallis applied his own power of logic, convinced that his fine mind could encompass all relevant issues and draw valid conclusions. All were convinced of the infallibility of their forensic technique, resorted to because the one type of witness which could conclude the matter was unavailable to them: none of them saw who put the poison in the bottle. I did.

My Lord Bacon, in his *Novum Organum,* discusses this point, and investigates with his habitual brilliance the various categories of evidence, and finds them all flawed. None conveys certainty, he decides, a conclusion which (one might think) would be devastating for scientists and lawyers alike: historians and theologians have learned to live with this, the former modestly tempering their claims, the latter resting their glorious edifice on the more reliable foundations of revelation. For without certainty what is science except glorified guesswork? And without the conviction of certainty, total and absolute, how can we ever hang anyone with an easy conscience? Witnesses can lie and, as I know myself, even an innocent can confess to a crime he did not commit.

But Lord Bacon did not despair, and claimed one instance of a fingerpost which points in one direction only, and allows of no other possibility. The perfectly independent eyewitness, who has nothing to gain from his revelation, who is, in addition, schooled in observation and report through a gentlemanly status and education, this is the nearest we can get to a reliable witness and his testimony may be said to be conclusive, overwhelming all lesser forms. I claim here that status, and assert that what follows eliminates all possibility of further argument on the subject.

I sent a brief note to Dr. Grove, begging the favor of an interview, and in due course received a note saying that he would see me that evening. Thus, perhaps some two hours after Mr. Cola had left the college, I knocked on the door.

Naturally, I did not refer to the purpose of my visit immediately; I might be a beggar, but I did not wish to appear an uncivil one. So we talked for a good three-quarters of an hour, which was interrupted frequently by Grove's belching and farting as he complained loudly of the food that his college chose to serve up to its fellows.

"I wish I knew what that cook did to it," he said after a particularly bad attack. "You would not have thought a good simple roast could be so massacred. I swear it will be the death of me in the end. Do you know, I had a guest in this evening. Young Italian man, about your age, I'd guess. He chewed his way through with no complaint, but the look of shock about him was so great I almost felt like laughing straight in his face. That's the trouble with these foreigners. Too used to fancy sauces. They don't know what real meat's like. They like their food like their religion, eh?" He chuckled at his metaphor. "All dressed up and elaborate, so you can't tell what's underneath. Garlic or incense. It's the same thing."

He chuckled again at his little sally, and I could see he was wishing he had thought of it earlier, the better to irritate his guest. I did not point out that his attitude to the food seemed to me a little contradictory.

Here he groaned again, and clutched his stomach. "Dear God, that food. Pass me that little packet of powder, dear boy."

I picked it up. "What is this?"

"An infallible purgative, although that pompous little Italian says it's dangerous. It isn't; Bate says it is safe, and he is the king's physician. If it's good enough for a king, it's good enough for me, I should think. It is vouched for both by authority and by my own experience. Then this Cola tells me it is useless. Nonsense; two pinches and your bowels empty on the instant. I bought a large amount four months back against such occasions as these."

"I believe Mr. Cola is a doctor, so possibly knows what he says."

"So he says. I don't believe it myself. He's too Jesuitical to be a real physician."

"I understand he is treating Anne Blundy of a broken leg," I said, seeing my chance of bringing the conversation around.

At the very name, Dr. Grove's face darkened with displeasure, and he growled menacingly, like a dog warning a rival for a bone.

"So I hear."

"Or was, for she cannot afford the treatment, and Mr. Cola, it seems, cannot afford to work for nothing."

Grove grunted, but I did not take the warning, so eager was I to do my business and depart.

"I have pledged myself for two pounds and five shillings."

"Good of you."

"But I need another fifteen shillings, which I do not possess at the moment."

"If you have come here to ask me for a loan, the answer is no."

"But . . ."

"That girl near cost me eighty pounds a year. I nearly lost the living I have been promised because of her. I don't care if her mother dies tomorrow; it would be no more than she deserves, from what I hear. And if she cannot afford treatment, then that is the consequence of her own behavior, and it would be a sin to obviate the punishment that she has brought on herself."

"It is her mother, I think, who is being punished."

"That is not my doing, and no longer my affair. You seem to concern yourself greatly with this servant of yours, if I may say so. Why is that?"

Perhaps I blushed, and that gave the man the hint, for he was quick-witted in his malice.

"She works for my mother and . . ."

"It was you who recommended that she come to me as a

servant, was it not, Mr. Wood? You who are the *fons et origo* of my troubles with her? And you pay her medical bills as well? That is very caring, unusually so, if I may say it. Perhaps these rumors that have been circulating about her sluttishness should properly refer themselves to you, rather than to me.''

He looked carefully at me, and I saw a slow, unmistakable look of understanding spread across his face. Dissimulation has never been a skill I have either cultivated or perfected. My face is an open book to those who can read, and Grove had that sort of malice which delights in other men's secrets, tormenting and persecuting by his possession of them.

''Ah, the antiquarian and his servant, too wrapped up in his learning for a wife, contenting himself with some sluttish rubbish between his books. That's it, isn't it? You possess this little whore, and think it love. And you play the gallant with this grubby little bug, thinking her in your mind a veritable Eloise, pledging money you do not have, and expecting other people to stand you credit so you can impress your lady. But she is no lady, is she, Mr. Wood? Far from that, indeed.''

He looked at me again, and then laughed outright. ''Oh, dear me, it is true. I see it on your face. This is the perfect joke, I must say. 'The bookworm and the slut,' almost the subject for a poem. An heroic epistle in hexameters. A theme worthy of Mr. Milton himself, for no subject is too hideous for his pen.''

He laughed again, for my face was burning red with shame and anger, and I knew that no denial would persuade him, nor deflect him from his entertainment. ''Come, now, Mr. Wood,'' he continued, ''You must see the joke. Even you must see that. The meek little scholar, dedicated only to his learning, mousing away in his nest of papers, eyes red from never seeing the light, and we wonder why all this endeavor produces nothing. Is it some great work that is taking shape in his brain? Is it the difficulties of conception that delay the birth of a masterpiece? Is it the sheer magnitude of his task that means the years pass by with no result? And then we find out. No, 'tis none of these. It is because, while everyone thinks he is working away, he is instead rolling in the dust with his servant. Better still, he has persuaded his mother to have the girl in her house, turning his servant into a harlot, and his mother into a bawd. Now, Mr. Wood, tell me that is not perfect.''

The theologians tell us that cruelty comes from the devil, and this may be the ultimate cause, for it is most certainly evil in intent. But in its immediate cause I do believe that true cruelty comes from a perversion of pleasure, for the cruel man enjoys the torment he inflicts on others and, like an experienced musician with his viol or virginal, can play upon his instrument and make all manner of harmony, exciting torment and humiliation, distress and empty anger, shame, regret and fear at will. Some can produce all of these, together or singly, with the most delicate touches, sometimes playing more loudly on his subject until the motion excited in the mind is all but unbearable, then more softly so that the misery is summoned gently and with seductive delight. Such a man as Grove was an artist in his cruelty, for he played for the pleasure of his creation, and the delight of his skill.

If Thomas Ken (as I suspect) had regularly been subjected to such treatment, then I could only admire his humility in bearing such constant assaults, all (no doubt) made unseen, and unknown to any of his fellows. For private torment is still more delicious to the tormentor, and more intense for the sufferer, who cannot describe his Calvary to others without seeming weak and foolish, and thus coming to suffer still more cruelty, only this time self-inflicted. I make myself seem ridiculous by recounting this, I know. But I have to retell, and can only hope I will be understood. All men have been shamed and tormented in some degree, and so all know the way in which it unbalances the judgment and fuddles the head, so that the sufferer feels like a beaten animal on a leash, desiring escape, but not knowing how to slip the rope that keeps him in place.

For my trial was not yet over; Grove saw all too well what easy quarry I was, and how simple it was to impose himself upon me, for I had none of those skills which enable others to shrug off attacks, or mount defenses against those who wish them ill.

"I cannot imagine," he said, "that Dr. Wallis will continue to welcome the presence of a man such as yourself in the archives in which you take such pleasure. It is often the case that men do more damage through their lusts than others can ever accomplish. Think of the condemnation your mother and whole family will be forced to endure when it becomes known that she was running a whorehouse for her son, and paying his slut out of her own money."

"Why are you doing this?" I asked in desperation. "Why do you torment me?"

"I? Torment you? Why do you say this? In what way do I torment you? I am merely stating the facts, surely? 'We cannot but speak the things which we have seen and heard.' Acts 4:20. The words of St. Peter himself. Is it right for sin to go unpunished, and fornication undiscovered?"

He stopped talking, and his face darkened all of a sudden, as the air of humor vanished and was replaced by the blackest anger, like the sky in those moments before the heavens are torn by thunder. "I know you, Mr. Wood; I know it was you who sent that girl to me as my servant, so your friend Mr. Ken might calumnize me. I know it was you who spread stories around the town to blacken my name, and so deprive me of my rights. Mr. Prestcott told me all this, as honest a man as you are deceitful. And then you come here to ask me for money, like some grubby little beggar with his ink-stained hand out? No, sir. You deserve, and will receive, nothing but my hatred. You expect to conspire against me and receive no retribution from my hand? You pick a bad enemy, Mr. Wood, and you will soon discover that you have made the worst mistake of your life. I thank you for coming, for I now know how to respond; I have seen the guilt on your face for myself. And believe me, I will pay you back in full. Now get out, and leave me in peace. I hope you will excuse me for not seeing you to the door. My bowels will wait no longer."

And with a monstrous fart, he levered himself up, and walked into the next room, where I heard him pull down his breeches and settle with a loud sigh onto his chamber pot. I could do nothing, and had failed most miserably to defend myself from his attacks on me. I had sat there, reddened in the face like an infant, and made no attempt to reply in any but the most feeble of fashions. And yet I was man enough to burn with rage at his words and contempt. But instead of reacting like a man, I behaved like a child; bereft of any noble reply made to his face, I instead played a foolish prank on him behind his back, then sneaked out like some school jester, fooling myself that I had at least done something in my own defense.

For I took the packet of powder on the table, and poured it entire into the bottle of brandy which stood next his chair.

"Drink that," I thought as I left his room. "And may your entrails torment you."

Then I left him, hoping he would be up all night with the most violent stomach aches. I swear to God and by all I hold true that I meant him no other harm. I wished him to suffer, and to be racked with agony, it is true, and hoped fervently that I had not put too little of the powder in, or that it would not prove too weak to serve. But I did not wish him dead, nor had I any intention of killing him.

chapter six

IT WAS LONG SINCE DARK WHEN I LEFT, AND THE night was cold with a north wind and the suggestion of rain in the air. A miserable night for any man to be out, and yet I could not bring myself to go home and had no craving for the company of my fellows. There was only one thing on my mind and I could not possibly talk of it; in such circumstances all other conversation would have seemed petty and pointless. Nor could I summon the calm necessary for music. There is, usually, something immeasurably restful about the unfolding of a piece and the perfectly sweet inevitability of a well-conceived conclusion. But any piece of music formed in that way repelled me that night, the turmoil of my mind was so far distant from any harmony.

I found myself instead wishing to see Sarah, and the desire grew on me despite all my attempts to quash it. But I did not want her company or consolation or yet her conversation; rather I found a resentment deep within me that sprang from unknown depths, as my mind became convinced that she, and she alone, was the source of the troubles which had been visited upon me. I revisited, once more, all those old suspicions and jealousies which I thought had been suppressed forever. Instead they burst up once again, like tinder in a dry summer forest that catches a spark, and turns into a conflagration at the gentlest of breezes. My fevered mind imagined that my apology had been farcical, my regret misplaced. All my suspicions (so I told myself) were true, for the girl was cursed, and anyone who befriended her would pay heavily for his affections. All this I told myself as I walked, wrapped up in my heavy winter cloak, my feet already damp from the mud only just beginning to freeze over in New College Lane. Even more did I assure myself of my ill fortune as I crossed the High Street into Merton Street, and then turned away from the door of my house, unwilling to see my mother, and disguise the hurt I might well cause her if Grove made good on his promises to turn my family into a laughingstock.

So I walked on, out into St. Aldate's, thinking I might go into the countryside and walk along the river, for the sound of running water is another sure way of calming the soul, as is well attested by innumerable authorities. But I did not walk by the river that night, for I had barely passed Christ Church when I noticed a slight figure on the far side of the road, wrapped up in a shawl that was too thin to be of much use, with a bundle under her arm, walking purposefully along at a rapid pace. I knew instantly from the appearance and the bearing that it was Sarah, going off (so I thought in my delirium) to some secret assignation.

The opportunity finally to satisfy all my suspicions was there and I took it almost without thinking. I knew, of course, that she was in the habit of leaving Oxford either in the evening or for an entire day and night if she was free, and I had believed once that it was to go to find business for herself in those small towns where she would not be recognized; the penalties for whoredom were such that it was foolish for any woman to ply such a trade in her own town. I knew, also, that this was merest nonsense, but the more I told myself that she was a woman of rare goodness, the more the demons within laughed, so that I thought I would go as mad as Prestcott through the contradictions which fought to possess my imagination. And so I decided to carry out my own exorcism, and discover the truth, since she would not tell me herself, and her refusal only stoked my curiosity.

In recounting this, I will give another example of how, proceeding from faulty assumptions, a false conclusion can be drawn from the assembly of indisputable fact. Dr. Wallis states that his theory of a deadly alliance between Cola and the discontented radicals was confirmed by the behavior of the Blundy girl, who spent much time traveling from Burford in the west to Abingdon in the south, carrying messages to sectaries who, he was sure, would in due course rise up as one when the murder of Clarendon had thrown the country into turmoil. When he questioned her, Sarah denied doing any such thing, but in such a way that he (so surely could he penetrate deceit) was convinced she was lying to cover her illegal actions.

She was lying; this is true. And she was trying to cover illegal actions; this is also true. In this respect Dr. Wallis's understanding of the situation was perfectly accurate. For the girl was terrified that he would discover what she was doing, and knew full well that the punishment would be severe, not only for her but for others as well. She was not one of those who sought out martyrdom through pride, but rather was prepared to accept it in humility if it could not be honorably avoided: this, indeed, was her fate. In all other respects, however, Dr. Wallis was wrong.

My decision made all unthinking, I swiftly retraced my steps to my cousin's tavern and begged the use of a horse. Fortunately I knew that part of the world well, and it was a simple matter to take tracks, out to Sandleigh and then back into Abingdon, which enabled me to arrive long before she did. I wore a dark cloak, and a hat pulled down over my forehead, and (as everyone always tells me) I am an inconspicuous person, not one to be noticed in a crowd. It was easy to place myself on the Oxford road, and wait for her to pass, which she did a half hour later. It was also simple to follow her and see what she did, as she took no pains to conceal her movements, or hide her destination, and had no suspicion of being followed. The town has a small quay on the river, used for landing goods for market, and it was to this place that she headed and knocked boldly on the door of a small warehouse that normally stored farmers' produce the night before market. I was undecided about what I should do next and, as I stood there, I noticed first one, then more people also come up to the door and be given admittance. Unlike Sarah, these people were furtive in their movements, and were bundled up so that their faces could not be seen.

I stood back in a doorway for some time to consider this, and found myself entirely perplexed. I should say that, like Wallis, my instant thought was that this was some meeting of radicals, for Abingdon's notoriety was considerable and virtually everyone in the town, from the aldermen down, were persistent offenders—or so reputation said. Nonetheless, it was strange: the town was infamous for the brazen way it defied the law, yet these people were acting in a secretive fashion, as if they were doing something of which even sectaries might disapprove.

I am neither courageous nor daring, and placing myself in a position of peril is strange to my nature, yet my curiosity was all-consuming and I knew that standing outside, waiting for the rain to fall, would answer nothing. Might I be attacked? This was a possibility, I thought. These people had no reputation for placidity in those days, and I had heard so many stories over the years I believed them capable of anything. A sensible person would slip away; a responsible one would make a report to a magistrate. But although I consider myself both, I did neither. Instead, my heart beating heavily in my chest, and my bowels churning from simple fear, I found myself walking up to that door, and the dour man who guarded it.

"Good evening, brother," he said. "Welcome."

It was not the greeting I had expected; there was no suspicion, and instead of the caution I had anticipated, I was received with openness and friendship. But I still had no idea what all this was about. All I knew was that Sarah, among many others, had gone into that building. Who was she seeing? What meeting was she attending? I did not know but, strengthened by the lack of suspicion, I became more determined to find out.

"Good evening . . . brother," I replied. "May I enter?"

"Of course," he said with some surprise. "Of course you may. Although you may not find much room."

"I am not too late, I hope. I have come from out of town."

"Ah," he said with satisfaction. "That is good. Very good. Then you are twice welcome. Whoever you are."

And he nodded for me to go into the warehouse. A little

easier, but still conscious that I might be putting my neck into a fiendish trap, I walked past him.

It was a small, dingy room, scarcely lit, with huge dark shadows playing on the wall from the few lamps which provided the only illumination. It was warm, which surprised me, as there was no fire that I could see and it was cold outside; only gradually did I realize that the heat came from near forty people, who sat or kneeled on the floor so quietly, and with so little movement, that to begin with I didn't realize they were alive at all; I thought that I was seeing bales of hay or corn, packed tightly together on the floor.

Somewhat at a loss, and more perplexed than ever, I made my way to the back of the room and squatted down myself in the darkness, making sure that my cloak was covering much of my face, as everyone there, I saw, had bared their heads in some gesture of commonality; even the women, I noted with some disdain, were similarly exposed. It was strange, I thought: such people were known for refusing to doff their hats even in the presence of the king, let alone any lesser man. Only God, they said with typical conceit, deserved such respect.

I thought that perhaps I had tumbled into a meeting of Quakers or some such, but knew enough of them to realize this was quite unlike their gatherings. Rarely could they manage more than half a dozen people, and even less frequently did they gather in such a fashion. Then I considered that perhaps these were radical sectaries, gathered together to plot some uprising; the thought made me queasy as I knew that, with my habitual ill fortune, the magistrate's men would undoubtedly surround the place and cart me off to prison as a spreader of sedition. But the women? And such quietness? Hardly so; such people are characterized above all by raucous shouting as each and all express their opinions and damn all others. This tranquil mood was not what I associated with such devils.

And then I realized that all eyes in the place, every single person, were focused with extraordinary attention on a dim figure at the front, the only person standing, although as quiet as all the others. It took some time for my eyes to become accustomed to the gloom and I realized that this shadowy figure was Sarah herself, perfectly immobile, with her thick black hair falling loose around her shoulders and her head bowed so that her face was almost entirely obscured. Again, I was mystified; it was not as if she was doing anything, nor was there any expectation in the audience that she should. I think I was the only person there not wholly content with the proceedings.

How long she had stood like that I do not know; perhaps from the moment she came in, which was now nearly half an hour; I do know that we all sat there for another ten minutes in the most perfect of silence; and a strange experience it was to be so very still and immobile with all others in equal quietude. Had I not been perfectly in command of myself, I would have sworn I had heard a soft voice in the roof beams, telling me to be patient, and calm. It frightened me until I looked up and saw it was only a dove, fluttering from beam to beam as the presence of people disturbed its rest.

But even that did not alarm me as much as when Sarah moved. All she did was lift her head, until she was looking at the roof. The shock, and ripple of excitement that went through the audience was quite extraordinary, almost like being hit by lightning; a groan of anticipation from some quarters, a hiss of breath from others, and some shuffling, as many of the present leaned forward in anticipation.

"She will talk," came a soft murmur from a woman close by, followed by a hushing sound from a man next to her.

But she did not. Merely moving her head conveyed quite enough dramatic effect for the audience; any more excitement, it seemed, would be too much for them. Instead she gazed at the roof for a few more minutes, then looked down at the assembled throng, who reacted with even more tremulous emotion than before. Even I, caught up in the fervor despite myself, found my heart beating faster in my chest, as the moment (whatever it was to be) drew nearer.

When she did utter, she spoke so softly and sweetly that her words were hard to hear; instead everyone there had to lean forward intently to catch what she was saying. And the words themselves, set down on paper with my pen, give nothing of the mood, for she entranced us all, bewitched us even, until grown men were crying openly, and women were rocking themselves to and fro with expressions of angelic peace such as I have never seen in any church. With her words, she gathered us all to her breast, and gave us comfort, reassuring us of our doubts, calming us of our fears and convincing us that all manner of things was good. I do not know how she did it; unlike actors she had no technique nor any manner of artifice in her address. Her hands remained clasped in front of her and made no gestures; she scarcely moved at all, and yet out of her mouth and her whole body came balm and honey, freely offered to all. By the end I was shaking with love for her and God and all mankind in equal measure, but had no idea why this was. All I know is that from that moment I consigned myself, freely and without hesitation, into her power, for her to do as she wished and knowing it would be nothing ill.

She spoke for well over an hour and it was like the finest consort of musicians, as the words flowed and turned and played over us until we too were like sounding boxes, vibrating and resonating with her speech. I have read the words over again. How much I disappoint myself, for the spirit is entirely lacking from them, nor have I in any way managed to encompass the perfect love she spoke, or the calm adoration she evoked in her listeners. I feel, indeed, like a man who wakes from sleep after a wondrously perfect dream, and writes it all down in a frenzy, then finds that all he has on the page are mere words bereft of feeling, as dry and unsatisfying as chaff when the corn is removed.

"To all men I say, there are many roads which lead to my door; some broad and some narrow, some straight and some crooked, some flat and commodious while others are rough, and pitted with dangers. Let no man say that his is the best and only road, for they say so out of ignorance alone.

"My spirit will be with you, I will lay stretched out on the earth, licking the dust and breathing in the earth; I will give milk from my breast for the earth, mother of our mother, and for Christ, father and husband and wife. I held him at night as a bundle of spice between my breasts, and knew it was myself. I saw my spirit on his face, and felt the witness of fire on my breasts, love's fire that burns and heals and warms with healing like sunshine after rain.

"I am the bride of the lamb and the lamb itself; neither angel nor envoy, but I the Lord have come. I am the sweetness of the spirit and the honey of life. I will be in the grave with Christ, and will rise after betrayal. In each generation the Messiah suffers until mankind turns away from evil. I say, you wait for the kingdom of Heaven, but you see it with your own eyes. It is here and is always within your grasp. An end to religion and to sects, throw away your Bibles, they are needed no more: cast out tradition and hear my words instead.

"My grace and my peace and my mercy and my blessing are upon you. Few see my coming, and fewer still will see my going. This evening the last days begin, and men move to entrap me, the same men as before, the same as always. I forgive them now, for I will remember sins and iniquities no longer; I am come to give absolution in my blood. I must die and all must die, and will keep on dying to the end in every generation."

As I say, such as I remember are but a few fragments of the whole discourse, which ranged from sensible practicality deep into madness and back again, swinging from simplicity into incoherence in a way which made it impossible to tell one from the other. It made no difference to any in the audience, and it made no difference to me either. I take no pride in my captivity, and recall it with pain, and do not intend to defend or excuse myself. I state it as it was, and to those who scorn me (as I would do myself, were I another) I can only say this: you were not there, and do not know what magic she wrought. All I can say is that I was sweating as if I had the most violent fever, was not alone in feeling the tears of joy and sadness rolling down my cheeks and, like all others present, scarcely even noticed when the words stopped dropping from her mouth, and she walked out a little side door. It took perhaps a quarter of an hour before the spell dissipated and, one by one, like an audience when a play ends, we came back to ourselves and discovered that all our limbs and muscles were as stiff as if we had labored in the fields for an entire day at harvest time.

The meeting was over, and it was obvious that the only reason it had assembled was to hear Sarah speak; in that town, and amongst those people, she had a notoriety that had already spread far. The merest mention that she might make an utterance was enough to bring men and women—the poor, the rough and those of low breeding—out in all weathers, and risk all manner of sanction from the authorities. Like everyone else, I scarcely knew what to do once it had finished, but eventually pulled myself together sufficiently to realize I must collect my horse and go back to Oxford. In a daze of the most complete peacefulness I walked back to the inn where I had left it and headed home.

Sarah was a prophetess. Only a few hours earlier the notion would have elicited the utmost scorn from me, for the country had been benighted by such people for years, thrown into the light of day by the troubles in the way that wood lice become visible when a stone is overturned. I remember one who had come to Oxford when I was about fourteen, a man spitting and foaming at the mouth as he raved in the street, dressed in rags like some early saint or stoic, damning all the world to hellfire before falling to the ground in a convulsion. He made no converts; I was not one of those who threw stones at him (which attacks pleased him mightily, as proving the Lord's favor) but like all others, I was disgusted by the display and could easily see that, whatever he had been touched by, it was not by God. They locked him up and were then merciful in throwing him out of the city rather than imposing any harsher punishment.

A woman prophet was much worse, you might think, even less likely to inspire anything but contempt, yet I have already shown that it was not so. Is it not said that the Magdalen preached and converted, and was blessed for it? She was not condemned, nor ever has been, and I could not condemn Sarah either. It was clear to me that the finger of God had touched her forehead, for no devil or agent of Satan can reach into the hearts of men like that. There is always a bitterness in the devil's gifts, and we know when we are deceived, even if we permit the deception. But I could say for a moment only what it was in her words that conveyed such peace and tranquillity; I had the experience of it merely, not the understanding.

My horse clopped along the empty road, better able than I to see where the track led in a darkness only lifted slightly by a moon which occasionally peeped from behind the clouds, and I let my mind wander over the evening, trying to recapture that feeling that had been mine so recently and which I felt, with the greatest of sadness, to be ebbing slowly away. So preoccupied with my thoughts was I that I scarcely noticed the shadowy figure on the road, walking slowly in front of me. When I did, I hailed it without thinking, before I realized who it was.

"It is late and dark to be on such a road alone, madam," I said. "Do not be afraid but mount up here, and I will take you to your home. It is a strong horse, and will not mind."

It was Sarah, of course, and when I saw the moon on her face, I was suddenly afraid of her. But instead, she held out her hand, and allowed me to pull her up, and she sat comfortably behind me, her arms around my waist to avoid slipping.

She said nothing, and I did not know what to say; I felt like telling her that I had been at the meeting, but feared to come out with some foolishness, or have my words taken as a mark of deceit and mistrust. So instead we went along in silence for a half hour, before she began to talk herself.

"I do not know what it is," she said in my ear, so quietly that a man not three paces away would not have heard. "There is no point wondering, as I am sure you do. I have no recollection of what I say or why I say it."

"You saw me?"

"I knew you were there."

"You did not object?"

"I think that what I have to say is for anyone who wishes to listen. It is for them to judge whether it is worth the effort."

"But you keep it secret."

"Not for myself; that does not matter. But those who listen to me would be punished as well, and I cannot ask for that."

"You have always done this? Your mother, too?"

"No. She is wise, but has nothing of this; her husband

neither. As for myself, it started shortly after his death. I was at a meeting of simple people, and remember standing up to say something. I recollect nothing more until I found myself lying on the floor, with them all gathered around me. They said I had spoken the most extraordinary words. It happened again a few months later, and after a while people came to hear me. It was too dangerous in Oxford, so now I go to places like Abingdon. I often disappoint them, as I stand there and nothing comes over me. You heard me this evening. What did I say?''

She listened as though I was reporting a conversation which she did not hear, then shrugged when I was finished. ''Strange,'' she said. ''What do you think? Am I cursed or mad? Perhaps you think I am both.''

''There is no harshness or cruelty in what you say; no threats or warnings. Nothing but gentleness and love. I think you are blessed, not cursed. But blessings can be even heavier burdens, as many people in the past have discovered.'' I found that I was talking as quietly as she, so that I might have been talking only to myself.

''Thank you,'' she said. ''I did not want you of all people to scorn me.''

''You really have no idea what you say? There is no preparation?''

''None. The spirit moves in me, and I become its vessel. And when I awake, it is like coming out of the most gentle dream.''

''Your mother knows of all this?''

''Yes, of course. At first she thought it was just a prank, because I had always been scornful of fanatics and all those who run around pretending to be possessed to get money from people. I still am, and that makes it worse to have become one myself. So when I stood that first time, and she heard of it, she was shocked by my impiety; they were not our people in the conventicle, but they were good and kind and she was distressed I might make fun of them. It took quite a lot to convince her that I had not been deliberately offensive. She was unhappy about it, and still is. She thinks that sooner or later it will lead me into trouble with the law.''

''She is right.''

"I know. A few months back it nearly did; I was at Tidmarsh's, and there was a raid by the watch. I only just got away. But there is not a great deal I can do about it. Whatever is sent me, I must accept. There is no point in doing anything other. Do you think I am mad?"

"If I went to someone like Lower, and told them what I have just witnessed, he would do his very best to cure you."

"When I left that hall this evening, a woman came up to me, fell down on her knees in the ice and kissed the hem of my dress. She said that her baby had been dying, the last time I came to Abingdon. I walked past the door and it was instantly well.".

"Do you believe her?"

"She believes it. Your mother believes it. Many others in the past few years have held me responsible for such deeds. Mr. Boyle heard of it as well."

"My mother?"

"She was wracked with pain with a swollen ankle; it made her very ill-tempered, and she tried to beat me. I held her hand to make her stop, and she swore that at that moment the pain and the swelling went."

"She never mentioned it to me."

"I begged her not to. It is a terrible reputation to have."

"And Boyle?"

"He heard something, and thought I must have knowledge of herbs and potions, so asked for my recipe book. It was difficult to refuse him, as I could hardly tell him the truth."

There was a long silence broken only by the sound of the horse's hooves on the road, and the snuffle of its breath in the cold night air. "I do not want this, Anthony," she said quietly, and I could hear the fear in her voice.

"What?"

"Whatever this is. I don't want to be a prophet, I don't want to cure people, I don't want them coming to me, and I don't want to be punished for something I cannot prevent and do not will. I am a woman, and I want to marry and grow old and be happy. I don't want humiliation and imprisonment. And I don't want what will happen next."

"What do you mean?"

"An Irishman came to see me; an astrologer. He said he had seen me in his charts, and came to warn me. He said I will die, that everyone will want me dead. Anthony, why would that be? What could I have done?"

"I'm sure he's wrong. Who believes people like that?"

She was silent.

"Leave, then, if it worries you," I said. "Go away."

"I cannot. Nothing can be changed."

"You will have to hope this Irishman is wrong and you are mad, then."

"I do hope so. I am frightened."

"Oh, I am sure there is nothing to worry about, really," I said. I shook myself to cast off the atmosphere of ominous terror that had grown around us, and when I did so, I saw more clearly the foolishness of our conversation. Set down here, I suppose it seems even more so. "I don't hold with Irishmen or astrologers and from my limited experience, prophets and Messiahs these days tend to rush around telling all the world of their powers. It is most unusual to hope that the cup be taken from you."

She laughed, at least, but noticed my allusion, for she knew her Bible well, and looked curiously at me when I spoke it. For my part, I swear I did not notice till later what I had said, and it passed from my mind easily as we plodded on.

As I look back, I think that time on the horse was the happiest in my life. The return of the easy intimacy which I had so wantonly destroyed through my jealousy was such a blessing that, had it been possible, I would have continued on to Carlisle simply to preserve and lengthen our time together, the conversation of perfect amity and the feel of her arms around my waist. Despite the freezing chill in the air, I felt no cold at all, and might have been in the most commodious parlor, not on a muddy, wet road near midnight. I suppose the tumultuous events of that evening and night had fuddled my mind, and so shocked me out of my normal caution that I did not set her down on the outskirts of town so that we were not seen together in such a fashion. Rather, I kept her with me all the way back to my cousin's tavern, and even then could not let her go.

"How is your mother?"

"She is in comfort."

"You can do nothing for her?"

She shook her head. "It is the only thing I have ever wished for myself, and I cannot have it."

"You'd best go and tend her, then."

"She is in no need of me. A friend who knows me well offered to spend time with her, and only leave when she was sure she was asleep so I could attend that meeting. She will die soon, but not yet."

"So stay with me still."

We walked back to Merton Street, and went into my house, mounting the stairs quietly so that my mother would not hear, and then, in my room, we loved each other with a passion and ferocity I have never before, nor since, felt for any living person, nor has anyone shown such love to me. I had never before spent a night with a woman, had someone lying by my side in the quietness of the dark, hearing her breath and feeling her warmth beside me. It is a sin, and it is a crime. I say it frankly, for I have been taught so all my life, and only madmen have ever said otherwise. The Bible says it, the fathers of the church have said it, the prelates now repeat it without end, and all the statutes of the land prescribe punishment for what we did that night. Abstain from fleshly lusts, which war against the soul. It must be so, for the Bible speaks only God's truth. I sinned against the law, against God's word reported, I abused my family and exposed them even more to risk of public shame, I again risked permanent exclusion from those rooms and books which were my delight and my whole occupation; yet in all the years that have passed since I have regretted only one thing: that it was but a passing moment, never repeated, for I have never been closer to God, nor felt His love and goodness more.

chapter seven

WE WERE NOT DISCOVERED; SARAH AROSE AT DAWN, and slipped softly downstairs to begin her duties in the kitchen, and only after the fire was going and the water brought in did she leave to see her mother. I did not see her again for two days, and did not know that she discovered her mother abandoned by the friend, and in need of the assistance which prompted her to apologize to Cola and submit to his experiment with transfusion. She was sworn to silence and was a woman of her word in all respects.

For myself, I went back to a blissful sleep and awoke late, so it was several hours before I walked to an inn for some bread and ale, an occasional extravagance I indulge in when I am feeling at ease with the world, or wish to avoid my mother's conversation. It was only then, as I was sitting dreamily over a pot, that I heard the news.

There are countless tales in myth to warn us of our heart's desires. King Midas wished to be so rich he desired that everything he touched might turn to gold, and legend has it that he died of hunger as a result. Euripides talks of Tithonus, whom Eos loved so well she begged Zeus to give him eternal life. But mistakenly she asked not for youth as well and he suffered an eternity of decrepitude until even the cruel gods took pity on him.

And I wished to be spared the scandal which Grove in his malice threatened to visit on me. The memory of him cut into my mood, and I prayed that his mouth might be stopped forever, and that I should not suffer for what I had done and said, however deserving I was of punishment. I had scarcely finished my ale when I heard that my wish had been granted.

The moment I heard the news my blood ran cold with horror, for I was absolutely certain that my own prayers and private vengeance had been responsible. I had killed a man. I believe there is no crime greater, and I was tormented with remorse at my deed, so much so that I felt as though I should instantly confess. Cowardice soon overcame this urge, as I thought of the shame of my family should I do so. And I convinced myself that I was not really to blame. I had made a mistake, that was all. The intent was lacking, my guilt was limited, and my chances of discovery small.

So speaks the mind, but the conscience is not so easily quelled. I recovered from the shock as best I could, seeking out all the information available in the attempt to discover some small detail to convince me that I had not, in fact, caused this awful event. I persuaded myself for a brief while that all was well, then tried to return to my labors, and found all my concentration gone, as my rebellious soul confronted me with what I had done. And still I could not take any step to relieve myself; my contentment vanished, my sleep soon after and in the days and weeks that followed I grew haggard and sickly in my struggle.

I aim for sympathy but do not deserve any, for it was easy to remedy and cleanse myself of disquiet. I merely had to stand and say, "I did this." All else would be taken care of.

But to die myself, and make my family live under the obloquy of having engendered a murderer? To have my mother hooted through the street and spat on, my sister living out her old age in spinsterhood as no man would attach himself to her? My cousin's trade dry up into failure because no one would drink in his tavern? These were real concerns. Oxford is not London, where all sin is forgotten within a week, where criminals are celebrated for their deeds, and thieves rewarded for their endeavors. Here all know the business of all, and the desire to maintain good morals is acute, however great secretive breaches might be. My greatest loyalty is, and always has been, to my family. I have lived to bring what little luster is in my power to my name, and maintain our position of respectability. I would have accepted that the courts might punish me, for I could not deny that it would be deserved, but I recoiled in horror at doing such great injury to my people. They struggled as it was, due to our losses in the troubles, and I would not add to their burden.

I nursed my guilt to myself for the next few days, and kept to my room in miserable solitude, refusing food and conversation even with Sarah, whom I dared not look in the face. I had told her I had been to see Grove, but dared not tell her what I had done as I could not abide her disgust, nor could I burden her with information she would be obliged to share. I spent much of my time in prayer, and even more staring blankly at empty pieces of paper on my desk as I failed to get my mind to concentrate on even the dullest and most mechanical of tasks.

And in those few days I missed much of importance in my tale, for it was in those days that Lower discovered the bottle of brandy and took it to Stahl; dissected Dr. Grove to see if the corpse accused Cola through bleeding; and performed the experiment of transfusion on Anne Blundy. It was also in these days, it seemed, that the finger of suspicion first began to point at Sarah, but I swear I was totally unaware of this. I was aware only of Lower's growing discomfort with the Italian, and his fear that Cola was out to steal his glory.

MY OWN OPINION OF THE DISPUTE BETWEEN THE TWO is a complicated one, yet I think it will serve. Both, I think, tell the truth even though their conclusions be opposite. Nor do I think that this is necessarily a contradiction. I do accept, of course, that there is one truth, but except on rare occasions we are not given to know it. Horace says, *Nec scire fas est omnia,* it is not God's will we should know all, a sentence taken (I believe) from Euripides. To know all is to see all, and omniscience is God's alone. I state the obvious, I suppose, for if God exists, so does truth and if there was no God (a thing not to be imagined in seriousness, but as a philosophic jest alone), then would truth disappear from the world,

652

and the opinion of one would be no better than that of another. I might also reverse the theorem, and say that, if men come to think all is merely opinion, then they must come to atheism as well. " 'What is truth?' said jesting Pilate, and would not stay for an answer." I do believe that the fact we know in our hearts there is truth without having to reason about it is the prettiest proof of God's existence there can be, and as long as we strive to discover it, so we also strive to know God.

But, with Lower and Cola, we have no assistance from the divine, and must reason it out as best we can. Cola has put his account on paper for all to see; Lower told me (and many others) his version, although he disdained to enter the lists by publishing any sort of justification for his claims. He had published his account in the *Transactions,* he told me, because he was assured by Dr. Wallis that Cola had drowned in an accident when leaving the country. And even had he been assured of the man's health, he would have done so. In his recollection, Cola's notions were only of the vaguest sort; he spoke of rejuvenating blood by some magical means, but said not a word about transfusion. It was only when Lower described his own experimentation with injections that Cola hit on the idea of transferring new blood, and accomplishing the desired aim in that fashion. Lower had had this possibility in the back of his mind for months by then, and it was only a matter of time before it took place. He points out that, even by Cola's own account, it was he who performed most of the technical labors. Consequently, the credit should be his.

When I received this account and compared both versions I was, frankly, astonished that the dispute could arise at all, for it seems to me that it was the meeting of the two men which produced the result, and that both were responsible in equal part for the idea. When I wrote this to Lower, he ridiculed the idea with some asperity and made it clear that (he put it as kindly as he could, but his irritation showed through) only an historian, who has no ideas, could imagine such an absurdity. He repeated this assertion a week or so ago, when he made one of his now very rare visits to Oxford, and called on me to pay his respects.

The transfusion of blood, he said, was a discovery. Did I agree?

I did.

And the essence of an invention or discovery lay in the idea, not in the execution.

Agreed.

And it was whole and entire, not consisting of parts. An idea was like one of Mr. Boyle's corpuscles, or Lucretius's atoms, and could not be reduced further. It is the essence of the conception that it is entire and perfect in itself.

It was an Aristotelian concept that sounded strange on his lips, but I agreed.

One cannot have half an idea?

If it cannot be divided, then obviously not.

Therefore they all must have a single point of origin, as you cannot have one thing in two places at the same time.

I agreed.

Therefore it was reasonable to assume that it could arise in the mind of only one man?

I agreed again, and he nodded with satisfaction, convinced he had disproved my attempt to restore amiable agreement between the two men. His logic was impeccable, but I must say I still do not accept it, although I am incapable of saying why. Nonetheless he proceeded to his next theorem that, if one of the pair had conceived the idea of transfusion first, then the other must be lying when he claims its authorship.

Given his starting point, I agreed this was again an inevitable conclusion, and Lower rested content with the notion that, in a choice between himself and Cola, then he had the higher claim, for who would take the word of an Italian dilettante above that of an English gentleman? Not that it was unknown for the latter to lie, or miscomprehend the truth, but because the chances of it were very much smaller. This is well known and accepted. I did not enquire whether it was equally accepted in Italy.

chapter eight

ALTHOUGH I SCARCELY VENTURED OUT DURING those days, on the few occasions I left either my house or the library, I encountered the Italian; the first time our meeting was deliberate, for I sought him out in Mother Jean's cookhouse the day I heard of Grove's death, the second time it was by accident, after the play. On the first occasion, in particular, the conversation threw my mind into the utmost confusion.

He has recounted this talk between us in his memoir, and it was clear at the time that he believed he had deceived me. I found him to be sober and courteous, with an intelligent air and of moderate conversation. He was clearly gifted in tongues, for although the conversation tended to be in Latin, it seemed to me that he missed very little when we lapsed into English. Despite his skill, however, he gave himself away badly to anyone with the sense to listen; for what doctor (or soldier, for that matter) could talk so knowledgeably about heresies long dead, could refer so learnedly to the works of Hippolytus and Tertullian, or had even heard of Elchesai, Zosimus or Montanus? Papists, I grant, are more interested in such obscurities than Protestants, who have learned to read the Bible for themselves and thus need less knowledge of the opinions of others, but few even of the most devoted Romanists would have such matter readily to hand for use in dispute.

Cola did not act like a physician when he searched the Blundys' cottage; now he did not talk like one either; I found my curiosity about him getting ever greater.

Even so, this was a minor matter in comparison to the substance of the conversation, and the direction he gave me so unknowingly. I have often thought about this phenomenon which occurs so frequently in the lives of all men that we almost fail to notice it anymore. How often have I had a question on my mind, and picked a book at random off the shelf, often one I have never heard of before, yet found the answer I seek within its covers? It is well known that men feel impelled to go to that place where they are to encounter, for the first time, that woman who is to be their wife. Similarly, even peasants know that letting the Bible fall open where it will, and putting a finger randomly on the page thus revealed will, more often than not, give the most sound advice that any man could wish to hear.

The thoughtless call this coincidence, and I note amongst philosophers a growing tendency to talk of chance and probability, as though this was some explanation rather than a scholarly disguise for their own ignorance. Simpler people know exactly what it is, for nothing can happen by chance when God sees and knows all; even to suggest anything different is absurd. These coincidences are the visible signs of His manifest providence, from which we can learn well if we will only see His hand, and contemplate the meaning of His actions.

So it was that I was driven against my will to Sarah's house that night Cola searched it, came across her on the Abingdon road and followed her, and so it was also in my conversation with Cola. All those things which the scoffers call chance and accident and coincidence show the direction God takes in men's affairs. Cola could have taken any example at all to illustrate his point, any one of which would have done as well or better than a tale of a long-extinct and forgotten heresy. So through what inspiration did he mention that most obscure branch of the Montanist heresy? What angel whispered in his ear and directed his mind so that, by the time I left the cookhouse, my limbs were trembling and my body sweating? "In each generation the Messiah would be reborn, would be betrayed, would die, and be resurrected, until mankind turns away from evil, and sins no more.'' These were his words, and they frightened me greatly, for Sarah had said precisely the same only the night previously.

For the next few days, it was my greatest obsession, and all thought of Dr. Grove passed from my mind. I read what little I had at home first of all, then went to New College to ransack the small library of Thomas Ken, and scarcely noticed that poor tortured man's look of grief and anxiety. I wish I had, for had I attended more he might have spoken, and Sarah perhaps would have been spared. But I ignored his misery, and later it was not possible to make shift: he had gone to Grove to beg his forgiveness for the calumny he had spread, but found only that he was trapped in his falsehood, as he discovered Prestcott but did nothing to alert the magistrate or the watch. He could not retract his lie about seeing Sarah going into Grove's room without risking also being forced to confess that he aided a felon in his escape. Between facing the wrath of God after death, or the vengeance of Dr. Wallis in this life, he preferred the former, and has paid dearly for it ever since. For he stood by while an innocent was hanged that he might enjoy eighty pounds a year. I cannot condemn too harshly; my own sin was scarcely the less, for when I did speak, it was too late.

He lent me such books as I wanted, and when I had done with them, I went to the Bodleian, where I searched for the tale that Cola had told me. Fragments in Tertullian and in Hippolytus were all as he said, I found references in Eusebius and Irenaeus and Epiphanius as well. And the more I read the more my reason revolted against what I saw; for how was it possible that Sarah, unlettered as she was, could have quoted, almost word for word, a whole series of prophecies made more than a thousand years ago? There was no doubt about it; time and again the words were the same, almost as though it was the same person talking, this long-dead woman prophesying on a hilltop in Asia Minor and the girl who talked so strangely in Abingdon of her death.

It was an effort, but I put it all aside; it was a mad time, and the air was still filled with lunacies of all sorts, even after two decades which had all but exhausted men's appetites for enthusiasm in religion. I told myself that she was deluded, caught up in the corruption of the age, and that in due course, when she was less concerned with her mother and her own future, then she would cast off these foolish notions and endanger herself no more. It is often the case that men succeed in persuading themselves through the exercise of reason that what they know to be true is not so, merely because they cannot understand it.

To recover from this melancholy, I forced myself back into society, and in particular agreed willingly to Lower's suggestion that I accompany him and Cola to the play. I had not seen one for near four years, and much as I love my town, I admit it has few diversions to occupy a brooding mind when it needs distraction. I had a splendid day, I recall, for despite Mr. Cola's criticisms, I found the story of Lear and his daughters both entertaining and moving, as well as most excellently acted. And I also enjoyed passing the rest of the evening in good company and again had my interest in the Italian aroused. I spent a considerable time talking to him, and used the opportunity to probe him as much as I dared. Whatever there was to be discovered, however, remained elusive to my intelligence; Cola parried my questions about himself with ease, and forever returned to matters in which his own beliefs and opinions played no part. Indeed, he seemed more than aware of my curiosity, and amused himself in avoiding any answer of substance.

I could not, of course, ask him directly about my interests. Much as I would have liked to know why he had searched Sarah Blundy's cottage, it was impossible to put the question in any fashion which would have produced a useful reply. But, by the time he left he was aware of my suspicions about him, and he looked at me more warily, and with greater respect, than before.

Once he and Lower had gone, Locke and I spent another hour in agreeable conversation before we too left the inn and retired. I wished my mother good night and passed some time in my daily reading of the Bible and was on the verge of retiring for my night when a hammering on the door brought me back down the stairs to open up the door I had just laboriously closed up. It was Lower, apologizing greatly for the disturbance but asking for a moment of my time.

"I am at a complete loss," he said when I had ushered him into my room and asked him to keep his voice down. My mother detested any sort of disturbance in the evening, and I would have had to endure many ill-humored days thereafter if Lower's conversation or boots had awoken her.

"What did you think of Cola?" he asked abruptly.

I gave a noncommittal reply, as it was clear to me that it mattered not at all what I thought of him. "Why do you ask?"

"Because I keep on hearing shocking tales about him," he said. "I was summoned by Dr. Wallis, as you know. Not only is this Cola a man who habitually steals the ideas of other people, but Wallis now seems to believe he may have had some involvement in the death of Dr. Grove. Did you know that I anatomized the man? The point was to see whether his body accused Cola."

"And did it?" My heart was beating faster as this subject was raised. My worst nightmares were coming true before my eyes, and I had no idea how I should best react. Until that moment I had no idea that Grove's death was under investigation, and had not only persuaded myself that I was safe, but had even reached some conviction in my mind that his death was in no way connected with myself.

"No. Of course not. Or maybe it did; by the time I'd cut him open it was impossible to say whether he was bleeding in accusation or not. Either way, the test produced nothing."

"Why does Wallis think this?"

"I have no idea. He is a close man, and never says anything unless he has to. But his warnings have alarmed me. And now, it seems, I have to take Cola off on tour with me. I shall lie awake every night, convinced he will slip a stiletto into me."

"I wouldn't concern myself too much," I said. "He seemed a perfectly ordinary man to me, for a foreigner. And I know from experience that Dr. Wallis gets a strange pleasure in appearing to know more than other people. Often it is not the case, but merely a device to encourage confidences."

Lower grunted. "Still, there is something odd about the

man. Now it has been pointed out to me, I can feel it. I mean, what is he doing here? He's meant to be sorting out his family affairs, but he should be in London for that. And I know that he has done nothing whatsoever about them. Instead, he has attached himself to Boyle, and is remarkably obsequious to him, and is taking on patients in the town.''

"Only one, surely," I pointed out. "And that scarcely counts.''

"But what if he decides to stay? A fashionable doctor from the continent. Bad news for me, and he is remarkably keen to hear all about my patients. I do believe that he may be thinking about trying to steal them from me.''

"Lower," I said sternly, "for a wise man, you are the biggest fool I know sometimes. Why would a man of means, the son of a wealthy Italian merchant, want to set up in Oxford to take your patients? Be reasonable, man.''

With great reluctance he conceded the point. "And as for having anything to do with the death of Dr. Grove, then I must say I think that total fantasy. Why on earth would he, or anybody else, want to do such a thing? Do you know what I think?''

"What?''

"I think Grove killed himself.''

Lower shook his head. "That is not the point. The point is that I am to spend the next seven days in the company of a man whom I increasingly distrust. What am I to do about it?''

"Cancel the trip.''

"I need the money.''

"Go on your own.''

"It would be the height of discourtesy to withdraw an invitation once given.''

"Suffer in silence, condemn not on the word of others, and try to establish for yourself what he is. Meanwhile," I said, "as you are here and know him better than anyone, I must ask your advice on something. I do so reluctantly, as I am loath to excite your suspicion still further, but it is a curiosity which I cannot explain.''

"Go ahead.''

So, in as unsensational a way as I could manage, I told of

my visit to the Blundy cottage, and how I had seen Cola come in, establish the woman was asleep, then search the entire premises. I decided to leave out what happened thereafter.

"Why don't you ask Sarah Blundy if anything is missing?"

"He is her physician. I do not want to undermine that trust, nor to have him refuse again to treat her mother. What do you think?"

"I think I will sleep on my money bag when we are in the same bed," he said. "It seems odd that you spend considerable effort trying to assuage my suspicions, then reignite them again at the last."

"I apologize. His behavior was strange, but I hardly think your own fears have much substance."

The conversation reawoke my own concerns and, I must note, at no point did Lower mention that the magistrate had already begun investigating Sarah as a possible culprit. Had he done so, then I would have behaved differently. Rather, my thoughts as Lower left me to peaceful solitude once more turned more to Cola's strange behavior, and I decided to reach the bottom of the matter. Before I did so, however, I decided it would be best to question Sarah on the matter, physician or no.

"From that shelf?" she said when I had recounted the incident. "There is nothing of value there. Only some books which belonged to my father." She examined the books carefully. "There is one missing," she said. "But I never read it as it was in Latin."

"Your father read Latin?" I asked in some surprise. He was a man of parts, that I knew, but I had not realized his self-learning had proceeded that far.

"No," she said. "He thought it a dead language, and of no use to anyone but fools and antiquarians. Begging your pardon," she added with a faint smile. "He wanted to create a new world, not revive an old. Besides, he once told me he did not think we had anything to learn from pagan slave-masters."

I let my disapproval pass without comment. "So where did all these books come from?"

She shrugged. "I only ever thought of them when I considered selling them. I asked a bookseller, but he offered me very little. I was going to give them to you as a gift for your kindness, if you would accept them."

"You know me better than to think I would easily turn down a gift of books," I said. "But I would refuse. You are in no position to be so free with your possessions. I would insist on paying you."

"And I would refuse the offer."

"So we could fight a good long while over it. And there are more pressing things to accomplish. Not the least of which is that you cannot give, and I cannot buy, what may be in the possession of Mr. Cola. I think I should see if I can get it back first of all."

To start with, I walked all the way down to Christ Church, and made sure that Lower and Cola had indeed set off that morning on their tour. Then I walked over to Mrs. Bulstrode, Cola's landlady in St. Giles.

I had known this lady since I was at least five years old; I had played, before I exhausted puerile occupations, with her son who was about my age and is now a corn merchant in Witney. On many occasions she had given me an apple from her garden, or a lick of delicious honey from the hives she kept on a minuscule plot of land she, with great pomp, was always pleased to call her country estate. For she was a woman of pretension, despite the dourness of her religion, and liked to play the lady of quality. Those who knew her enough to see the fraud ridiculed her without mercy; those who knew her better saw the generosity within, and forgave a failing which, though grave, never once stopped her from an act of charity, nor a word of kindness.

I was welcomed into the kitchen—I was old enough an acquaintance to knock on the kitchen door—and greeted with great warmth. Half an hour's conversation was required before I could bring myself and her round to the matter at hand. I explained that I was a close acquaintance of Mr. Cola's.

"I am glad to hear it, Anthony," she said gravely. "If he is a friend of yours, then he cannot be so bad to know."

"Why do you say that? Has he misbehaved?"

"Not exactly," she conceded. "In fact in all respects he

is a man of great politeness. But he is a papist, and I have never had such a person in the house before. Nor do I want one again. Although I do believe we may yet win him over. Do you know, he prayed with us the other night? And went to church with Mr. Lower last Sunday, and said he found the experience very uplifting?''

"I am gratified to hear it. And for my part I can confirm that he is a man of kindness, since he is treating the mother of our servant at moderate cost. I think you can sleep easy in your beds at night. However, what I wish to ask you is this: could I go to his room, for he borrowed something from me which I need badly in my work. And I hear he has gone off for a week.''

It was no sooner asked than agreed and, as I knew where the room was, I was left in peace to mount the two pair of stairs to the little attic which Cola rented out. Inside, all was as spick and span as I would have expected from a room under the tutelage of Mrs. Bulstrode, who regarded dust as the devil's seed, and never ceased her campaigns of exorcism. Cola's belongings were few and for the most part contained in a great traveling trunk. And that trunk, unfortunately, was securely locked.

Having come so far, I was determined not to go away empty-handed, and I examined that great traveling lock with the most particular attention, in the hope that it would suddenly spring open before my eyes. But it was designed not only to ward off the attentions of thieves, but also of the likes of Mrs. Bulstrode, who was certain to have examined it if an easy opportunity presented itself, for her curiosity about the unknown was as great as that of the most diligent experimentalist. Violence or the key were the only options, and I could employ neither.

My long hard glaring at the chest made little impact in persuading it to open up to me, and eventually I accepted that no amount of wishing would make the slightest difference. With the greatest reluctance, and no small amount of resentment, I rose from my haunches, and made to leave. But first, out of simple irritation, I gave the chest a powerful kick, to demonstrate that I was not best pleased.

And the lock sprang open with a heavy thud, the clasp

being very ingeniously spring-loaded, a device I had never seen before. I was astonished at this, and at a loss to explain how it might be that a man could be so rash as to leave all his possessions unprotected in such a fashion—unaware until I read the manuscript that the heavy fall endured on the journey from London had broken the lock in such a way that it could no longer be relied upon.

Gifts from God should never be spurned. It had pleased Him to grant my wishes, and I was sure that it was for a good reason. With a prayer of thanks on my lips, I knelt down in front of the chest as though it were an altar, and began to search in as methodical a fashion as Cola himself had used to search the house of Sarah Blundy.

I will not list his possessions, comment on the quality of the clothing or the bags of money which gave the lie to his stories of poverty. For he had in his possession at least one hundred pounds in gold; far from being reduced to having to take patients to survive, he had enough to live as a gentleman for well over a year. No; I will merely mention that I swiftly discovered three books, wrapped up in a chemise near the bottom of the chest as though they were the most precious objects on earth, and accompanied by a sheet of paper which gave the name of a tavern in Cheapside called the Bells, and several other scribbles which seemed also to be addresses.

The first book was particularly gorgeous, tooled in gold, with a fine metal clasp, intricately carved and chased. It was my passion as a bibliographer which made me pause and examine it, for it was the finest Venetian work, and such splendid workmanship is only rarely seen in this country. I had a pang of the greatest envy when I saw it and I swear that, had I been only a fraction less honest, I would have taken it as well. It is a fine thing, no doubt, that so many books are now printed and that their cost steadily falls, even for the best scholarship. I count myself lucky that I live in this country, where books can be had at moderate expense (though still more than the Netherlands; had I a longing for travel I would go there, for I could buy many books and have the cost of the travel in the money saved). But sometimes it is borne in on me that there are disadvantages to this happy situation.

Of course it is the learning which is important. Of course the quality of scholarship must come first, and it is better that wisdom should reach the most people possible, for *sine doctrina, vita est quasi mortis imago,* says Dionysius Cato; without learning life is but the image of death. And of course, were it other, I could afford many fewer books. But sometimes I regret the days when people valued books properly, and spent lavishly on them. Occasionally, in the Bodleian, when my concentration deserts me, and my spirits flag, I order up one of those wonderful codexes that have found their way into the library. Or I go into a college and look through a book of hours, marveling at the love and skill which went into the creation of such glorious works. I imagine the men who made them, the scribes and the paper makers and the illustrators and the binders, and contrast them with the poor sad works I have on my own shelves. It is like the difference between a Quaker meeting house and a Catholic church. One is devoted to the word, and nothing but; it has its virtue, I suppose. But God is more than mere word, although He was that in the beginning. The speech of man alone is all but dumb in the task of expressing His glory, and the meanness of the Protestant constructions is an insult to His name. We now live in an age where the houses of politicians are grander than the houses of God. What does that say about our corruption?

So I sat awhile and feasted my eyes on this little book of Cola's, and traced my finger over the complexities of the binding. A room—no, merely a shelf—of books like these would give me the greatest possible joy, although I knew I might as well aim to become Chancellor of England as hope to possess such a wonder. It was a Psalter, and a fine example, and I flipped open the little clasp and opened it up to see whether the printing matched the binding, for I knew well that Venetian work was the finest to be had.

And received a tremendous shock; for inside, the book had been hollowed out into two carefully cut cavities. Initially, my distress was for the book, as to butcher such a wonderful object was the nearest thing to sacrilege I could imagine. Then I concentrated on the three little bottles that nestled so carefully in the hollows, each sealed by wax at the top. One contained a dark, thick liquid like oil, one a clear fluid which might as well have been water. The third, however, was the most interesting, for it was the most elaborate bottle of all, covered in gold and jewels and worth, in my inexperienced estimation, many dozens of pounds. This contained nothing except a thick, ill-shaped lump of old wood. What it meant was obvious, even to a dolt like myself.

So I placed the book aside and, consumed by curiosity for the first, examined the others with only a casual eye until I realized what they were. It was several minutes, as I flicked through and considered, before it dawned on me that here was something of great and strange significance. For both volumes were the same, one from Sarah's house and the other, I assumed, Cola had already. Each was a volume from Livy's history, in the same edition as the one which Dr. Wallis had so urgently entreated me to find for him many months previously.

SARAH BLUNDY WAS ARRESTED THE NEXT DAY, I NOW know at the instigation of John Wallis, and the news rippled through town and university like a tidal wave running up a creek in high wind. Everybody knew that she was guilty, and applauded the magistrate for his decisiveness as much as they criticized him for the delay in reaching a conclusion that had, in retrospect, been obvious to every single citizen since the moment they heard of Dr. Grove's death.

Only two people, I think, dissented from this opinion— myself, who knew the truth, and my mother, whose belief was the more virtuous for being founded on nothing at all. But, as she said, she knew the girl. And she would not accept that anyone in her household could act in such a fashion. Had she known the truth, I say, it would have killed her.

She was a strange woman, that blessed mother of mine, as good a mother as any man had. For she was strict and punctilious in all matters, jealous of her rights and watchful of the obligations of others. No woman or man was swifter to condemn sin, or pass comment on a moral failing. No woman was so careful in her devotions, praying not less than ten minutes in the morning when she rose, and more than fifteen every night before she retired. She attended the best church and listened with care to sermons which she often did not understand, but which she found uplifting nonetheless. And she was charitable with the greatest caution, so that neither too much, nor too little, was given from her pocket to the deserving. Careful with money she undoubtedly was, and jealous of her reputation, but not so much that either substituted for her duty to God.

And so confident was she of her knowledge of God's mind that, when public opinion and her own differed in point of detail, she had no doubts whatsoever that she knew best. When she heard of Sarah's arrest, she waited not a moment before announcing to all in our great kitchen that a serious injustice had been committed. Sarah (for whom she now had a proprietorial affection) was without blame in the matter, she said. She had not laid a finger on that fat prelate, and if she had it was undoubtedly well deserved. Not content with mere words either, she straightaway packed a hamper with food and her own homemade ale, walked boldly off to Mrs. Blundy's cottage to fetch warm clothes, took my best blanket (in fact, my only blanket) from my bed and marched in full public gaze to the prison, where she did her best to give comfort to the poor girl, and ensure that she was as guarded as clothes and provisions and stern words to the jailer could make her against jail fever.

"She has asked to see you," she said to me gravely on her return. She was in no good humor, as she had been jeered at by several low folk who habitually hang around outside the jail in the run-up to the assizes, taking perverted pleasure at seeing the prisoners arriving in chains. Why such people have nothing better to do I do not know, but I am sure that any well-run town would send them away, or punish them harshly for their idleness. "And you must go directly."

My heart sank at this, and I felt like a bull on a rope, being dragged into the butcher's yard for slaughter with all its efforts to escape the inevitable coming to naught. Before I heard of the arrest, I had convinced myself that the worst danger was over; if no one was ever blamed for the death of Grove, then it would be foolish to volunteer my own neck. The moment I heard about Sarah, I heard also the rustle of the rope and my bowels tightened as I saw the inevitable looming up in front of me.

Of course I had to go to the girl. I even managed to make myself angry at her, as though it was her fault she had fallen quite unfairly into suspicion. But as I walked up the stone steps to the jail, I knew as well that this was merely distress at my situation, and the trap I was now firmly in. Sooner or later, I would have to own my deeds, for if I had committed a crime in killing Grove, I would not have any other souls weighed in the balance against me as well.

Sarah was surprisingly cheerful when I saw her; the women's cell had not yet filled with the congregation of crones who would soon be brought in from all over the county to await the judge's pleasure, and she had only been there a few hours. The dark and the damp had not yet begun their deadly work on her spirits.

"Stop looking like that," she said, when she saw my sorrowful countenance looming up at her out of the dark. "I'm the one in jail, not you. If I can be cheerful you can manage to look a little more lighthearted."

"How can you be so, in such a place?"

"Because my conscience is clear, and I believe the Lord will look after me," she said. "I have done my best for Him in my life, and refuse to accept He will forsake me now."

"And if He does?"

"Then it will be for a good reason."

Sometimes, I confess, such humility tired me excessively. But I had come to give courage, and finding it already present, I could hardly settle down to convince her that her optimism was misplaced.

"You think me foolish," she said. "You are wrong. For I know that I had nothing to do with this business."

"Indeed, and God knows it too. As I do. Whether the courts will be in His confidence is another matter."

"What can they say? Courts have to produce evidence, do they not? And you know as well as I where I was that night."

"And, if necessary, you must say so," I told her.

But she shook her head. "No. That would replace one scandal with another, and I will not. Believe me, Anthony, it will not be necessary."

"Then I will."

"No," she said firmly. "I suppose you think you are being kind, but you will not be the one to suffer. The law on this would hardly touch you, but I would have to leave, and I cannot with my mother in such a condition. Nor could I expose those people in Abingdon and elsewhere to sanction. Believe me, Anthony, there is no danger. No one could possibly think I would, or could, behave in such a way."

I did my best to persuade her she was wrong, that not only could the town think it, it was already convinced. But she would have none of it, and eventually told me either to talk of something else, or to leave her in peace, an imperious command, which was strange in her circumstances, but quite like her.

"You will say nothing of this to anyone," she said. "It is my wish and my command. You will say what I permit you to say, and no more. You will not interfere in this matter. Do you understand me?"

I looked at her strangely, for serving girl though she was, she looked and spoke like one born to command: no sovereign could have given orders with as much resolution, or with as much confidence of being obeyed.

"Very well, then," I said, reluctantly after a long pause in which she waited for the assent she knew I must give. "Tell me about this Cola."

"What is there to say you have not seen with your own eyes?"

"It may be important," I replied. "And what I saw confuses me slightly. I saw him approach you, then recoil. It was not your doing that made him pull back; it was more as though he had horrified himself. Is that true?" She admitted it. "And you would have let him have his way, had he not removed himself?"

"You had already told me I had nothing to lose, and I suppose that is the case. If he insisted on payment, there was little I could do to prevent him taking it. Nor would any protests before or after have helped me. I have learned this with others." She touched my arm as she saw my face fall. "I do not mean you."

"And yet he pulled away. Why?"

"I suppose he found me disgusting."

"No," I said. "That is not possible."

She smiled. "Thank you for that."

"I mean, it does not fit with what I saw."

"Maybe he had a conscience. In which case he joins you as the only two men in my acquaintance so equipped."

I bowed my head at those words. Conscience I had indeed; scarcely a minute went by that I was not aware of it these days. Listening to its warnings, and acting upon them, however, were different. Here I was, the author of this girl's misfortunes, able with one word to bring them to an end, and what was I doing? I was giving her comfort, and acting the part of the sympathetic helper. I was so generous, and so helpful that it entirely covered my turpitude, so no one suspected the depths of a guilt which daily grew ever deeper and more monstrous. And still I lacked the courage to do as I should. It was not for lack of desire: many times, I imagined myself going to the magistrate and telling him what had happened, and exchanging my life for hers. Many times I saw myself standing as the stoic, making my sacrifice with unflinching honesty and bravado.

"I have recovered the object he stole," I said, "and I am mightily puzzled by it. It is a book by Livy. Where did it come from?"

"I believe it was with the bundle my father left, just before he died."

"In that case, I would like to open that package. I have never touched it, because you asked me not to, but now I think we must; it may contain the answer."

She gave her permission with some initial reluctance, then I made to leave; but before I did I once again implored her to let me speak, hoping that there might be a way for her to escape without my having to confess. But she would not allow it, and I was bound to her wishes; in the circumstances I could hardly hope to escape by inflicting more hardship on her.

chapter nine

I MUST TALK ABOUT THIS BOOK, I THINK, FOR I HAVE
forgotten to mention my examination of it. To look at there
was nothing especially worthy of note; it was an octavo,
bound in only inferior calfskin, with tooling done by a man
of skill, but who was no master in his trade. There were no
markings to give its ownership, and I was sure it had not
come from a scholar's library, for I knew of none who did
not mark meticulously his ownership, and the place on the
shelves where it might be found. Nor were there any of the
marginalia I might expect to have found in a book that had
been well-read and studied. It was battered and bashed, but
my practiced eye told me that this was more due to the ill-
treatment of movement and abuse, rather than excessive reading; the spine was in perfect condition, and was the most
undamaged part of the whole.

Inside, the text was untouched, except for some small ink
markings, which underlay certain letters. On the first page a
''b'' was so marked on the first line; an ''f'' on the second,
and so on. Each line had one letter marked and, knowing
that Wallis was interested in puzzles, I thought perhaps they
made up some acrostic. So I wrote them all down, and came
up with the merest jumble, which had no sense in it at all.

I spent a good half-day on these fruitless pursuits before
admitting defeat, placing the volume on my shelves behind
some other books so that it would not be noticed should

anyone come alooking. Then I turned my attention to the packet, still secured with unbroken seals. Even now, it is strange to consider that such a small object could unleash such fury in the world, that so many people could contemplate such cruelty to gain possession of it, that I could have had about me such a powerful weapon all unknowing for so long a time. Nor did I even realize this until I opened it.

Half a day's careful consideration opened up all the secret history of this realm to my eyes, but it was not until I read Wallis's account that I understood fully how these matters fully affected the tragedy unfolding before me, and grasped the extent to which the mathematician was deceived by John Thurloe, still perhaps the most powerful person in the kingdom despite his lack of position. What he told Wallis was, to some extent, true: his account of how Sir James Prestcott and Ned Blundy, both fanatics though for different causes, formed an alliance was confirmed in every particular, for half of the documents or more consisted of letters between Thurloe and Clarendon, Cromwell and the king, in which their mutual courtesy was as striking as their knowledge of each other's characters and aspirations. One letter in particular would have caused uproar had it been publicly known, for it expressly said that the king had instructed Mordaunt to pass on details of the rising of 1659; and an accompanying piece of paper listed some three dozen names, many locations of arms and details of gathering places. Even I knew that many of those named were subsequently killed. Another was an outline of an agreement between Charles and Thurloe sketching out conditions for a restoration of the monarchy, saying who was to be favored, what limits were to be placed on royal power, and outlining details of laws to control Catholics.

It is clear that had Sir James Prestcott recovered these and made them known at the time, the royal cause would have been utterly blasted, and the career of John Thurloe as well, for both sides would have rejected absolutely those people willing to abandon principles established at the cost of so much blood. This was, however, the lesser part of the bundle and, although it would have been of considerable danger in 1660, I doubt it would have shaken the throne in 1663. No;

the more dangerous documents came in a separate package, and those were undoubtedly provided by Sir James Prestcott himself. For just as saltpeter and niter can cause little harm when separate, but can bring down the strongest castle when conjoined to make gunpowder, so these two groups of papers drew extra power from their association.

For Sir James Prestcott was a Catholic, and a member of that papist conspiracy to bring England back into the thrall of Rome. Of course he was; why else would his son attract the support of the papist Earl of Bristol? What else explains the horrified silence of his family, the refusal to talk of the unspecified injuries he had done them, which Jack Prestcott notes but treats as another example of their callousness. His wife's family was most fervently of the Protestant persuasion, and to have one of their number embrace Rome was to them quite unforgivable. Why else would they refuse to help Sir James in his trouble against all instincts of obligation? Why else pack young Jack off to the Compton family where he could be placed under the tutelage of the resolutely Anglican Robert Grove? It is in the nature of papists to entrap their own family, to wheedle their way into their minds and corrupt them. Could there be any hope that a youth as easily led as Jack Prestcott would withstand his adored father's blandishments? No; whatever else happened, it was essential for his safety and the family's standing that he be kept safe and that, having given up his estates, Sir James should not recover them. In my opinion, the family stands acquitted of greed and mendacity, although I leave it to others to disagree with my verdict.

Sir James's conversion came, I believe, during his first exile, a period in which many Royalists, weakened by misfortune and adversity, embraced popery with a most despairing anguish. He entered the service of the Venetians at the siege of Candia, and in his time abroad came greatly into contact with many people of substantial influence in the Roman church, eager to spy out any advantage for themselves in England's misfortunes. One such was the priest with whom he corresponded in these letters.

I will explain this later; at the moment, I will merely point out the shock that must have been felt by any Catholic who had given near twenty years of his life in fighting for the throne, to discover that the king was prepared to agree to the most ferocious measures of persecution against him and his kind. The news he had that the king was preparing to reach a deal with Richard Cromwell and Thurloe pushed him into action, and also pushed him from loyalty into his final treachery.

For Pestcottr knew that at the same time Charles, that most duplicitous of men, was also negotiating with the French, the Spanish and with the pope himself, soliciting their support and money in return for a promise to ensure complete toleration of Catholics when he was reestablished. He promised all things to all men, and reneged on all his agreements when he was on the throne once more. Even his advisers did not know the full extent of his duplicity, I think, for Clarendon knew nothing of the discussions with the Spanish, while Mr. Bennet was kept in ignorance of the talks with Thurloe.

Sir James Prestcott alone knew it all, because Ned Blundy told him of one side, and his correspondent, a priest deeply involved in these discussions, told him of the other. That priest was called Andrea da Cola, whom Prestcott must have met while in the service of Venice.

chapter ten

IT GRIEVED ME GREATLY LATER ON, BUT EVEN NOW I do not see how I could have pieced together events in such a way that I might have prevented Sarah's death. Had I known that Wallis and Thurloe were looking for those documents and would have given me anything I wanted for them, had I realized they were even involved at all in the machinations which put her on trial, had I understood the full significance of Cola's presence in this country, I could have gone and said, stop this trial immediately, set the girl free. They would have obeyed me, and granted my every wish, I think.

But I did not know this, and did not realize it until I read the words of Wallis and Prestcott and understood for the first time that Sarah's trial was no mere miscarriage of justice, but had instead an overarching inevitability to it that could not be avoided.

Many people have over the years talked greatly of the rewards and punishments God metes out to His servants to show His approval or disfavor. A battle lost, one won: both are signs from God. A loss of fortune when a ship sinks in heavy seas; a sudden illness, or a chance meeting with an old acquaintance who brings news, these too occasion prayers of lamentation or thanks. Perhaps it is so, but how much more is it when countless deeds and decisions, secretly taken and only half known, slowly accumulate over the years to produce the death of an innocent in such a way. For had King Charles not been duplicitous, had Prestcott not been a fanatic, had Thurloe not been concerned for his own safety, had Wallis not been vain and cruel, had Bristol not been ambitious, had Bennet not been cynical, had government, in sum, not been government and politicians not what they are, then Sarah Blundy would not have been led to the scaffold and the sacrifice would not have been made. And what can we say of such a victim, whose death is the culmination of so much sin but is accomplished so quietly that its true nature is never known?

As I say, I did not know this, and at that moment, sitting in my room surrounded by these bits of old paper, I upbraided myself instead for my cowardice, for taking refuge in a matter which then seemed of no importance to me at all: for I did not care at that moment whether King Charles of England kept his throne or not, nor did I care about his policies, or whether Catholics were persecuted or given complete toleration. All I cared about was Sarah in jail and the fact that I was running out of excuses, and would soon have to confess.

To prepare myself and work up my courage, I decided to talk to Anne Blundy, for I was sure she could give me the strength I needed. Cola mentioned that she had been placed in the care of John Locke during his absence, and this man performed his duties with the utmost punctiliousness, although with little enthusiasm.

"Frankly," he said, "it is a waste of my time although, no doubt, good for my soul to act in a way which will bring no reward to either of us. She is dying, Wood, and nothing will change that. I perform my tasks because I promised Lower I would do so. But whether I give her herbals or metals, practice new or old medicine on her, bleed her or purge her, it will make no difference at all."

This he said in a low voice in the street outside the cottage, where I met him. He had just been in to pay his daily visit which, as he said, was more for form than anything else. My mother came down every day with food, as Sarah had insisted that this be done, rather than the food coming to her in prison, and the old lady did not want for a blanket or sticks in the fire. More than that could not be done.

The stink of corruption inside was severe, and caught in my throat as I went in. All the doors and windows were fast shut to keep out the bad winds; which was necessary, but had the unfortunate consequence of allowing none of the foul air to escape from the chamber. And the old lady, who had always been perverse in having the shutters and doors wide open except in the most icy weather, complained bitterly of this. Locke had closed everything up the moment he arrived, and her inability to move from her bed made it impossible for her to open them again. She begged me to oblige her, and although reluctant to do so, I eventually agreed, on condition she permitted me to close them all again when I left. I did not want a fight with Locke about countering good medical practice on a whim.

Whatever the reasoning, I must say that I also was greatly relieved when the winds began to sweep the foulness out of the room and natural light replaced the darkness; Anne Blundy also seemed to benefit from the sweetness of the cold air. She breathed deeply, and sighed as though a great torture had come to an end.

I had not been able to see her in the gloom, and was shocked when I had opened the shutters and turned round to look properly at her. The wasting of her face and the deathly pallor were the most noticeable, of course, and I saw her for the first time without a covering to her head, so that the thinness and wispiness of her hair was most obvious. She looked twice the age of a few months previously, and my sadness bore in on me so much that my throat tightened and I could not speak.

"You are a strange young man, Mr. Wood," she said after I had asked her how she was and said all the usual things that one says in these circumstances. "So kind and so cruel by turns. I pity you."

It was strange to my ears to have this pathetic bag of bones pity me, and insulting to be called cruel, for I never was so with deliberation.

"Why do you say this to me?"

"Because of what you have done to Sarah," she said. "Do not look at me like that, you know what I mean. For several years now, you have given her something which has been of the greatest value. You have talked to her, and listened to what she has to say. You have been her companion and as near to friend as man can be to a woman. What do you mean by that? Don't you know that the world has changed, and that a girl of her sort must learn to remain silent, especially in the company of gentlemen?''

''This sounds strange from your mouth.''

''I see what is going on around me. Who cannot, when it is so obvious? But you are too blind to notice, it seems. So I thought, at least. I thought you were a simple scholar who was so enthusiastic about his learning that he would share it with anyone. But that is not the case. For having taught her that she can be listened to, and made it so this becomes the one day in the week she looks forward to, you then cast her off, and will have nothing to do with her anymore. Then take her back again. What will you think of to hurt her now, Mr. Wood? I should never have let you into my house.''

''I never intended her hurt. And as for the rest, I think that I have taught her nothing. She seems to be the teacher now, I think.''

She looked immeasurably sad, and reluctantly nodded. ''I am very frightened for her. She is so strange now, I think she must come to harm.''

''When did she start speaking at meetings?''

She looked at me sharply. ''You know of this? Did she tell you?''

''I found out on my own.''

''When Ned came back that last time, and then we heard he was dead, we talked time and again about him; it was our memorial for him as we could not bury his body. We talked of his parents and his life, and his battles and campaigns. I was grief-stricken, as I loved him very much; he was all the world to me and my greatest comfort. But my grief led me into indiscretion and Sarah never misses anything. I talked about the Edgehill campaign, when Ned commanded a platoon, and ended with a whole company of his own, and I told how he was away for more than a year, and how much I missed him.''

I nodded, thinking there must be a point to this, for she

was not a woman to ramble in speech, even when ill.

"Sarah looked at me very quietly and gently, and asked the simple question she had never asked before. 'So who, then, is my father?' "

She stopped until she was satisfied that my face did not register disgust.

"It was true, of course. Ned was away for a year, and Sarah was born three weeks before he returned. He never questioned or reproached me, and always treated Sarah as his own; the matter was never referred to again, but sometimes, when I saw them sitting together by the fire, with him teaching her to read, or telling her stories, or just holding her to him, I could see a sadness in his eyes, and I felt grief-stricken for him. He was the very best of men, Mr. Wood. He truly was."

"And what was the answer to the question?"

She shook her head. "I will not lie, and cannot tell the truth. I spend my days and nights considering my sins to prepare for my death, and I need all the time I have left. I have never claimed to be a good woman in any way, and there is much to repent. But the Lord will not reproach me for fornication."

Still not an answer to my question, but I hardly wanted to know in any case; I take little pleasure in such gossipy matters at the best of times, and Anne Blundy in any case was beginning to drift from me into her memories.

"I had a dream, the most wonderful dream of my life, that I was surrounded by doves, and one dove perched on my arm, and spoke to me. 'Call her Sarah, and love her,' it said. 'And you will be blessed amongst women.' "

I found myself shivering strangely as she said this, then smiled bravely at her. "You have done as you were told, at least."

"Thank you, sir. I have. Shortly after I told her this, Sarah started traveling and talking."

"And healing?"

"Yes."

"Who was that man? The one I saw leaving the house a few months back?"

She thought for a moment, to decide how much to say.

"His name was Greatorex, and he calls himself an astrologer."

"What did he want?"

"I don't know. I was here when he knocked on the door. I opened it and he was standing there, white as a sheet and trembling with fear. I asked him who he was, but he was so frightened he could not say anything to me. Then Sarah called from inside that I was to let him in. And he came in, and he just went down on his knees in front of her and asked her blessing."

The memory still alarmed the mother, and the telling of it alarmed me.

"Then what?"

"Sarah took him by the hand, and told him to stand as if she was not at all surprised, then led him to the seat by the fire. They talked for more than an hour."

"What about?"

"Sarah asked me to leave them alone, so I didn't hear. Just the beginning. This man said he had signs of Sarah in the stars, and had crossed the sea and traveled here to see her, as they had directed him."

" 'For we have seen the star, and are come to worship,' " I said quietly, and Anne Blundy looked sharply at me.

"Do not say things like that, Mr. Wood," she said. "Please do not. Or you will turn as mad as I am becoming."

"I am well past the stage of madness," I said. "And I am frightened beyond speech."

I NOW HAD ONLY A SHORT TIME TO FOLLOW THE URG-ings of my conscience, for the trial was due to begin, and the preparations for the assize were already under way. I drank a certain amount before I could force myself to act, and I still recoiled from my task. But eventually I succeeded in overcoming my cowardice and walked to Holywell to ask for an audience with Sir John Fulgrove, the magistrate. Though it was his busiest day of the year, he granted my request, but did so with such brusqueness that I became even more nervous, and stammered and shook as I tried to speak.

"Well, man? I don't have all day."

"It is about Sarah Blundy," I said eventually.

"Well? What of her?"

"She is innocent, I know it." A simple sentence, but it cost me an agony to come out with it, to step over the cliff and willingly cast myself down into the inevitable perdition that must follow. I claim nothing for my courage, my honor or my fortitude. I know, better than most, what I am. I was not born to be a hero, and will never be one of those to whom future ages look for example and instruction. Other men than myself, better men I should say, would have said these words earlier, and with more dignity of manner than the poor, sweating, shaking performance that I put on. Yet we must do as we can; I could do no more than this and, though it might elicit a sneer from those stronger than myself, I say that it was the most courageous act of my life.

"And how do you know it?"

As best I could, I repeated my story, and said that I had placed the poison in the bottle.

"She was seen in the college," he said.

"She was not there."

"How do you know?"

To this I could not reply, having given my solemn word that I would not betray her on the matter of her prophesying. So I lied instead, and in the lie, ruined all.

"She was with me."

"Where?"

"In my room."

"When did she leave?"

"She did not. She stayed with me all night."

"And your family will say this?"

"They did not see her."

"They were in the house, I imagine? I can ask them, you know."

"I'm sure they were in the house."

"And did not see her enter, did not see her climb to your room, did not see her leave again?"

"No."

"Heard nothing all night long?"

"No."

"I see. And you took this powder to his room for the purpose?"

"No. He had it there, and asked me to add it to his bottle for his stomachache."

"But not half an hour before, he had been told it was useless, and said he would never use it again."

"He did not mean it."

"Everybody who heard him believed he did, and was grateful to the Italian for the advice."

"He was not."

"That is corroborated by witnesses who were present."

"I cannot help that."

"And can you tell me how Dr. Grove's gold signet ring came to be discovered in her hands? Did you steal from his body and place it there?"

"No."

"So how did she come by it?"

"I know nothing of this."

Sir John leaned back in his chair and eyed me gravely. "I do not know what you are trying to accomplish, sir. It is clear to me that you are lying to protect this creature and it is a serious business to deflect justice from its true path. I beg you to think more carefully, and stop acting in this foolish fashion."

"But it is true; it is all true."

"It is not. It cannot be so. You cannot explain away the evidence proving her guilt, and those facts you cite to demonstrate her innocence are in no way convincing."

"You will not help me?"

"What do you want? She has been before the grand jury, and a case was found. If you persist in this nonsense, I cannot stop you from rising in court, and saying your piece there. Although if you do so, I tell you it will make no difference, and the judge may well see fit to punish you as well."

So I went to Dr. Wallis, hoping to persuade him to use his secret influence on the girl's behalf, not knowing he had already determined on her death. And I told my story a second time and for a second time it seemed I was not believed.

"I owe you no favors, Mr. Wood," he said, "and can in any case do nothing for you. It is for the judge and the jury to decide the girl's fate. I know you have heard stories of my works for the government, but they are exaggerated. I can no more stop her trial than I can start it."

"Do you at least believe me?"

We were in his room, and the interview was a strange one: there was a weariness about the man that I had not noticed before. I did not know, of course, how much this matter was plucking at his conscience, and how aware he was of the wrong he was doing. He had convinced himself that he was acting nobly, and when a man does this to assuage his soul, it is a rash person indeed who seeks to persuade him otherwise.

"I do not. I believe this tale comes from your selfishness. I think you would rather have your pleasure with this girl than see justice served. I know more about her than you think, and I am convinced that if she hangs then no great injustice will be done."

"She did not do this."

Wallis took a step toward me, overwhelming me with his bulk, and the sheer power and malice of his personality.

"That whore you like so much, Mr. Wood, is helping a conspirator, a subversive and an atheist. She is helping the most dangerous man in the country commit a monstrous crime, and that man has already slaughtered my servant. I will have my revenge, and that man will die. If Sarah Blundy's death helps me to my revenge, then so be it. I care not whether she is innocent or guilty. Do you understand me now, Mr. Wood?"

"Then you are the greatest of sinners," I said, my voice shaking in shock at what I heard. "You are no priest and are not fit to hold the bread in your hands. You are not . . ."

Wallis was a big man, powerfully built and very much taller than me. Without any more words he stood up and grabbed me by my collar, and began dragging me to the door. I tried to protest, and say this was no behavior for a priest, but when I began to speak he shook me like some dog, and pushed me hard against the wall before opening the door onto the street.

"Do not meddle, sir," he said coldly. "I care nothing for your concerns, and have no time for your whining. Leave me in peace and say no more, or you will pay heavily for it."

Then he pushed me out of the door, and kicked me hard with his foot, so that I tripped down the stone steps into a cold, muddy puddle, which splashed up all over my clothes.

As I knelt there, with the water seeping into my shoes and breeches, I knew I had failed. Even if I shouted from the rooftops, it seemed, people would stop their ears and refuse to acknowledge what was so obviously the truth. I do not know whether it would have been different had I spoken earlier, but it was certainly too late now, and the realization made me sink my head into that puddle and weep with anguish as the rain spattered more mud onto me. It was as though heaven itself had intervened, and made me like some lunatic in the street, shouting out to all the world but finding people averting their eyes and pretending not to notice. In the deepest rage, I beat my fist on the muddy earth and cried in despair at God's cruelty and, for my reward and solace, heard two passers-by laugh with disgust at the raving drunkard they saw on his knees before them.

chapter eleven

THE START OF SARAH'S TRIAL BEGAN THE MOST ANguishing, wonderful two days of my life, in which I felt with full force both the power of God's punishment, and the sweet grace of His forgiveness. Again, Cola has described the proceedings, and does so with perspicacity. I will not repeat his account, but rather must add to it, for he has quite naturally omitted certain events which he could not know.

Sarah had commanded me not to interfere, and I had already done so, but could not bring myself to disobey in her presence. This will seem weakness on my part, but I do not care if it does: I speak the truth and say that no man who knew her as I did would have acted differently. I was hoping someone else would speak for her, or present evidence of her innocence, yet they did not. Sarah herself said nothing except to admit her guilt so that her body could go to Lower and her mother receive treatment, and when she uttered that word, ''guilty,'' so quietly and with such resignation, my heart broke, and I determined that I would try for the third time to persuade people of the truth. Then I heard the judge say those words, ''Does anyone have anything to add? For if there is one who will speak for the defendant, then he must do so now.''

''My Lord,'' I said. I was going to cry out to the whole room that this poor girl was as innocent as Christ himself, that she had no hand in Grove's death, and that I was responsible for his end. I was going to demonstrate the truth of my assertions with every scrap of evidence and eloquence I had, and was confident that while the latter might let me down, the former would carry conviction. I was going to save her.

And I hesitated, tongue-tied in my anguish and my indecision, and in that moment, the opportunity was lost. I know many in the town, even in the university, hold me in contempt, and ridicule me behind my back, and I have always taken care not to allow the opportunities for humiliation to be created. This time I disregarded all thought of my dignity, and in my brief pause, some fellow made a ribald remark, and others laughed, and this encouraged still more. For the court as a sentence of death is to be passed becomes a solemn place full of apprehension and dread; men leap eagerly at anything which will break that atmosphere, and render it less awful. Within seconds, the court erupted in jeers and, even had I shouted at the top of my voice, I would not have been heard. Red-faced with embarrassment, and consumed by shame at my failure, I felt Locke pull me down, hoping as I resumed my plea the judge would restore order, and call on me once more to say my piece.

He did not. Rather, with a supercilious smirk on his face, he thanked me for my eloquent words, and deliberately encouraged more laughter. Then he sentenced Sarah Blundy to die.

When I heard those words, I ran out of the courtroom to avoid further misery, and took myself to my room where I locked myself in and prayed for guidance. I had no idea what I should do, and I stayed, in mute immobility, until my mother put her head around the door and told me there was a visitor who would not take no for an answer. She had told him to go away, and he had refused absolutely to budge until he had seen me.

And, a few moments later, in marched Jack Prestcott, as cheerful as he was insane. He frightened me greatly, for his deterioration since I had last seen him was very great indeed, and the look in his eyes, to my mind, suggested a man who could fall into violence at any moment should he be crossed or contradicted.

"Ho there, my friend," he said as he walked in, for all the world like a seigneur condescending to pay a call on one below his social rank. "I hope I find you well."

I neither know nor care what reply I made; I could have recited an extract from the Bodleian catalogue, I think, for all the difference it would have made. Jack Prestcott was not interested in anything but the sound of his own delusions, which poured from his mouth in a thick torrent. He kept me there for half an hour, as he recited to me all his ills, and how he had overcome them. Every detail was put in, much as he later put it down in his manuscript. Indeed, some of the words and phrases and sentences, some of the little asides and comments, were precisely the same and I believe that in all the years that have passed between that visit and his putting pen to paper, he has done nothing except go over in his mind the self-same account, repeating endlessly in his delirium the same events. When he dies he may go to hell; it would be no more than deserved. But in my opinion he is in it already, for Tully says true, *a diis quidem immortalibusquae potest homini major esse poena furore atque dementia,* what greater punishment can the gods inflict upon a man than madness?

I was at a loss to understand his purpose in coming, for I knew he hardly recognized me as a friend, and I had certainly done nothing to encourage any intimacy. I thought perhaps he wanted to consult me on matters of historical fact, and did my best to indicate I would not assist him in any way. But instead he held up his hand to silence me in a gesture of the most perfect condescension.

"I have come to provide you with material, not to ask your opinion," he said with a sly smile. "I wish you to keep these papers, if you will. I will certainly reclaim them some day, perhaps if my suit still has to go formally to law, but I shall be on the move in the next few months, and am in no position to guard them carefully. If you keep them, you will be doing me as much a favor as I am doing you, for Dr. Wallis would surely want them back if he knew where they were."

"I do not want them and have no desire to help you in any way," I said.

"Yes," he said, nodding his head with the gravest satisfaction. "When your life of my father comes out, and people see through your pen the great man he truly was, then your career will be made. And let me assure you that I will not abandon you. All the expenses of publication I will bear. A thousand copies at least, I think, in the finest bindings, and on the best paper."

"Mr. Prestcott," I said more loudly, "you are a liar and a murderer and the foulest person I have ever encountered. You are killing the dearest person I know, the best person in the world, for no reason. I beg you to consider what you are doing; it is not too late to change, and undo the damage. If you go to the magistrate now . . ."

"And to do the job perfectly," he said as if I had merely muttered some conventional appreciation of his kindness, "you must have these. But on condition that you say nothing to anyone about them until the book is ready for press."

More paper. I took the proffered sheets and looked at them. Complete nonsense written on them.

"I leave it to you to detect their importance," he said. "It can serve as a puzzle for you."

Then he laughed outright at the look of consternation on my face. "I must explain," he said, "for I see your perplexity. These all come from the drawer of Dr. Wallis. I stole them a few weeks back." Prestcott leaned forward on his chair and said in a conspiratorial whisper: "They are in a most cunning code, and have all defeated the good doctor. He is properly mad about it."

"Please," I said, "Stop talking like this. Can you not hear me? Can't you understand?"

Mr. Boyle conducted his experiments with his vacuum pump, Cola mentions some of them, and noted that as the air was sucked out, the sound of the animal inside it becomes fainter and fainter, until it can be discerned no more. As Prestcott stood before me, conducting the conversation he wished to have, hearing answers which were in his mind alone and oblivious to my words, I felt like some poor experimental beast, banging my hand against an invisible wall and shouting out at the top of my lungs, but receiving no response or understanding for my efforts.

"Yes. He prides himself on his skill, and yet these letters elude his mind completely." He chuckled. "But he told me the key, even though he thought me too stupid to notice. Apparently, you need a book of Livy. And with it, all will be revealed, he thinks. I must say I do not mind him reading his own, but I no longer want him reading my father's letters. Which is why you must have them. He will not think of looking here."

And with this remark, Prestcott bade me farewell and went off to amuse himself before his fateful interview with John Wallis the next day. Both of them have given their accounts, and Wallis's is obviously the correct one, for Prestcott's assault on him caused something of a stir, and there was a great crowd in the High Street a few weeks later to see the young man escorted from Bocardo jail by his uncle, and carried off so wrapped in chains he could scarcely move. It was a kindness to all, especially for him, that he should be so confined. He was too murderous to be free, and too mad to be punished. I hope it will be understood that I thought he received more consideration than he deserved.

But he left me those letters, and in particular that one crucial letter which Wallis intercepted on its way to Cola in the Low Countries; the only copy indeed, and the only proof of that Italian's purpose here. I put it aside with scarcely a glance, even though I now knew something of how to read it; I cared nothing at that moment for intellectual puzzles. Instead, I tidied up my room with methodical precision, added the papers to my collection under the floorboards, and thus occupied my body in useless tasks while my mind resumed its melancholic reverie. Then I left the house to visit Sarah one last time.

She would not see me; the jailer instead told me that she was on her own for her last evening and wished to see nobody. I insisted, and offered him a bribe, and begged, and finally persuaded him to go back and ask again.

"She will not see you," he said, with a look of sympathy. "She said you will see her tomorrow well enough."

Her rejection saddened me more than anything, and I am so selfish that all I could think of was my own sorrow at being deprived of an opportunity to give consolation. I confess I drank more than I should have done that night, and also that it soothed me not at all. Tavern after tavern and inn after inn I went to, but could scarcely abide the company of all those happy and cheerful faces. I drank in solitude, and turned my back when even people I counted as friends approached me. Everywhere I went, people who knew who I was came up to me, and asked me about Sarah and what I thought of her. And every time I was too miserable to speak the truth. In the Fleur-de-Lys, then in the Feathers and finally in the Mitre, I shrugged, and said I did not know, that it was none of my concern, she might have done it for all I knew: all I wanted to do was forget it all, so self-pitying had the drink made me.

Eventually I was thrown out for having drunk too much, and slipped over and fell into the gutter once more; this time I stayed there until I found myself being bodily picked up.

"Do you know, Mr. Wood," said a soft sing-song voice in my ear, "I do believe I just heard a cock crow. Is that not strange for this time of night?"

"Leave me alone."

"I think perhaps I would like to talk to you, sir."

So this stranger, this Valentine Greatorex, led me to his room and sat me down by the fire and dried me, then sat opposite and regarded me seriously but with great calm until I spoke myself.

"I went to the magistrate, and told him she was innocent," I said. "I told him that I had killed Dr. Grove, not Sarah. He did not believe me."

"Is that so?"

"Then I went to Dr. Wallis, and told him, and he would not believe me either."

"I expect not."

"Why do you say that?"

"Because otherwise she might not die tomorrow. You know her well, I think?"

"Better than anyone."

"Tell me, please. I want to know everything about her."

Jack Prestcott talks of this man, and how his voice fascinated and soothed, so that those he spoke to almost fell into a dream of tranquillity and obeyed his every command. So it was with me, and I told him everything I knew about Sarah, everything I have put in this manuscript and very much more, for he was fascinated by her conversation and wished to hear every word she had ever uttered. As I spoke of her words at the meeting I had attended, he gave an enormous sigh, and nodded with satisfaction.

"And I must save her," I concluded. "I must. There must be something I can do."

"Ah, Mr. Wood, you have read too many chivalrous romances," he said kindly. "Do you see yourself as Launcelot du Lac, perhaps, sweeping down on your charger and rescuing your Guinevere from the pyre, fighting off your enemies and taking her to safety?"

"No. I thought if I went to the Lord Lieutenant, or the judge . . ."

"They would not hear you," he said. "Any more than the magistrate, or this man Wallis, or even the entire court could hear you. They hear ye, indeed, but understand not; see ye indeed, but perceive not. It says so in Isaiah, and so it is."

"But why do so many people want her dead?"

"You know full well already, but will not accept it in your heart. You know what you have seen, you know your Scripture and you have heard her own words. There is nothing you can do, and nothing you should do."

"I cannot live without her."

"That is your punishment for your part in this."

I had no spirit or energy to say any more, and the drink had so fuddled my brain I could barely have spoken even had I wanted to. It was Greatorex who eventually pulled me out of the chair, and took me into the cold air outside, which revived me enough to walk steadily.

"It is a purgatory, my friend, but not of long duration, you will see. Go and sleep if you can; pray if you cannot. It will soon be over."

I DID AS HE SAID, AND SPENT THE ENTIRE NIGHT IN THE deepest prayer, for myself and for Sarah, begging God with all my might that he should intervene and stop the madness He had visited on the world. My faith is weak, a disgrace to anyone who has in life been favored as I have. I have been spared riches and fame and power and position, just as His goodness has saved me from poverty and great illness. Whatever dishonor is mine I have brought on myself, and whatever accomplishment is by His grace alone. Despite that, I did not believe enough. I prayed fervently, I used every device I knew to achieve that peaceful sincerity of submission that I had felt but once, when on a horse in dead winter with Sarah behind me. One small part of my soul, at least, knew that I was doing nothing but filling out the hours until the inevitable took place. Again and again I threw myself back into the struggle, getting ever more desperate in my attempts to force my rebellious spirit into calm. But I had spent too long amongst the rationalists and those who told me that the age of miracle was past, and the signs of the divine given to the fathers of the church had been taken from the world, never to come again. I knew it was not the case, and knew that God could and did intervene in men's affairs still, but I could not accept it with my whole heart. I could not say those simple words, ''Thy will be done,'' and mean it. I meant, I know, ''Thy will be done if it agrees with what I want,'' and that is not prayer, nor is it submission.

My prayers failed. And shortly before dawn I lifted up my head and abandoned the attempt, and knew that I was alone. I knew that I would receive no help, and that the one thing I desired most of all would not be given me. I would lose her, and at that moment knew that Sarah was the most precious part of my life, and the most precious thing that would ever be in my life. I accepted my punishment and in the quiet of dawn and despair perhaps then I prayed truly for the first time. All I know is that the darkness lifted from me, and a feeling of the most profound peace came to rest on my soul, and I found myself on my knees once more, thanking God with all my heart for His goodness.

I did not know what would happen, and could not understand how it could possibly be that the inevitable march of man's cruelty could be thrust aside. But I no longer questioned or doubted. I dressed myself as warmly as possible, took my thickest cloak—for although spring had come it was still frosty at dawn—and joined the throng of people walking down towards the castle to see the execution.

There was only one person to die that day; the judge was as merciful with others as he was vengeful with her, and the affair would be over in only a short time. As I approached the mob gathered round the big tree in the courtyard, the rope already hanging from the thick bough and the ladder in place, my heart sank and the doubt came upon me once again, but with a mighty effort of will I pushed all such thoughts from me. I did not even know why I was there; certainly there was no purpose in it, and I did not wish Sarah to see me. But I knew that it was necessary, somehow, and that her life depended on my presence, although I could not begin to comprehend how.

Lower was also there, with Locke and a few burly fellows, one of whom I recognized as a porter from Christ Church. Strange company, I thought, before it dawned on me what he was proposing. I had not seen him now for several days, but I should have realized he would not readily pass up an opportunity to get more material for his book. He was a kind man but dedicated to his work; the look of grim determination on his face as he paced up and down was not that of someone who anticipated any enjoyment from imminent events, but he was certainly not going to flinch from them.

I avoided him; I had no desire for conversation and I scarcely even noticed another small party, standing to one side, talking loudly and making coarse jokes, which clustered around the Regius professor. Had I paid more attention, I have no doubt I would also have given more significance to the whispered conference between Lower and his associates, to the way they positioned themselves next to the hanging tree, and the look of grim satisfaction on Lower's face as he surveyed the coming battlefield and the disposition of his forces.

And then Sarah was brought out, in heavy chains and between two large guards, although scarce any were needed, so small and frail and weak did she look. It made my heart break to see her; her eyes were heavy and the blackness of the rings around them was made more visible by the deathly pallor of her face; her beautiful dark hair was uncovered, but seemed beautiful no longer; she had always combed it lovingly, it was her greatest—indeed her only—vanity. Now it was matted and unkempt, and was bundled up coarsely above her neck, so it would not get in the way of the rope.

I merely repeat what Cola has already documented from my lips; she did indeed dismiss the priest in a way which brought loud applause from the crowd, said her own prayers and then made a brief speech which, while she confessed to sins, did not confess to the one sin for which she was about to die. There was no ringing heroism or defiance, or appeal for the crowd's sympathy, such as would be appropriate for a man in similar circumstances. Her common sense, I am sure, told her that it would be unseemly from her lips, and win her no admiration. Rather, the way to the mob's heart lay through courage and submission and, as these two greatest of human qualities were in natural conformity to her nature, she won their applause merely by being herself—and to be that in such an extremity is, to my mind, the greatest of achievements.

Once all was over, she mounted the ladder after the hangman, and then waited patiently as he fumbled around her with the rope. I do not know why hangings have to be so coarse and crude; the last moments should be more dignified, not this welter of legs and arms up a rickety ladder propped uncertainly against a tree trunk, and to submit without exciting laughter is rare. But the crowd was in no mood for laughter that morning; her youth, her frailty and her calm stilled any ribaldry, and they watched with greater quiet and respect than I have ever seen at such an event.

Then the drums sounded; only two drummers, both boys aged about twelve whom I had seen many times playing in the street; the days when a proper troop would perform the ceremony were gone now, and the magistrate had decided there was no need of soldiers that morning. He did not anticipate any trouble from the crowd, as might have been the case if a popular figure in the town, or a highwayman of standing, or a man with a family, was being hanged. Nor was there. The crowd fell absolutely silent, the drums followed suit, and the hangman—with a movement of the most surprising delicacy—pushed Sarah off the ladder.

"God have mercy." This was her cry, and the last was lost as the rope pulled tight under her weight, and ended in a strangled sob that brought a sigh of sympathy from the crowd. And then she swung there, her face turning purple, and her limbs twitching and the stench spreading as the telltale stains on her shift showed that the noose was having its usual foul effect.

I will not continue; there can be few who have not seen such a sight, and even now the memory pains me beyond belief, although I recall that I watched it all with the most remarkable calm, despite the sudden and terrifying clap of thunder and darkening of the skies which broke from heaven as she fell. I prayed for her soul, and for my own, once again and lowered my eyes that I should not see the end.

I had reckoned without Lower, and his determination to beat the Regius professor to the body. He had, of course, bribed the hangman in advance; this accounted for the nods and winks that passed between them, and the fact that he was suffered to be so close to the tree; I did not realize he had purchased Sarah's permission with a promise of treatment for her mother, nor indeed that the mother at that very moment lay breathing her last only a few hundred yards away from the castle. Sarah had only just stopped twitching and convulsing when Lower cried in a loud voice to his little army, "Right, lads," and surged forward, giving a sign to the hangman who straightaway pulled a large knife from his belt and sliced through the rope.

Sarah's body fell the three feet to the ground with a heavy thump, accompanied by the first muttering of disapproval from the crowd, and Lower bent down to see if she still breathed. "Dead," he shouted after a proper examination, so that all might hear, and signed for his comrades to come forward. The porter from Christ Church picked up the body and threw it over his shoulder, and before anyone could react at all, began to head off, almost breaking into a run as the protests from the crowd grew. Two others in his party stood back to head off the Regius professor's men should they try to intercept, and Lower looked around once before following his prize.

Right across that open patch of land our eyes met, and in

mine he can have seen nothing but disgust. He gave a little shrug, then cast his eyes down, and would look at me no more. Then he too turned and ran off, into the rain which was already falling heavily and with appalling ferocity.

I hesitated for only a brief moment before leaving myself, but unlike the crowd, who attempted a pursuit and became blocked in the narrow gateway by all trying to run out at the same moment, I left by the other entrance. For I knew where Lower was going, and did not need to keep him in my sight in order to catch up with him and his gruesome prize.

He must have moved quickly, and knew that the faster he went the better, for the crowd was now in an unforgiving mood. They accepted the hanging as God's will and the king's justice, and went to see all the proprieties maintained. What they did not accept—for crowds have a fine sense of right and wrong—was any meanness of behavior. The condemned must die, but must be treated well. Lower had offended victim and town, and I knew it would go hard with him should he be caught.

They did not, however, for he had planned well; I only just caught up with him myself before he slipped in the back of Boyle's elaboratory and mounted the stairs.

I was still cold with shock at what he had done. I knew all his arguments in advance, had heard them all before and even agreed with most of them, but this I could not countenance. You may say that, considering all I had done and not done, I had long since resigned any right to make judgments. I did so nonetheless and mounted the stairs so that, if I could not ensure justice was done, I could at least maintain appearances.

He had already posted guards on the stairs, lest the crowd realize that he had come here rather than to Christ Church, and was on the verge of bolting the doors so that no one could disturb him in his horrible labor. I, however, managed to burst in by pushing all my weight against the door before the bolts were shot.

"Lower," I cried when I stopped and briefly took in the hellish scene in front of me. "This must stop."

Locke was there already to assist, as well as a barber to attend on the more mechanical aspects of the dissection.

Sarah had already been stripped naked and that beautiful body which I had held so often lay on the table as the barber roughly washed it down and prepared it for the knife. That she was dead no one could doubt for a moment; her poor broken body was as drained as a corpse is, and only the thick red weal around the neck, and strangled expression of anguish on her face, destroying all beauty, showed all too well what had become of her.

"Don't be absurd, Wood," he said wearily. "She's dead. The soul has gone. I can do nothing to hurt her further. You know that as well as I. I know you were fond of her, but it is too late for that."

He looked at me kindly, and patted me on the back. "Look, my friend," he said. "You will not like this. I don't blame you, it takes a strong stomach. You should not stay here to watch. Take my advice and go away, old fellow. It will be better. Believe me."

I was too mad to listen, but angrily flung off his kindly touch and retreated, daring him to act in the bestial way he intended in my eyesight, thinking, perhaps foolishly, that my presence would make him see the evil he did, and desist.

He looked at me for several moments, uncertain about how to proceed, until Locke coughed in the background.

"We have little time, you know," he said. "The magistrate gave us an hour only, and time is going. Quite apart from what will happen if the crowd finds out where we are. Make up your mind."

With difficulty, Lower did, and turned away from me, and back to the table, signing for all others to leave the room. I sank down on my knees, begging the Lord, anyone, to do something and stop this nightmare. Even though it had served no purpose the night before, I went over all my prayers and my promises. Oh Lord God incarnate for our sins, have mercy on this poor innocent, if not on me.

Then Lower picked up his knife, and placed it on her breast. "Ready?" he asked.

Locke nodded, and with a swift, sure movement he began to make his incision. I shut my eyes.

"Locke," I heard him call through my darkness, suddenly

angry, ''what on earth do you think you're doing? Let go of my hand. Is everyone gone mad here?''

''Stop a moment.''

And Locke, whom I had never liked, pulled the knife away from the body, and bent over the corpse. Then, with a puzzled look on his face, he repeated the movement, so that his cheek rested on her mouth.

''She's breathing.''

I could scarcely restrain my tears at those few simple words, which said so much. Lower gave his own explanations later; how she must have been cut down too early in his efforts to get hold of the corpse first, and how, rather than life itself, merely the appearance of it had been extinguished. How the fall had merely strangled and brought temporary oblivion only. I know all this; he told me his reasons time and again, but I knew differently, and never bothered to contradict him. He believed one thing; I knew another. I knew that I had witnessed the greatest miracle of history. I had seen resurrection; for the spirit of God moved in that room, and the soft wings of the dove that attended her conception returned to beat on Sarah's soul. It is not given to man, and certainly not to physicians, to restore life when it is extinguished. Lower would argue this proves she was never dead, but he had pronounced her so himself and he had studied the question more carefully than anyone. People say the age of miracles is past, and I believed that myself. But it is not so; they do occur, only we are getting better at explaining them away.

''So what do we do now?'' I heard Lower say, a tone of the greatest bafflement and surprise in his voice. ''Should we kill her, do you think?''

''What?''

''She is meant to be dead. Not to kill her would merely postpone the inevitable, and ensure I lost her.''

''Well . . .''

I could not believe my ears. Surely, after witnessing such a marvel, my friend could not be serious? He could not go against the manifest will of God and commit murder? I wanted to stand up and remonstrate with him, but found that I could not. I could not stand, I could not open my mouth;

all I could do was sit there and listen, for I think the Lord had still more purpose that day as well; He wanted Lower to redeem himself as well, if only he would take the opportunity.

"I'd hit her on the head," he said, "except that would damage the brain." And he stood awhile in thought before scratching his chin nervously. "I'll have to cut her throat," he went on. "It's the only solution."

And again he picked up his knife, and again he hesitated, before quietly laying it down again. "I can't do this," he said. "Locke, advise me. What should I do?"

"I seem to remember," Locke said, "that we physicians are meant protect life, and are never meant to kill. Is that not the case?"

"But legally," Lower replied, "she is already dead. I am merely doing properly what should already have been done."

"Are you a hangman then?"

"She was condemned to die."

"Was she?"

"You know very well she was."

"I remember," Locke said, "that she was sentenced to be hanged by the neck. She has been so. There was no mention of her being hanged by the neck until dead. I admit this is normally understood and stated, but as it was not in this case, it cannot be counted a necessary part of the punishment."

"She has also been condemned to burn," Lower said. "And the hanging was merely a way of sparing her pain. Are you telling me we should now hand her over to the pyre and let her burn alive?"

Then his attention was brought to Sarah herself, who issued a soft, low moan as she lay all unattended while they conducted their dispute.

"Bring me a bandage," he said, the physician once more. "And let me bind up this cut I made in her."

For the next five minutes or so, he worked steadily on the wound, fortunately only small, before he and Locke used all their strength to raise her up into a sitting position, resting her back against their shoulders, and swinging her legs down off the table. Finally, while Locke instructed her on deep breathing, so that her head might steady itself, Lower fetched a cloak, and with the utmost gentleness, covered her up.

A living, sitting woman is more difficult to contemplate killing than a corpse flat out on a table and, by the time the movement was finished, Lower's attitude had entirely changed. His natural kindness, kept at bay on many occasions by his ambition, swept all before it and, whatever he thought he should do, he began to treat the girl as his patient almost without being aware of it. And he was always ferocious in the defense of those whom he considered to be under his protection.

"But what do we do now?" he said, and all of us in that room were aware that while this had been continuing, the noise from the street outside had insensibly grown, so that now there was the roar of a substantial number of people outside. Locke poked his head out of the window.

"It is the crowd. I told you they wouldn't like this," he said. "Just as well it is raining so hard, it keeps most of them away." He peered up into the sky. "Have you ever seen rain like this before?"

Another groan from Sarah, who bent her head down and was violently sick, heaving and retching, distracted their attention once again. Lower brought some spirits, and patted her on the head as he forced her to drink some, although it only made her retch the more.

"If you tell them this, they will only say it was a sign of disfavor at what you intended. They will take her away and put her on the pyre, then stand guard to make sure you get nowhere near."

"Are you saying we shouldn't hand her over?"

Through all this, I had said not a word, but merely stood in the corner and watched. Now I found my voice was given back to me. I could make a difference in this balance, for it was clear that all must agree to whatever action was taken.

"You must not," I said. "She has done no wrong. She is entirely innocent. I know it. If you hand her over, you will not only abandon a patient, you will abandon an innocent whom God has favored."

"And you are sure of this?" Locke said, turning and apparently noticing me for the first time.

"I am. I tried to tell the court, but was hooted down."

"I will not ask you how you know," he said softly, and his penetrating look made me realize, for the first and only time, how it was that he subsequently achieved such a place in the world. For he saw more than other people, and guessed more still. I was grateful to him for his silence, and have been ever since.

"Very well," he continued. "The only problem is that we may take her place on the gallows. I am a generous man, I think, but even I have limits to what I will do for a patient."

Lower, meanwhile, had been pacing up and down in the greatest agitation, occasionally sneaking a glimpse out of the window, then looking in turn at Sarah, then Locke, then me. When Locke and I had finished our exchange, he spoke:

"Sarah?" he said softly, and repeated it until she lifted up her head and looked at him. Her eyes were bloodshot and ill, for the little vessels within them had ruptured, and gave her the air of a very devil, and the whiteness of her complexion made this seem even more frightening.

"Can you hear me? Can you speak?"

After a long pause, she nodded.

"You must answer me a question," he said, coming and kneeling on one knee before her, so that she could see him clear. "Whatever you have said in the past, you must say the truth now. For our lives and souls depend on it, as well as yours. Did you kill Dr. Grove?"

Even though I knew the truth, I did not know the answer she would give. And she did not give one for some time, but eventually she shook her head.

"Your confession was false?"

A little nod.

"You swear this by all you hold dear?"

She nodded.

Lower stood up, and heaved a heavy sigh. "Mr. Wood," he said. "Take this girl upstairs to Boyle's chamber. He will be indignant if he discovers, so try not to make a mess. Dress her as best you can, and cut off her hair."

I stared uncomprehending, and Lower frowned. "Now, Mr. Wood, if you please. You must never query a physician while he is trying to save a life."

And I led Sarah out by the hand, hearing Lower murmur:

"In the next room, Locke. It is a long shot, but it may serve."

Although there seemed little wrong with her, Sarah was still unable to speak or do anything except sit, staring into space as I followed my instructions. It is hard cutting off hair without a scissor, and the result would have done no credit to a woman of fashion. That, however, was not Lower's intention, whatever else he had in mind, and within a short while I had done as I was told, then tried my best to clear up the mess.

Then I sat down beside her, and took her hand. There were no words I could say that would have answered my need, so I said none. But I squeezed lightly, and eventually felt the very slightest of squeezes back. It was enough; I broke down in the most complete of sobs, bending my head down across her breast while she sat there immobile.

"Did you really think I would leave you?" she said in a voice so soft and weak I could barely hear her.

"I could hardly hope for anything better. I know I did not deserve as much."

"Who am I?"

It was the most glorious moment of my life. Everything before built to that question, everything after, the years of life which I have had since and still hope to have, are the merest coda to it. For the first and the last time, I had no doubts and had no need of thought or calculation. I did not need to consider, or assess evidence, nor yet to use any of the skills of interpretation needed for lesser matters; all I had to do was state the manifest truth without fear, and in perfect confidence. Some things, indeed, are so obvious that examination is redundant and logic contemptible. The truth was there to be believed, the most perfect gift because so undeserved. I knew. That was all.

"You are my Savior, the living God, born of the spirit, persecuted, insulted and abused, known to the Magi, who died for our sins and is resurrected as happened before and will happen again in every generation of man."

Anyone who heard me would have thought me mad, and in that sentence I stepped forever out of the full society of my fellow men and into a peace of my own.

"Tell no one of this," she said softly.

"And I am afraid. I cannot bear to lose you," I added, ashamed of my own selfishness.

Sarah seemed scarcely to pay any attention, but eventually leaned forward and kissed me on the forehead. "You should not be afraid, and should never be afraid. You are my love, my dove, my dearest and I am your friend. I will not forsake you nor ever neglect you."

They were the last words she spoke to me, the last I ever heard from her lips, and I sat by her side, holding her hand and staring in awe at her until a noise from below roused me once more. Then I rose from the bed where she sat, staring blankly across the room, and went back down to Lower. Sarah now seemed completely unaware of my existence.

The carnage in that room downstairs was truly diabolical, and even I, who knew the truth, was appalled by it. How much greater must Cola's shock have been when he forced his way in, and saw what he thought to be Sarah's body. For Lower had taken the corpse he had acquired in Aylesbury, and roughly hacked it into unrecognizable fragments, so brutalizing the head that it was scarcely recognizable as human. He himself was covered in blood from a dog Locke had slaughtered to complete the illusion, and the stench of the alcohol in the room was unbearable, even though the window was wide open to allow the winds into the room.

"Well, Wood?" he said, turning to me with a grim expression. Locke, I saw, had resumed his languid, absent pose, and was standing idly by at the door. "Will anybody spot our imposition, do you think?" And with a knife, he levered an eyeball out of the skull on the table, so that it hung by a thread from its socket.

"I have cut her hair, but the experience has so affected her she is hardly capable of moving, I think. What do you suggest we do with her now?"

"Boyle's servant has some clothes in the cupboard next the chamber," he said. "At least, he normally keeps them there. I think we must borrow them. Dress her up, and get her out of the building so no one will recognize her. Meantime, keep her upstairs and quiet. No one must see her, or even suspect there is anyone there."

Again I mounted the stairs, found the clothes and began the lengthy process of getting Sarah into them. She spoke not a word during the whole operation, and when I was finished I left her and went out by Mr. Crosse's back door and followed a little lane down to Merton Street and my house.

First, however, I called into the Feathers, as I needed a few moments to steady my nerves and collect my thoughts. And was approached by Cola, looking tired and worn out himself, who wanted news of the execution. I told him the entire truth except for the one detail of importance and he, poor man, took it as confirmation of his theory about blood transfusion, that the death of the spirit in the donor must inevitably cause the death of the recipient as well. I could not, for obvious reasons, illuminate him on this point, and demonstrate that his theory had a fatal evidential flaw.

He also told me of the death of the mother, which grieved me greatly, for it was yet another burden for Sarah to bear. But I forced myself to put it aside as Cola went to remonstrate with Lower, and I went myself to my house to discover my mother in the kitchen. She had been greatly affected by Sarah's fall, and had taken to sitting quietly by the fire when she was not praying for the girl. This morning, as I arrived— for despite everything it was still scarcely eight—she sat all alone in the chair no one else was allowed to occupy, and I saw to my astonishment that she had been crying when no one was there to see her. But she pretended not to do so, and I pretended not to notice, as I had no wish to humiliate her. Even then, I think, I wondered how something of normal life could continue despite the wonders I had just witnessed, and could not understand how no one had noticed anything, except myself.

"And it is done?"

"After a fashion," I replied. "Mother, I must ask you something in all seriousness. What would you have done to help her, had it been in your power?"

"Anything," she said firmly. "You know that. Anything."

"If she had escaped, would you have assisted her, even though it meant breaking the law yourself? Not given her up?"

"Of course," she said. "The law is nothing when it is wrong, and deserves to be disregarded."

I looked at her, for the words sounded strange on her lips, until I realized it was something I had once heard Sarah say herself.

"Would you help her now?"

"She is beyond my help, I think."

"No."

She said nothing, so I continued, my words blurting out once I had gone too far to retract. "She died and is alive again. She is in Mr. Boyle's apartment. She is still alive, Mother, and no one knows of it. Nor will they ever, unless you say something, as we have all decided to try and help her away."

This time even my presence did not provide enough incentive to spare her dignity, and she rocked back and forth in her chair, clutching her hands together and muttering "Thank God, thanks to God, all praise to God," with the tears welling up in her eyes and rolling down her cheeks until I took her by the hand and got her attention once more. "She needs hiding until we can get her out of the town. Do I have your permission to bring her here? If I hide her in my study, you will not betray her?"

Of course she gave her absolute promise, and I knew it was better than any I might make, so I kissed her on the cheek, and told her I would be back after nightfall. I last saw her bustling about the kitchen, dragging out vegetables and our last winter ham for a celebratory feast when Sarah should come again.

It continued a strange day, that one, for after all the frenzied activity of the first few hours, all of us—Lower, Locke and myself—found ourselves with time on our hands, and little to do until night came. Lower realized that the events at least had made up his mind about journeying to London, for his reputation amongst the townsfolk would never be the same again, such was the disapproval of his supposed activities. He now had no choice but to risk all and begin the long task of establishing himself elsewhere. The remains of the girl he had bought in Aylesbury were taken off to the castle and burned on the pyre—Lower's humor returned sufficiently for him to remark that she had been pickled in so much alcohol it would be fortunate if she did not blow up the entire building—and I had been given money by Cola to ensure the decent burial of Mrs. Blundy.

Organizing the burial was a simple, if painful, process; there were plenty of people who were now prepared to do something, so great was the revulsion felt for the fate of the girl, that they were happy to make some amends by treating the mother as well as possible, especially as they were to be paid for their kindness. I had the priest at St. Thomas's undertake to perform the rites, and set them for that evening, and he also sent his men round to collect the body and prepare it. It was not either the priest or the church the woman would have chosen for herself, but I had no clear idea who should do it, and as asking anybody but an established minister would create untold difficulties, I decided it was best to avoid unnecessary complications. The service was set for eight o'clock that evening and, as I left, the priest was already shouting at the sexton, telling him to dig a grave in the poorer, more neglected part of the churchyard so that a more valuable plot, such as is occupied by gentlemen, was not used by accident.

I had entirely put out of my mind the unwelcome task of telling Sarah what had occurred. It would have to be done, of course, and I knew I would have to do it, but I simply postponed it as long as possible. Lower had already been told by Cola, and looked greatly upset by the news.

"I cannot understand it," he said. "She was not well, and was very weak, but when I saw her she was not dying. When did she die?"

"I do not know. Mr. Cola told me of it. He was with her, I think."

Lower's face darkened. "That man," he said. "I'm sure he killed her."

"Lower! That is a terrible thing to say."

"I don't mean deliberately. But his grasp of theory is better than his practice." He sighed heavily, and looked mightily concerned. "I feel bad about this, Wood. I really do. I should have attended the woman myself. You know Cola planned to give her more blood?"

"No."

"He did. I could not stop him, of course, as she was his patient, but I refused to have anything to do with it."

"It was the wrong treatment?"

"Not necessarily. But we had a falling out, and I did not wish to be associated with him. I told you that Wallis said he has in the past stolen other men's ideas."

"Many times," I said. "So?"

"So?" Lower repeated, greatly affronted. "Is there anything worse?"

"He might have been a scheming Jesuit, here in secret to rekindle civil strife and subvert the kingdom," I suggested. "That might be accounted worse."

"Not by me."

And the remark broke the tension which had been building up all day, and all of a sudden both Lower and I found ourselves collapsing in gales of laughter, roaring until the tears rolled down our cheeks, gripping each other tightly as our bodies shook with the most strange merriment. We ended on the floor, Lower flat on his back, still heaving, I with my head between my knees as the laughter made my head spin and my jaw ache. I loved Lower dearly then, and knew that, whatever our differences and whatever gruffness of character he might have, I would always love him, for he was a truly good man.

When we recovered and wiped the tears from our eyes, it was Lower who brought up the topic of what to do with Sarah. No laughing matter, that.

"She must obviously leave Oxford immediately," I said. "She cannot stay in my chamber forever and even with her hair cut, she is easily recognizable. But where she should go, and what she should do, I am at a loss to suggest."

"How much ready money do you have?"

"About four pounds," I said. "Much of which is the money due to you and Cola for her mother's treatment."

He waved that aside. "Another patient defaults. Not the first, and not the last, I'll be bound. For my part I have two pounds, and in a fortnight I am due my annuity from my family. Out of that, I can afford another two."

"If you make it up to four, I will repay you the difference when my own quarterly comes in."

He nodded. "Ten pounds then. Not a lot, even for a girl of her condition. I wonder . . ."

"Hmm?"

"You know my younger brother is a Quaker?"

He said it quite naturally, and without evident shame, although I knew it was a topic he touched on with only the greatest reluctance. Indeed, there were many who knew him well who were entirely unaware that Lower even had a brother, so greatly did he fear being damaged by the association. I met this man once, and did not dislike him. Just as his face was like Lower's without the same expression, so his character was like that of his brother without the merriment and easy laughter, for laughter, I am told, is forbidden among them as a sin.

I nodded.

"He is in business with a group of like-minded people who wish to go to places where they will not come under attack; the countries of Massachusetts and suchlike. I could write to him, and ask him to get Sarah Blundy sent there. She could leave as a servant, or as someone's relative, and would then have to make her own way when she arrives."

"It is a harsh punishment for one who has done no wrong."

"Few who go there of their own volition have done anything wrong. Yet they go nonetheless. She will be in good company, and will find more people there of her like than she will ever do here."

After all that had happened, the thought of her leaving, of never seeing her again, tore at my heart and I know that I argued against the plan for selfish reasons. But Lower was right; if she stayed in England, then sooner or later she would be discovered. Someone—an old comrade of her father, or a traveling man from Oxford, or an old student—would see her and recognize her. Her life would be in the balance every day and so would ours be. I had no idea what, technically, the law said about what we had done, but I knew that few judges looked kindly on anyone who presumed to interfere with their prerogatives. She had been condemned to death, and was alive. All of Locke's cleverness in argument would have a hard time explaining that one away.

And so we agreed; or at least, we agreed that it should be put to Sarah, as the scheme was impossible if she would not give her consent. Lower undertook to suggest the plan, as it was his idea and he would have to do all the arranging with the dissidents. I took myself back to St. Thomas's to ensure that the preparations for the funeral were going well and fully expected that I would be the only person there at the service itself.

Sarah was not content because she did not wish to leave her mother, and it was only Lower informing her that the woman was dead which brought her to sense. All her own trials she had borne with fortitude; the loss of this woman brought out all her weakness. I will say no more, except that Lower was not the best of people to deliver comfort. He was kind and desired the best for all; but he did have a tendency to become gruff and unsympathetic when confronted with a misery he could do nothing to alleviate. I have little doubt that his tone—matter-of-fact to the point of being brutal— only made matters worse.

Sarah insisted on coming to the funeral, even though Lower remonstrated with her forcefully about the foolishness of such a desire, but she insisted and was quite impossible to divert. The fact that my mother backed her up, and said she would bring the girl to the church whatever Dr. Richard Lower said, decided the matter.

I was distressed when all three of them arrived, Lower looking anxious, my mother grim and Sarah blank, as though some vitality had left her body, never to return. They had done their best to disguise her appearance and had dressed her as a boy, covering her head with a cap pulled down low in front of her eyes, but I was terrified that at any moment the priest would look up from his book, and stare goggle-eyed before rushing off to call the watch. But he did nothing of the sort; merely droned through the service faster than was seemly, refusing to make the slightest effort for the soul of a woman who was not a lady, not a rich parishioner, nor indeed anyone who should attract the condescension of someone as grand as he. I felt, I must say, like slapping him, and telling him to do his job properly, so ashamed I was. With priests like that, no wonder so many people turn elsewhere. When he was over, he snapped the book shut, nodded at us, held out his hand for his fee, then stalked off. He would not, he said, finish the rest of the ceremony at the graveside as the woman was all but a heathen. He had done his legal requirement, and he would do no more.

Lower, I think, was even more furious than I at this callousness, although I like to believe the man would have been more considerate had he known that a member of the woman's family was present. But he did not, so made no effort, and the result was one of the most painful events I have ever witnessed. And for Sarah, it must have been many times more anguishing. I did my best to comfort her.

"She will be sent on her way by her daughter, who loved her, and her friends, who tried to help her," I said. "That is far better, and more appropriate. She would not have liked to be intoned over at the graveside by a man like that in any case."

So Lower and I picked up the bier ourselves, and carried it out of the church stumbling across the yard in the dark with only one taper to guide us. A more different occasion than the one which attended the burial of Dr. Grove could not be imagined, but we were, at least, all at one now the minister was gone.

It fell to me to make the speech, for Lower did not know her well, and Sarah seemed unable to speak. I had no idea what was appropriate, but simply spoke the first thoughts that came into my head. I said that I had known her only in the last few years, that we were not of the same faith, she and I, and could not be further apart in matters of politics. Yet I honored her as a good woman, and a courageous one, who did right as she saw it, and was also a seeker after the truths she wished to know. I would not say she was the most obedient of wives, for she would have scorned to be described in such a way. Yet she was the greatest support for her husband, and both loved and helped him in all the ways he wanted and expected. She fought herself for what he also believed and brought up a daughter who was courageous, true, gentle and good, better than anyone could conceive. In this best of fashions she honored her Creator, and was blessed for it. I believed she had no faith in the afterlife, for she distrusted anything that came from the mouths of priests. Yet I knew she was wrong, and that she would be welcomed into God's embrace.

It was an inarticulate mish-mash, that speech of mine, delivered rather to give such comfort as I could to Sarah, than to paint a true portrait of the dead woman. Yet I believed it all then, and believe it still. I know it is inconceivable that a woman like her, of her religion and her opinions, of her status and her deeds, could ever be accounted worthy or noble or virtuous in any form. But she was all of these, and I do not trouble any more about reconciling my beliefs with those of other men.

When I had done, there was an awkward pause before my mother led Sarah up to the body, and pulled back the cloth so that the face was exposed. It was raining heavily, and inexpressibly miserable as little spots of mud were thrown up by the rain, spattering on the dead woman as she lay there on the damp, cold ground. Sarah knelt down, and we all stood back while she muttered a prayer of her own; she finished by leaning over and kissing her mother's forehead, then gently tidied away a wisp of hair that had come loose from the old woman's best bonnet.

She stood up once more. Lower tugged me by the arm and together we lowered the corpse into the ground as gently and decorously as we could manage before Sarah performed her final duty as a daughter and scattered the earth over the grave opening. We all followed suit, and finally Lower and I wielded the shovels ourselves, filling up that hole as swiftly as we could. When it was all completed, and we were all thoroughly drenched and muddy and cold, we simply turned and walked away. There was nothing else to be done, except attend once more to the living.

Lower, as usual, had been busier and more effective than I. He had taken it upon himself to borrow Boyle's coach— reasoning correctly that the vehicle of such a man would not be stopped or even examined by the watch, however late it was to be found on the road—and hired two horses to pull it. He proposed to take Sarah himself to Reading, sufficiently far from Oxford to be safe, especially as relations between the two towns were bad enough to ensure that there was, at present, little communication between them. There he would lodge Sarah with associates of his brother, a family of dissenters whom he could guarantee would guard her secret, or what little they were to be told of it. When his brother returned and passed through the town on his way back to Dorset, he would be informed of events and would certainly take the girl under his wing, putting her on the first ship available taking dissenters away from England. So it was agreed by all of us.

I cannot bring myself to write of my final parting from her, my final look at her face, and will not do so.

Sarah left ten days later in the company of his brother, made her way under his guidance to Plymouth and there took passage.

It was the last anyone ever heard of her. She never arrived in America and it was assumed she had fallen overboard. But the boat was becalmed at the time and was in any case so crowded it was difficult to imagine anyone coming to grief without being noticed. Yet she simply disappeared one day in full sunlight and without any sound, as though she had been taken up bodily into the heavens.

chapter twelve

THERE THE STORY, SUCH AS I KNOW IT, OF SARAH
Blundy comes to its end and I can say no more: those who
wish to disbelieve me can do so.

It remains now for me to recount the last portion of the
story, and show what the Italian had as his business in England. I confess I do not find it important, for in comparison
to what I had witnessed, the errors of men who squabble in
such ignorance of the truth, cannot but excite the most complete disdain. Yet as it is both part of these events, and a
cause of them, so I should set all down that I might complete
my labors and rest.

I traveled to London the day after Sarah left Oxford, still
very much in a mood of most profound dismay and reverie;
it was Lower's idea to go, and he recommended it forcefully
as a treatment for melancholy and brooding. A change of
scenery, different company and a bit of entertainment, he
insisted, would help shake off the sadness that had settled
over me. I took his advice because my lassitude was such it
was easier to do so than to resist. Lower packed my bag for
me, walked me to Carfax, and put me on the coach.

"And enjoy yourself," he said. "You must admit everything has turned out better than you could possibly have expected. It is time to put it behind you."

Naturally, I could not do so quite so easily, but I tried to
follow his advice as much as possible, and spent time forcing

myself to visit people with whom I had corresponded over the years, trying hard to be interested in what they said. I did not succeed very well, as my mind kept drifting off to more important matters, and I fear I may have aroused some resentment among my colleagues because of a distance which they surely took as disdain and arrogance. Matters which ordinarily would have produced the liveliest fascination could generate no interest at all; I was told of the discovery of huge bones, turned to stone in a quarry in Hertfordshire, proving that the Bible spoke true when it said that once giants walked the earth, and I was less than fascinated. I was given hospitality by John Aubrey, at that time my good friend, but could display no enthusiasm for his ingenuity in discovering the purpose and nature of Stonehenge and Avebury and other such sites; I was invited to attend a meeting of the Royal Society, but turned this great honor down with ease, and never cared that I was not invited again.

And one evening, after I had been there but two days, I found myself walking past an inn in Cheapside called the Bells, and remembered I had seen the name in Cola's chest, and felt the need to go in search of someone who had also known Sarah and seen something of what I had seen. And I had this great urge to know the answers to many questions, to understand the apparent chain of human events which had brought her end.

He was easily found, even though the innkeeper—whom I later knew to be a papist—did not know the name; all I had to do was ask for the Italian gentleman, and I was immediately shown to the grand room—occupied by himself alone—where he had lodged himself since his arrival.

His astonishment at seeing me was very great, but no more so than when I began to talk to him.

"Good evening, Father," I said.

He could not deny it, could not bluster or protest or insist, for priests cannot do so. Instead, he stared at me in terror, thinking that I was sent to trap him and that armed men would soon be pounding up the stairs to take him to his martyrdom. But there was no sound, no noise of boots or shouts of urgent command, just the silence in the room as he stood by the window in shock.

"Why do you call me Father?"

"Because that is what you are." I did not say, who else would go around with holy oil and holy water and a sacred relic hidden away in his belongings? Who else but a priest bound to celibacy would react in such horror when he realized the strengths of his carnal desires? Who else would secretly and in goodness give extreme unction to a woman he thought was dying, to intercede for her soul despite herself?

Cola sat down cautiously on his cot, and looked at me carefully, and with much thought, almost as if he was still expecting me to launch some surprise assault on him.

"Why have you come here?"

"Not to do you harm."

"Then why?"

"I wish to talk."

I felt sorry for putting him into such a dangerous situation, and did my best to assure him that I intended him no ill. I believe it was my face, rather than my words, which convinced him of my sincerity. Both can lie, but not in my case, for I have said already that the merest simpleton can see straight through me. Had I been lying, Cola would have known it, and yet he saw nothing of the sort on my face. So, after a long and very tense wait, he sighed and bowed to the inevitable, and asked me to sit.

"Is your name really Marco da Cola? I feel I should know whom I am addressing. Is there any such person?" I asked.

He smiled gently. "There was," he said. "He was my brother. My name is Andrea."

"Was?"

"He is dead. He died in my arms on his return from Crete. I grieve greatly for him still."

"Why are you here?"

"Like you, I can say I wish no harm on any man. Not that many would believe me; hence my subterfuge. Your government does not greatly approve of foreign priests. Certainly not Jesuits." He said it deliberately, eyes on my face all the while to see my reaction to his admission.

I nodded. "You have not answered my question."

"Mr. Wood," he continued, "you are the only person to have divined who I am, and you are the only man of your faith I have encountered who does not react as if I were the devil himself. Why is this? Are you, perhaps, drawn to the true church in your heart?''

'' 'Let no man say that his is the best and only road, for they say so out of ignorance alone,' '' I said and the words were out of my mouth before ever I remembered where I had heard them.

Cola looked disturbed at this: "A generous, though erroneous sentiment," he replied, and I hoped he would not query me too much on it, for I knew I could neither defend it nor even explain it. Either the bread turns to flesh, and the wine to blood, or it does not; it cannot do so in Rome, but not in Canterbury. Either Christ made Peter and his successors the foundation stone of faith, conferring on them all authority in matters spiritual, or he did not; Our Lord did not tell Peter he would have authority over all the world except for those parts of Europe which think differently.

But Cola said no more on this subject, glad only that he had the fortune to have been discovered by perhaps the one person in the whole country who felt no need to betray him to the authorities. Nor was my mind in the spirit for theological debate, even had I a chance of winning it. Such discussions had always given me great delight, but I was overburdened with the knowledge I carried within me, and in no mood any more for what I could now only consider trivial.

Instead he asked, with exquisite kindness, about the funeral of Anne Blundy, and I told him as much as was seemly. He seemed satisfied that his money was well spent, and expressed sorrow that Lower had behaved so ill.

"You seem to have recovered from your distress at the girl's death," he said, with a penetrating look in my direction. "I am glad of that. It is not easy, I know; it is hard to lose someone who is important in your life, as she was in yours, and my brother was in mine."

And we talked of such matters, Father Andrea with such sense and kindness that, even though he knew little of what had occurred, he soothed my loss and did something to reconcile me to the loneliness I already knew would be my fate. He was a good man and a good priest, though a papist, and

I was lucky to find him, for such people are rarely encountered. It is hard to be a physician of the body and even though many try, few have the skills or the sympathy for success. How much more difficult it is to give physick to the soul, to guide a man in sorrow to calmness and acceptance, yet Father Andrea was one who could. When we had finished, and I had no more to ask him and he had no more comfort to offer, I told him of my appreciation and decided to give him something in return by way of recompense.

"I know why you came to Oxford," I said, and he spun round quickly to stare me in the face.

"You were in correspondence with Sir James Prestcott, and those letters were lost when he died. They would greatly damage the cause of your religion in this country, and you wished to recover them so that they might not become generally known. That is why you searched the Blundys' cottage."

His eyes narrowed. "You know of this? You know where they are?"

"I know you need have no fear about them. I give you my word no one will ever see them, and they will be destroyed."

He was in two minds about trusting me, I could see, but knew he had no choice, and that he was profoundly fortunate. After a while he nodded. "That is all I ask."

"And you will be given it. Now, I must go."

He descended the stairs with me, resuming his disguise with each step, and while he had blessed me as a priest upstairs, he bowed to me as a gentleman in the street, before we went our separate ways.

"I suspect you will never come to Rome, Mr. Wood," he said with a smile. "You are not a man for traveling. It is a pity, for you would find it the most extraordinary of places, and there are many fine historians and antiquarians there who would delight in your company as much as you would delight in theirs. But, should the urge to travel ever come upon you, then you must write to me, and I will ensure you the finest of welcomes."

I thanked him, we bowed to each other one last time, and I walked off, never to see him again.

But I did hear of him; for I had gone no more than a few yards when I encountered my friend John Aubrey again, a man whose abilities as a gossip were as great as my reputation for such nonsense is undeserved.

"Who *is* that man?" he asked curiously, peering over my shoulder at Cola as he walked away. "Are you not going to introduce us?"

"He is a physician," I said. "Or at least, a gentleman interested in physick. Why do you ask? You talk as though you have seen him before."

"Indeed I have," he said, still peering, even though Cola by now had disappeared around the corner. "I saw him in Whitehall yesterday evening."

"A man may walk without arousing interest, I expect."

"In the palace itself? Not easily. And not when you are being accompanied by Sir Henry Bennet to the king's bedchamber."

"What?"

"You seem excessively surprised by this. Might I ask why?"

"No reason," I replied hastily. "I did not know he had such illustrious connections in this country. I am afraid that in Oxford we have all been patronizing him mightily as an impoverished foreigner, down on his luck. What is more, he never sought to enlighten us. We must have come across as very dismal people. But tell me exactly, when did you see him? And where?"

"It was late, well after dusk, possibly as late as eight o'clock. I had the great boon of being invited to a supper—very private and informal—with my Lord Sandwich, and his lady, and a cousin of his who receives his patronage. A bumptious man who works in the Navy Office, forever discoursing on subjects he knows nothing about, but very enthusiastic, and quite likeable in his simplicity. His name, as I recall, is . . ."

"I do not wish to know his name, Mr. Aubrey. Or what you ate, or the details of my Lord Sandwich's table. I wish to know about my acquaintance. You may tell me of your good fortune later, if you wish."

"I left his lodgings, you see, and walked back to my small

abode, and when I was almost there I remembered I had forgotten a box of manuscripts that the chancellor had said I could look at for my work. As I was not tired and had scarce drunk a quart of wine, I thought I would read them before sleeping. So I went back and, rather than walking across Whitehall to the office, I went via St. Stephen's yard. There is a corridor there, and at the end it turns right and leads into offices that contain my papers, while a left turn leads to a back entrance to the king's apartments. I will show you later on today, if you wish.''

I nodded, impatient for him to continue. ''I got the papers I wanted, and tucked them under my cloak, then walked back. And coming toward me down the corridor was Sir Henry Bennet—did you know he is now Lord Arlington?— and this man, whom I had never seen before.''

''You are sure it is the same man?''

''Absolutely. He was dressed in exactly the same fashion. The thing which attracted my attention as I bowed to let them pass before me was that he was carrying what looked like a lovely book. I am sure I had seen something like it before, Venetian work, very old indeed, in gold on a calfskin base.''

''How do you know it was the king he was seeing?''

''Nearly everyone else is away. The Duke of York keeps separate apartments and in any case is at St. James's with the king's mother. The queen is at Windsor with all her attendants. His Majesty is still there until he leaves in a few days. So unless Bennet was bringing this man, late at night, to visit a footman . . .''

And that, tantalizingly, was all I ever discovered for certain of the last few days that this Venetian spent in London, before he took ship for the continent once again. I cannot work it all out precisely, but it must have been a few days later that, again leaving by the same route, he was seen by Dr. Wallis and arrested. And all the while Sir Henry Bennet was organizing the search for him, and concealing the fact that he had himself taken him to visit the king in the greatest secrecy.

Clearly there were murky affairs of state involved, and I knew that the innocent never emerges with credit if he involves himself in such matters without good reason. The less

I knew, the safer I would be, and although it was hard, for once, to rein in my curiosity, I nonetheless left London on the university coach that evening, and was glad to be away.

I SAY "DISCOVERED FOR CERTAIN," BECAUSE I DO KNOW what happened with as near to certainty as is possible without having been present at that most secret of interviews. Now that I have read the manuscripts by Cola, Prestcott and Wallis as well, I take great pleasure in them, for the reasons behind Cola's decision to write is plain and clear. All the purpose lies in the intent to sow uncertainty, and the dispute with Lower—real though it was to him—is presented simply to deflect attention from those matters he wishes to remain in the dark.

The manuscript was produced to establish the continued existence of Marco da Cola, who has been dead now for so many years, and prove that he, a soldier and a layman, came to England and was seen in Whitehall that day. Because if Marco da Cola was in England, the Jesuit Andrea da Cola was not. Therefore what I believe took place at Whitehall could not have occurred, because it could only have happened if a priest, a Catholic priest, saw the king that day. And at a time when hatred of papists is greater than ever, and any man tainted with the merest hint of popery is at risk, that is of the utmost importance.

Dr. Wallis came very close to seeing the truth; indeed, he had it in his hands but threw it away as incidental. I refer you to his manuscript, wherein he quotes his traveling picture dealer in Venice that Marco da Cola *"had no reputation for learning or diligence in study at that time"*; yet the man I met was learned in medicine, with a fine knowledge of many of the best authors, and an ability to discourse interestingly on the philosophies of the ancients and the moderns. Add to this the account of the merchant Wallis interviewed, who described Marco da Cola as *"gaunt and thin, gloomy of attitude,"* and contrast that with the stout, cheerful man who came to Oxford. Add to it Cola's refusal to discuss soldiering in Crete when at Sir William Compton's, then tell me what soldier you have ever met who would not talk endlessly

about his heroism and actions. Think of those articles I foun
in his chest, and consider their meaning. Think again of hi
reaction when confronted with the power of his lust at Sara
Blundy's that night and say how many soldiers you know
who are so delicate. Truly the man was like one of thos
puzzles, so difficult to comprehend, yet so simple when th
truth is finally known.

I knew by then that the book in my possession was on
of the copies of Livy that Wallis and Cola both sought, an
that it was the key to at least some of the letters that Jac
Prestcott had handed over to me. Reading those scripts, how
ever, was no simple matter; by recounting my ultimate suc
cess, I do not desire to undermine or in any way denigrat
the achievements of Dr. Wallis.

At first I hesitated, and not only because I was certain tha
any knowledge thus won would do me no good; the event
of those days still bore so heavily on my mind that I los
myself in lassitude for months. As is my habit, I console
myself among my books and my papers, reading and anno
tating with a fury I could scarcely contain. The activities o
the long-since dead became the greatest consolation, and
became almost a hermit, noting with only passing interes
that my reputation for strangeness grew to the point that i
became unshakeable. I am, I think, held to be a queer, un
mannerly sort of fellow, ill-humored, irascible and of a sou
disposition, and I think this character grew in those day
without my even noticing. And it is true, now: I am dead t
the world, and delight to converse more with the dead tha
the living. Being so ill at ease with my own times, I seek
refuge in the past, for only there can I show the affection
am unable to give to my contemporaries who do not know
what I know, and could not see what I saw.

A few things only kept me from my books, and so careles
was I of human society that I hardly noticed how my ac
quaintanceship was diminishing. Lower slowly transferre
himself to London and was so successful that (favored by
the patronage of Clarendon and the death of many serious
rivals) he soon became the most successful physician in the
country, was given a place at court and took to having no
only a fine house but even a coach with his family crest on

the door—for which he was criticized greatly by those who thought it a presumptuous display. It did him no harm, however, for the wealthy and well-born like to be treated by those they consider of proper background. On top of all this, he even paid his sisters' dowries and reestablished his family in Dorset, for which he was greatly admired. But while he published his great work on the brain, he never did any serious investigation again. All that he considered truly noble, the pursuit of knowledge through experiment, he abandoned in search of worldly gain. I alone, I think, understood the sorrow of this, that what the world considered success was, in Lower's mind, waste and a failure.

As for Mr. Boyle, he also went to London and, I think, came to Oxford only twice more in his life. A greater loss to the town could not be imagined for, even though he was never of the university, yet his presence illuminated it, and brought it renown. That fame he took with him when he left, and in London he built on it incessantly with a never-ending stream of ingenuity which has guaranteed that his name will live forever. Locke also left, once he found himself a suitable sinecure, and he too abandoned experiment for the world, although in his case he became so involved in the most dangerous form of politics that his position is forever shaky. He may, one day, achieve fame through his writings, but he may equally become so swept up in events that he ends on the gallows if he dares return to these shores from his exile. That remains to be seen.

Mr. Ken, as was inevitable, gained the living that would have been Dr. Grove's had that man lived, and thus was perhaps the only man to benefit from the tragedies I relate. He became a good man, of moderate religion and noted for his charity. All this came as something of a surprise to me, but occasionally, I feel, people rise up to match the dignity of their office, rather than dragging its honor down to their own level. It happens only rarely, but often enough for reassurance. And, for the general good of all mankind, he gave up playing the viol through being too busy with his duties, and we must all thank those who gave him a bishopric for visiting this kindness on God's creation.

Thurloe died a few years after, and took his secrets to the

grave—except for those which, I believe, are among the papers he hid somewhere when he first felt illness coming upon him. He was the strangest of men, and I regret very much not knowing him. I am convinced that he not only knew all the secrets of which I talk, he was instrumental in guiding many of the government's actions in those days. This may seem remarkable considering his devotion to Cromwell, but he served that great man because he brought order to our poor country, and he worshiped order and civilized quiet far more than he reverenced men, king or commoner.

Dr. Wallis changed little, but became ever more irascible and violent as his eyesight deteriorated. Apart from myself he is the only one, I think, who is still living the same life now as then. Publications—on English grammar, on how to teach the mute to talk, on the most obscure and incomprehensible forms of mathematics which no one but he and a half-dozen others in the world can understand—flow from his pen, and from his mouth comes a matching stream of criticism and abuse of those colleagues that he always believes to be his worthless rivals. He has many admirers, and no friends. I have no doubt he continues his work for the government, for his skills in decipherment are as great as ever. Now Thurloe is dead, and Bennet has faded from power as all men of politics are bound to do, only the old king knows the true secret of how Wallis was deceived, lied to and made a fool.

And myself. For, on my own and unaided, I deciphered that letter which Wallis intercepted on its way to Cola in the Low Countries, and laid bare the entire secret it contained. It was not easy, As I say, I avoided even looking at it for a long time, and did not seriously engage myself until well after the plague and the fire of London, which filled Oxford once again with poor frightened people trying to escape destruction. I was frightened myself, and it was only when I was certain from long inactivity that the matter was forgotten by all concerned that I removed the papers from my secret hiding place underneath the floorboards in my room, and began to examine them.

That was only the start, of course. What Dr. Wallis could have done in a few hours took me many weeks, as I had to search out books in many places before I understood the principles involved. The simple explanation which Wallis gives in his manuscript would have saved me much pain and labor had I possessed it then, but he was the one person I could not ask. Nonetheless, I eventually grasped what was required through my own efforts. The letter starting the code every twenty-five characters was not the next letter in the text, nor the first letter of the next word, but the next letter which had been underlined. It sounds simple, and thus explained it is so: so simple a soldier on campaign could write it up in an instant, given the right book. That was the point of it.

And so, once this marvelous discovery had come to my mind, the whole secret of those letters was revealed to me after a morning's labor. And it took many months more before I could believe what I had read.

I have destroyed everything, as I promised. Only one copy of the translation I made is in existence, and I will destroy that, along with this manuscript of mine, when I know my last illness is upon me. I have asked Mr. Tanner, a young librarian and scholar of my acquaintance, to arrange my estate on my death and this will be part of his duties. He is a good and honest man, who will keep his word. Let it not be said that I have broken faith with anyone, or revealed anything which should be kept in the dark.

The letter, written in code to Andrea da Cola by Henry Bennet, Secretary of State and (the greatest joke of all) employer of Dr. Wallis, read as follows, after the usual introductory remarks:

The matter discussed in our recent correspondence is now come to fruition, and His Majesty has indicated his desire to be received, as soon as possible, into the Church of Rome, this being in full conformity with his true faith and belief. I am instructed that a priest who can be relied on be sent in the most total secrecy to fulfill his wishes, and I very much hope you will take this task on yourself, since you are already well known to us and trusted. It will be understood that the greatest disaster would result should any of this become known;

rather, a steady policy to loosen the ties which bind Catholics will be adopted, and hatred insensibly reduced over a period of years, before any public acknowledgment can be made. At present, all that can be done will be done, as a gesture of intent. The king will try to persuade Parliament to allow greater toleration of Catholics, and is confident that this first step will lead to many others, before the reunification of the churches can proceed. An emissary, Mr. Boulton, will travel to Rome once the reception is accomplished, to discuss the manner and style which will be needed.

As for yourself, dear father, you may travel in peace to this land; although no official protection can be offered you for obvious reasons, we will endeavor to ensure your safekeeping, and make sure your identity does not become known.

The king of England, the supreme governor of the Protestant Church of England, is, and has been since 1663, a professed Catholic, acknowledged in secret and taking the rites of the Catholic church. His chief minister, Mr. Bennet, was also a Catholic, and had as his secret policy the destruction of that national church he was sworn to protect. Far from a failed assassination attempt, Cola came to England to receive the king into the Church of Rome and, I believe, did so when he went to Whitehall that evening with his holy oil and his crucifix and his relic.

And all along, Wallis had his obsessions, and Henry Bennet listened, and encouraged him, so that not only did the story never emerge into the light of day, it would be more obscured than ever. I am sure (but have no proof) that it was Bennet who ordered the destruction of Wallis's servant Matthew to ensure the secret was guarded, for I do not believe that Cola could have done such a thing: he was not a man of violence, while the cutting of throats had all the hallmarks of the man John Cooth whom Wallis himself employed on occasion.

If I published this letter, or even delivered it in secret to someone like Dr. Wallis, the monarchy of this country would come to an end within a week, consumed by civil war, so great is the present public detestation of all things Roman. Wallis's wrath at the humiliation he suffered would be so great he would whip up a campaign of such vitriol that the Protestants of England would soon be on the march, baying for the blood of another king. If I went to the king himself I could become a wealthy man, living in comfort for the rest of my days, for the value of this paper—or its continued obscurity—is beyond price.

I will not do so, for how paltry all this is to a man who has seen such marvels, and felt such grace, as I have seen and felt. I do believe and know that I have seen and heard and touched the incarnate God. Quietly, out of sight of mankind, divine forgiveness descends again, and we are so blind we do not even realize what inexhaustible patience and love is ours. Thus it happened, and has happened in every generation and will happen again in every generation to come, that a beggar, a cripple, a child, a madman, a criminal or a woman is born Lord of us all in entire obscurity, and is spurned and ignored and killed by us to expiate our sins. And I am commanded to tell no one, and I will keep that one commandment.

This is the truth, the one and only truth, manifest, complete and perfect. Beside it, what importance have the dogma of priests, the strength of kings, the rigor of scholars or the ingenuity of our men of science?

Mr. Tanner sorted all the papers, some of which Mr. Wood laid by in order to be burnt when he himself should give the sign. When he himself found himself ready to leave this world, he gave the sign, and Mr. Tanner burnt those papers which were put by for that intent.

—THOMAS HEARNE,
ACCOUNT OF ANTHONY À WOOD
IN *ATHENAE OXONIENSIS*, 3RD EDITION
(LONDON 1813), VOL. 1, P. CXXXIV.

dramatis personae:

JOHN AUBREY, 1626–97—Antiquary and gossip, a man of great knowledge and few publications. Best known now for his ''Brief Lives,'' a set of character sketches of contemporaries. He was interested in all branches of learning, lived in constant financial difficulties and was a member of the Royal Society from 1663 onwards.

HENRY BENNET, 1628–85—Created Baron Arlington, 1663, then Earl of Arlington 1672. ''A man whose practices have not left his character free from reproach. The deficiency of his integrity was forgotten in the decency of his dishonesty . . . he lived a protestant in his outward profession, but died a catholic.'' Ambassador to Spain, then appointed Secretary of State (effectively foreign minister) in October 1662; impeached for promotion of Catholicism in 1674 and dismissed from office.

SARAH BLUNDY—Fictitious; the account of her trial and execution is based on that of Anne Greene, hanged in Oxford in 1655.

ROBERT BOYLE, 1627–91—The ''Father of Chemistry,'' fourteenth child of the fabulously wealthy Earl of Cork, discoverer of ''Boyle's Law,'' describing the relationship between the elasticity and pressure of gases. In the *Sceptical*

Chemist used the word element in its modern sense for the first time; speculated about the existence of atoms. Thought himself to be as much a theologian as a scientist, and was keenly interested in alchemy as well as modern chemistry.

GEORGE DIGBY, Earl of Bristol, 1622–77—Longtime supporter of Charles II who was denied office on the Restoration because of his Catholicism. Formerly a close friend of Clarendon, he spent the 1660s plotting against him, and in particular launched a badly planned and abortive attainder on corruption charges in 1663 after failure to secure a Spanish alliance. No one supported the move and Bristol had to flee into exile. Returned to conspire in the downfall of Clarendon in 1667.

CHARLES II, 1630–85—Succeeded by the openly Catholic James II who was forced off the throne by the Glorious Revolution of 1688. Lived in exile in France, Spain and the Low Countries until the Restoration of 1660. Charles's negotiations of 1663 to be received into the Catholic church were first published in the *Monthly Review,* 13 December 1903.

EDWARD HYDE, EARL OF CLARENDON, 1609–74—Lord Chancellor and effective Prime minister after the Restoration of Charles II. Clarendon was the king's most loyal supporter, having been with him throughout his exile. His position weakened when his daughter Anne married the king's brother without permission, but he survived in power until 1667, when he was forced into exile and supplanted by Henry Bennet, Lord Arlington.

GEORGE COLLOP, d. 1682—Of Dorset, receiver-general for the Duke of Bedford from 1661 until his death, and overseer of the later phases of the drainage schemes which converted huge parts of Lincolnshire into farmland.

SIR WILLIAM COMPTON, 1625–63—Royalist soldier and conspirator, knighted 1643. Described by Oliver Cromwell as ''a sober young man and godly cavalier.'' Imprisoned for plotting against the Commonwealth in 1655 and 1658, died

London 1663 and buried at Compton Wynyates, Warwick-shire.

JOHN CROSSE—Oxford apothecary, now mainly known to history as Robert Boyle's landlord while in the city.

VALENTINE GREATOREX (A.K.A. GREATRAKES)—Irish faith healer, who came to England and used a technique of stroking to heal victims of scrofula and other ailments. Believed his ability to cure was a special gift from God. His success impressed Boyle and others, and he achieved some success among the English aristocracy. "A strange fellow, full of talk of devils and witches." Subsequently resumed career in Ireland as Justice of the Peace and landowner.

ROBERT GROVE, 1610–63—Fellow and "amateur astrologer" of New College, Oxford. "Mar 30, being Munday, Mr Robert Grove, senior fellow of New Coll., died. [He] was buried in the west cloister of that Coll."—Anthony Wood, *Life and Times,* vol. I, p. 471.

THOMAS KEN, 1637–1711—Bishop of Bath and Wells, lecturer in logic and mathematics New College, Oxford, 1661–63, then presented to living of Easton Parva by Lord Maynard, and built up a reputation for piety and charity. A noted preacher, he was made a bishop in 1684. Opposed James II's Catholic policies, then also opposed his deposition, for which he was deprived of his see by William III after the revolution of 1688.

JOHN LOCKE, 1632–1704—Probably the greatest philosopher in the English language, Locke's work defined English political thought for more than a century. He was trained as a doctor, before becoming tutor in the family of the Earl of Shaftesbury—a man who was imprisoned for opposition to the government in the 1670s. Locke lived in Holland from 1683 to 1688, when the accession of William III made it safe for him to return. Author of *Essay Concerning Toleration, Essay on Human Understanding, Two Treatises on Government.*

RICHARD LOWER, 1631–91—Physician and physiologist, friend of Anthony Wood and the most successful London doctor of his generation. One of the kernel of the Oxford group that founded the Royal Society but not a member until 1667. Fellow of the Royal College of Physicians 1675, but career damaged by his political affiliations and did not recover properly until the revolution of 1688. Conducted experiments on transfusion in the 1660s, published *Tractatus de Corde* 1669.

THOMAS LOWER, 1633–1720—Brother of Richard and Quaker, married stepdaughter of George Fox; imprisoned 1673 and 1686, had interest in Quaker settlements and property in America.

COUNT PATRICIO DE MOLEDI—Spanish ambassador to England 1662–67. Known for his learning and courtesy.

JOHN MORDAUNT, BARON MORDAUNT, 1627–75—Second son of the first earl of Peterborough, sent abroad for his education, then became leading Royalist conspirator. Arrested 1658 and acquitted at his trial. Appointed Constable of Windsor Castle at the Restoration, but was impeached in Parliament in 1666 and never attained high government office. Spent his last years embroiled in a legal dispute with members of his family.

SIR SAMUEL MORLAND, 1625–95—Diplomat and inventor, clerk to Secretary of State Thurloe 1654 and accredited by Cromwell to lead mission to Savoy in 1655. Switched sides in 1659 by identifying traitor in Royalist ranks, knighted on the Restoration. Made calculating machine in 1663 and experimented with pumps and early steam engines from the 1660s onwards. Consultant on water supply to Louis XIV at Versailles, 1681.

JACK PRESTCOTT—Fictitious; his story, and that of his father, is based on the disgrace and exile of Sir Richard Willys for treason in 1660. Willys's son later died insane.

SIR JOHN RUSSELL, d. 1687—Leading member of the "Sealed Knot," a group of active Royalists in England which plotted ceaselessly and fruitlessly in the 1650s to overthrow Cromwell and bring back the king.

PETER STAHL, d. 1675—''The noted chimist and Rosicrucian Peter Stahl of Strasburgh in Royal Prussia was a Lutheran and a great hater of women, [and] a very useful man . . . he was brought to Oxon by Mr Robert Boyle, an. 1659 . . . About the beginning of the year 1663 he removed his elaboratory to a draper's house in the parish of Allsaints. In the year following, he was called away to London, died there about 1675, and was buried in the church of St Clement Danes.''—Anthony Wood, *Life and Times*, vol. I, p. 473.

JOHN THURLOE, 1616–68—Lawyer, secretary to the Cromwellian Council of State in 1652; thereafter organized Cromwell's espionage system. Escaped all punishment on the Restoration and lived in Great Milton, Oxfordshire, until moving back to London shortly before his death. Hid all his state papers, which were discovered embedded in a plaster ceiling and published in the eighteenth century.

JOHN WALLIS, 1616–1703—Professor of Geometry at Oxford, founder-member of the Royal Society and the greatest English mathematician before Newton. A great xenophobe, who carried on lengthy and vitriolic disputes in print with (among others) Hobbes, Pascal, Descartes, Fermat. Cryptographer for Parliament, 1643–60, for Charles II, James II and William III. Published *Arithmetica Infinitorum* 1655, *Mathesis Universalis* 1657, *Treatise of Algebra* 1685. Complete *Sermons* published 1791, *Essay on the Art of Decyphering*, 1737.

ANTHONY WOOD, 1632–95—Antiquary and historian, author of *Historia et Antiquitates Universitatis Oxonienses* (1674) and *Athenae Oxonienses* (1691). A bachelor who lived a hermitlike existence and gained a reputation for unsociability and rancour in his later years, although until the

1660s had a wide range of friends and acquaintances. Chiefly known through his diaries and papers, which were not published until this century.

MICHAEL WOODWARD, 1599–1675—Warden of New College, Oxford, 1658–75; rector of Ash in Surrey and "a man of few scholarly attainments and fewer political or religious sentiments." But tireless in restoring the college's finances after the disastrous loss of revenues during the Civil War.

SIR CHRISTOPHER WREN, 1632–1723—Professor of Astronomy at Oxford, Surveyor of the King's Works and architect. Classed by Newton as Wallis's equal as a geometer, worked on spherical trigonometry, produced a measured map of the moon, was a founder-member of the Royal Society, and performed important anatomical work with Lower and others of the Oxford circle. Mainly known for design of St. Paul's Cathedral, his London churches and Hampton Court Palace.

chronology

1625 Death of James I, accession of Charles I.

1629 Charles begins experiment to rule without Parliament.

1640 Parliament recalled; Charles defeated in war against Scotland.

1642 Outbreak of Civil War in England; Charles wins victory over Parliamentary army at Edgehill; Oxford becomes Royalist headquarters.

1644 Battle of Cropredy Bridge, Charles's army wiped out at Marston Moor.

1645 Battle of Naseby; decisive defeat of Royalists.

1646 Oxford surrenders under siege.

1647 War ends with defeat and capture of Charles.

1648 Visitation of the Universities and purging of Fellows with Royalist sympathies.

1649 Execution of Charles I; Charles II in exile. Establishment of Commonwealth.

1650s Dominance of Oliver Cromwell, "Lord Protector" of England. Boyle, Wallis, and others form the kernel of the Royal Society in Oxford.

1658 Death of Cromwell; brief succession of his son, Richard, as Protector.

1659 Resignation of Richard Cromwell; Parliament recalled; fall of John Thurloe as Secretary of State. Attempt at rising by Royalists crushed.

1660   Recall of Charles II from exile; Earl of Clarendon as Lord Chancellor.

1661   Brief and unsuccessful rising of London Fifth Monarchists. Charles marries Portuguese princess and earns enmity of Spain. Second Purge of Universities.

1662   Acts passed by Parliament to enforce conformity of religion, despite Charles's desire for tolerance; persecution of Quakers; plots by Spain against Charles.

1663   Perpetual rumors of assassination plots against Charles. Earl of Bristol attempts to impeach Clarendon. Experiments by Richard Lower and Christopher Wren on blood transfusion. Formal foundation of Royal Society.

1667   Fall of Clarendon. Ascendancy of Henry Bennet, Earl of Arlington.

1678   The "Popish plot"—widespread hysteria caused by fictitious accusations that foreign Jesuits were planning massacre of Protestants.

1685   Death of Charles, accession of his Catholic brother, James II.

1688   The "Glorious Revolution": James expelled, constitutional settlement ensures primacy of Parliament and supremacy of Protestantism.

acknowledgments

With thanks to Michael Benjamin, Cathy Crawford, Margaret Hunt, Karma Nabulsi, Lyndal Roper, Nick Stargardt, Felicity Bryan, Eric Christiansen, Dan Franklin, Anne Freedgood, Julie Grau, Mih-Ho Cha, Nicole Wan, Maggie Pelling, Charles Webster, and (most important of all) Ruth Harris.

about the author

Born in 1955, Iain Pears has worked as an art historian, a television consultant, and a journalist, in England, France, Italy, and the United States. He is the author of six highly praised detective novels, a book of art history, and countless articles on artistic, financial, and historical subjects. He lives in Oxford, England.